Rex Tjin's life has never been normal. It just took him a while to notice the difference.

Not every kid spent their summer vacations learning survival tactics on rural Pennsylvania paintball fields, could fieldstrip a .9mm and slap it back together with military speed, or had really good instincts for just *knowing* things—including when to get out of the line of fire.

Most of the time.

When Rex finally realized his family was different from his friends and neighbors in Kutztown, he didn't care. He's the third of eight kids who are all crazy. They drive each other nuts, but they love each other. To every single one of them, that's the most important part.

Four of them go into the military, thinking long-term careers. Then Rex's younger brother dies in Iraq in 2005. It's a disaster that isn't his fault, a loss he can't stop blaming himself for. He bows out after only eight years instead of the planned twenty.

Rex spends the next decade trying to figure out what to do with the rest of his life. He attends a college he can't remember graduating from; doesn't even know if he collected a diploma. He didn't care. School was something to fill the empty spaces left behind by his dead brother and the mental inertia of leaving the intensity of Special Forces.

Picking up available contracting work through the Department of Defense starts to fill those empty spaces. Rex has a conscience and the ability to say "No thanks" if he doesn't like the job; he gets to shoot things again (or turn them into craters); and the pay is great. Awesome.

On his thirty-sixth birthday, Rex goes to a bar looking for nothing more than brandy and a chance to mourn another loss in peace. Instead, he meets a fascinating redhead who also works for the DoD. Rex wasn't planning to get involved with anyone, but sometimes you just *fit* with someone. Rex's new favorite redhead is also the reason why 2016 decides to push the envelope on what's normal, even for him.

If he's going to make an enemy out of an organization within the federal government, it might as well be one that's been up to sci-fi levels of weird since 1951...the same organization th̶a̶t̶ i̶s̶ ultimately responsible for Rex's eerily n̶e̶w̶

Also by Jer Keene:

Awaken the Stars Trilogy

Ashlesha आश्लेषा

Vishakha विशाखा in Winter 2018

Aparajita अपराजिता in Winter 2019

ASHLESHA

First story in the *Awaken the Stars* trilogy

Jer Keene

Edited by
Joy Demorra, Jules Robin, & Ashlee Tessier

Altered Nature Press

Altered Nature Press, 11 Pleasant Pl., Waterville, Maine
Ashlesha. Second Edition.

Cover art by Rumiana Ruseva; cover design/layout by Jer Keene.

Please purchase only authorized paper or electronic editions of this story—or at least consider purchasing a legal copy if you liked it. Your support of the author is appreciated. Fanfiction, however, is another matter entirely. Have fun! I'll be watching from the sidelines.

Obligatory Disclaimer: the author and Altered Nature Press do not have any control over and do not assume responsibility for third-party websites or their contents.

First published in the United States and worldwide October 31st 2016 by eBook distribution and print copy. Printed in the United States. Second printing published November 21st 2017.

Fonts: Linux Libertine Font, Libertine Open Fonts Project; Charis SIL; Annapurna Devangari v.1.001 SIL OFL; Constantine, Quintessential, & Marcellus by Astigmatic One Eye Typographic Institute, SIL OFL.

Ashlesha, by Jer Keene.

Library of Congress Control Number: Data Pending

Rex was career military until his brother died in Iraq. He left the service and spent ten years trying to figure out what he was supposed to do with the rest of his life...until he stumbles over the cliché of meeting a redhead in a bar on his birthday.

1. Action/Adventure Fiction. 2. Science Fiction. 3. Romance Fiction. 4. Magical Realist Fiction. 5. Paranormal Fiction.

I. *Ashlesha.* 444 p.

ISBN 978-1-945932-10-6 (Pocket Paperback)
ISBN 978-1-945932-09-0 (Hardcover)
ISBN 978-1-945932-18-2 (Trade Paperback)
ISBN 978-1-945932-58-8 (ePub)

Ashlesha is available at most bookstores and eBook sellers by title or ISBN.

A Pocketbook Mature Readers version of *Ashlesha* is available under the ISBN 978-1-945932-08-3,

This is a work of fiction, but the trouble with setting your story on modern Earth is that it has to be *real*. Without that element of recognition, that spark, the story doesn't make your heart quicken or your thoughts dance with possibility.

Thus, you can find these roads and towns, buildings and business with a decent map and a good sense of direction. You might even be able to visit them, but doing so without permission can get you shot for trespassing in the United States. We're a twitchy, violent sort of people. It's quaint except for the body count.

Liberties have been taken. People have wished that the restaurant in the second chapter actually existed. Others live where I've put fictional homes; please leave them be, since they were living there first.

Public places are public and I borrowed them shamelessly without permission, but I put everything back where it belonged when I was done. In that same vein, the pop culture references in this book are vast, varied, and a hell of a lot of fun.

Lastly: references to historical events, real people (living or dead), locations, myths, religion, or legends are used fictitiously. Other names, places, and incidents are the product of the author's imagination, and any resemblance to actual events, locations, or persons, living or dead, is entirely coincidental.

Anne Rice, *Interview with the Vampire* (Knopf Doubleday Publishing Group, New York, NY, 1976). Anne Rice, *The Vampire Lestat* (Knopf Doubleday Publishing Group, New York, NY, 1986). Anne Rice, *The Queen of the Damned* (Knopf Doubleday Publishing Group, New York, NY 1988). Ann Rice, *Pandora* (Knopf Doubleday Publishing Group, New York, NY, 1998). Seth Grahame-Smith, *Pride & Prejudice & Zombies* (Quirk Books, Philadelphia, PA 2009). Robert Bryndza, *The Girl in the Ice* (Bookouture Digital Publishing, UK 2016). King, Stephen, "The Langoliers" *Four Past Midnight* (Viking Press, USA, 1990). Lloyd Alexander, *The Chronicles of Prydain* (Guild America Books, US, 1991). Terry Pratchett & Neil Gaiman, *Good Omens* (Gollancz, UK & Workman, US, 1990. J.R.R. Tolkien, *The Hobbit*, "Misty Mountains" (George Allen & Unwin, UK 1937). James O'Bar, *The Crow* (Kitchen Sink Press, Northampton, MA 1994). Jack Kirby and Joe Simon, "Captain American Comics" (Timely Comics, New York, NY 1941 and Marvel Entertainment, LLC 2016). Captain America©, Wolverine©, Punisher©, and all associated characters are property of Marvel Entertainment, LLC & Walt Disney Studios.

"Baby Got Back" by Sir Mix-A-Lot. © 1992 and 2012 under American Recordings, LLC. "The Sound of Silence" recorded under the Creative Commons License by Disturbed. © 2015 Reprise Records and ℗ 1964, 1966 Sony BMG Music Entertainment. "All Along the Watchtower" recorded under the Creative Commons License by Lisa Gerrard. © 2009 Gerrard Records. Written by Bob Dylan and © Columbia Records, 1967, 1968. "Song of the Lonely Mountain" written by J.R.R. Tolkien, Plan 9, & David Long, composed by Howard Shore, performed by Neil Finn. © 2012 WaterTower Music, Inc. of Universal Music Operations LTD. "I Have Seen the Rain" written by Jim Moore and performed by Pink and Jim Moore. ℗ 2006 LaFace Records LLC. "Bad Blood" by Alison Mosshart and Eric Arjes. ℗Eric Arjes and Domingo Recording Company, Republic Records, UMG Recordings, Inc. "Welcome Home (Sanitarium)" written by James Hetfield, Lars Ulrich, & Kirk Hammett, by Metallica. © 1986 Blackened Recordings.

Star Wars© and all associated characters belong to Lucasfilm Ltd., 20th Century Fox, and Walt Disney Studios Motion Pictures. *Star Trek*© and associated characters belong to CBS and Paramount Pictures. *Indiana Jones and the Kingdom of the Crystal Skull*, 2008. © Paramount Home Entertainment. *Indiana Jones*© and associated characters belong to Paramount Pictures and Paramount Home Entertainment. *Pokémon* is © by Nintendo, Game Freak, & Creatures; (®) by Nintendo & managed by The Pokémon Company. *The Hobbit: An Unexpected Journey*, 2013. © Warner Brothers Pictures. *The Hobbit: The Desolation of Smaug*, 2014 and *The Hobbit: The Battle of the Five Armies*, 2015. © New Line Home Video. *Gremlins*, 1984. © Amblin Entertainment and dist. by Warner Brothers. *Gremlins 2: The New Batch*, 1990. © Warner Brothers Pictures. *Se7en*, 2006 & 2011. © New Line Home Video. *Highlander*, 1986. © Cannon Films, Highlander Productions Limited. Dist. by EMI Films & 20th Century Fox. *Interview with the Vampire*, 1994. © Geffen Pictures and Warner Brothers Pictures. *Deadpool*, 2016. © Marvel Entertainment, Kinberg Genre, The Donner's Company, and TSG Entertainment; dist. by 20th Century Fox; *Deadpool*, *Wolverine*, and the *Punisher* are all ©Marvel Entertainment. *Silent Hill*, 2006. © Davis Films; dist. by Tri-Star Pictures. *Silent Hill: Revelation (3D)*, 2012. © Konami Davis Films; dist. by Universal Pictures, Open Road Films, Alliance Films, and Metropolitan Filmexport. *Pandorum*, 2009. © Overture Films, Constantin Film, Icon Productions, and MGM. *Sharknado*, 2013. © Syfy Films; dist. by The Asylum. *History of the World, Part I*, 1981. © 20th Century Fox. *Robin Hood: Men in Tights*, 1993. © Brooksfilms & Gaumont; dist. by 20th Century Fox. *Young Frankenstein*, 1974. © Mel Brooks & John C. Howard; dist. by 20th Century Fox. *Halo: Nightfall*, 2014. © Scott Free Productions with 343 Industries. *Return to Oz*, 1985. © Walt Disney Pictures; dist. by Buena Vista Distribution. *The Wizard of Oz*, 1939. Metro-Goldwyn-Mayer; dist. by Loew's, Inc. *Pearl Harbor*, 2001. ©Touchstone Pictures & Jerry Bruckheimer Films; dist. by Buena Vista Pictures Distribution.

Bugs Bunny© and "Loony Tunes" are 1933—current. © Warner Brothers Animation, subsidiary of Time-Warner. "The Brady Bunch" released 26th September 1969—8th March 1974, and is © Redwood Productions and Paramount Television via CBS Television Distribution. "Star Wars: The Clone Wars" and all associated characters belong to Lucasfilm Ltd., Lucasfilm Animation, Lucasfilms Singapore. Dist. Cartoon Network Studios & Disney ABC, 2003—2014. "Doogie Howser, M.D." released 19th September 1989—24th March 1993, and is © 20th Century Fox Television and Steven Bochco Productions. "Doctor Who" is 1963-current, and © BBC One/BBC One HD.

Call of Duty, 2003—2015. © Activision. *Silent Hill*, 1999—2012. © Konami Digital Entertainment. *LEGO Indiana Jones: The Original Adventures*, 2008. © LucasArts Entertainment Company, LLC. *LEGO Star Wars: The Complete Saga*, 2007. © Lucasarts Entertainment Company, LLC.

Girl Scout "Thin Mints"© cookies are really that bloody good and can start riots if not stocked in sufficient amounts. They're made by the Girl Scouts of the USA in New York, NY. www.girlscouts.org. The girls are awesome and do great work.

Introduction

There is something magical and utterly consuming about this story.

Ashlesha gave me something that I dream of. While the beginning is gentle, building the characters and their world, I was hooked within the first few pages.

For the first time in years, I'd found a book that I couldn't put down. I took it with me everywhere, reading it again and again.

It haunts my dreams and enlivens my days. It leaves me speechless and looking to find words to answer the emotions that it calls forth.

It feels like I'm reading something that could have happened. It feels *real*.

While immersed in Ashlesha, I can find myself. I can be uplifted—be inspired. Certain scenes resonate deeply within me; they make me *wish*. Emerging from the book always feels like waking from a dream, leaving me with a feeling of, "That's right. I'm not there." (It's a bittersweet thing.)

Like a cocktail at the end of a long day, the story balances action and romance with hints of science fiction in a wonderfully refreshing way. Its flavor is intoxicating, vivid and raw, while the supporting notes have their own unique charms. The little details contribute to a savory sound, full and rich and real. Some writers can make their words sing, and this is like a symphony embedded in my soul.

At its heart, *Ashlesha* is a story about family. It shows how amazing that bond can be. Every time I turn to the first page again, I fall in love just a little bit more.

There are so many stories mentioned in these pages, stories yet to be told. I want to hear them all; I have faith that the next two books will deliver those stories and more.

I know that however *Awaken the Stars* ends, I will be immensely satisfied...and ready to reread them all again.

The best books feel like coming home.

—Chelsea Bickley
1st November 2017

NAMES ARE IMPORTANT; NAMES HAVE POWER.

They affect us throughout our lives; they affect those around us. *Ashlesha* is laced with symbology, so it seems appropriate to be mindful of it here and now, before you turn the next few pages and find yourself in a different world:

Rex Vis (ɹɛks viːs; rehks veeS-eh): Latin *rēx*, n., for "king" or "ruler." From the Proto-Indo-European *hrég̑s*, the Sanskrit rājan, and Old Irish *rí*. The name reached its modern height in popularity in the U.S. in the 1950s. Vis, n., from the Latin *volo* "wish" meaning force, power, strength, or violence; a root word meaning "to look at or observe." Also see: Rex Stout.

Django (dʒãŋgo; zhain-gho): Romani Sinti name that most likely means "to awaken." Previous variations before the 20th century include *dszangewo* or *dszangewau*. The name reached the height of its popularity in the U.S. during the 1920s. Also see: Django Reinhardt.

Xãwuth (baouwu; bah-oh-woo): from Thai meaning "weapon" originating from the Devanagari, from the Sanskrit *pāli* "line" and *pālibhāṣā* "language of the sacred texts." Also see: Avudha.

Khỏi khôn đi Som (khôɛn khỏaɪ-đaɪ sʌm; kon koh-ee-dee sum): *Khỏi*, n., from Vietnamese meaning "smoke," *đi*, n. meaning "departing," *khôn*, n., meaning "wise," and Sanskrit *soma*, meaning "moon;" as a whole, it means "Wisdom comes from the moon." Also see: Khodī; see also "*Chưa khỏi vòng đã cong đuôi.*"

Ella (ˈelːɑ; el-lah): 19th century short form of Eleanor, from the Latin *ali*, "other" and the French *énor*, meaning "grantor." Aliénor is also translated as "pitying light" in the sense of charitable giving. Also see: Ella Fitzgerald.

Eric (ɛɹɪk; eh-rihk): Old Norse for Eirrik, from *ei* "always, eternal" and *ríkr* "ruler" from Proto-Germanic *ríkijaz*, a cognitive of the Latin *rex*. Also see: Eric Dolphy.

Wesley (wɛsli; wehs-lee): an Old English term for *west* and *lēah*, a "wood" or "a clearing in the wood." Also see: Wesley C. Skiles.

Brian (ˈbraɪən; Bry-ahnh): Irish name, possibly Proto-Brythonic form of *Brigonos*, meaning "high" or "noble." Also see: Brian Boru.

Ki te Muri kā (ki tɛ muri kɔ; Kee Teh Moo-Ree Kay): *Ki te*, particle., Māori for "to" or "in"; *Muri*, n. meaning wind ("breeze"); *kā*, stative., "the state of being alight, burning, or being ablaze." Also see: Kai Manne Börje Siegbahn.

Makani (məkɑni; Mah-kAh-nee): an uncommon name, makani, n., is Hawaiian word for "wind." Also see: Lévy Makani.

Whetū (ˈfwɛɪtu; Vweh-too) n., Māori, "star," used as singular or plural form. Earlier "Vweh" pronunciation, not the modern "eff."

Som (sʌm; Suhm) n. "moon" from the Sanskrit root *soma*. Enjoyed a resurgence in popularity in Cambodia during the 1970s.

Tjin (ʧiaɪn; Cheyn) p.n. alt. of Tjhin, Hakka Chinese of Chinese-Indonesian origin, from the Mandarin *Chen* (Chén) derived from *Gui*, surname of Emperor Shun and passed along to his many descendants.

Bùi (ˈbui; boo-ee) n., a Vietnamese surname originating from the Hoa Binh Province of northern Vietnam. Potentially comes from the Korean word *bae*, meaning "pear."

Ngata (kGæt ɑ; kGAT-ah) 1. South Island Māori, n., satisfaction or gratification. v., to be satisfied; appeased. 2. Māori surname most often found among the Ngāti Porou of North Island. The Tongon word for "snake" is also *ngata*.

ʻAukai (ɑukəi ; Ah-oo-kah-ee) *ʻAukai*, n. Hawaiʻian for "seafarer;" one who travels the water.

This book is lovingly dedicated to Norcumi, an amazing individual. Without her, this book would not exist.

Rachel, יַקִּיר: you and your sister are aunts to my children; your parents are my children's grandparents. לך רבה תודה

Special thanks to Ashley Soucar, who made it possible for Altered Nature Press to become a publishing imprint in truth; to Susan Smit, who never once doubted I could do this; to Alix Ayoub and Gail Ayyūb, who have both madly encouraged all of my ongoing projects; to Emmaleia deWolff, who babbled until I started writing more about Django's life. Thanks a lot, wench.

There are more of you, but there are also a lot of you— you're behind the story, my lovely minions. I've not forgotten you.

This book is also dedicated to the men and women who are serving, or have served, in the armed forces the world over. You're all completely terrifying, and it's awesome.

Last, but never least—to everyone who ever felt like there is no story out there for them; for everyone who has stared at the library shelves, wondering where the person wearing their face resided; for those who never found representation anywhere:

Welcome home.

Ashlesha, Asleshā, or *Ashlesās* in Sanskrit.
Aayilyam in Tamil and Malayalam: the 9th *nákṣatra*
Ashlesha, the Ascendant sign of the *nagas* entwined
as they mimic the double helix of a DNA molecule.
Overseen by Ahi, the naga serpent of wisdom,
Ashlesha's group of stars breaks the eastern horizon
in the constellation of Hydra:
Epsilon, Delta, Mu, Rho, Sigma, and *Zeta-Hydrae.*

ఆశ్లేష

ஆயில்யம்

आश्लेषा

Much of the world sees the snake as something to be
feared: mysterious, cunning, hypnotic, false creatures—
the death-bringers of folklore, the bane of Adam and Eve.

Yet snakes are also intuitive and perceptive, with the
wisdom, calculation, and concentration to devote
themselves to their chosen task.

They are astute observers, yet always so difficult to
grasp.

It is often conveniently forgotten that snakes are also
viewed by many cultures as symbols of sexuality.

Part I

"What is learnt is a handful of sand,
while what is unknown is the size of the world."

—A ஔவையார் poet of Tamil Literature in the
Sangam Period, 100-300 CE.

Chapter 1

:)O(X)(C:

This, Rex reflects, is an actual disaster. A travesty. He's going to kill Arram Haervati for doing this to him.

"Portland, Maine? Are you actually kidding me?"

"You've complained about your destination eight times now," the man on the other end of his cellphone says. "I've been keeping count."

"Goddammit, Haervati!" Rex flinches as his voice echoes off the walls. The terminal for Portland International is massive, and there are maybe five people around, total. This is not what an airport is supposed to be like.

Rex switches tactics, trying to appeal to Haervati's sense of logistics. "Do you have any idea how long it takes to drive from Portland to Trenton, Haervati?"

"No," Haervati returns promptly, "because I am a smart person who never leaves D.C., Tjin."

Rex rolls his eyes. "Haervati, you never leave your desk."

"My desk is awesome. You're just jealous." Haervati pauses; Rex can hear him pounding away at his keyboard. "Stop blaming me, by the way. You asked for the fastest flight back to the States from Bahrain, and I got you one, right to good ol' PWM. The thanks I'm getting sounds like the pissing and moaning of crying teenagers going through Basic."

Rex glances up at a sign and switches direction, searching for a ticket counter that's manned by an actual human being. The last time he tried to use a kiosk when he hadn't slept for two days after a transatlantic flight, he ended up in South Korea. Again.

"Let me put it another way," Rex says. "It's 8:00 a.m. on a Saturday morning, an ideal travel day with great weather, and there is *nobody* in this stupid airport. It's fucking creepy."

"So, *The Langoliers* is real? Awesome!"

Rex comes to an abrupt halt. "Haervati, that didn't help anything. At all. Ever."

"Made you think about it, though!"

"Fuck. You."

Haervati laughs at him. "Come on, you know there's no such thing as those giant anti-Pac-Man things eating stuff."

Rex finally sees a living person manning a ticket counter. Awesome. "That's the mini-series. You've never read the short story, have you?" he asks, veering directly for the agent before they can disappear and go hide wherever the hell else the rest of this airport's population is lurking.

"Nope, can't say that I have."

"I really think you should," Rex tells him. "At night. In an airport terminal. Talk to you later, Haervati."

"Hey, wait, no, I need you to report in officially on Bahrain—" Haervati tries to say, but Rex has already disconnected the call and is smiling at the middle-aged man at the counter.

"Mornin'," the gray-haired man says with a weird accent that Rex can't place right away. "What can I do for ya?" His skin is weathered; his eyes are the same shade of blue as the ocean Rex just flew over. Rex suspects the agent may be a former lobsterman who correctly decided that the ocean sucked.

"Hi, there." Rex tries for a smile that isn't a grimace. "Please tell me there is a flight out of this creepy airport that would put me in Trenton, New Jersey before 8:00 p.m."

The airline agent gives him a neutral once-over, one that says he's thinking about calling the TSA on Rex. Then he notices the obvious dog tags hanging out in full view over Rex's t-shirt. "Ah. In a hurry, are we?"

"A little bit of one, yeah," Rex says, dropping his duffel on the ground so he can get to his wallet more easily. He doesn't rely on the dog tag cheat unless he's desperate, and desperate is right now. He'll tuck them back under his shirt once he has a flight out of here.

"Well, I have bad news for you—Portland doesn't have a damned thing going to Trenton."

Rex bites back an angry sigh. Haervati is so dead. Haervati is paying for his fucking car rental. "Princeton?" he asks, even though he knows it's even less likely than Trenton.

"Not a chance in hell." The man's accent is pure Bostonian, Rex realizes. It's as weird to hear in this empty airport as it would be to hear full Southern twang in Mexico. "Got Newark listed, though."

"When, where, how much, how long?"

The agent seems amused. "They pull out at eight-thirty. Doesn't leave you much time, but you don't have to deal with security again. United Airlines Express flight, nonstop to Newark. Arrives around ten in the mornin'. Not a bad price for a one-way ticket on short notice."

"Excellent." Rex pays for the flight—$239.00, what the hell, that is not cheap—collects his ID along with the printed ticket, and hefts his bag up onto his shoulder again. "Thanks for helping me out."

"No problem. You have yourself a good day there, soldier."

Rex hides a wince. Technically, he hasn't been a soldier since 2005, but the Department of Defense is good at ignoring that shit. "Have a good morning," he manages in a pleasant voice, and bolts at a socially acceptable pace for the terminal and his flight home.

While he waits the ten minutes before boarding, he dials up Haervati again. "You owe me a rental car out of Newark, ready at 10:00 a.m."

"You hung up on me. I'm going to find you the shittiest vehicle that airport has ever rented," Haervati retorts.

"I don't care as long as it drives." Rex picks up his bag and goes to stand by the observation window when too many people sit near him, trying to be neighborly or something. No, assholes, he is *on the phone*.

God, but he needs to sleep.

"Bahrain, Rex," Haervati insists.

Rex drops his duffel at his feet and leans against the glass. "They're not letting much out. I think I cleared my entire stipend for the job just paying out bribes to collect the information I *did* get."

"They still think Iran is behind the bombings?"

"I don't even think Iran knows what the hell they're doing," Rex says. "I've got rumors about arms shipments successfully smuggled in to insurgents; the kingdom itself says they've claimed an arms shipment; there is evidence galore; there is no evidence; everyone knows who bombed the station; nobody knows who fucking bombed the station."

"Didn't get to shoot anyone, huh?"

"No." Rex thumps his head against the window. "The stress relief would have been great." He has one checked bag with a gun inside, properly bagged and tagged per TSA standards, and it better be waiting for him in Newark when he arrives. The inspecting agents have a bad habit of "losing" his bags when there are weapons involved.

"Well, you've told me three things that we didn't know stateside, so it wasn't a complete waste of time. Wanna go back in October, see if you can stir anything up? It's always good to send some familiar faces back to the locals, and you're the only active contractor I have available right now who isn't lily white."

Rex thinks about it. "Maybe. We'll see if they actually announce anything. At least if I go in, Bahrain is aware that our interest is Iran. Politically, anyway. Dad blames Reagan."

"Everyone with half a brain blames Reagan," Haervati replies dryly. "Have a nice flight—look, I can have a car meet you at Newark and take you home. I know you're running on fumes, Tjin."

Rex almost takes him up on it. If it were any other day, he probably would. "No thanks, Haervati. I can make the drive."

Non-stop flights are great, especially when it means he's away from the creepy Stephen King Airport in two hours. His arrival is 10:30 instead of 10:00, but Rex doesn't care about the delay. There is a car waiting for him at the rental booth, his checked luggage is where it's *supposed* to be, and home is only an hour away.

Usually. Goddamn traffic.

He hates Pennsylvania drivers who flounce around on the interstate, pretending they know what they're doing. He's allowed to hate PA drivers; he is one, even if the rental and his own car at home both have plates for New Jersey.

He gets off I-95 and swaps over to US 1 going south, then drives with his knees long enough to dial in his brother's phone number. His Bluetooth picks up the signal in time for Rex to put his hands back on the wheel as someone veers across two lanes of traffic without signaling to make their exit. Masshole.

"Hey!" Wesley answers after five rings. "You're stateside again. Or you fucked up."

"I'm stateside, but not via fuckery," Rex says, smiling a little. "Hey, look, when you were still playing pro ball, did your team ever fly into Portland, Maine?"

Wesley doesn't even need to think about it. "Nope. Too far north. There isn't any football in Maine. They root for the Patriots, and they're out of Boston."

"Got it," Rex replies, cutting off any further details. He doesn't really care for the game, but kept up with football just enough to know where Brian and Wesley were playing and when, just in case he needed to find them. Or help them hide a body. Whichever.

"Why?" Wesley asks.

"Gigantic international airport with no one in it on a prime travel day," Rex says. "Nobody wants to find that in Maine."

"Creepy as hell," Wesley agrees. Finally, someone with a sensible reaction. "You headed home?"

"Working on it. Making better time now that I got away from I-95, but I'm still north of Princeton. It's like someone let out all of the asshole drivers at once."

Wesley snickers at him. "That's because they all know the lead asshole driver is out on the road, and they're welcoming you home."

Rex scowls. "I love you, too," he says, and disconnects the call.

*　　　　*　　　　*　　　　*

He parks in front of his building ten minutes before 1:00 p.m. and takes a satisfying minute to rest his head against the rental's steering wheel. He needs to shower; he needs to *sleep*. Then he has to find a bar that doesn't reek of alcohol and piss so he can observe his yearly tradition. He's getting desperate enough for watering holes that aren't also hellholes that he'll even skip the music aspect. That's getting a lot harder to find these days.

Then again, he lives near Princeton. He might get lucky.

Rex's apartment is in an old brick duplex that someone converted into four apartments back in the 1940s. His half is painted red; the other half is painted an obnoxious shade of blue for reasons known only to a long-dead landlord. Their current landlord is good about taking care of the inside of the building, and none of them gives a shit about exterior eyesore blue.

His apartment is in a terrible neighborhood by society standards, but his neighbors are awesome. They are also nosy busybodies who lie in wait for him to get out of the car. "Hi, Lois."

Lois grins at him from her doorway on the blue side of the duplex. "Welcome back, baby. Did you have a good trip?"

Rex lifts his bag out of the trunk. "Well, I got paid for it, so I guess that makes it okay."

"They oughta pay you better," Lois says frankly. "Then you could afford to move out of these crappy apartments."

"I happen to like my crappy apartment, thank you," Rex retorts, smiling as he shoves the trunk closed. He can afford to live in a better building, but when he first got out of the military, the upstairs apartment in the duplex suited his needs. Close to the river (escape) and close to the train tracks (noise), with clean water from the tap. Everything else was a fringe benefit.

Lois Blackburn is definitely one of the nicer benefits, a white-haired black lady who's lived in the other downstairs apartment for forty years. She's eighty-six and refuses to act like it, even though her fashion sense is trapped somewhere around 1982. She never goes out on warm days unless she's wearing ankle socks with the little round bunny tails sewn on the back. Those went out of style when Rex was five, and he never lets her forget it.

"You always say you like this place." Lois plants her hands on her frail hips and gives him a narrow-eyed, suspicious inspection. Today's aqua-colored bunny tail bobs are visible under the hem of her lavender skirt. "You need to gain weight. Want one of my cookies before you head upstairs?"

Rex unlocks the outer door on his side of the building. "Lois, your cookies are diabetes waiting to happen."

"Boy, I've been making cookies that way my entire life, and my blood sugar is just fine!" Lois shoots back, grinning wide enough to reveal the edges of her upper palate dentures.

He hesitates after shuffling his keys around to get the next one ready. "Maybe tomorrow," he says, and Lois's eyes brighten. She doesn't get much company, he doesn't have plans, and Rex will exchange a cookie for some of the stories Lois tells when she's in a good mood. Her time in the WAC during World War II was a prime breeding ground for drunken debauchery and shenanigans.

Lois nods. "If you're going out like your usual for the nineteenth, head into Princeton, baby. Rumor's on the wind that the cops are hitting Trenton bars tonight, sniffing out underage drinking."

Rex frowns. That definitely cinches the idea about searching Princeton. He doesn't like dealing with cops unless he's related to them. "I'll keep that in mind. Thanks, Lois."

"Tomorrow, boy. Cookies!"

"Yes, ma'am."

Rex passes the locked door to the first floor apartment. They all know Janice lives there; it's just that she refuses to come out unless it's a special occasion, like aliens invading. He still raps on her door and says hello as he passes by, and hears her cantankerous voice tell him to Fuck Off Unless He's the Poh-Leece.

"Nice to be home, Janice!" Rex yells back. She swears at him some more, which makes him smile as he climbs the stairs up to his door. He slides in the second key and turns the deadbolt, then swaps to a third key to unlock the doorknob. Always confuses potential thieves when they need two different lock pick sets to try to break in.

A Glock is also a great deterrent. Nobody's tried to rob the mutant duplex in years.

The goal had been to shower first. Rex gives up on that idea once the door is locked behind him and he gets hit by a wall of exhaustion. He drops his bag onto the bedroom floor's rug, faceplants onto his bed, and sleeps until some jackass rings his phone four minutes before his alarm is set to go off.

Oh, god, I'm stupid, Rex thinks blearily, trying to make his fingers work so he can answer the call. He didn't even take the Bluetooth earpiece off when he went to bed.

"Rex, man! You made it home in time!"

He blinks a few times while staring at his bed's spare pillow. His eyes feel gritty, like he faced down a sandstorm and lost. "What?"

"It's your birthday, dumbass!" the cheerful male voice on the line tells him.

Rex sits up and runs his tongue along the roof of his mouth. Instant regret. It tastes like coffee died in there. "I know it's my birthday. Why are you calling me?"

"Because it's your birthday," his caller repeats patiently. "We go out, we drink, we have a good time."

Right; he remembers this man now. David Polansky, friend from Princeton U.

No, friend is the wrong word. Polansky is just an acquaintance with the intelligence of a rounded brick. "I'm not available tonight, David. I've told you why for at least three years running now."

"Rex, man, you really can't keep mourning some dead wicked stepmother forever. It's your birthday, not a funeral."

Rex grits his teeth, one hand clenching into a tight fist. "David, when you ask our other friends why I don't speak to you any more, tell them about what you just said to me. They'll understand," he says, and hangs up.

The rest of Rex's admittedly small social circle, left over from university and the military? Not that fucking stupid.

A shower helps him feel awake, human, and less likely to murder the first person he sees. Rex washes off Creepy Stephen King Airport leftovers along with Bahrain sweat, dries off, and uses the towel to wipe the fog from the bathroom mirror. His hair is getting long enough to curl again. He can't make up his mind about leaving it alone or shaving it all off. He compromises and buzzes it down to fine blond fuzz, then goes to find a clean t-shirt and a pair of jeans.

Princeton has a bad habit of opening a swank new bar and then having it shut down six months later when the newness fades and the college crowd looks for the next trend. Finding one that actually serves hard liquor is difficult, but the power of Google nets him a place north of campus, a bar and grill combo that doesn't close until 2:00 a.m. The neighborhood is really nice, which means expensive drinks, but that's Princeton all over: cookie-cutter neighborhoods and pretentiousness with some trees mixed in.

He still hasn't been over to the local airport to get his car back, so he's back in the rental, and Saturday night traffic sucks. It takes Rex almost forty minutes to get north of campus and find a place to park.

He walks to the bar in cool night air that is paradise after a week in Bahrain, weaving his way through the groups on the sidewalk. Most of them are college kids, either returning for the semester or just starting out. Most of them have no real idea of what they're in for.

The name of the bar-and-grill joint is Maritimes. It's a nice pun, even if it's the wrong town for it. Rex walks in the door and is assaulted at once by crashing waves of noise. The tables in the joint have all been claimed, the floor is crowded, and the lineup at the bar is shoulder-to-shoulder. Music is playing loud enough to be heard over the din, and the moment Rex makes it out, he knows he's in the right place.

Robert Miles. Mid-'90s electronica. Thanks for that, universe.

It takes him five minutes to get the bartender's attention. Rex is honestly starting to wonder if he should just flag the bald bastard down with money before the man finally deigns to acknowledge Rex's existence.

"Brandy, top shelf, tumbler on the rocks, please." Rex places a twenty down on the bar to prove that yes, he can pay for it. His t-shirt and cargo-pocket jeans aren't exactly fitting in with the rest of the bar's clientele, which is a lot closer to high-end preppie than he'd expected.

"Salignac, Honey Bee, Martell XO, or Hennessy?" the bartender asks.

Rex glances up at the liquor racks in surprise. "Holy shit, you guys have Honey Bee? Definitely that." It's pretty much impossible to get the brandy in the U.S. unless you can import it yourself, in bulk, straight from Delhi. "Why do you have it?"

"Owner likes it," the bartender explains in a curt voice as he takes down the bottle.

"Then I'm really glad someone in this town has decent taste," Rex replies, which earns him a noise that's either an amused snort or an irritated grunt. Hard to tell, and the bartender isn't big on speaking. He does his job instead: doesn't go overboard on the ice, pours brandy almost to the rim of the glass, and then leaves Rex the hell alone. Excellent. No one committed the sin of watering down the brandy, either.

Rex's cell phone vibrating against his thigh rouses him from what must have been a blank-eyed stare at the bar's shiny racks of alcohol. He reaches for his ear, remembers leaving the Bluetooth at home, and fishes the phone out of his pocket instead, checking the caller ID before he answers.

"I hear the dulcet tones of shitty, shitty music, little brother."

Rex sighs. "Khodî, you lived through this musical era, too."

"But then I became a grown-up and started listening to Viking metal," Khodî replies. "How many sheets to the wind are you?"

Rex looks down at his glass. The ice has melted, but the water is clear. At least he drank the brandy before he spaced out.

Khodî might have a point about the music, too. Robert Miles was replaced by C+C Music Factory, and not everything they produced is glittering gold. "Just the one, so far."

"Then I caught you in between the birthday tradition of two drinks. My timing is awesome."

"What do you want, Khodî?" he asks, signaling the bartender for another drink. The surly bastard ignores him. Rex behaves himself and does not chuck the empty glass in the bartender's direction to try and get his attention.

"I was just calling to say happy birthday, and to remind you that other people celebrate their birthdays doing much more normal things than listening to bad music from the early '90s. I mean, you've got the drinking part right—"

"You really need to go get fucked," Rex says, scowling. "Seriously, you are a lot more chill when you've been laid sometime this millennium."

"Like you've done any better," Khodî grouses.

Rex feels a wide, vengeful grin spread across his face. "I know something you don't know, fucker." He hangs up to the delightful sounds of Khodî demanding to know what the hell he's talking about.

Rex shoves the phone back into his pocket, grin fading. Yeah, he's actually been in a relationship this millennium, but it sucked. Nobody got what they wanted, and it literally ended in a hail of gunfire.

A new personal rule came out of 2012: no dating Russian *bratva*.

To be fair to Russians, Rex went specific and made it a rule not to date anyone who wouldn't be happy about the fact that he works for the Department of Defense. He just didn't realize that

8

was going to narrow down his potential dating pool to what feels like a billion-to-one odds.

Goddammit, Rex still hasn't managed to get Surly Bartender's attention again. He's giving this asshole one more chance, and then Rex is climbing over the countertop to get his own damned drink.

"Excuse me."

Rex gives up on flagging down the bartender when the words are repeated. He turns around, curious, and gets an eyeful of vibrant hair so red that it looks like someone set it on fire. The illusion is helped by the fact that this man has grown his hair down to his shoulders in one sleek, flaming wave. Pretty eyes, too—perfect Caribbean ocean blue, vivid and inviting. He's wearing jeans with an unbuttoned black long-sleeve shirt over a gray t-shirt. The man's age is hard to pin, especially with the beard in the way, but it's trimmed fashionably short, all precision and sharp angles. Rex pegs him as younger than forty, older than twenty. He's smiling— flirting, maybe?

"Yeah?" Rex asks, keeping his tone polite by the barest margin. He doesn't come out on the nineteenth of September to socialize.

To Rex's surprise, the man's hopeful look crumples into severe disappointment. "My apologies. I thought you—for a moment, you reminded me of someone else."

It's not a pickup line, even though it easily could have been. Fire's voice is as warm as his hair, just shy of too deep for someone his size, which is probably an inch or two shorter than Rex. There are faded Oxford notes in the man's accent that capture Rex's attention, too.

Curiosity gets the better of him—and he doesn't want to be responsible for someone else's unhappiness. Not tonight.

"You British?" Rex asks.

Fire pulls himself together. "Technically, American. Childhood transplant, earned my citizenship with military service." He looks surprised, like he hadn't meant to be that specific. "Again, I apologize for bothering you."

Rex shakes his head. "Nope, sorry. You can't leave."

Fire gives him a bewildered look, which is a nice improvement over that sudden, absolute misery. "I'm—I'm sorry?"

"You have to buy me a drink first."

One fire-gold eyebrow rises, as does a corner of Fire's mouth. "Oh, really?"

Rex smiles. The man might turn out to have the personality of a dull crayon hiding out in a knife drawer, but he's damned pleasant on the eyes. "Sorry, I don't make the rules. It's my birthday, and it's required."

That earns Rex a smile just touched by polite disbelief. Definitely not a dull crayon. "I do believe I've heard that one before."

Rex holds up one finger. "Give me a sec and I can prove it."

Fire waits with that same amused almost-smile, watching as Rex pulls his wallet out of the pocket of his jeans and flips it open. "September nineteenth, 1979," Fire reads, drawing out the year like he's savoring it. "I stand corrected; it is, indeed, your birthday. I'm glad. You didn't strike me as the sort that played games."

Rex frowns. "Those sorts of games are stupid," he gets out, and then flinches as his new friend bellows at the top of his lungs.

"HEY, FRANCIS, YOU HALF-DEAF WANKER!"

It's an actual miracle. The bartender turns around, a glare on his face that lessens when he identifies the shouter. "What the hell do you want, Ambrus?"

"For the last goddamned time, it's Am-*briss*," Ambrus corrects Francis, his tone only slightly less loud than the initial bellow. "This veteran has a birthday today! Get your ass down here and help him celebrate!"

"Veteran?" the college-aged kid at Rex's right shoulder asks.

Rex glances at him: blond-haired, brown-eyed, and definitely too young to have served before coming to college. "Yeah."

"Wow. Sucks to be you, man," the kid says, and turns back to his friends.

Ambrus decides it's time to sit down, shoving against Rex's sort-of sympathetic bar mate until he's captured the seat on Rex's right. The kids in the group shift further down the bar, used to the constant shuffle.

"Vet?" Rex repeats while Francis makes his slow, resentful way down the line.

"Your military ID was visible in the slot behind your driver's license," Ambrus says. He's giving Rex a curious inspection that doesn't necessarily feel like dating interest, but he manages not to be impolite about it. "And nobody keeps their hair that regulation-short unless they've been in the habit for a long time."

"Maybe I just like it this short," Rex counters.

"Dog tags." Ambrus says the words like he's singing them. Nice tenor, too.

"Point." Rex's hand goes to his tags out of habit. He tucked them in properly under his t-shirt, but up close, there's a distinctive outline of their shape. "You always that observant?"

Ambrus nods. "It's my job," he says cryptically, which does nothing to diminish Rex's fascination in his newly discovered Brit transplant.

Francis seems less sour by the time he's standing in front of them. "Same as before, then?" he asks Rex.

Rex glances at Ambrus. "Expensive," he warns.

10

"I'm buying it anyway," Ambrus replies. "I'll take one, too. I think I'm going to need it—oh, Honey Bee. You are definitely not getting rid of me until this drink is done."

Rex is already making notes about Ambrus's arms (muscled but not heavily so) the military-grade Timex on his right wrist (worn upside down) the mispronunciation of his name, which probably means Rex is guessing right on the correct spelling (Remember: Am-*briss*) while also wondering where a name like Ambrus comes from. It's a hobby born of his own odd background. Almost no one knows where Tjin originates from unless Rex tells them.

Bonus: Ambrus likes one of the rarest brandies available in the United States. Holy shit.

Ambrus pays Francis in cash taken from a small roll in his pocket, not a wallet. He says something that Rex doesn't catch, but it seems to make Francis act like less of a walking asshole.

After Francis wanders off to resume his surliness at other customers, Rex takes a guess. "Where did you serve?"

"Multiple posts. I've never really had a stable base assignment long enough to point out one posting over another." Ambrus sips brandy and smiles without looking at Rex. "You?"

"Some early work with the UN, followed by Afghanistan and Iraq." Rex feels guilty sympathy when he notices some of the light leave Ambrus's eyes. He knows that look. "I thought I'd be career when I first started, but I lost a brother in Iraq. Got out in late 2005, haven't looked back."

"I'm sorry. For your brother's loss, not for your decision to get the fuck out of active service," Ambrus clarifies.

Rex never knows what to do when offered sympathy about Eric, so he just nods. He didn't miss the clarification on active service, so he reverts back to the original subject. "Are you still active military? You sound like someone who's not fond of their job."

"In a sense, yes." Ambrus grabs a saltshaker, adds perhaps three grains to his glass of brandy, and blends it in with a swizzle stick. Weird. "I work for a department within the Department of Defense."

Rex glances at Ambrus again. The man's hair is nowhere near regulation short; he's been DoD for a long time. Technically, that's against DoD regulations if you're working in the Pentagon, but some of the brass remember that it's less about appearance and a hell of a lot more about who can do the damned job.

"You were in Iraq," Rex says. "How bad?"

Ambrus looks at Rex from the corner of his eye before nodding. "Standard levels of bad, I suppose. Saw combat I wasn't supposed to see, but that's pretty much my entire military career. Combat where combat should never be."

11

अश्लेषा

"What the fuck kind of DoD work are you doing that firefights sound like a common thing?" Rex doesn't really expect an answer, even though he's curious. There is shit his own father can't tell him about his time with the DoD, or his active service before that, and it's all been over and done with for twenty-four years.

"Uh, well." Ambrus's smile is self-deprecating, and a lot hotter than it has any right to be. "I have actually hit the limit of what I'm allowed to say about my work."

"NDAs?"

A faint line appears between Ambrus's flame-red eyebrows. "Non-disclosure agreements make it very difficult to talk to people."

"Yeah, they do," Rex agrees. Ambrus is startled by that, as if he hadn't expected any kind of solidarity. "I've been picking up DoD contracts since I finished college. When friends ask, 'So, what did you do this weekend?' the answer they want does not involve a stack of papers to sign and a blood oath that they won't repeat anything I tell them."

Ambrus's laugh is a near-silent chuckle that ramps up Rex's interest in the other man. He never thought he'd go for the bearded type, or the vaguely British type, but he's quickly discovering that he can make exceptions.

"How do you discuss anything with your friends if you don't talk about work?" Ambrus asks.

Rex feels a cold chill, a warning that he could easily say the wrong thing in this moment. He suspects Ambrus doesn't have a lot of people outside the DoD to talk to, and that's depressing. Rex isn't great with people, but he still speaks to his neighbors, the few friends he made in college—not David Polansky—his father, and his asshole siblings.

"Well, there are movies, music, video games...uh, music." Shit, maybe Rex needs a real hobby aside from DoD contracts. He couldn't name anything else right now to save his life.

The only subject he hasn't mentioned yet? It's *way* too early for that one.

"Music actually does give me a place to start," Ambrus says as Reel to Real gives way to Loreena McKennitt. Someone needs to fire this stupid DJ. "'90s Nostalgia Night is a hell of a choice for a first trip into a club. Maritimes doesn't even advertise the occasion. Why choose it?"

"How do you know it's my first time?" Rex refuses to wince after asking. Yes, brain, he is aware of the fact that it was innuendo. Shut up.

Ambrus lifts one shoulder in a shrug that is barely gesture at all. "I'm in here often; I've never seen you before; Francis didn't know you. That man is a dick, but he doesn't forget a face. Tip well, and you'll never have to fight for his attention again."

Useful information on how to get more Honey Bee. Awesome. "So noted. I'm here because the joint I used to go to in Trenton lost their liquor license about eight months ago, so they shut down. I had to find a new place for the birthday tradition—two drinks and a trip down memory lane."

Ambrus runs his finger along the rim of his glass. Most of the brandy is already gone. "Nobody should have to spend their birthday grieving what's been lost."

Rex refuses to stare at Ambrus, even if he's a little bit creeped out. It isn't just the accurate guess, but the other man's posture and voice. "Insightful."

"Grief and I are very well-acquainted." Ambrus raises his glass, shaking off the mournful air.

Rex suspects he already knows, but asks anyway. "Why are you here, then? Fair is fair."

Ambrus smiles at Rex. "I'm here because the liquor is of good quality and close to home. I can drink myself all but unconscious and still walk back to my apartment."

Rex congratulates himself on his accuracy while grimacing at the idea of being that wasted. "Nobody waiting at home, huh?"

"Not even a cat." Ambrus pauses thoughtfully. "My schedule's far too erratic for any sort of pet, anyway."

"Is it too erratic for dating?" Rex asks, and then tries not to bury his face in his hands. He hadn't meant to ask that. Fuck.

Ambrus looks surprised by the idea. "You know—I don't—I don't know? I can't even remember the last time I dated anyone."

"That's depressing. Unless it's by choice," Rex adds. His eldest brother is definitely in the "Hell no, not ever" category when it comes to dating people.

"Not by choice." Ambrus puts his empty glass down on a coaster, slides a twenty and a ten underneath, and hops off the bar stool. "Thanks for the company, Birthday Veteran."

Rex quickly swallows what's left in his tumbler, copies the bit with the twenty and the ten, and stands up. "Holy shit, you're dense."

Ambrus is already turning to leave, so when he pauses mid-motion, he's stuck twisted around, which is way more endearing than it has any right to be. He's shorter than Rex initially thought, too—maybe five foot eight to Rex's five eleven.

"I'm what?" Ambrus asks.

"Dense," Rex repeats, crossing his arms. "Like a fucking brick, I swear."

Ambrus's eyes widen. "Oh, you meant—dating. You meant *us* and dating. I don't—I mean—"

Rex is bracing himself for "I'm straight," but what he gets is, "That's probably not a good idea."

Rex lowers his arms. "Why? It's not like I don't understand what the hell an NDA means. Or is the problem a lack of interest?"

Ambrus's eyebrows go up. He purses his lips as he gives Rex a more specific version of that original curious inspection. "Oh, lack of interest is definitely not the problem."

He can keep it simple. Exchange cell phone numbers and walk away for the night.

Rex is really bad at keeping things simple. See: hail of bullets.

"You said you can walk to your apartment." Walking is good; he's definitely over the DUI limit for New Jersey. The rental will have to cope with being parked for the evening.

"Yes?" Ambrus draws out the question.

"Do you have a Blu-ray player? Pay-per-view? Netflix?" Ambrus gives Rex a cautious nod. "Great! It's way too late in the day to actually go to a theatre. We walk to your place instead, find a movie we haven't seen, and watch the fucking thing while sitting in the same space. No expectations. Just two guys watching a movie."

"Just a movie." Ambrus tilts his head, that little half-smile making another appearance. "Don't you think you should know my name first, Rex Vis Tjin?"

Holy shit, he said my entire name correctly, Rex thinks, thrilled. Most Western tongues can't capture the faint, musical J-sound that lurks in the middle of *Cheyhn.* Usually they're too busy assuming that Tjin is pronounced *Chin.*

Rex holds out his hand. "Nice to meet you, whoever you are."

"Euan Ambrus." Ambrus takes Rex's hand in a gentle but firm grip. His fingers are warm; his palms are heavily callused. That is the hand of a man who either has weird hobbies, or he fires a pistol. A lot.

"*Yo-an?*" Rex repeats. "What kind of a name is that?"

"Spelled E-U-A-N, derivative of É—O-G-H-A-N, Scots Gaelic," Ambrus explains, grinning. His eyes light up when he's happy, a bright ocean blue that Rex could get used to seeing. "Well, not a derivative. It's just that someone felt like modernizing the spelling. I stick with the early 20th century pronunciation, though. Rest of Scotland seems dead-set on *You-an.*"

Rex grins back. "So is this a yes, or should I fuck off?"

Ambrus pretends to think about it. "I suppose I can handle watching a movie with a strange man in my apartment," he says, and leads the way to the door.

Rex sucks in a surprised breath at Ambrus's sudden acceptance before following him. "How far?" he asks once they're outside on the sidewalk.

"About a mile and a quarter," Ambrus answers. Rex estimates the time at twenty minutes if they're not in a rush, which isn't a bad walk. The weather's nice, and Princeton is a firm believer in pedestrian-friendly sidewalks. The crowds thin out quickly as they trek up North Harrison Street.

"Bunn Drive." Rex bites his lip as they turn onto the road. "You live on Bunn Drive."

"Technically, I live on Red Oak Row," Ambrus says crossly.

Rex snorts. "Nope. Bunn Drive. *'My anaconda don't—'*" is as much as he gets out before Ambrus shoves into him, his eyebrows sunken down in a truly magnificent glare.

"I have lived here for several years, and I finally—*finally*—managed to stop thinking about that damned song every time I drove down my street. Then *you* have to go and reference it!"

"I was a kid in the '90s." Rex grins, unrepentant. That angry glower is just as fun as Ambrus's bright smile.

"I hate that fucking song!"

"Too bad," Rex sings back, and ducks away when Ambrus mock-swings at him.

Oh, yeah. He is in so much trouble, and it's kind of awesome.

Rex almost balks when he realizes where they're going. Right; he'd forgotten that Bunn Drive hosts an apartment complex so upscale that it makes him cringe to think of what the rent must be.

Ambrus lives in an upstairs unit of the apartment block on Red Oak Row, as claimed. Rex climbs the stairs behind Ambrus, doing his best to be polite and not ogle the man as a distraction.

To Rex's relief, the apartment itself isn't ritz and glam, just understated affluence. Thick carpeting in the living room under his feet after he ditches his shoes, open floor plan to the kitchen, which has granite countertops and cabinets that are probably solid wood from front to back, not wood facing over particleboard. Higher end appliances without overdoing it, good lighting. A hallway that probably has a bedroom or two at the end, not to mention the bathroom.

"Drink?" Ambrus asks.

"Sure," Rex says, still looking around. "Thanks."

The furniture choices definitely offset the apartment's expensive features. Cheaper couch, microfiber in a dark burgundy. Flat panel widescreen television on a black stand with two cabinets. Not much else in the living room, and there are only some standard wooden stools for the bar top in the kitchen.

One side of the television stand hosts a Blu-ray player and a couple of movies. Rex is nosy and glances at the titles. Lots of science fiction, including *Pandorum*, which was a great movie until they killed off everyone who wasn't white. Lots of Tolkien. Rex gives the collection general approval and moves on.

The other side of the stand hosts a cable box...and of all the fucking things, a VCR.

"Why?" Rex asks, trying not to laugh. He can't remember the last time he saw a VCR in a stateside residence. Even his father saw sense and upgraded, though Rex's youngest brother had to goad him into it.

"Because the federal government still doesn't know what the word 'upgrade' really means. Job-related necessity." Ambrus brings Rex a soda with an organic label slapped on the side.

Rex eyes the can like it might bite. He's not really on the organic train, even if he understands some of the necessity. "Really?"

"I can't stand the taste of corn syrup. Ruins everything," Ambrus explains. "Besides, this is a lot closer to how a Coke used to taste."

"Except for that whole cocaine part they took out." The soda's not bad, and the war taught him not to have a preference. Soda was a thing you drank so you could stop choking on desert sand.

Come to think of it, his dad hates corn syrup soda, too. Maybe Rex should consider finding a case of this stuff and taking it home the next time he visits.

Ambrus smiles. "South America, a sprinkle of white powder into a Coke produced in Mexico using real sugar—good times. Also very illegal times, but that was sort of the point."

"I do not even want to know, except I do, but I really don't. Got popcorn?"

"Uh..." Ambrus goes back into the kitchen while Rex pushes buttons on the Blu-ray remote until he gets a Netflix menu via the box's Wi-Fi connection. It's cheaper than most other options, and Rex can log in with his own account and hit the Suggested Titles bit.

"No, there is no popcorn in this apartment," Ambrus announces. He comes back and hands Rex a sealed Jell-O cup and an undecorated spoon that still has pretty good heft. Not cheap silverware.

"Are you fucking serious?" Rex gives cup and spoon a bemused look. There isn't a flavor name on the foil cover, but all red Jell-O tastes about the same.

"Meat may rot in the fridge when a three-day trip turns into four months in a steaming jungle, but Jell-O is forever," Ambrus quips, peeling his open. "Oh, hey, the fourth Indiana Jones movie," he says as it pops up on the list. "I haven't seen that yet."

"Sounds good. I haven't seen it yet, either." Rex selects it, glad they found a movie so quickly. He loved the first three Indiana Jones movies, too. Nostalgia that isn't steeped in depression feels like a good idea for a change.

Sitting next to Ambrus on the couch feels weird for about a minute before it feels normal. Comfortable-normal. Rex takes it as a good sign and then tries to focus on the movie.

He almost tosses a Jell-O cup in utter horror about ten minutes into the film. "Did they just *nuke* Indiana Jones?" he squeaks in disbelief.

Ambrus stares at the screen in blatant disbelief. "Well, that was a short movie," he says just as the refrigerator comes flying out of the mushroom cloud and lands with a horrible thud in the desert sand. "A *very* short movie."

"HOW THE FUCK DID HE WALK OUT OF THAT FRIDGE?" Rex shouts two seconds later.

Ambrus's jaw hangs open. "Maybe drinking from the Grail cup makes you immune to the laws of gravity and inertia?"

"What the shit did I just witness?" Rex keeps staring at the screen, hoping they'll get an explanation for why one of his and Khodî's childhood heroes isn't so much goop in the bottom of a magical lead-lined fridge.

No, there is no explanation. The magic fridge is a warning about what lies ahead.

Colonel? Bullshit. Jones would have gone into the war as a captain because of his doctorate, but he *definitely* wouldn't have been military long enough to earn a colonel's rank. That shit takes over twenty years to earn.

"If the Grail cup made him immune to the laws of physics, why the hell is his father dead?"

Ambrus has his elbow propped on the arm of the couch, resting his face against his hand. He seems to be watching the movie the same way Rex is: train-wreck fascination. "Sean Connery retired after a pet project flopped, so he wasn't available."

"Then what about Marcus?" Rex asks, still outraged over nukes and magical refrigerators and bullshit military rank.

"The actor died." Ambrus's eyes twitch as the movie makes some cringe-worthy blunders for the sake of humor. "Early '90s, I believe."

"Shit." Rex hadn't known that, and it makes the movie worse. He eats the stupid Jell-O so he doesn't resort to flinging it at the screen. Not his apartment, not his electronics. "You're not allowed to choose the next date movie, not if this is the result."

"Next date?" Ambrus's expression is stone dry as a fistfight starts in a 1950s diner while bad music blares. Rex is appalled; it takes more effort to start a bar fight in the worst dives in Trenton.

"Hey, I'm eating your expired gelatin," Rex points out. "You owe me."

Ambrus looks affronted and picks up the discarded foil label from the coffee table resting in front of the television. "Oh, shit. Sorry. I'm glad I'm right about Jell-O's immortality."

"Do you know how to keep real food in the house?" Rex asks so he doesn't scowl at the movie. Mutt? Seriously?

Fuck it. Rex decides that this is a parody movie. The real Indiana Jones died in World War II while saving Europe from Nazis and some doomsday archaeological treasure.

Ambrus shrugs. "Random long trips, remember? I have take-out menus for every restaurant in delivery range. I gave up after the fifth time I had to clean out the fridge in a single year. Did you know that cucumbers turn into a tiny little puddle of pink goo if you leave them in the refrigerator long enough?"

"Nobody wants to know that, Ambrus."

By the time the movie gets to South America, Ambrus has his legs stretched out across Rex's thighs, and Rex is resting his arm over the man's shins. He has no idea when that happened, but he's not complaining.

"Did they just use vines to keep up with a car chase?"

Ambrus started laughing ten minutes ago and hasn't stopped yet. The vines aren't helping. "This is the fucking funniest thing I have seen in years. Actual years. This is amazing."

Rex loses it laughing when the amphibious truck goes over the waterfall. "Well, at least they made it a lot farther into the movie before dying again."

"No such luck," Ambrus says, pointing at people as they start to surface. Damn.

"OH, THAT SHIT IS NOT RACIST AT ALL!" Rex roars when the "tribe" shows up. What the actual *hell!*

"Did—did no one inform the directors and writers of this film that the movie was set in the 1950s, and most tribes in that region had regular contact with other cultures and visiting Western anthropologists?" Ambrus's eyebrows are scrunched together in disbelief. "Just—what?"

"See, now I really do want everyone in this movie to die," Rex grumbles. He's glaring at the characters as they enter the stupid alien temple. At least aliens would have explained Magic Fucking Fridge if the movie had *started* that way.

"John Hurt is the only thing making the movie bearable at this point," Ambrus says, shaking his head.

Rex frowns. "John who?"

"First guy to die in *Alien.*"

Rex peers closer at the man onscreen. "Oh, yeah! I thought I knew who that was, but he was busy being crazypants."

"Crazypants," Ambrus repeats softly, smiling. "Rex, do you care about what happens during the rest of this movie?"

"Not particularly, not unless they all die horribly soon," Rex answers, curious. "Why?"

Ambrus's smile widens. He swings his legs down from their perch, crawls over, and sits in Rex's lap, facing him. "This is why," he says, and leans down until their lips are just shy of touching.

Rex considers it for about a millisecond before he covers the rest of the distance, finding lips that are soft and pliant, and warm breath that is sweet—and not because of Jell-O.

Fuck, he's in trouble. He is in so, so much trouble, and he doesn't care at all.

"Oh, you are absolutely lovely," Ambrus whispers, "and I don't deserve you in the slightest."

Rex rolls his eyes before shoving his hand into Ambrus's hair, pulling him back in for another kiss. That one is long and deep, and makes him feel like he's drowning in bliss.

"My hands are not free of blood, Euan Ambrus." Rex speaks the words against Ambrus's parted lips. "If that's what you're worried about—don't be."

Ambrus gazes at him, one hand trailing along Rex's scalp, fingertips sliding through the short blond fuzz of Rex's hair. His other hand traces the planes of Rex's face, finding the faint scar that decorates his chin. "If I were a good person, I would tell you to leave, to never come back. I would move halfway across this country to ensure it."

That gives Rex's heart a painful jolt. It should be way too early in the game for that, too, but... "I'm good at finding people," he chooses to say.

Ambrus's smile is sad, but there is a possessive glint in his eyes. "And I am a terrible person," he says, and kisses Rex again. There's something different in this, heat and intensity that was missing before, and it makes Rex groan aloud.

"Oh, that sound—" Ambrus licks at Rex's lower lip. "Gorgeous."

Rex smiles and removes Ambrus's button-down shirt, then yanks up the man's t-shirt so he can put his hands on Ambrus's bare back. Ambrus's skin is smooth under his hands, and he's built like someone who gains all of their muscle by swimming.

Ambrus jumps a little at the touch, but his eyes flutter closed, his mouth parting at the gentle contact. "Oh, lovely."

Rex bites his lip in dismayed realization. "You're touch-starved."

Ambrus nods without opening his eyes. "Probably."

Rex continues to run his fingertips up and down Ambrus's back, tracing his spine and creating swirling nonsense patterns. No one should have to experience that lack of tactile sensation unless it's by choice, and it seems for both of them, it wasn't choice at all.

"That is amazing, Mister Tjin," Ambrus purrs.

Rex grins. "Technically, I still hold a major's rank."

Ambrus raises an eyebrow and cocks his head to one side. "You made major in only eight years of service? It's supposed to be ten."

"I am very, very good at my job." Rex tries to be utterly serious when he says it, but his lips twitch. It's true, but he has no idea why someone decided that promoting his mouthy, insubordinate ass was a good idea. There's also his cheat of entering the service as a second lieutenant, an early promotion that's sealed under an NDA. Ambrus isn't the only one with limited conversation material.

19

"Interesting." Ambrus's lips curve up in an inviting smile. Rex has never seen someone embody the word sultry before, but Ambrus does it as his blue eyes turn to smoke and fire. "Major," he says in a low voice, and Rex can't help it—he shivers.

Ambrus treats him to another long, lingering kiss in response. "Oh, that will be so much fun later." His hands trace the corded lines of Rex's neck before he reaches down under the collar of Rex's shirt, flicking at the dog tags lying against Rex's skin. "And I am truly regretful that it does have to be later."

"Later?" It takes a moment for Rex's brain to translate what Ambrus means. "Oh."

Ambrus rests his finger over Rex's lips. "Not a denial, I just—I wasn't prepared to—I don't actually—" He blushes, which makes his skin flush from the top of his cheeks all the way down his neck. "I don't have any of the supplies for safe sex. I don't really...do this."

"So, I'm an exception?" Rex asks, a thrill racing up his spine.

"You are an amazing exception," Ambrus replies in blunt honesty. "But unless you are carrying around condoms and lube in one of the many pockets of these trousers you're wearing..."

"No such luck. I wasn't planning on date-related activities, either," Rex admits. "It's been a while since I've had to worry about it."

Ambrus takes Rex's hand so that he can lick Rex's thumb. Rex lets out a startled whimper. "But on the plus side, 'out of practice' does not mean 'inexperienced.'"

"Nope, no, it does not, no," Rex babbles, his eyes rolling back as Ambrus proceeds to suck on his fingers, one after the other, treating each one to a final lick at the end that goes from palm to fingertip. "Fuck, that's evil."

"Perhaps," Ambrus agrees, grinning at him like a smug Cheshire cat.

Rex bites his lip and then decides to bite the bullet, too. "Look, I have to get tested monthly during DoD contracts. I tested clean two months ago, and I haven't had sex or encountered blood since then."

Ambrus lets out a regretful sigh. "I took a spray of blood across the face that included eye contact last month. I still have another round to go on the blood-borne disease testing before I'm rated clear. I'm probably fine, but I am not risking your health and life for a fucking orgasm."

Rex swallows. There is real concern in Ambrus's eyes. It's such a rare thing to see on someone outside of family that it makes his chest hurt a little. "So, uh—second date. Any thoughts?"

"Many, but I'm saving them for after you leave," Ambrus says blithely.

Rex's eyes widen. Shit, he's going to be thinking about that later, too.

"Not a movie," Ambrus continues, expression turning thoughtful. "Not after the disaster we forgot to finish watching."

Rex glances at the television to find that the credits are rolling, already listing soundtrack information that comes at the end of the reel. He can't find it in himself to regret missing the last fifteen minutes of the movie. Stupid magic fridge.

"Do you like sushi?"

Having real sushi in Japan kind of ruined the experience for Rex in most stateside places. "Depends on if it's done right."

"There is a small restaurant a town over, run by a chef who worked and trained in Japan for twenty years before moving to the U.S.," Ambrus says. "Reservation only, and probably one of the most well-kept secrets in the entire region. I assure you, he's doing it right."

"Okay." Rex takes a breath, trying to think about scheduling and not about how really distracted he is right now. "When?"

Ambrus leans back, which leaves space between them and makes it a bit easier for Rex to think. "I have a job I'm scheduled to begin on Monday. It's supposed to take five days, so…Saturday?"

"Saturday is good," Rex agrees, and then pulls Ambrus back down for another kiss, one that leads to a steamier ten minutes than he had necessarily been planning, but it's worth it. Ambrus is wide-eyed, his pupils blown out, when Rex finally releases him.

Rex reaches up to brush his fingers through the short ginger beard on the man's cheek, enjoying the prickly sensation beneath his fingertips. The simple touch just seems to melt Ambrus even more.

"That is the best acceptance ever," Ambrus declares, nuzzling against Rex's hand. "Saturday. No Jell-O, I promise."

Rex smiles, pleased and thrilled. "Saturday," he agrees, pulling out his cell so they can swap phone numbers.

He's also a little bit nervous. It feels like he's rushing into a relationship, and at the same time, it doesn't. Much like the couch, it just feels normal. It feels *right.*

Ambrus winces before he tells Rex not to text until Friday evening. "It's supposed to be a milk-run, an inspection of an office building overseas, but just in case."

"Not a problem; I get it." Rex lives that life, too. Unless he knows that it's only a reconnaissance job, Rex leaves his phone at home. Ambrus isn't the only one who lucks his way into firefights that aren't supposed to happen. See: *bratva.*

"Where do I find you? The sushi joint?"

"Sushi joint." Ambrus snorts. "I'm not telling the chef that you said that. It's called Makase Itamae Erabu, and it hides out in Kingston. I'll make a reservation for eight, after the initial dinner rush. We can meet in front of the building here around seven thirty and drive over."

"Sounds good."

Ambrus hesitates in a way that instantly puts Rex on guard. "If I'm not here, text me. If I don't show at all, call me the next day. If I still don't answer, try again in a week. If six months go by and you don't hear from me...someone will be by to clean out the apartment."

Rex's stomach lurches. "Hey, no, that shit's not allowed. Expired Jell-O, asshole—you owe me non-expired fish, and you're not allowed to dodge that debt!"

Ambrus stares at him like he's seeing Rex anew before he smiles. "Fair enough. I'll be there, Major."

Rex shivers again. There is far more to this than Jell-O debt. "You'd better be."

Chapter 2

:)OC)OC:

Rex knocks on Lois's door after noon the next day, once he's had time to head out to the airport, turn in the rental, and reclaim his car from long-term parking. Both bills are added to the folder he uses every year to figure out his taxes. There have been times when he's wondered if an IRS audit might actually be easier than dealing with all of that shit, but he keeps doing it anyway.

Lois waves him inside while using her foot to keep one of her three cats from escaping. Rex isn't sure why the orange monstrosity keeps trying, since all he does is turn into a terrified ball of frozen fluff the moment he realizes freedom is at hand.

"How did things go last night?" Lois asks once she has molasses cookies and sweetened iced tea on the table. They're both okay, but it makes Rex wonder how the entire Southeast quadrant of the U.S. isn't dying en masse from a sugar overdose.

Rex appreciates that Lois only ever asks how things went, not if things went well. She knows why he keeps up that tradition. "You know...it wasn't that bad."

Lois narrows her eyes at him while denture-mauling a cookie to death. "Someone got laid."

"I did not!" Rex protests, but Lois just grins. "Make-outs and sex are not the same thing, dammit!"

She laughs at him. "But I was headin' in the right direction, baby! Is he cute?"

Rex has to stop and think about it. He hadn't been considering "cute" last night so much as enjoying individual aspects of the man. "Yeah, I guess he qualifies as cute. Scottish too, I think, by way of England, but he's childhood transplant and American citizen."

"Not a lot left of that sexy, sexy accent, huh?" Lois asks, pushing another cookie at him.

Rex takes it with the resignation of a man on death row. "Plenty enough, you gossipy old bitch."

"Damn straight." Lois eats the rest of her cookie. "Didn't figure you for the white boy type."

"Lois, right now my type is narrowed down to 'probably won't kill me in my sleep,'" Rex says, which makes Lois cackle. His date for Saturday is DoD, yes, but he also wants to feed Rex expensive sushi, so chances are high that Ambrus is not going to kill Rex in his sleep any time soon.

Rex realizes by evening that Ambrus is a dirty cheat. He doubts the DoD job is a lie, but now Rex has to wait a full damned week to look forward to (or dread) their date.

About halfway through the movie he's watching, Rex realizes that no, he will not be dreading this date. He started thinking about Ambrus and got distracted, and now has no idea what in the hell

23

happened in the last twenty minutes of the film. He might also have forgotten its title.

Rex hits the information button and sees that he's been trying, for some reason, to watch *Sharknado*. He did not notice he was watching a horrifically bad movie. Yeah, he's screwed.

Rex gets his ridiculous act together and spends the rest of the week doing the adult work of catching up on the mess that always develops if he's away from home for more than a week. He gets his held mail from the post office, recycles three-quarters of it as junk, and files or pays off the rest. His apartment is clean except for a layer of dust, which is easy to get rid of. He has about as much perishable food in his fridge as Ambrus, but he's better about keeping the non-perishables stocked.

He never forgets to have popcorn around, either. Seriously.

Rex goes up to the second floor on the other side of the duplex on Thursday to fix Juan's sink when the faucet pretty much disintegrates in the poor kid's hand. "I should have had the landlord fix it last month, but I—you know. People." Juan fidgets in his kitchen while Rex unscrews what's left of the ex-faucet and pulls it free of its very old moorings. "And now he's on vacation."

"Plumbing always has good timing like that, kid," Rex says, cleaning away ancient cracked plumber's putty and what looks like someone's half-assed repair job from about thirty years ago. Caulk is not a fix. It's amazing the sink lasted this long.

Juan can't keep still, but he does watch Rex's work with careful, evaluating eyes, learning as he watches each step. Rex shouldn't call Juan a kid, but he's known the man since he was ten years old and can't break the habit. Juan has lived alone since his mother died when Juan was seventeen. The entire building banded together—even Janice, by phone—to claim Juan as a legal guardian entity until the kid turned eighteen a few months later. None of them really stopped keeping an eye on him even after he was legal. Habit.

"What do I owe you?" Juan asks once the new faucet is installed and tested, proving that it can spit water from the tap without leaking or exploding.

Rex gives him a stern glare. "What do you think?"

Juan lifts his head and lets out a frustrated sigh, dark eyes rolling towards the ceiling. "Yeah, yeah, I know. *Manaaki* hospitality crap."

"Damned fucking right," Rex retorts. "You can go to the store for Lois when she has a bad hip day if you really feel like you've got a debt to repay."

"Yeah, but then she owes *me*." Juan's thin brown eyebrows come down in a sulky tell that reveals he's still not quite done being a teenager.

"Lois gives you cookies afterwards. Problem solved."

Rex does call the landlord afterwards, leaving a message saying that he owes Rex for the cost of the faucet repair. There's hospitality, and then there is the sense of knowing who really should be footing the bill.

When Rex picks up his cell phone to turn off the morning alarm and observes that it is finally Saturday, it's a huge relief. If the date goes badly, at least it will be over and done with, and Rex can move on with his life.

Besides, if the DoD chatter from Haervati and Llamas is any indication, Rex will be in Bahrain again soon, anyway. That will be another fun round of not learning anything useful, and not getting to shoot anyone because diplomacy.

"You nervous?" Lois asks Rex when she catches him sitting on the outside steps around six that evening. He's gauging traffic, trying to estimate a travel time that means he won't arrive at Ambrus's apartment creepy-levels of early.

"No-yes," Rex replies. He is and he isn't, which is weirding him out. His instincts are good, but he's not certain what this particular sort of warning is for.

"I like your shirt, but you should tuck it in. Gentlemen who aren't wearing coats should tuck in that mess," Lois tells him sternly.

Rex glances down at the dark red, short-sleeved collared button-down he pulled on after staring at his wardrobe of boring shirts for ten minutes. They're boring for a reason; this is literally the nicest thing he owns that's not a firearm. "New Jersey doesn't need to know that I'm also taking a gun to dinner, Lois."

Lois's stern look doesn't fade. "You aren't Special Forces anymore, honey."

"No, but I'm DoD," Rex replies, while thinking, *Also, I made the* bratva *angry.* No one likes the *bratva* when they're angry, and that includes the fucking *bratva* themselves.

Granted, it's been four years since that hail of bullets. Maybe he could try being less paranoid.

He could also try being really fucking stupid, too, but he wasn't raised to be that naïve.

"See you later, Lois."

Lois waves him off. "Have a nice time, baby."

*　　　*　　　*　　　*

Rex gets to the apartment building's guest parking area about ten minutes early. It gives him time to walk the distance to Red Oak Row without feeling rushed. The local weather is holding onto early fall's cooler temperatures and warm breezes, but not the rain that sometimes comes with it.

Ambrus doesn't show at 7:45. By 8:00, Rex is a bit irritated, but Ambrus did warn him. Military schedules often don't mean shit. He texts Ambrus's phone, waits another thirty minutes while sitting on the curb out front, and gets nothing.

Dammit. Sushi is nice and all, but he'd been looking forward to what might come *after* dinner.

"You get stood up?" Lois asks him when Rex gets home far too early.

Rex glares at her after he gets out of his car. "Don't you have anything better to do?"

Lois smiles. "I'm eighty-six years old and retired, baby. Course I don't. Well?"

"Not deliberately stood up, no," Rex says. "He's DoD."

Lois rolls her eyes heavenward. "Can't you find someone to date with a normal job?"

"My job *is* normal," Rex responds, miffed, and goes upstairs without saying goodnight.

He puts the shirt back in his closet, sulks about it, and finally decides to call his father. "My job is normal, right?" he asks without bothering to say hello.

"Normal? No," his dad replies immediately. "Necessary; yes. You called me on a Saturday night just to ask me about this shit? How was Bahrain?"

"Dad, you don't have the security clearance anymore for me to tell you how fucking boring it was in Bahrain."

"That's okay. I'll ask David."

Rex pulls the phone away from his ear when he hears it click. "Well, I love you, too," he mutters, and goes back downstairs.

Lois answers her door after he raps on the doorframe so she'll know it's him. "What's normal?"

"Normal, or accepted?" Lois counters. She's holding and petting one of her cats, which is shedding clouds of white hair with every pass of Lois's hand.

Rex gives up. "Never mind. Night, Lois."

He tries texting Ambrus again a couple of times on Sunday, but still no dice. On Monday he tries calling Ambrus directly, though he limits himself to one voicemail and a single text.

By the time Wednesday rolls around, Ambrus hasn't responded at all and Rex is starting to freak out. He's up to four phone calls and five texts a day, though still only one voice mail. Late is one thing, but this is heading deep into "shit went south" territory. The fear curdling in his gut is what *really* tells Rex he's already vested in this relationship, and it's not even officially a fucking relationship yet!

It's Thursday afternoon when he finally gets a voice on the other end of the phone. "Ambrus," the man slurs. He is either very tired, or very, *very* drunk.

"Thank god," Rex whispers, and then clears his throat. "It's me. Where are you?"

"I'm...Rex?" The hesitation is what tells him that it's exhaustion, not alcohol. "I'm—I'm home. You can..."

Rex hears a puff of air through the phone that isn't a sigh, and then the line disconnects.

There are government tags on his car, and Rex rarely takes advantage of them. Today is an exception. He doesn't obey a posted speed limit in Trenton, Princeton, or the township between. He bolts up the outer stairwell and skids to a halt in front of Ambrus's door. It's locked, which isn't a surprise, and knocking doesn't get him an answer.

Ambrus didn't tell him to come inside, but an implication of an invitation is good enough. Rex uses that as today's convenient excuse as he pulls out a credit card and slides it along the inside of the doorframe. The deadbolt isn't thrown, so he catches the latch and unlocks the door. He isn't above breaking down doors when necessary, either. He's glad he didn't have to resort to that.

The living room is dark, but he already knows the layout. "Ambrus?" he tries, bites his lip, and then calls, "Euan?"

The click of a gun's safety halts him in his tracks. Rex winces and raises both hands. "Not a threat."

"That remains to be seen," a strange man says. "Turn around and let's see you, Not-A-Threat."

Rex does so, palms spread wide. If Ambrus has a boyfriend on the side that Rex wasn't informed of, he might consider homicide as an acceptable option.

Okay, so maybe his lack of dates is also related to Rex's utter intolerance for bullshit.

The person in Ambrus's kitchen, hidden from Rex's initial threat-check by darkness and the room's corner wall, is a tall kid holding a Glock in a steady, two-handed grip. "Hi, there," the kid says. At least he's wearing clothes—a rumpled t-shirt and faded jeans.

"Yeah. Hi." Rex glances at the gun. It's a Glock SIG, but not a .9mm barrel. That's a .357. That...could hurt. A lot.

"Who the fuck are you?" the kid asks. Rex's eyes are adjusting to the lack of light. The kid has brown eyes, brown hair, and pale skin. He looks utterly nondescript American until you notice the very East Asian shape of his eyes.

"Rex Tjin. Ambrus stood me up for a date, but when I called, he did invite me over." Maybe.

"You're Tjin?" The kid smiles and lowers the gun, which makes some of the tension leave Rex's shoulders. "Not quite what I expected Euan to have picked up, but it's nice to meet you. I'm Jasper Fox."

"Nice to meet you too, now that you're not pointing a gun at me," Rex replies, and the kid's smile widens. "Please do not be that man's boyfriend."

Fox laughs and shoves the gun into the back of his pants. "Nope, don't swing that way. I'm Euan's partner," Fox explains, and then he grimaces. "Shit, you're probably not—damned stupid NDAs. Come with me, okay? But don't freak out."

Rex frowns as he follows Fox down the hallway. "I'm not going to freak out."

That earns him a look of confused disbelief, but the kid was right. Rex almost does freak out when he sees Ambrus.

Ambrus is lying in bed curled up on his side, pale as hell. His hair is dark with sweat, its bright fire guttered under damp. His cell phone is next to his hand, making Rex suspect that Ambrus passed out mid-sentence. The phone means that Rex notices the intravenous line in Ambrus's arm at his elbow, leading to a saline bag hung above the bed on a 3M plastic hook.

"What the hell *happened*?" Rex asks, staring at Fox in shock. "Did you two go out and pick up fucking malaria?"

"It's not malaria!" Fox sits down on the edge of the bed near Ambrus's hand, grabs the phone, and puts it down on the nightstand. "Hey, asshole. Wake up."

Ambrus's eyes flicker open when Fox gives him a firm nudge. They're red-rimmed and bloodshot, like he hasn't slept in days, and it takes Ambrus a disturbing amount of time to focus on Fox.

"Hey."

"You went and called me a second-shifter," Fox says to Ambrus, smiling. "I appreciate it, but some warning would have been nice. I almost shot your date, jackass."

Ambrus seems puzzled before his gaze shifts upwards and finds Rex. "Oh. Sorry. Very late."

"I'm just glad you're not *dead*." Rex hears fear in his voice, something that he didn't plan on admitting to feeling.

Ambrus closes his eyes. "No such luck, Major," he whispers, which makes Rex's blood run cold. "Couch, Jas. Orders."

"Yeah, yeah." Fox glances up at the saline bag, which is about half-full. "I'm not sleeping until you agree to a Rex-shaped babysitter, and vice versa."

Rex looks down at Fox. "I don't mind staying, but what the hell is going on?"

"It really helps that you're DoD." Fox rubs at his face, where brown bristle is growing on his chin, slightly darker than his eyes and hair. That's what makes Rex finally realize that while Jasper Fox is not the pile of wrecked human being Ambrus is busy portraying, he's really damned tired. "After we sleep, one of us has to hand you a pile of NDAs to sign, and half of those are because we met."

Fox's gaze is sharp and intent, which means not a bit of what he's saying is horseshit. "As for Euan—it's a type of exhaustion. He saved a lot of lives a few days ago."

"You helped, dumbass," Ambrus grumbles.

Fox snorts. "I'm not the one who almost did myself in during the process, genius. He needs someone to stay with him. Make sure he doesn't...keep him hydrated, mostly. Stir him out of bed for bathroom trips once the saline bag is empty. Euan will be fine with sleep, but he'll be a grumpy wreck for most of it."

"Fuck. You."

"See?" Fox points out while smiling, which causes Ambrus to repeat the endearment in a quieter, mulish tone.

Rex breathes out, like he's getting ready to take a shot. The trick always steadies his nerves even if there's no gun involved. "All right. I'm good for this. Anything else?"

Fox looks a little embarrassed. "Uh—physical contact helps. You're not one of those macho types that thinks it's girly to hold hands, are you?"

Rex is tempted to roll his eyes. "No. Go back to wherever you were sleeping when I broke in, okay? You look like shit." Fox's head keeps listing forward when he's not fighting to be the most dominant thing in the room. "I'll make sure he's fine. I swear."

"I was sleeping in here, so that would be awkward." Fox grins at Rex, a sunny expression that lights up his dark eyes and makes him seem even younger. "I knew he liked you for a reason. Thanks, Tjin." Fox gets up and makes the trek back down the hallway. A moment later there is a thump as a solid weight lands on the living room couch.

"Shit," Rex whispers. He takes off the light jacket he wore against potential rain, hangs it on a coat hook next to the door, and then slips off his socks and shoes. The Glock and its holster he puts on the bureau across from the bed, farther out of reach than he's normally comfortable with, but Fox seems capable of dealing with anyone else who tries to enter the apartment.

Lying down next to Ambrus is like trying to embrace a furnace. Rex throws an arm over the man's chest anyway and discovers that Ambrus has also managed to sweat through his t-shirt.

At Rex's touch, some of Ambrus's fever-twitching lessens and his breathing evens out. Fox was definitely not kidding about physical contact.

"What the hell." Rex tries to make himself relax. He's been tense and on-edge for days, but at least now he knows why.

Rex doesn't realize Ambrus is still awake until he speaks. "I fucked up." He's staring up at the ceiling, and his eyes seem more storm-cloud-muddied than perfect ocean blue.

"I doubt it," Rex says. There are genuine notes of distress in Ambrus's voice. "You came back. Your partner came back. You both saved lives. That doesn't sound like a fuck-up to me."

"Shouldn't have happened." Ambrus closes his eyes, tears leaking from beneath closed lids. "I should have gotten out when a friend told me to at the end of the war. I just...I didn't. I didn't, and I'm so fucking stupid. I'm so tired of this stupid fucking job, Rex."

Rex feels like this is a lot more honesty than either of them were ready for. They still haven't even managed a second date. "So leave," he suggests, propping himself up on his elbow. He brushes wet strands of hair away from Ambrus's eyes and forehead. Some of the distressed lines on his face ease, but not all of them. "You're DoD, but I bet you're not contract-locked. Quit."

"I can't, I—" Ambrus's eyes open again, but he's looking at the open door and the darkened living room beyond the hall. "Jasper. He's not ready to solo. He—he trusts the wrong people too easily. I'm trying to teach him, but God, he's so young..."

"You can only teach people so much before they have to learn it on their own." Rex offers Ambrus a wry smile when his fever-glazed eyes finally turn in Rex's direction. "Yep, voice of experience. I went into Afghanistan convinced it was the right thing to do."

Ambrus gives him a tired look. "Afghanistan was bullshit."

"Yeah. I know that now, but I had to learn it. Fox seems smart—he'll learn it, too. Now, forget all of that shit for a while," Rex orders. "Chill. If Jasper has orders to sleep, then so do you."

Ambrus smiles in gratitude at the subject change. "I'm so sorry, this is...I'm terrible at this, but even I know this is a miserable second date."

Maybe it's too soon, or the wrong time for it, but Rex still leans down and presses a soft kiss against Ambrus's lips. "Believe me, I've had worse."

Ambrus is definitely less distressed when Rex pulls back. "I really, really need to be informed about how this is not your worst date," he says, humor starting to surface in his blue eyes.

"Iraq. Mortar rounds ruin everything, trust me."

*   *   *   *

Rex falls asleep with his left arm still resting on Ambrus's chest. When he wakes up later, Ambrus has rolled over onto his side so that they're facing each other, and his fingers are curled in a lax grip around Rex's right hand.

Circumstances aside, it's a nice way to wake up.

After throwing off the grog of an unplanned afternoon nap, Rex gives Ambrus a quick once-over. He's no longer sweat-soaked, but he's still too pale.

The saline bag is empty, so Rex sorts through the mess on the nightstand until he finds packaged gauze pads but no gloves. He adds extra gauze and its waxed wrapper to act as a blood barrier while pressing down on the end of the IV line to pull it free. A torn strip of surgical tape then holds the makeshift bandage in place. Rex caps the bloodied end of the IV line with its original plastic cover, removes the empty saline bag from the wall, and tosses it, capped tubing and all, into the trash bin.

Ambrus wakes up at the sound and looks baffled about no longer being tethered. "Didn't know they taught IV procedures during basic military first-aid courses." His voice is slurred again, but from just waking, not supreme exhaustion.

"Well, they updated the CLS bags in 2009 for intravenous lines, finally," Rex says while making sure blood didn't drop onto Ambrus's sheets, carpet, or nightstand. "I'm formally 18A *and* 18D certified, though, not just cross-trained." Before Ambrus can contemplate that, Rex starts tugging the man to his feet. "Come on, get up. You have an appointment."

Getting Ambrus upright is one thing. Keeping him stable is another; Ambrus staggers like he's drunk. Once inside the bathroom, however, Ambrus insists that he can piss on his own, he's been doing it since he was a toddler, thank you very much. Rex makes sure that Ambrus has a wall to brace against and leaves him to it. Then he catches Ambrus on the return trip when Ambrus loses his balance and almost face-plants into the wall.

"Good job."

"Get fucked," Ambrus retorts, and Rex grins.

Rex waits until Ambrus is in bed and asleep again before he goes to the kitchen. Fox seems twitchy, so Rex uses the overhead LED on the stove, getting enough light to search for the pile of take-out menus Ambrus claimed to have. Sleep is great, but these men need food. Jell-O doesn't count.

He finds a menu for an Asian fusion restaurant, offering the best of both worlds when it comes to soups—a gentle miso broth and an egg-drop soup. Those get written down, along with a hot-and-sour soup made right, no stupid pork crammed where it isn't supposed to be. Then he adds a hell of a lot of spring rolls, a side of boneless spare ribs, and a carton of fried chicken strips because fuck, he is starving.

Rex hesitates and walks over to the couch. Fox is lying on his stomach with his face pressed into one of the throw pillows. "Hey, are either of you Jewish?"

"Th' fuck—no," Fox mutters without lifting his head. "If you're ordering food, wontons. I'll pay for them. Just get me motherfucking wontons."

"Got it." Rex writes it exactly as Fox specified, contemplates the menu, and throws in two quarts of fried rice.

The phone call goes well until Rex mentions the delivery address. The lady taking his order makes a scoffing sound. "Your boyfriend, he no fucking cook!"

"He's not my—okay, he kind of is my boyfriend," Rex admits. He did just spend an entire afternoon sleeping in the man's bed. "*Qǐng nín bǎ wàimài sònglái.*"[1]

"Oh, you Chinese!" she gushes. Rex congratulates himself for guessing right on the Mandarin. She could have spoken Cantonese or Min —or worse, Hokkien, the Singapore Chinese Rex was supposed to learn as a kid. "*Zhènme shuō de nàme zhèngshì?*"[2]

"*Wǒ de wàipó jiùshì zhème jiāo de,*"[3] Rex says before switching back to English. "Can't break the habit."

"*Nǐ shì cóng nǎr lái a?*"[4]

Nosy woman. There can't be so few Mandarin speakers in the area that she has to try and claim him, too. "Singapore. Grew up in the States, though."

"I give you discount, not your fault you from Singapore," she says.

"Hey!" Rex blurts indignantly, but she just laughs and adds two free bottles of Sierra Mist to the order.

"Your boyfriend crazy, but he my favorite customer. Love for Ginger, Singapore!"

Rex has to give the place credit; delivery is prompt and in less than thirty minutes. The Chinese guy stares at Rex's blond hair and hazel eyes before giving Rex a baffled look.

"*Nǐ jiù shì xīnjiābō dè?*"[5] he asks in disbelief.

Rex sighs. "Just give me a receipt to sign, okay?"

Fox sits bolt upright the moment the smell of Chinese food starts wafting out of the open bag. "Oh, god, food. I love you and I will have your babies."

Rex gives him an appalled look as Fox tears through the bag on his wonton hunt. "I'm not even having *his* babies. Keep your weird mating quirks to yourself, kid."

"I'm not a kid," Fox mumbles, biting into a wonton that's still steaming. "I'm twenty, asshole."

"And I'm thirty-six. Kid." Rex grins at Fox's annoyed scowl. Yanking this man's chain looks like it's going to be a fun pastime. "Where are you from, Fox?"

"Mother's Dutch. I'm from Korea," Fox answers, and then stuffs his face with a spoonful of egg drop soup that still looks hot enough to scorch his tongue off.

---

[1] F. Mandarin: "Please send the takeout over."
[2] C. Mandarin: "Why're you speaking so formally?"
[3] F. Mandarin: "That's just how my grandmother taught it."
[4] C. Mandarin: "Where're you from?"
[5] C. Mandarin: "*You're* the one from Singapore?"

Fox doesn't give him any more than that, but Rex can infer a lot from those two sentences. Whoever Fox's father had been, he probably hadn't been the parenting type.

Rex goes to haul Ambrus out of bed. Once he's shaken off sleep fugue, Ambrus wobbles his way down the hallway to the kitchen, but at least he no longer walks like a man on the verge of alcohol poisoning.

"Hot and sour soup. Oh, I love you, Rex." Ambrus pries off the lid and drinks straight from the plastic container.

Rex tries not to be thrilled and fails miserably. Little early to hear that, and it's not meant in the romantic sense, but...

Fuck, he is in so far over his head already. Still doesn't care. "There's miso, too."

"Ugh. Seaweed soup." Fox shakes his head at the idea of miso and crams another wonton into his mouth with his fingers.

"Fuckin' Philistines," Rex tells them both, not surprised when they ignore him. At least he has some table manners, and eats tiny cuts of spare ribs with chopsticks like a civilized human being.

There aren't any leftovers. It's just as well; if Ambrus gets called away again, there would be rotten Chinese food in his fridge when he returned.

It's not a plan so much as a natural migration—Rex sleeps with Ambrus again that night, and somehow in the twists and turns of getting situated, he winds up spooning the shorter man. Ambrus isn't complaining, so Rex throws one of his arms over Ambrus's chest and pulls him in close.

"This is lovely," Ambrus whispers, sounding like he's on the verge of passing out.

"Hey, you guys said touch is a good thing," Rex reminds him, a wide smile on his face. He feels...this feels comfortable. It feels like it's something he always should have been doing.

"Sleep well," Rex offers, only to realize that Ambrus is already a slumbering, boneless lump in his arms.

*　　　*　　　*　　　*

The next morning, Fox looks spry, healthy, and way too damned energetic for 7:00 a.m. Rex fumbles at a too-small coffee pot in the kitchen, trying to make it provide caffeine. Fox is nice enough to take pity on him, finds Rex a mug, and then pours coffee that's too pale. Still coffee, it counts, do not care.

All right, he cares a little. He likes military-grade coffee, thank you very much.

Also, there is food in the fridge—bread and eggs. Fox must have gone shopping and found some godforsaken place that opens before the sun comes up.

Ambrus isn't nearly as spry or talkative, but he can walk and shower without assistance, though Rex insists on standing paranoid guard outside of the bathroom door. Fox gives him an approving look before he's distracted by a laptop that apparently needs to be glared into submission.

"You feel better?" Rex asks, when Ambrus wanders out, dressed except for the t-shirt he's pulling on over his head. Ambrus's hair is still wet enough to darken the fabric, but Ambrus doesn't seem to notice.

Rex was very good, and did not sneak glances at the man's bare skin. No. He did not.

Lies. He catalogs at least three different scars before the shirt covers everything. Two of those scars are old bullet wounds, probably .9mm. Ambrus also has freckles, and they look like fun.

"Much." For a moment there is a confused look on Ambrus's face, as if he expected differently. "Jasper!"

"I am having fucking breakfast!" Fox yells back, as if Ambrus interrupted him in the middle of painting the Mona Lisa.

Ambrus shakes his head in resignation. "I would prefer not to be the one traumatizing you, but it has to be done." He leads Rex to the only other door in the hallway, opening it to reveal a small office.

"Have a seat," Ambrus instructs absently. He's opening a filing cabinet that has a fingerprint scanner instead of a lock and key. That kind of necessary security makes Rex glad that his contracts through the DoD usually involve shooting people. Kind of like the military, except he often gets paid more for a single contract than he did per year in active service.

Rex sits down in a chair that's more comfortable than most office furniture, but he feels like he's invading someone's personal space. It's an odd sensation, especially considering that he doesn't feel that way anywhere else in Ambrus's apartment.

Ambrus pulls out a manila folder about four inches thick and brings it over to the desk. "Here we are." He drops the entire stack in front of Rex.

Rex opens his folder, unsurprised to see the cramped legalese of an NDA form sitting on top of the pile. "You keep this many of these fucking things at home?"

Ambrus's expression twitches, a wince just barely held at bay. "Uh, no. These are the forms that you need to sign for knowing that I work for the DoD, that I have a partner who does the same, that you've seen us both in desperate post-mission state and assisted with recovery without asking questions, that you know where I live, that you won't tell anyone anything about us beyond our status as DoD employees..."

"Wait—I have to sign this entire fucking *stack?*" Rex stares at Ambrus in shock. "Just for that?"

"Yes. If I told you anything else about my job, you would have to sign another mound of NDAs and possibly accept a job offer. I am begging you: don't even consider it."

There is a grim set to Ambrus's jaw that looks a bit too much like fear. "Hadn't even considered it. I already have a job," Rex says, and Ambrus seems to relax. He wants to ask what the hell Ambrus and Fox do for a living, but NDAs. He can resist that temptation, thanks.

Rex resigns himself to an hour of scribbling his signature on every single stupid NDA in the pile. "Is any of this going to cause you problems?"

"No. You know nothing else, and it will stay that way." Ambrus lowers his gaze. "The offer to get the fuck away from me still stands."

Rex snorts and shakes his head. "I'm not going to ditch you because of an NDA, Euan."

The gratitude on Ambrus's face is so intense that Rex thinks his heart might actually crack in half. There is no doubt at all that Rex isn't the only one invested in what is still not an official relationship.

So, push for it, Rex thinks, smiling. "We could always try for sushi again."

Both of Ambrus's eyebrows go up in surprise. "You're right. We could do that, couldn't we?"

"Nothing stopping us except our failure to make reservations," Rex points out.

"Jasper!" Ambrus yells again. Fox seems to be feeling more sociable, since he peers around the office door instead of yelling obscenities from the kitchen.

"What's up?" Fox asks, and then gives the pile of NDAs the disgruntled stare of someone who's already signed far too many.

"Go home," Ambrus says. "I have a date."

"You mean you—yeah, okay, I am totally gone." Fox's grin is a mile wide. "You have fun, and remember that you can't have a party without the balloons!"

"That—that saying is so fucking old!" Ambrus sputters as Fox bolts.

Rex can hear Fox laughing as he navigates the living room. "Yeah, but so are you!" Fox yells, and then the door shuts behind him.

Rex pauses in the midst of one of his signatures. "I like him," he says in a mild voice. Ambrus props his face in his hands and gives vent to exhausted giggling.

Ambrus picks up a landline phone while Rex is still signing NDAs, dialing a number from memory. "*Hai, kon'nichiwa, koreha Euan Ambrusdesu. Watashi wa Itamae Isamu to hanashimasu, onegaiitashimasu.*" There's a pause before Ambrus rolls his eyes. "*Akage no shinshi, hai[6].*"

Rex's grasp of Japanese is poor, at best. He picks up the introduction, the part about Ambrus's hair color, and that's about it, especially as the conversation becomes more animated as this Isamu gets on the phone.

Ambrus hangs up after a few minutes, grinning in triumph. "There! Reservations for eight tonight."

Rex stops what he's doing to stare at Ambrus again. "It's four in the afternoon. On a *Friday*. That is some seriously short notice, especially if this is the sushi place you talked up before."

"I know the man. He probably dumped some poor visiting celebrity from the reservation list just to get us in." Ambrus looks unapologetic, and Rex decides to enjoy the opportunity. He doesn't get to outrank a celebrity every day.

"Go take a nap," Rex suggests instead. Ambrus starts to protest and yawns right in the middle of what was already a weak argument.

After Ambrus curls up on his bed for a nap before dinner, Rex calls his father. He checks in regularly; all his siblings do. Family tradition of justified paranoia.

"Yeah?"

"Hi, Dad," Rex says, hearing his father's familiar, gruff voice. The military killed Django Whetū's phone manners, and nobody was ever able to domesticate him back to saying "Hello" like a normal person. He spent too many years in the service with a job that gave him absolutely no time to deal with bullshit. "How are you?"

"No complaints, except for fucking weeds refusing to die like they're told," Django answers. "How're you doing, Rex?"

"Uhm..." Rex swallows as he realizes that saying the words makes it real. "I think I might have a boyfriend."

His father's tone is full of mocking disbelief. "You think? Come on, Rex. You know yourself better than that."

Rex scrubs at his hair. "Yeah, I do. It's just...it's been a while."

"Your mystery relationship from 2011 into early 2012 is still the only one this decade, huh?"

"Sure is." Rex hesitates. "Did you ever—did you ever feel like you fit with someone? Like, you're lying next to them, and it's as if everything in the universe has fallen into perfect alignment?"

The pause he gets in response makes Rex bite his lip. "Yeah," Django finally says in a quiet voice. "Yeah. It was like that with me and your step-mother."

---

[6] Japanese: "Yes, hello, this is Euan Ambrus. I will speak to Chef Isamu, please." .... "That redheaded gentleman, yes."

"Wow," Rex whispers. Django and Makani's relationship was one of the best examples Rex has ever known of how to share a life with someone.

God, but Rex misses her. Makani 'Aukai Whetū was the closest thing to a mother he's ever known. (His own birth mother had *not* wanted the job.) 1999 was a long time ago, but Rex does not forgive or forget, not easily. He still has an intense hatred for inattentive semi-trailer truck drivers.

"If this plays out right, then you are a lucky son of a bitch," Django tells him in complete seriousness. "You hang on to this new boyfriend of yours, and don't let go. When do we get to interrogate the poor bastard?"

"Maybe during the holiday, after Brian and Nari come back from New Zealand and Kai is on break from school." Rex says. "Might as well let everyone have their turn at interrogation all at once, right?"

"Good plan. What does Khodî have to say about the boyfriend?"

"Dad, I know better. I'm not telling Khodî a thing about this boyfriend situation until he's meeting the boyfriend face-to-face," Rex replies, grinning.

"Smart. Hope the new boyfriend isn't another *bratva*, Rex. One was bad enough," Django says, and hangs up.

Rex lowers his cell phone and gives it a confounded look. "I don't even want to know how the hell you found out about that."

*   *   *   *

Dinner is superb, as advertised. It's the best sushi Rex has had in the entirety of the United States. The fish is as fresh as you can get without pulling it out of the ocean yourself. There is no menu, just a talkative chef who gauges his customers with jokes and teasing before he puts completed dishes in front of them.

"For you, yellowfin from the cheek," Noboru Isamu says to Rex, sliding over a fresh plate five minutes after he finished the previous one. This one has beautiful slices of yellowfin on a stack of rice layered with strips of fresh kombu. Flavors bloom across his tongue.

"Oh, my god, that is sex food," Rex declares once he's finished chewing the first slice. "You're a damned genius."

Noboru grins at him. "I see sparks between the two of you, I do what I must to encourage such flames."

"You're a troublemaker is what you are, Noboru." Ambrus lifts a piece of sashimi, using chopsticks with graceful, practiced ease—not the fumbling he and Fox demonstrated while demolishing an entire order of Chinese food.

Rex waits until Noboru is distracted by another customer at the bar. "Is he wrong?"

Ambrus glances up from his plate in surprise. Then his expression melts into one of the warmest smiles that Rex has ever seen, just touched by an amorous spark in the man's eyes.

"No. He's not wrong."

The moment the apartment door is locked behind them, Rex has Ambrus pushed up against the wall, kissing him with gentle abandon. Ambrus opens his mouth, their tongues gliding together. Rex moans at the unexpected contact, hot and slick, and Ambrus shivers against him.

Rex smiles and puts one hand on Ambrus's arm, the other on Ambrus's shoulder, pinning him in place so that he can investigate the long, freckled line of Ambrus's neck. The man gasps aloud, all but vibrating in place.

"Fetish, huh?" Rex asks, noting Ambrus's glazed, wide-eyed stare.

"Not until right that second," Ambrus replies, staring at Rex in amazement. "I normally don't—oh, wow. Bedroom, Rex. Bedroom, now, there are things, I am not doing this in the *hallway.*"

"Things, huh?" Rex feels a flush of warm, lazy amusement as they slowly make their way past the kitchen and down the hall, kissing and exploring. Hands roam under shirts; fingers dip below waistbands but venture no further. Not yet.

"Things, yes," Ambrus confirms.

Ambrus has more musculature on his frame than Rex expected to find. He'd guessed right on swimmer's form, but this is a swimmer who could probably also run five miles without a problem. There are more scars, bullet wounds, and knife scrapes, including what looks like a legit slice from broken glass. Ambrus follows his eyes and nods in confirmation to the unspoken question, which makes Rex wonder about the circumstances.

Ambrus had to be military before he was DoD. Even contractors with shit luck don't pick up this many scars unless they've walked into an explosion.

Rex has more than a few scars himself, along with his own knife scar—the thin white line that climbs the left side of his chin from jaw to cheek. Ambrus kisses that scar as his fingers trace old bullet wounds. Then he kisses each of those, too, as if in benediction.

He really hasn't done anything like this in a long time, but this chest-bursting sensation of intense excitement is reminding him.

Except...Rex has never felt like this. Not with anyone.

Ambrus nudges him. "Bedside table, in the drawer."

Rex gives Ambrus another exploratory kiss, plants a teasing peck on the end of Ambrus's nose, and goes to investigate the mysterious "things." Inside the drawer are condoms, the sealing tape on the box already sliced open. The bottle of lube isn't a cheap sort—and it's unscented, which Rex prefers. New box of nitrile gloves, which aren't as prone to tearing as latex. That's definitely the hoard of someone who believes in being prepared.

Ambrus cups Rex's face with one hand. His fingertips caress the faint bristle on Rex's cheeks like he enjoys the texture. "Approval?"

"Definitely," Rex says.

"You're not allergic to latex, are you?" Ambrus asks in a sudden rush of concern. "I forgot to ask."

Thank you gods, no, I am not. "Nope."

"Good. Cellophane *really* was not meant for sex," Ambrus says cheerfully, and Rex bursts out laughing.

*   *   *   *

Ambrus's shower is a tiled, glassed-in space with a square rain-style showerhead. It's a tight fit; they're embracing just to be able to stand under the spray of hot water. It's a situation that could easily lead to more sex, but instead it melts into intimate touching. Rex enjoys the sensation of water-slick skin under his hands as they roam Ambrus's body. Ambrus sighs into every caress, as touch-starved as Rex suspected.

The water turns Ambrus's fire-bright hair into darker red skeins that gather in loose curls on his back and shoulders. Rex touches one of those silken red strands and wonders how he ended up in this moment.

Ambrus's head rests against Rex's shoulder, and his voice emerges in a low murmur. "I know this wasn't ideal."

Rex lets his head lean back until it's pressed against the cooler tile of the shower wall. "I don't actually give a fuck about ideal. Ideal is kind of boring. You're not...I like you," he finishes lamely.

Ambrus snorts. "Ah, so verbal."

"Hey, fuck you. I'm still orgasm-stupid."

"I like you, too, Rex Vis Tjin," Ambrus says a few minutes later. "More than I should."

Rex straightens in place, feeling intuition strike. "You're scared because you can feel how well we fit together."

Ambrus lifts his head and stares at him, brows drawn together, lips parted. "Yes," he admits. "I really am."

"Don't be." Rex kisses him, a closed-mouth molding of lips, soft and gentle. "I survived two miserable damned wars, Euan Ambrus. I don't scare easily."

Ambrus cups Rex's face with his palms, looking at Rex with something akin to wonder shining in his eyes. It's a mirror reflection of the way Rex feels. "No, you really don't. Stay the night again?"

Rex smiles, a renewed flutter of that same wing-beating excitement in his breast. "I'd love to."

Chapter 3

They don't move in with each other, not at first—or at least, not officially. Rex spends a lot of his time at Ambrus's place, and belongings just sort of shift over. Neither of them really notice the difference until one day in the first week of December, Rex looks around and wonders why half of his stuff is in the wrong apartment.

It's second Friday in October when they have their third official date, hunched over a table at Maritimes while demolishing an entire bottle of Honey Bee Brandy. Francis is still a surly bastard, but he does remember being tipped well. Enough deep-fried food is sent to their table to keep them both from discovering the joys of legitimate alcohol poisoning.

Rex admits why he was in the bar on the nineteenth. He tells Ambrus about his stepmother, and the first gift she ever gave him— a cassette tape of '90s dance music, all she could afford at the time.

"How old were you?" Ambrus asks. There is sympathy in his eyes, but also remembered grief.

"Nineteen." Rex prods half-heartedly at a piece of chicken with a celery stick. "I know it's not the worst age to lose a parent, but it's still hard to let go."

"My mother died when I was sixteen," Ambrus says, and Rex glances up at him in surprise. That explains a hell of a lot about the sorrow dimming the shine in his eyes. "You're right. It's hard to let go."

Rex and Ambrus both have jobs during the third week of October. Rex is back in Bahrain (hurray) trying to get information. He tells Haervati and Llamas during his few calls out on burner phones that it would be easier to shove a live turkey up an angry cat's asshole. Neither of them are impressed by the analogy.

He finally gives up and just pretends to be investigating. Once the royal family decides that information isn't getting out, nobody is getting jack shit. He leaves when someone in their government takes a shot at him. If Uncle Sam really wants to play ball with Bahrain that badly, they can send someone else. He's done with this country.

Rex decides that their fourth date needs to be a hell of a lot less depressing. After Ambrus sleeps off whatever he was doing overseas, Rex brings Ambrus to Trenton and introduces him to Lois.

"Nice to meet you." Ambrus shakes Lois's hand while they give each other evaluating looks over Lois's doorstep. "Rex tells me that you are the purveyor of terrifying cookies."

"That boy wouldn't know a good cookie if it bit him," Lois says, beginning to smile. "What about you, English? Do you like cookies?"

Ambrus blinks a few times, an odd expression on his face. "Yes, but I'm Scottish. Or Scottish-American, I guess."

Lois takes them into her kitchen, where Rex gets mauled by the white cat and its permanent cloud of trailing white hair. Ambrus is claimed by orange-haired foolishness, who yowls while weaving around Ambrus's legs. Lois's third cat, a Siamese, glares at them all from her perch atop Lois's old olive green refrigerator.

"You figured out how to combine a ginger snap with a molasses cookie," Ambrus says, after Lois has doled out her diabetes fare. "There's usually too much of one and not enough of the other."

Lois beams at Ambrus. "Most people never notice."

"I like them. Do you share recipes?"

"Maybe on my deathbed, honey," Lois retorts, grinning, and that's enough to get Euan Ambrus into Lois's good graces, probably for life.

Ambrus's introduction to Rex's apartment becomes the reason why Rex spends most of his time in Princeton instead of Trenton. His boyfriend isn't offended by the neighborhood, which is run-down and looks rough, or the building, which is old. It's the noise that sets him off. Ambrus's hands clamp down over his ears as the entire building rumbles when the train goes by.

"Not your thing, huh?" Rex teases him, while Ambrus stares out of the living room window in bewilderment.

"How the fuck do you sleep here?" Ambrus rubs at his temples. "That was obnoxious levels of train-loud. The tracks are that close?"

"Just up the street," Rex says, pointing in the right direction. "River's that way. I can go for a swim and be in Delaware in five minutes."

"Yes, but then you would actually have to contend with being *in* Delaware." Ambrus tilts his head to look in the other direction, the view offering enough space between buildings to reveal the dark blue of the Delaware River. "Why do you live here? You take DoD contracts. I know you can afford better."

"I..." Rex has to swallow down nerves. Talking about this isn't hard with family, but Ambrus is still new. "After the war, I couldn't—the quiet made me nervous. Therapy and school helped, but by then I was used to the noise. Neighbors are great, and the rent's cheap."

"Lois is nice," Ambrus agrees. "Have any of you ever actually seen Janice?"

Ambrus met Janice by way of Rex knocking on her door as he escorted his boyfriend up the staircase. Her greetings don't vary much from obscenity-laden standard.

"Oh, she had to come outside in 2008 when the fire department evacuated the building for a possible electrical fire." Rex fights back a smile. "She was not impressed, especially when it turned out to be a false alarm."

Ambrus wanders around Rex's apartment, looking at the furniture, the art on the walls from Princeton U that Rex won't admit are his unless directly asked, running his hands along the old plaster walls. Rex follows him as Ambrus makes his way into the kitchen.

"I don't really need much, anyway," he says, trying not to feel like his living space is being evaluated. "I put most of the money away. Bank accounts, lock boxes. Rainy day money."

Ambrus nods, but he's standing in the center of the kitchen, a wistful expression on his face. "Wise idea."

"Yeah, I know the kitchen's old."

Ambrus shakes his head. "Oh, I wasn't—it's not that. This is a 1930s build."

"That's what the paperwork said, anyway." There had also been the obligatory warning about lead paint, but Rex didn't plan to lick the walls, so he didn't care.

"I grew up in a house that was built around that time," Ambrus explains. "It's nice to see something like it again."

Rex doesn't like the distant, lost look in his boyfriend's eyes. "I didn't bring you to my apartment to depress you."

"Oh?" Ambrus shakes off the past, ghosts fleeing his eyes as he smiles at Rex. "Why did you bring me here, then?"

"Christening." Rex cups Ambrus's face with both hands before kissing him. Ambrus wraps one arm around Rex's neck and melts against him, pressing their bodies together. Rex chuckles and lifts him up, seating Ambrus on the edge of the kitchen's old Formica countertop.

"Oh, you are happy to see me," Ambrus murmurs.

"At least you skipped most of the stupid joke." Rex sighs as tension melts away. He can forgive the stupid Bahrain job when it means coming home to this.

"Hey, I have a surprise for you." Ambrus leans forward to whisper in Rex's ear. "Blood work's clear. So, unless you've been doing sordid things while I'm away…"

Rex grins. "I'm only doing sordid things when you're home. Are you sure?"

Ambrus gazes at him with a wide, naughty smile on his face. "Oh, believe me, I am very, *very* sure."

"We have made an absolute mess of your kitchen," Ambrus says later. His voice is low and lazy, rich with sated pleasure. They're both lying on the floor naked, but the weather's been weird this year. It's eighty degrees outside, and Rex's apartment is almost too warm.

Rex is gazing at Ambrus. He's still entranced by the difference in their skin tones; Rex's dark brown hand gripping Ambrus's pale hand with his red-blotched skin is a dichotomy that Rex kind of likes. "It needed a good cleaning, anyway."

"Cleaning, my ass," Ambrus mutters. "This floor is so spotless you could eat off of it. The table, now—that probably needs cleaning at this point."

Rex's brow furrows in realization. "I didn't really have much else to do." Before Ambrus found him in Maritimes, he hadn't been doing anything except marking time, going from one day to the next, one job to another, because that was what he was *supposed* to do.

"Well, now you can just do me, instead," Ambrus says blithely. Rex inhales wrong, coughs, and starts laughing.

Technically, date number five happens on Halloween in Jersey City, but then Fox turns up and it becomes a not-date. At least Fox is an interesting kid, even if he absolutely refuses to take the hint and fuck off.

Rex briefly considers bodily removing Fox from the dive bar they're boxed into, but Ambrus seems happy about Fox's presence, so Rex gives up on the idea of getting laid that evening.

El Día de los Muertos fills the street outside with costumed throngs, tourists and genuine celebrators of the holiday mingling together. Rex prefers this holiday over American standards of cheap costumes and trick-or-treaters. He's been attending since 2010—at least if he's in the country at the time. He'd rather watch people enjoy an evening that has more significance than running door-to-door like cranked-up little addicts.

Also, candy skulls are delicious. He'd hoard them like Girl Scout Thin Mint cookies if there were ever enough available.

After midnight, Rex always stops by one of the local churches, which are filled with people quietly murmuring prayers. The church gathering isn't quite on par with Latin American traditions, but most of the area's Hispanic population is a hell of a long way from home. They don't have gravesites to visit. Hell, neither does he. Makani was cremated; Eric has a stone in Arlington that Rex refuses to visit because it's just a damned rock with no body underneath.

The church's lights are off, the darkness pushed back by the flames of hundreds of candles spread out across the altar, taking up every available bit of space. If Rex participates in another culture's holiday, then dammit, he does all of it, not just the fun touristy bits.

Rex lights two votive candles with a long taper: one for the friends he lost in the military, and one for Eric. His stepmother has Rex's birthday for remembrance, but *Día de los Inocentes* is for his brother, and all of the other men and women he couldn't save. It always feels like the list of names he murmurs under his breath is far too long.

He doesn't realize that the candle tradition is why Fox and Ambrus are still hanging around until Ambrus gently takes the taper from Rex's hand. He relights it from one of Rex's candles before touching it to the wick of a new votive on the next row.

"Family?" Rex asks, his voice sounding cracked and raw. He isn't crying, but it *feels* that way, grief crawling into his throat and lodging itself there.

"Usually." Ambrus shakes out the taper's flame before handing it to Fox, who seems familiar with the tradition, too. Fox lights the taper from Ambrus's candle before seeking out an unlit votive of his own.

"For my father," Fox tells Rex without being asked. He stares into the new and bright candle flame, a distant look on his face. "He didn't know that he and Mom had—he didn't know he had a kid. I was eight when I met him, and that's when he found out that Mom and I were in trouble. The moment he realized it, he told someone. The wrong someone, but..."

"High-profile murder always attracts attention," Ambrus says. Fox nods, but doesn't say anything else about his parents.

That church visit signals the end of the evening. They say goodnight and walk away in three different directions. Rex is taking the train back down to Trenton, but he's pretty sure Ambrus and Fox drove out to Jersey City in separate cars.

What has always made Rex good at his job is his ability to pick up little bits of information and then put those seemingly random pieces together. What he realizes tonight makes his stomach turn over in a sour lump.

Jasper Fox was a human trafficking victim. Jesus.

Rex doesn't ever say anything to Fox or Ambrus about it, but sometimes he catches Fox watching him, something akin to gratitude on his face.

*　　　*　　　*　　　*

The next time Rex gets a call from Llamas, he opens it with, "If you send me back to Bahrain, I will set your desk on fire without removing your chocolate stash first."

Llamas laughs at him. "You don't know where my desk is."

Rex grins as he shuts the door to his fridge, two beer bottles in one hand. "Third floor, two-one-eight." He knows she's somewhere in that area, at least.

"Son of a bitch! You win this round, Tjin. What cruel monster would do that to chocolate?"

"The kind of cruel monster who doesn't want to go back to Bahrain," Rex hands a beer to Ambrus, who is giving him a look of curiosity mixed with the utter bafflement of someone wondering what anyone would even be doing in Bahrain aside from pissing people off.

"Not Bahrain, I swear."

Rex sits down on the couch, resting his ankle across his knee. "I'm listening," he says, but cuts her off a few seconds later in disbelief. "Why in the entire name of *fuck* would I want to go Romania?"

"Don't you watch the news?" Llamas asks.

Rex scowls. "Of course I don't watch the news. I don't like torturing myself. I read the news on the internet like a civilized human being. What did I miss?"

"Prime Minister resigned," Ambrus murmurs at the same time that Llamas says, "The Romanian PM just resigned because of a nightclub fire's. We want someone on the ground assessing the political situation. Should be a smooth transition, but nobody has forgotten what it's like in Eastern Europe when the political transition *isn't* smooth."

Rex sips his beer. "You know, I miss the days when you sent me out to shoot people."

Llamas has zero sympathy. "It's your own fault for being one of our more observant contractors. Is tomorrow morning all right?"

"If it's before 6:00 a.m., the offer to set your desk on fire still stands. I have a date tonight."

"Is he hot?" Llamas asks shamelessly.

Rex glances over at Ambrus. "Are you hot?"

Ambrus raises an eyebrow, utterly deadpan: "So hot my hair is on fire."

"I heard that. I did hear that, yes? You found a ginger and didn't tell me? You're a selfish bastard, Major Tjin."

Rex is still staring at his boyfriend. "Oh, I can't fucking wait to introduce you to Khodî," he says, hoping his tone does a very good job of conveying the fact that he'd like to keep Khodî Som and Euan Ambrus on opposite sides of the continent. "Sofia Llamas, please give me a flight time and an airport. I have to deal with a troublemaker."

"Oh, those are the best kind. Newark, 10:00 a.m., on a United overseas flight. Take your ID to a kiosk and the computer will hook you up with the tickets. Enjoy the business class bed, Tjin."

"Thanks, Llamas. Have a nice night."

"You, too, Tjin. Condoms, sweetie!" she reminds him, and then hangs up before he can yell at her.

Ambrus seems amused by the exchange. "Do I need to sign an NDA about Romania?"

"Why, are you planning to visit?"

Ambrus frowns. "Fuck, and also, no."

"Then I don't give a shit," Rex says. "Beer and movie night, remember?"

"Beer, movie, and sex," Ambrus corrects him.

"Deal," Rex agrees, and they return their attention to the first *Star Wars* prequel from 1999. He'd been in the middle of SFQC, so he hadn't seen it. Ambrus skipped the prequels because of sentimental attachment to the original trilogy. Rex's father was so pissed off by the second prequel that he refuses to watch the third. Rex is not looking forward to finding out what put Django Whetū off of a movie with a Māori actor playing a character that sort-of shared his first name. Kai was still in school and living at home, so he saw it in the theatre with their dad. He is also an utter troll who won't tell Rex what went wrong—he just keeps making "Seeding the South Pacific" jokes.

The Phantom Menace destroys Rex's enjoyment of the film when they kill off the two most interesting characters outside of Amidala, or Padme, or whatever her name actually is.

The sex makes up for it. Hell, the sex is great enough that Janice pounds on her ceiling, yelling at them to stop making out like howler monkeys. Rex ends up lying on his stomach, giggling into his pillow while Ambrus stretches out beside him, sulking.

"Howler monkey." Ambrus is indignant. "I do not sound like a *howler monkey.* Do I?"

Rex shakes his head, still laughing. "No. I don't think they make incredibly sexy noises. Janice is just jealous."

"You should have warned me that you had paper-thin floors," Ambrus grumbles.

"I didn't actually know that my bedroom was above hers," Rex replies. "Heh. Howler monkeys."

"Please, you are actually starting to hurt my considerable ego." Ambrus rolls over and begins tracing patterns on Rex's back. "You know, until I saw this, I didn't realize you were Māori as well as Chinese."

"Half-and-half," Rex says, trying not to squirm when Ambrus hits a ticklish spot. "Well, mostly. My birth mother's family is from mainland China, and my grandmother was a huge proponent of Chairman Mao even after they moved to Singapore. My dad's family is Māori."

Ambrus runs his fingers through Rex's hair, which is on the verge of curling again. "I know there's blond hair in the South Pacific, but this doesn't quite fit the profile."

"European grandparent and genetic quirks." Rex sighs into the caress. One of Ambrus's hands is still petting his hair, and the other has gone back to following the lines of his tattoo, which is centered along his spine and stretches from his shoulder blades down to the waistline of his jeans.

"Hence those beautiful hazel eyes of yours," Ambrus's voice is full of warm affection. "When did you get the *moko* done?"

"I left the service in 2005, but I didn't get it done until the summer of 2006." Rex turns his head to one side so he can look at Ambrus, who is studying the tattoo on his back the same way he studies books or the government files that Rex pointedly doesn't look at. "Khodî had just gotten out that spring. He wanted to see our family and have the *moko* done properly, I guess. At that point, we'd both earned the right to wear it."

"Combat rights, and...Moana is in here, yes? One of the family names?" Ambrus asks.

Rex nods. "If you can figure out the rest, I'll definitely make it worth your while."

Ambrus grins. "You're on. There's a serpent here, and one of the guardian spirits watching over it. The serpent's done with *pakati* patterning, and the guardian spirit is filled in with *unaunahi.*"

"You are a walking fucking encyclopedia," Rex says, impressed. "What's the point of a guardian spirit watching over a serpent?"

Ambrus lifts one eyebrow and gives him a smug look. "Your *taniwha* doesn't have *pūkana* —so it's being subtle, lying in wait. Combine that with the *pakati*, and someone is commenting on your ability to be a sneaky bastard. The *manaia* watches over the *taniwha* to ensure that it behaves itself, and the *unaunahi* gives it strength. The *koru* twirls bound with whale teeth tie them together. This must have taken hours, Rex."

"Try days." Rex sighs again when fingernails start sliding along the patterns. He really wants to know who taught Ambrus so much about Māori symbology. "Even though we're not doing it by carving anymore, it's still a lot of work."

"Six stars at six points." Ambrus brow furrows. "The compass?"

Rex nods. *"Raki, Matariki, Whitinga, Tonga, Atutahi,* and *Tomokanga.* For those who don't want to lose their way."

"You knew you were staying with the DoD," Ambrus guesses. "Or at least, you were definitely considering it."

"Sort of. Figured if I did decide to go back, I could use the extra moral shove, y'know?" Rex rolls over and runs his hand down Ambrus's bare leg.

"Did I win a prize?" Ambrus asks, starting to smile.

"Maybe more than one," Rex says, and settles in to drive his boyfriend back to shouting again.

Janice pounds on the ceiling some more. Rex ignores it; he has way better things to do with his mouth than respond to her howler monkey bullshit.

Rex leaves Ambrus sleeping in a happy, exhausted heap in his bed and locks the apartment door on his way out. That was definitely not the worst way to spend the night before heading out on a job.

*　　　*　　　*　　　*

Romania is restless, but Rex doesn't think they're going to see a war out of it. The president of the country is lining up elections as scheduled, and there are people on the docket that the kids roaming the streets seem to like.

In short, Romania is boring as hell. Thanks a lot, Llamas.

*   *   *   *

They've hit the end of November when Rex dares to voice the idea. "So, uh, winter holiday—you doing anything?"

"Not particularly. I usually spend a few days with Jasper and his mother if we're not working, but they have another invitation this year that I don't want to intrude upon. Why?" Ambrus asks.

"I, uh—I have family," Rex begins, trying not to be nervous. Introducing boyfriends to family lost him his first two boyfriends. Granted, that meant they were spineless fucks, but still. "The winter holiday is pretty much the only time during the year that we can all figure out how to be in one place. I'd like to introduce you. To them. If you want."

Ambrus is bemused by Rex's hesitation. "Is this where I sing about the Inquisition?"

Rex winces. "Maybe?"

"Oh, now I'm intrigued." Ambrus grins and takes Rex's hand. His fingers are cold, but Ambrus hates wearing gloves unless the weather drops into the Arctic glacier range. "Sure. It sounds like fun, Rex."

Rex lets out the breath he's been holding. "Fun. Okay. Awesome. I usually head out on the twenty-fourth or the twenty-fifth for about a week, if I can get away with it."

"Fabulous. I'll block that off on the calendar at work. Nobody fucks with my vacation days unless there is a potential apocalypse in the making."

On the thirteenth of December, the apocalypse rears its ugly damned head. Or something does, anyway. When Ambrus comes slamming into the apartment, Rex knows at once that his boyfriend is beyond pissed.

"What is it?" he asks, tossing his Kindle onto the coffee table. Terry Pratchett was a grand author, and Neil Gaiman is one of his father's favorites, but this sounds far more important than reading *Good Omens* for the fifth time.

"Holiday plans are fucking blown." Ambrus's glower could set entire nations on fire as he rounds the corner. New Jersey is on crack this month; it's hot and humid outside instead of cold and spitting snow, so Ambrus's hair is a curling, wind-blown mess.

"Job?" Rex asks in a neutral voice, biting back a hell of a lot of swearing. Ambrus looks disappointed enough for both of them, but Rex's siblings *and* his father have been riding Rex's ass about meeting The Boyfriend. The grilling has gotten so bad that Rex doesn't dare tell any of them his boyfriend's name. They'd hunt Ambrus down just to satiate their own rabid curiosity.

49

"Fucking cock-up of a job that I'm going to kill someone over," Ambrus snarls, and then tries for a smile. Rex's boyfriend can be mercurial, but there's still a lot of murder lurking in his eyes when he asks, "How do you feel about signing another stack of NDAs?"

"Depends on the reason," Rex ventures. Ambrus is worth it, and Fox is a neat kid, but Ambrus told him that there wouldn't be any more NDAs to sign unless Rex tried to join up.

Some of the anger fades from Ambrus's eyes, and his smile seems more genuine. "Jasper wants to introduce you to someone."

Rex can read that tone. "Wait, Fox found someone desperate enough to date him?" There is an immediate, indignant shout of, "HEY!" from the hallway. Rex grins. "Sure, bring them in. Let's meet the newest addition to your crazy family."

"New addition? Not so much," Ambrus says. Rex resigns himself back to "cryptic shit" for a while as Fox and a shorter woman enter the living room. "I introduced them, so it's my own damned fault."

Fox's companion pulls off her hat, which kept her long brown hair from ending up in the same condition as Ambrus's tangled mess. "Hi!" she says in a bright, friendly voice, looking up at Rex with eyes the color of dark blue velvet. "You must be Major Chin."

Rex ignores the mispronunciation of his name, knowing it means that Fox didn't coach her. Asshole left himself open for immediate revenge, though.

"That's me," Rex agrees before glancing at Fox. "Did you drug her? Hypnotize her?"

"Tjin, you're an asshole," Fox grumbles. "I was nothing more than my charming, adorable self."

When Fox turns away to put his girlfriend's shoes and hat in the hallway closet, she mouths, "Awkward, stuttering, adorkable self," at Rex, who is hard-pressed to keep a straight face when Fox comes back.

"And you are?" Rex asks, hoping someone will finally tell him the girlfriend's name. She probably works in Ambrus and Fox's department, which explains the fresh stack of NDAs.

"I'm Ziba Banner." Rex shakes the hand she holds out. More pistol calluses, something Rex can recognize at the merest touch. Almost everyone in his social circle spends a lot of time with guns. Banner has a girlish smile that's just shy of impish, and appears to be in her early twenties, but her eyes are older.

Rex is a bit unnerved by that. His father's eyes have that similar shine of age that doesn't quite fit.

Fuck. Come to think of it, Ambrus's eyes are the same way.

"Ziba's a Persian name, yeah?" Rex asks, trying to find a safe subject in the midst of having a lot of uncomfortable realizations at once. Banner looks like she could be white, but Rex is walking blond proof that all it takes is one set of genetics in the mix to screw up an entire racial heritage.

Banner's smile eases down into something that feels a lot more genuine. "Yes! Most people assume Israeli."

"No, that's usually Ziva. Banner is what's throwing me," Rex says.

"Banner is the result of my grandfather's trip through Ellis Island." Banner rolls her eyes. "He said that the clerk who processed the family through was an illiterate goat, so part of our family name is missing. It's supposed to be Bannerjee."

"Family had kids late, huh?" Rex asks, using curiosity as a mask.

"Pretty much." There is only a slight flicker in Banner's eyes to tell Rex that while Banner isn't lying, it isn't quite the entire truth, either. "My grandfather married a white American woman, and my father married another white American, and now I'm only one-quarter my original heritage, anyway. What about you, Major? Chins can be found across the entirety of Asia, but I don't see many blond ones without a hell of a lot of bleach involved."

"Not Chin. Tjin," Rex corrects, emphasizing the slight change in pronunciation that most Western ears never hear. "*Cheyhn* with a silent J sound lurking in the middle. Singapore variant."

"Neat!" Banner repeats the proper pronunciation of Rex's name until she has it right. "Now—you promised me food, Euan. We have swapped boyfriend meetings, and now you have to feed me!"

Ambrus gives Fox a pointed glance. Fox sighs and trudges towards the hallway beyond the kitchen. "I'll go get the stack of bullshit."

"He means paperwork," Banner interprets, and then spies Rex's Kindle. "Oh! I've thought about getting one of these, but I keep talking myself out of it because I have books. Can I play with it?"

"Sure." Now Rex gets why Banner and Fox hooked up—they both like shiny electronic toys. Rex had to buy another damned Kindle just to get Fox to leave his alone. He also blames Fox about the necessity of upgrading to the newest model. Rex saves his place in *Good Omens* and hands it over, showing Banner basic Kindle navigation, along with the joy that is a good tablet connected to reliable Wi-Fi.

Fox brings him another folder of NDAs. "Sorry," he apologizes, putting the stack down on the coffee table. "It's stupid, but most of the others claim that paranoia's saved their lives so many times that it's just good sense."

"That's okay," Rex assures him, snagging a pen and turning to the first page. "I still do not want to fuckin' know about your job."

"I'm sold. I'm buying one," Banner proclaims of the Kindle, just as Ambrus announces, "Food!"

Food turns out to be pizza from a joint close to campus. Fox, Banner, and Ambrus demolish a pie like they haven't eaten in days, while Rex watches in amused silence. He only has to slap Fox's hand once to keep him away from the slices Rex has claimed. Dammit, he gets to eat, too, no matter what shit they've gotten up to today. It can't have been too bad, and Rex hasn't witnessed anything like that epic second date...but he's starting to have suspicions about who the trio work for.

Dad is probably going to kill me, Rex thinks, but he can't see himself walking away. He knows that Ambrus and Fox are good people. His intuition is never wrong, not about that. Fox cheats at video games like nobody's fucking business, but he's the first to smile, the first to laugh, and often has the brightest, most unclouded eyes in the room. The kid's seen combat—Rex knows those types on instinct, too—but Fox hasn't let it weigh him down.

Ambrus's temper can be vociferous, if he lets it slip, but Rex has never seen him direct it at the undeserving. The man is kind even when he doesn't have to be, polite in the face of supreme irritation, with a god-awful sense of humor that's salvaged into awesomeness because of his damned sense of timing.

Every word Ambrus has ever spoken to Rex has been true, and meant with every fiber of his being. He does nothing by halves.

Also: sex. Rex is not ignoring that aspect.

Banner feels like good people, too. She seems pushy, but that's the unfortunate side effect of being a woman in the U.S. military, dealing with manly bullshit all the time. His sister is the same way.

Rex realizes that Ambrus is determined to make a nice evening out of the apocalyptical cock-up. He pointedly avoids discussing whatever has blown their holiday plans to smithereens, and Fox brought an entire pile of older model PlayStations over. The four of them spend the entire night playing through all of the *Silent Hill* games, scaring the shit out of each other. When it's 4:00 a.m. and they're still keyed up, Rex finds the first movie for the franchise on Netflix and queues it up.

That is a terrible idea. The movie actually manages to be *worse than the fucking video games*.

Banner is curled in close to Fox. She buries her face against his shoulder for an immolation scene that Rex unabashedly covers his eyes for. Nope, been there, done that, bled through the t-shirt, no fucking thank you. Oh, two immolation scenes for the price of one! That does not help anything, ever.

"Well, I did not need to see that," Ambrus says in a faint voice. Fox doesn't seem to have shied away from any of it, but his jaw is still hanging open in bewildered horror.

The sequel is far less traumatizing. The sun is already bright in the sky when the credits roll, but Rex is happy about the fact that he didn't need to hide from the fucking television at any point during the movie. It's Ambrus who did that, leaping behind the couch and refusing to come out until the mannequin-spider-thing is over with. Rex *really* does not want to know what prompted that reaction.

Rex's jaw pops as he yawns. He doesn't feel his age most of the time, but he hasn't done anything like this in years that wasn't combat-related. Even Fox looks peaked.

He turns off the television before he asks, "Now that we're all adrenaline-cranked and punch-drunk, does anyone wanna tell me why we stayed up all night and halfway through the next morning?"

Ambrus sighs. "The three of us have to get on an airplane in a little over two hours. We'll be gone for...fuck." He rakes his hand through his hair, shoving long ginger strands back behind his ear. "I have no idea, Rex."

"I'm estimating about a month." Banner rests her chin on her clasped hands. "I was really looking forward to being home with my family. Nothing beats the yearly tradition of American Christmas blended into Deva-Diwali."

"How the hell does that work?" Rex asks.

Banner thinks about it. "It's kind of like Hanukah, but with a lot more gods, bloodshed, astrology, and astronomy involved. The candles are pretty, though."

"And this is the year that Ziba finally convinced my mother to try out the, uh, difference in tradition," Fox says. "She's Dutch, the American holiday's commercialism kind of freaks her out, and I grew up surrounded by people celebrating Korean or Russian holidays depending on how drunk they were. We don't really do stuff for Christmas, not once we got past Sinterklaas. It's too weird."

Banner grins. "*Krampusnacht.*"

Fox scowls. "He's not fucking Dutch!"

Rex says goodbye to Ambrus in his bedroom, sharing a thorough kiss that leaves him breathless. "Come back in one piece, yeah?" he suggests, gently untangling his fingers from Ambrus's long hair.

Ambrus smiles. "That's the plan." He touches Rex's lips with his fingertips. "I'm finding that I have a very important reason to come back—wait, that reminds me." Ambrus goes over to his bureau and returns with a silver key, holding it out to Rex.

"The apartment?" Rex asks as he takes the key, a nervous hollow pit in his stomach. This is a hell of a lot more significant than turning up when Ambrus is home.

"Yeah, I uh..." Ambrus shoves his hands into his pockets, looking sheepish. "I mean, it's—I know you're going out to see your family for the holiday, but I, uh..." He swallows. "I want you to know that you're welcome here. Any time you like. Whether I'm here or not."

Rex's stomach swaps over from hollow pit to solid pretzel knot. "My apartment," he blurts, because he has no idea what else to do. "Around the backside of the building, there's a brick about seven feet off the ground with a smear of green paint on it. It's loose—there's a spare key to my apartment behind it. If you need…I know you hate the place, but if you get out of the airport in Trenton and that's the farthest you can't—"

Ambrus interrupts him with another kiss. Rex sucks in a deep breath through his nose, surprised, and then laps at Ambrus's lips with his tongue. The result is a blissful sigh, not quite a moan.

"Dammit. They will never let me live it down if I miss this plane." Ambrus pulls back and smiles at Rex. "I'll see you soon."

Rex grips Ambrus's hand, forcing a smile onto his face. "You'd better," he says, even though he's suddenly consumed by the terrible feeling that he'll never see this man again.

*   *   *   *

As anticipated, Rex gets so much shit from his family for showing up on Christmas Day without The Boyfriend. "Did you manage to get dumped already?" Khodî asks, a merciless grin on his face.

"Fuck you, Khodî," Rex replies genially. It's Christmas. You don't strangle siblings on Christmas. "He had to work. Fucking DoD."

"Military schedules aren't," his father agrees, hugging Rex. Then he joins everyone else in mocking him, but Rex expects nothing less.

Home is a weathered clapboard Pennsylvania farmhouse built by Rex's great-grandparents on the Norwegian side. The house is supposed to be white, but the paint never lasts more than a season before fading to a silvery gray. Their father gave up on the insanity of painting a house over and over again, like they were going to get different results, and claims the boards are so old they're probably petrified, anyway.

The second floor was added on by Rex's grandparents, a slew of upstairs bedrooms built in hopeful expectation of filling them with children. Instead, there had just been two: Django and his younger sister, Kaia. His grandparents and aunt are long dead; Rex's father was the only one of the two siblings to have kids. Rex's grandparents got what they wanted—a generation too late.

Django passed on his mother's Māori black hair, dark eyes, and South Pacific skin to seven of eight kids. Rex has the same dark brown skin, but he's also the one who had to go and ruin the lineup by being born with their grandfather's Norwegian blond hair and hazel eyes.

Somehow, the house had fit all eight of them—nine when his stepmother joined the menagerie—without bursting at the seams. It's one of those weird houses Rex finds on occasion that always seems to be just the right size, even when it fucking well *shouldn't* be, crammed with warm bodies and flying elbows and harsh language.

Their late afternoon dinner is excellent. Rex's father was cooking for himself long before the kids came along to turn things into a clusterfuck, and he can make a turkey turn out like a gourmet bird.

Django sits at the head of the table, less tradition and more about the fact that it's the chair that directly faces the kitchen door. The rest of them jockeyed for position over the years before finally settling into specific chairs along the sides. Makani got the opposite end of the table by default.

Her chair isn't empty, at least. It's been claimed by Neumia Anari, Brian's eight-year-old daughter, who is busy trying to make mashed potato and turkey Tetris structures out of her food instead of eating it. She has her father's golden brown skin, but her mother's bright blonde hair. Then she ruined it by deciding that she needed to dye her hair dark green, and Rex went back to being the only blond. Traitor.

There is another empty chair that nobody's ever been able to remove from the table, even though their father never gets enough houseguests to need it. Brian is the only one of them that's accidentally managed to procreate, so there aren't any other kids to put there. Sometimes Neumia's mother uses the empty chair if they've managed to cajole or bribe her into visiting, but that's not often. Bonika de Lacy of Los Angeles is not impressed with Kutztown, Pennsylvania.

The problem right now is that the chair next to Eric's old spot is *also* empty.

"All right, I give," Rex says at last. "Where the hell is Ella?"

"Nari, please eat your food instead of building with it," Brian says before he glances at Rex. "The last time I got Ella to answer her cell phone, she said she was out of the country on an unplanned excursion. Then she said, 'Fuck off and Merry Christmas' and hung up on me. I'm assuming she meant that last part for all of us."

"Out of the country on an unplanned excursion," Rex repeats, thinking of his own recent, boring trips overseas. He really doubts that the Department of Defense is desperate enough to hire his sister for any job ever again, so this is probably Ella-levels of shenanigans.

God, he misses his brother for many reasons, but Ella is definitely one of them. Eric could at least keep Ella...managed. On her own, there is no "Getting in over her head." Ella ties a rope around her ankle, attaches the other end to a rock, drops the rock into the ocean, and follows it down while giggling the entire way.

"Do any of us ever want to know what she means?" Rex asks. There is a simultaneous, shouted, "NO!" from almost everyone at the dinner table, even Neumia, who smashes a potato block on accident when she tries to wave her fork in agreement.

Wesley's the one who doesn't yell. He lifts an eyebrow, grinning. "Ten-to-one odds that whatever she's doing, the police are involved."

Rex rolls his eyes. "Please, I'm not taking a sucker bet."

"I'll take the bet," Kai says, surprising them, "but only if you'll agree to my twenty-to-one odds that she didn't get caught."

Wesley thinks about it for a moment before lifting his hands in surrender. "Nope, I'm out."

Django sighs, his mouth twisted to the side in a way that means he's trying not to smile. "Thank you for not betting on whether or not your sister pissed off a police force."

"Way more fun to bet on what the escape vehicle was, anyway," Khodî adds thoughtfully.

"No," Django orders, but his mouth is still twitching.

There is a rule for presents: every adult receives only one thing, and the siblings trade names every year as to who's getting what for whom. Rex is easy to buy for; he always winds up with a gift card for Amazon.com, and his Kindle gets two more SD cards full of eBooks. He hasn't needed to set foot into a pathetic airport bookstore in years.

Neumia, being the only available kidlet, gets one thing from all of them, and revels in her haul. "Thanks for the chart, Grandpa!" she says in delight.

Brian sighs in resignation. "A practical guide to human pressure points and how to manipulate them. Thanks, Dad."

Rex bites back a grin. Last year it was arterial weak points. Their father is extremely practical. Neumia's been taking self-defense classes since she was old enough to walk around without falling down every few feet. It's one of the things that makes Neumia's mother tolerable. Bonika didn't just agree to the lessons—she pays for them, along with anything else Django suggests might be useful for Neumia's physical education.

"Hey, you never know when she might need it," Django replies.

"Yes, but she practices on *me*," Brian complains.

Django smiles like a happy shark. "Then you'd better learn how to avoid those tiny fingers."

The entire family conspires together in what to get their father, which often ends up being weaponry. This year is no exception.

Django disables the small pistol by pulling back the slide before he sights down the barrel at an old stain. No one has ever managed to get that Ella-created smear of paint off the living room rug, but it's good to use as a relatively safe ground-point target.

"She is damned pretty," Django says of the Glock 43, a single-stack .9mm that holds six rounds and weighs in at a whopping twenty ounces fully loaded. Rex wants one in the worst way, but he doesn't *need* one.

Khodî grins. "She's a lightweight fucker, too. Paintball pistols are heavier."

The weather is still utterly out of whack, so there's no snow on the ground as they filter outside. Sixty degrees is too damned warm for Christmas Day, but it does mean that no one has to shovel a path to the farm's gun range. It's an old earthen berm that the family keeps shored up properly for safety, and the firing lines are clearly visible against the dead grass.

They take turns breaking in the lightweight little pistol, which becomes a competition between Rex and Khodî over who can make the most headshots in a row without veering off-target. Rex wins and tells Khodî that he's out of practice. Khodî tells him to go get fucked; he is a county sheriff and headshots are frowned upon when dealing with drunks and lost cattle.

Django has to go and ruin the argument by heading out about one hundred yards past the three-hundred yard line before putting six shots through the target's head in the exact same place. "You're both out of practice," he says, pulling the slide back. "Fuckin' amateurs."

"I hate you all," Wesley announces, pulling his earplug collar and letting the plastic rest around his neck. His turn with the gun had resulted in a lot of flying dirt from bullets striking the berm instead of a paper target. Give the man a rifle, though, and you get some damned good results. Wesley is the one who took Khodî's place as champion for long-distance shots when he grew up. He'd treated a football the same way, and still holds a record with his former team for launching a ball that had landed in a teammate's hands in the end zone—a touchdown from eighty yards across the field.

"Not bad for a linebacker," Wesley said to the press, and that was the quip that followed him for the rest of his career.

"She is a nice tiny beast," Neumia announces after taking her fingers out of her ears. "Can I try her?"

Django ruffles Neumia's collection of green braids. "Handling them is one thing, kiddo, but you're still a bit too small for firing one. Even that tiny little beast kicks. A rifle, though..."

Brian rubs at his goatee as he stares down at his daughter, who is eying the 43 like it's the best thing ever. She understands firearms safety, but Rex also understands her point of view: shiny is *shiny.*

"Fuck," Brian mutters, sounding like a man who has given up. "Whatever you buy her, I approve it first," he says. Their father just nods, as if he expected exactly that.

"Give me the tiny beast," Kai says, and Django hands it over after Kai shoves his hearing protection back into place. He's another family member with a different preference—in his case, shotguns that put very large holes in things with a single blast. Kai 'Aukai is a big fan of overkill.

For a medical student in his last year and thus potentially out of practice, Kai is still damned accurate with a pistol. Six torso shots are still six bullet holes that are probably making someone very fucking dead.

None of them name their weapons very often. You never know when you're going to have to ditch one, but Tiny Beast ends up being the 43's name by default. General family agreement is that the new 43 is awesome, and Rex has resolved that he'll make up an excuse to buy his own. Fuck it. It's not like he doesn't have the money.

".22?" Brian asks, glancing at their father.

"They make them child-size and lightweight for beginners," Django answers. "Hell, they make the fucking things in *pink*."

Neumia scowls. "I don't want pink. I want green!"

"That's my girl," Brian says with a grin, proud that his daughter still favors his old team colors over anything else.

*   *   *   *

Rex gets back to Trenton early on the second of January, and wishes Lois and Juan a Happy New Year when they greet him from the other door. He left them presents before heading out to the farm. In return, he comes home to a tin of dangerous diabetic cookies from Lois and an extremely nice wooden carving of an *El Día De Los Muertos* skull from Juan.

"You guys know me too well," Rex says, grinning. The skull is definitely Juan's woodwork. He has serious carving skills, even if the kid is still half-convinced that he doesn't. "Thanks."

"You share those with Euan," Lois orders him sternly.

Rex's good mood falters. "I'd love to, but he's out on a job. Not sure when he's getting back."

"Put a piece of waxed paper over the cookies in the tin, stick them in the freezer. They'll keep just fine, baby," Lois says. "Works on berries, too."

"Genius," Rex replies, and goes into his side of the building. "Happy New Year, Janice!"

"I didn't get you shit!" Janice yells through her closed door.

Rex just smiles. "I didn't get you a present, Janice. What the hell would you even do with it?"

"KINDLING!"

Rex grins as he heads upstairs. He has no idea what makes him like Janice, who does her absolute best to be the most unlikeable person on the planet.

Nothing happened in his absence, except a dish on the counter sprouted new life because Rex forgot to wash it before he left for Ambrus's apartment in December. He cleans the dish, puts it away, flops down on the couch, and stares at the blank TV screen.

Honestly, every time Rex comes home, he's glad the building is still standing. It's an old duplex, and it wouldn't surprise him if faulty wiring finally lit a real spark that gutted the place. He keeps a few valuable items, mostly paperwork like his birth certificate and immigration information, in a fireproof safe. Those same documents for himself, his family, and all the family photos are digitally stored on encrypted tiny flash drives he keeps on his keyring. There's a backup of all of his official documents in one Cloud account; the photos are stored on another. Rex doesn't trust Cloud security, but he didn't register the accounts under his real name, either. They're just backups of backups.

His father might be paranoid, but crap happened to them in 1991 that did a very good job of proving to Rex that sometimes they really *are* out to get you. Rex was twelve years old the first time someone shot at him. That was also the first time Rex fired on another human being, happy and willing to kill the shit out of whoever was trying to make his family dead.

Special Forces just seemed like a logical choice after that. Rex and Khodî followed in their father's insane footsteps; Ella and Eric went Range. Brian and Wesley decided that the four of them were all nuts during childhood and chose careers in pro ball. Kai's mother, who'd specialized in large animal veterinary medicine, but Kai went the people route, claiming that Rex's 18D specialization convinced him it was a good idea.

Their eldest sibling stayed overseas, raised by his Thai mother instead of Django. Xāwuṯh is a little bit off-kilter and doesn't fit in well in the United States, anyway. Django says Xāwuṯh took after their great-aunt Tahiri, a woman with itchy feet and no concept of settling down. Tahiri once had her canoe; Rex's brother has his boat and a nickname based on the fact that Westerners mispronounce his name as Beowulf, every fucking time.

Khodî, Ella, and Eric are Cambodian. Khodî looks like their dad; Ella is like a younger, more narrow-faced version of their mother, Chanthavy. Eric only looked like himself until you stood him next to Ella, where it became very obvious that they were twins. Brian and Wesley are the offspring of two different Māori women; Kai was Makani's only son.

His siblings' mothers are varying levels of kind and snarky. Much like the blond hair lottery, Rex had the great misfortune of being born to a semi-decent Chinese woman with an absolutely batshit mother. Rex does his best not to think about his early childhood, living in his grandmother's house in Singapore. They aren't happy memories, and it always makes his head hurt to try and recall toddlerhood, anyway.

Rex blinks a few times, realizing he zoned out and is still staring at a television that's not showing him anything but a black screen. He feels restless in a way he hasn't experienced since getting out of the service in 2005. He needs to *do* something, and right now all he has are movies he's not interested in watching and books he's not interested in reading.

He holds out for another hour before giving up and calling in. "I need a short contract and something to fucking shoot at."

Rex gets Llamas instead of Haervati, which means the latter is still on vacation. "Hi, Rex. It's nice to hear from you. How was your holiday?"

"Hi, Sofia," Rex replies, sensing that he's not getting anywhere until he remembers that manners are still necessary, no matter how damned twitchy he's feeling. "My holiday was fine. We ate food, exchanged gifts, shot at things, and nobody got arrested." No one has heard about Ella being incarcerated anywhere, so he's probably not lying. "How about yours? Did you get arrested?"

He meant it as a joke, but he can all but hear Llamas wincing. "Nooooo," she draws out, "but my idiot brother did."

Rex grins. "Congratulations; you owe me money. I told you he'd manage to get nailed again before the year was over with."

Llamas coughs out something rude. "You said you wanted a short-term contract that involved shooting things?"

"Yeah." Rex rests his head against the back of his couch. "I would really prefer that they're people who deserve to be shot at."

"You're in luck. We just got line on an ISIS cell establishing itself on the border of Turkmenistan and Iran."

Rex lifts his head, scowling. It's always fucking ISIS lately, but he likes shooting terrorists, and these particular fucks are nothing but trouble. The American Press has jumped on the ISIS IS EVIL bandwagon like it's going out of style, and they have a bad habit of conflating those pricks with Islam. It's giving some of Rex's Muslim friends from the service a bad name. Getting rid of ISIS assholes helps balance the stupid scales.

"That's a disaster waiting to happen, Llamas. Things in that area are fucked up enough. They don't need it to get worse, especially after this last year."

"That's why we need to get in there and get rid of that new cell before they have the locals coerced into believing that life under terrorist rule is the best thing ever," Llamas says in a sour voice. "Do you want a team, or do you want to handle this solo?"

Rex taps his fingers on his thigh, thinking. "Do we have intel on the size of the cell?"

"Nothing solid," Llamas answers. "We think twenty, but it could be as many as fifty, Major."

Those are numbers he can handle. "Llamas, you get someone to meet me on the ground in Ashgabat with all of the shiny weaponry they have available, and I won't need a damned team. Get me a flight, a gun, and some damned stress relief."

"Bad day?" Llamas asks in surprise.

"No, it's just—boyfriend is DoD, different department, and he's off doing fuck knows what for another few weeks."

"Understood," Llamas says with genuine sympathy. She and her girlfriend often deal with the same bullshit runaround. Military life doesn't really make dating easy. "You head out to Newark, and there will be a flight waiting for you at fourteen hundred hours. Show your ID at the kiosk to get your tickets. I would advise traveling light."

Rex smiles in relief as that damned sense of restlessness begins to fade away. "Thanks, Llamas. You're the best."

"Flattery means nothing to me. Send me more chocolate, Tjin."

"Yes, ma'am," Rex says, and disconnects the call. He has packing to do.

अश्लेषा

Chapter 4

Rex flies into Ashgabat International at 21:30 EST, only about a half-hour behind schedule. It's 06:30 local time on the third of January, with the sun just starting to break the horizon line.

He easily finds a cab with its mandatory government escort riding shotgun, but Rex isn't going wandering, he's going straight to his hotel, intent on a nap. Even with business class flights and chairs that turn into decent beds, Rex does *not* sleep on planes without some serious alcoholic intervention. Seven hours' flight time is too short for that when he's on a job.

The hotel is a decent one, definitely designed with tourists in mind. The concierge manning the desk has a Western-style haircut with a crisp white dress shirt and trousers, but he's wearing the traditional open-front red robe of the Turkmen. "Good morning."

"Good morning; *As-Salâm Alaikum*,"[1] Rex says, and hopes he's stumbled across someone who understands one of the few languages in the region that Rex actually knows. He spent way too much fucking time in the Middle East back in the day. Proper manners stick with you when everyone is armed and twitchy.

He gets a beaming smile from the concierge. "*Assalamu Alaikom warahmatu Allahi wa barakatuhu*,[2]" he replies.

"I'm checking in under the name Tjin." Rex gets out his wallet and pulling out his ID to give to the concierge, his brain chanting, *Right hand, right hand, right hand,* at him. He's normally ambidextrous, but that isn't exactly kosher over here.

Oh, man. He's got a friend in Israel who would stab him for making that joke.

"I am Yusup Nýazow, morning manager for our establishment," Nýazow says, and then looks at Rex's U.S.-issued driver's license. "Ah, yes, the spelling. That makes things so much simpler. I would not have thought to check for your name under T."

Rex smiles. "Nobody does, but I'm used to that."

He receives his identification back, along with an honest-to-god *key* with his room number engraved on it. It's a nice bit of nostalgia, and it's not like card-based hotel room locks are more secure than a key, anyway.

"Would you like to be seen to your room, or would you prefer breakfast?" Nýazow asks, and then smiles. "I am assuming that I will not hear complaints from you about our lack of bacon."

"Not a word," Rex promises. "Breakfast sounds great. Just point me in the correct direction."

---

[1] Arabic: "God's peace be upon you."
[2] Arabic: "...peace be upon you and God's mercy and blessings."

"*Alhamd li'Llâh,*"[3] Nýazow mutters under his breath. "You will find the dining area in that direction," he instructs, pointing at a room to Rex's right that has a brilliant shaft of sunlight illuminating the floor in front of the open doorway. "Do you have bags that need to be taken to your room first?"

"No, I only have what's on my back," Rex says, tilting his head to indicate his backpack. "*Mushkoor.*[4]"

Nýazow tilts his head, another genuine smile on his face. "*Aafwaan,*[5] and please let me know if you require anything during your stay."

"I will," Rex replies, and heads directly for food. There are three different breakfast choices based on religious preferences—no pork on any of them—and to his surprise, they included Israeli.

Maybe they get a lot of Jewish tourists, Rex thinks, and orders from that menu. It's been a long time since he's had that sort of meal without it being affected by the differences in available American cuisine.

Afterwards, Rex goes up to the third floor, finds his room, and checks out the stylized finish that was modern ritz in the '80s. He shoves a chair up under the doorknob as an extra security measure and searches the room for monitoring devices. He doesn't find any, which is almost disappointing. Either this hotel is high-end enough that they prefer their guests not to be paranoid, or someone in this friendly local police state is not doing their job.

He takes a nap in a bed big enough to hold three more people. It's official; he loves this hotel.

Rex's contact shows up a half-hour before noon. Mergen Garayev is still fiercely Russian in a country that officially disapproves of its remaining Russian population. According to Llamas, he makes a living by taking U.S.-based jobs, usually acquiring weaponry for agents on the ground.

Garayev and Rex exchange pleasantries that are modified ident-and-confirm phrases before Rex lets the man inside his hotel room. Garayev has an innocent-looking sports duffel with a popular brand name on the side, but Rex can see by the flex of the man's arm that he's carrying some serious weight in that bag.

There is a case inside that Rex goes for immediately, unsnapping the catches and throwing open the lid. "Oh, a sniper rifle. You do love me." Rex runs his hands along the disassembled pieces of the M24. There are two different scopes included, day and night, that can also be used independent of the rifle. Excellent.

"I do not love you," Garayev retorts. His mustache makes his frown look pronounced and fluffy, which sort of spoils the effect of the expression. "We just want problem dealt with."

---

[3] Arabic: "Praise be to God."
[4] Arabic: "Thanks."
[5] Arabic: "You're welcome."

"That's why I'm here." The bag also holds a Glock 26 double-stack with two extra magazines, an M27 that looks like it's in superb condition, a vest, a few packs of C-4—it's a damned good kit. Someone was even smart enough to throw in water bottles and MREs, things Rex usually has to ask for. Those will hold him for several days if he conserves resources.

There are a couple of items he'll grab in the market on his way out of town, but otherwise, Rex is good to go. The exchange rate is about one to three at the moment, definitely in his favor. Garayev is probably making out pretty damned well, too.

"What was the cost of the bribe to get me a vehicle out of Ashgabat without a government guide?" Rex asks.

"Not bad. Many would rather stay home than drive out to the middle of nowhere, no matter the reason." Garayev shrugs. "Another bribe goes further up the chain, and then: What unaccompanied driver?"

"Pre-paid, or do you need a tip?"

Garayev looks at him like he's stupid. Rex shakes his head and puts two hundred-dollar bills into the bastard's palm, which are quickly tucked away. Pre-paid bribes are more likely, but it's always a good idea to keep your contacts happy. Also: not his money. He just has to account for it later.

Rex zips up the bag. "Any updates on the potential number of targets?"

"The most recent count estimates thirty, but no one will go closer to this camp to confirm the number." Garayev gives Rex a suspicious glower. "Fucking Americans. You think you will handle these men all by yourself? They are armed, trained, and rumored to have armor-piercing rounds. That vest might not save you if you are foolish."

Rex grins. "Want to put money on it?"

Garayev's anger dims a bit. "Twenty American says that someone finds your bones in the desert, and I will be retrieving my winnings from your rotting wallet."

"Forty American says that I'm back here in less than thirty-six hours, and your little ISIS nest is a smoking crater."

Garayev's lips lift at the corners in a challenging smile. "Thirty."

"Deal," Rex says, slapping palms with Garayev. "See you in two days, asshole."

"Fucking American," Garayev mutters again on his way out. Rex is happy to see him leave. His accent is way too close to the region where Hail-of-Bullets-Ex-Boyfriend used to reside.

*   *   *   *

Rex leaves Ashgabat after the midday prayers have concluded. It's strangely comforting to be back out in the desert, even if he's driving alone in a car that was manufactured before he was born. The air conditioning still works, but he's going to be running around in the desert later in the day, so fuck that—all of the car windows are rolled down. It's over seventy degrees in the region when it should be in the forties, nothing but blue sky and harsh sunlight. Fucking global warming.

He takes the M-37 east until the highway veers south. It's a two-hour drive to Kaakhka, and his friendly local ISIS cell is supposed to be establishing itself southwest of the city, in spitting distance of the Iranian border. It's the middle of fucking nowhere, just desert sand, rock, migrating herdsmen, and the occasional nutcase wandering through...or in this case, an entire cluster of nutcases.

Rex parks the car on a side street that Garayev mentioned and leaves it there for someone else's eventual use. Then he goes hunting for his next mode of transportation.

One of the migrating trade groups has set up a sheep-or-camel shopping center outside the ancient city walls. Despite the heat, the men are wearing red or buff-colored striped robes. The women are wearing long red dresses emphasized by different types of beadwork from collar to bodice, with accompanying glittering headdresses that emit faint chimes as they move. Rex has found a family of true traditionalists, a dying breed due to Turkmenistan's strict policies on acceptable culture. Maybe they'll escape it all; maybe the country's borders mean nothing to them.

Rex honestly can't fucking remember who he should speak to first when the eldest man makes the decision for him, coming out of a tent to greet Rex with a smile on his face. Rex introduces himself and explains what he's looking for—a camel, so that he can make a trip out to some of the more remote archaeological spots.

The man glances at Rex's short-bristled hair, his navy blue clothing, the heavy sports bag slung over his shoulder, and nods. "Archaeology. Of course," he says, not convinced by the archaeology line at all. He shows Rex to a camel that's stomping its feet, itching to travel because of the unseasonably warm temperatures. Perfect.

"How much?"

"For rent or for buy?" the trader asks in English, his accent making the words sound smooth instead of abrupt.

Rex sighs. "I'll buy him. If something goes wrong during my archaeology visit, you have already been compensated."

"Compensated." The old man says the word like it's foul, sighs, and then asks for an exorbitant sum of money.

Rex counts out fifties in U.S. currency and hands it over without bothering to haggle, which earns him some audible teeth-grinding from his camel-selling friend. Haggling might be tradition, but it's Uncle Sam's dime, and Rex has no patience for that type of arguing right now. He's got people to kill and a bet to win.

He hangs around the old outer wall on the edge of the city until evening before slinging his bag over the camel's back and mounting up. The camel snorts at the extra weight, but obligingly heads in the direction that Rex indicates. They travel southwest so the glare of the setting sun isn't shining in their eyes. The camel all but prances like a show horse, he's so eager to be moving.

Rex pats the camel's neck. "Well, Bait, my friend: here's hoping you survive the night."

The sun sets at 18:00, giving him about a half-hour of twilight before darkness falls. As the temperature cools, Rex pulls out the dark blue robe and scarf he bought on the way out of Ashgabat. The scarf hides the shock-blond of his hair, and the robe insulates him against encroaching chill. Dark blue is awesome for night-work, and his friend the camel seller knew it. Rex doesn't think he's ISIS material, or stupid enough to sell Rex out—not when the women and girls in the man's family are still in glittering Turkmen dress.

When Bait has spent another half-hour wandering forward into full darkness, Rex pulls on the camel's lead, halting Bait's progress. He doesn't see anything, doesn't hear anything, but he *knows* he's right on the edge of someone's sentry lines.

Rex dismounts, pulls down the sports bag, and nudges the camel's knees until Bait obediently folds himself down to park on the ground. "You stay here. Be good," Rex instructs. Bait snorts at him in derision. "I mean it. I don't want your name to be a bad omen." When Rex heads out, the camel makes no attempt to follow him. Maybe he's lucky and it's camel naptime.

He creeps along in the darkness and finds a rocky outcropping thick enough to provide cover from the rumored armor-piercing bullets. Then he pulls the night vision scope from the M24's kit and takes a look around.

"Oh, hello," he murmurs, finding the first sentry about a quarter-mile from his position. The man is wearing night-vision goggles and carrying a cheap Chinese reproduction of the classic AK-47. Rex sweeps the scope around the area until he finds eight sentries total, surrounding a central point in a pretty standard defensive pattern. The camp itself is just that—multiple tents set up in the desert. He can make out the square edges of munitions containers, hidden from overhead satellite view by a layer of thick canvas that's probably the same color as the sand.

Rex puts down the scope, tapping it thoughtfully against his leg. "Really? You're going to make it that easy?"

He double-checks the munitions containers, estimating the full pile's contents by average size per case. Yes, they really are going to make it that easy. Holy shit, this is going to be fun.

Rex checks his watch and finds that it's 21:00. Moonrise is around 01:00. That gives him four hours of darkness. He's about to use most of that time getting into camp without being noticed, but these sentries are looking for vehicles, people riding in. Blatant ground assault.

Rex is not that fucking stupid. He's grinning as he sets up the M24's tripod for his return, but leaves it and the rifle itself behind the rock, out of sight until he's ready to use it.

He strips off the robe; the Glock gets holstered at his hip. The strap of the German M27 IAR goes over his shoulder so that the gun rests on his back, and then he puts the robe back on to cover the distinct shine of metal, detectable even by starlight. If he needs the M27 after emptying the Glock, he can get to it quickly enough.

He blows out a breath before turning his watch face so it lies against the inside of his wrist. He doesn't need light shining across the quartz, giving away his position. One of his early squad mates in Afghanistan learned that lesson the fatal way.

The crawl towards the camp is a tense adventure of hoping he doesn't find scorpions with his bare hands. He hates the fuckers. Checking his boots for them every day had gotten old so fast. At least a snake will actively try to avoid you.

The sentries swap out when Rex is about halfway to the camp. He has to wait in stillness, blending in with dark desert sand. The group has set sentry positions, which is stupid, but it means no one comes near the lump of not-desert, whose heart is hammering so loud it should be audible from space.

By the time Rex makes it into camp, lying a few feet away from that convenient munitions stack, the old sentries are in their tents for the night, sleeping or passing time with other members of the cell. He overhears several different conversations while counting the shadows cast by warm bodies illuminated by lamp light. Most of it is gossip, but he takes note of someone muttering about another cell setup in Afghanistan. That country *also* does not need another fucking ISIS problem.

Between the known sentries, the shadows, and one asshole with a snore that could wake the dead, Rex puts the camp count at thirty. Nice to know Garayev was correct.

Rex crawls the last few feet to the plastic cases, labeled with varying types of munitions from at least five different governments. Resourceful little bastards. He reaches in between the stacks and slaps a pre-set C-4 package into place, shoving it in far enough so it won't be noticed unless the camp suddenly decides to re-Tetris their shit in the middle of the night.

He waits in the shadows as someone passes from one tent to another, gives them time to settle, and then crawls to the other side of the pile to place the other package. He only has two C-4 blocks, but each one has a touch of AN/FO, with added monomethylamine nitrate to give the AN/FO extra kick.

Rex crawls back to his rocky outcropping without incident, scorpions or otherwise. The temperature has finally dropped low enough for his breath to come out as thick plumes of steam.

He makes sure he's settled in behind the rock, out of sight of sentries that might be smart enough to notice rising mist in the air, before he guzzles down a full bottle of water. He eats an MRE that tastes like cardboard crawled up a sheep's asshole before someone added pepper for flavor. The longer he's been out of the service, the worse an MRE tastes, which honestly makes him wonder what the fuck he was eating for eight years.

The downside is that the crawl, the C-4 placement, and his trip back took longer than Rex estimated. He did it in safety, yes, but now he's got thirty minutes to take out an entire group of assholes before moonrise. The moon phase is waning crescent, but that will still provide enough light to reveal the entirety of the desert floor.

Rex pops the night vision scope into place and makes himself comfortable behind the tripod mount, snugging the stock up to the correct place on his shoulder. The M24 is an old friend, a veteran of both stupid wars, and reliable as all hell. He tests its range of motion, making certain he can direct a shot at every sentry position, and then pulls out the remote detonator for the C-4 bricks.

Rex flips up the safety cover with his thumb. "Good morning, assholes," he says, and presses down on the trigger.

Thanks to his pre-prepped chemical cocktail, he gets a very nice explosion. Munitions crates fly in all directions, bullets spark and fire, tents are blasted over by debris, people scream, and fabric turns to flame. Chaos is useful and awesome.

Rex's first eight shots take out the sentries that are shouting in the dark, trying to find the threat while still half-blinded by Rex's improvised bomb. Nope, sorry. Better luck next life.

He pulls the night vision scope and replaces it with standard so the fire won't blind him. Then he nails every target in the camp foolish enough to be standing upright when a firefight is happening. He's up to fifteen bodies within two minutes of the explosion.

Fifteen isn't thirty. Rex breathes in slow, steady inhalations and exhalations, all of his senses keen and alert for movement and sound. There—he finds a bent-over body hiding behind a table. The sniper round from the M24 goes straight through the cheap plastic, netting him a cry, a thud, and nothing else. Sixteen.

There is a lull when he finds no one, and Rex tries to ignore the feel of passing time. He might have to swap clothes for moonrise, but at least the sun won't come up until 06:00.

Seventeen, eighteen, and nineteen are a trio that suddenly spring up, machine guns blazing fire out into the desert night. They get their direction correct, smart enough to figure out bullet trajectory, but Rex is behind a rock, and they're stuck in a hard, flaming place.

Twenty, twenty-one, twenty-two. He counts off each one as people escape burning tents, trying to find better cover that's not also on fire. Twenty-three. Twenty-four. Twenty-five.

That's when all movement stills, and for ten solid minutes, there is nothing. Fuck. He has five more bodies to account for, which means going back into the camp. If he doesn't clean up the entire nest, some surviving ISIS asshole will pack up and take their bullshit rhetoric somewhere else.

Rex sighs. "Goddammit."

He dismantles the M24 and its tripod, packing the weapon back into its hard-shell case. He strips down to his underwear, swapping out navy blue for dun-colored cargo pants, t-shirt, the bulletproof vest, and a matching scarf and robe. He's dressed in less than ten minutes, but moonrise happens fast. In short order, the desert has gone from almost complete darkness to moon-bathed sand. There's nothing to do but try to blend in as much as possible, or at least try not to present as a blatantly obvious target.

Fuck, he's probably going to get shot.

Rex goes in at a run, soft-soled shoes making almost no noise as he bolts across rock and sand. The IAR is a comforting weight on his back, but the Glock is what he has in his hands, safety off and ready to fire. The M27 is fun, but Rex is faster with a pistol, more precise.

Twenty-six and twenty-seven are lying in wait near the guttering flames of what used to be a hell of a lot of ammo. Rex nails the first one in the head when he stands up, cheap AK-47 already sputtering bullets that strike the ground at Rex's feet. Instinct guides Rex's hand to the next man in line, a center mass shot. He's down and gurgling out his last breath as Rex spins in place, searching for targets.

Rex's heart is hammering in his chest, his pulse pounding in his ears. Every sound is amplified, every glint of metal a potential weapon, every lick of flame a light that gives away his position.

Twenty-eight and twenty-nine are corpses already, killed in the explosion via tent proximity to C-4 and the munitions stack. Thirty is trying to crawl away, both of his legs showing severe burns and at least one compound fracture. Rex feels a moment's sympathy before nailing him high in the back along the spine, putting the poor bastard out of his misery. Even if Rex thought the man would survive those injuries without dying of shock, the DoD doesn't want prisoners. Not that Rex is in any great hurry to send someone to Gitmo. Bullets are kinder.

Rex then gets to contend with uncounted, lucky number thirty-one. Son of a bitch.

What should be an easy confrontation becomes a prolonged firefight that is pissing Rex the hell off. He's emptied the IAR, no rounds left in the Glock until he gets the chance to reload, and still he's got a fucking problem walking around the flaming camp, doing a very good job of trying to make Rex dead.

Rex flings himself to the ground and rolls as bullets strike the sand, following him to cover. He ends up behind a fuel barrel that's still burning off its contents. The metal singes his shoulders when he leans against it, trying to mentally calculate position and shots—

No, you shit, armor-piercing rounds! Rex is already moving again, but takes a single bullet that passes through the jacket he's wearing like the metal plates don't exist, exiting high in his chest.

Rex gasps in pain, gritting his teeth as he keeps rolling. Shit, shit, shit. He was right; he got shot, and it's his own stupid fault.

This time he rests his back up against the wheel well of a deflated jeep tire. The lack of bullets tells Rex that Thirty-One has lost track of his position. Small fucking favors. He glances down and realizes he got lucky. It looks like the bullet took him under his left collarbone, but he doesn't taste blood. Small caliber round, too, or he'd be dealing with one hell of an exit wound.

"Who are you? Afghani? American? Israeli?" Lucky Thirty-One asks in English. He has a deep tenor voice verging on bass, one that turns his accent into something that's probably sexy-swooned many.

"*Ahau he Māori, fuck-upoko!*" Rex yells back, grinning. He's bleeding and in pain, but man, adrenaline is a wonderful thing.

"A fucking *Māori?*" Lucky Thirty-One sounds baffled, and kind of insulted. Music to Rex's ears.

He triggers the magazine release and drops the empty clip from the Glock, using the pop and crackle of still-burning fires to cover the sound of reloading: the clack of the slide being pulled back, his last clip going in, slide release triggered. One round in the chamber and fourteen to go.

If he needs more than his last fifteen bullets to kill this asshole, he's going to be really fucking pissed.

Rex closes his eyes, ignoring the pain from his shoulder, and waits. His patience is swiftly rewarded. "When I kill you, I will leave your corpse out for the scavengers."

"That's what I was about to say about you," Rex murmurs. He rolls out from cover, gun raised and aimed right at the source of Lucky Thirty-One's voice. The man is already halfway to Rex's position. He gets out a single shot that bounces off the front of the jeep before Rex puts a bullet in his head.

"Thirty-one assholes." Rex drops down into the sand, trying to catch his breath. Fuck, that better be all of them.

Rex wakes up to the feel of something snuffling along his neck. He tries to lift his arm to shove at whatever is bothering him, but that only sends a jolt of screaming pain through his chest. The

---

[6] "I'm Māori, fuckhead!"

resulting surge of adrenaline wakes him right the hell up and earns him a mouthful of dirt when he gasps for air.

Rex spits out sand before rolling over to look up at Bait, who is still nosing at Rex's clothes. "I thought I told you to stay put."

The camel snorts and then licks at his hand. Rex sighs and rubs the camel's head. "Thanks for not listening."

He uses the camel's lead to haul himself up from the ground. Bait tolerates that, but stomps his feet in irritation when Rex does nothing more than slump against the camel's side.

"Hey, I'm working on it," he mutters. He finds a smoldering box that used to hold .50 caliber rounds, using it as a mounting stool so that he can get on top of the fucking camel.

Bait takes him out to his original rocky outcropping. Rex slides off the camel, drops to his knees, and gets the first aid kit out of the bag. Ibuprofen, Paracetamol, bandages, antiseptic—who the hell packed this kit, a kid from the *Brady Bunch*? There is nothing in here with enough strength to deal with the pain from being fucking shot!

Rex swallows about 2000mg of the Paracetamol, adds 1000mg from the ibuprofen bottle, and then starts stripping down. He can't wait for the drugs to kick in, not when he needs to plug up two different damned holes. He's panting from exertion by the time he gets off the robe and pulls the strap for the IAR over his head, and he still has to remove the vest.

That involves creative swearing and movement that leaves him all but sobbing. Fuck, he hates being shot. It sucks and he deserves it. He forgot fucking *basic intel* about enemy fire. He was so pleased by the rest of the kit that he didn't check the first aid supplies, so that lack is *also* his fault. His father is never going to let him hear the end of this shit.

Removing his bloodied t-shirt pushes Rex to the point of vomiting into the desert soil. He squeezes half a bottle of iodine-laden wound wash over his back, which stings just as much as it feels really damned soothing. The other half of the bottle washes the exit wound, which is *not* soothing. He's fortunate it's a high shot, or else he wouldn't be able to reach the entry wound on his back to gently press a pressure bandage over it.

Pressing the second, larger bandage over the exit wound makes him pass out again for another few minutes. Bait rouses him with snuffling hot breath against Rex's neck.

Rex inspects both bandages to make sure they held while he was unconscious, puts the dark blue t-shirt back on, and chugs another bottle of water. He's honestly thrilled when he doesn't vomit it right back up, and grateful that he has yet to taste blood. That means the bullet made a mess, but didn't tear a hole in his lung. Excellent; that probably means he'll survive this.

He packs the clothes, food, water, and Glock, which still has fourteen rounds in it, all that's left of the ammunition he came out

72

into the desert with. He can't lift the weight of the other equipment. Some wandering desert soul can have it. Maybe selling the M24 and the M27 on the black market will feed someone's family for a while.

Dammit, even without the extra weight, Rex still can't lift the bag up over his shoulder to load the camel. He stumbles his way up the uneven incline of the rocky hillside so he can scramble onto Bait's back, nearly dropping the bag off the side in the process.

"Okay. Go...home, I guess," Rex tells Bait, who flicks his ears. "Uh—fuck. *Ead lilwatan.*[7]" he tries hopefully, and gets nothing. Rex wracks his brain until he pulls up half-remembered Kazakh. "*Üyge barw?*[8]"

Bait paws at the ground before moving forward. If Rex is judging the moon's position correctly, the camel is headed in the right direction, back to town and the trader's camp.

He falls asleep, lulled by Bait's swaying gait, and doesn't wake up again until the camel bumps him against the old stone wall on the outer edges of Kaakhka. The sun is up in the sky; his watch tells him it's already after 09:00. The air feels cooler against his exposed skin, too. Maybe Turkmenistan is going to remember that it's winter in the northern hemisphere, not late spring.

Rex slides off Bait, ignoring the painful jolt of landing, and takes the animal back to his original owner. The women don't seem all that surprised by his return, but the old man who sold the camel looks at Rex as if he's seeing an apparition.

"That's a good camel," Rex says, handing over Bait's lead. "Don't eat him."

"Wait—this is paid—you rent!" the old man stutters.

Rex waves him off. "Keep it," he says, and trudges determinedly in the direction of the tourist areas where all of the government-approved cab drivers lurk. He finds a taxi with a man willing to overlook Rex's blatant lack of government-mandated companion, happy to take Rex back into Ashgabat in exchange for a handful of American twenties.

Rex leans back in the car's seat, trying not to pass out again. OTC painkillers only go so far, and he feels awful. The driver asks him a question, probably in Turkmen, but that's a language he never picked up.

"*Tüsinbeymin.*"[9]

The driver side-eyes Rex before nodding. "You have good accent, but not quite right. American?"

Rex smiles. "Yeah."

"Soldier?" the driver asks, giving Rex's chest a pointed look.

Rex glances down to find that his tags are showing and blood is beginning to leave a dark, glistening patch on his shirt. Rex tucks

---

[7] Arabic: "Home" (Verb)
[8] Kazakh: "Go home?"
[9] Kazakh: "I do not understand."

his tags back under his shirt where they belong. Then he bites his lip while using his fingers to gently press the edges of the bandage back into place. He's not bleeding heavily, but he'll need to change the bandage in Ashgabat, if not sooner. He hopes the driver isn't squeamish.

"I think this counts as mercenary work, but it's sanctioned U.S. government mercenary work, so who gives a fuck," Rex says, closing his eyes.

"Should you not be in hospital?"

"Ashgabat has a decent one," Rex replies. "But hotel first, please. I have to win a bet with a Russian asshole who believes I should be dead by now."

The driver chuckles. "I will have you to your hotel in record time, soldier. Then you tip well, yes?"

"Always, my friend."

The driver calling for his attention causes Rex to jerk awake, hissing in pain. The man is nice enough to open his door, but it takes stubborn effort to crawl out of the cab and stand up. There's an alarming moment where everything swims in his vision before the lightheaded wooziness settles.

Better. Rex absolutely refuses to pass out on the street. He has a hotel room for that.

The driver gets a nice tip, another handful of twenties, and offers Rex a polite bow before he drives away. Rex watches him go, trying to remind himself of his goals. Right—he's going to find whoever stocked that shitty first aid kit and beat the hell out of them.

Priorities first, though. He enters the hotel and goes straight to the bar, the most likely place in the world to find a Russian man in a country whose favorite alcohol is vodka.

The bartender isn't nearly as friendly as the desk concierge. He gives Rex and his dirty bag a disgusted glower as he looks him up and down.

"I'm a fucking guest," Rex snarls, his temper trying to loosen itself as pain and exhaustion kick his ass.

"Very well," the bartender says. His English is accented, but it's not local or even Kazakh. Actual Russian, maybe, for all that he dresses as the concierge did, Western shirt and pants covered by the robe of a Turkmen. "Fucking Guest it is, then. What can I get you, Fucking Guest?"

Rex lowers his head to laugh in silence. "Okay, I deserved that. I'm just looking for someone, but hell, I would not say no to a smooth martini. Bill it to room 302, yeah?"

"Done." The bartender moves with the swift professionalism Rex likes to see in someone handling his alcohol. It almost makes him nostalgic for Francis.

Rex sits down and rests his face on his hand, staring down at the bar top until a drink is slid under his nose. Except for a bitter aftertaste reminiscent of the local tap water, the martini slides down his throat like velvet. Awesome.

"You haven't seen a man named Mergen Garayev lately, have you?"

"Not today. Would sir Fucking Guest like for me to arrange a message?" the bartender asks snidely.

"Yeah. Tell Garayev that he owes an asshole American soldier thirty dollars, since I'm not fucking dead."

The bartender offers Rex a thin-lipped smile. "I will be sure to pass the message along, exactly as you have given it to me."

Rex puts a twenty down on the bar top. "I know the exchange rate; that's good for your fee." He can afford more, but he ran out of patience sometime around getting shot. Francis at Maritimes might be a grumbling jackass, but he's not a dick.

"Very good, sir. Enjoy your drink, Fucking Guest."

"Up yours," Rex returns with a cheerful smile, raising his glass. He can hear the soothing vibration of afternoon prayers through the walls as people indoors and outside perform them. Twenty-four hours on a job, start to finish. Not bad.

Rex is enjoying a pleasant buzz and the pain-dulling effects of good booze when someone claims the barstool on his right. Rex ignores them, swirling the last remnants of martini around in his glass before polishing it off, putting it down on a coaster decorated in the hotel's Soviet-based motif. It's occurring to him that drinking more water might also be a good idea. He'll go upstairs and have room service bring it to him, swallow more acetaminophen, and try to sleep before tending to this stupid bullet wound.

"Why is it that I keep finding beautiful blond men in bars where I least expect to find them?"

Rex's heart skips a beat in a way that actually hurts. He turns his head, feeling a lurching echo of *déjà vu* when he encounters his boyfriend's Caribbean-blue eyes and flaming hair.

"What—the fuck?"

"That is exactly what I'm wondering." Euan Ambrus is staring at Rex like he's just encountered a mirage. "Rex?"

Rex frowns. "If I'm not hallucinating, then neither are you."

"Right." Ambrus swallows, still looking bewildered. "I—we have had discussions about you not following me, yes?"

"Following you—fucking shit, Ambrus, I am fucking working!" Rex growls back. "You sure you're not following *me*, jackass?"

Both of Ambrus's eyebrows go up in a way that's kind of entertaining to watch. "Oh, wow, that's—no, never mind that. Rex, I'm well aware of the fact that the military expects us to bleed for them, but this seems excessive," he says, tilting his head at Rex's chest.

Rex glances down long enough to see that the pressure bandage gave up again. He shrugs with his right shoulder, even though it hurts and pulls on both sides of the bullet wound. "Got shot. Perk of the job."

"Perk." Ambrus presses his lips together, eyebrows starting to come down in a piercing scowl. "And you're drinking, which thins the blood and makes you bleed." He shakes his head. "Goddammit, Rex."

"No decent meds in my kit. Sue me," Rex grumbles. "Besides, I was lying in the dirt for a while. Extra blood pushes out any potential bacteria that made it through."

When he looks at Ambrus again, there is a faint, sad smile on his face. "Rex. Have you even seen a doctor yet?"

"No." Rex feels his eyes narrow as his brow comes down in what he hopes is a truly impressive glower. "I am sitting at this bar, waiting for a motherfucker who owes me money for *not being dead.*"

"I don't think said motherfucker is going to turn up." Ambrus waits for the bartender to pass by on his way to serve another customer at the end of the bar. "Rex. Medical treatment. Please."

"Aren't you working?" Rex asks, irritated as all hell without any idea why.

"I was." Ambrus turns away from him to face the mirrored wall of alcohol. "My assignment was to deal with a fucking bastard who was conspiring with enemy combatants to kill DoD agents and their teams. You didn't hear me say any of that, by the way."

Rex isn't stupid, even if he's a little drunk from having a martini after being fucking shot. "Garayev. You owe me thirty dollars, asshole."

"You bet Garayev thirty dollars that you wouldn't die." Ambrus closes his eyes and presses his fingers against the bridge of his nose. "Dear God, my boyfriend is completely fucking nuts."

"Yeah, but I'm still alive, and there are a bunch of motherfuckers out in the desert who aren't." Rex puts his hands on the countertop as he slowly stands up. "Now if you'll excuse me, I'm going to leave and pretend our paths didn't cross while you were at work."

"Rex, wait," Ambrus says, which quickly becomes a much louder shout of, "REX!" as the world tilts sideways. Rex blacks out and comes to lying on the floor, dizzy as hell, with fire burning in his veins.

Ambrus's hands are cupping Rex's face, his eyes far too bright. "Oh, fuck, Rex," he whispers.

Rex tries smiling. "Didn't think I'd lost enough blood for that."

Ambrus shakes his head. "You didn't. Hang on," he instructs, and then stands up.

The last thing Rex hears is a gun firing twice, accompanied by a hell of a lot of undignified screaming. He really wants to know who's shooting at who, or if anyone's shooting back, but blackness hits hard.

*   *   *   *

When Rex wakes up again, it's a slow, gradual process, like the aftereffects of surgery when he's trying to shake off the anesthesia. He can feel the vibration specific to a car driving down a long stretch of highway. Rocks bounce off the bottom of the car on occasion, with little bumps here and there that jar him but don't make him feel like he's going to be swallowed by pain. That part feels pleasantly distant. It's...nice. Better than waking up dead, anyway.

Rex's head is pillowed on someone's lap, and a hand is stroking through his short-buzzed hair, over and over. He's stretched out on a bench seat, knees folded up enough that his boots are brushing the passenger side door. Old car, then—you can't get a bench seat in a vehicle anymore unless you buy a van. Light is shining through the driver's side window, highlighting the top of the passenger door. It has to be sunset, and the car's headed north.

There is an intense electronic hush before he hears music coming from above, probably an iPod with good speakers. It's a piano in minor key, soft and lulling. Rex almost falls asleep again before there are lyrics, words whispered like they're coming out of graveyard fog.

Rex swallows against a dry mouth and forces himself back to fuller awareness, entranced as the music continues. He knows the song. A lot of bands have done remakes over the years, but he's never heard a version like this before.

Then another voice joins in, and Rex looks up in surprise. It's Ambrus's lap his head is resting on; Ambrus's hand stroking his hair; Ambrus driving the car. His left arm is draped over the steering wheel of a model so old it doesn't even have a rudimentary air bag in the center. His lips are moving as he sings along to the words in the third verse, a gentle tenor that sounds like it has the potential to be a hell of a lot more vibrant.

Rex swallows again. He feels overwhelmed by the vehemence lacing Ambrus's voice. That's a lot of frustration and sadness bundled up together, one hell of an angry cocktail for a song like "The Sound of Silence."

"Who—who is that?" he asks after the final notes fade away.

The hand on Rex's head twitches before Ambrus glances down at him. "The band's called Disturbed. I didn't think anyone could make a version of this song that would hurt more than the original, but they sure as hell managed it." Ambrus's eyes go back to the road, but he seems melancholy, or maybe just distracted.

Rex doesn't know how to respond to what Ambrus told him. There are implications in that statement, but he's so goddamned tired it's a minor miracle he remembers his own name. "Where are we?" he goes with instead.

Ambrus lifts his hand from Rex's hair long enough to rub at his eyes. "About thirty minutes out of Nukus."

"Nuk—uh, *why?*" Rex asks, trying to sit up in surprise. That's a miserable failure, one that leaves him biting back a groan of pain. He feels better, yes, but there is still a bullet wound in his shoulder. He can't figure out how he's managed to lie on his left side without fire and agony clawing its way into his brain. Good drugs, maybe.

"Stay still," Ambrus murmurs, running his fingers back through Rex's hair in a soothing gesture. The pain fades back to the dull ache he'd felt upon waking.

Not sitting up sounds like a great idea, but Rex still needs to know what's going on. Nukus is in fucking Uzbekistan, which is *definitely* not Turkmenistan. "Why Nukus, Euan?"

"Well, I might have shot a bartender for poisoning you." Ambrus gives Rex a quick down-and-back-up inspection before he refocuses on the road. "Is there a reason I killed a member of the *bratva* today, Rex?"

Rex closes his eyes and tries to use his right hand to cover his face in dismay. "It's...kind of a long story." His words are already trying to slur together. Good drugs at work; he'll be out again soon. "I sort of dated a *bratva* without telling him about my job. I didn't want him panicking, thinking I was investigating him or his family."

Ambrus makes a sound of amused dismay. "And he found out anyway, and did not take it well. Holy shit, Rex. I can't tell if this is alarming or hilarious."

"Go with hilarious," Rex whispers, his eyes beginning to flicker shut. "Hail of bullets for a send-off. You're the only person I've ever told."

"I'm flattered, and also horrified," Ambrus replies in a dry voice. "Stay put. Try to rest. Hotel soon. I have desperately got to sleep, or I'm going to drive us off the road and kill a goat."

"Why a goat?" Rex asks in bewilderment.

Ambrus lets out a brief huff of laughter. "They're everywhere today. I expected sheep or camels, but no, it's like goat season, the horror movie."

Rex gives up. "Okay." He's been shot, he's in the wrong country, his boyfriend is driving a car while singing along to one of the most haunting remakes Rex has ever heard in his life, and a fucking *bratva* bartender tried to poison him.

What the actual fuck. 2016 is already going down as the weirdest year he's ever had, and it's only the fourth of January. Or...maybe the fifth? Shit.

"What day is it?"

"I don't fucking know," Ambrus replies, followed by the high-pitched laughter of the exceptionally overtired. "Go back to sleep."

Rex doesn't really want to, but it happens anyway.

*　　　　*　　　　*　　　　*

Rex is on his feet the next time he's conscious, but he wouldn't call it functional. He's standing in a strange building, his right arm supporting him as he slumps against a wall.

Somewhere nearby, around a corner, he can hear Ambrus speaking in some Slavic-based language. He has no idea what's being said. Not his specialty; even his Russian is fucking awful.

Then Ambrus returns, gently coaxing Rex away from the wall with nothing more than gesture and touch. It takes getting into the elevator for Rex to put enough pieces together in his head to recognize that they're in a hotel.

"Sorry for the wait." Ambrus is leaning against the wall, head tilted up at the ceiling, eyes closed. There is sweat dampening his hairline in a way that's familiar, but Rex can't remember why. He's still stringing together the off-kilter memory of car trip, goats, Uzbekistan, Nukus, and *bratva* bartender.

"I think I missed most of it," Rex says in a cracked voice.

"Mmm. Maybe." Ambrus doesn't move. "Had to convince the proprietor that you just got out of a hospital, and that I'm your acting nursemaid, to keep the paranoid bastard from calling the police 'for homosexuals daring to step foot in his hotel.' Not that it took much, since you do actually look like you just left a hospital."

Rex thinks about it and finally dredges up a vague memory about Uzbekistan's president making a huge stink about homosexuality being part of the Gay Western Agenda, like the Middle East's version of Fox News. He glances down and discovers there is a dressing over his left shoulder and a sling supporting his left arm, one he didn't even feel until he saw it.

Rex looks at Ambrus. "You don't look much better."

"I'll be fine." The elevator dings, allowing Ambrus to pull back the old accordion gate to reveal their floor. The carpet is a beautiful old Persian runner in maroon and blue, and the hall is white plaster. Bright electric light from converted, yellowed gaslights on the walls makes everything seem touristy and surreal. "Go. I've got the bags."

"Bags?" Rex glances down and sees one desert-scuffed sports duffel, his own backpack, and another pack that has to be Ambrus's. "How did you get—"

"I'm good at not being noticed," Ambrus says blithely.

Rex stares at his boyfriend's fiery hair as he follows Ambrus down the hallway. "*How?*" he asks, but if he gets an answer, he loses it when consciousness checks out on him again.

The next time he opens his eyes, it's to the feel of soft cotton against his skin, and the pleasant realization that he's lying down—not standing, not sitting in a car seat while bleeding, and not waking up while still astride a fucking camel. He also feels like he's floating, which means someone finally introduced some really good pain meds into his life.

For a few minutes, Rex does nothing more than lie still. His chest hurts, bruised from rolling around while getting shot at. Rex's left shoulder aches, but without the sharpness of a fresh wound. Another few bruises on his arms and legs announce themselves as he's taking stock. His eyes feel too dry and his mouth tastes like sand, but he's indoors, in a bed with damned nice sheets, and he feels...safe.

Safe. That's weird.

Rex turns his head to the right and finds Ambrus sprawled out on the bed next to him, sound asleep. He's pale, and sweat has soaked the hair on his head a darker red, but he doesn't look desperately ill. This seems more like heat stroke, even if the weather's wrong for it. Rex can't hear any sort of climate control system running, but the room feels temperate—in the low seventies at the highest.

Ambrus's eyes flicker open while Rex is still watching him. His eyes are red-rimmed, yes, but he really isn't suffering that same terrible exhaustion. There's too much awareness in his gaze, humor and sadness and a sort of wistful peace that makes Rex's chest hurt worse than it already did.

"Hi." Rex's voice emerges as an attractive, dying toad croak. When he smiles, it makes his lips feel like they're going to crack and bleed. "You're still here."

"Still here." Ambrus smiles back, sounding almost as wrecked. That makes no sense at all—except maybe it does. Rex just isn't ready to contemplate that yet. Besides, the drive from Ashgabat to Nukus is...is...

Fuck, math is hard. Rex concentrates until he pulls a legitimate-sounding estimate from his foggy brain. Nine hours. He has no idea how long Ambrus was awake before bartender-shooting and long drive. That would also be a valid reason as to why Rex's boyfriend looks half-beaten to shit.

Rex gives his left shoulder an experimental wiggle and feels only that same ache of a healing wound. Shit. Not the drive, then—or at least, not only the drive.

He reaches out with his right hand. The pain in his chest eases when Ambrus takes it so that their fingers curl together. It's an awkward grip, but it's reassurance and physical contact, two things he desperately wants right now.

"Why?" Rex asks, swallowing against the sand-taste that makes him sound like he tried to swallow a square cheese grater on a dare. He means the rescue, the bartender, medical treatment, or anything else that comes to mind. "I'm not...ungrateful. But why?"

Ambrus either doesn't pick up how many subjects Rex is trying to ask about, or decides to try and answer one at a time. "If you'd waited a moment longer before trying to leave the bar, I'd have told you that my current job was officially over," Ambrus says. His voice is soft, but there's no blame or censure in his tone. "Your job was also completed, and then we would have been out of NDA territory. Sort of, anyway."

"Oh, dinner and dating in Turkmenistan. That would've gone over well with the locals," Rex teases. "What happened to Mergen Garayev?"

"Left him out in the desert to rot. No *bratva* tattoos on that one, which made the bartender a complete surprise." Ambrus sighs. "I was only waiting in Ashgabat to find out if the DoD agent that Garayev sent out to Kaakhka would return, or if I was going to send Jasper and a team out into the desert on retrieval to bring another body home."

"Not when I'm behind the scope," Rex grumbles.

"I had no idea you were involved." Ambrus's fingers tighten around Rex's hand. "They weren't even ISIS, this bunch, just a group of vengeful Taliban-esque assholes. Moved around often, seeded different information on what type of terrorist *du jour* they were to attract United States military attention. They took out eleven contractors and a full unit in six months, Rex, and this wasn't their first long-term play."

"Hey, I'm fine." Rex says, running his thumb down one of Ambrus's fingers when he can't quite mimic the hand-squeeze. "Got bored, asked for a job, drew the lucky straw."

Ambrus's concerned look doesn't change. "You almost weren't. Thirty men, Rex? Solo? Seriously?"

Rex manages to get a hint of moisture onto his lips before he grins again. "Pfft. Easy job. Also, thirty-one. Learn to count, asshole."

Humor is not helping. His boyfriend just seems more distressed. "You got *shot*, Rex."

Rex's grin widens. He refuses to let Ambrus wallow, not when they're both fine. Also, he won that stupid fucking bet, thank you. "Not for the first time. More like the sixth time. Or seventh— might've lost count somewhere in there. Also, three plane crashes, a car chase, and two car accidents, one of which was totally my fault, but the other driver deserved it."

"Three plane crashes." Ambrus seems to be bracing himself. "Military?"

"First two were. Third was Dad's fault."

That's when Rex hesitates. This is definitely wandering into confirmation, not to mention NDA gray area. Rex still thinks that Khodî looks the most like their father, but Rex has been told often enough that except for his hair and eyes, Rex and his father mirror each other a lot. It's their posture, gesture, their way of moving— something like that, anyway.

"Pretty sure it was him you thought you'd found in Maritimes."

Ambrus's expression twists a bit with guilt. "I shouldn't say." Rex waits, giving him a level stare that invites no bullshit. "Okay, yes, fine! But I wasn't going to hit on him!"

"You wouldn't even hit on *me*," Rex reminds Ambrus, grinning. "Dense motherfucker. I love you."

Ambrus freezes in place, staring at Rex with shock-wide eyes. It would be funny if it wasn't alarming. "What did you say?"

With the potential damage done, Rex decides to go for broke. "Uh, I'm apparently drugged out of my fucking skull," he says with a wry smile. "But I do. I love you. You don't have to say it back," he adds when Ambrus keeps staring at him. "I am not kidding about the drugged part. I just wanted to say—"

Ambrus surprises him by covering the distance in one swift movement to kiss him. Their lips are too dry, like they're both on the verge of a bad, peeling sunburn. It's not a deep kiss, either, but it's comfortable, and it's...

Oh, god, his dad's right. It's like something falling into place, like it's *always* meant to be this way.

"I love you," Ambrus murmurs against Rex's cheek, and then pulls back enough to stare at him. The early morning light in the room is at the perfect angle for Rex to make out the faint reflection of his own hazel eyes in that beautiful Caribbean blue. "I wouldn't have given you a key to my home if I didn't. I just—the idea that anyone would—Rex, I'm a terrible person."

"No," Rex says in a terse, angry voice, and then grits his teeth. Ow. "You aren't. Ambrus. Euan. I have *met* bad people. I've shot quite a number of them. I know the fucking difference."

"Rex—"

"You saved my life," Rex reminds him. "I do remember that comment about the poison, and we're both politely ignoring how this bullet wound is far more healed than a single car trip and a hotel overnight can manage. I'm pretty sure that terrible people don't bother saving other less-than-shining examples of humanity unless there's some personal gain involved."

"Sex is a personal gain," Ambrus tries to point out.

Rex snorts. "Have you looked in a mirror, dumbass? You could practically go get sex down at the corner market whenever the mood struck."

Ambrus starts laughing. It's dry, exhausted chuffs of air, but Rex will take that and run with it, thank you very much.

Their conversation comes to a temporary halt, but it's not discomfort or avoidance. Rex has the feeling that Ambrus has a hell of a lot of thinking to do, but that's good timing, as Rex has some serious *showering* to do. The water is tepid more than hot, but it still removes several days of travel, desert grit and grime, and flaky bits of dried blood from his skin. It also reveals that the bullet wound under his left collarbone is surface-healed. Only redness marking where that particular messy hole had been. Rex touches it with curious fingers and can feel the heat of still-mending tissue beneath. The floating sensation from the drugs is fading, but pain doesn't come spiking back in its place.

"Wow," Rex whispers. That is definitely a useful fucking trick.

There is a drab, short-sleeved gray button-down shirt in his bag, along with a pair of jeans. Rex dresses in the jeans and gets through about half the shirt's buttons before giving up. He's wearing pants and most of a shirt; it counts.

At some point while he was showering, room service stopped by. The room's old wooden table is set with a spread of breakfast and early lunch items, enough food to fill every available space while still leaving two place settings available on opposite sides of the table.

A huge perk of traveling to other parts of the world is the blatant reminder of how much American hotels suck unless you're willing to throw around thousands of dollars per night. The rest of the world might have governments struggling with human rights concepts, but a lot of those same countries still remember that hospitality is a large part of being civilized.

Ambrus is already seated, gripping a mug of something that smells like a good strong black tea with mint involved, but he's not touching the food. Rex lets him be; Ambrus will eat after caffeine, but not usually before that. Leftover weird-ass Scot-British upbringing or something, he claims, but Rex can't name a time when the British *aren't* guzzling tea.

Rex's stomach is convinced that yes, food is a great idea. Coffee, not so much, but water and maybe several thousand calories in food? Fuck, yes.

"I didn't know."

Rex glances up from his plate in surprise. "Know what?"

Ambrus sips at his tea to hide part of his expression. "I didn't know who your father was. I thought—I thought that moment in the bar was a coincidence."

Rex puts down his utensils and finds a cloth napkin tucked neatly beside his plate. "When did you figure it out?"

Ambrus smiles, amused and nostalgic at once. "When you were bitching me out in the hotel bar while calling me by my last name. God, you looked and sounded just like Django Whetū."

Rex is sort of wishing someone had captured that moment on video. He doesn't sound like his Dad. No way. That's Khodî's job. "When did you meet him?"

"Oh, we worked together a few times." Ambrus lowers his gaze back down to his tea. "Don't—don't push beyond that. Not yet, anyway. Fuck, Rex, I can't even go meet with your family right now."

Rex pauses while mid-bite of what he's pretty sure is a northern-migrated and adapted spanakopita. "What—*why?*"

"Because Django would strangle the life out of me if I brought him a three-foot stack of NDAs to sign," Ambrus replies, shaking his head.

Rex is disappointed, but he nods. He knows these strictures; he works under them. "Khodî is going to accuse me of making up a boyfriend when I never bring you around."

"Oh, I didn't say never, I just..." Ambrus puts the tea down and then places both of his hands, palms flat, onto the tabletop. "I'm retiring."

It takes a minute for Rex to realize that he's staring at Ambrus, waiting for a punchline that never came. "What?"

Ambrus stares at the table. "Not right this second. I mean, I can't. It's a process."

Rex can hear glass beginning to chime, a very low-pitched sound. He puts his fingertips on the table's wooden edge and feels a faint vibration against his skin. His boyfriend is on the verge of freaking the hell out.

Oh, shit—he's serious.

"It takes a few months, and I think by then I will have finally gotten certain lessons about trust through Jasper's thick skull." Ambrus swallows visibly. "My goal is to be done in June, July at the latest."

Pretend it's normal, because it is, Rex thinks. "So, summer," he says casually.

Ambrus bites his lip before nodding. "Summer," he agrees. The glass chiming slows and stops. The table seems less like it's going to vibrate itself to bits. "Then your father can mock me all he fucking well likes for not getting out when he suggested I should."

"When was that—sorry. NDAs," Rex says, but Ambrus is tilting his head.

"You don't have any trouble with the idea of an older boyfriend, do you?"

Rex shrugs, smiling. "Mom didn't have issues with the idea of an older husband. I think I can cope." He does kind of want to know *How much older?* but it's not like it really matters.

"Right. I'll—when it's official, when I'm out, I...I don't have the originals anymore, they were lost to a fire, but I'll..." Ambrus seems to be forcing a smile. "I'll show you a copy of my immigration paperwork. It has my original name on it."

Original name. Huh. "Is it NDA territory to ask what that used to be?"

Ambrus's forced smile becomes a real grin. "Éoghan Beathan Kellagh-Ambrus."

"Fucking bless you?" Rex offers in horror. He can speak four languages fluently, understands at least six more, knows basic phrases in at least a half-dozen after that, and he still has no fucking idea what Ambrus just said.

Ambrus laughs and slows down his pronunciation. "*Yo-an Beh-an*, first and middle name. Child of life, born of the yew tree— the immortal child, basically. *Keh-lagh-Am-briss* is Manx, not Scots, but my father had already been Scot for several generations when he married my mother, so we all just pretended it was native. Fuck, why not, right?"

"What does Kellagh-Ambrus mean, then?" Rex asks. The *gh* sound is more like a guttural *gk*, which is neat. It reminds him of how South Island Māori groups treat the *Ng* sound, which is like a sharp and angry *kG*.

Ambrus props his elbow on the table and rests his face on his right hand. It's a gesture that reminds Rex that he's slipped and gone right back to ambidextrous. Oh well; at least they aren't out in public. "It means 'divine strife.' My parents' families—they paid attention to the whispers in the backs of their minds, their instincts. They named all of their children on the third day, not the first, and with a hell of a lot of careful consideration."

Rex looks at Ambrus in disbelief. "Your parents named you 'immortal child of divine strife.' Were they *trying* to curse you?"

Ambrus lifts one finger from his propping hand and points at Rex. "Your name means 'violent king.'"

"Yeah, but that's because my mother thought it was a crime against humanity to name another child 'Also,'" Rex retorts, and Ambrus bursts out laughing. "And dammit, it's Latin, you jackass. *Strong ruler!*"

Ambrus shrugs. "Like that's supposed to make it mean something different."

The coffee that comes after the meal could probably kill someone with a weaker digestive tract. It's a sharply bitter counter to what feels like a real conversation, one that isn't as fraught with as many NDAs. They're still skipping around a lot of subjects, but loopholes are awesome.

"Eight kids. Eight," Ambrus repeats, when Rex tells him about his father's final tally count of offspring. "What the fuck?"

"A lot of coincidental failures of birth control, me included," Rex says, and leaves it at that. Those were birth control failure rates that abandoned the norm and definitely entered "entirely improbable" territory, but Rex would rather watch Ambrus make fun of his father in person.

Ambrus tells Rex about his parents, Ciaran Kathal (Shadowy might of the divine battle? Fuck, but Gaels are terrifying bastards) and Murieall Mùirne Lìos (Arran's sea-bright affection, which at least isn't fraught with horrible implications) and their three children. They lived in mainland Scotland before Ciaran landed a lucrative job with the British government and moved the family to London. That ultimately led them to transplanting to the United States under something consulate-based, but Ambrus doesn't remember the details.

"I was eldest." Ambrus points at himself. "My two younger sisters were Mùirne—Moira—Aileen and Nessa Rose. She was born in London. We used to tease her about being English."

Had. Were. Rex gets an unsettling realization. "They're all dead, aren't they?"

Ambrus nods, but if there's grief in his eyes, it's old and faded. "Everyone died before I turned eighteen."

"Fuck," Rex whispers in shock. He'd suspected Ambrus didn't have a lot of family, not that there was a complete lack. "I'm sorry."

Ambrus shrugs. "It's just been me for a very long time now. I'm used to it."

Bullshit. Rex doesn't voice that opinion aloud. Ambrus is probably well aware of his own lie. "No wonder you didn't ditch when Dad told you to. You didn't have a reason to."

"No. I guess not." Ambrus's cell rings, interrupting them. "Shit, hold on," he says, pulling it out of his trouser pocket. "Oh, this should be a fun conversation. Hello, Jasper."

The response is so loud that Rex can hear it from across the table. "Where the *fuck* are you?"

"Uzbekistan," Ambrus replies. "Please stop shouting and calm the hell down. Garayev had a partner that poisoned our DoD contractor when he got back in from the desert. Sorry about the lack of contact, but I needed to get our half-dead contractor the hell out of the country in case Garayev had yet more friends we didn't know about."

Interesting cover, Rex mouths, and Ambrus grins at him.

"Well, that does explain why we've got thirty-one bodies, but no Americans among them." Fox sounds calmer, but his voice is still carrying clearly—*oh.* Ambrus put him on speaker.

Rex raises an eyebrow. Ambrus nods, holding one finger to his lips.

"That poor bastard. I bet his life is nothing but NDAs as it is," Fox says, and Rex bites down hard on his lip so that he won't laugh.

"I'm sure signing a few more won't hurt him," Ambrus responds, sounding just the right touch of bored and guiltless. "I'm taking him down to Urgench International this evening, and I was going to fly out from there, too—"

"Nooooooope," Fox interrupts. "You actually need to fly back down here, instead."

"Shit, hold on." Ambrus gives Rex an apologetic look and turns the speakerphone off. "What is it?" There's a pause. "You are fucking kidding me. Aw, Goddammit. No, we're already a fucking *week* overdue—no, I do not give a shit about overtime, some of us remember how savings accounts and investment banking works!"

Rex shakes his head and reminds himself that Fox is twenty. Still learning.

He waits until Ambrus says, "Fine, I'll see you sometime after midnight," and hangs up the phone before he pours more coffee for both of them.

"That sounds like it'll be entertaining."

"Entertaining, my ass. I'm going to set a motherfucker on fire, is what," Ambrus grumbles, lowering his phone to glance at Rex. "Trenton? Or did you fly out of Newark? I've got to get you the fuck out of here before I fly back down to sandy doom."

Rex almost says Newark before he realizes it's a terrible idea. "Better make it Allentown—Lehigh International. I'm not ready to drive the car back from the airport without lots of painkillers and swearing. Besides, if I'm not the first one to tell Dad what happened, someone else will, and then it's endless late night phone calls and mockery."

Ambrus's smile makes his eyes light up like sun-dappled waters—there it is. That's what his boyfriend looks like when it's fond nostalgia, not grief, at the forefront of his thoughts. "Nice to see some things haven't changed."

"Not really, no," Rex agrees.

Ambrus selects a number from his contact list that's in a Cyrillic font, puts the phone to his ear, and launches into fluent Russian. Rex picks up on "flight" and "United States" before he loses the thread completely. The end result is an evening flight back to the States with a transfer at La Guardia.

Their farewell is a shared nap in the hotel that rucks up the other bed, proving to their suspicious proprietor that both beds were slept in. One last kiss happens behind a closed door before they put on their own distinct masks of distance and professionalism. Nobody's in the mood to risk three fucking years in jail for an accidental graze of the hand, especially when the DoD wouldn't be in any great hurry to bail them out.

At the airport, Rex's sports duffel is a hell of a lot lighter when he pulls it from the trunk of the old car Euan found—or stole. "All the contraband's gone, huh?"

"Can't put you on a plane to the States with a gun in the carry-on, not without pulling a hell of a lot of strings. Unless you're willing the check the bag?"

Rex tightens his grip on both the duffel and his backpack. "Not after the assholes 'lost' the last two." He'd been in the midst of breaking in that Beretta90two[10] properly, dammit. It might not have stayed on his list of go-to weaponry, but fuck, the thieving bastards could have at least let him finish making the decision before stealing his shit!

Ambrus nods. "Fucking 9/11 ruined air travel forever." He helps Rex stuff his smaller travel bag into the larger duffel, giving Rex only one bag to haul around. His left arm isn't riding in a sling

---

[10] Author's Note: Yes, they really called it that.

anymore, but his shoulder is starting to ache again. He isn't fond of the idea of carrying both bags when he doesn't have to.

"I'm good," Rex says after he gets the duffel settled over his right shoulder.

Ambrus glances around before resting his hand on Rex's right arm, just below his elbow. "I'm estimating another week or two. Please try not to get bored again before I get back."

"Video games and terrible movies only," Rex promises. "You try not to come home looking like a malaria victim."

Ambrus rolls his eyes, but he's smiling. "If I come back with actual malaria, I'm blaming you."

Chapter 5

January 8th 2016:

Allentown is always a crowded disaster. Today it feels worse for no reason other than it's fucking *Allentown*, and being a drunken clusterfuck is what it's famous for.

Django Whetū sips coffee that tastes burnt, watching as the herds from Arrivals traipse through on their way to baggage claim. He's already been here two hours longer than planned thanks to a weather delay that turned out to be a false alarm, like most of them have been this year.

Django finally spies the familiar buzz of Norwegian-pale blond hair above skin that's currently sun-bronzed several shades darker than his own. Rex looks exhausted, a slump to his shoulders that he only gives into if it's been one day too many plus debilitating injury. Django finds obvious signs right away; Rex's left arm is resting in a sling that looks like it was made from a t-shirt and sheer desperation. He doesn't even see Rex's bag until he realizes that Rex is pulling the thing by a single broken strap, giving no fucks about the fact that the duffle is sliding along the floor behind him.

"Oh, now what the shit is this?"

Rex looks up and grins when he sees him. "Hi, Dad."

"Rex." Django hugs him, feeling heat radiating out from Rex's left shoulder. Rex's right hand grips Django's back almost uncomfortably tight, fingertips digging in, before they release each other. "What the fuck did you do to break an arm?"

"Break?" Rex shakes off a few seconds of bafflement. "No, my arm's fine. It's the healing bullet wound that's causing issues."

"A fuckin' *bullet* wound?" Django glares at Rex before he grabs the duffel and slings it over his shoulder. There's not much weight in the bag, but the poor damned thing has definitely put in its last trip.

Rex looks resigned to incoming parental interrogation. "Can we wait until after we're in the car before you start that shit?"

Django nods in wary agreement, unsettled by some odd tone in Rex's voice. Discussing bullet wounds in airports makes people nervous, anyway.

He keeps an eye on his son, watching as sheer stubbornness carries Rex from the Lehigh Valley public terminal and out to short-term parking.

"Your flight was out from La Guardia." Django drops Rex's bag into the trunk of his car. "Nobody in New York has a gun anymore unless they're a cop. You didn't piss off a cop, did you?"

Rex slowly lowers himself into the passenger seat, swearing under his breath until he manages to get the seatbelt buckled. "No, because then there would be a dead cop, and I'd be hiding in the sewers like a damned ninja turtle." Django gets in the car, buckling up as Rex leans back in his seat. "Fuck, I think I've decided that I hate flying," Rex says.

"That's not my fault," Django mutters, starting the car. It's a *little* bit his fault, but he did manage to land the damned plane. Several pieces of it, yes, but it was still a landing. The problem came down to the fact that it had been plane crash number three for Rex, and three is too often the magic fucking number.

Rex winces when they hit a hole in the street carved out by last year's ice and shoddy street maintenance. Django makes a note of that pained response and does his best to avoid the others, which is like trying to avoid televised news of Bill Clinton's blowjob in 1998.

It's the second week of January, but Allentown traffic is still insane. All of the holiday sales are over; please go home, assholes.

Django gets them onto the interstate west before he glances at Rex. "Talk."

"There anything on the news about an ISIS nest getting wiped out in Turkmenistan?"

Django frowns. "Nothing detailed, just a nice overhead shot of a crater—" He breaks off and smiles. "I should've known. How many?"

"Wasn't actually ISIS, but they were still assholes, so there are thirty-one less terrorist fucksticks in the world." Rex tries to settle himself more comfortably in the seat. Django has been assured by multiple passengers that it's an impossible job.

"And you got shot...why?" Django asks. "You're better than that."

"Armor piercing rounds." From his peripheral, Django can see Rex shaking his head. "Went straight through the fucking vest, delivered by the last asshole standing. He didn't stand for much longer after that, though."

Django nods. Sometimes you can't account for all the variables, even if you know about them. He's just glad the bullet didn't hit anything vital. "Did anything else fun happen while you were out in the desert?"

Rex pretends to think about it. "I met a very nice camel, and a bartender who could make the best martini I've ever had. Downside: he also poisoned me. Weird fucking day."

Django's hands tighten on the steering wheel. "He did what, and is he fucking *dead?*"

"Oh, way dead," Rex assures him. "And I'm not dying. Chill."

"Poison, Rex!" Django snarls. He downshifts long enough to pass an obnoxious driver cruising along in the center lane, walking their damned car. "How are you not actually dying?"

"Oh, it ended up being a cross-department sort of operation." If the tone of Rex's voice hadn't been warning enough, the way his kid is determinedly staring straight ahead is a huge fucking tip.

Anger and fear curl together in Django's gut. "Details. Now."

"Took a DoD contract for that supposed ISIS nest, just wanting something to shoot at." Rex is still not looking at him. "My contact agent on the ground in Turkmenistan was selling out servicemen and contractors for money. A DoD agent from a different department was also on-site, trying to ferret out the troublemaker. He succeeded while I was off in the desert shooting people, and we met in the bar by chance when I came back."

Django rolls his eyes. Went for a drink before hitting up medical—he can almost guarantee Rex did exactly that. Django would probably have done the same. "And the bartender?"

Rex shifts in his seat again, but this time Django is picking up on physical discomfort mixed with embarrassment. "He was, uh, *bratva*. They're still a little pissed off."

The chuckle breaks free before he can stop it. "A little? Poisoning someone who's DoD in public is more than a little pissed off, Rex."

"Yeah, yeah. Shut up," Rex grumbles. "Anyway. That same DoD agent was nice enough to make sure I didn't die. Also, he shot the bartender through both eyes after I went down. Still sorry I missed that part."

Both eyes. That plucks a random string of memory, but whatever it is won't come to him.

Django concentrates on driving instead, trying not to embed his fingers in the car's steering wheel in a restrained panic. "Are they recruiting?" he manages to ask without growling.

"Oh, fuck no," Rex replies at once. When Django has a moment to look again, Rex is frowning. "So many NDAs, Dad. So. Fucking. Many. Hell, I've been actively discouraged from joining up."

Django tries to pretend that he's not letting out a relieved sigh as he focuses on the road again. Some serious fucking concerns were just eased by the certainty in Rex's voice. "You must have run into someone decent from that mess."

"Yeah. Pretty sure I did."

He's distracted for a while, dealing with a patch of idiotic fucking traffic. It's not even snowing, and still drivers are acting like January means it's the end of the world.

When Django gets clear of the mess—two accidents, what the actual fuck—he looks over to find that Rex fell asleep while Django was cursing at traffic.

That's a hell of a surprise. Rex doesn't like to sleep in moving vehicles, a trait from childhood that developed even before Rex kept finding planes and cars with a bad tendency to strike other objects.

His son's hair is starting to grow out enough to get the curl distinctive to Django's side of the family. Rex is fine, if tired, but a few days ago it was definitely a different story.

"Shit, kid," Django whispers, and concentrates on getting them home safe.

A county sheriff's car is waiting at the house when Django pulls up in front of the closed garage. He has another project going on inside, and it's not like there's any fucking snow to worry about, so he parks there and pulls the e-brake. Rex is, by some miracle, still asleep—he didn't wake up from the transition to county roads, or during the trip down their own long, meandering, bumpy driveway. His plane ride from overseas must have been a crapshoot, and the delays didn't help.

Django gets out of the car and stretches his arms upwards. The drive from Allentown is usually an hour, even with snow, but everyone turned extra-stupid and made it two hours of complete fuckery.

"Aren't you supposed to be at work?" he asks his visiting sheriff.

Khodî is leaning against his car with his coat stripped off. It's half-covering one of the blue bubble lights on top. "Hey, when Rex comes here instead of going back to Trenton, then I'm going to be a nosy sibling and come find out why."

Rex pushes open the other door, stands up, and immediately bends over. "If I throw up, nobody is allowed to say a damned word."

"What the fuck did you do, get shot again?" Khodî teases, grinning.

"Yes," Rex retorts.

All of the humor vanishes from Khodî's face. "Shit. How the hell did you manage that in New York?"

"Not New York. Tried to make friends in Turkmenistan. Didn't work out well," Rex says, slowly standing back up. He's biting his lip, but his color's still good. Django thinks Rex will make it through the rest of the day without a repeat of wanting to vomit up his insides.

"And you didn't take me with you?" Khodî asks indignantly.

"You have this thing called a job and a schedule, Mister Sheriff Som, sir."

"It would have been fun, though. My job's so goddamned boring when it's not tourist season," Khodî grouses.

Rex starts to look unhappy. "Shit, I just realized how much paperwork I'm going to have to take to a doctor's office to get physical therapy. I'd rather go get shot again."

"NO!" Django and Khodî both shout at once.

"Aw, come on." Rex grins at Khodî. "It can't take nearly as much paperwork to explain an accidental weapons discharge."

"Blow me," Khodî retorts. He grabs his coat before following them to the porch. "You couldn't pay me enough to have to fill out that pile of bullshit."

"I'm so glad it's paperwork that keeps the two of you from killing each other." Django shakes his head. "Come on, you stupid shits. There's coffee on."

Khodî's eyes light up. "Coffeeeeee."

"Fuck coffee," Rex mutters. "You can have *all* the coffee, Khodî. I just want a beer."

"You've been shot," Django points out.

"Which is exactly why I want the fucking beer!"

Django smiles and slides the key into the lock of the kitchen door. "Not before noon."

"That is in *ten minutes,*" Rex whines.

"You can wait." Django pushes the door open when it wants to stick. The frame is starting to warp again as the house settles, age and weather taking their toll. He enters the kitchen to a ringing phone and picks it up while Rex and Khodî are still toeing off their shoes. "Yeah?"

"Colonel Whetū, sir."

Django's blood runs cold, making it feel like the temperature in the house dropped forty degrees in an instant. "That's Mister Whetū, whoever the hell you are," he corrects them, trying not to grind his teeth. He's been fully retired since 1991, and he will remind these damned D.C. government fucksticks of that every single chance he gets. Colonel is a courtesy title he earned with his retirement, but D.C. bureaucrats don't have good manners in mind when they call him that.

"Ah, yes, of course. Forgive me. I see you've been retired for quite some time now," the voice says in a blatant lie. Male, perfect enunciation—sounds like a complete prick. Django already wants to put a bullet through the man's head, and he's only known the fucker for thirty seconds.

"What do you want?" Django asks, aware that his kids are watching. He must be a lot more pissed off than he realizes, since Khodî's eyes are narrowed, prepared to deal with another problem while his hand rests damned close to the gun on his belt. Rex looks prepared for more government bullshit.

"We here at the Department of Defense are aware of your son's final destination this morning, *Mister* Whetū. We just need to speak with him to clear up a few final details."

More than one bullet, Django thinks while handing the phone to Rex. "It's for you."

*   *   *   *

"What the fuck?" Rex asks, once he's sure that his father's hand is still covering the receiver of the old landline phone.

"DoD," Django mouths, and Rex wants to bang his head against the nearest wall. Shit.

Rex takes the phone while gesturing for Khodî to get him a damned beer, because fuck noon. Noon just became *now*, especially if he has to talk to someone from Ambrus's department.

"Hello."

"Ah. Mister Chin, sir."

The man's voice shoves Rex's temper right out onto a knife's edge. "That's *Major Tjin*," he corrects through gritted teeth. Fuck, no wonder their dad looks so pissed off. "How can I help you, whoever the fuck you are?"

"Your entire family is so crude of language." The man makes a *tsk*-ing sound like some irate school taskmaster. "The Department of Defense wishes to know of your current state of health."

"Not dead," Rex says. He tucks the phone between his ear and his right shoulder so he can grab the beer Khodî brings him, taking a swig the moment it's in his hand. "Get to the point."

"Fine." A lot of polish disappears from the caller's voice, but not the precise delivery of his words. "I represent a certain department within the DoD. I'm sure you're aware of our existence, especially given the number of NDAs you've signed in recent months that acknowledge your willingness not to reveal our existence to others, including your own family. Trust me, we've made certain of that."

Rex feels his lips curl back from his teeth. That sounds like a threat, and he isn't in the mood. "Yeah. Lots of those to sign."

"You worked well with one of our agents in a field capacity. Given your excellent military service, past and present, as well as...certain family history, my department wishes to extend a formal offer of employment to you."

Rex takes another sip of beer before scowling. "No."

"Now, Mister Chin—"

"See, now you're doing that on purpose." Rex falls back into an easy, relaxed speech pattern that's put a lot of jackasses off their guard over the years. "It's Major Tjin. If you're so impressed with my record, get my fucking rank correct, asshole."

"Very well, Major Tjin." The prick's pronunciation of his name is suddenly perfect. "Potential animosity aside, the offer being made is sincere. We here in the department can make it worth your while, I assure you."

Rex puts the bottle down on the narrow side table near the door so he can take the phone in a firm grip again. "You heard my answer, but you don't seem to believe me, so listen up. The last time someone tried to coerce my family into doing government bullshit after being told no, a whole lot of bureaucrats ended up in body bags. It was a great fucking week, and some of it even made the news. So, unless you want to become another stupid dead shit residing in a shiny new body bag, you will kindly fuck the hell off."

"You do not know who you're refusing, Major."

"I don't care," Rex replies. "I'm not stupid, and I know what I'm turning down."

"And if I made the offer to other, equally qualified members of your family?"

"You'd get the same answer." Rex smiles. "Piss off, don't call back, and maybe go die in a fire. I don't care, but leave us the hell alone."

"Major—"

Rex slams the phone back down into its cradle. "Motherfucker!" he declares, and chugs down half the beer before turning around to face his father and brother.

Khodî gives him a genial golf-clap. "My little brother just told the U.S. government to go get fucked. I'm so proud."

Django has a flat, grim look on his face. "I just hope they take no for an answer."

"If they don't, bullets are very good at also affirming my refusal," Rex counters, polishing off the beer. "Fuck them—shit. I may have blown my spotted career as a DoD contractor, though."

"Probably," Khodî agrees, smiling. "You penniless?"

Rex smiles. "More flush than you, Mister Sheriff, sir."

"Bite my ass, brother," Khodî shoots back while rubbing at the scar on his right temple, earned during his last year in the service. The car accident embedded glass into Khodî's face, leaving him with scars that healed up to look like fracture lines down his cheek and along his forehead. The weather's been doing weird shit; Khodî says that sometimes the swift pressure changes make the old injury hurt like hell.

Django sighs, but he looks like he's trying to smile. "Khodî, get me a fucking beer, would you? It's 12:01."

Rex has two glasses of water instead of more beer, because he really isn't stupid, and then takes a nap upstairs in his old bedroom. He wakes up a few hours later feeling a hell of a lot better. Food even sounds appealing again, and the overseas flight had done a damned good job of destroying his appetite. He's calmed down, too—he doesn't want to take every weapon in the house to the range out back and blow through a year's worth of ammunition.

Khodî went back to work, so dinner is himself, Django, and Wesley, who is very good at turning up at seemingly random moments when he might be needed. Wesley listens to the non-classified parts of Rex's Turkmenistan adventure, but seems more interested in Bait the Camel than in dead terrorist assholes.

Rex does not mention the *bratva,* and neither does Django. His father is either being nice—doubtful—or saving that blackmail for a truly vile moment in the future.

"All right, show me your range of movement," Wesley orders after dinner. He spent so much time playing physical therapist for his teammates that he went to school for it after retiring, and he knows his shit.

Rex sighs and removes the mock sling, holding up both arms. It makes his left arm burn like a motherfucking forge, but he can hold it there for a five-count before giving up. He lifts his arms again after a minute's relief, pointing both hands at Wesley, fingertips out, rotates them in a brief circle, and then drops his arms to his sides again when it hurts too fucking much. "Well?"

Wesley frowns at Rex while running one hand through his short-buzzed hair. "I think you're good," he says at last, "but I'd still call Kai, just in case. I usually deal with torn ligaments and idiots who don't know how to lift properly, not bullets."

Rex dials up Kai the next day, after he knows his baby brother is done with classes but not yet distracted by Perelman's other prospects. He gets a stranger on the line instead of Kai or Kai's roommate and decides he's in the mood to fuck with someone.

"Looking for Ki te Muri kā 'Aukai," Rex says, grinning.

"Who the hell is that?" Rex's victim asks in a high-pitched male voice.

"Kai 'Aukai. He never told you he's walking around using his aunt's nickname, did he?"

"I don't fucking blame the dude." The kid lowers the phone and shouts for Kai.

"Hey, there," Rex says, once he gets Kai on the phone. "How's the slicing and dicing?"

"Dicey," Kai replies happily. "That shit you pulled off in the desert is on the news, by the way. Awesome job."

"Why do you think it was me?" Rex asks, feeling his grin widen. He knows his name isn't attached to the news footage. The government doesn't like to admit it when private contractors clean up their messes. They prefer to claim all the credit for themselves.

"Crater in the desert? Please. I know your signature when I see it," Kai says dryly. "How shot up are you?"

"Just one hit, under the left collarbone, above the lung. Wesley already says my basic range of motion looks good, but he wants you to confirm."

"Hooo." Kai whistles. "You lucky bastard. That's a narrow margin for error." He makes a humming sound. "What happens when you move your arm around in a full circle?"

"Hurts like fuck, but otherwise there's no motion restriction," Rex answers. "At this point, I'd rather get physical therapy advice from you and Wesley instead of some dumb shit that scraped their way through medical school to get a license."

"That's because all of my siblings recognize my genius." Kai gives Rex a set of professional instructions to follow to make sure he heals up properly: yoga stretches, physical therapy exercises, a few balms to apply that are Eastern-based but work a hell of a lot better than most Western alternatives, times for ice, times for heat, and so on. Rex knows most of this already, since he trained for it, but sometimes Kai reminds him of something he forgot, or Kai has new ideas that are fucking brilliant.

"That reminds me—you still graduating in May?" Rex asks.

Kai lets out a glum sigh. "No. My advisor finally did his job and discovered I missed two classes back at the beginning, so I need to get them taken care of during the first summer session. Perelman won't let me test out so I can graduate on time. The advisory board likes to point out like snide fuckers that I'm graduating medical school at twenty-three, and thus have no right to bitch."

"Dickish of them," Rex agrees. Kai's been hounded by ten different hospitals for the last two years, all of them wanting to give his baby brother a residency. It's not entirely unheard of for someone to get through medical school before twenty-six, but it's not common, either. The only reason Kai's been delayed this long is because their high school refused to advance him at the right pace. Kai would be a practicing doctor already if they hadn't held him back, but it's just as well. Doogie Howser jokes were starting to creep into consideration.

"Hey, hold on a sec," Rex says before Kai has the chance to pry him off of the phone and go perform an evening of mischief, or whatever the fuck students at Perelman do when they're not in class. "Summertime is boyfriend-meeting time."

"Legit this time, and not more random work excuses?" Kai asks. "You know if the dude doesn't show, Khodî's going to start with the accusations that the man's not real."

Rex glances over to see Wesley and Django both staring right at him, almost identical looks of polite disbelief on their faces. "Yes, *legit* this time," he emphasizes for the assholes in the room. "He's retiring in July. No DoD bullshit schedules to deal with after that."

"Awesome!" Kai exclaims. "That means you get laid on a regular schedule, too!"

"Kai!" Rex sputters, but Kai laughs and hangs up. Dammit, his baby brother does *not* need to learn bad habits from Khodî!

Rex hangs up the phone and goes back to the kitchen table for a welcome beer. "Well?"

Wesley grins. "Can't wait. Interrogation of the innocent always gives us something to thrive on."

"Too bad—I warned him in advance," Rex says. "He can deal with all of my asshole siblings *and* Dad."

Wesley shrugs. "Fine. We'll just sic Nari on him," he says, which makes their father grin like a damned shark.

Shit. Ambrus is maybe a little bit doomed if they put Neumia to work. Still worth it, though.

* * * *

Django doesn't need to insist on keeping Rex at the farm for a few more days. Rex is willing to wait for his shoulder to heal well enough to handle the drive from Newark to Trenton. It's not a long trip on a good day, but it's Jersey traffic, and thus completely fucking unpredictable. His kids heal up fast, though, so it's only the twelfth when they head out.

That also happens to be the one day the weather decides to remember that it's Pennsylvania in fucking January. Rex is screwing around with his cell phone while Django has his eyes glued to the road. The ground's too warm for the snow to stick; it's the wind that's the damned problem. Sudden gusts keep blowing loose snow over the highway and into the air, obscuring his line of sight and hiding the asphalt until another blast clears it away again.

He has no idea what Rex is up to until his son clears his throat. "So, uh, I know you don't like a lot of the music that was popular during Vietnam, but uh...I heard a remake that I thought you might actually like."

Django's eyes narrow at once. There were a lot of anti-war songs during Vietnam, yes, but many of them are tied to some really awful memories.

Rex is giving him the chance to say no, too. He appreciates that, but none of his kids have ever brought up the subject quite like this before. Curiosity wins out over the desire not to think about the war.

"Okay," Django says, forcing his grip on the steering wheel to relax a little. "Go for it."

"The band is called Disturbed."

Django cocks his head in surprise. "I've heard some of their music on the radio. Are you sure—"

"Trust me," Rex says, and plays the song.

The first piano notes hit Django hard, even though he doesn't recognize the song until the lyrics start. Then "The Sound of Silence" is just haunting as all hell. He's mouthing the words without even realizing it until he notices that Rex is doing the same.

He used to sing. It's a part of his culture, one his mother made sure he knew and understood.

He hasn't been able to get a musical word out of his throat since his wife died. Even this silent repetition is more than he's managed in sixteen years.

"Fuck," Django whispers as the song hits the end of the third verse. He can feel his eyes burning as he clenches his jaw against way too many emotions that want to hit at once.

"Should I turn it off?"

"It's fine," Django manages to say, gruff without meaning to be. Rex falls silent, letting him focus on the words in the last verse.

Django swallows hard when the notes fade away and Rex shuts off the music. "Shit. That asshole gets it."

"Yeah. I thought so, too," Rex says. When Django glances over, Rex is partially slouched in the passenger seat, his thumb resting over the dark screen of his phone. His eyes are focused on the swirling white drifts of snow, but Django doesn't think it's snow that he's seeing.

"You all right?" Django asks, taking a moment to wipe his eyes.

"Me? Sure." Rex looks over at him. "What is it?"

"Is there anything else like that?" Django asks hesitantly. If a band that slides towards the metal side of rock can grasp that fucking concept, maybe others have, too.

"Remake, or just the feel?"

Django shrugs. "Either."

Rex stumbles across someone named Lisa Gerrard covering "All Along the Watchtower." Django doesn't know what to expect, but it isn't *that,* and his eyebrows keep climbing as the song progresses.

"Well, that was fuckin' creepy," Django declares when the song ends, and they both start laughing. "Fuck, forget that idea. Find something modern, okay?"

Rex nods and scrolls through a music listing until he pulls up a song called "Bad Blood." It's all moody guitar and smoky voices coming out of the darkness, looking for redemption.

"Alison Mosshart and Eric Arjes," Rex tells him without being asked.

Django nods. Bad blood—now there is a theme that fits his mood. He passed bad blood along to eight kids, and he never wants any of them to have to pay for it.

Before he gets out of the car in Newark's long-term parking lot, Rex says, "Still not joining up with the fucking department."

"I know." Django nods and tilts his head in the direction of Rex's car. "After that phone call bullshit, I'm still following you home."

Rex frowns and looks to be on the verge of arguing before something stops him. Common sense, maybe, or a hell of a lot of experience kicking in. "Yeah, fine. Waste of gas, Dad."

Django shrugs. "My gas to waste. Move your ass, kid."

It isn't only about the gas, or potential pricks out of D.C., and Rex knows that, too. Bullet wounds, blood loss—that can fuck with your perception even days later. Your body gets tired and forgets to check in to let you know, and then shit can turn sour in a damned hurry. Django's not happy until they get off the freeway and he sees Rex parallel-parked in front of his duplex in Trenton.

Django double-parks next to Rex's car, ignoring the jackass who honks as he drives around. The street ends a few houses down; the other driver can cope.

Nosy Lois isn't home, but the Hispanic kid, Juan, peeks out from an upstairs window on the other side of the duplex. He smiles at Rex, but only gives Django a tentative, fearful wave before he disappears again in a blur of pale skin and dark hair.

Django sighs. He isn't that terrifying.

No, be honest. He is *usually* not that terrifying.

Rex already has his door open before Django's gathered enough courage to ask the question that's been eating at him since Rex told him about department involvement in Turkmenistan. "The agent who helped you out—was she shorter than me, ginger hair that can compete with a lit match?"

Rex's shoulders hunch in an immediate line of tension, which is all the answer Django needs. "See you later, Dad," he says, and closes the door behind him. Django listens to his kid slowly clomp his way up the old wooden staircase, and doesn't get back in his car until he hears the upstairs door open and shut.

Django fucking hates NDAs. They ruin everything, including his son's ability to talk to him about what really went down near Iran.

So: he cheats.

Once he's out of Trenton and on the highway heading northeast, away from Pennsylvania, he dials a number he's known from memory for over a quarter-century. "Merrill residence," a bubbly female voice says.

Django smiles. "Hi there, Martha. How are things?"

"Colonel!" Martha Bellamy sounds thrilled. Django suspects she has a minor crush on him. It's flattering, but that's not a complication he needs right now, thanks.

"Things are actually very well today," Martha continues. "My patient has been behaving himself, ate both meals, and swore at me about how he needed me around when his wife was still alive because she couldn't cook. You know; the usual."

"No, Helen Merrill could not cook," Django agrees. Scrambled eggs, coffee, and toast had been about the limit of the good doctor's repertoire. "Listen, I know it's afternoon, and that's usually naptime, but I need to speak to our favorite grumpy General. Can you get him on the line for me? Use one of those Bluetooth things so he doesn't have to hold up the phone."

"You got it, Colonel!"

Django pulls into a random travel plaza on the Jersey Turnpike, sets the e-brake after shifting into neutral, and waits. He can hear Martha's chirpy birdsong voice in the background, and faint responses coming from someone else. The brief, noisy clatter signals that the line is being swapped over to something a hell of a lot more secure than Django's cheap prepaid cell phone bought off a truck stop rack.

"General Merrill," Jason Merrill snaps. "Martha is being a bitch and won't tell me who this is, so I hope it's fucking important."

Django grins. "Well, look who's full of piss and vinegar today!"

"I'll be damned. Django Whetū," Jason replies, his voice getting breathy as he gives up on sounding like a man about to wreak havoc on the unsuspecting. "How are you?"

"Doing all right," Django answers, trying not to flinch. He hates it when Jason asks him that, because asking Jason the same question in response feels redundant, stupid, and cruel. His friend is fucking dying of cancer. A good day is not puking up your lunch after you eat it, and they both know it.

"Good to know. Saw where one of your kids blew the shit out of something in the desert," Jason says proudly.

"Blame Rex. He's the only one still crazy enough to take DoD contracts." Django hesitates. "There were...certain individuals involved."

Jason is suddenly a lot more alert. "Are they recruiting?"

"The agent on the ground actively discouraged Rex from taking a job in that particular department," Django says. "It was a prick that called out of D.C. who tried the recruiting bullshit. Rex told our friend on the phone to fuck off. Probably dried up his contract list in the process, but my kids know better, Jason."

"Of course they do. Some asshole raised them right."

Django bites back a smile. He'd done his best, even if his best had left him with a lot of baffled teachers resorting to heavy drinking in order to cope with an entire clan of Whetūs in their school system. "How you doing, Jason?" he makes himself ask.

Jason drags out a minute of silence before sighing. "You never call to talk shit about my health. You need something."

Django thumps his head back against his seat's headrest. "That isn't the only reason I call."

"Bullshit," Jason says fondly. "I know why you don't, and it's okay. However, I know there's nothing wrong with your writing hand, asshole. Send me some gossipy letters. Dying is a hell of a lot more boring than I expected it to be."

Django bites on his hand until he knows he can talk without emotion slipping into his voice. "Gossipy letters. Roger," he agrees. "I need a secure contact phone number for a man with his hair on fire, Jason."

"Him, huh? Well, that's been a while," Jason muses aloud. "Might have to talk to David. That's not going to be an easy thing to get. You got any favors left in D.C. that you can call in, Colonel?"

"A few. If David has to push, your son can remind the man who was Director of Central Intelligence in 1991 that I cleaned up that mess," Django says.

"You got paid for cleaning up that mess, Django," Jason reminds him dryly.

"It wasn't about the money, and he knows it. Use the favor and text me a phone number. I need to—it's just to talk. I swear."

Jason sighs again. "All right. Give me about an hour, huh?"

"Sure," Django agrees. "One hour. I—I'll talk to you later, Jason."

"Won't be dying tomorrow, so you'd damned well better," Jason retorts, hanging up.

Django gets out of his car, sliding the phone into his pocket. One of the overcrowded, overpriced joints in this place should have coffee. He needs something that kicks like a fucking mule. That's already three hits too many today, and he's about to take one more.

He's caffeinated and knows the route he's taking back home—longer than necessary, but paranoia keeps him alive—when his phone finally beeps an incoming text. The number has a D.C. area code, but Django doubts that D.C. is the phone's current location.

Django gets back in the car, seatbelt on, and starts the engine to cover up the sound of conversation for anyone passing too close. He dials the number, trying to ignore the way his stomach is knotting up, and waits.

The phone picks up when he's pretty sure it's on the verge of going to voicemail. "It is midnight where I am," he hears, the words spoken in a grumpy, sleepy mumble. "This is an unfamiliar United States number calling me, and if you are a telemarketer, I absolutely do swear that I will hunt you down and kill you."

Django finds himself grinning. The man's lost a hell of a lot more of the Brit accent, but he knows that voice. "Only thing I have to sell is bullets, and they're not cheap."

"Oh my God—*Django?*" He listens to the rapid shift of moving fabric. "What the hell—how the fuck did you even get this number?"

"Called in a favor," Django says, enjoying the pun.

"You've been retired for over twenty fucking years. How many favors can you possibly have left?" Kellagh-Ambrus asks in disbelief.

"Not many. Saving them for a rainy day. Listen, I won't keep you for long. I only wanted to say thank you."

He can all but hear Kellagh-Ambrus tensing up, just like Rex did. "Thank me for what?"

"Oh, you know how it is. There's a big-ass crater on television in the Middle East. Something about an ISIS cell. Or maybe it was *bratva*," Django adds. He knows he's right when he hears a swift intake of breath.

"You're welcome, but I didn't do it for you."

Django decides to push, especially with that kind of bait dangling. "Didn't know any of you lot were tracking my kids, not at this stage."

Kellagh-Ambrus's response is genuine; Django always knows when it's not. "I didn't even know that you *had* kids until very recently. I put off the resemblance to a coincidence."

"A Māori man with blond hair?" Django smirks. "Really? You gettin' that bad at your job?"

"He said he had a European grandparent," Kellagh-Ambrus mutters. "I was willing to let it be. Call it a coincidence. You didn't seem like the Dad type. Fuck, did I feel stupid the moment I realized whose kid he had to be."

"I'm still saying thank you. And I—" Django lowers his head, clenching his jaw until his fucking traitorous feelings calm the hell down. "I'm glad you're still around, Kid."

"I haven't been that stupid kid in a long damned time, Django," Kellagh-Ambrus replies quietly. "But I'm glad you're still around, too."

Django glances up at the car's dull gray ceiling, breathing through another hammer coming down on way too much ancient history. "I should go. Anything else I need to know?"

Kellagh-Ambrus lets out a quiet snort of amusement. "Ask me again in July," he says, and disconnects the call.

Django slowly lowers his phone down to rest on his lap. July. That's important, someone mentioned it recently—

A minute later, Django puts his hand over his eyes and starts howling with laughter, scaring the shit out of a tourist walking past his driver's side door.

*   *   *   *

Rex holds out for about a day before he decides he can't stand his empty apartment right now. His shoulder is hurting from the colder weather, a dull, annoying throb. He swallows three acetaminophen before packing a few days' worth of clothes. Ambrus has a stacked washer and dryer in the hallway alcove, so that's enough to last him a while. The washing machines in the duplex's murky basement are coin-op and they work, but some days it's not worth fighting the spiders just to have a clean shirt. Rex doesn't have anything against spiders, but he also knows when he's strategically outnumbered.

Thirty-one against one, a voice in Rex's head reminds him, sounding an awful lot like his boyfriend.

Still wasn't strategically outnumbered, thank you very much. He doesn't hear any further twinges from his conscience, or common sense, or whichever part of his brain decided to whine about being shot.

Rex finds Lois sitting on her concrete doorstep, feeding a stray cat. "You'll be up to four cats by February."

"Baby, that's the goal," Lois replies, but the black cat bolts the moment it realizes that Rex is standing about six feet too close. "Poor pussy cat. He used to live 'bout two streets over. Bastards tossed him out on the street when they moved away. Now he's shy, doesn't like people."

"Don't blame him at all. See you in a couple of weeks."

"Did you pack those cookies?" Lois yells after him.

Rex doesn't break stride. "Sure did."

"You're a bad liar, baby!"

Rex grins. "You're the one who said they'll keep in the freezer!"

Ambrus's place is just as empty, making Rex wonder why he wanted to come here. Then the soft whisper of the central heating system kicks on, and the tension all but oozes out of Rex's shoulders. The apartment is quiet in a way that he needs after Turkmenistan. Weird. Usually it's the other way around.

Rex reprograms the thermostat back to habitable levels instead of the balmy fifty-eight degrees Ambrus leaves it set at if he's going to be out for a long time, going for broke at seventy. The desert wasn't hot, but he got used to that temperature fast, and he damned well wants it back. There hasn't been any more snow since the flurries on the twelfth, but it's finally sort-of-cold outside.

He leaves his bag on the side of Ambrus's bed that somehow became his, checks to make sure nothing broke in their absence, hits the local hippie-whole-foods market to put something in the fridge, and then runs out of things to do. Dammit.

Oh, well, Rex thinks, picking up the television remote to turn on both it and the Blu-ray box that gives him Netflix options. They never did get around to watching that second *Star Wars* prequel movie. Maybe he can tell Ambrus about it when his boyfriend gets back from whatever the fuck he's still doing out in the desert with Fox and Banner.

An hour and fifty-three minutes into the second prequel, Rex is staring at the screen in angry amazement. "You have got to be fucking kidding me."

He rewinds the movie and lets it play the scene again. No, they were not kidding.

Then he watches it a third time. Yes, he is indeed witnessing a supposed Jedi Master perform an onscreen, unnecessary decapitation of a bounty hunter that had already been literally disarmed. A Māori bounty hunter, one with a kid to raise.

Fuck, no wonder his father hates this movie.

Rex waits out the rest of the film—yep, there goes a protagonist's limb—just to finish what he started. The only good thing he gets out of the flick is an understanding of why Kai wouldn't stop with the "Seeding the South Pacific" jokes when the movie came out.

He gets a phone call from Ambrus's cell as the credits are rolling, so he turns down the volume and answers. "Hey. Wasn't expecting to hear from you."

"Hi there. What are you up to?" Ambrus's voice warms Rex in a way the central heating can't, all the way through to his core. He hadn't realized how much he'd needed that until it happened.

"Watching movies. Trying to figure out if I'm going to be rooting for Darth Vader in the third *Star Wars* prequel."

"Oh, that's not a good sign." Ambrus pauses. "I, er, got a phone call the other day. From your father."

Rex puts his hand over his eyes and resists the urge to sink down into the couch cushions. "I didn't give him the number."

"Oh, I know. He's not without his own resources, the cheating motherfucker," Ambrus says. It takes Rex a minute to realize that he's hearing fond annoyance, not anger.

Rex tries to figure out if he's angry or relieved that one potential July landmine has already been disarmed. "Okay. Now what?"

"I'll be home in about a week. We can discuss it then. I just..." Rex can hear Ambrus swallow. "You're all right. Yes?"

"Still hurts, but yeah, I'm fine." He can't resist. "Why, did you manage to get shot after I left?"

"No," Ambrus retorts, miffed. "I'll see you in a week, Rex."

Rex grins. "Must've been a stab wound, then."

"Fuck you and your accurate guesses. I love you." Ambrus hangs up before Rex can reply.

Rex shuts off the television and goes to the bedroom, plugging in his phone to charge before he lies down. He feels better than he has in days, and all it took was a three-minute phone call that left a doofy smile on his face.

He might have been drugged and pain-loopy when he said it, but yeah: he really does love that man. He's not sure how this became his life in such a short amount of time, but Euan Ambrus is one of the best damn birthday presents Rex has ever received.

The rest of the week passes in a blur of books and interesting visual entertainment. At one point, Rex grabs his Bluetooth and dials his phone with one hand as the show on the television keeps playing, volume muted.

"Hello, you have reached the dorm of Kai 'Aukai, and I may kill you for interrupting my studying," Kai says in greeting. It's so similar to the message Kai has set to voice mail that it takes Rex a moment to realize it's actually his brother talking, not a recording.

"Hey, slicer-and-dicer."

"Rex! Didn't expect to hear from you again so soon. Did you fuck up your shoulder?" Kai asks suspiciously.

"Nah. I was wondering if you knew they'd made cartoons about the war that happens during those *Star Wars* prequels."

"I know that there are two different cartoons, but I never got around to watching them. I was dealing with high school bullshit during the first cartoon, and the second started up when I was in my first year of college," Kai says. "Why?"

"Be prepared for more 'Seeding the South Pacific' jokes." Rex sighs. "Two of the main character clones are named Cody and Rex."

Kai laughs until he sounds like he's wheezing. "I knew about Cody because of the third movie, but Rex? Really?"

"Yep." Rex doesn't want to comment further than that. For a kid's show, the animators really didn't hold back on the battle sequences, and some of it has really set off his PTSD. He's just about hit his limit on what he can watch, and that's without the other characters shouting his name all the time. If there was one thing he never had to worry about growing up, it was someone else having Rex's name in his classroom—hell, not even the same state. Sharing a name with a fictional character is fucking *weird*.

"Sooooo, do you think they meant Rex as in the Latin, or Rex as in dog?"

"I got the impression someone was thinking about dogs." Rex watches as a clone soldier is randomly eaten by a gigantic fucking worm, because...reasons, or something. "I know Dad's famous in military circles, and maybe some of his history got spread around through the gossip chains when it shouldn't have been, but this is just getting ridiculous."

"At least Dad's name isn't said even remotely the same way," Kai points out. "First *or* last."

"Most people can't even *pronounce* Dad's last name." Rex flinches when the friendly's base goes up in a fireball. This went on television with a PG rating? How?

Kai snorts. "Should I be watching this or what, Rex?"

"Don't turn it into a drinking game. Your liver would shrivel up and die." Rex turns off the show when the credits roll. He just—he can't. There are too many men dying, and a lot of the battle tactics look to be designed for high body counts. He'd rather watch the old *Ewok* movies from the '80s, or even the fucking holiday special, than try to wade through this shit.

"I'm not sure if that's a yes or a no. Gotta go, Rex. Time for me to literally dice someone up. The challenge is on to find out what killed our recent scientific donation."

"Have fun," Rex says. "Bye, kiddo."

"Farewell, seed of the South Pacific!"

"*You're* a seed of the South Pacific," Rex reminds his baby brother.

"Yeah, but I was actually born in the States, unlike the rest of my lovely siblings," Kai sings out, and then disconnects the call.

Rex turns off his Bluetooth and tosses it aside, shaking his head. He's got to give Kai that one; he's also the only one of the siblings whose mother married their father. Granted, the wedding happened well after Kai was born, so he goes by her name, not Dad's.

Nope, his thoughts going in that direction is not helping at all. He finds *Robin Hood: Men in Tights* and watches it to cleanse his mental palate.

On Friday night, Rex has been asleep for maybe two hours when he hears a key in the lock of the apartment door. His hand automatically goes to the .9mm he has hidden under Ambrus's pillow as he sits up and listens. The door opens, doorknob thudding into the doorjamb, and then someone slaps the entry wall three times.

Rex relaxes when he hears the agreed-upon signal, one they both use even if they're not sure the other is around. He slides the gun under his own pillow before Rex goes out to meet his boyfriend while wearing only a pair of thin cotton shorts.

Ambrus is in the middle of dropping a bag onto the couch and trying to shrug out of his coat when he spies Rex. His eyes go comically wide. "You're—you're here?"

"Yeah. You didn't see my car?" Rex asks. He takes the coat and helps Ambrus out of it before Ambrus manages to tangle himself into a knot. His boyfriend looks like he's seen the ass-end of too many airports in too-few days.

"Didn't drive past the visitor's lot," Ambrus explains. "I didn't know if you—I know we discussed keys and—"

Rex grasps the man's face with both hands and kisses him. Ambrus whimpers, latching on like an octopus as he opens his mouth to deepen the kiss. That feel of connection, of belonging, fills Rex's chest again. He has no idea where this relationship is going, but god, he loves this feeling.

"Hi there. Bad day?" Rex asks, when they break apart.

"Terrible month, hated it, thought someone I loved was going to die," Ambrus whispers, and manages a wobbly smile. "Hi."

"That does sound awful," Rex agrees. "They must be really fucking lucky that you decided to be in the neighborhood."

"Lucky." Ambrus's fingers touch the red mark just below Rex's collarbone. There's an uneven splotch like it on his back, the only remaining visible evidence of his Turkmenistan souvenir. Rex's shoulder still aches a bit, but he can raise his arms over his head now without wincing.

Ambrus lets his fingers drift away from the scar, resting his palm flat on the center of Rex's bare chest. "Yes. Yes, he was. I have to say that being greeted at the door like this? I feel almost as fortunate."

Rex grins. "Not a lot of men greeting you at the door half-naked, then?"

The confused look on Ambrus's face quickly turns into baffled dismay. "Uh—no. Not for a long time."

"Gotcha." Rex starts unbuttoning Ambrus's shirt. "Then it definitely needs to be memorable."

"What are you—oh, *fuck*." Ambrus gasps out as Rex presses him against the living room wall. Rex removes Ambrus's long-sleeved shirt before pulling off the t-shirt Ambrus is wearing beneath it. The moment the shirt is out of the way, Ambrus lunges forward, locking their mouths together. The level of enthusiasm he's displaying definitely counts as delighted consent.

Rex runs his free hand along Ambrus's bared chest, fingers brushing through the sparse, dark red curls that line his torso from mid-chest all the way down to his pelvis. On Rex's way back up, his hand encounters the distinctive stainless steel ball chain that usually bears dog tags.

"Didn't know you had any of these," Rex says, skipping the tags to run his thumb along Ambrus's neck.

"Shit, I forgot." Ambrus yanks at the steel chain until it pops free and drops his tags on the carpet. "No peeking."

"Not a problem. Not only do I have this great distraction in my arms, I turned down the recruitment call I received the day I got home," Rex says.

Ambrus rears back until his head thumps against the wall. "They did *what?*" he asks in outrage.

"Relax." Rex kisses Ambrus again, his lips coming to rest against Ambrus's skin in different places between every sentence. "Turned them down. Not interested. Told them to fuck off and die in a fire."

Ambrus chokes on barely restrained laughter before he grins at Rex. "Well, I'm glad you're certain."

"Hey, my boyfriend is retiring. Got way more important things I'm going to be doing."

"So I see," Ambrus murmurs as Rex swears about the stiff leather belt Ambrus is wearing. "Bloodwork?"

"Clean," Rex answers. "It was just my blood I had to deal with, no infections afterwards. Why, do we need to go back to black-gloved kink because you made a mess?"

"Well, if your bloodwork is clean, then noooo," Ambrus draws out, "because the only blood I had on my hands in the last month was yours. Oh, and my own, but at least it was a clean knife."

"Considerate of the asshole who stabbed you. Hope he's dead."

"Very much so, yes," Ambrus confirms, sounding amused.

There is a faint red line on Ambrus's thigh, a scar from being stabbed, but it looks like it's been healing for months, not days...just like Rex's shoulder. He knows why, but the visual evidence stalls him out for a few seconds.

Then Ambrus's hand is on Rex's head, his fingernails scratching through Rex's short hair to graze his scalp. Rex turns his attention back to far more important matters.

When Rex looks up at Ambrus's face again, his skin is blotched red, his eyes shining with euphoria, and he's gasping for breath. "Holy shit, Rex. What would it take to convince you to move in with me?"

Rex gets to his feet, licking at one of the bite marks he left on Ambrus's neck before placing another gentle kiss on his boyfriend's reddened lips. Ambrus whimpers again. "Retire first, Euan. You've got to get all of that department shit out of your office before there's room for me."

Ambrus gives him an odd look. "I've seen your apartment, Rex. What you own could fit in the corner of the living room."

Rex's fingers touch the strands of his boyfriend's long hair that escaped confinement before he tugs on the ponytail as a hint. Ambrus obliges and tilts his head forward, letting Rex remove the elastic band that kept his hair tied back. The strands, once free, are like flames that fall around Ambrus's face, fire laid against a piercing ocean of blue.

"One thing my grandparents knew, something Dad learned from them? Everyone needs their own space, Euan," Rex says in a soft voice, kissing Ambrus's forehead. "Otherwise you're up in each other's shit so often you drive each other crazy."

Ambrus's gaze saddens. "They were wise people," he whispers. "I'm so sorry you never got to meet them."

Rex draws back in surprise. "You did? But—"

Ambrus puts his finger against Rex's lips, releasing a long sigh. "NDAs. July, Rex. But—yes. I did. Your aunt Kaia, too."

Rex swallows. He has only ever seen one really good picture of his aunt, a color photo that resides on the mantel next to Django and Makani's wedding picture. "Do NDAs keep you from telling me what she was like?"

"Brilliant," Ambrus whispers. "Shower."

"She was a shower?" Rex asks, trying for an awful damned joke.

"No, *I* want a shower," Ambrus corrects testily, and then his expression softens. "She was so goddamned intelligent. It made Kaia's eyes shine like the stars your family line is named for."

Rex nods in response, not sure what else to say. He gathers up Ambrus's discarded clothing and then nudges his boyfriend down the hallway, and into the bathroom.

"You need this," Rex explains as Ambrus gives his own shower a baffled stare. "Airport funk does not belong in the bed."

"No, it does not," Ambrus mutters while turning on the water full blast. Rex rescues Ambrus's wallet and keys before putting his travel clothes into the hamper.

Ambrus snags Rex by the arm before he can leave. "Company?" Ambrus asks, still with old, muted grief visible in his eyes.

"Sure." Rex shucks his shorts and joins Ambrus. Warm water strikes him, and it's soothing, like he was both too cold and too hot at once. After Ambrus's hair is soaked through, Rex grabs shampoo to wash sweat and desert grit from Ambrus's hair. Ambrus purrs under his hands, already half-asleep.

Rex finally gets them both dried off and into bed, where Ambrus presses in close against Rex's side. Rex never liked crowded bed conditions before, but Ambrus feels so right plastered up against him that he doesn't mind at all. Ambrus offers Rex a brief, tired smile, kisses Rex's left shoulder, and immediately passes out.

Rex lies awake for a while, staring up at the dark ceiling. Its texture is visible, illuminated by the streetlamps outside that force light through the thick window blinds.

He really doesn't mind having an older boyfriend, but the dates bother him a little. Kaia Aweite Whetū died of tuberculosis in 1956. His boyfriend would have to be almost as old as Rex's father, if not the same age, to have known her.

What the department did to them is on sci-fi levels of fucked up, which is one of the many reasons Rex and all of his siblings know to tell the department to fuck off if they come calling. Rex's father looks like he's in his late thirties, tops. Ambrus averages out at around thirty on bad days, but looks a bit younger when he's happy.

Django hated the department; he got out the moment he had the opportunity to do so. Kaia's death gave Rex's father the excuse he needed to transfer back to regular army. Django was originally going to retire when his last set of four was done, but instead he went on to Special Forces as the first Groups were forming.

Everything his father has ever told him about the department paints it as a complete hellhole. It makes Rex wonder why Ambrus stayed behind.

* * * *

"I need to practice some of my wording," Ambrus tells him the next day.

Rex, still in the middle of trying to wake up enough to figure out which part of his face gets the coffee, gives Ambrus a blank stare. "What?"

"Wording," Ambrus repeats, but is merciful enough to let Rex tank up on caffeine before he tries again. "I don't wish to spend the rest of my life unable to discuss my sordid past with my boyfriend, so I wanted to practice...oh, skirting the legal limits of what existing and upcoming NDAs say I can and can't speak of."

"Look, I don't need to know about your job," Rex says in complete honesty. He's never hounded his father for specifics of the shit he got up to, and Rex got up to enough of his own military shenanigans that curiosity really doesn't bite. "There are plenty of other subjects we could discuss that aren't military."

"Oh?" Ambrus raises an eyebrow. "Try me."

"Okay." Rex smiles at the challenge, even if he's going to use it as the chance to fish. "When was your last legit, serious, long-term relationship?"

Ambrus stares at him. "If I didn't know better, I'd accuse you of calling Django and asking for details."

Okay, so Rex hadn't expected that. "Stumbled right onto more NDA stuff anyway, huh?"

"You couldn't have come up with something more useful for NDA-avoidance practice if you'd tried," Ambrus mutters. He grabs dirty dishes from the countertop to put in the dishwasher, still grumbling under his breath. Rex watches, mostly because he's not about to skip the opportunity to stare at his boyfriend's ass.

Ambrus hip-checks the dishwasher closed and leans against the counter, crossing his arms. "Just...give me a moment, will you?"

"Sure." Rex uses it as a chance to get more coffee. "Hey, if I really do move in with you, you've got to let me buy a bigger damned coffee maker." He's never seen a four-cup machine outside of cheap hotel rooms.

"Okay," Ambrus agrees absently. "My last relationship involved someone who also worked in my department, so I can't give you a name. He was oversight, though, not..."

"A guinea pig," Rex supplies. That's what his father called it.

Ambrus scowls but doesn't refute the point. Then the expression turns into something much more thoughtful. "Huh. I think I'm also realizing I have a type."

"Yeah?"

Ambrus glances down at the floor, a faint flush on his cheeks. "He was half-Irish, half-Japanese," he admits, which makes Rex snort coffee out of his nose as he starts laughing. "And fuck you, too."

Rex picks up a paper towel and wipes his face, still laughing. "Yeah, yeah. Another blond?"

Ambrus rolls his eyes. "No."

"Still haven't told me when," Rex says when he's done cleaning up the mess.

"It's difficult to talk about, but not because of NDAs." Ambrus's mouth settles into a grim line that looks like anger and grief mingled together. He's studying the contents of the living room instead of facing Rex. "We never lived together. I guess you could classify it more as long-term dating."

"Broke it off?" Rex asks, but he doesn't think that's it.

"Never officially. We started to argue about whether or not we *should* break it off." Ambrus sighs. "He was getting older."

"And you weren't."

Both of Ambrus's eyebrows go up in surprise, as if he hadn't expected Rex to be so blatant about the subject. "No," he admits. "I suppose it's hard to think long-term when evidence of your mortality isn't being reflected by your partner. Either way, it became a moot point."

Rex studies the flicker of memory in Ambrus's expressive blue eyes. "He died."

"Yes." Ambrus drops his arms and finally looks at Rex again. "The coroner could never make an official determination, but he was only in his early forties. I've always doubted it was natural causes."

Rex thinks of the phone call he received from a pushy bureaucrat and can't blame Ambrus for doubting. "Funeral must have sucked."

"I wouldn't know." Ambrus gives him a tired smile. "I was already in Vietnam, Rex. One did not request time off to attend the funeral of another man unless he was a relative. Not in 1968."

"Shit. I'm sorry." Rex has another sip of coffee before his brain catches up with him. "Wait. You mean to tell me that you haven't been in a long-term relationship in forty-seven fucking *years?*"

Ambrus frowns and looks away again. "There were a few failed attempts—badly failed, at that. A few one-night stands, some more awkward than others. Otherwise? No."

Rex pushes back his chair and stands up. "That explains a hell of a lot."

"It does—Rex?" Ambrus doesn't have time to escape the kitchen before Rex has snagged Ambrus around the waist and slung his boyfriend over his shoulder. "Hey! What the hell are you doing?" Ambrus yelps.

"This requires a lot more sexing," Rex tells him, and strolls down the hallway to the sound of Ambrus's bright peal of laughter.

*   *   *   *

Ambrus slams his way through the apartment door in mid-February, startling Rex so badly that he falls off the couch. He picks himself up from the floor just in time to watch Ambrus stalk by like a vicious storm cloud that's ready to start spitting tornadoes.

All right, then. Rex retrieves his Kindle, puts it on the coffee table, and peers down the hallway. If the office door is closed, he knows not to push, but all three doors are standing open.

He finds Ambrus slumped over his desk, his face buried in his hands. Rex feels a twinge of guilt, which is stupid; whatever went wrong can't be his fault. "Guess I don't have to ask how your day went."

When Ambrus drops his hands and looks at Rex, his eyes are red-rimmed and watery. "Before I had the chance to tell him myself, Jasper found out about my retirement."

Okay, maybe it's a little bit his fault. Shit.

"And he didn't take it well." Rex sits down as Ambrus shakes his head. "He wasn't in the mood to be talked down, huh?"

"If by 'talked down' you mean both of us screaming at each other for ten minutes before stomping away in opposite directions?" Ambrus rests his forehead against his left hand. "Sure. Let's go with that."

"He'll get over it. He's a kid. They're flexible that way," Rex says.

"Oh, I know. It's—that's not how I wanted him to find out." Ambrus smiles wearily. "Also, Jasper can hold a grudge like nobody's fucking business, Rex. It's a good thing I'm not retiring until July, or we still wouldn't be speaking to each other when the paperwork gets stamped."

Ambrus is right about Fox and grudges. The kid doesn't visit, call, or pester Ambrus the way he usually does, which makes Rex roll his eyes. Rex has five younger siblings. This is amateur levels of sulking, and he tells Ambrus so.

"Yes, but you're all Django's children." Ambrus pauses in the middle of unpacking a bag of take-out to look at Rex. "All seven of you in the same place. What's that going to be like in July?"

Rex grins at him. "Eight, if someone can convince Xāwuṭh to set foot on U.S. soil again for a day or two."

Ambrus sighs and turns his attention back to the food. "I reserve the right to wear a bullet-proof vest."

"Please. It's not the bullets that you've gotta worry about."

"I am *highly* aware of that."

When Ambrus heads out on another assignment at the end of February, Fox is still being a standoffish, spoiled brat. Ambrus thinks it'll be another month before he calms the hell down. Rex isn't above tracking the kid back to his house, tying him to a chair, and making him act his damned age, but he never gets the chance.

Rex goes back to Trenton on the second day of March. Ambrus called the day before, filling the airwaves with a hell of a lot of profanity as he explained that he'll be back in fucking mid-March at the fucking earliest and fuck everyone and everything.

"That's an awful lot of fucking," Rex replied, trying to hide the fact that it was taking every single bit of willpower he had not to crack up laughing in the audible face of his boyfriend's wrath.

"God, I hope so," Ambrus said, and the conversation had more or less ended there. Either way, it made Rex more aware of the fact that March is a lot closer to July than January had been. He doesn't have a lot of things to move, but he hates last-minute jobs. He'd prefer to get a head start on tossing shit that he doesn't want to take over to a new place.

Rex also considers it his personal duty to make certain that whoever next rents his part of the duplex isn't a complete asshole. He lets the landlord know of his moving date, and that yes, he damned well *will* be sitting in on the rental interviews. He's not leaving Janice, Lois, and chronically shy Juan to be abused—or ignored—by his replacement.

"You gonna marry him, baby?" Lois asks, chewing on one of her cookies while the black stray twines around her ankles. Rex gives it another week before the black cat is once more a housecat.

Rex shakes his head. "We haven't even known each other for a year yet, Lois."

"Yeah, but you're the one moving in with him," Lois points out.

"In *July*," Rex insists.

"And you agreed to that when, last month?" Lois grins at him. "It's legal now, baby."

"I solemnly swear that it shall be a personal quest to make sure that whoever replaces me as your neighbor will be as horrific a gossip as you are," Rex tells her, but Lois just laughs. Unsuitable revenge; must think of something else.

His cell phone rings late that night and jars him out of a deep, dreamless sleep. Rex rolls over and feels around for it on the nightstand, squinting against the bright display. It's two in the damned morning, and he doesn't recognize the number. That either means it's a wrong number, a telemarketer with no fucking sense, or an emergency.

The last part is what convinces him to actually hit the answer button and put the phone to his ear. "Tjin," he tries to say. It sounds more like a snore, he slurs his own name so badly.

"What the *fuck* did you ask my partner to do?"

Rex blinks a few times. Maybe he answered a wrong number, after all. "What?"

"Euan," the caller repeats in a pseudo-patient voice. "Retiring. What did you tell him?"

Oh. "Hi, Fox," Rex says, propping himself up on his elbow, trying to figure out what deity he angered to make Fox call *him* instead of dialing overseas and yelling at his partner, instead. "How are you?"

"Fucking pissed!" Fox yells back. "What the fuck, Rex?"

"I didn't tell him a damned thing," he snaps. "I didn't ask him to do anything, either. Euan Ambrus is what's known as a grown adult. You know, people who are capable of making their own fucking decisions?"

"Shit."

Rex nearly pulls the phone away from his ear. He's pretty sure that's a sniffle he just heard.

Aw, please no. Please don't be calling me to bear witness to your premature nervous breakdown.

"Look. Jasper—" Rex tries, but is interrupted by what sounds like a minor scuffle. He waits, bewildered, until the sound of breathing through the phone's speaker is different.

"Hi, Rex. Sorry about that."

"Banner—Ziba?" Rex rubs at his eyes, trying to get the last few seconds to make sense. He hasn't had a chance to hang out with Ziba Banner since the great *Silent Hill* debacle, and they still don't know each other very well. "What's going on?"

"Oh, it's—shit." That makes both of Rex's eyebrows fly up in surprise. Military or not, Banner struck him as too prim-and-proper to swear.

"Can you come over?" Banner asks. "I think this should be done in person for it to be of any help."

"What am I helping with?" He's honestly starting to wonder if it involves burying a body.

Banner lets out a deep sigh. "Trying to convince my idiot fiancé that he's capable."

Fiancé? That's new. Or it's old, and Rex has been out of the loop because of Fox's snit-fit.

"Please, Rex."

Rex gives up. He's not sleeping any more tonight, anyway. "All right. Tell me where I'm going."

Banner and Fox share a place across the Jersey border into New York, but not on the Manhattan side. Rex drives up I-87 until he's south of Woodbury and finds an apartment complex. The main office building is covered in aging stucco, but the apartment blocks themselves are sleek, modernized lines.

Rex knocks on a door on the fourth floor of the second building. It's Banner who answers, looking bleary-eyed, frustrated, and sad. "Hi, Rex."

"I—hi, Ziba." Rex comes inside when she motions, wiping his feet on a mat decorated in bright fall leaves. The theme is out of season, but the mat matches the avocado green paint on the kitchen walls. The color could make the place way too damned dark, but everything else is stark white to make up for it. Even with the lights dimmed to about half-strength, it's still a bright room.

From what Rex can see, it's a nice place—pale hardwood floors, new stainless steel appliances, a gas fireplace in the living area beyond the kitchen. Someone definitely took Ambrus's advice when it came to living spaces, but Rex is going to be living in Ambrus's place by summer, so he no longer has any right to feel weird about upper-class apartments.

Jasper Fox is sitting on the floor at the far end of the kitchen in a long-limbed sprawl. His brown eyes are red-rimmed, and one of his hands is buried in his shaggy brown hair. Banner sits down on a white wooden stool at the opposite end of the kitchen, resting her elbows on the countertop. That leaves Rex to figure out what in the hell to do next.

Rex studies Fox for a minute before shucking his jacket, tossing it onto the countertop, and sitting down on the kitchen tile across from him. "You couldn't have waited to have your mental breakdown until after the sun was up?"

Fox snorts out a weak laugh. "Sorry. I've always had bad timing."

"No shit," Rex agrees, which earns him a rueful smile to go with the laugh. "What's going on, Kid?"

"I have no idea how to do this job without Euan." Fox covers his eyes with his free hand. "I'm not—I'm not *ready* to do this without him."

I thought I was ready to do the job at twelve, Rex thinks. At least Fox is smart enough to have doubts, but the man's twenty now. It's time to blast Fox out of this stupid fucking hole he's dug for himself.

"Kid, if you're ready to stick your dick in someone else, you're ready to do this job," Rex says bluntly. Fox drops his hand to stare at Rex in wide-eyed horror, which sets Banner off in a fit of laughter.

Rex waits until Banner's giggling dies down. He knows exactly what's going on with Fox now. This isn't about a lack of skill—just confidence. "You think you'll make the wrong call if Euan isn't there, and that people will blame you for it—people like Ziba, maybe."

Fox bites his lip before he nods. "Yeah. I'm fucking twenty, Rex. What the hell do I know?"

I know you're blaming yourself for something you shouldn't. Rex has no reason to suspect it; he just knows. "Let me tell you a story," Rex says, and immediately has their full attention.

"Back in 2005, I'm still in the fucking sandbox known as Iraq. My older brother Khodî and I, we were Special Forces, since we were always sensible about our insanity." Banner lets out an amused snerk of laughter. Fox is definitely unconvinced as to how Special Forces is supposed to equal sanity.

"Our younger siblings, the twins, went Ranger, 3rd Battalion from the 75th Regiment. Eric liked the structure, and Ella is..." Rex frowns for a moment. "Ella is a force of fuckin' nature."

"She was in active combat in 2005? They didn't lift the ban until last year," Banner says.

Rex nods. "Officially, Ella was down on paper as a driver, but every one of those bastards knew better. She would have been lead for her squad if it hadn't been for that fucking combat restriction."

"Sandbox, 2005," Fox prompts, like Rex and Banner are going too far off-topic.

"The morning of April twenty-third, I wake up to a man in my company telling me that my brother is on the radio, and he needs to talk to me. Khodî says..." Rex hesitates. Banner and Fox don't know about his father, but soldiers have their instincts. "He says he's got a damned bad feeling about the twins, but he's stuck with his battalion up north near the Triangle. He asks me to go find out what the hell is happening near Baghdad. We're not that far away from the city, and my crew actually has a day of downtime, so I tell Khodî that I'll go check on them. I order my company to sit tight while I technically go AWOL."

It hadn't quite been that easy. His company, every single man and woman, had all been willing to ditch with him. Rex had to point out that a) he outranked them, and b) a full company on the move is *going to be noticed, you stupid shits.*

"I get as far as a road near the airport and I...I didn't know what I expected, but it wasn't to walk into the last big highway firefight of the decade," Rex says, trying not to curl his hands into fists at the memory. "It's full dark and shit is *still* going down. Every time we tried to get lights on the situation, a sniper from the insurgents would take them out."

Rex goes mute when the words stick in his throat. "What happened?" Banner prompts him in a soft voice.

"I found Ella. I think that was part instinct, part blind fucking luck," Rex admits. "Also, force of nature. She'd collected every squad in her platoon and badgered the assholes into setting up a real defensive perimeter. She nearly shot me before she realized who I was."

Where's Eric? Rex remembers yelling above the din—gunfire and IEDs and grenades and screaming, so much of it. The scent of copper was riding the air, competing with gunpowder and smoke. Ella had the combat part handled; Rex was about to put his 18D certification to a hell of a lot of use.

I don't know! Ella shouted back, her dark eyes wide with what looked like something very close to panic. *There was an IED, I didn't see what happened—I haven't seen him in an hour!*

Rex covered Ella before they turned as one, nailing a small cluster of insurgents trying to crawl up the perimeter's backside. Like Ella would be so stupid as to leave a blind spot on their asses. *Is he alive?*

The barrel of Ella's rifle had dipped for a second. *I—I don't know.*

"People were overheating because the water was gone. No one expected an extended shootout that day. If someone dropped too far from a defensive line, the insurgents would tag them, bag them, and take them—strip their gear, steal their supplies, and leave the bodies behind to rot in the sun if we couldn't find them afterwards.

"When things finally calmed down, we went hunting for Eric based on his last known position." Rex has to swallow back the grief that always wants to choke him when he talks about this, and that hasn't happened often. "There was nothing. We followed tracks out from the highway, and there was still nothing. Full daylight, and there was fucking *nothing*.

"We both knew—we both knew he was gone."

Ella had screamed the opposite at him, but fuck, they'd known how the fucking war was playing out. Either they'd find a body one day, or they wouldn't.

"I'm sorry," Fox whispers, a sentiment echoed by Banner. Rex nods, trying to look like he's not being disrespectful about their sympathy. He just doesn't handle that sentiment very well when it comes to Eric.

"It was my job to cover Eric's ass, and I wasn't there." Rex stares Fox directly in the eyes. "I was so goddamned certain that my family was going to blame me—our eldest brother on down to the youngest."

"Did they?" Fox asks, after taking a deep, sniffling breath.

"There was this one moment when Khodî finally got in from the Triangle...I thought he would. Maybe he even really did blame me for a second, but Khodî's a good man. The next thing I know, he's hugging me, telling me he's fucking sorry, that he should have been there—that it wasn't my fault. Ella said the same, when she woke up from the sedation that kept her from bolting off into the desert to look for Eric. It was the same way when we all got back stateside for the funeral. Not my fault."

Fox rubs his eyes again and stares right back at Rex, almost oozing defiance. "You do, though. You blame yourself. You've never stopped."

"Nope," Rex replies. "That's the thing, though—nobody made the wrong call, Jasper. There wasn't even a right call to make in the first place. Things can go to shit, and it's nobody's damned fault. It just *happens*."

"It shouldn't, though," Fox says, shoving his hand back through his hair again to get it out of his eyes.

"Nothing's ideal, nothing's perfect, and there are a lot of assholes in the world." Rex studies Fox and decides to go for broke. "What is it that you won't forgive yourself for, Kid?"

Fox winces and closes his eyes. "Asshole."

"Yep. That's why your fiancée told me to come and see you."

"No, I told Rex to come here because Jasper has the bad habit of listening to men more than women," Banner says dryly.

"I was too listening!" Fox protests, but Banner makes an amused sound and shakes her head.

"He'll learn," she says. "Rex?"

"Talk, Kid. The sun isn't even up yet, and you owe me breakfast, so you owe me this, too," Rex orders.

Fox drags out the silence for a few minutes before he can say it. "My father."

Rex almost leans back in surprise. That hadn't occurred to him, but maybe it should have. "Why?" he asks. No censure, no blame, no anger—only gentle curiosity.

This time both hands get shoved into Fox's hair, which turns it into a complete mess. "I was eight. Grew up in a fucking brothel. Great childhood, right?"

"There are probably worse, but not by much," Rex says in a mild voice. A human trafficking ring's base of operations was one of his infamous craters.

"My mother tried to make it as normal as she could, but childhood only lasts so long. By then, I'd figured out that things weren't normal at all," Fox whispers. "I knew she was starting to worry about me."

"Sounds like a good parent."

Fox smiles at Rex. "She is—she—I'd like to introduce you, one day. Anyway, uh...she gets this client. She called them friends instead of clients, but even *I* knew that friends actually came back for repeat visits. Most of those assholes never showed up again. This guy, though—he comes out afterwards and joins me in one of the sitting areas I'm allowed to be in. He was Korean, which wasn't so weird for the area. A lot of families booked it out of North Korea into Primorsky Krai after the U.S.S.R. fell in the '90s and things started to go to economic shit. North Korea couldn't keep up, so even Russia looked greener in comparison.

"At first, I felt weird about him talking to me. I was wondering if I'd hit my product expiration date." Fox looks seriously wry for a kid who'd been worried about childhood rape in a brothel. "He asked me what I liked, what I didn't like. He was trying to get to know me."

"Then he came back, again and again. He'd go see my mother, and then he'd come out and talk to me. He finally told me..." Fox turns his head so he's not looking at either of them. Tears squeeze out from beneath closed eyes and make glittering trails down his cheeks. "Fuck. Cheul-Su Yeou told me that he was my father."

"Elegant Fox," Rex translates quietly, giving Fox the chance to compose himself.

Fox nods, faint smile on his face. "Yeah. Mom's name is Dutch, and afterwards...anyway, I did something I shouldn't have. I told Cheul-Su how everything really was. See, he thought Mom had chosen the job. She spoke Russian, blonde hair and blue eyes—fit the stereotype perfectly, which is why the fuckers grabbed her in the first place. The brothel was set up to look government-approved, even if it was illegal as all hell. You had to, or else the *bratva* got pissy about people horning in on their territory.

"I told him we were slaves." Fox swallows hard enough for his throat to bob up and down. "I said that Mom was worried about me being turned into someone's cheap toy, that I wanted her safe, and—I told him everything I shouldn't have."

"You were eight years old," Rex says in a flat voice.

Fox shrugs. "Cheul-Su Yeou came from a family with money, so he thought—and this was before Putin got that really creepy iron grip on Russia—he thought the police were the best place to go. He just happened to find someone who was part of the brothel's infrastructure, someone who stood to lose a lot of money if the brothel was officially noticed. He had my father murdered."

"Murdered someone with money and influence," Rex murmurs, remembering what Ambrus said on *Día de los Inocentes.*

"It got attention, yeah." Fox has a bitter smile on his face. "I got what I wanted, and we were rescued, but I got someone killed for opening my fucking mouth. Now you know why I'm freaking out."

"You were still only *eight years old,*" Rex emphasizes. "Naivety isn't the same thing as making a bad call. It's a terrible goddamned learning experience, but it's not the same thing. Not even remotely."

"Fine." Fox crosses his arms and glares at Rex. "I'll stop blaming myself for my Dad when you stop blaming yourself for your brother."

"That was a low blow." Rex points at Fox. "Now you owe me double-breakfast, you cranky little shit." Fox rolls his eyes.

"What's double-breakfast?" Banner asks, sensing the break in tension.

"Rex means bad diner food, lots of it, and maybe a gift card for more on the way out," Fox replies. "I bare my soul, and you want food."

"Tell me that you don't," Rex challenges him.

Fox pauses before his mouth twists up in annoyance. "Dammit. Ziba, I hope you like waffles at 4:00 a.m."

"I like waffles all the time, genius."

Rex doesn't bring up Fox and Ambrus's long-standing match of pre-school Quiet Game until after he has waffles, coffee, and bacon between himself and the mutual kitchen confessional. "Have you and Euan spoken since you decided that yelling at each other in a hallway was how grown adults communicate?"

Fox scowls and then steals Rex's bacon. Thieving fucker. "No, but not because we're bad at talking. We're not!" he insists, when Rex raises an eyebrow and Banner snickers under her breath. "We've just been working different jobs. Trial basis shit. You didn't hear me say that."

"Selectively deaf," Rex assures Fox, which makes Banner smirk before she plows her way through a fourth waffle. The woman is terrifying him; she's eating more than they are.

"Hey, so we both have a week off after Saint Patrick's Day," Fox says. "Euan does, too."

"Okay, and?" Rex asks when Fox looks at him expectantly. Rex will probably have that week off, too. He hasn't had a DoD contract call since he told that department asshole to go die in a fire.

"So, *LEGO Indiana Jones* and *LEGO Star Wars* on the Wii. All nine games," Fox retorts, like it's supposed to be obvious. "A week of all four of us contributing to each other's OCD."

"Cleaning a weapon daily isn't OCD, it's SOP," Rex points out.

"Yeah, when you're using it every day, it is." Fox shakes his head. "Seriously, we're all varying levels of nuts. She's just as bad for that."

Banner smiles. "I like gun oil."

Rex feels his eye twitch. There is a different sort of lube out there with that name. "Uh—"

"Not like that!" Banner laughs and spews waffle crumbs across the table as Fox buries his face in his hands. The tips of his ears are glowing bright red.

"You'd better not be bringing the fourth *Indiana Jones* movie in with that mix," Rex warns Fox after Banner cleans up and Fox can look at them all without bursting into embarrassed flame. "Even if it's just in LEGO video game form."

Fox snorts. "Chill, wuss. I won't contaminate your life with the horror that is supposedly *Kingdom of the Crystal Skull.*"

"Have actually you watched that travesty?" Rex asks, but Fox laughs at him. Asshole. "Seriously, you've gotta watch it. I need to know that you've suffered the way we have suffered."

"I won't watch *Temple of Doom*, either." Banner rests her chin on her hands. "Why yes, I'd love to see my entire cultural heritage completely misunderstood and slathered in tar for good measure, even if I do get to watch an admittedly pretty white man save the day."

Rex winces. He'd forgotten that *Temple* was almost as bad, if not actually worse, than *Kingdom*. "Sorry."

"S'okay," Banner replies, unconcerned. "At least they tried for redemption with that whole 'betraying Shiva' line. They just ignored the fact that Kali is the divine mother of the universe, who also happens to be one of Shiva's wives, and he's actually okay with the fact that sometimes she's kind of nuts."

Rex almost chokes on a corner bite of waffle. "I didn't know that. What about the Thuggee bit?"

Banner shakes her head. "The Thuggee didn't even exist after the 1830s, and that's if they ever existed to begin with."

"Good ol' American racism," Rex says, raising his coffee mug. Banner nods wry agreement.

Rex and his siblings grew up lucky, and they know it. Anyone in town who didn't like Django Whetū also lived in mortal terror of him. Anyone else who was stupid enough to try shit at school usually got the snot beaten out of them—and it wasn't necessarily Khodî delivering the beat-downs. Rex fondly recalls the time his still-tiny sister rode down some overgrown junior-high dickweed in the hallway before smashing his face in with a textbook for trying to throw a punch at her older brother.

"So?" Fox kicks Rex's shin under the table. "Video games all week. No other responsibilities. Skipping *Temple of Doom* to make Ziba happy, if necessary."

Rex gives up. "Sure, Kid. It sounds like fun." The swearing should be creative, anyway.

They go outside the diner to find it chilly and spitting rain as the sun comes up. "I have to go to work," Banner announces as she twirls her way down the sidewalk, on a sugar high from way too much pancake syrup. "You two have fun!"

"What's *really* bugging you about Euan?" Rex asks the moment she's out of earshot.

"The other stuff was totally valid," Fox says, but he shoves his hands into his jacket pockets and sighs again. "NDAs, man. I'll still be doing the job, and he won't. How do I know I'll even get to see him again? He's practically my brother at this point—a very

Scottish, annoying, asshole brother, but Ziba says that's the definition of a sibling, so I guess it counts."

"Yeah, that definitely counts," Rex agrees. "I still have six of them; I know."

"Geeze, didn't your Dad know about birth control?"

Rex bites back a smile. Nope, too complicated, and it's way too early in the morning to try and explain that. "Look, NDAs didn't stop visitation rights in Turkmenistan. You'll be fine, Jasper. That man probably has NDAs to keep an NDA from affecting your ability to be caught by an NDA, anyway."

Fox is still watching his girlfriend. "No, that's Ziba. If you ever hear her start cackling, it's because she's about to kill a tree and bury someone in bureaucracy. It's her favorite weapon outside of just shooting some prick—wait, what about Turkmenistan? What do you know about that?"

Rex grins. "Fill out an NDA and I'll tell you."

"Oh, fuck you!" Fox blurts in genuine horror.

Rex sends Fox off down the street to catch up with Banner when the kid remembers that he's also supposed to be working that day. He watches them go, hands shoved into his pants pockets against the damp chill.

Okay. Crisis averted. Now Rex has to survive a week of Ambrus's maddening "must collect all the LEGO things" habit during gameplay. Then he'll move in with his boyfriend in July, and the Whetū clan will descend. It should be a fun summer.

Brian snorts awake, aware that something in his bedroom isn't the way it should be. He's already reaching underneath the spare pillow when he realizes it's just Neumia. His heartbeat starts slowing down to a normal rhythm; his daughter is really good at jumping him. Wesley keeps teaching her bad habits, the complete asshole.

"Nari, baby? What's wrong?" Brian pulls his hand back from the tiny little Beretta 71 he keeps in the bed. Dear god, it isn't even light out yet. "Did you have a nightmare?"

Neumia shakes her head, which sends her long green braids flying out in a whiplashed circle. "No, Dad. Well...maybe? But it didn't *feel* bad."

Brian sits bolt upright in alarm, brushing strands of his hair away from his face. "Did your mother call?"

His daughter looks at him like he's stupid. "It's 4:00 a.m. here, and way earlier than that in California. Mom's probably still playing Warcrack."

Brian lets out a sigh without trying to be obvious about it, still trying to figure out how so much of his hair escaped from its ponytail. It's gotten long enough that tying it back for sleep has just become necessary, but his hair refuses to be confined if he's not paying strict attention to it.

"Don't tell Bonika I called it that, squirt." His sort-of-ex-girlfriend calls the game stress relief, and Brian approves of anything that makes Bo less tetchy.

He runs his tongue over his teeth, grimacing at the fuzzy feeling. "Okay, I give up. What's up, sprat?"

Neumia's expression turns serious. "I think we should have a video game weekend. For Saint Patrick's Day."

Brian almost starts laughing, but something glimmering in his kid's bright green eyes stops him. "Any particular reason, Nari?"

"Uncle Wesley's bored," Neumia explains. "Also, Uncle Kai might stab his roommate if he doesn't get to come home from school for the weekend."

Brian frowns. The former is often true; the latter is a bit unusual. Kai has the most easy-going temper out of all of Brian's siblings, so said roommate must really be working the asshole angle. "Okay, but why Saint Patrick's Day?"

"I dunno." Neumia shrugs, her eyes darting away. "Maybe because it matches my hair?"

No, that is not the reason. "Baby girl," Brian says quietly, "I know your mother pretty well—well enough to know when she's pulling bullshit. That is her exact 'I am lying through my teeth' face. Why, Nari?"

Neumia's expression crumples into disaster-and-tears territory. "I don't know!" she bursts out. "I just know we should! They should be here! It's important!"

Brian tries not to sigh. He's not awful at parenting—gets it from Dad—but sometimes he has no idea what magic his father performed to get them all through childhood.

"You could have just said that, baby." Brian holds up the covers in blatant invitation. Neumia knows better than to go pillow-fishing for weapons, anyway. He trained her on that when she was still learning to walk. Granted, she also knows the rules for when it is completely acceptable to go pillow-fishing, but Brian hopes she never has to.

Neumia rushes to fill the offered space in bed, cuddling in close to Brian's chest. The extra heat makes it too hot, so he tosses a blanket from the bed. He desperately wants to go back to sleep, but he has more important things to worry about—like finding out why his kid is on the verge of panic.

"I know you guys *say* I can just tell you," Neumia says once she's settled, "but sometimes you look really nervous, so I was trying to not-say it."

Brian sighs, feeling stupid. His kid is smart, and probably figured out her father's *Everything Is Fine* mask a long time ago. "I'm sorry, Nari. It's not that I—we—don't want you to say it. I just worry about it. That's all."

"Okay." Neumia hesitates in a way that actually makes it feel like time slows down. "Game night, though, right? Game weekend? Saint Patrick's Day?"

He's going to say yes and she knows it, but now they're past the panic. Time for a show of reluctance. "Well, I don't know..."

"Dad, all they'll have otherwise is green beer, and you already said that green beer is stupid," Neumia says in her too-serious voice.

Brian grins. He stands by that opinion, thank you very much. "Okay, sprout. Game weekend, Saint Patrick's Day, no green beer, and nobody is required to wear green, either." He pauses. "House owner picks the first game, though."

"I don't *care* if you wanna shoot virtual people all weekend!" Neumia huffs. "Seriously, Dad. Uncle Wesley's the one who wants to play *Pokémon* all the time."

"And I get to mock him for it, no matter how old we are," Brian replies, trying and failing to sound just as serious. "By the way: vengeance."

"What vengeance?" Neumia starts to ask, but begins shrieking with laughter as Brian tickles his kid within an inch of her life for waking him before dawn.

Part II

"Take care of those who are under your protection."

–Tamil Proverb

Chapter 6

⦂)(X)(X⦂

Rex grew up very much aware of the fact that he is many things, but Irish is not one of them. His only concession to the day is to put on an aging pair of BDU trousers in the phased-out traditional camouflage pattern. It's more military than he prefers when he's not on a job, but it has pockets. More importantly, they're *green*, which means people will leave him the hell alone.

He hates Baltimore, but he hasn't seen his boyfriend in a month. The two-hour drive south is worth it.

Finding Ambrus in the disaster that is a proper international airport on a Friday afternoon is like trying to find an actual needle in a damned haystack. He gives up on facial recognition after about thirty seconds and just starts looking for gingers.

"Happy Saint Patrick's Day," Rex says in a dry voice when he finally finds Ambrus at BWI's baggage claim. His boyfriend looks like he's sleeping upright.

Ambrus jerks his head up, startled. "Fuck!" he gasps out, and then he smiles as he recognizes who woke him. "Rex!"

"Hi there." Rex hugs his boyfriend—and then staggers when he's suddenly supporting Ambrus's full weight. "What the hell, Euan?"

"Fuck this holiday," Ambrus mutters, getting his feet beneath him again. "Stupid, stupid holiday."

Rex frowns when he notices Ambrus's eyes aren't focused. "Hey!" He snaps his fingers in front of Ambrus's face until the man looks first at Rex's fingers, and then at Rex's face in confusion. "What's wrong?"

It takes almost a full minute for Ambrus to produce an answer. "I'm just...I'm really tired."

Rex puts his hand on Ambrus's forehead, feeling heat beneath his palm and the faintest hint of sweat. Not September levels of tired; he's still upright and not exhibiting signs that mimic malaria. "You must have had one hell of a trip."

Ambrus leans forward and rests his head on Rex's shoulder. "Yeah. I really need to sleep, Rex," he says, voice cracking three different times within six syllables.

Rex puts his arm around Ambrus's shoulders. "Okay. I'll get us home, all right?"

"Fuckin' queers!" someone shouts.

Rex sighs and turns his head. Some asshole in a camouflage hat is glaring at them from about ten feet away. "Can you please fuck off?"

"Not when there's two disgusting perverts standing in front of all these kids and God's followers, spreading their sick—OW!" the man yelps, as someone's cane collides with his elbow. "What the hell?"

Rex looks at the shriveled old white man in an army baseball cap covered in European military service pins. He's using a walker with a cane that hooks over the front bars, and he's brandishing said cane at the noisy bastard's head. "I didn't fight in World War II just to listen to you brats mouth off to other servicemen!"

"But they're fucking queers—OW!"

"And they're better behaved than you are!" the old man retorts. "Go on, mouth off again. You can explain to security why you're yelling slurs and obscenities in an airport full of kids!"

Rex decides he likes this old bastard. "Hey, yeah. We're pretty close to D.C. I bet half the TSA agents working here used to be in the service."

Camouflage Hat and his bigotry both hesitate, which makes Ambrus sigh in resignation. "Asshole: I have a concealed carry permit and enough weight in the government to shoot you in an airport without concern of arrest or conviction. Please go the hell away."

The threat of being shot still doesn't convince the man, who seems dead set on being a shit stain on humanity. Then he realizes that the crowd isn't on his side and scowls at them one more time as he slinks away.

"Time was they'd at least respect a vet," their grumpy savior mutters, scowling like his face might cave in. "Fuckin' ignorant kids."

"There are a lot less ignorant children about than there used to be," Ambrus says. The crowd goes back to paying attention to the baggage carousels instead of them, and the tension in the air is gone.

Rex feels his shoulders relax. He hasn't had a confrontation like that in years, and he didn't miss that bullshit. New Jersey has some bad features (Newark), but at least he can walk down the street with his boyfriend and not get screamed at.

"Amen to that." The old man's chin juts out a bit as he looks up at them. "Where'd you serve, boys?"

"Afghanistan and Iraq," Rex answers, which makes the old vet swear some more.

"Similar." Now that there isn't potential trouble to deal with, Ambrus is starting to droop again. "Still work for the Pentagon. Just got off of a very long flight."

"And I bet you ain't armed, either." The old man chuckles. "The shit some people will believe, huh?"

"Uh huh." Rex smiles. "Gay?"

"Queer as the damned day is long," the vet admits sunnily. "Met m'boyfriend in the service. Then the peckerhead had to go and die on me before they make it legal to get married. He always did say he hated weddings."

"How inconsiderate of him. Thanks for, well..." Ambrus trails off, words failing him.

"Thanks for hitting that asshole so I didn't have to," Rex says. There are kids around, after all.

"My pleasure. What's the point of being old if you can't use it as an excuse to hit people who are too dumb to know how to breathe properly?" the old geezer asks, giving them another wide, toothless smile before going on his way.

Rex grabs Ambrus's bag when it finally makes its slow way around the carousel. He carries it with one hand while keeping the other on Ambrus's shoulder, steering his boyfriend towards the doors, outside, and onwards to short-term parking to find the car. By the time Rex gets the bag into the trunk, Ambrus is in the passenger seat, buckled in, and has already passed out.

Either someone called in a minor miracle, or everyone hit the bars early. Rex only finds a few hang-ups in traffic on his way out of Maryland. He taps his fingers along the top of his steering wheel in time with the music he's playing on low volume, waiting for everyone to realize that they've all come to a standstill on the highway because a single asshole flashed their brake lights about two miles ahead for no reason.

Rex skirts Philadelphia using I-295, just like any every wise individual living on the east coast with a driver's license. They're about twenty minutes south of Trenton when Ambrus jerks upright, drawing in a sharp breath.

Ambrus startles the hell out of Rex, but he breathes through it and keeps his voice even. "Hey. It's just me over here," Rex says.

Ambrus's eyes stay wide and panicked for a few seconds before he slumps back into the seat. "Sorry. I've been having bad dreams for days now."

Rex is about to ask Ambrus if he wants to talk about it when he realizes that his boyfriend has already fallen asleep again. He glances over a couple of times when traffic allows before making a decision. They haven't had a chance to discuss the bits and pieces they can of Ambrus's last job, but it looks like the department tried to run his boyfriend into the ground. It makes Rex wonder if it's supposed to be revenge for Ambrus's pending retirement.

Ambrus subjects the mutant duplex to the owl-like blinking of the exceptionally sleep-deprived. "Here? But—trains, Rex."

Rex snorts out a laugh as he puts his palm on Ambrus's shoulder again to keep him from falling over backwards. "Yeah, I really don't think a train is going to be keeping your ass awake right now." He prods Ambrus up the outer steps, waving at Juan out of habit without looking when he hears the upstairs window slide open. Princeton is quieter, but Trenton was closer.

He hasn't forgotten Fox's specific instructions about physical contact, not after his deep-end introduction to it last fall. It doesn't take much to convince Ambrus to lie down on the couch in front of the TV and use Rex's lap as a pillow.

Rex doesn't mind at all. He gets to run his fingers through his boyfriend's unbound hair while watching a *Halo*-branded movie called *Nightfall*. Honestly, it's not all that bad—sci-fi enough not to hammer on his PTSD, but full of enough wartime poetry to make him want to bawl his eyes out. Thanks, United States Army career.

He's watching *Return to Oz* for lack of anything better available when Ambrus stirs. "Oh, I remember this one," he says in a sleepy mumble.

Rex doesn't stop carding his fingers through Ambrus's hair. "This movie scared the shit out of me as a kid."

"Why?"

"Dunno. Might have had something to do with all of the fucking stolen heads that were still alive," Rex replies, trying not to wince as the scene in question plays out. "Also, I was six. Terrifying shit."

"I still think it's terrifying shit." Ambrus rolls over onto his side so that he can watch the flickering screen. "Also, freefall and reliance on a talking moose."

Rex clenches his jaw until the stupid moose starts flying. Even knowing that it'll happen never stops the reaction. Too many fucking plane crashes in his career. "How are you?"

"Is it still the seventeenth?"

"Yep." Rex glances down just in time to see his boyfriend's brow furrow. "Okay, spill. Why do you hate Saint Patrick's Day?"

"Aside from the fact that it's a stupid, American, co-opted Catholic holiday based upon a man with a terrible penchant for book-burning?" Ambrus sighs. "My mother died on Saint Patrick's Day. I disliked it before, but afterwards, I...I hate this day."

"I'm sorry," Rex says, trying to swallow back guilt and his own remembered grief.

"It's—it's been so damned long. You'd think it wouldn't bother me anymore," Ambrus whispers. "I hate dwelling on it. Tell me about your siblings, Rex. I'd rather hear about a family that's alive."

Instead of one that's dead, Rex can hear, even if Ambrus doesn't say it aloud. He shoves his own feelings ruthlessly aside and fills the air with ridiculous childhood anecdotes. Then he tosses in a few stories from the Army that pre-date 9/11, ones that focus on Ella and Eric's special ideas about rules and how to circumvent them all.

Ambrus falls asleep again sometime during that hour, but it's the deep, boneless slumber of someone who isn't going to be disturbed by much short of a bomb going off. Rex takes the opportunity to use the bathroom, find a beer, call out for pizza, and have dinner. The fact that Ambrus didn't smell pepperoni and bolt for the kitchen says a lot about how tired he really is.

Rex saves half of the pie for later and sits back down on the couch. Ambrus grumbles at him for daring to move without even bothering to wake up first, which makes Rex smile.

He is so damned screwed. It needs to be July already.

He queues up *Young Frankenstein* when it catches his eye. It's a good movie, and he likes it, but he's fallen asleep every time he's tried to watch it from start to finish.

Case in point—Rex jerks awake when he hears the vibrating buzz of a cell phone. It's fully dark outside, and the only light in the apartment is from the kitchen overhead he left on earlier. Ambrus's phone is the one ringing, not his, which is sitting peacefully on the coffee table next to Rex's foot.

Ambrus fumbles around at his pants pocket, half-awake and swearing under his breath. Rex rubs his eyes and checks his watch to discover that it's after 1:00 a.m. He slept through the movie and half the fucking night, too.

"If this isn't important, I'll kill someone." Ambrus pulls his phone free of confinement and answers it before it has a chance to stop ringing. "Ambrus." His scowl turns into complete bafflement. "Jasper? Jasper—wait—what fucking time is it?"

"After one," Rex supplies, trying not to crack his jaw on a yawn.

"Okay, it's an hour after midnight, I just got into Trenton this afternoon, and I've had less than eight hours of sleep. What's so important that it can't wait until morning?"

Rex can't hear what's being said; there's only a delay as Ambrus listens before sighing in regret. "Fine. Okay, no—calm down, Jasper. It's fine. I'll be there in about twenty minutes, since it'll take me a bit to walk over—because I'm not driving on six hours' sleep after being awake for two damned days, that's why!"

Ambrus disconnects the call and drops the phone onto his chest. He covers his eyes with both hands before groaning, *"Why?"*

Rex is in full agreement with that sentiment. "What the hell was that about?"

"He's citing work. For all I know, someone dug up fucking Jimmy Hoffa," Ambrus complains.

"That's Michigan, not New Jersey," Rex points out, rotating his neck and listening as tendons pop when tension is released.

"I know." Ambrus drops his hands and stares up at the ceiling, still blinking away sleep-fog. "It's probably something legitimate enough to warrant the call, but minor enough that Fox is using it as an excuse to talk before I go back to D.C. tomorrow. Besides, he promised me alcohol, and I'm easily bribed."

"I'm keeping that in mind," Rex says.

Ambrus smiles up at him, his hair a flaming mess that covers Rex's lap. It's a view that Rex adores as much as it gives him terrible, awesome ideas. "It shouldn't take long, even with the drinking part. You could go finish sleeping in bed instead of spending the night on this couch."

Rex pretends to think about it. "I might, but you have to come join me when you get back."

"Oh, such a hardship," Ambrus drawls, which always emphasizes the Oxford tones in his accent. "My boyfriend wishes for me to join him in bed. Whatever shall I do?"

"Asshole." Rex gives up and yawns. "You going to be all right for that kind of walk? There are taxis."

"Taxis mean witnesses. I wouldn't have agreed to do it if I wasn't capable, Rex." Ambrus sits up and shoves his feet back into the black leather steel-toed shoes he wears when flying, tying the laces with swift precision. Twill pants and long-sleeved button-down shirts aren't necessarily the most comfortable airline wear, but Ambrus says that he either has to look business-casual presentable when he gets off a flight, or he has to worry about keeping blood off his skin.

The one time Rex tried to point out the sheer amount of clothes Ambrus seems to go through, Ambrus had lifted one eyebrow and said, "*Bratva*."

"Yes, but they weren't into human trafficking," Rex shot back, irritated. "They had rules."

"Rules." Ambrus had shrugged. "True, sometimes."

Rex thought about how his ex-boyfriend's family didn't turn to crime until the U.S.S.R. fell and Russia's economy tanked with it. Working for the mob was better than starvation, but Vladimir's family, Greek Orthodox in a land that had banned religion for decades, had put their feet firmly down on the ground against certain human rights abuses.

Still hadn't stopped the hail of bullets—or the poisoning attempt, for that matter. Fuck his luck, anyway.

Ambrus is opening the door before Rex gets up from the couch to follow him. "Fox is underage. Where the hell is he getting alcohol, Euan?"

Ambrus smiles. "NDA, Rex."

"That is such bullshit," Rex replies, but Ambrus probably means it. Then again, Fox has an older girlfriend.

"See you in a few hours," Ambrus says, and turns to go.

"Wait." Rex touches Ambrus's shoulder to get his boyfriend's attention, and gives him a deep kiss that is probably going to lead to some serious masturbation before bed. That might have been a miscalculation. Now he doesn't want Ambrus to go.

Ambrus's kiss-dazed look becomes a smirk. "Leaving now; sex later."

"Yeah, yeah." Rex gives him a nudge out of the door before he watches Ambrus trek down the staircase. Janice yells at Ambrus as he passes her door, but Ambrus only raises his hand and flips off her closed door using the British standard, not the American.

Ambrus has been gone maybe two minutes before Rex's skin starts prickling. He rubs at his arms, but it's not gooseflesh. This is something else, something he literally hasn't felt in years.

"He's fine," Rex mutters defiantly, rinsing out two empty beer bottles before dropping them in the recycle bin. "Stop being paranoid, jackass."

Three minutes later, his heartbeat has picked up, joining the electrical tingle trying to crawl all over his skin. Rex grips the countertop, cursing. This isn't paranoia. Every instinct he has is screaming. Every mental alarm bell is blaring that something is *wrong*.

Rex lets go of the countertop, stands up, and takes a breath. He lets it out slowly, shoulders easing down, chin coming up. His nerves steady; his pulse evens out to a smoother rhythm.

Good. Now he can think.

Euan.

Rex gets his old M1911 from beneath the mattress, dropping the magazine from the pistol long enough to double-check that he reloaded it after its last use on a public range. The 1911 used to be his father's service pistol, long before Django decided upon the love of a Browning High-Power, then the Beretta 92 when it was brand new, and finally the double-stacked awesomeness of a good .9mm Glock.

The 1911 is a .45mm, which is technically overkill, but Rex's skin is still trying to crawl away. He wants to be carrying something capable of putting down a bear.

If there is an actual bear wandering around in Trenton, Rex is going to be seriously confused. The bear too, probably.

"Forget the damned bear. Get your shit together, asshole." Rex straps the holster for the 1911 in place on his left side for a right-handed draw, trying not to grind his teeth as he feels the seconds tick away. A coat light enough for spring weather hides the bulk of the gun, and his good boots are already waiting by the door.

Rex double-checks that his military ID and concealed-carry permits are still in his wallet, muted cell phone in his pocket, and heads out. Then he turns right back around and unlocks the door again as instincts nudge him hard. Inside the coat closet is a bag with a change of clothes, ammunition for his usual Glock and the 1911, and a damned fine first aid kit that Rex and Kai put together from scratch. Kai brought the additional medical-school-learned skillsets. Rex added the wartime experience of how sometimes you really *did* need special equipment in the field to keep someone from bleeding out in front of you. The first time that happened, Rex's military kit and his 18D classification hadn't meant shit. He always went above and beyond the standard after that, spreading out the medical load among his company in 3rd Battalion, 5th SFG. There was non-stop bitching about the extra weight until it kept seven of them from dying during an ambush in 2002. The complaints about the weight dried up afterwards.

Rex swallows hard as he hoofs it down the old wooden staircase. Please, let him not need the first aid kit.

He's trying to check his watch for the time when Janice's door flies open. Rex is so surprised he nearly plows into it. "Janice? What the fuck?" She never steps foot outside her door. *Ever.* The fire department had to pry her out last time.

"You tell me, boy." Janice sounds a lot less cranky when she's not screaming through the door, and she has the rough-sultry voice of someone who used to smoke at least a pack a day. She's tall and willowy, somewhere between forty and eighty years old—nobody's been able to figure it the fuck out. Her hair is white, her brow sunken, but otherwise she stands like someone that osteoporosis wouldn't dare approach. "You're damned well vibrating."

He checks his watch again, this time able to register the time and remember it. It's almost 01:30. He's ten minutes behind Ambrus, and when that man decides he's going somewhere, he does not fucking linger.

Rex doesn't trust this not to be department fuckery, not after January. Ambrus isn't the only one potentially in danger if they're involved, and neither is Rex. Goddammit.

"Clear the building, Janice," Rex tells her. "I know you packed a bag, just like I taught you, even if you yelled at me the entire damned time. Get the others out of range of...of..."

Fuck, he doesn't know. "Just. Out of here. Please."

"You still ain't told me jack shit about what's going on," Janice points out in narrow-eyed irritation, crossing her arms. She actually pulls off intimidating pretty well, but Rex grew up with Ella. He's seen better.

"I don't fucking know." Rex's grip on his bag tightens. "I hope it's nothing, but if not? I don't want anyone here if some asshole comes knocking."

Janice glances down at Rex's bag before staring him in the face again. "I'm agoraphobic."

"We all figured that out years ago." Rex has to resist the urge to shove her aside so he can go. "Lois and Juan. Please."

Janice sighs and half-closes her door, clearing his path. "Ain't leavin' them behind to be eaten by whatever bogeymen you stirred up. Go find that jackass howler monkey boyfriend of yours."

Rex nods at her. "Thanks, Janice. See you soon."

"Don't think you will," he hears her say as the outer door closes, and that shit doesn't help at all. Now he's not just on the verge of panic, he's fucking bewildered, but at least the latter helps offset the former.

Rex stands outside in the cool night air, breathing it in. It's in the mid-50s, maybe, with a breeze that smells like molding damp and fresh green mixed together. There isn't much traffic on his street, but the noise increases north towards US 1.

By logic and reason, he should have no damned clue where Ambrus went, but he still turns left and heads for the highway. Rex just *knows*, the same way he knows that something is about to go pear-shaped and completely FUBAR.

Please be all right, both of you. Rex is focusing on Ambrus's casual cheer and wicked smirk when he's up to no good. He's seeing Fox's gentle, adoring smile as he watches his girlfriend twirl in circles as she traipses down a New York sidewalk.

Rex crosses the freeway and cuts across traffic to merge onto South Broad Street. He wades through spots of pedestrian traffic on the sidewalk as the first crowds start stumbling out of bars, wearing stupid green hats and emitting their own personal clouds of cheap American beer. Rex only has to deal with them for a minute before he hooks a right onto Greenwood Avenue. It's not much more than an overgrown alley, but the trees are great for covering the road in shadow. It also means he's back in the real part of Trenton, away from the downtown area and its slapped-on shiny overhaul. *If the neighborhood isn't run down, it's not the real town,* Lois is fond of telling people.

Rex knows that there was a row of houses lining part of one of the side streets last fall, edged up next to Market Street and richer traffic. Now there's a solid block of new construction jutting out of the suburban landscape, destined to become apartments that half of Trenton can't afford, or rental offices for businesses that can. Class warfare—his father says it hasn't changed in forty years. Rex doesn't think so; he thinks it's gotten worse.

It doesn't make Rex feel any better to realize that instinct is guiding him in that direction. The new building is ugly even for modern architecture. It looks like it's going to max out at six stories, and the sixth floor isn't finished. It's a clear night with decent light coming from the moon, so Rex can see that electricity is still being run up from lower floors by secured groups of industrial-thick extension cords. The steel I-beams are all in place, but there are no partitions up to define the space, leaving it open to the air.

Movement catches his eye, shadows tall enough to be people moving around on the top floor. He can't hear voices, but that doesn't mean anything, not at this distance.

Rex swears under his breath when he skirts the enclosed yard and finds the site's only entrance guarded by a big motherfucker wearing a fitted three-piece suit. Tailor didn't do a good job—Rex can pick out the outline of the man's gun holsters, one on each side.

Rex hides his bag in the shadow cast by an upright CAUTION sign and twists his watch around on his wrist. Nobody needs a guard in a cheap gray Armani knockoff watching over a construction site in the middle of the night. Regular security should be patrolling the place, men and women in uncomfortable polyester uniforms armed with flashlights, paranoia, and not much else.

He uses years of military training and sibling avoidance to sneak up on the oversized guard and choke him into unconsciousness, then double-checks that the man's pulse remains steady. It isn't the nicest thing to do to someone, but if nothing's wrong? Someone wakes up embarrassed as all hell instead of never waking up at all.

Rex is halfway across the yard, making his way from shadow to shadow, when he hears the first sharp pop-crack of a gunshot. He draws the 1911 on swift, war-honed instinct just in time to hear more. Low caliber .9mm rounds have him tracking muzzle flash to the sixth floor.

The shots have stopped at six—single stack, Rex decides—when a body falls from the unfinished edge of the top floor. It crashes down on a tarp-covered stack of drywall on the ground about ten feet away from Rex's position. Half of the stack shatters, blowing thick clouds of gypsum dust in all directions.

Rex's heart is hammering in his chest. He feels like he can't breathe. He can't even move.

A white-blue security light mounted a few stories above him had illuminated fire-bright hair as the body fell.

No.

No, no, *no!* He did not just watch his boyfriend die!

Shock keeps him locked in place until Ambrus rolls off the obliterated drywall pile and hits the ground face down. Rex bolts across the lot and into the drywall cloud. His boots slide on the tarp as he comes to a sudden halt next to Ambrus.

His stupid boyfriend is actually trying to push himself up with his hands. "Stop, stop," Rex orders in a harsh whisper, relieved and horrified that Ambrus is still alive. He can't rush this, he'll make it worse—

Then he hears the distinct rack of a slide release. There isn't going to be time for gentleness. What he's about to do may finish what the bullets started.

In war, there are never any great choices, just less bad ones. He hates that lesson to this very fucking day.

Rex hauls Ambrus to his feet, wincing at what he finds. "Oh god, Euan." There is blood at Ambrus's nose and lips. Red is spreading out from four different, distinct stains on his torn white shirt, turning to mud as it mixes with drywall dust.

Ambrus's eyes are open, tiny slits of awareness. "Followed me?" he asks in an amused mumble.

"Had a bad feeling, broke the rules, not sorry." Rex pulls Ambrus's right arm over his shoulders, gripping Ambrus's wrist with his left hand so he can keep the 1911 available for firing.

Hearing Ambrus say, "M'glad," makes Rex's blood turn to ice. He still has to find Fox, not to mention the asshole with the gun who'd just attempted to murder his boyfriend.

Rex swallows down fear and dust. "Please just keep fucking breathing," he says as he lifts the 1911 back up to sight at the sixth floor again.

For the first time in his life, a weapon falters in his hand.

Jasper Fox is standing on the open edge of the sixth floor, staring down at them. Rex can't make out the shadowed expression on his face, but he knows two things at once:

There is no other shooter.

Fox is the one who shot Ambrus.

"What the fuck?" Rex whispers in shock. His skin is once again crawling with the unpleasant electrical tingle that precedes terrible potential outcomes.

Fire. Fire the gun, Rex orders himself, but he can't. That's Fox. Jasper. He can't—

Then another figure behind Fox moves. He's nothing more than a black shape in the darkness, but Rex can hear the mystery man's instructions as clearly as if they're spoken next to his ear:

"Kill them."

Fox doesn't hesitate. He lifts his arm, the snub barrel of an older model .9mm in his hand.

It's instinct that saves him. Rex doesn't think; he fires. His ears ring as he squeezes off all seven rounds at Fox and his mystery asshole friend, driving them back from the building edge. He hears a cry of pain but doesn't stick around to find out what or who he hit. He shoves the 1911 back into its holster and swings Ambrus up and over his shoulders in a fireman's carry. Knowing he hit someone is great, but gaining time was far more important.

Rex runs for the exit, ignoring the repeated *thud-thud-thud* of bullets striking the ground behind him. He ducks low enough to grab his bag, knocking the yellow sign over onto its side.

He goes south until he finds two houses without fencing, blows through the narrow alleyway between them, gets honked at by a car on the next street as he crosses worn asphalt, and then shoves his way past an aging fence with accompanying barking damned dog. The alleyway and its shadowy safety are only a lunge away when he emerges onto the next street. He crosses Greenwood and shoves his way into the trees that line US 1.

He halts for a precious few seconds to decide on his escape route. He memorized all of his options the same month he moved into Trenton, and he knows these neighborhoods better than a bunch of assholes working out of D.C. Fox and his department friends don't have a chance in hell of catching him. Not here.

Is it the department, though? Rex wonders, crossing the freeway the moment he can do it without getting clobbered by a car or a semi rig. No train, so he shoves his way through the brush between the freeway and railway to cross the tracks.

Rex feels his jaw clench in sudden anger that grinds his teeth together. *Of course it's the department. Don't be fucking stupid.*

He just doesn't know *why*.

He stumbles just once when gravel shifts beneath his feet, but Ambrus doesn't make a sound of complaint. The only assurance Rex has that the man is still breathing is the steady rise and fall of Ambrus's chest against Rex's back.

He hides in a tiny patch of darkness cast by the Broad Street overpass. Pounding feet are traveling over his head, at least six individuals, heading south. It's really damned inconvenient that he needs to go south, too. Fortunately, he knows of other ways.

Rex follows the train tracks until a people-created trail between houses gets him onto Ferry Street. He runs southwest until he can take a sharp left onto Asbury, nothing but quiet residential homes and no damned green-beer-guzzlers to speak of. That puts him five streets over from Centre Street and his apartment, with a hell of a lot of sound-muffling homes in between.

He hopes Janice did what she said, that the duplex is empty. He has no idea what the department would do to anyone they found inside. Shit, he's even hoping they got the damned cats out.

Rex chances the overhead lights and cuts through Streamboat's playground. Noise strikes his ears; he bolts over to Lamberton Street to avoid the night shift at the processing plant. He cuts between houses again, scaring the shit out of a pair of teenagers necking on an old porch swing—"Sorry!"—and keeps going south by following the next alley. He has to wait, ignoring the way his breath is steaming into the air like a fucking bellows, for traffic to pass by on Cass Street. Then he's finally back on Centre Street, still going south—right to Trenton's biggest cemetery.

Rex is wheezing for breath by the time he makes it to Second Street, which back-ends the cemetery's main offices. Oh, fuck. Motherfuck. Fuck a rabid goddamned duck, he feels like he's going to vomit. He ran two miles with a dying man slung over his shoulders who tops out at one-sixty. Rex's stomach curdled about halfway across town, from the run or panic about Ambrus or bafflement over Fox—hell, pick one. Any reason fits just fine.

He walks the rest of the way down Second, listening hard for any hint of pursuit. He hears nothing except the song of birds confused by city lights, crickets chirping their confusion about the too-warm weather, and Ambrus's rasping breaths.

Always have a fallback. Always have a way out. Don't trust someone else to do it for you.

His way out is parked behind the smaller office building, an old Ford truck that rusted a solid uniform brown over the years. There isn't really a place to hide a getaway vehicle in Trenton unless Rex wanted pay outrageous parking fees or risk it being stolen, but letting someone borrow it on permanent loan? It breaks his father's last rule, but it worked out pretty damned well. Rex paid for the truck's upkeep and yearly fees. The groundkeepers had a free vehicle to do their jobs with, a win for both parties—except for the part where Rex actually needs it now, and those same workers are going to arrive at sunup to find their tools on the ground in an empty parking spot.

Ten years of free vehicle, though. As far as he's concerned, that's one hell of a donation.

Rex uses his free hand to pull the latch on the tailgate and lower it, wincing as the hinges whine about their need for oil. The truck bed smells like raw earth from recently dug-and-covered graves. It's a stretch to snag the end of the outdoor carpet that's used to cover dirt mounds and pull it close. Rex feels the burn in his arm as he unrolls it one-handed, green plastic side up.

He's gasping again as he gently lowers Ambrus onto the carpet, which will be kinder than a cold, grooved metal truck bed. Then Rex leans over, elbow propped on the side of the truck, and tries to decide if he really will have to throw up before climbing in.

Rex gets past the nausea, pulls off his coat, and then climbs into the truck bed to kneel down on the earth-scented plastic next to Ambrus. His eyes are closed, his breath is coming faster as his body tries to compensate for blood loss. Rex looks at the full blossom of red soaking Ambrus's white button-down, then glances down at his own ruined t-shirt. That's about a liter and a half of blood if Rex is calculating it right, and Ambrus's body size puts him in the not-quite five liters category. If Rex can't get the bleeding stopped...

He rolls Ambrus over onto his side and searches for exit wounds, finding none. That's as beneficial as it is concerning. Bullets fucking tumble.

Rex rolls Ambrus onto his back again and closes his eyes, forcing himself to calm the hell down. He's no good to Ambrus if his hands start shaking. "I'm so glad you're a tough fucker."

"Rex?"

He glances down to find Ambrus staring up at him in confusion. "What—the fuck?" Ambrus asks.

"Kind of what I'd like to know, too." Rex unzips his bag and pulls out the first aid kit, unfolding it a section at a time until it's stretched out next to Ambrus. There's a single saline bag but no place to set it up out here—that will have to wait until they're in the truck cab, which still has an old rifle mount across the back window.

"I don't..." Ambrus swallows with a dry-sounding click. "How bad?"

"Four shots, center mass." Rex keeps his voice even. He's honestly terrified that he's still watching his boyfriend die. "Two in your left lung. Definitely missed your heart, since you're still talking to me. One near the hollow of your throat, and it's a fucking miracle it didn't tear out your esophagus. Last one's in your right shoulder. Hold still."

Rex uses the kit's razor-sharp scissors to slice through both layers of Ambrus's shirts, right down the center. Then he peels the drywall-muddied layers back to reveal four bullet holes and bloodstained skin. Rex quietly says one of the few prayers he's ever genuinely meant, glad he was the one holding the .45mm and that Fox only had a .9mm.

"Still have one good lung," Ambrus says in a faint voice, smiling. His teeth are stained red, which isn't helping Rex's state of mind at all.

Rex grips Ambrus's wrist, feeling a pulse that's running faster and fainter under his fingertips. "You staying with me?" he asks in a light voice, trying to keep fear at bay. The last time Rex asked someone that question, he was still wearing an officially sanctioned uniform.

Ambrus lifts his left hand in a slow, trembling motion, stilled when Rex grabs ahold with his free hand. "Staying." Ambrus squeezes Rex's fingers in a brief, tight grasp. "Promise."

Rex squeezes back before placing Ambrus's hand back down on the plastic grass. "You allergic to iodine?"

"No." Ambrus looks like he's wincing as Rex pours out most of a container of basic wound wash over each bullet hole. "Didn't we just do this?"

"I slept through it," Rex replies, biting his lip as the ridiculousness of the situation strikes him. They really did just do this, but it was the other way around. "Any other allergies?"

"Fucking bullets," Ambrus mutters.

Rex gives in and smiles while filling a syringe from the strongest painkiller the kit contains. "Yeah. Me, too."

The fentanyl kicks in faster than Rex expects. Ambrus's eyes go glassy in short order, but he doesn't pass out. Rex properly cleans all four wounds with straight-up iodine, not in the mood to take chances with bacteria. The shoulder hit and the wound near Ambrus's throat start trickling blood again the moment he's done; Rex packs gauze into place and seals both wounds with pressure bandages.

The bubbles that form around the shots perforating Ambrus's left lung do not make him happy. Between that and the bleeding— shit. Rex packs and pressure-seals the first wound, but the second one he leaves clear as he preps for what he's going to have to do.

Rex leans down close to Ambrus's ear. "Listen to me. You have a sucking chest wound and a goddamned bleeding problem. If I don't put a stent in this, you're going to fucking drown before we find help."

Ambrus gives him a pained nod. "Understood," he whispers.

"Okay." Rex takes another breath and releases it to steady his hands again. "Breathe in," he instructs.

The moment Ambrus complies, Rex pushes the stent line through broken skin and destroyed tissue. Ambrus's gasp is high-pitched, pain overriding the fentanyl, but then the stent's in and it's over with. Rex seals three of four corners of the pressure bandage around the wound. One more thing.

"Breathe out," Rex orders. "All the way."

Ambrus listens better than a hell of a lot of soldiers Rex treated during wartime. The moment he hears the last bit of air leave the man's lips, Rex presses down, hard, sealing both the wound and the area around the stent line.

"There. Now you can fuckin' breathe," Rex tells Ambrus with forced cheer. Ambrus thanks him by finally passing out. No damned manners.

Rex eyes the end of the stent line, which is leaving drops of red on the plastic mat. He doesn't even have a stupid fucking bottle to let that drain into. They'll just have to suck it up and deal with the mess.

God. He blames Ambrus for that awful pun.

The driver's side door accepts Rex's key and opens without the unhappy creak the tailgate emitted. The cab light comes on after a few seconds, casting grudging amber light over the old bench seat.

Attached to the metal frame beneath the bench seat is a license plate for Pennsylvania, secured in place with neodymium magnets. It's as old and beaten-up as the truck itself, but the sticker is still good through April.

Rex pulls out his multi-tool and removes the Jersey set of plates from the front and rear, then screws the Pennsylvania replacement onto the back bumper before he rests his head against rusty metal.

Breathe. In and out. Keep it together.

Rex grabs the saline bag and tubing from the kit and crawls into the truck, hanging it from the rack by tearing a larger hole into the plastic on top of the bag. Not the best solution, but the only one he's got. He pulls the tubing line and sealed port into the front seat and leaves it dangling there while he goes to collect his passenger.

It takes a combination of swearing and creative, gentle shoving to get Ambrus into the truck, stretched out along the bench seat. It isn't lost on Rex that this is *also* a mirrored reflection of what Ambrus probably did for him in Turkmenistan.

Rex drops the repacked bug-out bag on the floor next to the gearshift, shuts the door, and goes back around to the driver's side. By the time he's seated, there is fresh blood at Ambrus's nose.

Dammit.

Rex grabs the bag and shoves it in snug against his right leg, then pulls Ambrus towards him, using his lap and the bag to elevate his boyfriend as much as he can. When Rex cleans the red smudges away from Ambrus's nose, they don't come back. Better.

Ambrus sleeps through the IV insertion, which is another minor miracle; Rex turned the air blue trying to find a decent vein under the crap lighting provided by the ancient overhead dome. It's the grumbling roar of the old truck's engine starting up that wakes him. "What the hell?" Ambrus rasps.

"Hey, don't mock the family icon," Rex says, teasing words that probably fall flat. With the cab light off, it's too dark to really make out Ambrus's expression. "1974 Ford F-series extended cab. Truck of champions, or people who like contributing to global warming."

"Right." Rex can feel when Ambrus swallows; he hears the shift of cloth as he explores the new IV line taped to his hand. "Where?"

"Safe, at the moment." Rex rolls down the window with the hand crank so he can adjust the driver's side mirror. The passenger side mirror has been gone for years. Inconvenient, but he would have to crawl over Ambrus to fix the stupid thing, anyway.

Rex tilts the rearview into the best position to make sure he can see exactly what might try to crawl up their ass. "The truck used to be Dad's. I borrowed it for potential emergencies. Been letting the local cemetery use it so it wouldn't sit and rot. Plates are borrowed, pursuit doesn't know where the fuck we are, and there isn't GPS tracking on this old heap of shit."

"No. I meant..." Ambrus draws in a pained breath. "Where?"

"Oh." Rex puts the truck in gear, backing it out of its spot. Headlights shine on the heap of left-behind tools before they cut away to illuminate Second Street. He hits Lamberton long enough to turn onto Lalor Street, which will take him to 129. That gets him back to the freeway, and from there it's I-276 into Pennsylvania. "We're going home."

"Oh," Ambrus echoes him. "Rex, you can't—"

"Got any other suggestions that aren't stupid?" Rex asks, his eyes darting around as he drives. He sees at least one government-type car, but it ignores the old truck and keeps going in the opposite direction. Awesome.

"No," Ambrus admits.

"Good." Rex glances down at Ambrus when the streetlights along the freeway give Rex enough light to see his face. "You're not allowed to fucking die, either."

Ambrus looks utterly mystified. "I just...was shot!"

"Exactly!" Rex retorts. He turns his attention back to the road, feeling the reassuring weight of the 1911 in its holster. He's lost everything in his apartment, maybe for good, but all of his flash drives are safe on his keyring. He still has everything important in his life aside from the bleeding man at his side. "If you can get shot four times, fall six stories, and survive that shit, you can survive an hour in this fucking truck!"

*   *   *   *

"How many drunks out of Allentown have we collected so far?" Khodî watches as Scotty pushes another cuffed, cursing, red-cheeked man towards temporary holding. The last one smelled like too much cheap beer. This one just smells like vomit.

"Fuckin' eight," Scotty replies, still growling under his breath every time his new friend so much as twitches in the wrong direction. "Tasing them would be so much easier."

Khodî rolls his eyes. "No, jackass. Don't make me confiscate your shiny little electronic toy."

"No fun," Scotty mutters under his breath, disappearing around the corner. Howls of welcome come from the other seven inebriated souls Khodî's people have picked up since ten that evening.

"They've slacked off from last year." Khodî glances down at the boards. He's due to go out in a half-hour to replace John on patrol. "It was sixteen by midnight last time." There are reasons why he pulls night shift this time of year, and Saint Patrick's Day are all of them.

"Maybe they decided to go bother Philadelphia instead of us," Genni offers hopefully. "Hell, Khodî, we haven't even gotten any calls about cows."

"I don't trust it. The cows usually pull their shit around four in the morning," Khodî replies, and then twitches when he feels a cell phone vibrate against his chest. Odd; he remembers putting that in his belt catch earlier—

Wrong phone. Shit.

Khodî removes the phone from his breast pocket, glances at the unfamiliar number, and flips open the older-model cell. "Hello." He knows his voice sounds normal, but Genni is still giving him a suspicious look. She knows where his cell phone lives, and it's not there.

"Khỏi Khôn đi Som."[1]

Khodî feels his heart try to drop directly into his stomach. "Hi there, Trenton warrior. How much drinking have you done tonight?"

"Fuck, not nearly enough." Rex sounds stressed to the max. "I need you to go get Kai and meet me at home."

"Look, I don't care if you're broken down on the side of the road," Khodî says, which makes Genni roll her eyes and start paying attention to her booking paperwork again. "That's what Triple-A is for, asshole."

---

[1] Butchered Vietnamese: pronounced: Kon Koh-ee-dee Sum.

"Four GSWs and a six story fall, Khodî. I can't—I don't have that kind of fucking training," Rex whispers.

The only thing that keeps Khodî from giving the game away right then and there is practice from before, during, and after the military. "Okay, okay. Fine. I'll come and get your dumb ass. You're going to owe Genni and Scotty beer, though."

Khodî smiles when Genni makes a quiet, delighted squeal under her breath. She's well aware of the fact that Rex never brings deer piss in to share.

"Oh, god, thank you." Khodî hears Rex swallow just before it sounds like he's trying to cough up part of his lungs. Jesus. "It has to be fast. All right?"

"Fuck, what are bubble lights for if I can't abuse the speed limit?" Khodî retorts, grinning. "I'll see you soon, okay?"

"Okay. Thanks," Rex says, and the call disconnects. Khodî doesn't bother to try and save the number, not from what is probably the only burner Rex has on him.

Fuck and damnation. What in the hell did Rex do? This sounds like it's going to escalate Ella's goal posts in her bid to be the family's worst offender at getting into shit.

"Scotty's gonna kill you," Genni says, looking up at him with her chin parked on both of her hands.

"Scotty can wank off and cope." Khodî grabs his hat while Genni cackles aloud. "You guys can fight over who takes John's lunch break, all right?"

"Sure. When can we see you back, Illustrious Leader?" Genni asks.

Khodî hesitates with his hand on the doorknob. "Trenton traffic is going to blow, so between the trip there, back, and the need for sleep...tomorrow afternoon, most likely," he says, aware that he's probably lying through his damned teeth.

He has no idea when he's going to make it back. At least he's got vacation time saved up.

*   *   *   *

Kai hears the chirping twice before he figures out where the hell it's coming from, but Wesley still beats him to it. "Go answer your phone, man," he says, right before nailing Brian's game avatar with a really nasty headshot. "It's driving me bugshit."

"SON OF A BITCH!" Brian roars, but Neumia's been asleep on the couch for the last two hours and doesn't even twitch. She's used to game nights being loud.

"Nothing drives you bugshit, Wes," Kai replies, heading over to the two bags he left at the bottom of the stairs. "You are one of the chillest bastards to ever chill."

"So that's why this asshole tries to sweat me out of the house during the winter," Brian mutters, grimly waiting through respawn time so he can go back to stalking Wesley in revenge.

Kai grins at them both while digging through his bag. Brian and Wesley sort-of-share a farmhouse about two hours out from their father's place, and by sort-of-share, Kai means that Brian owns it, Brian and Neumia live there, and Wesley turns up whenever he feels like it for extended periods of time.

Oh, well. It's not like they don't all do the same thing to Dad.

Kai pulls out his regular cell and finds that nope, it's not that phone. Then the one in the bottom of his backpack starts cricket-chirping again.

He feels his stomach turn over. Not that phone. Not that phone. Not that phone. Especially when he doesn't recognize the number.

"Hi," Kai answers it, feeling his voice crack. Please let no one be dead.

"It's me," Khodî says, which doesn't make Kai feel much better.

"Hi, bro." Kai gestures a knife-cut over his throat to get his other brothers to pause the game and pay attention. "What's up?"

"I'm sitting out in my patrol car with a burner in my hand I had to fish out from underneath the seat. Rex called me a few minutes ago and requested you special out at the farm, so I'm trying to find out where you are so I can break speed limits."

"Rex called you?" Kai repeats, sounding stupid.

"Rex called me by my *full* name," Khodî clarifies, which nope, not helping. Hell, most people don't even realize that Khodî is a fucking nickname.

"So, I...need both bags, then?" Kai asks, and hears an affirmative sound. "How the fuck did he get shot twice in one year?"

"Got the feeling it wasn't him. We need someone Hawaiian with good sense."

Kai tastes bile in the back of his throat. Shit. That particular code was created because of Mom. They just never stopped using it for the next doctor in line.

"Okay." Kai draws in a sharp breath through his nose, lets it out through his mouth, and shakes out his free hand. Surgical trick, but he learned it for a gun well before that. Whichever; it works for both. "You don't need to head out to Philly. We're all at Brian's place. We can load up and meet you there."

"I'm almost disappointed." Khodî says it in a way that Kai knows he isn't disappointed at all. "Tell Wesley to drive. He's the one with the lead foot."

Speed needed. Heard and understood. "All right. See you in about an hour, I guess," Kai estimates. "Excluding cows."

"Too early for those assholes," Khodî reassures him, and then hangs up.

Kai stares at the cell in his hands before he powers it down, yanks the battery, pulls the SIM card, snaps it in half, and then shoves the phone and broken card into his pocket. The battery goes into the trashcan. He can toss the phone and the broken bits of card from the vehicle on the way, but he can't leave them here. Phone's got internal memory.

He had no reason to tear that phone apart. He has every reason.

Dammit, he hates when his instincts refuse to be specific.

"Sup?" Wesley asks, giving Kai a partially raised eyebrow. He knows shit's going down. He just wants details.

"Uh—Rex phoned Khodî and called him by his full name. We need to go to Dad's."

Wesley reaches over to turn off the game system and the television. "I'll get the bags."

"I've got Nari," Brian adds, scooping up Kai's niece. Neumia rolls over in her father's arms and goes back to sleep, still young enough not to care about being hauled around unexpectedly at night.

Brian's car and Wesley's van are both outside, and Wesley goes straight for his favorite. "I'm driving," he says without Kai needing to suggest it.

Brian opens the door and buckles Neumia into the rear, where a spare booster seat has had a place of honor since she graduated out of a full car seat. "If you get a ticket, I'm not paying for this one."

Kai crawls into the seat next to Neumia and buckles up without saying anything, trying not to bite his lip. He has a feeling that Khodî has the cop part taken care of.

Chapter 7

:XXXX:

Django always knows when he's dreaming. It's a leftover from life in the program, which eventually became the department—one he wanted absolutely nothing to do with.

Knowing he's dreaming doesn't mean he can make it stop, or even necessarily change it, but Django can tell sleep from reality. He fought in several wars; knowing the difference has probably stopped him from accidentally killing someone more than once.

Sometimes the dreams are fucking silly, the results of a brain unwinding from a long day. Other times it's the replay of a distant memory.

Then there are the dreams that belong to someone else. Those are the most frustrating because they usually make no damned sense whatsoever. It isn't a natural talent. He doesn't go seeking these people out. Some assholes are just really damned *loud.*

Especially this one, a dream he's had several nights in a row. Always, always, there's a song in the background. It sounds familiar, like something his kids might have liked back when they were first broadening their musical horizons and trying things other than what local Pennsylvania radio had to offer.

The name crops up like an unwelcome weed in a rose garden. "Welcome Home, (Sanitarium)." Metallica, mid-1980s.

Django flinches in his sleep. His sister died in one of those fucking hospitals. Not his fault. Completely his fault.

His dreamer has been mulling over the song's lyrics as if they're embedded with meaning. They fear imprisonment, not life.

Good start, Django thinks, irritated because he can't wake up from this fucking mess. He doesn't even like the damned song.

Why?

The first bit of sympathy leeches into Django's awareness. This poor person dreams like they took too many hits to the head, and there's a hell of a lot of damage to their thought process. No wonder they're so loud.

Can't kill my way out. Innocents. Patients. Staff. They...care. Never hurt anyone unless they believe they need to *stop* a hurt.

Django waits, curious. Someone might actually be making some progress. Maybe then they won't be so damned loud.

All right then, you stupid song that never stops: why is that the only way to reach out again?

No. Not reach out.

Django gets it at the same time his mystery dreamer does, and smiles in his sleep.

Not reach out. *Get out.*

It's the long, angry wail of an older-model car horn that wakes Django from the dream. He's grateful at first, then irritated. It's still

145

dark out, and the alarm clock on the bedside table shows that it's three in the goddamn morning.

Then the long wail repeats itself, followed by three short honks. Django is out of bed, Tiny Beast in his hand, before he realizes he's on the move. He peers out of the side of the bedroom window and finds a truck in the driveway. Older model, looks like it should have been retired about twenty years ago and put out of its misery—

Shit. Now he knows why he was dreaming about getting out.

Rex.

Django dresses in a hurry, pulling on yesterday's jeans and t-shirt. He tucks Tiny Beast into the waistband of his pants before he rushes down the hall and into the kitchen to unlock the door. By the time he gets outside, Rex is standing in front of the pickup, his right arm resting on the hood as he bends over. Either he's thrown up, or he's giving it some serious thought.

His kid is also covered in blood. Dark red and brown stains mar Rex's t-shirt, face, and hair. Even the old camouflage trousers he's wearing are splattered with red.

"Did you fucking get shot twice in one year?" Django asks in disbelief, hopping off the porch. The ground is cold beneath his bare feet, but not like it's supposed to be in mid-March. The land should still be thawing from winter, but they never got one.

Rex looks up, and the expression on his face is so reminiscent of the way he looked during Eric's funeral that Django nearly panics. "No, I didn't—oh, fuck, Dad."

"Did the *bratva* decide to finally creep stateside and stalk you?" He's trying to break the tension that's now weighing down his shoulders. Something has gone badly wrong, and he knows it.

"That would at least make some fucking sense!" Rex straightens up, wiping his mouth and nose to clear away blood mixed with what looks like mud or dirt.

Django tries one more time. He wants this to be a hell of a lot less *wrong* than it feels. "Okay, then who the fuck did you kill? I told you guys—we're not burying any more bodies on this farm until the last ten have had the chance to rot."

Rex visibly tosses shock aside, his shoulders going back as his chin comes up in angry defiance. "I'm not responsible for some of my siblings' bad habits!" he snarls, skirting around the front end of the truck to yank open the passenger side door.

Django is considering making a crack about the family's white (blond) sheep when the truck's cabin light reveals Rex's passenger. The bottom falls out of Django's stomach. For a brief, horrible moment, it feels like the earth tilts beneath his feet.

He knows that hair, even if it's badly illuminated by old yellowed lighting. He knows that face, even if the features are smeared with as much mud and blood as Rex's are.

"Bad habits," Django repeats in a shocked whisper. "Rex, what the fuck happened?"

"If I knew that, I'd be a lot less fucking confused right now. Just help me!" Rex shouts, getting ahold of his bleeding passenger and half-carrying, half-dragging him off the bench seat until he's cradling the man in his arms.

Django can see that Rex's arms are shaking. "No, here," he says softly, and convinces Rex to let him carry the poor, bloodied bastard instead. "Go open the door, kiddo."

"Django?" It's just above a sleepy mumble, with a wet quality that Django doesn't like hearing at all.

"Hi, Kid." Django slides sideways through the open doorway, letting Rex close the door behind them. "This is a hell of a lot earlier than July."

"I know. I'm—" Django thinks he's going to receive an apology, or an explanation, but the man's already unconscious again. Dammit.

Rex sweeps the kitchen table clean of what little detritus it picked up since the holiday, mostly pens and paperwork. Django lays his bloody burden down onto the hardwood tabletop, glad that it's long enough to support him from head to foot. The table will hold anyone except Xãwuṭh, who insisted upon growing up to be mutant-levels of tall compared to the rest of the family.

For a moment, Django stares down at the man Rex brought home. "Éoghan Beathan Kellagh-Ambrus," he murmurs.

"You know his whole name?" Rex asks, and suddenly bends over, coughing in short, harsh barks. The sound reminds Django far too much of Khodî's medical leave after Ground Zero.

"He was still using it when we last met. Why, did you decide to switch it up?" Django asks, seeing the flicker of motion behind closed eyelids. "Let me hear you sing it, English."

Kellagh-Ambrus opens his eyes and gives Django a tired, narrow-eyed glare. "Fu—fuck you, and your little dog, too."

Rex is still hanging onto the edge of the table as he stares at them in disbelief. "*The Wizard of Oz*? Fucking seriously?"

"We were all really damned drunk when choosing those first ident-confirms." Django pulls open Kellagh-Ambrus's ruined shirt to investigate the damage. "C'mon, tell me about the name change," he pesters, trying to keep the man conscious. These are not good wounds to have, even for someone out of the fucking program.

"I shortened it," Kellagh-Ambrus whispers. "Euan Ambrus. Few years ago."

"Good choice," Django says in mocking approval. The bastard doesn't look like he's aged a day since Vietnam. Then again, he had to do his aging fast and far too young. "Easier to say while still capable of confusing the fuck out of everyone. The person who shot you had good aim, by the way."

"Can't decide if that's—if that's good or bad." Ambrus blinks up at him, his eyes filled with the sort of desolation Django thought he would have left behind a long time ago. "Taught him to go for a headshot if he—if he wanted someone dead."

"Guess you really didn't stay stupid, after all, Kell—Ambrus." That's going to take a while to get used to. "What the hell did you two get into?" Django asks, noticing an uneven jut to Ambrus's collarbone.

"Fucking drywall dust." Rex wipes his eyes and gives Django a brief, tired smile. "Hold on," he says, and disappears down the hallway.

Django picks up Ambrus's arm, the one without the IV stent, and presses his fingers against the pulse point at his wrist. Fast and a hair too faint; he's lost a lot of blood, given how much of it Rex and Ambrus are wearing, but not a fatal amount. Django suspects the half-empty saline bag resting on Ambrus's chest is the reason why it's not worse. Ambrus isn't going to die—not today, at least.

Rex comes back with an armload of old towels, stuffing them up under Ambrus's head, neck, and shoulders to prop him up at an angle that will probably make breathing a hell of a lot easier. "I need to hang the bag again."

"Yeah. Here." Django reaches up and removes a small skillet from one of the pot rack hooks, putting it on the stove. Rex uses the free hook to hang the bag, letting gravity help it do its job again. "About how long is left on this one, Rex?"

"Fifteen minutes or so." Rex leans against the table, breathing in a wheezing undertone. He must have swallowed a hell of a lot of dust to still be struggling. "I called Khodî on a burner phone after I got out of Trenton. He's going for Kai."

"Kai has a few more saline bags stashed in the garage," Django says. Kai also has bags of human blood stored in the garage fridge, and Django made a point of not asking where the hell they came from. Having a kid in medical school has its perks anyway, but Kai is like his mother—a hell of a lot of conniving hidden behind a cute, innocent face.

Django reaches over to flip the wall switch, turning on the overhead for the kitchen. The bright light throws Ambrus's pale features into stark relief, which only serves to highlight the amount of blood that's darkened and dried in his mustache and beard. Four pressure bandages; four hits. The lowest lung wound is sealed with a stent line at the base, letting fluid drain so that Ambrus won't fucking drown while waiting for surgical care.

Django gets a bucket out from under the kitchen sink to put the stent line into. That gives the blood a place to go that's not the floor, but it doesn't take long at all for the bottom of the bucket to start turning red.

Rex coughs a few more times. "Everything's still sealed up?"

"Yeah." Django glances over at him. "You did good, Rex."

"Hey, what was the point of getting the full 18D classification on top of the 18A if I don't fucking use it?" Rex smiles. "Your fault I went through that shit twice, anyway."

Django refuses to comment. It wasn't his fault he'd gotten shot. What had really influenced Rex into confounding the military and insisting on the double classification while still in SFQC was Makani 'Aukai, who'd had enough medical training to keep Django from bleeding out from a lung wound.

God, he misses her. There are days when he wakes up and feels like he can't breathe, the grief is so damned suffocating.

"What happened to the right collarbone here?" Django asks, prodding at the uneven spot. Ambrus jerks back to consciousness and hisses a litany under his breath, nothing but variations on the word "fuck."

"I didn't notice. Was too worried about the bleeding." Rex leans over to see what Django is pointing at. "It must have happened when he fell."

Ambrus's lips twitch. "Sorry, I—didn't fall. Jumped."

That one surprises Django, but Rex is infuriated. "You did fucking *what?*" he growls. "And you think *I'm* nuts?"

"Nowhere else to go. Didn't want to get shot again." Ambrus blinks up at the overhead, his pupils blown too wide for the bright light. "Took my chances with—with gravity."

"Six stories, asshole." Rex closes his eyes for a moment. "That pile of drywall probably saved your life."

Django frowns. "Where the fuck was your gun, Euan?" Shooting back is an excellent means of self-defense.

Ambrus seems to think about it before he moves his head back and forth in negation. "The shooter—startled me. Then...then the drywall. Rex?"

"You didn't have it when you hit the ground. I didn't see it, but there was such a goddamn cloud of dust I could have walked right by without noticing." Rex leans over again, coughing in deep, ratcheting hacks as he tries to get gypsum dust out of his lungs.

"You never did do shit by halves," Django says. "You know how it is, Kid—can't let broken bones sit for long, not with us."

Ambrus winces. "Yeah. I know."

"Seriously, where the hell did you find him?" Django asks Rex, mentally preparing for what he's going to have to do.

"Club," Rex says in a curt voice, his eyes on the bucket and the stent line. The bottom of the bucket has vanished beneath a layer of red. "Bar and grill. Whatever the hell you want to call them."

"A club?" Django snorts and grins down at Ambrus. "You are eighty years old."

Ambrus rolls his eyes. "Screw. You."

"Eighty." Django looks over to find Rex staring at Ambrus, wide-eyed. "Are you fucking serious?"

Ambrus glares up at Django. "Eighty-one. Learn to fucking count, Whetū."

Django shakes his head when Ambrus jerks back from his fingers. "It's healing wrong, you stupid shit. Either I set it now, or my kid resets it in an hour by breaking it again."

"Eighty-one," Rex repeats in a cracked voice.

Ambrus sighs, closing his eyes. "And a half. Do it, Django."

"Deep breath," Django orders, and then presses the edges of the collarbone into the correct alignment. That nets him one hell of a shriek, which makes Django feel a lot better about waking up to 3:00 a.m. emergencies and blood and the fucking department back in his life.

Rex pulls Django's hands away, wincing at the blood that wells up from broken skin. The collarbone break was a compound fracture that didn't show exterior damage. Now it's more like a mutant oblique, if Django's remembering his fractures correctly. It's been a while. "Good work on that one, too, Dad."

"We learned a lot in those first years," Django replies, feeling tired. Ambrus's eyes are wide open, spiked into full awareness from the adrenaline surge of having bones reset without painkillers.

Painkillers. Shit, he's a complete asshole. "You got any more drugs in that kit?" Django asks Rex.

"Yeah." Rex shoulder-pushes his way outside, letting the kitchen door slam shut. Django uses the time while Rex is gone to fold up the kitchen towels in the room, stuffing them beneath Ambrus's head and shoulders to give him more literal breathing room.

Rex comes back and unfolds the kit along the table until he comes to the collection of tiny glass vials and two remaining sterile syringes. "Not much left, not after the initial drug injections for the ride out here."

Django nods, picks up the fentanyl, and loads up a syringe with double the maximum dose for an adult male. Then he finds the surgical-strength ibuprofen and adds it to the mix. "You ready?" he asks Ambrus.

"Dad?"

"He's program. Department." Django looks at Rex, who is gazing back at him in exhausted concern. "I don't think any of us want your boyfriend to be conscious when Kai starts pulling lead out."

"Program." Rex closes his eyes and nods. "Dosing him like we'd have to do for you. Shit—I probably undercut him."

Ambrus tries to smile at Rex in reassurance. "Slept through the trip."

Django decides his kid needs a minute to pull his ass back together. "I left the bike in the middle of the second garage bay. Move it aside and park the truck in there. If they figure out your escape vehicle and send out drones, I don't want them to see shit."

Rex nods. "They're going to suspect I came here anyway."

"We'll deal with that when it becomes a problem, but not before," Django agrees mildly. "Go on. Hide the fucking truck, all right?"

Rex's eyes drop back down to Ambrus, who is watching him in cautious silence. "Don't murder my boyfriend while I'm gone."

"You're the one dating him. If anyone makes him dead, you get first dibs," Django says. Rex rolls his eyes, but that finally gets him moving.

"Maybe eighty-one is too old." There is a painful, lost quality to Ambrus's voice that Django is also familiar with.

"He'll get over it." Django knows Rex; this was a surprise, not a deal-breaker. He takes a quick look at the IV line and finds the injection port clogged with dirt and blood. "Your shirt is fucked, by the way."

Django gets the kitchen scissors and cuts a line almost the entire way up the ruined white sleeve, pushing cloth aside. Then he clamps his hand down on Ambrus's arm above the crook of his elbow, waiting patiently for a decent vein to reveal itself before he slides the needle home. Ambrus jerks a little as the drugs go in, but he doesn't complain about the burn.

Ambrus's eyes go glassy in less than two minutes. "Wow. That's...that's a lot."

"Trust me, you want to sleep through this surgery." Django begins pulling strands of Ambrus's dust-caked and blood-stiffened hair away from his face. "You poor bastard. I told you to get out after Vietnam."

"Tried." Ambrus looks a touch rueful. "I got bored. Went back."

Django raises an eyebrow. That isn't quite the entire truth of it, but hell, NDAs. "Adrenaline junkie," he teases instead. He's got maybe three more minutes before Ambrus is unconscious. Time to try and get answers before Rex comes back. "I know you were retiring. What went wrong, Euan? Shifting political climate?" Django hasn't heard anything concrete, but enough rumors are circulating that Jason's son David got in touch with Django to share tidbits of weirdness. David knows something is off, and in the DoD, that means things might be turning foul.

"I don't...maybe?" Ambrus blinks a few times in obvious confusion. "After tonight, wouldn't...put it past them. Not anything."

Damn. "Knew the person who shot you, huh?"

"Yeah." Ambrus cracks another tired, beaten smile, but his eyes are leaking tears that trail down his temples to soak into his hair. "Rescued Jasper and his mother from human trafficking when Jasper was eight. Practically my baby brother. Only reason I stayed in the department the last few years was...was him."

Django grimaces. He'd suspected the department had lost its shit and hit the betrayal button hard when Rex turned up with Ambrus. He just hadn't considered the fact that they would make it that fucking personal. "Christ, I'm sorry. Why the hell did he do it?"

"I don't know." Ambrus's smile fades into utter distress. "Only thing they said was...traitor. That I'm—betrayed them. I don't—I haven't—I don't know what happened, Django. No sense. Nothing makes sense."

"Is there anyone else you need to worry about?" Django asks, keeping his anger under control by sheer force of will. Traitor, his ass. Ambrus would sooner eat his own hands than betray his service vows. When this man said he was going to do something, he fucking meant it.

"Everyone's military, either department, or...department-aligned. Everyone except..." Ambrus looks at the closed kitchen door.

"Seriously?" Django asks, and Ambrus nods. "Huh. If you live, I'll buy the two of you a silverware set."

Ambrus huffs out a laugh. "No. Buy us a car, asshole."

"Spoiled shit." Django smirks at him, glad to have at least gotten some of that despondence off Ambrus's face. "Fuzzy dice."

"Still a...cheap fucker, Django Whetū," Ambrus murmurs, his eyes fluttering closed.

Django waits until Ambrus's breathing evens out as the drugs ease pain and tension. Then he rests his head in his hands. "Shit."

Only a few seconds after the rumble of the old truck's engine dies, Django hears the distinct, panther-prowl growl of a police cruiser coming down the drive. His hand drifts towards his gun automatically before there's a quick double-tap on the car's horn. Khodî. Not more trouble.

Khodî and Rex's voices mingle together before they both enter the kitchen. Khodî pulls his hat, glances at Rex, and then looks down at the kitchen table. "Dad, I've told you—you can't have me out here when it's time to bury a body."

Rex glowers at Khodî before punching him in the arm hard enough that Khodî flinches. "I told you not to say it."

Django smirks at Khodî's really bad attempt at lightening the mood. "We're not burying this one." *We're not, dammit.* "Meet the boyfriend."

"Really?" Khodî stares at Ambrus, head canted to one side. "Gotta admit, this is not how I expected this meeting to go. I mean, usually it's us shooting them first. People start coming in pre-shot, we're all going to be spoiled."

Rex sighs. "Please stop being an asshole for at least five seconds."

"Okay, then." Khodî gives Rex a truly magnificent commanding-officer-style glare, reminding Django that Khodî retired from the service as a lieutenant colonel, even if he hadn't been one for very long. "Go take a fucking shower. Rinse out your sinuses—you don't need the shit they put in drywall these days to sit in your lungs."

For a few seconds, Django wonders if Rex is about to slug his older brother, either because of the orders or out of sheer damned frustration.

"Fine," Rex snarls. He picks up the bag he brought from home and disappears down the hallway to take over the first floor bath.

Tiny Beast is back on his lap without Django thinking about it when another vehicle turns onto the driveway. It's too early to be—

"That's Wesley's van," Khodî says. Django eases his finger away from the trigger guard of the pistol. "Kai was at Brian's place. Pretty sure the entire bunch drove out."

Django makes himself put Tiny Beast down again, trying to breathe normally. "Good idea," he says, listening to doors slam and hearing three different, recognized voices.

Kai is in the lead as they enter the house. "Hi Khodî, Dad—holy *shit!*" he blurts when he sees Ambrus. "Khodî, you were not fucking kidding."

Wesley pushes Kai gently into the kitchen when surprise keeps Kai in the doorway a second too long. Brian is right behind him; Neumia is sleeping in his arms with her head resting against her father's chest.

"Thought you were supposed to be at school, Kai," Django says.

Kai nods. "Yeah, normally, but I really needed a weekend away from my fucking roommate. Then Brian calls up and says video game weekend. There was no way I was turning that down, even if I can't play the games worth shit."

"Yes, he can," Wesley counters in amusement. "We've discovered that if you get really drunk, *Call of Duty* is the fucking funniest shit that has ever digitally existed. So many pricks whining about campers and lurkers and how it's not fair that we snuck up on them. You'd think they'd never seen a spy movie in their lives."

Brian shifts in place before looking at Django. "Getting Kai home for this particular weekend wasn't my idea. It was Nari's."

"Was it." Django resists the urge to react to that information. Neumia seems completely normal most of the time, but when she pulls a rabbit out of her hat, it's usually the type that bites hard.

"Bro, I'm wide awake," Brian says, abandoning the previous subject like it's on fire. "You want to take Nari upstairs? I can assist for Kai and Dad."

Wesley extracts Neumia from Brian's arms, a process that she stubbornly refuses to wake up for. "The driver gets to take a nap. Awesome."

Once Wesley and Neumia are climbing the stairs, Django scowls at Brian. "You played that stupid game in front of Nari?"

Brian shrugs, his eyes still on Kai's new patient. "It's not like she hasn't heard those words before, directly from all of us. She knows they're for adults only. Besides, we're way more violent than a video game."

"Point," Django admits. Brian picks up Kai's familiar duffel bag of medical supplies and brings it to the table.

Kai is checking out his patient while walking around them, making a full lap of the table before he lets out a low whistle. "This man should be dead. Like, really, really dead."

"He's program, Kai."

Kai's eyes widen. "Seriously? Shit. Okay. In that case, I will probably be able to save this man's life, and not have to go into hiding from Rex for the rest of my existence." Kai goes out to the garage for saline and blood from the fridge, muttering under his breath about blood types, body sizes, and fluid limits.

"What the hell happened to this guy?" Brian asks when he hears the garage door open and shut. "Who the hell did he piss off?" Khodî looks up from where he's been leaning against the kitchen wall next to the phone, curiosity a bright spark of interest in his eyes.

"Someone with power and influence." It was bad enough when the program became an official part of the DoD, but to be so secret that they didn't even have a real name? No thanks; not for him. After you hit a certain level of military secrecy, nobody gives a damn about your morals.

Django rubs his face with his hand, needing to shave—needing for this to be a bad fucking dream, even though he knows better. "I don't think anyone ever expects this level of betrayal, though."

Khodî's eyes narrow. "His own people did this to him?"

Django nods. "The department. Nobody knows what the hell is going on," he adds as Kai comes back into the kitchen, carrying a literal armload of saline and blood bags.

Khodî shrugs out of his coat and hangs it on the coatrack before he sits down next to Django. "We're in deep shit, aren't we?"

"Yeah." Django glances down at Ambrus before his gaze drifts over to Kai, who is scrubbing up at the kitchen sink with his head cocked to listen. Django looks at Brian again, whose expression is turning hard and wary.

"Yeah, we're in trouble."

*　　　*　　　*　　　*

When Rex strips off his clothing behind the closed bathroom door, he has to stop and stare at it all in disbelief. His keyring, multi-tool, and flash drives fared all right; he only needs to wipe stains off the steel exteriors of the tiny silver drives. His boots are leather that can be scrubbed clean.

The rest is goddamned ruined, all of it. The amount of blood and drywall dust that his t-shirt, pants, underwear, and socks picked up during a pretty brief amount of time is just shy of unbelievable. He's glad he was smart enough to put clothes in the bug-out bag, but also angry at himself for not thinking to make Ambrus put a bag together to leave in Rex's apartment closet as a matched damned set.

Ambrus and Dad are pretty close to the same size. That could work, Rex thinks. Definitely better than nothing at all.

When he climbs into the shower, though, he isn't thinking about clothes. He's wondering about bad omens.

The bike was easy to move. The truck went into the garage without a hint of some of the temperamental fussing it used to pull when Rex and his siblings were kids. It's when Rex got out of the truck that a snarl of *wrongness* curled up from his gut and sat in his stomach, refusing to leave.

Neumia plastered a stupid happy-faced green frog sticker onto the bumper of his dad's car last summer. Despite Django's best efforts, it had stubbornly refused to be removed...until the moment Rex touched it as he walked by. The doofy frog crumbled under his hand, littering the dusty garage floor in faded bits of green.

Ignore it and hope it's bullshit, Rex tells himself. Pennsylvania winters are harsh...except it snowed maybe a handful of times. The weather has been pretty damned mild.

The entire drive out to the farm, Rex had divided his attention between the road, Ambrus, and the sky. He hadn't seen the flashing lights of a plane at night, and the window had been cracked to listen—drones are fucking loud—but there was nothing. Just dark highway, the occasional startled deer, and shitty country music, the only station the ancient radio would pick up.

They can't stay here. The department knows his father's address. Rex debates impossibilities, things that are already too late to change. He shouldn't have brought Ambrus here; Rex couldn't have taken Ambrus anywhere else. At least he knows everyone in his family has the training to survive if the department comes calling, but Rex isn't going to stop being paranoid about his family's safety until they're maybe all living in a third-world country in a fucking cave.

He doesn't realize he's fallen asleep standing upright in the shower until he drains the last reserves of hot water from the furnace boiler and gets blasted in the face with ice-cold water. "Fuck!" Rex screeches. He hurries to turn off the water before he leans over, panting out shock, impending panic, and maybe the desire to simply vomit up last night's pizza just to clear out his system.

Despite the shower, he still has bloodstains on his hands. Dammit. That means it's lurking in other places.

Rex unsnaps the chain from his neck and catches his dog tags in his hand, staring down at them. There are red splotches on the steel thick enough to hide parts of his name and service number.

He removes the black silencers and scrubs everything down with soap and water, douses it all with rubbing alcohol, and dries them off. The silencers go back on; the chain is clipped in place around his neck again. He doesn't usually wear them unless he's going on or coming off a sanctioned op. Having them on display in Baltimore International had been useful in attracting an old geezer with a cane and the fearlessness that accompanies old age, but it still isn't—it isn't something he usually does. It's not something *any* of them do. He doesn't even remember putting his tags on yesterday morning.

Rex gets dressed, pulling on an old olive-green t-shirt that was probably issued in the early 2000s. It's cotton that was meant to last as long as you didn't run out and fill it full of bullet holes. The cargo pants are dark gray denim. He wants pockets right now, spaces ready to stuff extra ammunition boxes, magazines, knives— hell, right now, he wouldn't say no to a grenade, and he was never a fan.

He gets a washcloth out of the bathroom closet, soaks it in the sink, and starts scrubbing foulness off his boots. By the time he's done, three washcloths are varying shades of gray, black, and brownish-red. He uses the least filthy cloth to wipe stains off the silver flash drives; another dab of alcohol removes a lab's ability to pull a blood sample from the steel. The ruined washcloths go into the bathroom trash to join his destroyed clothes.

His keyring and flash drives go into his uppermost pants pocket, and the empty magazine for the 1911 goes in a lower pocket. The multi-tool actually snaps in his hands when he opens it up to clean it, so it joins everything else in the garbage.

That feeling of curled-up *wrong* won't go away. Rex straps the 1911's holster back into place on his left side, its spare magazine already shoved into place. He'll give it a proper fieldstrip cleaning in a while, but for now it will still do its damn job, dust or no dust.

When Rex returns to the kitchen, he looks at Ambrus first and breathes out a quiet, relieved sigh. Ambrus's color is so much more life-like than corpse-like. His boyfriend's eyes are closed, and there are unhappy-looking bruises forming beneath his lashes, but he's breathing easily, newly bandaged, and a hell of a lot cleaner. Two hooks on the pot rack are supporting a new bag of saline and another bag that's just emptying itself of blood.

Kai is the only other person still in the room, and he's guzzling coffee straight from the carafe. "You've been in college too damned long. Share that, asshole," Rex says. Kai flips him off without looking before lowering the empty pot.

Rex shakes his head. "Hi to you, too. How's school?" he asks, a question he never neglects. None of them do; Kai probably wants to strangle them all at this point for being nosy fuckers.

"School-like." Kai looks tired right now, but once the caffeine hits his system, he'll be hyper and verbal enough to make his siblings consider the values of duct tape. "Irony and shit—one of the electives I chose for module five is advanced GSW understanding and treatment. Good teacher, but man, it was hard not to giggle my entire way through every class. I knew more about GSWs when I was twelve."

Rex manages to smile. "Kai, not everyone approves of the way our family does things."

"Not everyone has family members who get *shot* on a regular basis," Kai counters, pointing at Rex's left shoulder. Rex is so damned glad that they all heal up fast. Otherwise he'd be in some serious pain from running almost two miles with one hundred sixty pounds slung over his shoulders.

"Khodî still wins for getting shot by a drunk with a cheap .22 rifle during his first year on the county force," Rex says.

Kai thinks about it. "Yeah, okay, but he totally earned that mockery, especially since I'm the one who got to the scene first and outdid the paramedics. Made him look ridiculous."

"Hey, if things don't go to complete shit, maybe you can put my boyfriend down as extracurricular credit or something." Rex glances at Ambrus again. No change, but it's still so damned reassuring to hear him breathing without having to fight for it.

"Maybe. If I wasn't almost done with school—and it wouldn't make Dad paranoid—I'd transfer outside the U.S. to a real damned university that pays attention to what you don't know instead of what you can already do in your sleep." Kai rinses out the carafe and starts filling it at the kitchen sink. "I'll make more coffee. You go try and get the rest of that blood off your hands. If feds come calling who *aren't* the enemy, it'd be nice for us all to be clean, presentable, and not covered in blood."

Under the sink in the bathroom is a half-empty gallon jug of mechanic's orange scrub, and to Rex's relief, a stiff boar bristle brush. His freshly washed sinuses are clogged with citrus scent right away, but at least the orange scrub removes what soap and hot water left behind. He doesn't look up from his work until someone raps on the doorframe.

"Heard you dug yourself up a fossil."

Rex glances into the mirror to look at his brother. "Khodî, please don't start. Not again and not now."

Khodî smirks at him. "Found someone as old as Dad, too. I'm impressed."

"Isn't some asshole I know going to turn forty this year?"

"Hey, fuck you," Khodî retorts.

Rex grins. If Khodî didn't want him to cheat, he shouldn't have started the war. "Didn't you find a gray hair last November?"

"Double-fuck you," Khodî grumbles. He waits until Rex has finally gotten every bloodstain off his skin and out from beneath his fingernails before turning serious. "Are you all right?"

Rex looks at the reddened bristles on the brush and tosses it into the trashcan with everything else. "I'm fine."

"You don't look fine," Khodî says in a flat voice. "You look fuckin' pissed off."

"Well, my boyfriend was almost murdered last night by his best friend for no damned reason. My boyfriend also used to work with Dad, which is really fucking awkward. But mostly, it's the whole boyfriend-nearly-murdered thing." Rex leans over the sink when he feels nauseated again. At this point, he's not sure if it's exhaustion, nerves, or potential food poisoning from the stupid pizza.

"Fair enough. I imagine it must be weird, getting stuck with parental sloppy seconds."

Rex grabs the soap from the dish, turns, and chucks it at Khodî, who ducks while laughing. "I will fucking stab your ass!" Rex yells. By the time he retrieves the broken soap from the hallway floor, Khodî has disappeared, but that's because his brother is a smart man who knows when to retreat.

Please be lying your ass off, Rex thinks in dismay. Please let Khodî be fucking with him. His father and his boyfriend—no, he isn't going there. He has things to do that do not involve dwelling on that possibility. Nope. Not doing it.

Rex gathers up the bathroom trash, ties it off, and takes it out to the garage using the door opposite the guest bedroom doorway. The garage is colder, reminding him that outside the air is still holding onto the morning chill. He finds the burn barrel in the corner of the garage standing empty. Rex drops his armload inside for later incineration.

Incineration. He has no idea why that reminds him, but he doesn't question his instincts. Kai's right—they need to at least be capable of passing a basic visual inspection, if normal feds show up. Cleaning the blood off the kitchen table and floor should be fun.

Rex goes back to the truck and opens the unlocked passenger door. The door's edge thumps into the wooden sidewall of the garage and wedges itself there. It's a tight squeeze to climb into the cab, but Rex gets his bloodstained coat, tossing it out of the truck and onto the garage floor.

It's swearing, frustrating work to remove the old cloth cover for the bench seat. If any blood soaked through the old woven fabric, it's not visible on the cracked black leather, or on the ancient foam that's pushed its way through.

Once the cover is out of the cab, the truck just smells like old leather, dust, motor oil, and dirt. Much better.

Coat and seat cover join the trash in the burn barrel before Rex goes back into the house. In the guest bedroom on the bed are four different stacks of folded laundry. One of the smallest stacks has a dark blue short-sleeved button-down shirt that Rex left behind at some point, probably last fall when the weather insisted on being too damned hot. It's not a coat, but if he leaves it unbuttoned, it has enough room to mostly hide the outline of the gun holster. It's not like it's going to be all that cold outside, anyway. Before Rex ditched his smartphone along the highway, piece by piece, the weather forecast for Kutztown was pegged in the mid-sixties for the day.

His father is emerging from his bedroom next door, still in the midst of pulling on a long sleeve dark blue shirt with enough length to hide the Glock holstered at his back. Not Tiny Beast, but a double-stack.

They're both wearing dark blue. Night-work colors. Nice to know Rex isn't the only one feeling paranoid. They'll have to swap out after dawn, but it's always good to be prepared.

"Morning," Django says, his focus already on the kitchen.

Rex wants to get back there, too, but he needs to know—aw, fuck. He braces himself. "Khodi's not wrong, is he? About you and Ambrus being a thing."

Django grimaces and continues walking down the hallway without saying anything. That is *not* the answer Rex wanted. That's far more awkward than he was prepared for. Ever.

"Please tell me it wasn't serious."

Django glances over his shoulder, a chagrined expression on his face. "It was just one time, it was over forty years ago, and there was a hell of a lot of drinking involved after what had been a stressful fucking week. No, it wasn't—that."

Rex tries not to cringe. "Right." So much awkward; this much awkward should not be allowed to exist in one place.

"Hey, look what asshole's awake," Django says as they enter the kitchen. Kai is still there, and Brian turned up in the meantime, but Rex's breath hitches for another reason entirely.

Ambrus is sitting up on the end of the table, his head still tilted forward in a tired slump. His fingers are wrapped around the table's edge in a white-knuckled grip, but he's breathing, one slow inhale and exhale at a time. The intravenous line is already out, a wad of gauze taped over the place where it had been plugged into his hand.

Kai is leaning against the kitchen counter, glaring daggers at his patient. "I told him not to sit up. If you start bleeding again, don't come crying to me."

"If I start bleeding again, it's probably from another gunshot wound." Ambrus lets out a dry chuckle and then winces in pain.

Django shakes his head, looking like he wants to put his face in his hands. Kai is less than impressed. "I pulled five bullets out of your chest. Try not to add a sixth right away."

"Five?" Rex looks at his brother. "Four holes, five bullets?"

"Two taps to the same spot," Kai confirms. "I thought the upper lung hit was a single, too, but Brian saw light bounce off the second little lead bastard."

Rex goes to the table, leaning in close to Ambrus so that his boyfriend can rest his head against Rex's chest. "Hey." Rex puts his hand on the back of Ambrus's neck, where his skin still feels drywall-sticky. "How are you?"

Ambrus swallows, reaching out to hold onto Rex's arm in a loose grip. "Ow, fuck everything, and five is pretty close to my record number of gunshots received in one day."

"Shit. What's the record?" Brian asks, intrigued. "You've already beaten Dad's record for one day."

Django snorts. "That's because I know how to fucking duck."

"Uh—eight," Ambrus tells Brian, after thinking it over. "That was a bad day."

"Liar. It was nine," Django says. "Your memory's going already?"

Ambrus slowly lifts his hand and flips off Django much the same way Kai had greeted Rex over coffee. "I've been enjoying meeting your offspring, Django. Tell me: did you actually find the time to father them all, or did someone just get you wet after midnight?"

Rex laughs at the wrong moment and tries not to choke on his own spit. His father is scowling, Brian is cackling, and Kai just looks mystified.

"What the hell does water have to do with anything?" Kai asks.

"Oh, you poor and deprived younger sibling," Brian says, patting Kai's shoulder. "We've all failed in our duty if you haven't seen that movie yet."

Kai is still confused. "Seriously, what movie?"

"I like him already," Khodî announces before Brian can answer, pushing his way in through the outside door. That also happens to be out of range of Rex and potential retaliation unless Rex wants to start tossing pans at his brother. It's not as if he doesn't have plenty nearby.

"Double pun for the win," Khodî adds.

"Someone noticed." Ambrus sounds pleased. "I'm glad that didn't go to waste."

"Not a lot of them did, no," Khodî agrees cheerfully.

Rex's face scrunches up in disgust as he closes his eyes. "Khodî, for pointing that out, I'm no longer going to stab you. I'm going to fucking shoot you instead."

Khodî shrugs. "Hey, he started it."

Rex decides to be the better man and just gets Ambrus a glass of water when he notices his boyfriend giving the faucet a plaintive look. "Here."

Ambrus's first sip makes his lips pucker in revulsion. "Oi, fuck, it tastes like drywall." He wipes his mouth, his shoulders shaking with silent, pained laughter, before he rinses down last night's construction remnants with the rest of the water.

"Better?" Rex knows he's really close into Ambrus's personal space, and he's not sure if Ambrus needs the reassurance, but Rex sure as hell does.

Ambrus lifts his head so that Rex can see his face. The light in his eyes seems brighter as they dart around the room while he mentally collects himself. "I think I can actually remember names now."

"For the fourth time, then: I'm Kai 'Aukai," Kai says, and shoves at Brian. "This is Brian Ngata."

"My brother Wesley is upstairs with my daughter, Neumia Anari," Brian says.

Khodî taps the badge on his uniform. "Khodî Som." Not even his badge is engraved with his full name; too many people tripped over their own tongues trying to say it.

Ambrus gives Khodî a wry look. "There might be an A.P.B. out for my arrest."

Khodî shrugs. "I'm off-duty right now. I don't give a fuck."

Ambrus nods and leans against Rex again. "You had a bad feeling, huh?"

"Hey, I wasn't wrong," Rex points out. "I'm not sure what in the entire *fuck* happened, but I was there when I was supposed to be."

"Huh." Ambrus's hand drifts down Rex's arm until it's covering Rex's hand. "It's genetically transferable. I didn't know that."

"How the hell could you *not* know that?" Django asks. Rex doesn't hear scornful disbelief from his father often. Mockery? Hell yes, but this is something different.

"Not a lot of people in the department have children," Ambrus replies without lifting his head. "The ones that do, the few of those children I've met previous to this? Their parents never mentioned anything about that particular part of their heritage being passed along."

"You don't have to dance around this bullshit," Khodî grumbles. "We're all aware that we have certain talents we're not supposed to."

Ambrus shakes his head. "I'm still trying to take a large number of NDAs seriously. It would be a shame to survive this, be proven innocent, and then go to jail for treason anyway because I violated one of those fucking things."

Rex puts his arm around Ambrus's shoulders and gently pulls him in close. "What happened?"

"Still have no idea," Ambrus says. "Skirting around the logistics? I knew something was wrong when I got the top floor of that building, just not what. Those particular warnings aren't always clear and useful."

Khodî snorts out a bitter laugh. "We're aware."

"There was someone else there, and I couldn't see them—they didn't *want* to be seen." Ambrus lifts his head again, a baffled frown on his face. "I was still trying to figure out what I'd walked into when Jasper started shooting."

Django crosses his arms. Rex glances over at his father, who looks really uncomfortable. "You think maybe this mystery asshole pushed the kid into shooting you? And that 'traitor' bullshit was only a trigger?"

Ambrus licks his lips as he considers it. "Maybe. I—I hope to God you've stumbled onto the truth of it. Otherwise, it wasn't...it just wasn't *like* him, Django! Not at all."

"He still shot you," Brian says. "Maybe he didn't plan it, but it would probably be a good idea to avoid this person for a while."

"Don't think I'm going to have much choice." Ambrus's grip tightens on Rex's hand. "Help me stand up, please. I desperately need to walk around."

"No, you desperately need to fucking rest!" Kai retorts. "Preferably in a bed instead of on the stupid table."

"I can't—!" Ambrus hunches inward again, hiding his face against Rex's chest. "Kai. I appreciate the lead removal, I really do, but I can't settle right now. If I don't move around, my blood pressure is going to spike from the sheer fucking bewildering *stress* of the situation, and that's just as bad as not resting, isn't it?"

"I hate medically smart assholes," Kai mutters, narrowing his eyes. "House only. No stairs. Not outside."

"House only," Ambrus agrees. Rex isn't happy about the deal, but if he doesn't help, Ambrus will do it on his own.

Rex eases Ambrus the rest of the way off the tabletop and onto his feet. Ambrus wobbles for a moment before Rex can tell that he's got his balance. Once he's walking, his steps are a lot smoother than Rex expected them to be, but Rex can feel that Ambrus is all but vibrating. Stress, hell—Rex is pretty sure Ambrus is on the verge of a major damned breakdown.

Rex's father heals faster than normal. They all do. Shit. "I hope you used dissolvable stitches," Rex says to Kai.

"Duh," Kai replies. "Dad just had to say was 'program,' and I was all over that. Give me some fucking credit, asshole. I'm just three months out from being a doctor with a real residency instead of the module version."

"Help me to the living room, please," Ambrus requests. "The kitchen's changed too much."

That almost stops Rex in his tracks. "When was the last time you were here?"

"1956," Django says.

Rex and all of his brothers turn to stare at their father. "Fuckin' seriously?" Brian asks. Rex can't tell if he looks impressed or baffled.

Django rolls his eyes. "We were friends, you idiots. After '56, our schedules didn't really line up anymore. Lost touch."

Ambrus sighs. "Django."

"No fuckin' NDA I signed says I can't mention that shit," Django replies. "Suck it up and deal."

"Asshole," Ambrus says fondly.

Rex tries not to cringe again. So fucking awkward.

*　　　　*　　　　*　　　　*

Kai waits until the Rex and Ambrus disappear into the living room. "I'm just gonna clean up this mess." He starts clearing the table of used medical supplies, dumping them into the open kitchen trash bin.

Django nods, his thoughts already about an hour ahead and twenty miles down the road. It isn't just the need to move that got Ambrus out of the kitchen, but an understanding of what Django is about to ask family. Maybe he's even aware of the phone call Django needs to make. It's a given that Rex is in it for the long haul, seeing as he's dating Ambrus, but the others still have a choice.

"Going or staying?" he asks Khodî.

Khodî smiles. "I hate to leave Berks County's finest in the lurch, but family comes first. I'm in."

"Change clothes," Django orders, something Khodî was probably planning to do already. "We're heading out as soon as I get a solid confirm that Ambrus is ready to travel."

"How long?" Khodî asks.

Django considers the way Ambrus was moving when he got off the table. "Fifteen minutes. Maybe less." Khodî nods and leaves the kitchen; a moment later, Django hears his footsteps on the stairs.

Kai pauses in the middle of dumping bleach onto the tabletop. "Shit. That soon?"

"They know where I live, Kai," Django replies. "I'm not waiting around, presenting an obvious target. Brian?"

Brian heaves out a long sigh. "Dad, if they come after Rex, and after you? They're coming for all of us. I'm with you. Wesley and Neumia are, too, even if they don't know it yet. It won't be safe for them to stay. Are we getting Ella?"

"First stop after we leave," Django assures them. "Kai?"

"Brian's right. Not sure any of us have much choice." Kai shrugs. "Besides, someone has to be around to keep you assholes alive."

Django smiles at his youngest son. "Still proud of you, kid," he says, and goes to the phone.

He calls Ella first and gets an answering machine. She's either not at home or ignoring her phone. "Baby, two-seven-zero-zero," he says, and hangs up. Those are the last four digits of her twin brother's service number. If she gets the message, she'll understand.

Then he calls Virginia. "Merrill residence," a clipped female voice says.

Django tries not to visibly wince. "Mrs. Hudson." He hates this woman with a fiery passion, even if she's good at her job. He was hoping it would be Bellamy's shift. "This is Colonel Whetū, calling for General Merrill."

"General Merrill is resting at this time."

Django hardens his voice. "Then wake him up. It'll be brief."

"It better be. You stress out my patient, I will find you and beat your ass," Hudson threatens.

"You and everyone else, ma'am." Django cradles the phone against his shoulder and waits, resisting the urge to tap on the wall with his fingertips. He hates this sensation of time ticking away. He's never been able to tell if it's his imagination or his damned instincts at play.

"This is General Merrill," Django finally hears Jason say in a querulous, cranky tone. Jason's voice sounds like rasping sandpaper now, no matter how much Jason might be trying to project otherwise. "This better be so fucking worth it. That was the best sleep I've had in two weeks."

"Jason." Django hears a sharp intake of breath on the other end, and the guilt comes bubbling back up to the surface. "Sorry I haven't called since January. Hope you liked the gossipy letters."

"You're the worst damned gossip, and I mean it. Your letters were so damned boring I used them for nap fuel." Jason's retort is followed by wheezing laughter.

"Hey, you're the one who asked for letters," Django says. "I'm not allowed to plant live ordinance out in the field, not since the seventies and the incident with the cow. Retirement's pretty boring, and you know it."

"Fucker, I get it. Nobody likes watching a loved one die, even at a distance."

Django covers the receiver with one hand for a moment so he can swallow without being overheard. Goddammit. "Yeah. Doesn't make me less of an asshole, especially since...aw, fuck, Jason. Three-Zero-One."

"Shit." Jason's voice is heavy with regret. "You're sure?"

"Yeah." Django presses his forehead against the wall. He doesn't want to be, but he knows which way the wind is blowing. Right now, it's not in his family's favor.

"If you can, let me know when you're safe." Jason pauses. "If I'm not here..."

"Dammit, Jason—"

"I'm ninety-eight years old. I'm dying, you stupid shit," Jason replies amiably. "My wife is already waiting for me, and I know my time's coming. Now listen up, Colonel."

Django closes his eyes. "Listening."

"I've been looking after your ass since 1956. You're not my kid, but I would have been proud if you had been. You're a good man, Django Maha Whetū. Don't let anyone *ever* tell you otherwise."

Django blinks back tears that feel like emerging fire. "Fuck you, Jason."

"Love you, too, asshole," Jason replies in a gentle rasp. A moment later there is a click as the line disconnects.

Django puts the receiver back in its cradle and turns to his kids, who are kind enough not to mention the expression probably stamped upon his face. "Okay. Time to move."

अश्लेषा

In the living room, Ambrus tugs his arm free of Rex's gentle grasp. He makes a slow, shuffling loop of the room using the old wooden-edged art deco couch as a support. Ambrus's jaw is clenched the entire time, but Rex doesn't think he'll fall, even if he stays upright out of sheer stubbornness.

The original family parlor, their living room, is the only thing in the farmhouse that hasn't been remodeled. Its lines are all rural Edwardian—designed and built by his great-grandparents before World War I. The walls are still plaster; the ceiling is square-patterned tin. The far wall from the open entryway hosts the house's original brick-and-fieldstone fireplace, framed by large windows on both sides. All of the original woodwork is still whitewashed, which always helps make the room seem bigger than it is. The only thing his father ever changed was the windows, replacing the old single-panes with double-hung windows made from tempered glass.

Django and Rex's grandfather put a lot of work into the house over the years to make sure it never suffered structural issues as the wood aged and the ground changed beneath the house's basement foundation. Only a few floorboards squeak here and there, and the plaster walls in the living room never cracked. The old house's only problem has always centered on the stupid kitchen doorframe, which likes to warp out of shape once every decade or so.

When Ambrus finally lets go of the couch, he goes straight to the wooden mantelpiece above the fireplace. He holds onto the oil-smoothed wood with one hand while studying the photographs that line the shelf. Rex tries to ignore a twinge of discomfort when his boyfriend's eyes linger on the only blond kid among the lot of seven children trying to crowd into a picture. That was taken during Xāwuṭh's first visit to the U.S. in 1985, and it's obvious from the expression on his face that he had *not* enjoyed it.

Eighty-one. Rex has to keep reminding himself of Ambrus's age—it's completely unbelievable while still being believable. Rex knows his father has to be around the same age to have served in Korea, but Rex and his siblings were all raised with Django's unyielding rules about minding their damned manners: don't steal from those who can't afford the loss; say please and thank you even if you're really not in the mood; don't set shit on fire that isn't yours; don't ask people their age unless there is legit medical need; keep your finger off the fucking trigger of a gun until you're ready to fire. There were other rules, of course, tacked on as Rex and his siblings got older. Most of them still centered around firearms safety, but the ones about manners stuck pretty well.

They're all used to the fact that their father appears to be in his late thirties—early forties on bad days, when old grief or PTSD hits too hard. Rex cracked jokes about Khodî's hair, yeah, but his, Ella, and Eric's mother started silvering in her late twenties. A first gray hair at forty doesn't really mean much in comparison.

Rex and his siblings all look like they gave up on aging around their twenty-fourth birthdays. By the time Wesley and Brian hit the thirty-mark six years ago, they realized all of them had ditched the aging train. Even Kai looks like he's going to stall out at twenty-three, maybe twenty-four, but he's taken the least hits out of all of them and still has to argue with bouncers about his ID not being fake.

Six years ago, the siblings all came to silent agreement to just not talk about it. Not talking about it always seemed easier, or maybe safer. Hell, that's been the entire town's way of coping with Django's lack of aging since the late 1970s, anyway. Don't knock it if it works.

Rex casts about for topics that don't seem fraught, hypocritical, or stupid, and finally settles on something pretty obvious. "You know, Dad took a chest shot years back when we were all still kids. It took a full day's recovery in bed for him to be able to walk around the way you are right now."

"I've been active, and he hasn't. It makes a difference."

Rex feels his eye twitch. He does not want to be the one to tell his sister that. Ella is active enough as it is.

Ambrus is still studying the pictures as he moves along the mantel, one shifting handgrip at a time. There's a shot of Nari as a baby, one with Brian and Nari taken last year, and individual school photos of each of them. They were allowed to choose the photo, at least, so Rex can look at the photograph of himself in senior year and not cringe. Everyone went junior or senior except Ella, who chose a picture of herself in kindergarten. She's beaming at the camera with an innocent smile that is a complete fucking lie...which is basically Ella-speak for truth in advertising.

Kaia Awe Whetū is in the photograph next to Ella, taken in 1949 when she was twenty. Rex's aunt was a blonde-haired, blue-eyed woman who took after her Norwegian father instead of her Māori mother. There is a sharp bite in her eyes that's like veiled, intelligent rage.

Ambrus lifts his finger and touches the silver frame that holds one of the only existing photos of Rex's grandparents, Mereana and Tor. There are digital copies, but this is the original color print from the 1930s, a rarity from a time when color photographs were almost nonexistent. It helps to highlight that they were almost literally as different as night and day. Mereana Awe Moana Whetū. Maori, black-haired, black-eyed, bronze skin. Barely scraping in at five-foot-one. Tor Rikard Skjeggestad Whetū. Born in Norway to parents who immigrated to America and settled in Kutztown.

Blond-haired, blue-eyed, farmer's tan. Towering over his wife at five feet, ten inches tall.

Tor and Mereana still fit together in that photo like puzzle pieces that just happened to fall into the proper alignment.

"They wanted to adopt me," Ambrus says quietly. "I wasn't averse to the idea, but needed some time to think about it. Then Hurricane Hazel hit the east coast in '53, and..." He sighs. "You've heard the story, I'm sure."

Rex nods until he realizes Ambrus isn't looking at him. "Yeah. I know it." His grandparents were out of town on a day-trip, expecting nothing more than rain and maybe a bit of wind, leaving an insistent Kaia behind. Rex's wheelchair-bound aunt hadn't been fond of travel because it was, quoted his father of his sister, "a complete pain in the ass."

A flash flood took out his grandparents' car on a one-lane bridge. It was several days of searching until they were found nearly twenty miles downstream. Kaia went into an institution that would oversee her care until Rex's father finished his last set in the military, meant to wrap up in the summer of 1956. She died in the spring of that year, and Django has never forgiven himself for not being there.

Rex hasn't quite dared to ask Ambrus about his grandparents before this. He's heard a few stories from his father, but his boyfriend isn't family. This is someone who witnessed everything from outside that circle. "What were they—what were they like?"

"Devoted to each other," Ambrus says. "She was a bit terrifying, like your father, but they were also kind. A mixed-race couple who served in World War I, survived all the bigotry that life could throw at them from three different continents, the Great Depression, Kaia's battle with polio, World War II, and the start of the Cold War. It's more like...how could they not be kind in the face of all that?"

"Thank you," Rex says while ignoring how much more damned awkward things would have been if there had been no flash flood, no institution, and the informal adoption had proceeded. He has enough awkward stocked up now to last him through several dozen lifetimes. "Dad doesn't—he doesn't talk about them much."

"He never stopped blaming himself." Ambrus glances into the ancient silver mirror hanging above the mantel and meets Rex's eyes. "Hell, neither did I."

"When were you first here? If Dad says NDAs don't cover this, then I'm going to pester the shit out of you," Rex adds when Ambrus frowns.

"Ah. Asshole," Ambrus mutters, but he probably means Django. "My father wasn't a soldier, but he was deployed to the Pacific Theatre in a British ambassadorial role of some sort, I don't know. I don't remember the details, but the point is that he died on

May eighteenth in 1945 after an ambush put three bullet holes where they did not belong. My mother held the family together after that, fought to make sure we still received a monthly stipend from the British government. My father essentially died in battle, so she had fuel for that particular fire. Then she died in 1950, like I told you last night—complications from scarlet fever when the antibiotics were tried too late. The moment she was gone, we were all underage orphans. The stipend vanished overnight. None of us wanted to sell the house or get blasted family services involved, but I couldn't get work because I looked like I was twelve and weighed about one twenty sopping wet. Arguing that I would be sixteen soon was just...maybe if we'd been in a farming community instead of the middle of New York City, things might have been different.

"Moira and Nessie were too young to even make the attempt of getting a job, but they could handle things at home well enough. The moment we realized how dire the situation was, I enlisted so I could send all of the money home to my sisters. Lied through my teeth and told the military I was eighteen, but the Korean War was beginning. The Army was desperate for warm bodies that could hold a rifle, point it in the correct direction, and pull the trigger."

Rex bites back a smile. "Ah, young and stupid."

Ambrus points at Rex in the mirror. "If that's your father speaking, he has absolutely no room to say a damned word about being young and stupid."

"And I can't wait to ask him." Rex studies the way Ambrus's eyes have gone too narrow, his lips thinned out from emotion instead of pain. "What happened to your sisters?"

"It was after the first phase of the program was complete—shush on that detail, please—so I had the freedom to attend their funerals. Influenza Outbreak of 1951," Ambrus explains, head lowering until it's almost resting on the mantelpiece. "It barely touched the U.S., but it hit New York. Moira and Nessie died five days apart."

"Fuck. Fuck, I'm sorry," Rex whispers, feeling it like a punch to the gut. Eric's loss hurts enough. He can't imagine losing *all of them.*

"When the program was certain that we were all indoctrinated enough not to run off and never return, our first official shore leave was granted for the winter holidays. I didn't have anywhere else to go, not after selling the house to pay for their funerals. Hell, I didn't want to go back there, anyway. Nobody wants to go home to a house full of ghosts. When he realized I had nowhere to go, Django insisted I come here, instead. It became a tradition—for a little while, at least."

"If you've known each other that long, why hasn't he ever mentioned you?" Rex asks.

"Your father left the department, but that doesn't mean those talents simply shut off. To make sure the department ignored him, I stayed away." Ambrus smiles. "Made damned certain our schedules didn't line up. That's what you do to make sure the department doesn't pay attention. You leave people the hell alone."

Ambrus's early reluctance suddenly makes a lot more sense. "If Dad ever finds out you did that, he's going to be seriously pissed off."

"Probably," Ambrus agrees. He sounds normal enough, but all at once Ambrus is resting his head on his forearm, bowed over the old mantelpiece and its photographic lineup of history. "Oh God, Rex. What the fuck is going on?"

That's the break Rex has been waiting for. He goes to Ambrus and wraps his arms around him from behind. "I don't know. But we'll figure it out, okay?"

Ambrus turns around and clings to Rex, his face buried against Rex's shoulder. He's trembling, but Rex only knows Ambrus is weeping when dampness soaks through his shirt.

Rex glances up for a few seconds, gathering himself, and then runs his hands through Ambrus's hair. It's gotten longer since their September meeting, hanging down in ginger flames to mid-back. "Euan. I'm right here. So is my dad, and my family, and none of us are going to let anything like that happen. Not ever again."

"You can't fucking promise that," Ambrus retorts, his voice thick with grief.

"The hell I can't." Rex keeps his tone firm, just shy of the fierce protectiveness that wants to come out and play. "We'll figure out what happened to Fox—to Jasper—but it has to be after we get our own asses to safety."

"There really isn't any such thing." Ambrus straightens, tilting his head back so he can stare into Rex's eyes. Ambrus's own eyes are red-rimmed from exhaustion, injury, and crying, but his gaze is steady, and so are his hands when he grips Rex's arms. "You really shouldn't have brought me here, but I'm grateful."

Rex shrugs. "Too late to change it now. Besides, I'd do the same damned thing if I had the choice to do it over again."

Ambrus shakes his head, a faint smile on his face. Then he leans forward and kisses Rex.

Rex closes his eyes and enjoys the too-brief sensation of smooth warmth, their lips moving together in a kiss that is comfort, not passion. Ambrus's beard protects his sensitive skin from developing scratched red lines across his face from the stubble on Rex's cheeks. Shaving had definitely not been on his priority list that morning.

Besides, light scratches are for other times. It's both fun and awesome, even with the obligatory Tic-Tac-Toe jokes.

Like it's Rex's fault he can actually play the game on Ambrus's back just by using his fingernail.

"I love you," Ambrus murmurs against Rex's cheek. Then he deliberately scrapes his cheekbone along Rex's chin, like he's reading Rex's thoughts. Such cheating. "And I'm sorry that I've fucked up your life."

Rex grins back at him. "I'm really not."

Ambrus's smile is full of wry affection. "I know you aren't, but you come by your insanity honestly."

"Hey!" Rex protests, but Ambrus's attention had wandered to the last photograph gracing the mantelpiece.

"Wedding?"

"Yeah." Rex is a bit unsettled by the flip-flopping subject matter, but Kai did warn him that they gave Ambrus a *lot* of fentanyl. "1998. That's Makani 'Aukai—Kai's mom and my step-mother. She died in April of 1999. Car wreck."

"Only a year together?" Ambrus's expression shifts back to tired grief. "Your father looks so Goddamned happy."

"No, almost eight years," Rex corrects. "They met in 1991." Fun courtship, too, and by fun Rex means car chase.

"Still not enough—" Ambrus's head jerks up like it's been pulled by a wire. "Shit."

Rex resists the urge to scratch at the crawling sensation that immediately breaks out on his skin. "Euan?"

Ambrus takes a deep breath. When he lets it out in a long, gentle exhale, most of the pain-fueled stress on his face vanishes like it never existed. "Something's wrong."

"Got that impression," Rex replies, leading the way back to the kitchen. Ambrus is right behind him; even to Rex's senses, Ambrus is mission-ready. That is a hell of a neat trick, and Rex wants to learn it yesterday.

Django, Brian, and Kai are still in the kitchen. Khodî is coming down the stairs, dressed in a dark green t-shirt and jeans instead of his uniform.

For a handful of heartbeats, all they do is stare at each other. Rex can tell by the look in his father's eyes that whatever is wrong—he's picked up on it, too.

Fuck. Even by DoD standards, this is too damned soon!

Brian winces and rubs at his temple. "What the hell is that?"

"Empty the house," Ambrus orders. He goes right to Tiny Beast; Django left it sitting on the countertop close to the back wall, well out of reach of tiny Nari hands.

"Basement?" Django asks, tossing an extra single-stack for the 43 at Ambrus, who catches it one-handed without even looking. Brian is already halfway up the stairs, shouting for Wesley and Neumia. Rex hears a faint "What the hell?" from Wesley, and then all of Rex's attention is taken up by the sense of danger crawling up his spine like an unwelcome fucking scorpion.

Ambrus hesitates, but then his expression morphs into a battle-ready harsh ferocity that Rex had yet to witness. "No. EMPTY!" he yells.

"I've got Kai!" Rex yells, grabbing the sleeve of the person now closest to him.

"I've got the boyfriend. We'll go out the door," Khodî says in a rough voice, using his hand as leverage to leap over the kitchen table.

"USE THE ESCAPE LADDER!" Django roars up the stairs, and gets faint vocal acknowledgement from one of Rex's brothers.

Rex bolts down the hallway, towing Kai along with him. "Help me!"

Kai is wide-eyed, but they have drilled for this shit. Their father leaves nothing to chance. "Okay!"

One of the last wallboards before the garage door has a groove that looks like it was caused by an overenthusiastic kid with a hammer. Rex hooks his fingers underneath that gripping point and pulls hard, yanking the entire panel free before turning around long enough to drop it against the opposite wall.

Rex snatches the first bug-out bag and the rifle stored behind it. "Hurry the hell up, Kai." The sensation of danger is skyrocketing, making it feel like there's electricity trapped in Rex's teeth. "DAD!"

"FASTER!" Django yells back. "The others are almost out!"

"Don't forget to get yourself out!" Rex shouts back. He's angry and worried and tense as hell as Kai grabs the second bag, collecting the sawed-off paired with it.

"What in the entire fuck," Kai gasps out as Rex skips the garage door (too much clutter, bay doors sealed, too much time) and goes right for the southern window at the end of the hallway. "I didn't even *like* the drills, Rex!"

Rex lifts the window high enough to unlock it at the top edges, swiveling it inwards, and then yanking it free at its pivot points. Thank god his Dad upgraded the windows. "Yes, but unlike the drills, you might get to shoot something!"

Kai looks offended. "I am a fucking doctor, you fucking shit!"

"Get out of this fucking window before I throw you out!" Rex orders.

"Goddammit, *fine!*" Kai throws his bag through the open window and then leaps through, shotgun tucked properly in his arms for a safe landing roll. Rex tosses his bag out and follows Kai, hits the ground, and rolls across the dirt. Doesn't break anything, no sprains, probably won't even bruise that much.

Drills always have two possible goals: get to the vehicles if it's possible; run through the field and book it to the stream if it isn't. Kai is already standing, reaching for weapon and bag, but Rex feels like he can't breathe.

Basic. SFQC. Afghanistan. Iraq. Instinct. Rex doesn't care if it's one of them, all of them, or none of them. All he knows is that he's pinned Kai back onto the ground, protecting his baby brother, before Rex consciously recognizes the scream of a large incoming projectile.

The explosion is big enough to hit them with heavy debris. Rex loses track of Kai as hot wind and flame sear Rex's skin. His ears are ringing with the deafening hum of a thousand bells. Hot embers rain down on his face and neck.

He's seeing bright blue sky overhead, feeling heat beneath his back and sandy grit under his hands. His mouth tastes like dust. He can hear screaming, the injured—he has to get the fuck up. Rex is the one who argued SFQC into letting him qualify for the full 18D training to pair with the 18A, not just the standard cross-training that everyone in an operations group is normally subjected to in the field. He has a medic in his group, but you always need another pair of hands. It means he now has two jobs to do. Not one. Two.

Get up. Get up. Get up.

Rex's head rocks to one side, followed by one hell of a sharp sting from chin to temple. "Get the fuck up!" Kai shrieks at him, both of his fists bunched into Rex's shirt. "Freak the fuck out later, but I need you *here* right now, Rex!"

Rex puts his hand on Kai's arm. He hasn't had a bad flashback in years, even though he still takes DoD contracts into violent territory. "I'm here," he says, and can barely hear his own voice. "Where are the others?"

It isn't until he sits up that Rex realizes the enormity of what's happened.

Their house is rubble with fire still burning in the center. Flames lick along boards jutting into the sky, all that's left of the exterior walls. The only things still mostly intact are the house's old stone basement walls, the fieldstone corner supports, and the chimney. All of the gray fieldstone is burnt black.

Oh, fuck. What the hell— "Kai. The others!"

"I don't know!" Kai shouts back, just as deaf, and then he starts coughing.

"DAD!" Rex bellows.

The response is swift. "BUSY!"

Rex takes a breath before looking at Kai, pieces of their childhood home raining down around them. The rifle is still in his hands, so Rex flips off the safety, knowing it's loaded and ready—they check the bags twice a year. "Still a doctor right now?"

"Fuck no," Kai growls, popping open the shotgun to check the shells before he follows Rex to the house's rear-window exit.

Rex smiles in grim pleasure. He is going to kill someone for doing this to his home, and then line up the corpses of whoever dared to come after his family.

He always manages to forget that when he really means it, Django is a terrifyingly fast motherfucker, and that's *without* a gun. When they round what used to be the west corner of the house, two camouflaged soldiers in patterned navy—*Night work? The sun is up, you dumb shits!*—are already dead in the flaming dry grass. Django has a third in a chokehold. His free hand is pushing aside the barrel of asshole number four's rifle, who is desperately trying to regain control of his weapon so he can fire.

Kai mutters something rude under his breath and takes the fourth soldier out with the sawed-off. It's a wide shot that always makes a hell of a mess, but it also goes where Kai wants it to go. That's three dead assholes for the corpse lineup.

Rex lifts the rifle to his shoulder and gets the remaining soldier in the side, right between the plating of his bulletproof vest. Rex is firing small caliber rounds, but they'll still do a very good job of making sure that asshole bleeds out from the shot that tore through his heart.

Django drops the dying soldier and finally gets the chance to pull the Glock at his back. "You two all right?"

Rex glances at the flaming pile of destruction he used to live in. "I'm going to have flashbacks for the rest of the fucking year, but we're both okay." Kai nods his confirmation, busy replacing the single spent cartridge with a new one to keep his weapon loaded and ready for mayhem. "Have you seen the others?"

"Not yet." Django inclines his head to the left. "North side. Let's go."

They find Brian, Wesley, Neumia, and an actual pile of fatigue-dressed bastards on the ground with twisted limbs, necks, and a few bullet holes for good measure. Neumia is perched on Wesley's hip while Brian chokes the life out of some unfortunate bastard.

Neumia's left arm is wrapped securely around her uncle's neck, but she's not afraid. She looks like she wants to help Brian kill that asshole.

"Serves them right," she mutters vindictively as Brian drops the soldier the moment he stops twitching. "They blew up Grandpa's house."

"Everyone always underestimates the football players, don't they, sweetie?" Wesley asks her, kissing Neumia's cheek. Soot stains his face, including a long smear of a handprint that goes from his nose into his hair. Otherwise, he seems fine, as does Brian. Neumia has splinters of wood caught in her green braids.

"This is why *Call of Duty* is funny," Brian says with a tight smile. "Everyone thinks it's about camping or bulldozing your way through, like there's nothing in between."

"Instead, it's all about being good at your job," Neumia finishes primly, sounding a hell of a lot like her mother.

Kai just seems resigned to her attitude. "We really do raise the bloodthirstiest kids, don't we?"

Rex glances at him. "You're going to be carving people up for a living."

Kai shrugs. "Kind of my point. What the hell is going on?"

"No idea. Where are Khodî and Ambrus?" Django asks.

"We were looking for them, and the rest of you, but then someone aimed a weapon at my daughter," Brian explains. "Who are these people trying and failing to crawl up our asses?"

"Not Special Forces. We're not that fucking dumb." Rex is still mentally mocking them for wearing night gear for a dawn op. Stupid dead assholes.

Django drops down onto one knee long enough to check for tags or ID on the closest fatigue-clad body. "No identifying gear," he says, frowning. "Military's a possibility, but I think they're mercs."

"If they're mercs, then we don't have an accurate count." Wesley glances down at his slide-locked .9mm Beretta. "Clip, kiddo."

Neumia digs around in the bag slung over Wesley's shoulder and hands him one. Wesley drops the empty magazine from the Beretta and gives that one back to her. "Going to need a refill, sweetie. Get those clips full again."

"Got it, Uncle Wes," Neumia replies, a box of .9mm ammunition already in her right hand. She's so practiced at it, her fingers so strong and nimble, that she doesn't even need a speed loader unless it's the larger caliber ammunition.

Rex notices that all of them perk up, chins raised in almost the exact same way, when the echo of shooting comes from the east side of the house. "Kitchen exit," Django growls, and runs.

"Shit," Brian adds as they all follow. Rex counts twelve shots before they get around the last surviving fieldstone column that used to be a corner of the farmhouse.

Ambrus and Khodî are both kneeling in the dead grass, facing opposite directions. Tiny Beast and Khodî's M9 are putting bodies on the ground at a decent pace as idiot mercs try to storm their position.

Django snarls under his breath and raises his Glock. As if it's a signal, they all do the same. In seconds, the area in front of the house is clear of breathing blue-fatigued mercs; they're just left with the dead ones.

Rex listens intently, but he doesn't hear anything else. No rustling of grass, no footsteps, no rounds being chambered. He doesn't even hear any fucking sirens, which is definitely not right. They have neighbors down the road who would have heard that explosion and dialed 9-1-1 in a heartbeat.

Then Kai hisses in a breath. "Khodî!" he yells, running for their brother.

Rex can't see it at first, not when their father is right on Kai's six. Then they're bracketing Khodî and Ambrus, and Rex gets a good look at something that makes his stomach try to turn over.

"You are not supposed to catch fucking debris with your body!" Django yells. Several gory inches of wood are emerging from the bottom of Khodî's arm, leaving the other six inches to rise up out of the top of his arm like a broken flagpole.

"Oh, good job, bro. Our house blows up, and you manage to get staked by it," Brian says, staring down at Khodî's left arm. The splinter is about an inch wide and a foot long, embedded directly between ulna and radius. "You're about to start bleeding on the lawn."

Khodî glares up at Brian. "Fuck the hell out of you, too, jackass. This fucking hurts!"

"I was just glad it wasn't his weapon hand." Ambrus finally lowers Tiny Beast and lets his head fall forward. "Fuck all of this."

"I can shoot fucksticks with my left hand just as well, thank you," Khodî says before jerking back from Kai's touch. "Hey, hell no!" he protests, lowering his M9. "Someone reload me, I can't do it one-handed without making things worse."

Neumia wiggles to signal Wesley, who lowers her to the ground. She darts forward and collects the empty clip when Khodî triggers the magazine release. "Thanks, kiddo."

"Welcome, Uncle Khodî," Neumia whispers, but doesn't waste any time, claiming the empty clip and stuffing a new one into the M9. She uses the flat of Django's offered hand to slap the clip firmly into place before hitting the slide release, all while keeping her fingers well away from the trigger.

"Well done, kiddo," Django says. Neumia nods as she gives Khodî his M9 back. "Kai?"

Kai rubs his face before dropping his hand in distress. "I—this is surgical removal. My bag was in the house. I can't just—"

Ambrus puts his hand on Kai's arm, hushing him with gesture alone. "How are you with pain, Khodî?"

Khodî lifts an eyebrow in snide rebuttal. "Depends on if I get to live afterwards."

"Oh, well. It's nice to know that one of you is most assuredly just like their father," Ambrus replies. Rex bites back an inappropriate smile as Wesley starts cackling and Django glares at them all. Khodî deserves that comment. Belated revenge is still revenge.

Ambrus is studying the house-supplied stake. "Kai, I know you have no reason to trust me other than family history—"

Khodî starts grinning, the bastard. Not enough revenge achieved. Rex reserves the right to hit him later.

"—but when I tell you to, I need you to yank out this damned piece of wood."

Kai stares at Ambrus in disbelief. "Surgical. Removal," he repeats. "Are you trying to cripple my brother's left arm? I can stabilize the fucking wound and deal with it later—"

"Kai, shut up." When Rex looks at his father, there is an odd expression on Django's face. Disquiet, he thinks. Resignation.

Certainty.

"Do it, Kai," Django says.

Kai swallows, several shades too pale, and then wraps his hands around the top part of the gigantic fucking splinter Khodî just had to catch. "Okay. Khodî, please don't punch me for this."

"Yeah." Khodî's eyes are locked on Ambrus. "I really hope you know what the fuck you're doing."

Ambrus quirks one eyebrow, smiles, and gives Khodî no warning whatsoever. "Kai, *now!*"

Kai winces, but he's already moving, yanking the splinter up and out in one swift motion. Khodî lets out a shriek, followed by more high-pitched swearing as Ambrus clamps his hands around the jagged wound, ignoring the blood that immediately coats his hands.

Rex knows that Ambrus has some sort of weird program-created healing talent. He's alive because of it, after all. Rex just didn't expect *glowing fingers*.

"Dad?" Wesley whispers as they all stare in bewildered fascination. Khodî isn't swearing anymore, but his mouth is still twisted up in a pained grimace.

"I was never much good at it," Django says quietly. "Didn't experiment with it after ditching the program, either. I didn't want them convinced that they needed to dig those hooks in any deeper than they already had."

"Life or death, Django was good at." Ambrus pulls his hands free of Khodî's arm. Khodî's skin is still bloodied, but the wound is gone. "Smaller, less vital things? Not so much."

Khodî turns his arm around so he can see both sides, and then glares at Ambrus. "That fucking hurt!"

Ambrus gives him an incredulous look. "Worse than being staked by a piece of your own fucking house?"

Khodî grimaces. "No. Worse than having a bullet pulled without a numb shot, though."

"What did you do, dig it out with your fingers?" Ambrus asks.

"It was Iraq and everything sucked balls," Khodî retorts, and then glances at his arm again. "Thanks."

Kai isn't satisfied until he uses the edge of his own black t-shirt to wipe Khodî's arm clean. Some of the red staining won't go without some serious time with soap and water, but there is no hint any stake-driven damage. Rex's bullet hole stayed red for weeks afterwards—this looks like Khodî never received an injury in the first place.

"Healing." Kai sounds awed. "That would be so damned useful. I only get advanced notice of who's going to win basketball games."

"Why basketball?" Ambrus asks as Wesley and Brian pull Khodî to his feet. Khodî wobbles for a few seconds before waving them off. He's either fine, or he's faking it to hell and back, but Khodî will refuse to give in until he literally collapses from exhaustion.

Kai shrugs as he gets up from the ground. "No damned idea."

Ambrus stands up, staggers, and falls right against Rex when Rex steps into place to keep his boyfriend from meeting the ground again. "Hi there," Rex murmurs against Ambrus's cheek.

They'd just done this, less than ten minutes ago.

"Hi," Ambrus offers in shy response. It takes a few seconds before he puts his arms around Rex.

Rex smiles. "You are in so much fucking trouble, by the way." He means the words to be teasing, and knows they aren't taken that way when Ambrus sighs.

"I'm aware."

"Vehicles, now," Django barks before anything else can be said. "The barn's intact, so we've got options. Kai!"

Kai nods and runs for the barn, on his way to go shuffle through their collection of stolen license plates.

Rex puts all personal feeling aside and studies the smoldering remains of their home. That's too much devastation for an RPG or IED, and he'd heard the sound of something *large* incoming...

"Ground-to-ground missile," Rex says. The implications of that are not fucking good at all. You have to get some very specific clearance to launch those on American soil, and burning in front of him are all of the reasons why.

"Has to be," Ambrus agrees with him, his head resting against Rex's shoulder in a tired slump. "Didn't hear a jet for it to be an ATGM."

"Hey. Keep it together for a few more minutes," Rex tells him. Ambrus nods, but Rex is supporting more and more of his boyfriend's weight as the seconds tick by.

Brian returns from casing the vehicles. "Everything in the garage is toast—which should not be a surprise, considering how little is left of the place. Khodî's car is good, but kind of obvious. Tight fit, too."

"Nothing wrong with the van." Wesley looks far too thrilled by that. "It'll hold us all, too."

Django rolls his eyes. "Yeah, great. Always wanted to make a dramatic getaway in a family passenger van."

"Hey, do not mock the V8," Wesley counters in mock-offense. "Even if the gas mileage sucks."

"We'll have to ditch it soon, anyway." Django nods his approval of the set of New York license plates Kai brings out from the barn. "Different tags will throw pursuit for a little while, but not for long, especially if they catch a glimpse of the VIN with a drone."

"At least we're not hearing those noisy little bastards yet," Khodî mutters.

Brian pulls open the side door. "Everyone aboard. I'll get the bags into the back."

Django pauses with one hand on the passenger front door handle, eyes on the sky. "You're right—we're not hearing them. No planes, no drones. Either they weren't expecting survivors, or they thought the mercs would take care of any remaining problems."

Khodî snorts. "Then I'm glad our potential murderers were fuckin' dumb."

Django smiles in grim agreement before getting into the van. "Nari, tell your uncle that he's got shit taste in vehicles."

"Uncle Wesley, you have—" Neumia starts to repeat.

Wesley rolls his eyes. "I heard your grandfather, Sweet Pea."

Rex claims the far corner of the bench seat right behind the driver's side and almost has to haul Ambrus in with him. The minute they're settled, Ambrus's head comes down on Rex's shoulder. It would almost be romantic if Rex wasn't still keeping an eye out for more people trying to fucking kill them all.

Brian, Neumia, and Kai take over the back seat. Khodî sits down next to Ambrus as Wesley gets behind the wheel. "We're going for Ella, right?" Khodî asks.

Django nods. "Get us to Lavelle, Wesley."

Wesley turns the van around in the yard, driving over bits of dried, dead grass still burning. They travel the length of the driveway in silence until they hit the turn for the main road. "Ella is going to be so pissed that we blew up the house without her," Wesley says.

"Forget the house, Wes. Ella's going to be pissed that she didn't get to fucking shoot any of them." Khodî's hand is resting on his arm where the wooden shard tried to literally stake a claim. "Rex, your fossil boyfriend is drooling on your shoulder."

Rex glances down to find that Khodî is correct. Ambrus probably fell asleep before Wesley turned the key in the ignition. He's too pale, his hair a sweat-dampened dark red. This is a lot closer to last September than to Uzbekistan, and it's nerve-wracking. If they're on the run, none of them can afford to be physically fucked up.

"It always hit us hard, pulling that shit off," Django explains, but he won't look at any of them. "I wouldn't worry, though. Your sister is going to get plenty of opportunities to shoot people."

Khodî sighs and rests his Beretta M9 on his lap, his finger tapping against the trigger guard in a nervous tic. "Great."

*   *   *   *

Most of the hour's drive north to Lavelle is spent keeping an eye on the traffic around them, alert for patterns, for vehicles who stick with them too long. Ambrus sleeps through the trip; Khodî spends most of the time with his head between his knees, his hands laced over the back of his head.

"You just got stabbed by our house, and you're carsick," Brian says incredulously. "How, man?"

Khodî groans. "Please shut up about everything ever."

Wesley pulling the van into a crowded gas station is what wakes Ambrus. "Why are we stopping?" he asks without lifting his head.

"LUNCH!" Neumia yells from the back. Rex winces and rubs at his right ear. The explosion was bad enough. He does not actually need to be deaf by the end of this day.

"And bathrooms, oh my god," Kai adds. "Some of you also need shirts that aren't blood-stained."

"Mine's fine—" Khodî looks down at the red stains on the dark green. "Fuck, never mind."

"Asshole check," Wesley announces. He gets out of the van and strolls across the wide parking lot to the store. If they've been followed, people are going to start revealing themselves the moment someone recognizes Whetū genetics.

"You have to eat," Django tells Khodî.

"So. Fucking. Carsick," Khodî replies. "How many messes do you really want to clean up between here and Ella's place?"

"Nobody took the football player-sized bait. I'll go buy shirts for you guys while he starts nabbing food," Kai says.

"Nothing green," Ambrus mutters. "Fucking Saint Patrick's Day bullshit."

"Aw, but it's the day after! Everything green is on clearance!" Kai ducks when Khodî swings at him on Ambrus's behalf—or maybe he felt like Kai deserved it. "Fine, nothing green. Bunch of spoilsports."

Brian chuckles as he climbs out of the van. "You realize that just means he's going to feel challenged to find something so much worse." Neumia jumps into her father's arms when Brian holds them out, and he hefts her up so she can park on his hip. "Back in a few. Bathrooms so awesome."

"You are not gonna make me pee in the men's room again," Neumia tells her dad sternly, and then they're off across the parking lot.

Rex glances over and finds that Django has turned around in his seat to grin at Ambrus. "You're too English for Saint Patrick's Day?"

Ambrus lifts his head long enough to glare at Django. "I am fucking Scottish, you Māori prick, and you damned well know it."

Django laughs and turns around to face forward again. "Yeah, but pushing your buttons is always fun."

"Asshole," Ambrus mutters. This time he sounds less fond, but not *I will shoot you* levels of annoyed.

Khodî hesitates for a minute. "Okay, I'll bite. If you know better, why do you keep calling him English?"

"Aside from button-pushing?" Django glances out of the window as Wesley crosses the asphalt strip, carrying two full plastic bags. "When we first met, Ambrus sounded like someone had just rolled him off the Oxford assembly line. Teased him about being English, and even after we learned better—and had motherfucking fire ants put in our beds—the nickname stuck. Nice distraction for people trying to look up the kid's background, anyway. What self-respecting Scot will politely allow themselves to be referred to as English?"

"Military men with pricks for friends," Ambrus mumbles.

"Where did you get the Brit accent, then?" Khodî asks. "What's left of it, anyway."

"Went to school in London for a bit before my family moved to the States. I was at the right age where kids soak up accents, and it bloody well fucking *stuck*. It's just as well. Nobody understands my family accent, anyway."

"Oh, no. You can't just leave it there." Khodî sits up. "Examples, English."

"Oi—don't you fucking start," Ambrus retorts, and then releases one long slur of completely incomprehensible Scots that is either swearing or a comment on the weather, if not both.

Khodî scowls. "Was that fucking Gaelic?"

"Sadly, no." Ambrus sounds pleased. "*'S e seo na Gàidhlig.*"[1]

"I think that was easier to understand than the first bit you said." Khodî looks impressed right until Wesley opens the driver's side door and the scent of food hits the vehicle. "Oh, god, *no.*"

Brian, Neumia, and Kai return as a group, loaded down with drinks and more gas station fare. On a good day, it might feed all of them with a few snacks left over, but between Ambrus's potential need to fuel up and Neumia's presence, the meal doesn't stand a chance.

"It's god-awful gas station crap, but it's edible," Brian apologizes. "I did the best I could, but this is middle-of-nowhere Pennsylvania, even by our standards."

"I appreciate it, regardless," Ambrus says of the cheap sandwich that Neumia politely hands him. "I haven't eaten since yesterday, I was shot five times, and oh, yes, I also healed your arm."

"Still also appreciative of that," Khodî says, starting to turn green.

"Not since yesterday—how the fuck are you still upright?" Django asks, using the passenger-side vanity mirror to look at them.

Ambrus chews up his first bite of what Rex thinks is chicken salad, but that's pure speculation. Rex has the same thing, and even after he tries it, he still doesn't know what the hell he's eating aside from mayonnaise and bread.

"Motherfucking spite," Ambrus finally replies, and then gives Neumia an apologetic look. "Er—"

---

[1] "This is the Scots Gaelic."

Neumia pauses in the middle of clambering into the back seat and pats Ambrus's shoulder. "It's okay. I know I'm not s'posed to say Adult Words."

Rex glances forward again in time to see Django nod, a dry smile on his face. "Spite would do it."

Khodî gets a whiff from an open bag of chips and gives up. "You can have my lunch, kid," Khodî tells Neumia. "Food bad."

Neumia shrugs. "Okay. You can eat later, when we're not in the van. The last time you puked down the side with the window open, it didn't come off for days. Uncle Wesley was grumpy."

Khodî grins and puts his head back down between his knees. "Hurray, vengeance. Told you to slow down, asshole."

Wesley shrugs. "Not my fault you're a complete wuss."

"How the hell did you survive—"

"Twelve years," Django supplies without looking up from sorting through Wesley's discoveries.

"How the hell did you survive twelve years in the military if you get carsick so easily?" Ambrus asks in disbelief.

"When I was a kid, I didn't really get carsick. Then I got older, and along came the Dramamine," Khodî answers. "So much fucking Dramamine. It doesn't even work anymore."

"I got shirts!" Kai announces after Brian is settled and Kai can get into the van. He shoves the door forward until it clicks shut and then plops down in the backseat, a bag on his lap. "We can wait until we get there for Euan and Khodî to try them on."

"He's proud of himself," Brian warns Khodî. "Be ready for the worst that a Pennsylvania gas station has to offer."

Ambrus finishes off the sandwich so fast he may as well have snorted it up one nostril. "How much farther do we need to go?"

Wesley closes his door and starts up the van, but at least he finishes chewing and swallowing whatever is in his mouth before he speaks. "About thirty minutes. Less if I push it."

"Inconspicuous," Django reminds him. "Stick with traffic but don't follow a Masshole."

Wesley steers them back onto the highway, heading northeast again. "No Massholes. Got it."

"Should we be concerned as to your other sibling's well-being?" Ambrus asks. He takes a sip of a fountain drink that Brian assembled, makes a face like he just tried to cram a lemon into his mouth, and gives it right back.

Khodî shakes his head without looking up. "If they sent a team after Ella, we'll arrive to find her sitting on top of a pile of bodies."

Rex is pretty sure Ambrus falls asleep again during the long—and thankfully boring as hell—highway drive. It's when Wesley hits the first bump on Ella's long dirt driveway that Ambrus sits bolt upright, letting out a string of pained, whispered cursing. Neumia bounces in her seat to every sharp jolt, cackling with glee as they drive down a road that hasn't seen proper maintenance outside of a snowplow in at least five years. Khodî is still keeping his head down, but Rex is pretty sure he's whimpering.

Ambrus is white in the face by the time Wesley parks the van at the end of the driveway. Before 9/11, Ella and Eric sank a hell of a lot of money into making sure the building would survive long absences. The two-hundred-year-old farmhouse looks modern instead of the decrepit mess they initially purchased, shaded by trees that aren't even as old as the farmhouse's original foundation.

"You all right?" Rex asks in a low voice, meant for Ambrus alone.

Ambrus glances at him. "Still alive," he mouths. The smile on his pale face is sort of ghastly, but genuine.

Khodî bolts from the van the moment Wesley turns the engine off, muttering about finding a nice bush to vomit on. "We should make sure there isn't trouble!" Kai calls after him.

"Then I will fucking *vomit* on them!" Khodî shouts, disappearing behind a tall flowering shrub that's covered in spring buds. "That'll teach them!"

"Fine, he can play bird dog," Wesley says, shaking his head as he opens his door. They pile out of the van and stand in the too-warm March sunlight. Rex realizes how much he's been relying on his smartphone when he tries to find it in his pockets to check the weather forecast, and then remembers that it's in pieces along US 1.

Django glances around, his dark eyes seeking threats, but his head is cocked in a particular way. He calls it 'listening to the wind' and until he was eight years old, Rex thought his father was being literal. He still has no idea what it is that Django hears, but Django has always told Rex and his siblings that as long as they trust their instincts, the wind bit doesn't matter.

"Anything?" Brian asks while Rex checks the windows of the house for movement. He doesn't see the curtains twitch, no breezes blowing through open windows. Ella could be home; Ella could be in fucking Mexico and they wouldn't even know it.

"No, I think we're good," Django says as Khodî comes back, wiping his mouth with his stained shirt. He looks less green, at least.

"Tire swing!" Neumia proclaims, but she does wait for Brian to nod permission before she runs for the tire hanging from a nearby tree.

"Shirt time!" Kai announces. He pulls a dark blue t-shirt out of the gas station plastic bag, tags already snapped off, and hands it to Khodî.

Khodî's eyes narrow as he reads the text in bright white lettering on the shirtfront. "'Blow me, I'm a Veteran.' I hate you, Kai."

Kai's grin is bright with mischievous, manic humor. "You haven't been laid in forever. You could probably use the help."

Khodî sighs and pulls off his bloodstained t-shirt to swap over. "Hatred, Kai. Burning, fiery hatred."

Ambrus unfolds the dark red shirt Kai gives him and stares at it with a baffled look on his face. "'I survived Gettysburg.' Are you sure it's only basketball scores?"

Kai ignores Khodî's muttered threats and glances at Ambrus. "Huh? Why?"

"I got shot in that damned field—not in the fucking Civil War!" Ambrus snarls at Khodî, who grins wide, like a man who's smelled easy pickings. "Rex, can you help me get this disaster off?"

"Sure." Rex looks at the remaining mess of two different shirts before he takes the pocketknife Django offers and slices both shirts down the back, collar to hemline. The front is already destroyed, both sleeves sliced up past the elbows; it's not like any of it was salvageable. The cotton is stiff beneath his hands from dried blood and drywall mud, but this way Ambrus doesn't have to fight just to take the damned mess off. It's putting on the new shirt that makes Ambrus swear under his breath as he pulls it on over his head. It's barely long enough to hide the bloodstain on his trousers, but it's a hell of a lot less obvious than the ruined alternative.

Kai holds up two different sections of shirts. "We should burn these."

"Probably," Ambrus says, turning his head back and forth while wincing. "I wonder if Khodî found a nice bush. I'm thinking about helping him decorate it."

"Nope, sorry, find your own damned bush," Khodî replies. "Rex tell you about Ella?"

Ambrus nods. "And about Eric. I am sorry, by the way."

Khodî shrugs. "Desert Storm's bullshit sequel was a long time ago," he says, but Rex doesn't agree. Ten years, twenty years, one hundred years—he is not ever going to lose the clarity of that day.

"Ella kind of...didn't take it well," Brian says, his eyes still on Neumia's attempts to gain height with the tire swing.

"Ella kind of lost her marbles for a while," Wesley counters, shoving his hands into his pockets. "I wonder if she's home."

Rex winces when he feels the bore of a large-gauge shotgun jab him in the small of his back. "Yeah, Ella's home." She always was the best of them at sneaking up on people.

"Please don't shoot your brother, baby," Django says, glancing in Rex's direction.

"Unexpected family reunion. Don't mind me for being nervous," Ella replies in the low-pitched voice she uses when she's still judging a situation. "What'd I do to earn the honor?"

"Didn't check your messages, huh?" Django doesn't look surprised.

Ella's shotgun isn't prodding Rex quite as sharply. "I was working in the barn. What's up?"

"Someone blew up the house, there's a bunch of dead mercs in the yard, and you're the only one who knows where Eric reburied the bags that last time," Kai explains in a single breath. "Hi!"

"He never did like leaving them in one place for too long." Ella steps around Rex, the gun now resting against her shoulder. She's dyed her short hair dark brown, and it's all pushed up into curled half-spikes by a multi-colored stretchy cloth headband that is trying and failing to soak up sweat. She's wearing a tank top, a sports bra that looks capable of doubling as body armor, cut-off denim shorts, and no shoes. The barn story is legit, then—the mucking boots stay out there with the stench.

"Hi Kai, everyone," Ella says, ignoring the fact that Rex is still glaring at her for the gun-greeting. "Who's Whitey McPaleface?"

"Euan Ambrus." Ambrus raises an eyebrow. "I used to work with your father, and I'm dating your brother."

Ella grins. "Hoo, sloppy parental seconds."

Rex looks skyward while Khodî chokes on a snort of laughter. "Goddammit, Ella!" It does not help that one side of Ambrus's mouth is tilting up in what Rex is pretty sure is approval.

Ella ignores that, too. "Hi, sweetie!" she yells, raising her gun and waving it, barrel pointed skyward, to catch Neumia's attention. "How's tricks?"

"I'm good, Auntie Ella!" Neumia shouts, swinging the tire around in a high, wide arc.

"Was prodding me with that thing really fucking necessary?" Rex asks his sister.

Ella shrugs. "You guys are the ones out here saying the house is blown up and there are dead mercs everywhere," she counters, and then pauses. "Wait—someone *really* blew up the house? Like, actual crater levels of gone?"

"Yeah." Django's expression shatters for a second, letting grief shine through, before the moment is gone again. "Total loss."

"Fuck." Ella looks like she can't figure out what to do with that information.

"No pursuit that we know of. Probably didn't have time to get drones into the air before realizing they'd lost track of us. Given the lack of sirens after the GTG hit, pretty sure they were sitting hard on rescue services. Is the farm still listed under a fake ident?" Django asks.

Ella scowls, insulted. "Duh. It'll take people a while to carve their way through that pile of bullshit. Should give us about six hours of breathing room." She drops the scowl and turns to Brian. "Have you called her mother yet?"

"No." Brian glances back over at Neumia, still young enough to bounce back from just about anything. "We didn't keep burners in the house bags, and everything else went up with the house. I wasn't going to start digging through that burning mess trying to

186

find a phone that wasn't destroyed." Brian swallows hard. "At least we never got married. That'll slow down their search, too."

"Go call her, dumbass," Ella says, and gives Brian a sharp nudge in the leg with her bare foot. "Front door's unlocked, burners are stashed behind the fridge, and watch out for the cat."

"Why the fuck do you have a cat?" Khodî asks as Brian heads for the house.

"Because cats are awesome, self-sufficient creatures who keep my allergic brothers at bay so they're not invading my house, trying to find out if I'm nuts or not," Ella tells Khodî in a too-sweet voice. "Seriously, keep up."

Ambrus tilts his head and then looks at Django. "Wet *and* fed after midnight."

Django rolls his eyes in irritation. "Fuck you."

"Heh, *Gremlins*." Ella grins at Ambrus. "Are the mercs after you, or all of us?"

"Myself, originally, but I imagine it's now all of you simply by association." Ambrus lowers his head in apology. "Government-level mercs, by the way."

Ella frowns. "Not six hours then. Maybe more like two or three. Shit." Then she shrugs. "Dad made sure we'd be ready if this fuckery ever happened—justifiable paranoia and stuff. I'm just surprised you haven't booked it."

That makes Rex cringe. He hadn't even considered the idea that Ambrus might do exactly that. Ambrus admitted mere hours ago that he did it to Django in a bid to keep him safe from the department.

Ambrus pulls down the collar of his t-shirt just enough to show off the white edge of a bandage. "Shot five times yesterday."

"Wow, they really don't like you. Traveling with you should be fun—" Ella's eyes widen. "Fuck, I just finished paying the damned mortgage on this place!"

Ambrus smiles. "Ah, priorities. Rex, you didn't mention she was charming."

Ella grins back and points at Rex. "Okay, I approve of the boyfriend."

"You have fucked-up standards, Ambrus," Khodî says.

Ambrus gives Khodî a dry look. "I'm friends with your father. That should explain everything about my standards."

Django glares at Ambrus. "I haven't seen your ass since 1975!"

Ambrus raises both eyebrows in response. "And?"

"Oh, fuck you."

"Yep, you are totally friends with Dad." Ella laughs at their father's mulish look. "Who wants lunch? I want lunch. If you started the day with a blown-up house, I bet you haven't had lunch."

"We had gas station food, but I'm just realizing that was breakfast," Kai says.

Rex notices that Wesley is already scratching at his arms in preparation for Cat. He's pretty sure the allergy is psychosomatic, a response trained into them all from childhood by Khodî, who is *not* a fan of cats.

Shit, now Rex wants to scratch at his arms, too. No, dammit. He isn't allergic to cats. He's got the medical documentation to prove it!

Ella starts herding them towards the house. "I hope you like sandwiches, then, because I don't fucking cook."

Brian is standing in the kitchen, staring at a powered-off cheap cell phone cradled in his left hand. He already pulled the battery and the SIM card, but that's as far as he got before stalling out.

"You got ahold of her, right?" Django asks.

Brian shakes himself and looks up. "Yeah. I talked to her." He snaps the card in half and drops everything into the trash. "She's pretty sure they haven't looked in her direction yet."

Ella puts her shotgun down on the countertop, pushed towards the wall so Neumia can't reach it when she comes into the kitchen. "What'd she say?"

"*It had better not be typhoon season, Brian. I hate typhoon season,*" Brian quotes, and Ella laughs at him. "I told her that as long as we didn't need to shift plans on the fly, we'd see her in about a week."

"Is there another phone? One of us needs to call Xāwuṭh," Khodî says. "He'll be glad to see us."

"He'll be glad to mock us," Kai corrects. "Wolf's an asshole."

"Yeah, but that's genetic. There are more phones; I keep five." Ella waves her hand at the fridge and kitchen cabinets. "There should be something edible as long as I didn't forget stuff in the fridge and let it become some new kind of lifeform. I'm going to go dig up the fucking map."

"A map?" Ambrus asks.

"Yes, a map," Ella retorts, like it's obvious.

Ambrus blinks at her, some of his exhaustion starting to leech through. "How many bags are we talking about?"

Ella tilts her head back and forth as she thinks. "Probably a full set of three. Not sure if Eric finished updating the map before we shipped out again last time, so I'm not counting on finding more than that. Also, I wanted to be a pirate when I was a kid. Who the fuck says I can't fulfill childhood ambitions?" she asks, and heads outside using the rear screen door at the back of the kitchen. "I like your shirt, Khodî!" she yells over her shoulder.

Khodî is already in the middle of dialing Xāwuṭh's cell, so he only sighs and rolls his eyes. "Burning, fiery hatred, Kai."

"Whatever," Kai replies. "Taking turns on showers?"

"Good idea," Django agrees.

"Dibs," Rex says, realizing all at once that they smell like the worst elements of a house fire. He had one shower already today, but he wants this scent gone.

Kai bolts for the hallway. "Downstairs shower is mine."

Rex winces. He really is starting to feel bruised from the last twenty-four hours, and stairs...

Stairs are worth not smelling like tragedy. "Fine."

By the time Ella gets back with a dirty, laminated terrain map of the farm, most of them are clean, and Ambrus is taking his turn in the upstairs bathroom. On-demand hot water is definitely something Rex is going to miss, but it doesn't exactly get cold enough in the South Pacific for that to matter.

"That is still the plan, right?" Rex asks his father. "South Pacific, disappear and regroup until we know what the fuck's going on?"

Django nods, helping Ella pin the curling edges of the map down on the kitchen table with rocks. Ella's cat helps by sitting on one corner after Ella bribes the fluffy gray asshole with petting. "Still the same plan," he confirms. "Right now, we have no reason to change it, and it's best to go where most of us are going to blend in."

"What's the cat's name?" Brian asks. It hasn't escaped Rex's notice that Brian is on the opposite side of the room, away from the cat.

"Cut," Ella says, which for some reason prompts the cat to get up and abandon that corner of the map. Ella puts a rock on the spot that Cut vacated.

Wesley glances up from Ella's household first aid kit he's helping Kai sort through. Kai hasn't stopped muttering under his breath about why it's complete shit, but his full surgical bag went up with the house. "Why Cut?" Wesley asks.

Ella grins. "Because if you mess with my cat, he will cut you up."

"Fair enough," Brian says, and backs away from the cat when it walks by.

Ella marks up the map with a handful of crayons from her kitchen junk drawer. "These are still here, definitely," she says, circling three Xs on the map in waxy blue. Two more Xs are circled in red: "Gone. I had a bad spell and took off for Canada on a horse. Fun trip—and that was my fucking hair dye!"

Rex looks over and gets a bad jolt of shock, one too many on a day that's held nothing but horrible surprises. Ambrus is standing in the kitchen doorway, but he's dyed his hair and eyebrows the same dark brown that Ella's favored for the last few years, cut his hair short, and shaved off the beard. The change makes his eyes seem paler, less Caribbean blue and more hazel-gray. He also looks ten fucking years younger.

Ambrus lifts his shoulders, the barest twitch of a shrug. "I'll buy you another bottle, Ella."

"Definitely less noticeable than ginger," Django comments.

Ambrus shrugs again. "Not my first dark op."

"You think you know a man," Rex says. He meant it to come out as a joke, but it falls so flat the words might as well be burrowing through the basement.

"Yeah." Ambrus's smile is wry, lopsided self-deprecation. "Ella is right, you know. About the fact that I should leave."

Rex has to swallow before he can respond. "What?"

Django looks up from the map, eyes already narrowing in anger. "Excuse me?"

"I can take the van to the next town, swap it out, and go in the opposite direction that you're all going," Ambrus explains, though he doesn't look enthused. "Present them with an obvious target."

"Why the fuck would you do something that stupid?" Rex hears himself ask. He can't decide if he's infuriated or terrified that his idiot boyfriend is going to do exactly what he's suggesting.

Ambrus meets his eyes for a second before looking away. "One of me, eight of you," Ambrus replies. "Not exactly difficult math."

"This is not fucking *Star Trek*," Khodî growls. "All of us stick together. None of that 'Needs of the many' Vulcan bullshit."

"This is exactly the wrong time to run away," Rex spits, and regrets it when Ambrus flinches. It isn't a fair button to push, and Rex knows it. If his boyfriend wasn't fucking injured, it would be a good plan—distract and divide pursuit, meet up again elsewhere.

Ambrus *isn't* healthy. This is no fucking time for him to try to do his stupid mystery job.

Rex knows the words, the logic, but he can't get them past the anger crowding out everything else. "Fuck this," he mutters, and shoves his way outside so hard that the kitchen screen door slams against the outside wall before banging back into place.

"We should—" Khodî tries, but Ella cuts him off.

"Leave him the fuck alone. Never get involved in a lover's quarrel unless one of the lovers is already dead," she says.

Rex is grinding his teeth, because that's the damned problem. This is anger born of the fact that he's afraid Ambrus is going to end up dead. He nearly lost the man twice today. Right now he can't handle the idea of a third risk.

"Fucking...fuck." Brilliant articulation. Rex should have tried that thirty seconds ago. He rubs his face with both hands, angry, tired, and so damned frustrated it's a wonder that he's not bleeding all of that from his ears. He still can't even fathom the idea that his childhood home is gone, that Fox—

The creak of the tire swing's rope over the tree branch catches Rex's attention, sharp and piercing enough to make him snap his head around. The tire is empty, the swing moving from side to side in listless, recent abandonment.

Rex is about to turn around and ask if Neumia's come inside when all of his instincts light up, burning fire and crawling ants all over his skin. Not abandonment.

"Nari," Rex whispers. Then he's tearing hell across the yard, screaming her name while yanking the 1911 from its holster. He only has six rounds. That's all he needs. Please let it be all he needs.

There. Broken grass, an obvious trail into the brush beyond the dirt and rock border of Ella's yard. He hears the others pour out of the house like angry fucking hornets, shouts accompanied by the rack of at least one shotgun.

"Uncle Rex!" Neumia shrieks. Rex alters course and veers left. He's going to kill whoever touched his niece, even if he runs out of bullets and has to do it with his bare goddamn hands. Brian can have what's left over.

Rex breaks through tall grass that's still dead and dry from last fall and bursts into a clearing, sliding to a halt. A man in military fatigues and full facial gear has Neumia, one arm wrapped around her chest in a too-tight grip—and he's pointing a standard-service M9 at her head.

Rex feels rage coil in his chest, fierceness held ready to break free as he lifts the barrel of the 1911 to point at the sky. He can't risk a center mass shot on this asshole, not with Neumia so close.

He sees a flash of visible flesh between the asshole's glove and sleeve: white, adult male, mid-thirties probably, definitely with better training than the merc idiots back at the house.

Rex looks directly into muddy brown eyes. Stupid fuck should be masked for the op. "You are a dead motherfucker."

The soldier makes a derisive noise and points his M9 at Rex. "If I were you, I wouldn't move," he says in the long drawl that Fort Benning girls and boys pick up if they stick around too long. Ella's still desperately trying to get rid of hers.

"All I have to do is squeeze," the soldier drawls. "If I splinter her ribs, you'll really have something to worry about, won't ya?"

Rex bares his teeth in a feral smile. Soldier friend here already made a fatal mistake, and he doesn't even know it. "I'm not the only one who should worry."

With the M9 no longer an immediate threat, Neumia does what years of schooling have taught her to do. She goes right for the idiot's belt knife, yanking a serrated blade free. Before the soldier has a chance to realize he's not just coping with a wriggly child, Neumia buries the knife right into his groin.

The soldier squeals like a stuck pig, dropping both Neumia and his M9 as his hands go for the spurting femoral wound. Rex takes him out with a single shot from the 1911, putting a .45mm hole in the asshole's chest that lays him out on the ground.

Rex double-checks in a three-sixty for other dangers before he goes straight to Neumia, making sure none of that asshole's blood landed on his niece. "Fuck this day. You okay, sweetie?"

"WHAT A FUCKER!" Neumia shouts, and then bursts into tears.

Rex scoops her up with his left arm. "That's my girl. You're okay, it's okay." Neumia wraps her arms around his neck, her legs around his waist, and sobs into Rex's shirt. "Let's get back to the house."

"NARI!" Brian comes flying out of the dead brush the same way Rex had a moment ago, a Glock in his hands that he raises to point upwards the moment he realizes he's found friendlies. "Is she—?"

Neumia lifts her head, still sniffling. "I'm okay, Dad."

Rex gives her a quick squeeze with his left arm. "We've got trouble. That dead fucker on the ground there is active military."

"You sure?" Brian starts to ask, and then they hear shots fired back at the farmhouse. "Fuck, never mind," he snarls, and runs back in the direction he came from.

Rex follows, but slowly, worried about potential assholes trying to crawl up his brother's ass. He keeps the 1911 pointed at the ground, ready to lift and shoot the moment a target presents itself. Five rounds left in the 1911. "Earned two war stories in one day, huh Nari?"

"Sucks," Neumia mutters as she buries her face against his shirt again. "I just wanted to swing."

"I know." Rex listens to what sounds like a full-scale firearms war breaking out around the farmhouse. Dammit. Dead military asshole number one back there came with a full team. "We're going to have to dye your hair a different color," he says to distract Neumia.

"But I like green!" she complains at once.

"Yeah, but now they know you have green hair. Too easy to recognize." Rex peers around the tire swing tree. Part of his family is standing in the yard, upright and uninjured. There are a *lot* fatigue-wearing bodies on the ground.

That's not a single team. That is multiple teams, and Ella, Ambrus, and Wesley are unaccounted for. "I'm in the same boat. Not a lot of blond Māori men wandering around the U.S., Nari."

Movement on Rex's peripheral gets his attention just as instinct kicks in. He raises the 1911 and fires without turning his head, dropping two more men in fatigues. No, the other was female. Definitely *was*, considering the hole he put in that facial gear.

"Sorry, Nari," Rex says as Neumia cringes. "Your ears okay?"

"I hate those bells." Neumia lifts her head, an elegant sulk on her face that is definitely reminiscent of Bonika. "Owie."

"I hate them, too," Rex admits, glancing around. His ears hurt, but he's been trained to suck it up and cope. "Did my stupid boyfriend leave?"

He thinks Brian says no, but a twig snaps behind him and Rex whirls around, weapon raised—only to witness Ambrus drive a stolen serrated military knife through the neck of the fucker trying to sneak up on Rex and Neumia. Ambrus's mouth is open in a vicious, soundless snarl of rage as he rides the soldier down to the ground, twisting the knife to sever the man's spinal cord.

Ambrus yanks the knife free when the dead soldier stops twitching. "Your stupid boyfriend isn't that fucking stupid."

Rex can hear the apology in Ambrus's voice, even if he doesn't say the words. Right now, that's good enough.

"Django!" Ambrus shouts.

"Full count, two teams on this side!" Django shouts back. "If any of you see movement, be ready to kill another full damned squad of assholes!"

Rex is keenly aware that he has three rounds left, an empty magazine in his pants pocket, and no knife. Bare hands it is, then. He doesn't want to ruin the 1911 by using it as a damned club.

They all wait long, tense minutes, standing in a loose semi-circle in the yard. Rex isn't the only one all but holding his breath, straining his ears for any hint of incoming danger.

"CLEAR ON THE NORTH!" Wesley finally shouts.

"EAST SIDE, TOO!" Kai adds. "FUCK ALL OF THIS, BY THE WAY!"

"SOUTH IS DEAD!" Ella yells. "WEST?"

Rex, Django, Ambrus, and Brian all glance at each other. "WEST IS CLEAR!" Django finally replies. "GET YOUR ASSES OVER HERE!"

Brian stares down the length of Ella's driveway. "They must have parked miles away and hoofed it in. I didn't see or hear any vehicles, before or after."

"Aw, man," Wesley groans as he spies the van. There are three bullet holes in the windshield and two in the front grill, which is releasing a slow vent of steam. "Did they have to shoot my baby, too? That's just mean."

"What a fucking day. Who are these assholes?" Django asks.

Ambrus kneels down and quickly strips the nearest dead soldier of weaponry, ammunition, and all forms of identification with the ease of long practice. That kind of swift efficiency would be hot if everything wasn't currently insane.

He flips the dog tags over in his hand to read the engraved side. "Aw, dammit," Ambrus says in a low voice.

Rex catches the symbol engraved on the backside of one of the tags. "Rangers," he mutters. Ambrus confirms it with the military ID he pulls from the dead man's wallet, holding it up for Rex to see. "Fuck."

Django takes in the expression on Ambrus's face when he stands up. "Not department policy, huh?"

"We're assholes, but we're assholes with *standards*," Ambrus insists. "We have to get off the radar. This is—these men and women had no damned idea what they were in for. They were just following orders."

"Unlike the stupid mercs," Rex says.

"Usually," Django agrees. "Why the hell are they involving other branches—shit. I know why."

Rex looks at his sister and understands immediately. Her face is dry, but her eyes are red-rimmed, drowning pools of angry darkness. A bunch of bloodied dog tag chains are clenched in her hand.

"Guilt." Rex feels like he's going to help decorate Khodî's chosen bush. "Fucking bastards."

"Three full Ranger teams." Kai says, resting the shotgun over his shoulders. He's panting for breath and red in the face from exertion. "We are in such deep shit."

"Friends?" Rex asks Ella.

Ella shakes her head and drops the tags. "Knew some of them," she murmurs under her breath, kicking dirt over her stolen collection of tags. Like anger to cheer, she swaps back to fierce professionalism in less than a second. "They found the house faster than they should have. I know what the fuck I'm doing. It should have taken hours, not forty damned minutes."

Kai nods. "They would have nabbed me at school already if I hadn't been with Brian and Wesley last night. If they've surfed the records hard enough to find this place, then they're after everyone. Every connection we have." He pauses thoughtfully. "At least I fucking hate my roommate this year."

"Okay. Three burner phones left if we want to limit them to one call a piece," Django says, gaining everyone's attention. "We all know Xāwuṭh immediately passed on the message to Malai. She probably hit the gossip chain, and now half of Thailand knows to duck and cover."

"Malai and Moum[2] are friends," Khodî ventures. "She might tell her. Gives us a spare burner if we need it."

Django gives the idea brief consideration before shaking his head. "We can't take that chance. Chanthavy deserves the same warning Xāwuṭh and Malai received. Rin, Anahera, and Aroha put us at four calls, though, not three."

"It's five, then." Rex looks at Ambrus, but he's staring off in the direction of the dead field. "If we're warning parents, she deserves that, too."

Jasper's mother. Rex feels his stomach turn over. If Fox has lost his shit, he hopes the woman is still alive to warn.

---

[2] Cambodian term for Mom (English/French influence)

"My mother's the one who sticks closest to a phone," Wesley says. "I'll call Aroha, and she can tell Anahera. Down to four."

Django shakes his head. "Ultimately, it's not going to matter how many calls we make. It's how fast and *when*. Save the phone calls until we're ready to leave. We move out right after that."

"Well, we need a new vehicle, something a bit less obvious and dramatic than a passenger van." Brian bites his lip and refuses to flinch when Wesley slaps him upside the head.

Ella smiles. "Got that covered. There are just nine of us, so Nari will have to double up with Brian, though."

"ATVs?" Ambrus asks curiously. "Loud."

"Pfft, no. I'm a Ranger. I'm more subtle than that, especially compared to this pile of dead assholery," Ella replies, and tilts her head in the direction of the barn. "I raise trail horses. It's supposed to be my therapy."

"You don't raise horses, you raise insane hell beasts," Khodî mutters under his breath.

"They just don't like you. They *love* me," Ella singsongs.

Khodî glares at Ella. "Insane hell beasts love fellow insane hell beasts."

Rex shakes his head as he follows everyone to the barn. Ella's horses are placid, piebald creatures, even if they're prone to being sneaky when it's not called for. Ella says all smart horses are like that, which makes Khodî hate them even more.

"I keep everything out here, ready to go," Ella tells them, opening a storage room in the barn to reveal full kits for each animal, trail rations for human and beast alike, and ultra-lightweight camping gear to keep the horses from carrying too much weight. Rex loves his sister for many reasons, but always being prepared for weird-ass contingencies is definitely high on the list.

"Can you ride?" Rex hears Ella ask his boyfriend.

Ambrus looks at her as if she's insulted his mother. "Scottish man, served in Korea, Vietnam, the Philippines, the Middle East, and various points south. *Can I fucking ride a horse,* she asks."

Ella shrugs. "Hey, just checking. You're already leaps and bounds ahead of Khodî."

"Fuck you," Khodî retorts.

Rex is already looking, so he notices when Ambrus puts his hand on the bottom of his throat, but Kai reacts before he does. "Sit down," Kai orders.

"I'm fine—" Ambrus starts to protest.

Kai points at a bale of hay. "Sit the fuck down and let me check those fucking stitches. Or do you want to leave an obvious blood trail they can follow?"

Ambrus rolls his eyes and complies. "Wet and fed after fucking midnight," he mutters.

Relieved that Kai is making his stupid boyfriend behave, Rex turns around and finds Django in the middle of stealing a bridle from Brian. "Not like that, jackass," Django says. Rex doesn't think it's his imagination that the horse looks relieved to have a professional take over. The horse makes a show of blowing out a long, resigned sigh, but takes the metal bit that Django offers, which lets him slip the rest of the harness over the horse's head to be buckled into place.

"Stay put," Django tells the horse, who whickers and noses the ground. "You need a saddle, and we're not leaving yet." He loops the reins over the horse's neck and goes for more tack.

Rex bites his lip to hide a smile, watching the horse slowly shift closer. "OW!" Brian shouts a second later, yanking his foot out from beneath the horse's front hoof. "Fuck you, too!"

"I'm just gonna walk the entire fucking way," Khodî mutters.

Rex shakes his head and leaves Khodî to suffer. He keeps one eye on Kai and Ambrus while saddling up his own horse, a brown-and-white mare with random patches of dun-colored hair on her legs and face. She's a lot more antsy about the bridle process than Brian's black-and-white patched horse.

"What hurts?" Kai asks.

Ambrus smiles. "Everything." He pulls down the collar of his t-shirt with his fingers, revealing the bandage next to his throat. Rex winces when he sees the bright red stain.

"Not surprised." Kai tilts his head as he regards the ruined bandage. "You're not tasting blood, are you?"

Ambrus shakes his head, and Rex starts breathing again. "No. I would have mentioned that a hell of a lot sooner."

Kai nods. "Ella's kit isn't as awesome as the one I'd make, but I can replace that dressing, plus make a pain cocktail to counter trot-of-horse. Interested?"

"Gimme," Ambrus replies, which makes Kai grin.

While Kai works his particular brand of magic, Django and Rex glance at each other. Without saying a word, they both start the work of saddling the last horse, a white-and-dun gelding who watched the activity in the barn with interested eyes, but didn't nose around to investigate, bolt, or try to interfere in any way. If this is the calmest horse in the barn, then this is the animal that Rex wants his bullet-ridden boyfriend to be riding on their way out.

Ella comes back with an extra bag of supplies in one hand, a child-size sleeping bag and mat tucked under her arm, and Cut riding on her shoulder. "Nicely done," she says, doing a quick visual check of each horse. "I talked to Moum while I packed up, Khodî. She's heading into the city. You know the number."

Khodî nods. "Yeah, I remember. Fuck, I can't believe we have to resort to this shit."

"You do too believe it," Rex says as he accepts one of the phones Ella brought out. It takes a few seconds to recall the correct number. "We just don't want to have to fuckin' *do* it."

"Point," Khodî admits while Rex puts the phone to his ear and waits for the international call to connect. He's about to have an intensely formal, utterly creepy conversation with his birth mother.

"*Wéi? Shuí a?*"[3]

"Hello, Mother," Rex replies, giving Rin Tjin her first two major clues as to why he's calling. "How are you?"

He can almost feel her hesitation, like it's a tangible presence in the barn. "I am...sick," Rin says at last. Her English is stuttered, halting—and a complete falsehood. Rin worked out of Paya Labar United States Air Force base in Singapore for almost forty years. Her English is flawless. "I think often of—I think I must visit your sister."

Rex blows out a long breath. Message heard and understood. "That's a great idea. The visit north will be good for you."

"You are—yes, you correct. I will call when I arrive, dear son."

Dear son. Rex shakes his head, smiling. As if he'd ever been anything but an inconvenience until he grew into adulthood, when he'd become an amusing inconvenience instead. Rex understands all the reasons why Rin couldn't be his parent, but the fact that their coded conversation for trouble is built around things they would never say under normal circumstances is completely fucked up.

"*Zàijiàn le, mǔqīng.*"[4] Rex ends the call before she can respond. "Fuck."

Wesley hangs up from his own phone call a moment later with a heartfelt, "*Fuck katoa, tae atu ki nga tatou hoiho e haere ki te eke roto i runga!*"[5]

Brian waits until Neumia is distracted by the cat. "Bro, I'm not fucking a horse. I mean, I won't judge you if that's your thing—"

"Oh, piss off." Wesley rubs at his head; flakes of dried blood emerge from his short hair and stick to his fingertips. "I only got the answering machine. I hope my mother pays more attention to her phone than Ella did."

Brian claims Rex's phone to try calling his own mother. Ambrus holds out his hand and ask, "May I?" Wesley nods and hands over the cell phone.

Django frowns. "I thought you said everyone was department."

Ambrus nods. "Technically, she is, but if we're warning parents, then she deserves the same courtesy, Django."

---

[3] C. Mandarin: "Hello? Who's that?"

[4] F. Mandarin: "Goodbye, Mother."

[5] Māori: "Fuck everything, including the horses we are going to get out on!"

Django nods and gives his horse a light slap when she tries to sidle over and try the foot-stomping trick on him. "Fair enough."

The conversation serves as enough of a distraction for Kai to sneak up on Wesley. "Sit down and let me look at the cut on your head."

"What cut?" is Wesley's confused response, but then Ambrus is saying "Helena!" in a tone of complete relief.

"I need to speak to you about zero-zero-three-eighteen." Ambrus listens for a minute. "Yeah—it is that bad. I'm so damned sorry. The plan I told you to make, the one no one else is supposed to know, including Jasper and myself? Yes, that's the one. Do it now, Helena. Stay away from anyone in the department, even if you think they're trustworthy—yes, even if it's Jasper! Things have gone that damned sideways." There's another pause. "I—I don't— Helena. Good luck, and goodbye."

Ambrus ends the call, flips the phone over, yanks the cover, and then pulls both battery and SIM card. The battery and cell he tosses into the barn's large aluminum garbage bin. The card he snaps and buries in the dirt at his feet. Internal memory might net a unit some bit of intelligence, but it takes longer when the SIM card's gone.

"Damned answering machine," Brian informs them, fuming. "We'll have no idea what that means until we get new phones, or we go to fucking New Zealand."

Django nods. "We'll do what we can. In the meantime, let's get the hell out of here."

They ride out of the barn in sets of two, sticking to areas where horse hooves have already marred the soil into a useless map of prints. Ella doesn't look back, but Rex sees the forward curve of her shoulders, the flat line of her mouth, and knows exactly how much she wants to.

Ella leads them to a gentle slope of rock. With no horseshoes on her horses' feet, they can nimbly pick their way up the path without leaving a single metal-struck hint behind. If someone finds a really damned good tracker, then maybe they'll figure out which direction Ella and her horses went, but Rex doubts they'll think of it that way. When working on domestic soil, the military gets weird about how they consider ground movement. They watch roads and established trails, only patrolling forests via drone surveillance.

Ella is far too intelligent to lead them along any trail that a drone could map. "All three bags are in this direction," she says. "About five miles southeast. Convenient, right?"

"Yeah," Wesley says. He's looking up at the evergreen trees that shelter them from skyward view. "Right towards Philadelphia. Why'd you pick that way?"

Ella shakes her head. "I didn't. Eric did."

"That's my smart damned kid," Rex hears Django murmur, and his chest aches with renewed grief and guilt. Before he can say anything—what would he even say?—Django nudges his mount until he's close to Ella's horse. "I can't believe you're bringing the cat."

Cut is perched on the back of Ella's sleeping roll, looking for all the world like he rides a horse every day. Then again, this is Ella. It's entirely possible that the cat has been riding on a horse since kittenhood.

"Well, I wasn't going to leave my cat there for another string of fuckheads to find and kill," Ella replies. "Besides, I have to find Cut a new home if we're going overseas. Getting animals through impound quarantine is a pain in the ass. I don't even like doing that to people, and I hate people."

Rex tugs on his horse's reins and gives her a gentle nudge so that she'll increase her pace, drawing even with Ambrus's mount. "How's the ride?"

The saddle blankets are all thin for the season so the horses won't overheat, and the saddle leather is soft and flexible enough for Ambrus to guide his horse with his knees. The reins are looped around the saddle horn, leaving Ambrus's hands free to worry at a length of rope he salvaged from the barn before they left. "A horse on a hillside is kinder than Ella's driveway," Ambrus says.

"I fucking heard that!" Ella shouts.

Between Django and Ella, it doesn't take long to dig up the first bag once Ella matches its location on the map to the gnarled, lightning-struck tree it's buried near. Unlike the quick-and-dirty bug-out bags from the house, each of these three bags has a full set of false identification documents for every family member, with enough cash included to get them all out of the country.

"Very well done," Ambrus compliments them after the bag's contents are emptied. The only thing remaining are a pair of M9s—Eric and Ella's original service pistols. Ella packs them and their two boxes of .9mm away in her bag, a contemplative frown on her face.

"Between our rainy day accounts and the bags, we can set up nicely overseas as long as we stay out of Westernized parts of the world," Khodî says. "I was always hoping the bags and the accounts would never be anything except retirement money."

"Well, you just retired," Brian points out dryly. "Congratulations, Ex-Sheriff."

Khodî sighs. "Yeah. Good point."

Rex has no idea why the second bag has a box of .45mm ammunition but no .45mm weapon, and decides he ultimately doesn't care. It means that if shit happens on their long ride to Philadelphia, he can at least help to defend everyone. There isn't anything for Kai's sawed-off, but there is for the rifle from their father's house, along with a random box of .357.

"Why fucking Philly?" Brian asks while putting the .357 into his saddlebag. He's the only one carrying a weapon that can use it.

"Don't mock the town of my home team," Wesley retorts.

"We need an international airport," Ambrus says, probably interrupting an old football-based pissing match. "By taking the slow route, they might assume we're trying for the Canadian border, or going on to more distant airports. There might not be as many agents watching the city...or there could be a military blockade."

Django frowns. "They're not going to chance a military blockade of a major city, not yet." He's probably right, but Rex doesn't think any of them are going to be comfortable until they're on a damned plane over the ocean.

Well, the others might be comfortable. Rex will be busy spending time with his crash-related PTSD. Fuckers don't warn you when you join the service that PTSD comes in different colors and flavors.

From every bag they dig up, Ella claims all of the identification meant for Eric, tucking it away with her own. They all pretend not to notice, just like they pretend not to see Django doing the same with Makani's paperwork. The cash gets spread evenly around the group; everyone has enough to get on a flight and get the fuck out if they're separated. Even Neumia has a bundle of twenties tucked into her tiny backpack, along with strict rules about how it's for emergencies only.

They rebury each empty bag, which have outdated brand names that might attract attention. Ella trots her horse back and forth over each burial site to make the earth look naturally lumpy. A scatter of leaves from last fall completes the illusion of untouched ground. It won't hold up to close inspection, but the military will have to find these fucking places first.

"Sorry, no passports for strangers," Django says to Ambrus.

Ambrus rolls his eyes. "I have two stashes in Philadelphia. Even if I can only get to one box, that's two different sets of identification, along with a bit of my own rainy day money."

Ella takes the lead again. "Philadelphia is about three days' ride from here if we stick to the trails I know and avoid the highways. Takes longer than a straight shot, but it's less risk."

"Three days on a horse." Wesley wipes his still-dirty hands on his jeans before plastering them over his face as his horse follows behind Brian's. "Great."

"You're the one who wanted to fuck a horse, Wes," Brian says cheerfully.

"Whakamotitia shit, teina!"[6] Wesley growls back.

"Hey, horse riding beats dying," Brian replies, still smiling.

Neumia's eyes light up. "I didn't have to dye my hair!" she says gleefully.

---

[6] Māori: "Eat shit, brother!"

Brian smirks. "Not yet, anyway," he says, ruffling his daughter's green braids. "We'll compromise. Blonde first, then bright teal when we get overseas."

Neumia scowls. "Teal isn't green. Blonde *really* isn't green!" The last of her complaint is almost lost to a sudden, intense vibration that Rex can feel in his bones. It's followed a moment later by the harsh, echoing boom of a very large explosion.

The horses whicker nervously and stamp their feet, but Ella is actually good at her therapy job. None of their mounts try to bolt.

When Rex gets his horse turned around, he finds Ella sitting tall and proud with a broad grin on her face. "Aw, someone found my booby trap!"

Kai pulls on the reins so he can stop his horse and stare at her. "You booby-trapped your own fucking house?"

"Why not? It's not like I get to live in it anymore. Why the fuck should I let anyone else have it?" Ella counters. "And hey! House-blowing-up solidarity!"

Django smiles. "That's my girl."

"See?" Ella beams. "Dad approves."

"Am I the only person in this family who isn't a lunatic?" Kai asks plaintively.

"You *are* a lunatic, Kai. You're just suffering from baby sibling syndrome." Khodî awkwardly pats his horse, who is stamping her feet in irritation. "Please do not bite me."

Ambrus nudges his mount forward until he's alongside Khodî. "You're pulling on the reins too hard. It's pissing her off. Ease back. Don't pull unless you really want her to stop."

"Where's the reverse, then?" Khodî asks, annoyed.

Ambrus grins and nudges the horse with his knees again while lifting both reins, pulling them snug but not tight. The gelding obligingly shuffles backwards until he's following Rex's horse again.

Khodî turns in his saddle so he can glare at Ambrus. "I fucking hate you."

An hour of gentle riding later, Rex watches as Ambrus loops his stolen rope around the saddle horn and himself until he's bound in place. "Why?" Rex asks, baffled.

Ambrus turns his head and gives Rex a bloodshot stare. "So I can sleep without falling off."

Rex doesn't believe anyone can fall asleep riding a damned horse, especially over uneven, rocky ground, until he pulls even with his boyfriend five minutes later and realizes that Ambrus is fast asleep. What the actual hell.

"Is he out?" Django asks from the front of the line, where his horse is trotting nose-to-rear behind Ella's leading mount.

"Yeah," Rex answers, still baffled.

"Nari's asleep, too," Brian reports. "They're both insane."

They make camp that night near a stream that Ella confirms to be far from any known public camping areas. The horses get unsaddled, watered, fed, and spread out in a picket line around their camp. The tripwire with its tiny charm bells goes out to encircle the picket line out of horse-reach, invisible in the darkness. Kai makes a point of handing out ibuprofen like it's candy, which will save them all from becoming sore and unhappy bastards by morning.

Rex gets his idiot boyfriend to eat by shoving a self-heating MRE under his nose. Ambrus wolfs it down and then goes right to the sleeping roll he's already spread out on the ground. He passes out on it without even bothering to climb into the bag.

"More sleep will do him a hell of a lot of good," Django says while he helps Neumia lay out her own sleeping gear. "Tell me about Jasper Fox, Rex."

Rex looks up in surprise. "Dad?"

"Fuck NDAs, if that's what you're worried about." Django waits until Neumia is settled in her sleeping bag, her eyes already drifting shut. "Did Ambrus tell you that he knew that bastard for twelve years?"

"Yeah," Rex manages to say. "And why."

Django nods. "Human traffic rescue," he explains for the benefit of the others. "Ambrus probably got Fox into the program when the kid showed signs of having the potential to go through it and survive—or maybe it was Fox who insisted, but that doesn't matter.

"What *does* matter is that you need to tell us everything you know about this man," Django orders. "Right now, Fox is a threat to our survival. We'll help the poor dumb bastard if he's been suckered by the department, but our lives come first. Not his."

Rex settles down with the rest of his siblings in a semi-circle around their tiny campfire. It's enough light and heat to drive away the wildlife, and they're all well versed in building a fire so that the smoke diffuses into nothing before it can break through the evergreen canopy.

"I'm not sure anything I can say would be of much tactical use," Rex admits. "They all took those NDAs pretty damned seriously."

"Then tell us everything else," Kai says. "Anything can be a skill. Anything can be a weakness, right?" Kai ducks away when Khodî ruffles his hair. "Knock it off, asshole."

"I can be proud of you when you think like a smart soldier," Khodî replies, grinning. "Cope."

Rex thinks about it for a few minutes before he finally tells them about Jasper Fox and video games. How Fox cheats while playing them when it shouldn't even be possible. Fox and his sense of humor, and of his temper, roused only when he thinks he's losing something of great value. Fox calling Rex at two in the morning, afraid he can't do the job that Ambrus has trained him to do. That doofy kid and the absolute head-over-heels stars in his eyes whenever he looked at the agent he fell in love with.

Rex refuses to name her, just in case. Right now, Ziba is not a known threat, and he hopes it remains that way.

Then there is the obvious way that Fox cared for Ambrus. That's the part Rex still can't wrap his head around—Fox loved Ambrus. Rex can't even begin to figure out what could have been said to make someone that fucking stubborn change their mind so quickly.

The only thing Rex can tell them about the shooting is the way Fox stood on the edge of the building's floor, staring down at him. Rex couldn't see his face, and he doesn't say so, but he has a terrible feeling that there was no spark, no light, in Fox's eyes. Like the man standing there hadn't really been there at all.

"It sounds like you're describing two different people," Ella says when Rex runs out of words.

"Yeah." Rex swallows, reaching for a water bottle to rinse down trail dust and a choked feeling in the back of his throat that won't go away. "It really does."

अश्लेषा

Chapter 9

Around 5:00 that evening on the twenty-first, they ride up on a farm twenty miles outside of Philadelphia. Ella has passing relations with the owners, a couple of older women that Rex is about seventy-five percent certain are married. No matter how close they are to Philly, it's still rural Pennsylvania. These women are well-versed in never touching in public. Rex is good at doing the same; the military gave him lots of practice before Don't Ask, Don't Tell was repealed. Also, Uzbekistan—he did not get himself or Ambrus arrested.

What's really important to Ella is that they agree to babysit the horses (and Cut) for a week in exchange for several hundred dollars. By the time the women realize that they've just been bribed to take in free horses and an asshole cat, Rex and his family will be out of the country.

Another few miles of walking along the cracked old county road brings them to a much more run-down farm and its sole resident. Ambrus, Rex, and his siblings keep watch outside while Django goes into the house. Rex hopes the off-kilter building doesn't collapse from the weight of an extra person inside.

Django bribes the man who lives there to drive them all into Philadelphia inside a horse trailer. It's the only thing big enough to carry them all unless they steal another van—which would attract attention they can't afford. The trailer will also hide the group from traffic and prying eyes.

The moment Rex sees their new chauffeur, he understands why Django hired him for the job. This is one ex-farmer who is so out of his head on home-brewed meth that he won't remember any of them, let alone the trip into Philly. It'll be a miracle if the poor fucker finds his way back home afterwards.

After three days on horseback, they're all immune to the stench inside the old trailer. It's still a miserable trip spent huddled in their sleeping bags, trying to keep warm as highway speed turns cool weather into freezing wind. Bright side: Khodî is too exhausted from the long ride to get carsick.

Meth-Head leaves them in the parking lot of a boarded-up store. It's been out of business for so long that grass is growing through massive cracks in the asphalt.

"Yay, civilization!" Wesley crows tiredly once meth-head and his disaster-trailer have driven away. "I used to play ball here."

"College or pro?" Ambrus asks, but Rex thinks he's just making polite conversation. He looks dead on his feet—figuratively, at least, not literally. His boyfriend hasn't uttered a word of complaint, but three days on a horse after being shot *and* taking a header off a building can't have done him any favors at all.

"NFL, baby," Wesley answers, smiling. "Retired out before I let the game wreck my knees, unlike dumbass there."

Brian looks annoyed. "Only the one knee, surgery went great, and I still get royalty pay—well, I used to. Probably not anymore, if we've been declared fugitives while we were off the grid."

"This town sucks," Kai says in a low, dejected voice.

College, Rex mouths, when Ambrus gives him a confused look.

Ah. Ambrus nudges up against Kai. "Medical school?"

"Yeah." Kai shoves his hands into the pockets of his filthy jeans. "Perelman. Full scholarship."

"I am very, very sorry," Ambrus says in complete sincerity. Kai nods, mouth twisting up on one side in a horrible attempt at a smile.

"Let's find a motel," Ella suggests before awkward silence has the chance to descend. "We need to clean the hell up, or every federal agent in the city will know where we are by following the smell."

They find an aging motel strip about a mile down the road from the parking lot. Rex glances back and forth while they stand on the grassy hill overlooking the strip. "Don't see anyone."

"I really don't think they're searching for people who look like they've decided that homeless is the new chic," Brian says. "Besides, that motel is roach-level. Probably offers hourly rates. No one using that place is going to look twice at us, not when they're worried about getting arrested just for checking in."

Ambrus takes a breath and does that weird trick again. Most of his exhaustion falls away until he only looks disheveled and tired. "I'll go down and get us a set of rooms with connecting doors. I can make sure the office staff won't remember me. If there's a security camera inside, it won't capture my image, either."

"Neat trick," Ella says while Khodî, Brian, and Wesley stare at Ambrus like he just pulled a rabbit out of his ass. Rex refuses to be surprised, not after *glowing fingers*. "Don't take too long," she adds.

Ambrus nods and wanders down the grassy slope. He steps onto black asphalt and crosses the motel parking lot without anyone so much as glancing in his direction. Rex holds his breath until Ambrus is safely inside the office, and then finally releases it when there's no sign of an uproar.

"Once he has rooms, we're going down in groups," Django tells them. "You lot are going to wait for me or Ambrus to take you to a room."

"You can hide, too?" Khodî glares at their father. "You never taught us that!"

Django frowns. "I'm not sure I actually know how to teach it, Khodî. It was just something we sort of...figured out."

"Totally down on trying to figure it out," Ella proclaims, and Neumia nods in excited agreement. They grin at each other and high-five. Rex and Wesley trade glances, both thinking that Ella and

Neumia learning how to *hide* is probably the worst idea in the entire history of awful ideas.

Whether it's from being hidden, or because nobody gives a damn, they get a set of adjoining rooms without incident. Motels are bliss, even if they smell like mothballs came to the place to die. The bathroom sanitation is dubious, but the beds don't show signs of bedbugs and the sheets are clean.

Rex drops his dirty kit and faceplants on the bed farthest from the door without bothering to pull the covers back. "Fuck this entire week," he slurs into the bedspread.

Ambrus sits down next to Rex and nudges him. "Get back up," he says in an amused voice. "Do you want to sleep in a bed that smells the way that we do right now *after* we shower?"

Rex curses under his breath and rolls over to face the ceiling. "Our clothes smell like sweat and horse, and I bet this roach strip doesn't have a laundry room."

"Even if they did have a laundry setup, Ella's the only one of us with a change of clothes." Rex glances over to see that Khodî has mimicked Rex's faceplant onto the other bed. "Unless we do laundry in the nude, that doesn't help much."

"True." Ambrus slugs back the remains of coffee brewed so weak it looks like pale brown water. The motel staff can't even offer their guests decent fucking coffee; neither room has one of the little four-cup coffee pots endemic to the American hotel industry. Rex isn't going to complain (much), not for thirty bucks a night. He's in Philly. He can go buy a damned coffeemaker.

Django opens the connecting door to their room, glancing at Khodî and Rex before his eyes settle on Ambrus, the only one of them who didn't flop down onto a bed like a dying fish. "Plotting?"

Ambrus tosses the empty Styrofoam cup into the room's tiny trash bin. "Get me a piece of paper. There's a Target a few blocks up the street. If everyone gives me clothing sizes and preferences..." He pauses. "Clothes for how many days?"

"Clothes and luggage." Rex scrubs at his face with both hands. He was fucking Special Forces. He can tell sleep to fuck off so he can contribute to saving their asses. "Luggage tags and tourist gear. Gotta look the part."

"Clothes for about a week, then," Django says. "Rex is right. You take luggage to an airport, or you stand out like a sore thumb."

Ella pops into the room. "Are we plotting? We're plotting, I always know when we're plotting. Also, everyone already claimed the other beds, so Khodî, you're sharing with me."

Khodî shrugs without moving. "Not the first time. I don't care. Just please don't punch me in your sleep."

"Whine, whine," Ella returns cheerfully. "It's only happened like six times. If you guys are going shopping, I need to put together a makeup list. Some of you have distinctive scars that need hiding."

She disappears back into the other room while yelling at Kai to get out of the damned bathroom, it is *her turn.*

"The bathroom in here was free?" Ambrus says in puzzlement.

"That's Ella's way of claiming territory," Khodî mumbles into the bedspread.

Ambrus shakes his head and looks at Django. "Ella's right about scars. That line down your face is somewhat obvious. How the fuck did that happen?"

Rex lifts his head to look at his father, who is running his fingertip down the old scar that split his left eyebrow and created a faint, permanent line halfway down his cheek. "Never could remember if it was a knife or a bayonet that did it," Django says. "Happened when I was getting Khodî, his mother, and some of her family out of Cambodia in '76."

Ambrus glances over at Khodî. "You were born during that fucking disaster?" Khodî nods without lifting his head. "Fuck."

Khodî shrugs again, still refusing to move from his face-planted position. "Don't even remember it."

"I do," Django mutters.

Ambrus studies the expression on Django's face before turning to Rex with a too-bright smile. "Let's go shopping!"

Rex considers the merits of strangling his boyfriend. "I fucking hate shopping."

"Yes, but that means we won't linger. I'd rather take you than Ella," Ambrus says. "It should be a small group that goes, anyway, not all of us."

Django shakes off Cambodia-related memory and gives Ambrus a sharp-edged smile. "Ella doesn't like shopping, either."

"Oh, no, my opinion was less about female stereotypes and more about the fact that I think Ella would terrify everyone in the store," Ambrus replies wryly. "We're trying not to attract attention, after all."

Rex holds up his hand, raising one finger. "That is a valid point. Okay. Shopping. Why the hell not?"

Django is frowning by the time Rex convinces himself to sit up. "Take Nari with you."

"Uh—" Rex tries to process that. "Brian might kill us, Dad."

"He'll understand. Kids need toys." Django looks uncomfortable, which makes Rex blink in surprise. Django never acted weird about the Dad thing when they were kids, but then, he never actually had to explain it to them, either. "I don't trust you idiots to pick out something she'll like. Let her decide."

Neumia is thrilled to go to the store with them, which just makes Rex dread the trip even more. Brian gives him the obligatory warning about returning with his daughter alive and in one piece. Rex retorts that if they run into a problem, Nari can stab them in the crotch again.

Brian grins. "That's my girl. Euan?"

Ambrus shrugs, a bland look on his face. "If anyone tries to hurt her, Nari won't need to stab them, and Rex won't have the chance to shoot them."

Rex is about to ask, but the gleeful shark look is back on his father's face. He decides he doesn't want to fucking know.

It's another uneventful walk. Rex never feels any eyes watching them. Neither does Ambrus, if the relaxed posture of his shoulders is any indication. Neumia is content to stay between them, holding Rex's left hand so that his right hand is free to go for the 1911 if he needs it. Ambrus still has Tiny Beast tucked into the back of his twill trousers, which are now so filthy from the horse ride that Rex can't tell dirt and mud apart from the original bloodstains. Ambrus had to borrow Django's long-sleeved blue button-down to hide the gun from view, but at least they're armed.

They stop at the opposite end of the parking lot. The entrance to hell is a blazing, obnoxiously bright red bull's eye that lights up the dark sky. "You can do that clouding-the-cameras *Star Wars* shit in the store too, right?" Rex asks.

"I wouldn't have brought either of you with me if I couldn't. Stay close, though. It's got a pretty short range." Ambrus takes Rex's free hand in a gentle grip. "Remember: we're normal."

"Euan, we look like a gay couple out with their adopted kid, plus we are emanating an actual cloud of dirty horse stench. There is no 'normal' here," Rex replies.

Rex feels Ambrus's grip on his hand loosen. "Couple," Ambrus repeats, swallowing hard before he looks at Rex. "Are we? Still?"

Despite his exhaustion, Rex feels a wide, tired smile spread across his face. "Did you hear me break up with you, you stupid shit?"

Inside, it's all fluorescent lighting and far too many people for Rex's comfort when it comes to Neumia's safety. There isn't any canned music playing, but the entire front end of the store is full of green merchandise on clearance, waiting for some sucker to come along and buy it for next year's Saint Patrick's Day.

They need a full week's wardrobe of clothing for nine people. Luggage. Personal essentials in container sizes that won't piss off the TSA. Toys.

Rex grimaces at the length of the list and looks down at Neumia. "You're pushing the cart, kiddo."

"Awesome." Neumia grabs one that isn't trapped in a long cart string. "Can I hit people with it?"

Rex stares at her, trying not to grin outright. "What is Brian teaching you?" he asks, knowing full well that Brian used to ask their father the same question.

"That mean people suck and deserve to have carts rammed up their asses if they're rude," Neumia answers with a sweet smile on her face.

"Oh, shit." Ambrus puts his hand over his face and starts laughing so hard that he sounds like he's about to hyperventilate.

Rex, caught between Neumia's glee and Ambrus's lapse into hysteria, gets stealthed by an employee who is suddenly standing at his elbow.

"Y'all look like you need help," she says while Rex tries to convince his pulse rate that everything is normal. Her nametag reads Mary; she looks like someone's grandmother, with the thick, matronly build a lot of Pennsylvania farmwives seem to consider mandatory.

"We probably do," Rex answers, since Ambrus hasn't stopped giggling. "I hate shopping."

There is a brief flash of disapproval in Mary's gray eyes. "Well, I'd say y'all need Jesus, too, but the girl looks happy and healthy, so it can't be all that bad."

Oh, hell no. Rex is not going to put up with this fucking store, the fucking shopping list from hell, *and* a judgmental employee. "I'm her uncle. Her father's busy, and her mother's on an airplane, probably out over an ocean right now."

"Oh, it's that sort of thing." Mary suddenly seems a hell of a lot more sympathetic. "What do y'all need?"

Ambrus wipes his eyes with the collar of his t-shirt, which doesn't accomplish much more than leaving a dirty streak across his cheeks. "Clothing for nine people, about a week's worth. We were out camping, one of those extended group trips on horseback. Did you hear about that flash flood two days ago?"

"Oh, my." Mary presses her hand to her ample breast. "That was you all?"

"One of the groups, yes," Ambrus says, while Rex stares at him in utter bafflement. *What* flash flood? None of them have seen the news in days!

"We're in town for a few more days while we arrange for airline flights to go back home," Ambrus continues, lying so smoothly even Rex can't tell the difference. "God, the idea of replacing even just socks and underwear for nine people..."

"Yes, you'll definitely need help," Mary interrupts in a staunch voice. She grabs another shopping cart and gives Neumia a pat on the head. Neumia tolerates it, even though she gives Mary the scrunched-up look of a kid who is torn between politeness and biting. "Let's go. We are going to shop like professionals!"

Mary is true to her word, and absolutely fucking terrifying. She conscripts two other employees to help, one who runs off long enough to make copies of the clothing and supply lists. Then Mary puts everyone to work. The trip from hell is done in two hours, including Neumia's horrific walk through the toy aisles.

Rex is pretty sure that the glaze of the damned is clouding his eyes at that point. He doesn't miss being a kid, not at all. Also, he wants a vasectomy *yesterday*, and he's fucking gay!

On the way to check out, Rex makes no apologies about grabbing two full-sized coffeemakers, filters, and about five pounds' worth of Hawaiian-grown coffee as they pass small appliances and the grocery section. They're all going through caffeine withdrawal. Rex refuses to suffer anymore when there's a fucking solution at hand.

When they get to the register with two carts loaded to the point of overflowing, there really is a glaze of exhaustion in Ambrus's eyes. Ambrus stares at the numbers popping up on the screen as items are scanned, looks down at the cash in his hand, and shoves it all at Rex.

"Hey, Starbucks, you are shiny," Ambrus mutters, leaving Rex standing at the register with a pushy farmwife, all of their stuff, and Neumia—at least until Neumia scampers off to follow Ambrus, cuddling a stuffed teal dragon with purple accents.

"Uh, she has to uhm—pay for that?" the poor kid at the register ventures. If the boy is older than sixteen, Rex might honestly consider eating his shoes, and he knows where they've been for the past few days.

"Just ring it up as an item for $14.99. That's what's on the tag," Mary orders the kid. "Get these people packed up, Matthew. They need to be on their way."

"What the hell was that?" Rex asks Ambrus when he finally gets their shit paid for and meets Ambrus by the exit. His boyfriend doesn't answer, his face still buried in a coffee cup that smells like fragrant heaven. "Fine. Don't tell me."

Rex lifts up his niece and puts Neumia on top of the pile of bags in one cart for the ride back to the motel. He doesn't mind pushing both carts as long as they get to leave. All Rex wants is to be out of this store, out of horse-clothes, into a shower, and then into a bed with his face shoved against the pillow.

Ambrus earns a hell of a lot of points back by thrusting a sealed coffee cup at Rex once he has Neumia settled. Taking the other shopping cart to push evens the score. "Sorry," he finally explains. "I was getting so damned tired that I couldn't remember what numbers were. I didn't want to take the chance that I'd lose the ability to hide us."

"Okay." Saving their asses definitely trumps Rex's loathing of being left alone with shopping and carts and Terrifying Mary. He chugs down half of his coffee before he turns the cart and starts pushing it across the parking lot, following Ambrus. Neumia is starting to droop, but it still doesn't stop her from chortling over each bump the cart finds. "What flash flood, by the way?"

"You mean the one that I made up and pushed Mary into believing she'd seen footage of on television?"

Rex feels a chill climb his spine that has nothing to do with premonitions. The words were lightly spoken, but he'd have to be truly deaf not to hear the bitterness in Ambrus's voice. "Yeah. That would be the one. What the hell was your job, Ambrus?"

"Fucking terrible. There's a reason why your father made sure to get transferred out."

Rex glances down to check on Neumia, who is folding and unfolding the wings on her new dragon. "Then why the hell did you do it?"

Ambrus tosses his empty coffee cup into an open red-painted garbage bin as they hit the border of the parking lot. "For a long time, I thought I was doing the right thing."

Rex copies Ambrus's act with his own empty cup. He can't argue with that statement, not when he'd gone into Afghanistan with the same stupid mindset.

*   *   *   *

Rex was a military officer in SF for eight years, and spent most of that time far away from anything resembling modern conveniences. He must be spoiled rotten now, because *showers*. Hot water, soap, and showers are now his favorite things forever.

Fuck horses. He never wants to see another horse ever again.

One of the roach motel room's only positives aside from clean beds is that the designer was sensible enough to realize that not only should the toilet and shower be behind a closed door, but so should the sink area. Whoever popularized the lack of privacy for that part of a bathroom in American hotels was a thoughtless bastard.

The steam that escapes the shower fogs up the mirror. Rex grabs a coarse white towel and wipes it clear again, grimacing at his reflection. He's been living rough and definitely looks it. His beard and eyebrows grow in a much darker blond, and he needs to shave like nobody's business.

It's his bright blond hair that's the most distinctive, a trait easy to spot in a crowd. When Rex shaves off several days' worth of beard bristle, his hair is the razor's next victim. When he's rinsed off and toweled dry, it's like he's staring into a mirror at Basic all over again.

Bald wasn't Basic standard, but the first racist asshole with rank that Rex met during training had noticed his hair, the slant to his eyes, and immediately said unforgivable things about Rex's parents. Senior staff had been semi-lenient with him when they learned why Rex used his fist to remove four teeth from that asshole's head, but afterwards, it had been easier to keep his head shaved in an attempt to avoid necessary repeat performances. He also didn't need to rack up a record collection of demerits in the first week. Dad was the record holder for that, and Rex had been happy to let it stand.

Ella's the one who ultimately broke it, much to everyone's chagrined pride. Eric promised he would make certain that Ella would (finally) learn to be more subtle after that, but by subtle he had apparently meant blackmail. By then, none of them cared, because at least it *worked.*

Rex slips on a pair of loose cotton shorts to sleep in and exits the bathroom. Ambrus is curled up under the covers on their claimed bed, back facing the wall and sound asleep. Rex takes a moment to be exceptionally envious, but he was the one to volunteer for Dumpster duty, taking everyone's travel-stained clothes out to the overflowing container behind the roach strip. It also means he showered last, but that's where planning came in— Rex got to stay in the water as long as he wanted.

In the other bed, Ella is lying flat on her back, emitting a faint snore. Khodî is still sitting up, reading a dog-eared Dean Koontz novel he found in the room's shabby nightstand. The connecting door for the room is open, revealing the flickering light from a television dancing along the far wall.

Rex takes a quick glance inside, curious. Brian and Wesley are asleep in one bed with Neumia curled up between them. Kai and Django are sharing the other. Kai has trouble sleeping in strange places, so he and Django are both still awake, staring at the muted television.

"Anything interesting?" Rex asks in a low voice.

Kai shakes his head. His eyes have that low-angled tilt that says he'll be asleep in another five minutes from sheer, horse-created exhaustion.

"Nothing on the news that I could pick out," Django murmurs. "No closed captioning, and local channels only, so I can't hit CNN. This movie sucks, too."

Rex leans inside the room long enough to see that some network is playing a severely edited version of the second recent *Punisher* movie. "First one's better," he comments. "Night."

"G'night," Kai mumbles. Their father just nods, still giving the film in question a sour look.

Rex pulls the sheet back on his side of the bed. "Those books are awful," he tells Khodî.

"It's something to read. Too wound up to sleep, and one of us in each room has to keep watch, anyway," Khodî replies, turning a page with his thumb. "No fucking, by the way."

Rex crawls into bed before subjecting his older brother to the most indignant glare he can muster. "I don't know what superpower you inherited, but some of us do not get it up well when we are completely damned *exhausted.*"

Khodî grins. "I'll never tell."

"Read your fucking stupid book," Rex grumps, pulling the sheet over his head to block out the lamp light before pressing his face against the pillow, determined to pass out. Ella can have second watch. He refuses; he suffered enough by going into that damned store on everyone else's behalf.

Rex wakes up to the feel of fingertips stroking his head. He cracks his eyes open, ready to complain, when he realizes that it's Ambrus. His boyfriend is giving him a half-smile of contentment, one just touched by grief.

"Too distinctive," Rex mutters about his lack of hair. He's pretty sure that isn't what the grief is for, but it's too early for thinking. Rex feels like he blinked and missed out on sleep entirely.

"Good morning to you, too," Ambrus replies, leaning over to deliver a dry kiss to Rex's lips. "I made coffee."

"I love you, where is the coffee," Rex slurs, which chases the sadness out of Ambrus's smile.

"Sit up first, or you'll just pour it on your own head." Ambrus gets up so he can cross the room and deal with the store-purchased coffee machine. He's unwrapping a tiny Styrofoam cup when Rex remembers that he didn't buy anything to put the coffee *in*. Kai's college example aside, drinking from the carafe is still rude.

His boyfriend is also fully dressed, including shoes. Sunlight is filtering into the room around the blackout curtain. "What fucking time is it?"

"Seven." Ambrus brings him straight black coffee that is nothing like the pale sludge water the office staff brews for customers. "I woke up about an hour ago and couldn't get back to sleep. Went out and stole a laptop."

Rex stares at Ambrus, blinking a few times. "I know you're saying words, but they make no fucking sense. Please repeat them after I have at least three of these stupidly tiny cups of coffee."

"Okay." Ambrus reaches over Rex to pick up another Styrofoam cup sitting on the nightstand, taking a brief sip. "We forgot sugar, but the motel office now lacks their supply, so that problem solved itself. Ella, however, has not stopped swearing at me for forgetting the creamer."

"Creamer, asshole," Ella mutters to prove the point. "Who the fuck forgets fucking creamer?"

"People who don't use it," Rex replies, trying not to guzzle fresh coffee like it's a lifeline. Probably fails at it; does not care.

Rex gets dressed while drinking his second cup, slipping on new boots and regretting the lack of comfort. It takes a while to break in a decent pair, and they don't have that kind of time.

Ella dressed in the bathroom while Rex was still trying to get enough caffeine into his system to be functional. Khodî wakes up and glares at everyone in murderous displeasure until Ella rolls her eyes and gives him coffee.

Rex sits down on the end of the bed, cradling his third cup of coffee. Stupid Styrofoam and their stupid small cup sizes. "Okay. You stole what from where, now?"

Ambrus is sitting in the room's only chair with his booted feet propped up on the end of the bed. "I'd rather go into an airport with plane tickets already purchased. Thus, laptop."

Brian slips into the room and pulls the connecting door almost shut. "Everyone else is still sleeping. Might as well give them the extra ten minutes," he explains, and then his eyes alight on the laptop that has taken over the wobbly table by the window. "Hey, where'd you get that?"

"Stole it from a big-box electronic store," Ambrus says, and Brian's jaw falls open in early-morning disappointment. "It was nearby, easy to break into from the back, and has enough stock on-hand that the theft won't be noticed for a while. The miraculous part of the morning is discovering that the roach strip has free, *secured* Wi-Fi."

"Aw, yeah." Ella grins and makes grabby hands in the direction of the laptop. Ambrus smiles and passes it over. "That'll make things a hell of a lot easier. All I need is everyone's final choice on which ID sets they're going to use, and I can get us the fuck out of here."

"Which does mean I have to wait until a certain bank is open," Ambrus says. "I'll take a cab, and that gets me two sets of documents. The other documents are..." He trails off, frowning. "Compromised. I don't know how, just that they are."

"Then you're definitely not going alone," Rex insists. "Seriously, no. That would be stupid. Brian?"

Brian nods. "Sure, I'll go. Wesley might be recognized if he goes wandering around in public. I played in New York, and I can shave off the goatee and tie my hair back. I'm way less recognizable that way, even if I run into the worst NFL fanatic the city has to offer."

"We need to split up the group, too," Rex tells Ella. "We buy nine tickets at once for the same flight and destination, that's going to send up a flag."

"Ranger, baby," Ella retorts in reminder. "The only problem left is a valid credit card. Laptops don't take cash, and credit card generators on the 'net got cracked down on so hard that most of them are run by the feds. All they catch are dumb kids who want to watch porn, but it's a job, I guess."

Ambrus pulls out his wallet and flips it open. "I have one. The man it belongs to won't notice the charges until they do accounting at the end of the month."

Brian's eyes bug out comically when Ambrus hands the credit card to Ella. "Is that a black fucking American Express card?"

"Like I said: they won't notice," Ambrus returns dryly.

Khodî stares at the card that Ella is gleefully holding in both hands. "Where the fuck did you get that?"

"I might have stolen it from a South American drug lord, or he might have given it to me because he owes me a very large favor,"

Ambrus replies. "No matter which option you pick, the results will be the same."

"Don't even want to know," Khodî mutters under his breath, which is the option Rex is going with, too. Brian looks like he's afraid to ask, but Ella doesn't give a fuck where it came from, just that it exists and she gets to steal from it.

"Then I guess we need to make one more decision. Are we going to stay here for a while and try to recover from three damned days of horses?" Khodî asks. "Or do we leave today?"

"Today," Django says as he pushes open the connecting door. He's found coffee but not clothes, and is still wearing last night's t-shirt and shorts. "This afternoon—the earlier, the better."

Khodî sighs. "Okay," he agrees, but he doesn't look happy about it. "Today."

Ella looks up from the laptop parked in her lap. "We still sure about flying out of Philly International?"

"It's a huge, sprawling disaster that's hard to monitor, even after 9/11 and the fucking Patriot Act," Django says. "The DoD is more likely to monitor private charters, anyway."

"Fewer flights," Ambrus says.

Django nods. "Public flights give us more anonymity. It's harder to shuffle through thousands of people to find someone, especially if we fly international."

"The skin tones start to turn in our favor," Brian says.

"Fuck, at least something should," Khodî snaps, and then sighs again. "Shit. Excuse me. I'm going to go shower off Morning Asshole Syndrome."

"At least the TSA sucks at their job," Ella says, her eyes on the laptop screen again. "So many weapons smuggled through."

Ambrus grins at her. "It's even more fun when it's a complete accident."

"Yeah, but we go in assuming their best are on duty, not their worst," Django says, frowning. "We can't give these assholes any reason to look twice."

Rex almost wants to get the 1911 out from under his pillow and hug it. "That means all the guns stay behind. We can't check them without risking attention."

"Exactly." Django hesitates. "I'd almost tell you lot not to check your bags at all, but that also doesn't look right, especially with the travel bags we all have for the plane ride."

Ella whistles, both of her eyebrows climbing as she does so. "Wow, Dad. You are so damned good. There's a huge concentration of flights out of PHL this afternoon with connections to Ho Chi Minh. I can get us in split groups onto flights that have their first layovers outside the US. Even if something goes wrong at that point, we're already out of the country."

"Good. Make sure you're getting us onto land masses, though, not islands," Django says. "Trust me, it is really not all that fun to swim your way to safety when safety is at least thirty miles away."

"Why Vietnam?" Ambrus asks, giving Rex's father an odd look.

"Familiar territory." Django sips at the coffee clenched in his hand. "And I have contacts in the area that will happily resupply us on weapons, no questions asked. I'll be calling that request in from the first airport layover after I steal some poor bastard's phone."

Kai appears in the connecting doorway with the bleary-eyed expression of someone who feels like they were recently run over. "Kai, coffee, in the pot, on the counter," Brian instructs. Kai grunts in angry dismay before turning around and disappearing back into the other room.

Brian winces and glances at Rex. "Please tell me you remembered to buy tea."

"Shit," Rex says. "Wesley is going to kill us all."

"He's going to be too busy packing to kill anyone," Django counters. "Besides, I'm taking grumpy youngest down to a diner to get breakfast for all of us. Diners have tea bags. He'll cope."

Ella closes the laptop lid and gazes at their father in complete adoration. "Please buy them out of every single bit of bacon they have."

Django shakes his head and smiles. "Fine. Does anyone else have any requests?"

"Wesley's tea, and chocolate chip pancakes for Nari so that she'll eat them instead of whining about them," Brian says at once. "Also, all the food they have. If we're packing up and getting on a long plane ride today, I'd like to survive it without possibly eating a passenger out of desperation."

Khodî is dressed when he comes out of the bathroom, scrubbing at his wet hair with a towel when he hears Brian's plaintive threat. "Don't do that, man," he says, grinning. "You never know where some of those motherfuckers have been!"

Brian and Ambrus get back from the bank run with Ambrus smiling his success, bearing two different sets of documentation and a thousand dollars in fifties. "Lies," Brian announces once the door is closed behind them. "That wasn't a bank at all. It was the gym *next* to the bank."

"They both have secure locking boxes and they open their front doors at the same time. Close enough," Ambrus counters, giving Tiny Beast a look of pure resignation before he puts it into the motel garbage bin with the other weapons and ammunition. Rex is going to take it out back to the roach strip's Dumpster, which is due to be hit that afternoon by weekly service. If anyone backtracks them to the hotel, the evidence in that stinking bin will be long gone.

Ambrus flips open both passports, eyes flickering over details, before he chooses one to give to Ella. "That one will be safe. I'm not sure about the other, so I'll save it for less fraught circumstances."

"Got it." Ella's eyes track over the passport as she memorizes the information. "Brown hair, not ginger," she says, glancing at Ambrus's dark hair and its theft of a dye job. "Bonus time-saver. Who the fuck is Eugene Amber?"

Ambrus scowls. "Please read it again so that I can actually get on a fucking plane later today."

Ella rears back, nose wrinkling up, before she looks at the passport again. "Eugenes? What the fuck kind of name is that?"

"*Yew-zehn-ess*," Ambrus corrects her, eyes narrowed. "It's Greek. Most likely precursor to Éoghan."

Khodî pauses in the middle of hanging the clothes he'll wear on the plane. "Wait. Your name's Eugene?"

"No!" Ambrus snaps, and then puts his hand over his eyes, lowering his head. "It means *gentle*," he says, which is when Khodî, Ella, Brian, and Wesley start howling with laughter.

"And that's why I stuck with Euan," Ambrus tells Rex, his hand still over his face.

"Yeah, *born of a yew tree* does seem less, uh..." Rex bites his lip in something approaching desperation as he tries not to laugh. "Why'd you go with Eugenes Amber, then?"

Ambrus blows out a long breath. "Gentle Amber was my father's nickname."

"Your father," Rex repeats. Khodî, Wesley, Brian, and Ella stop giggling like lunatics as they catch the significance. Rex and his siblings are all assholes, but they're not insensitive bastards. "The man whose name meant 'Shadowy might of the divine battle' was nicknamed *Gentle Amber*?"

Ambrus shrugs. "Yeah."

"Scots are fucking weird," Brian declares.

"*Bite mo asail[1],*" Ambrus replies, a fierce smile on his face that looks like it could melt steel.

"What's that mean?" Neumia asks curiously, wandering into the room.

"I'll tell you in about six years," Ambrus promises her. "What happened to the cartoons?"

"I've seen that one Road Runner cartoon like, a zillion times."

Django and Kai return loaded down with breakfast. A multitude of white, grease-stained paper bags are crammed into four different plastic bags. It's a merciless feast with no survivors. Eating a meal with enough calories to put a cow into a coma makes them all far more cheerful about the fact that they're going to risk potential death just to get on a damned airplane.

---

[1] Scots Gaelic: "Bite my ass."

They're ready to go by one in the afternoon, three hours ahead of the first flight. Cabs are on the way to collect them, spaced about five minutes apart. Rex hates how they're dividing their forces, but it is, again, the best bad choice out of so many other worse ideas.

Either way, Rex can't delay any longer. He slips into a jacket that still smells more like preservative spray than leather before putting on a pair of oversized, amber-tinted aviator shades. "Well?"

Khodî laughs at him. "You look like a Navy man on leave, trying to figure out where Philadelphia keeps its hookers."

"Then I win points for getting exactly what I was going for," Rex says, "except for that 'hookers' part." The infamous rivalry between Navy, Army, and Air Force often means that there is an automatic overlook that happens if MPs are searching for one but think they've found the other. It came in handy a lot when Rex was still active military. He avoided the MPs searching for AWOL soldiers so many times by pretending to be in a different branch of service. Rex has learned since then that DoD agents often have the same mindset. Stupid of them, but right now it works in his family's favor.

Khodî puts on his beige suit coat and leaves it unbuttoned. The slightly darker dress shirt underneath is a quiet complement to both jacket and tie. One of Mary's assistants had a damned good eye for subtle color and detail.

Ella has already worked her magic with makeup and smudging sponges and voodoo. Khodî's scar on the right side of his face is reduced to a few faint lines that radiate outward from a now-invisible impact point at his temple.

"Monkey suit," Khodî grumbles, unfolding a pair of black-framed reading glasses from the pharmacy rack, the lowest magnification level the store had. He'll get a headache from wearing them, but they won't fuck up his vision.

Between the suit and the makeup job, Khodî looks utterly unlike himself. If Rex hadn't watched the process, he wouldn't recognize his own brother if he passed Khodî on the street.

When Khodî steps away to go put on steel-toed dress shoes that match his coat and pants, Rex takes a second look in the mirror. Ella and her voodoo sponges made the scar that climbed his chin vanish. Then she darkened Rex's eyebrows and eyelashes with a waterproof mascara that won't come off without make-up remover (or maybe a blowtorch) and somehow managed to alter the Chinese slant of his eyes to look less Asian and more Māori, which is actually kind of cool.

"Budge over," Ambrus says, walking up next to Rex and hip-checking him for sink space. He has the razor and tiny can of shaving cream from his travel kit.

"Already?" Rex asks, bemused. He knows his boyfriend shaved this morning.

"Grows in fast, and I can't exactly dye bristle," Ambrus points out. "I'll probably have to do this twice a day on the plane. I already had to borrow one of Ella's mascara tubes for my eyebrows."

"The fuck for?" Rex asks.

Ambrus smiles at him. "Same reason I didn't dye the beard. Facial hair grows out faster, and the red will be noticed sooner. Not taking that chance, even if I really, really loathe the feel of this stuff."

"Same," Rex agrees, lifting his eyebrows, which seem too heavy from the mascara coating. "Are you going to be okay for this? Truly?"

"Sleep is a wondrous thing," Ambrus says, lifting his shirt. There are two bright red marks over his left lung where Rex knows two bullets took temporary residence only four days ago. "Kai pulled the stitches for me a few hours ago. Everything's still a bit stiff, but I can handle a plane ride, Rex."

Rex touches the red scarring with his fingers. "Is this the same thing that you did for me? Speed-healing?"

Ambrus shakes his head. For an instant, a look of intense regret crosses his face, and then it's gone again. "No, uh—for other people, I have to concentrate. I have to *want* it," he emphasizes. "For those of us who went through the program...it happens naturally. You already know this. I can see it on your face."

"Yeah," Rex admits, as Ambrus pulls his shirt back down to cover the scarring. "We all—we all heal fast."

"And I'm very glad you do. I don't think you'd be alive right now otherwise," Ambrus whispers.

"You are dating a tough bastard," Rex says, leaning in to kiss his boyfriend. "I mean that literally, by the way."

Ambrus smiles against his lips. "I'm aware."

Rex kisses his boyfriend again and leaves him to shave off afternoon beard bristle. He's just now realizing that he's going to have to raid a plane bathroom to do the same thing, probably more than once. His Norwegian-gifted blond is as distinctive as Ambrus's fiery red.

They congregate in a single motel room, sitting on chairs or beds while waiting for cab number one to turn up. Brian went white collar for the trip, like Khodî, but with his hair slicked back he looks like he works for the mob. People are probably going to give him a wide berth without Brian needing to do a damned thing.

Ella has a ritz-hippie thing going. She's tamed her curly hair so that it lies in smooth brown strands almost to her shoulders. Between the pink-tinted round-rim glasses on her face, bohemian skirt, and high heels, she also looks *very* unlike herself. Ella the Ranger eschewed most of those things except for skirts. Her reasoning was that you could always hide things under skirts without anyone being the wiser—especially if they were guns.

"Thigh holders chafe," Ella admitted once. "But damn, the look on that asshole's face when I lifted my skirt and then shoved a gun into the side of his nose. Fucking priceless."

Kai, like Mom used to be, is very good at looking hapless and harmless. He's dressed in the kind of clothes Rex would find on a first-year college student, complete with a cheap-looking backpack as his bag for the flight. Kai already has his game-face on, wide-eyed and innocent, like a recently graduated high school student who is still trying to figure out how college works.

Wesley bitched about it the entire time, but he shaved his head and let Ella use a facial bleach on his eyebrows until they were bright blond instead of black. With the polo shirt, too-crisp jeans, rimless square glasses, and white sneakers, Wesley looks like a hapless suburban dad who is still figuring out Parenting—perfect, since he's traveling with Neumia.

Neumia complained about undoing her braids and stripping the green dye out of her hair with a conditioner-and-bleach combination until Django held up two sealed containers of Manic Panic, a bright teal that will dye Neumia's hair the same color as her new favorite dragon. Problem solved. Neumia grudgingly agrees to leave her curly blonde hair unbound, which makes her a closer match to Wesley's altered appearance. Except for her much darker skin, it also makes Neumia look a *lot* like her mother.

Ambrus is wearing jeans instead of twill, a maroon t-shirt, a navy blue sport coat that should clash but doesn't, and has a matching maroon scarf around his neck. Khodî already cracked an obligatory joke about Ambrus flying casual, which Ambrus refused to acknowledge. Ella trimmed his hair so it looks more like it was cut by a professional, not by an exhausted train wreck of a human being wielding dull scissors.

Rex's dad dressed in a t-shirt and slacks, and looks the most normal out of the entire group—which is funny as hell because Django is the least normal person Rex knows outside of Ambrus. Ella's makeup made Django's scar vanish, filling in the gap in his eyebrow where the scar cuts through and hiding the faint white line that marks his skin above and below. It's not a perfect job, but unless Rex gets really close, the dark mascara isn't noticeable at all. She also did something weird to his father's cheekbones that cause them to stand out in stark relief, an effect that makes his face seem longer and narrower.

Django is leaning against the wall, watching for traffic at the edge of the closed blinds. "First cab is here," he announces. "You're up."

Ambrus squeezes Rex's hand and stands, putting on a cross-body travel bag and grabbing the handle for his carry-on. "Ready to go, darling?" he asks Ella.

It's not the question that weirds Rex out. It's the utterly neutral American accent his boyfriend suddenly picked up.

Ella ignores the accent swap and bats her eyelashes at Ambrus, answering him in a Midwestern twang that makes Rex's head hurt. "Oh, sweetie, must we rush? I just *love* Philly."

"That's weird as hell," Kai says.

Ambrus puts on a pair of mirrored sunglasses and grins. "Django, scare the shit out of them."

Django chuckles and says, "You are so full of shit. Please leave," in *perfect Oxford.*

Rex feels his face twist up in horror, which is a match for everyone else's expressions. "Never do that again!" Brian orders, glaring at their father. "That was fucked up!"

Django grins. "No, that was fun," he says in his normal voice. "We'll see you in Ho Chi Minh."

"How's your Vietnamese?" Ambrus asks Ella as they leave.

"*Hút bóng của tôi,*"[2] Ella replies sweetly.

"Oi, fuck you, too!" Ambrus glances back, just once, as they load their bags into the back of the cab. Rex lifts his chin, but doesn't give any other sign that he noticed. The second cab is already pulling up, which means it's time to go.

Django nudges Rex with his shoulder. "Come on. We haven't flown together in a long time."

"That's because the last time someone let you fly a plane, you crashed it," Rex replies, grabbing his bag. He follows his father out of the dim hotel room and into bright sunlight that the amber aviators barely compensate for.

Rex puts his bag into the trunk, refusing to think about Ambrus and Ella, Khodî and Brian, Wesley and Neumia, or Kai, who will be flying solo and is doing a damned fine job of not freaking out about it. It's not Kai's first time running through TSA security with a fake passport, but those were always practice runs. The only real danger would have come from overenthusiastic TSA agents, not armed federal agents from the DoD.

Rex sits down in the taxi and tries not to clench his jaw as most of the group variables spiral out of his immediate control.

Everyone is going to be fine. If he repeats that enough, he might even start to believe it.

*   *   *   *

"Everyone's through security," Rex reports in a low voice. "Kai is already on his way to the gate." If the department or the DoD comes down on them, they all want the sibling with the least military training out of the country first. The others can more or less take on a small army by themselves. Hell, Rex recently made a point of demonstrating that skill.

---

[2] Vietnamese: "Suck my balls."

Django nods, wandering along the magazine racks in the airport bookstore. "Good to hear."

"What's our flight time?" Rex asks, trying to make conversation. He's seen at least three different federal agents in the airport so far, but they haven't given either of them a second glance. Rex thinks he might even have worked with one of those assholes a few years back. Either the man has gotten really unobservant, or is focused on blond, South Pacific mutant blend.

Stupid fucker, Rex thinks, just as irritated as he is pleased by his ex-compatriot's blind eye. *Please continue to be stupid.*

Rex suspects that Django is also using that weird don't-notice-me trick to make certain that DoD agents ignore him. His father worked for the military too long. Aside from Ambrus, Django is the most likely to be recognized, even with Ella's magic makeup job.

"Just over thirty hours, not counting gate time and layovers," his father answers, picking up a local newspaper to read. "How's your Vietnamese, Rex?"

Rex has to mentally shift gears to answer. *"Uh, chuyến bay dài như thế nào là?"*[3]

Django looks up from the paper and stares at him in disapproval. *"Im đi, và không nói chuyện với Hải quan."*[4]

Rex sighs. He has no idea how he fucked up that sentence, but it must have been spectacular. "Fine." He turns around to choose books for the flight, not willing to spend thirty damned hours twiddling his thumbs.

Ugh, Anne Rice—no, wait, classic Anne Rice. That will pass a plane ride. The movie version of *Interview with the Vampire* gave Rex his first clue that maybe girlfriends weren't in his future. He'd picked up *The Vampire Lestat* in his senior year of high school, but never got around to reading *Queen of the Damned* afterwards. Ella told him that it sucked the least of all the sequels, and she's extremely picky about her reading material. He grabs a copy of that as well as another sequel called *Pandora*. Rex shrugs and decides to give it a try.

He finds two more books that look interesting, or at least appalling enough to keep his attention, since he doesn't plan to sleep. After two military plane crashes and one bush plane crash because of Django, Rex is wondering how many tiny bottles of booze he can buy with the cash he has in his pocket.

He's about to ask his father for an extra twenty when he sees the headline on the newspaper Django is reading. A flash flood happened in upstate Pennsylvania, trapping a group of trail riders. Photos included, which is fucking creepy.

---

[3] Vietnamese: "Uh, how long flight was?"
[4] Vietnamese: "Shut up, and do not talk to customs."

"Euan mentioned that," Rex explains, when Django realizes Rex is staring at the paper and lowers it to find out why. "The headline."

"Did he." Django's expression goes utterly neutral, the way it usually does when he would prefer to ignore the subject at hand. "When was that?"

"Shopping trip," Rex says. "Last night. Ambrus said it happened two days before that."

"Huh." Django hesitates before he folds the paper and then holds it out for Rex to see, his thumb resting right below a paragraph on the top half of the front page. The date and time of the event is mentioned in the first two sentences.

The flood happened while they were setting up camp with the horses the night before arriving in Philadelphia, around eight in the evening. Not three days ago.

Rex frowns. They were already deeply involved in the mad shopping spree at eight o'clock. "What the hell does that mean?"

"It means that maybe...maybe I finally have confirmation on something." Django refolds the newspaper with perfect lines and puts it back on the rack. "Or maybe it's a coincidence."

Coincidence, his entire ass. "Spill," Rex says in a firm voice. It's not like they have anything else to talk about right now that doesn't revolve around paranoia.

"I didn't just leave the program because Kaia died." Django is still looking at the photos on the newspaper front, taken after the flash flood chaos. No deaths reported that Rex can see, but it was still a hell of a mess. "That only helped me make up my mind."

"Why?"

"There was an op about two weeks before the funeral," Django says, his brow furrowing. "Had to be completed at a specific time, but there were a hell of a lot of military types in the way. We needed a distraction. I went in posing as a senior official of that military group and told their CO a severe earthquake had just struck Afghanistan. Hundreds were confirmed dead; the country was calling in political and military favors for help in rescuing possible survivors."

Rex's skin crawls for a brief moment, but it's not a warning this time—just an echo. "There really was an earthquake."

Django shoves his hands into his trouser pockets. "Yeah, a pretty bad one. Four hundred people died."

"Okay, so you predicted an earthquake," Rex says, but Django shakes his head.

"That's not it. The dates—you couldn't get times down to the wire like you can today, or even like you could in fucking Vietnam. It was 1956, Rex. We could never confirm if the earthquake happened before or *after* I said that it did. The timing was too close."

Django gives Rex a worn, tired look full of guilt, one Rex is intimately familiar with from the number of times he's stared into a mirror and found that guilt glaring back at him. "We didn't know if I predicted it or if I caused it. That kind of potential, that possibility—that isn't the same thing as shooting someone in defense of your country. Those were innocent people. That's not shit I was prepared to deal with."

"What did Euan say?" Rex knows there has to have been a conversation about it. Ambrus wouldn't have let Django walk away with that much guilt riding his shoulders.

Django shakes his head. "He tried to tell me that it wasn't my fault, that even if I did cause it? We didn't know it was something we were even fucking capable of doing. It would simply have to be the warning we heeded from then on out, that we would have to be very careful of our words.

"He was still young enough to bounce back, but I wasn't. Not anymore." There is a hint of a smile on Django's face. "I told Euan to take that lesson to heart, but I wasn't taking a chance on repeating it. I was out. He didn't like it, but when I left the program, he's the one who escorted me back to the farmhouse."

The words leave such a vivid impression that Rex can almost see it in his head. "I'm with Euan, Dad. I don't think it was your fault—not if you didn't know."

"The first year of the program, I destroyed a radio tower just by thinking about it." Django's smile turns grim and terrible. "That's what should have been our warning, Rex. Not a fucking earthquake."

"Yeah. Yeah, I get that." Rex glances at his father again. "How the fuck did you destroy a radio tower?" he asks.

The PA speaker above them comes alive to announce that boarding is beginning at Gate D2. Django grins. "That's us, kid. Time to go."

Rex shakes his head and goes to pay for his books. "Our flight lasts hours. I bet I'll get an answer out of you eventually."

"No, you won't," Django replies as the PA crackles to announce boarding at Gates D8, A5, and E16.

Rex smiles at Django's stubborn tone. "We'll see."

*   *   *   *

Rex really, really does try, but his father wins that bet. Dammit.

*   *   *   *

Going through customs in Ho Chi Minh City sucks, mostly because Rex is into hour thirty-eight without sleep. He still feels half-hungover from Smirnoff that tasted like it had lived in the bottom of a cabinet for sixty years. Booze on the plane had not helped him sleep. At all.

Rex rubs his eyes and looks at his watch for the fourth time in five minutes, hoping this time the date and time will stick. It's the twenty-fourth of March, and it's 4:15 in the fucking morning.

Thursday, he reminds himself. *It is fucking Thursday. Just because you were drunk for part of it doesn't make it not-Thursday.*

Oh god, he's tired. Rex is so damned glad that the customs line he's in is moving along at a good pace. He's already next in line, and walks forward the moment the woman in front of him picks up her bag and steps aside.

The agent in the glassed-in booth smiles at him, her lips painted a dark maroon that reminds Rex, of all things, of his stupid date-night shirt. *"Doanh nghiệp của bạn tại Việt Nam là gì?"*[5]

"Killing everyone that gets between me and the first decent cup of coffee I find," Rex answers with way more honesty than is called for. Then he cracks his jaw yawning.

She laughs and slides his passport back over with the ink still glistening from the fresh stamp. "If you find a decent cup of coffee in this city, bring me one. Welcome to Vietnam," she says in English, and then waves the next man in line forward.

"What the hell did you say to her?" Django asks when Rex catches up to him. He's scratching at the bristle on his jaw, violet crescents starting to show beneath his eyes. Rex strongly suspects that his father didn't sleep, either, but not for lack of trying.

"I told her that I'd kill someone for a cup of coffee."

"Fuck, me too," Django admits. "Let's go see if Starbucks has continued its Borg-like conquest, huh?"

They find Kai already standing under a green sign with the company's symbol on it, his face pretty much buried in a large cup of coffee. It's such a strong reminder of how all this started that Rex feels like he's been gut-punched.

Django rests his hand on Rex's arm. "Keep your shit together," he murmurs, and then asks, "Straight black?"

Rex shakes his head, feeling his stomach knot up at the idea. "Oh, hell no. Right now I'd just vomit that back up. Tell them to add a hell of a lot of cow."

"Cow," Django repeats, frowning, and goes to order their coffee.

"Hi, Kai." Kai waves his hand at Rex in shushing gesture while continuing to chug coffee. "Fine, fuck you, too."

"No talking during coffee worship," Kai gasps when the cup is finally empty. "Fucking fuck fuckers fuck."

Both of Rex's eyebrows go up in surprise. "Have a nice flight?" Kai is in college; a global plane ride usually isn't enough to drive him into incoherency.

---

[5] Vietnamese: "What is your business in Vietnam?"

"Passenger in the seat next to me would not shut up for life, flaming death, or a fucking bullet to the head." Kai stares mournfully into his empty cup. "Have not slept. Hate everything and everyone."

Rex gives his brother a hug. "We'll find you someone to stab after naptime, all right?"

Kai's answering glare is pure suspicion. "Do I have to stitch them back up afterwards?"

"Nope. Free stabbing," Rex promises.

"Awesome-sauce—that's mine, right?" Kai reaches out with both hands when Django returns with two cups of coffee.

"Hell, no. You go buy another one of your own," Django retorts, handing one of the cups to Rex. "Extra cream, as requested, but I gotta tell you, the look on that barista's face was priceless when I asked him for extra beef."

"The fuck, Dad?" Rex stares at his father in horror. He doesn't even *like* steak and coffee.

"You said cow, and it stuck," Django explains, prying the lid off his coffee while Kai mutters complaints and gets back in line. "I'm getting too old for this shit."

Rex drinks half of his cream-and-sugar-laden coffee before he's pretty sure he can handle civil conversation again. The sugar was a good idea, something Rex forgot. The food on the plane was decent, but his blood sugar is probably shit right now. "You know, none of us have ever asked you how old you actually are."

"Good. That means I succeeded at teaching you miscreants some damned manners." Django waves at Wesley to gain his attention. Wesley turns mid-step and trudges over like a man on his way to execution. Neumia is slung over Wesley's back, her head on his shoulder, drooling onto his shirt and dead to the world. Kai rejoins them, slugging down another cup of coffee the size of his head.

"Manners," Rex repeats, feeling a pang of sympathy for Wesley. His brother does not look like he enjoyed his flight with their niece. "Right."

"Manners are important," Django stresses. To Rex's surprise, he adds, "I was born in 1927."

It takes Rex a moment to respond; he wasn't actually expecting an answer. They all grew up knowing that Django's birthday was on June sixth, but not what year. Their father has always been uncomfortable about handing out concrete dates for anything prior to Korea.

"Fuck," Rex mutters under his breath. Kai lets out a long, low whistle. "World War II?" Rex asks.

"I was seventeen," Django confirms, watching Wesley's forward progress. "It was god awful. I missed D-Day by three weeks, and that's probably the only good thing I can say about the entire damned war." He scowls, glaring into his coffee cup like it offended him. "Every time a movie comes out glorifying that shit-show, I have to remind myself that nobody puts bounties on movie execs."

"They do try to put emphasis on individual heroism," Kai points out hesitantly.

Django shakes his head. "Sometimes, but that's usually buried underneath a ton of propaganda fueled by bullshit. We don't *need* the damned propaganda. The U.S. did good things during the war. They can point that out without shoveling the fake patriotism all over our heads."

"I still remember when you told me about how you and an entire veteran's group walked out of that *Pearl Harbor* movie in 2001," Rex says, smiling.

"It was a stupid movie, but the shoveling wasn't the problem," Django says quietly. "We just couldn't handle the recreation of the ships sinking with everyone trapped inside. Hi Wesley," he continues in a louder voice.

"Hi." Wesley shifts Neumia upwards when she starts to slide down his back. "I have now experienced hell. I laughed at Brian when he said I had no idea what it was like to spend thirty hours on an airline trip with a kid. He was lying. *It's so much worse.*"

Kai tosses his coffee cup into a garbage bin. "Okay, now that I am conscious and no longer so bitey..." He draws in a deep breath. "Our schedule's fucked. Our flights are the only ones that didn't get hit by a weather delay. Euan, Ella, Khodî, and Brian are still stuck at their last transfer point, staring at the ass-end of a cloudbank. When I checked the boards, they were about four hours behind Wesley's flight."

"I was wondering why I hadn't seen anyone else," Rex says, and then grips his bag handle tighter when someone wanders too close, their eyes glued to it.

Find an easier mark, asshole, he thinks at the would-be thief. Their eyes meet; the man nods once and moves along, not bothering with any of Rex's family members.

"We'll go to the hotel," Django decides, unlocking his bag handle so he can tilt and roll it behind him. "We can come back when their flights arrive."

"Oh, please, *please*, yes," Wesley begs, catching Neumia before she can slip again. "This child needs a bed, and I want one, too."

Rex shoves his empty coffee cup into the trash. "You think your contact made the drop, Dad?"

"If he didn't, I will literally find that bastard and kill him," Django promises. "Let's go."

Wesley makes a disgusted sound as they pass by the fragrant Starbucks kiosk. Rex still has no idea how they ended up with a sibling that loathes coffee as much as Wesley does.

Customs, coffee, waiting for Wesley, and double-checking the boards ate up enough time that it's six before they get out of the airport. The sun is rising, an annoyingly bright and cheerful light. It's already hot enough that Rex shrugs out of his coat the moment a cab pulls up to the curb. "Euan told me that he lied about his age to get into the military."

Django slams the trunk door closed after double-checking that everyone's bags are inside. "Sixteen years old. Dumb damned kid."

"You went into World War II when you were seventeen," Kai says after they get into the cab. "Pretty sure enlistment age was eighteen at the time, Dad."

"Yeah, which makes me really fucking qualified to point out stupidity when I see it," Django retorts, and then looks at the driver. *"Khách sạn Thanh Hong. Bây giờ, xin."* [6]

The hotel they're taken to isn't posh, but it isn't another roach strip, either. Kai and Wesley wait near the elevators; Rex leans against a smooth white wall across from the front desk as their father checks them in. He nearly chokes on his spit when he hears what the cost of a single room is.

"What the fuck is 357,640.00₫ in US dollars?" Rex asks. Kai and Wesley make similar choking sounds at the huge number as they all pile into the elevator.

Django hits the door close button. "Sixteen bucks."

"You are fucking kidding me!" Wesley blurts out. "What's the exchange rate in this country for dong to dollar?"

"Forty-five millionth of a cent," Django replies. "The dong's been in decline for years. If I knew of a decent bolt-hole in this country, we could live like damned royalty just from what we've got on us."

"That is terrifying levels of math right now. I haven't had enough coffee or sleep for that kind of math," Kai says as the elevator doors open, depositing them on the third floor. "If I go shopping, I'm just gonna throw money at people until they give me stuff."

A keycard gets them into a hotel room that is clean, well-maintained, and does *not* smell like mothball death. The moment Django signals that the room is clear and safe, Wesley tucks Neumia into one of the beds and then flops down next to her.

"We can't stay," Django reminds him. "Once we get the others, we have to move."

"I know," Wesley replies in something approaching a gurgle. "If I can sleep for an hour, I'm good."

Kai drops his bag on the floor. "I saw a pharmacy a few minutes' walk down the street. I'll go see if they stock caffeine pills."

"Good idea," Rex says. Coffee is great, but caffeine pills will keep him going for a long time. He hopes they won't need them

---

[6] Vietnamese: "Thanh Hong Hotel. Now, please."

after today, though. Recovery from that kind of severe exhaustion takes a while, and it sucks balls.

"See you in a few. Please come rescue me if I'm not back in thirty minutes," Kai says. Wesley snorts awake when the hotel door opens, cracks one eye to see that it's only their brother heading out, and goes right back to sleep.

Django picks up the television remote and turns it on, muting the sound. "I'll be back in ten minutes." He hands the remote to Rex. "I know they get an American CNN broadcast here. See if we made the news," he says, and follows after Kai. Wesley doesn't even wake up for the second departure.

Rex flips through channels until he hits CNN, then pokes at the remote until it gives him subtitles in English. He's just in time to see an overhead shot of what used to be Ella's farmhouse, given the spread of debris around a massive crater. Ella loves going for overkill, especially when it comes to explosives.

"Hell, yes, we made the news," Rex tells his father when Django returns, carrying a long black duffel bag with his left hand. "We're terrorists rampaging across the Pennsylvania countryside, and we kidnapped my boyfriend. Oh, and they're hitting the Islam angle so hard that I'm seriously offended on the behalf of a whole lot of people."

Django puts the bag down on the bed, baffled. "We're not Muslim."

"All hail the great American media, where everyone who isn't white is ISIS or worse," Rex replies, somewhere between sarcastic and snarl. "No mention of our military service, or that we're second- and third-gen Americans—or that those are *our* destroyed homes they keep showing everybody."

"Figures." Django watches the talking heads for a minute, both of whom are awfully bright-eyed and bubbly for discussing suspected terrorism. The subtitle crawl is their useless blabber, but the station crawl is talking about Ambrus.

"*Distinguished serviceman*," Django reads. "Fuck. They want him alive."

"Looks like it." That concerns Rex a lot more than the initial shooting. Why would the department want him alive when they went to so much trouble to try and make Ambrus dead in the first place? "Doesn't seem like they're aware of the fact that we left the States, though."

Django slowly shakes his head. "Or they just don't want *us* to know. Terrorists watch TV, too."

Kai comes back with one hell of a first aid kit. It's built from individual pharmacy finds, *and* he somehow put together a makeshift surgical suite that rolls up in a tight bundle. Both easily fit inside his backpack. Kai also bought enough caffeine pills to fuel an army, which should last them a few days if they can't find a place to sleep.

"You're a fucking genius, kid," Django says.

Kai grins in pleasure at the compliment. "Gotta earn my keep. Besides, I've already removed five bullets from someone this week. Might as well be prepared."

Rex wakes up Wesley, who swings at him; Rex ducks out of long habit. Waking up any of them is chancing a beating anyway, even on good days.

Wesley goes into the bathroom, splashes his face with cold water, and comes out looking a lot more alert. "Okay. What have you got for us?"

Django unzips the duffel bag and hands Wesley the largest case. "Oh, you are so very shiny," Wesley croons as he opens the hard-shell case. Inside is a PDShP anti-material rifle, accompanied by several boxes of .57 caliber armor-piercing rounds.

"Is that legal to own in the States?" Kai asks, opening a box to look at the .57 casing.

"Depends on the state," Rex tells him. "Southern U.S. is pretty damned lenient. The PDShP is really popular in Eastern Europe, though."

"There's a hotel across from the airport's public exit, about a mile to the south," Django tells Wesley. "You need to be on the roof before those flights come in. Neumia will be up there with you. I want her out of the line of fire as much as possible."

Wesley glances at the ammunition. "That caliber puts me pretty close to its range limit."

"At that distance, it will still pierce body armor," Django replies, a humorless grin on his face. "I know you can make those shots. I'd put Rex up there, but he's got more experience on the ground, and if there's a fight..."

"Yeah, I can do it." Wesley glances over at Neumia, who is still asleep, one arm thrown over her eyes to block out the light. "If she's with me, she can watch my back and make sure nobody sneaks up on my ass. Is there anything in that duffel she can fire?"

"I'd really prefer that she didn't have to, but I'm not fucking stupid, either." Django gets out a small .22 rifle that looks like it's made entirely of plastic. "Lightweight, but it fires well. Neumia didn't get much practice after the holidays, but she knows how to load it and she can hit a target, even if it's not center mass. This is good for short-range combat, but it's not made for war."

"I don't want my niece seeing fucking war-levels of combat," Wesley mutters, checking the rifle over. "I feel like I'm holding a toy."

"She already knifed a Ranger in the crotch." Rex probably has more pride than he should in an eight-year-old's ability to stab people. "She severed the artery properly, too."

"Charts came in handy, huh?" Wesley asks, raising an eyebrow at their father.

Django nods, his eyes alight with the same kind of pride Rex is feeling. "Whetū girls are always terrifying."

"Ella is terrifying enough for all of us," Wesley replies dryly. "Why couldn't Nari be normal?"

Rex grins at his brother. "Brian should have thought of that before he had a kid with Bonika de Lacy."

Django pulls out a sawed-off shotgun and gives it to Kai, along with a box of shells. "See if that spring-weight duster in your luggage is long enough to hide this."

"On it." Kai goes to retrieve the coat in question. Rex always has to shake his head at the disparity—give Kai a medical tool and he's terrifyingly precise, but if you want him to have that same level of precision with a weapon, you give him something with spread and stopping power.

Django hands a pair of .357 compact SIG Glock 32s to Rex. Those are followed by four boxes of ammunition and four spare clips. "Might want to prep those in advance," Django suggests.

Rex glares at his father for pointing out the fucking obvious. "Thirty-six, Dad. Combat veteran. Been doing this for a while."

"Yeah." Django releases a tired sigh. "Sorry, I'm just—"

"Us, too," Rex says, and nudges his father until Django picks up the other two Glock 32s. "Why SIGs?"

"It was all they could get their hands on at short notice," Django replies. "A .9mm is safer for crowds, but fuck, Rex—if we're dealing with anyone from the department, we need to put them down and have them *stay* down. At least a .357 from a SIG will take out a target without blowing a hole through anyone standing behind them."

Kai puts on the coat, which hangs down to his knees, and tucks the sawed-off along his side. "Works," he announces. "I'll have to rig something to hold it in place. Maybe Velcro, so it gives easily if I really need to pull the gun fast."

"Velcro strips in the bag," Django says while fieldstripping the first SIG, laying it out on a t-shirt to protect the bedspread from stains. The smell of recently applied gun oil climbs into Rex's nose to say hello, an old and welcome friend. "Don't know if they included any way to sew it on, but it's in there."

Kai starts digging in the black duffel. "I have a fucking first aid kit. I can staple this shit into place if I need to."

Rex field-strips both of his new SIGs while Wesley practice-assembles the PDShP. Kai steals the sniper rifle's kit and starts cleaning the bores on the sawed-off, which are still blackened with residue from their last firing. For a while, there is nothing but the sound of weapons and work.

Rex breaks the silence first. "Euan really took nine shots once?"

"He was lucky they were .9mm shots." Django is swiftly loading one of the spare clips with .357 rounds. "A lot of people still carried their .45s as a service standard. Nine shots from one of those..." Django shakes his head. "Like I said, Rex: stopping power."

Rex nods. "Headshots it is."

Django glances at him. "They're not zombies."

Rex shrugs. "They'll still drop a motherfucker."

They finish prepping weapons in renewed silence. Neumia wakes up as Kai pockets the last shells for the sawed-off. She subjects them to a grumpy glare for interrupting her sleep.

"Go take a shower, kidlet," Wesley tells her, nudging Neumia in the direction of the bathroom. "You'll feel better." She doesn't look convinced, but she grabs her little rolling bag and disappears into the bathroom.

Django pops the lid from the first bottle of caffeine pills and dry-swallows three before he gets a map out of the bag. It's a really good terrain map of Vietnam and the surrounding countries that make up this particular Asian peninsula, with seaports and airports already marked in vivid yellow drops of paint.

"This is the only map, so memorize it, or find another if we get separated. We're already near the coast." Django points at a coastal area east of Ho Chi Minh. "When we get the others, we'll hit port in Phan Thiết. If things go to shit, head west into Cambodia. Chanthavy set up a temporary bolt-hole in Krong Ta Khmau. Khodî has her phone number. If things get so fucked that Chan can't be an option, keep heading northwest and disappear in Bangkok. Xāwuṭh will be able to get to you eventually."

"If things go according to plan, where is Wolf going to meet us?" Wesley asks.

"Maluku." Django scrubs at his face before pinching the bridge of his nose. "I don't want to go any further east than that, though. Even with the Philippines installations shut down, the U.S. presence in Japan and South Korea means that there are still an assload of American military ships in those waters."

"Singapore, too, the poor bastards," Kai says, but Rex shakes his head.

"No, they're Air Force. Not as many boats in the water, and Singapore is..." Rex hesitates. "We could hide in Singapore pretty easily, actually, even with U.S. presence." His birth country has dropped to about thirty percent local population, and now tops at seventy percent import. English is as common to hear on the street as Mandarin and Malay.

"Dad?" Kai asks, which makes Rex realize that Django is doing nothing more than staring off into the distance, eyes unfocused.

"You miscreants would have liked your aunt," Django says quietly.

Wesley, Kai, and Rex exchange nervous glances. "Daaaaaad?" Kai draws out the repetition.

Django blinks a few times and focuses on Kai, then Wesley and Rex. "The last time I felt this way, shit went sideways, and I watched a lot of people die."

Wesley grimaces; Kai goes pale. "We're not most people," Rex insists. "Shit isn't going to go sideways. Not fuckin' allowed."

"I hope you're right," Django says, rolling up the map. "Finish packing for the airport. We need to go as soon as Nari is ready."

Shit goes sideways, anyway. It just happens in a manner that's so fucked up that Rex has trouble processing it for days afterwards.

Chapter 10
:)(X)(X:

The weight of two compact SIGs resting against Rex's back is reassuring as he wanders through the public area of Tan Son Nhat International Airport, keeping away from security checkpoints and customs line-ups. Rex swapped out the annoying aviator sunglasses for a set of black-tinted wraparound lenses that allow him to check his peripheral, the movement of his eyes invisible to passersby. The original stinky leather coat he wore for the flight is stuffed into his luggage, riding in the back of the vehicle Wesley went out to acquire—by theft or by purchase, Rex has no idea. He just cares that they'll have a car that drives and will hold the entire family.

He's wearing jeans again, a black t-shirt, and a short-sleeved blue button-down with a long tail to hide the guns. The loose shirt gives him easy access to both SIGs if things go pear-shaped.

Rex still hopes that things won't turn sour. The problem is that he knows *something* will happen, and he's never trusted that fucking feeling. It's the same sensation no matter if it's "a hamster escaped" or "potential nuclear strike."

Django is off to Rex's left, chatting up the vendor running the media stands in fluent, fast Vietnamese. Rex is only grasping about one word in five. Then he heard something about chicken penis a few minutes ago and decided it was best to stop listening.

Kai is drift-pacing off to Rex's right, wandering in the opposite direction, his eyes glued to the open magazine in his hands. It looks like he's reading, but a small square mirror is resting on the right-side page, allowing Kai to see everything going on behind him.

Kai knows something's up, too, but if he knew what was wrong, he would have bumped into Rex to mention it. As time tick by, Kai's brow sinks lower and lower in irritated dismay. Between his professionally short hair, knee-length rain duster, and oversized glasses on his face, Kai looks like a young businessman getting steadily pissed off about how long it's taking someone to arrive.

Rex glances at his father, who is always aware of it when one of his kids wants his attention. Django meets Rex's eyes and lifts one shoulder in a vague shrug; he doesn't know what's coming, either. Just that it will.

Rex checks the boards to find that they've changed in the last few minutes. The flights that Ella, Ambrus, Khodî, and Brian flew in on have both arrived. Now they just have to wait for the two groups to get through customs and retrieve their luggage from the baggage claim area beyond the last security checkpoint. Then they'll be with Rex, Kai, and Django, who can keep an eye on everyone as they all leave the damned airport.

Rex feels a tension headache build and presses sharply along the pressure points on his forehead, trying to convince it to leave him alone. He's had enough caffeine pills to keep a full-fledged migraine at bay—he has no damned *reason* to have a headache!—but the pain refuses to fade.

When Rex looks back at the massive hallway that herds arriving passengers to the public side of the airport, he sees Ambrus and Ella making their way along the corridor, with Khodî and Brian trailing a few steps behind them. Brian is walking with his eyes downcast in a tired, listless trot, massaging his temples with one hand. Khodî looks like he's trying to figure out how to set things on fire with his eyes. Ella and Ambrus seem tired, but Ambrus keeps blinking and shaking his head, like he's trying to throw something off.

"Aw, fuck," Rex hears in English. He half-turns to see Django pressing his fingertips into the uppermost part of his eye sockets, trying to hit a different set of pressure points that can release muscle tension from a migraine.

That's one instance too many. Something's wrong.

Rex pulls his glasses and tosses them onto the floor, gaining Django and Kai's attention with the clatter of plastic against tile. His father gives the vendor a polite nod of farewell and heads in Rex's direction, hands loose at his sides in case he needs to pull a weapon from beneath his unzipped coat.

Kai mutters, "Shit," under his breath and drops the magazine before he turns around. He falls into step with Rex and Django as they move in a triangle formation towards Ambrus, Brian, Ella, and Khodî.

With every step they take, Rex feels intense pressure build in his head. It's like the world's worst goddamned migraine, and no matter how many physical pressure point or massage tricks he tries, he can't make it stop.

Ten meters away from the walkway that dumps new arrivals out into public airport space, Ambrus steps off the walk and presses his hands against his eyes.

Two seconds later, everyone in the entire airport is acting as if they've all come down with migraines.

"Goddamned *sideways*!" Rex hears Django snarl, and suddenly it's like a grenade explodes right in front of him.

Light blinds Rex's eyes. His ears are full of clamoring bells that won't go quiet. He thinks he hears gunshots. Definitely screaming.

He's on the ground. He feels like he's been slammed by a tidal wave, dragged under by riptide, and left half-drowned in its wake.

The sensation changes. It's the feeling of gravity returning too swiftly, pinning him in place as a plane nosedives in an uncontrolled descent. Again a change—his head is ringing from a blow he can't remember taking. Fire in the desert. Too much smoke and dust. No water. Weapons that are too hot but can't be put down or they'll be overrun. More screaming in the darkness.

"Hello, Euan."

Rex forces his eyes open, growling. No grenade, no explosives. Just flashbacks, most of them ones he hasn't suffered from in years. He turns his head with terrible, bone-grinding effort to seek out that voice.

Jasper Fox stands tall among a sea of prone bodies at the end of the Arrivals line. He's a mockery of still repose, clothed in a pristine three-piece gray suit. The shirt and tie are the exact same shade of gray, the perfect marriage of black and white.

Rex tries to make his arm move and he can't. His head is still spinning, his body half-convinced that he's drowning, falling, dying. Suffering.

Kai is down and out; Django is somewhere behind him. Everyone else Rex can see from his position is on the ground, too. Some of them are conscious; some are not.

Fox tilts his head as he gazes at Ambrus, who landed face down, one arm trapped underneath his shirt as if he'd tried to go for a weapon he forgot he wasn't carrying. Ambrus is bracketed by Ella on one side and Brian on the other. Ella is curled up with her hands clamped over her ears, her lips moving soundlessly. Brian isn't moving, but he's breathing, eyes open, at least semi-conscious.

Khodî is lying face down next to Brian, but he's far too still. What moves is the pool of dark red blood spreading across the floor in an arc from his head.

Rex feels the spit in his mouth evaporate. His gut clenches even as he tries desperately to get his traitorous limbs to cooperate. He has to go there, *right now*.

No. This isn't allowed to be. Please, no. Fucking no—not this!

Fox looks in Rex's direction, a smirk on his face as if he can hear Rex's thoughts.

Rex feels broken-glass fear try to clog his throat. That is not an expression he has ever seen on Jasper Fox's face before. That is an expression that doesn't fucking *fit*.

Then Fox ignores Rex, his attention back on Ambrus. "You're a very hard man to find, you know," Fox says, smiling in a way that screams pretense.

Ambrus lifts his face, his lips pulled back from his teeth in a wolf's warning growl, his eyes shining with complete fury. Blood paints his lips and streaks his chin from one hell of a nosebleed.

Rex and Ambrus's eyes meet for one too-brief second. *Run*, Rex hears in his head, a distinct echo of his boyfriend's voice.

Rex is torn between sudden panic and consuming rage. *NO!* That's something he won't fucking do.

"I can't have done a very good job at hiding, not if you're already riding my ass," Ambrus rasps at Fox.

Fox bends down and grasps Ambrus by the back of his navy blue sport coat. "I told you, Euan, that's not my thing. Up you come, brother." The way Fox speaks the word turns the endearment into an obscenity.

It happens so damned fast. If Rex hadn't been staring right at them, he would have missed the moment when Ambrus deliberately swipes his left hand through the spreading pool of Khodî's blood. Rex feels a cold chill trace its way down his spine as Fox lifts Ambrus into the air, turning him around with easy strength so that they're facing each other.

Fox still has that same Not-Jasper smirk on his face. "Time to go home—" he starts to say, and then Ambrus plasters his bloodied left hand over Fox's face.

Fox's high-pitched scream tears through the atrium, releasing a second pressure wave that makes the ceiling spin crazily overhead. Rex flashes on that second plane crash again, pinned to the ground with flames licking near his feet, he can't—

"FUCKING BASTARD!"

Rex is startled out of the flashback-hallucination by his father's animal-wounded howl of rage. That's followed by more gunshots, the much deeper cough of a .357.

Rex rolls over onto his side in time to see Fox drop Ambrus. He's still screaming, both of his hands covering terrible burns across his face. Two outer-edge torso shots are beginning to stain that gray suit a darker red.

Django yells something else that Rex doesn't catch and the SIG coughs again, gifting Fox with four more center mass shots. Fox stumbles but doesn't fall. Django swears in French-blended Khmer and adds one more bullet to Fox's upper thigh that makes him crumple, hitting the ground in a messy sprawl.

Rex pushes himself up with his hands and then gets to his knees. Everything hurts, but he refuses to miss witnessing his father walk up to Jasper Fox, arms trembling as he unloads the rest of the pistol magazine into Fox's chest. "That's for my son, motherfucker!"

"Holy shit." Rex glances over to see Kai rolling onto his stomach, gasping for breath like someone tried to drown him. "Shit, shit, shit. Oh fuck—Khodî—"

Rex hears the click of a safety disengaging. He turns, clumsy and too slow from whatever the hell Fox did to them all. He's still trying to pull one of the SIGs from the back holster on his right side when his eyes find the target. A man wearing a suit that looks *exactly* like the one Fox is wearing stands just a few meters away. The agent's weapon is raised, aimed directly at Django—and his finger is already squeezing the trigger.

Rex ducks on instinct when six shots are fired in rapid succession from behind him. The booming echo of a .44 is a lot louder than the .357, and the sound creates a wave of panicked whimpering from the civilians still lying on the floor.

"What the fuck," Rex chokes out, finally freeing one of his SIGs. He turns back to the Arrivals line, ready to raise and fire.

Instead, he almost drops the fucking Glock.

Khodî is up on his knees, pointing a stolen pistol at the dead agent now lying on the ground behind Rex. Blood stains Khodî's face and soaks his hair. The pale suit coat and shirt is a scarlet mess.

"Nobody gets to shoot at my dad but me!" Khodî bellows in rage.

Django stares at Khodî, so shocked he hasn't even reloaded his weapon. "Khòi Khôn đi Som?"

Khodî slowly lowers the .44. The light catches a ruby highlight that runs down the barrel; Rex knows at once that Khodî stole Fox's gun. "Yeah. Like I needed another fucking scar," Khodî says in a tone of complete disgust.

When Khodî turns his head to look up at their father, Rex can see a mess of blood but no damage. If Fox shot Khodî with that .44...then that gunshot has completely healed. In less than three minutes.

Rex swallows, still trying to get some spit back into his mouth. "Khodî, what the fuck?"

"What Rex said," Kai whispers, gazing at Khodî with huge eyes.

Khodî shakes his head. "Later—it has to be later." He uses the muzzle of the .44 to push himself up until he can get his feet under him. "Is that asshole dead?"

"No." Ambrus sounds half-strangled as he sits on the floor across from Fox. Ambrus is clenching his left hand to his chest as if he's cradling broken bones.

"Shit." Django steps over a few airport civvies, one of which cringes away from him. He reaches down and pulls Ambrus to his feet without bothering to ask first while Khodî yanks Brian up from the floor.

Brian looks like he's been slammed at least six times in the face with a brick, blinking and staring around like he can't quite figure out where he is. "Follow my lead," Khodî tells him. After a long moment in which Brian stares at him like Khodî spoke Greek, Brian nods his understanding.

Rex gets to his feet before taking a few unsteady steps over to Kai, hauling his baby brother upright. Kai is swaying like he's drunk, but Rex can look into Kai's eyes and see that he's at least coherent.

Fuck, what the hell did Fox *do* to them?

Django leaves Ambrus with Khodî and Brian before he goes to Ella. "Baby girl?"

Ella lets out a choked sob. "That fucker!" she hisses, grabbing her father's hands when Django offers them, letting him help her up. "Give me that fucking gun!" Ella yells at Khodî.

Khodî shrugs and hands it over. "Bet you he can survive a headshot," he says in a desert-dry voice.

Like you just did, Rex thinks, and feels another cold chill crawl up his spine.

Ella scowls at Khodî before adjusting her aim, emptying the rest of the ruby-lined .44's magazine into Fox's throat. "Heal a severed head, you skank fuck!"

"That's them!"

Rex looks up at the bellow and spies more gray-suited agents approaching. All three are armed, weapons up, but they're in the secured zone farther into the terminal. That gives Rex all the distance and time he needs. He lifts the SIG in his right hand and unloads half a clip into the glass ceiling above them. Shattered glass rains down on the agents, a distraction and weapon both. Rex finishes them off with the rest of the SIG's available rounds while they're distracted and bleeding.

"We're leaving." Django grabs Ella by the elbow. "Now, Ella!"

"HE'S STILL FUCKING TWITCHING!" Ella screeches, trying to stomp on Fox's head.

"Then let him twitch!" Khodî yells. Rex pulls his second SIG when Django points at the airport entrance. Another trio of agents are coming in through the doors, trying to block the exit.

Rex puts them down with ammo-conservative headshots, starting to get creeped out. They're *all* wearing those same gray three-piece business suit monstrosities, just like the guard at the construction site. Just like Fox. No camouflage, fatigues, or Secret Service black tie to be seen.

Kai whirls in place and buries a short scalpel in the eye socket of a fourth agent that was trying to crawl up their four o'clock. The agent makes a startled, gurgling squeak and drops.

Kai grins in delight. "I finally got to stab someone!"

"Promised that you would," Rex replies, a grim smile on his face. He doesn't want to know where Kai was hiding that scalpel. "There are more coming in through the doors. Clear our path, little brother."

"Hell yeah!" Kai pulls the sawed-off out of its hiding place and unloads both barrels on the set of incoming agents. He aimed low, so they're crippling thigh and groin hits instead of kill shots, but it still does the job nicely. Both agents are on the ground, howling in pain and too concerned with their multiple new lead-created wounds to be a threat. "Wasn't I just going to medical school like, five days ago?" Kai asks.

"And now you're fighting a fucking ground war in Vietnam. Congratulations," Django says in a rough voice as the others catch up to their position. Their father is all but dragging Ella, who is trying to go back and dismember Fox. Ambrus and Khodî are bracketing Brian, who's starting to show full sparks of awareness in his eyes again.

It helps that almost all of the people who were in the airport when Fox pulled his shit are still on the ground. Most of the men and women Rex walks past look shell-shocked. Some are weeping, like Ella had been, while others are unconscious. Rex has a bad, bad feeling that a few of them are dead.

Kai flinches when the wail of an alarm fills the building. "Oh, well, that took them long enough," Brian says, rolling his eyes before he shakes off Khodî and Ambrus. "I'm good now. Worst fucking alarm clock I've ever heard, but I'm good."

Khodî nods. "I'm glad. Move your ass!"

"If they still run drills, that alarm will keep everyone on the floor and out of the damned way." Django shoots a gray-suited agent that comes into view before he even enters the airport, nailing him through the window. The agent collapses on the exterior sidewalk with one hand on his throat, blood staining his fingers a glossy, vibrant red. The bullet hole creates a spider web pattern in the glass that's still spreading as they leave.

When they get through the half-shattered airport doors, Django and Rex are both on clip number three of four. Rex has nineteen rounds left; he's pretty sure Django has sixteen. Kai has reloaded his shotgun six times and is grinning like he's having a literal blast.

Another flood of agents is waiting for them. Khodî shoves the emptied .44 into his trouser pocket and grabs Django's spare SIG with the last clip loaded inside. Rex grits his teeth at the idea of giving up one of his guns, but they need more firepower. Ambrus is still acting like his left arm is out of commission, so Ella gets Rex's second SIG with the full clip.

"Please tell me we have other weapons," Ambrus says in a mild voice, the only one of them still weaponless. Nobody needed to say a word to make sure that Ambrus is sheltered by their loose protective circle.

"Yeah, but they're with Wesley," Django says, nailing another agent in the face. "How many of these fuckers are there?"

"Most of them aren't Specialists, they're standard agents." Ambrus lifts his right hand, one finger pointed behind them. "That way."

Khodî rolls his eyes and shoots the next two agents coming up their six. Ella nails an agent that was trying to lie in wait with an automatic rifle.

Then Wesley finally comes into play, nailing seven of the bastards in rapid succession from his position on the hotel rooftop to the south. "Told him he could make those shots," Django says proudly, clubbing a wounded agent in the face with the butt of his SIG when the bleeding man tries to grab at Ella.

"Nicely fuckin' done," Khodî says in approval, right before he points his gun at a terrified cab driver ducked down next to his car. "You. *Bạn không cần một xe taxi ngày hôm nay, đúng không?*"[1]

The cab driver shakes his head rapidly back and forth. "Keys in ignition!" he yelps.

"Thanks. Here ya go." Django tosses the driver a fold of twenties. "*Bạn nên để.*[2] There's a bunch of fuckers coming along who are a lot more dangerous than we are."

"Fucking Americans," the cabbie shouts at them. At least he's smart enough to run down the sidewalk, getting the hell away from the mess in front of the airport.

Django sighs. "Now there's a sentiment I've heard a lot over the years. Rex, you're driving."

"Awesome." Rex yanks the driver's side door open. It's a manual shift; thank you god, it's not a fucking automatic.

Django opens the passenger door and shoves Kai inside before he sits down and slams the door closed. It's a tight fit, but Rex still has room to shift. He starts the car, relieved to hear a well-maintained roar from an overpowered four-cylinder engine. Rex checks the rearview to watch as Ella, Khodî, Brian, and Ambrus cram into the backseat. It's barely wide enough for all of them, but they can shut the doors and still have room to shoot at things.

Rex looks at Ambrus, who is still holding his left hand to his chest, but his eyes are clear. That's a good sign, especially when Ambrus glances up long enough for their eyes to meet.

Here and alive. That's good enough right now.

Rex spies a car screeching into the Passenger Arrivals lane. "Oh, look, they still want us to shoot them!" Ella declares cheerfully.

"When's the last time you were in a car chase, Ella?" Rex asks, feeling a smile bloom on his face. Everyone's alive, they have a car, and he's willing to put a lot of money on the fact that he's a better driver than the asshole headed right for them.

"Uh, Canada?" Ella replies. "Not that long ago, really." She drops the magazine from the SIG long enough to do an ammo count. Khodî uses the butt of the empty .44 to smash out the cab's rear window. Nobody needs shattered glass blocking their vision, especially the driver.

Django pulls ammunition from his coat to start reloading the empty SIG clips. "How the hell did you end up in a car chase in Canada? Kai, get that shotgun ready!" he adds while Rex puts the car in gear. He slaps the bumper of the cab in front of him to get out of the airport lineup, and then they're free. Rex opens up the engine to give them some damned breathing room.

---

[1] Vietnamese: "You do not need a taxi today, do you?"
[2] Vietnamese: "You should leave."

"Got it, Dad." Kai pops open the barrel on the shotgun. Rex hisses when one of the still-hot shells bounces off his bare arm as he shifts into third. Kai gives him a brief, apologetic look.

"I pissed off a moose," Ella answers Django, using her hand on the ceiling to brace herself as Rex spins the car to speed the wrong way down the airport intake road. "Also, a whole lot of Mounties. It was a weird day."

They fly right past the car trying to come after them, but it's a decision that introduces a hell of a lot of traffic once they're clear of the airport. Fun times; Rex loved this shit in the military, much to his subordinates' unhappy screeching. Wusses.

The moment Kai has his weapon loaded, Khodî yells, "Give me the damned shotgun!"

Kai turns in the seat to give his brother an offended look. "You were just shot in the head, you stupid asshole!"

"And it hasn't affected my aim at all!" Khodî retorts. "GUN!"

"Goddammit," Kai mutters, and lifts the shotgun over his seat so Khodî can grab it.

Django slaps a fresh clip into the first Glock. "End this fast, kids. I'm not gonna wind up in some stupid Hollywood-choreographed car chase because you shits don't know how to stop a damned car."

Kai turns forward again just in time for his eyes to grow comically wide. "REX! BRAKES! THERE ARE BRAKES, PLEASE USE THEM!"

Rex drops the car into a lower gear to gain speed and fly around two airport-labeled passenger vans. "Kai, stop whining and let me fucking drive!"

"Always let little sister take first pick," Khodî says. Rex glances up long enough to see the shotgun exchange hands.

Ella grins, turns around, and takes aim through the rear window, blowing out two tires on their pursuit vehicle. It screeches off to one side and hits the back of a truck, folding in the front end.

"One down," Ella announces. "Another one's incoming. Want a turn, Khodî?"

"Fuck yes, I do," Khodî replies, taking the gun back. "Kai! Shells!"

Kai pulls fresh shells from his coat pocket and hands them backwards over the seat without pulling his eyes away from his train-wreck fascination of their speedy trip through Ho Chi Minh's northern end. The second car is close enough to start shooting, but Rex really enjoyed learning to drive under live fire conditions. It's damned hard to get a bead on a vehicle that's weaving around traffic.

Rex hears Khodî popping open the shotgun to replace the shells. "The moment we're out of danger, I would like everyone to know that I'm going to be vomiting out of this window," Khodî tells them.

"Oh, good. You can make the car look even more distinctive than it already is," Brian retorts.

"Just open the damned window!" Khodî orders.

"Distance shot, or up close and personal?" Rex asks his brother, using the car to nudge over a bus until it's up on the curb and out of the fucking way of potential gunfire. The driver yells at him as he passes by.

"Oh, give me up close and personal. I'm fuckin' pissed."

"Aw, shit," Brian mutters, reaching for the handle mounted to the car ceiling. "I hate you all."

Rex grins. "Hang on." He drops the car out of gear and slams on the brakes. Kai and Django both brace their arms against the dash before the inertia of deceleration hits. Rex gives it a three count and then lifts his foot off the brake, twists the wheel, and pulls the e-brake all at once, like a crazed teenager doing donuts across a snowy parking lot.

Okay, so his childhood had been fun, too. Good preparation, anyway.

Khodî already has himself braced in place, the shotgun aimed out of the driver's side rear window. There is a brief, wonderful moment when the car's spin brings them right alongside their tail, face-to-face with a shocked pair of male agents.

Khodî grins. "Hi there!" he says, just before he fires both barrels straight into the other car's passenger side window.

On the car's next spin, Rex sees that the shot took out both passenger and driver. The car veers sideways, tires squealing. Then it strikes a barrier and flips up onto its side, throwing sparks as it slides down the road.

Rex stomps down on the brake and brings the car to a perfect screeching halt, facing south again. "Everybody all right?" he asks as Khodî makes good on his earlier declaration.

"We're fine," Ambrus says, grabbing Khodî by the suit coat and yanking him back into the car the moment he finishes retching. Khodî gives the empty .44 a look of disgust before tossing it out the window to join the vomit. "Go!" Ambrus yells.

Rex nods and floors it, putting distance between them and any other potential tails. "Anyone see anything?"

"Nope," Brian reports, staring out of the broken back window. "I don't think they were prepared for everyone to clear out that fast."

"Good." Django's brow is furrowed, his jaw set with anger. "Get ready to ditch this piece of shit. Wesley's waiting for us."

Khodî sits back down in the seat, snugged up next to Ambrus. "What a fucking day."

Rex looks into the rearview to see a tight smile on Ambrus's face. "Fucking tell me about it."

"Our fucking luggage!" Ella bursts out. "Dammit. I had a really nice straight razor packed away."

"Buy you a new one," Django says absently, his eyes on the traffic around them. Rex isn't lingering, but he's also trying not to stand out as he gets them to the meeting point.

Ella scowls. "Ivory handle, Dad! It was a fucking antique!"

Django smiles as he reloads the final SIG magazine, emptying the last box of ammunition they brought to the airport. "Demanding brat. Bet it was fake ivory."

Rex checks the mirror again in time to witness Ella rolling her eyes. "Fine. We're in the fucking South Pacific. Mother-of-pearl handle replacement, Dad!"

They ditch the cab in an alley and approach the pre-arranged rendezvous on foot. Everyone who has a weapon is clutching it in their hand, pointed down and held against clothing or semi-hidden beneath shirts, trying not to draw any more attention than they already have.

Wesley is waiting for them, a van's doors already standing open and the engine idling. "Move your asses," he hisses as they jog forward to meet him. "I don't think we were followed, but no chances. Load up so we can go, right now."

"Works for me. Who needs two car chases in one day?" Kai asks.

Ella smirks at him. "Totally managed it."

"It's not supposed to be a fucking competition, Ella!" Wesley points at the van. "Inside, now. Brian! Your daughter would also very much like to be assured that you're not dead!"

"What took you so fucking long to start firing?" Django asks.

"Who the hell expects all of your targets to be wearing business suits?" Wesley responds, a baffled look crossing his face. "It's fucking weird."

Rex takes the bench seat right behind the driver's seat and grabs Ambrus's sleeve, encouraging his boyfriend to curl into place next to him. Ambrus gives Rex a look of intense relief before he presses in as close as it's possible to get without stripping naked.

Brian crawls into the back of the van, where Neumia latches onto him like an octopus. "DAD!"

"I'm still here, baby," Brian murmurs as Ella sits down next to him. "It's okay."

"It almost wasn't!" Neumia yells back, and then buries her face against her father's shirt.

"No. You're right. But it is okay," Brian insists.

Wesley grabs Khodî by the shoulder before Khodî can get into the van. "What in the entire name of fuck happened to you?"

"Got shot." Khodî shrugs. "Storytime later, okay?"

"Storytime, hell," Wesley mutters. He reaches out and pulls a red-stained ivory shard from Khodî's jacket. "What did you do?"

Khodî shoves Wesley's hand away before he climbs into the van. "Later!" he insists.

Wesley finally takes the hint and walks around to the other side of the vehicle. Django and Wesley take the front seats, with Wesley driving. Khodî waits until Kai has crawled into the back to sit with Ella, Brian, and Neumia before he shuts the door and then sits down next to Ambrus. The sound of doors shutting and locking is relieving to hear. Rex agrees with Kai; he's not actually in the mood for two car chases in a single day.

"V8 again?" Django asks, amused.

"Nah, V6. The less we stop for fuel, the better." Wesley pops the clutch and getting them rolling. "She's got decent top speed, though, and this model of van is everywhere. Blends in nicely."

"Good job, Wesley."

Wesley glances back over his shoulder at Khodî before he looks forward again and puts the van in gear. "Yeah. Thanks, Dad."

They're crawling along in Ho Chi Minh lunch hour traffic when Brian says, "My daughter just fell asleep. If anyone has any pertinent questions you don't want her to hear, now's the time."

It doesn't take long before Kai hisses, "How the *fuck* are you not dead, Khodî?"

Django's eyes dart up to the flipped-open passenger-side mirror in the sun visor, which gives him a view of almost everyone in the backseat. "I'd like to know that, too."

Khodî pulls a handkerchief from his coat pocket in a vain attempt to try to clean his face. "The scar on my face. I lied about getting it in a car wreck."

Ella gives him a sharp look. "What happened with the car, then?"

"I deliberately wrecked it so that I would have an excuse to have the scar afterwards." Khodî grimaces. "That wasn't any fun, either."

Wesley is shaking his head. "You were still in Iraq when you had the car wreck. You were a hot fuckin' mess when you came home."

Khodî's smile is pure bitterness. "Yeah. That's putting it mildly."

Rex looks at the way Khodî's scar twists out from his right temple, over his forehead and down his cheekbone, starkly visible after blood destroyed Ella's makeup job. "You fucker," he whispers, feeling like a hand reached into his chest, squeezing everything into an unbreakable knot. "You did *not* do what I think you did."

Khodî lifts both hands in a shrug before miming a pistol at his temple over the worst part of the scar. "Yep. Sure did."

"You bastard," Brian breathes out. He looks like he's taken another hit to the face. "What the hell did you do that for?"

"Hot mess, like Wesley said." Khodî sighs. "I pulled the trigger about an hour after I lost my entire team to that goddamned RPG strike. Even used a .44. Wanted to make sure that if I was going to do the job, it'd be done right."

"February," Django says. There is something about his voice that puts Rex on edge. "2006. February twenty-eighth." Khodî nods in confirmation.

"And it didn't work." Ambrus doesn't sound surprised, which makes the knotted feeling in Rex's chest feel even worse. "You went down, and you woke up again afterwards."

"Pretty much," Khodî says. "I lost about five minutes between right before I pulled the trigger, and when I finally realized I wasn't dead and looked at a watch. Bloody mess, everywhere. My face had scarred up on that side like I'd taken a side-header through a windshield." He pauses, smiling. "In my defense, I've never tried to do that shit ever again."

"You are such a fucking hypocrite!" Ella yells. The sound bounces around in the enclosed van, making Neumia whimper in her sleep. Ella winces. "Shit. Sorry, but—Khodî, you bitched at me about therapy, about not being a fucking psychopath, and then you went and tried to fucking commit suicide! You are an *asshole!*"

"Hey, that would be why I told you to go get fucking therapy!" Khodî snaps back. "What the hell do you think I did after literally shooting myself in the head? Therapy bills out my ass, sis!"

"The army covers psych time when you can get it," Ella says, eyes narrowing.

"Not if you don't want them to know you tried to put a bullet in your head," Khodî replies dryly. "Private therapy costs money."

Rex swallows down the bitter taste in the back of his throat. "How did you know, Euan?"

Ambrus lifts his left hand up and holds it out, fingers splayed. The red stain is dark and perfect, fingertip to wrist, as if he dipped his hand in a vat of dye. "Because—because what I did only works if you're using the power of someone's death. Khodî died. Clinically, it was perhaps a few seconds, maybe less, but it was still a death. I took that energy, and I branded it across Jasper's face."

"Good," Ella spits. "That fucker made me think about Eric—about Eric *dying!*"

"Bad things." Kai squirms in his seat, looking uncomfortable. "He was making everyone in the airport experience the worst things they've ever felt. Fears or—or actual events."

"Dad?" Wesley asks, glancing over at their father. Django is staring straight ahead, a grim set to his jaw. "We all know there are a hell of a lot of 'worst things' that bastard could have subjected you to."

Django smiles in a way that makes his eyes shine with rage. "Yeah, there's plenty of fuel in my head. But I'm used to facing it, all of it, every fucking day."

"That shit you did to Fox's face—will that heal?" Khodî asks Ambrus. "Or will it give me any weird problems in the future?"

"It won't heal, and no, there will be no weird...problems." Ambrus tucks his hand back against his chest. "Jasper might heal from multiple close-range gunshot wounds. He might even heal from Ella's attempt at removing his head from his shoulders via .44. The burns won't fade. They'll just scar in the exact same shape and color as the impression I left behind."

Ambrus swallows and clenches the stained fist closed. "While others were experiencing the worst times of their lives, I was busy creating another of my own."

"I'm sorry," Rex murmurs into Ambrus's hair. The rest of the family isn't ready to hear anything like that about Jasper Fox, but Rex knows his boyfriend needs that kind of sympathy right now. Twelve years. Twelve years, and now...fuck.

This is no simple department-created misunderstanding. Jasper Fox is their enemy.

Django turns in his seat to stare at Ambrus. "How the hell did Fox do that? That wave, that massive hallucination or whatever the hell you'd call it. Are you capable of that?"

"No." Ambrus shakes his head. "That wasn't—"

"Euan?" Rex asks, when Ambrus's explanation turns into silent shock. There is a strange light to his eyes, reminiscent of the odd wire-lift gesture that predicted their danger back at the farmhouse.

"They gave him a second dose." Ambrus draws in a breath. "Oh, God."

Django jerks back in surprise. "Oh. Oh—fuck!" he shouts. "Fuck a damned rabid badger. Those absolute fucking fools!"

"Second dose of *what?*" Ella yells over her father's swearing.

Django pinches his mouth shut, breathing harshly through his nose, before he uses the mirror to look at Ambrus again. "NDAs?"

"I think we're a bit past that point," Ambrus says quietly. "They need to know."

Django closes his eyes for a moment. "Fuck, but I want a drink right now. Kids, you remember what I told you about Korea, ETKC-51, and why you never mention either of them to anyone?"

Brian, Khodî, Ella, Rex, Wesley—they all glance at each other, nodding. Kai shrugs when Ambrus looks at him. "I wasn't born yet when it was an issue. 1991 was before my time."

"All they know is that ETKC-51 is the reason why I'm a walking, talking fucking fossil," Django tells Ambrus, who just raises an eyebrow at the description. "Nothing else. Tell them the rest."

"All right." Ambrus sighs. "During World War II, someone in the brass got a bug up their ass that the super-soldier bit in the *Captain America* comics was a great idea, and it should be recreated in real life."

Ambrus runs his right fingertips along the dried blood on his left hand. "They didn't succeed during the war, like that particular brass-topped officer hoped, but they didn't stop trying, either.

ETKC-51 was the fifty-first attempt. The previous fifty versions of that serum were...failures."

"Dead, or crackers like Fox?" Ella asks.

"Dead," Django replies. "ETKC-51 was the first version that ever did anything aside from resulting in some nasty deaths."

"And when it finally worked, they didn't get super-soldiers." Ambrus's expression twists up in a dry smile. "They got...well..."

"Super spies," Django finishes. He's glaring at the highway as they merge onto a new road and finally escape the capital.

"Spies with benefits," Ambrus corrects dryly. "What an awful abuse of modern slang."

"What the fuck happened?" Rex asks. He can almost feel his boyfriend's hesitation as decades of secrecy try to keep him silent.

"In 1951, the Korean War had been raging for eight months when the program in charge of exploring options for ETKC believed they'd finally made a breakthrough. They rounded up soldiers who seemed exceptionally stubborn, or exceptionally lucky. Of that original group, they whittled it down to fifty by introducing all of them to someone who could..." Ambrus hesitates. "He could convince you to do something you didn't want to do. If you could resist, or if you could, oh, push back, refuse, you were placed with the final fifty. Not that any of us actually had a choice if we participated or not. We'd all signed the paperwork that said our bodies belong to the United States military for the duration of our service."

"How old were you guys?" Kai asks, leaning forward so that he can rest his arm on the back of the bench seat.

Ambrus's smile is pure self-deprecation. "Sixteen. Yes, I'm aware that it was too young."

"Twenty-three," Django answers when Kai glances at him. "Twenty of us lucky fuckers received a single dose of ETKC-51. To this day I still have no idea what the fuck's in it, so don't ask. Twenty others received a double dose. The final ten men, acting as a control group, got nothing."

"Those who received double-doses lost their fucking minds." The first threads of anger enter Ambrus's voice. "It took anywhere from one to two weeks, but by the end of the first week, they were already fading. The control group was sent home at that point for their own bloody safety."

"Just imagine a group of lunatics, all of them capable of pulling off massive examples of the little things you lot have gotten up to over the years," Django adds. "The Army had to put the double-dose victims down—all of them were dead by the end of that second week. They were too dangerous, too out of control. Not that the Army didn't *try* to control them. Those attempts just ensured that a lot of people died."

"But they learned from those failures." Ambrus stares down at his bloodstained hand again. "Because of the original Twenty, the program's directors realized that the sort of mental growth the drug creates can't be rushed. It needs time—people need time to adjust. If you push the human mind too far, too fast…it breaks."

Ambrus lowers his head and wipes at his eyes with his right hand. "They killed my brother. It doesn't matter if he lives through today or not—those fucking bastards killed him the moment they gave him a second dose. He's got maybe a week left before he breaks completely."

"Forced, you think?" Django sounds sympathetic, though Rex thinks that sympathy is reserved exclusively for Ambrus, not Fox.

"I told Jasper about what happened to those who accepted a second dose," Ambrus replies. "Someone was either very, very convincing, or…no. Fox wasn't stupid. I think it was forced."

"Can it be reversed?" Rex asks. "Maybe make Fox *not* be fucking nuts?" Jasper Fox had been a bit naïve, but he was also a good man. He doesn't deserve this shit.

God, Ziba. Rex is suddenly terrified for her. He has no idea what a double-dosed Fox would do to his own fiancée.

"Rex, we don't even know how the serum works." Ambrus gives him a look that's full of grief, old and new. "It just does. They've had scientists studying that shit for almost seventy years, and still that's all we know. The drug works for some, but not for others. Later versions and experimental changes created the same results as the first fifty attempts."

Ambrus looks at Khodî. "How old were you were you decided a .44 was your best friend?"

Khodî grimaces. "Twenty-nine."

Rex swears under his breath, but Ambrus just nods. "I was fifty-one when I tried to get out via one hell of a pharmaceutical overdose, right after the Iran-Contra fuckery. That didn't work, either. I didn't feel good afterwards, but it didn't work."

"Got bored and went back, huh?" Django asks in a low, angry voice.

Ambrus shrugs, offering Django a faint smile. "At that point, I didn't know what else to do. But, as Khodî says: I never tried that shit again."

"Can I make *Highlander* jokes? This seriously deserves *Highlander* jokes at this point," Kai says.

"NO," Khodî insists, scowling. "Fuck you; no."

Ella frowns. "They killed the ones in the program, though, the double-dose fucks. You said they were dead."

"Yes, but they were killed after recent application of the drug," Ambrus tells her. "It changed them, but those were still new changes. Once ETKC-51 has been in your system for a while, doing its work…"

Wesley's hands twitch on the steering wheel, causing the wheels on the van to shriek for a second before he regains control. "Are you telling me we can't fucking *die?*"

Khodî rolls his eyes. "Gray hair, remember? Dad doesn't look twenty-three, and Ambrus here sure as fuck doesn't look sixteen. We still age, it's just..."

Ambrus smiles again. "Slow. Very, very slow."

"Like *Wolverine*, except no bonus claws." Brian looks down at Neumia, who is sleeping while curled up in his lap. "What about Nari? What does this mean for her?"

"I don't know. Django is one of the few of us who decided that trying to sow his genetics throughout the South Pacific was a good idea. The others wouldn't discuss it." Ambrus hesitates. "I wouldn't get any ideas about experimenting, either. ETKC-51 doesn't always create imperviousness. Some Specialists have died after years of service in the department from wounds that other Specialists easily survive."

"That's the second time you've mentioned Specialists. Who the fuck are they?" Django asks.

"Specialists have ETKC-51. Regular agents don't. Most of our now-dead friends at the airport weren't Specialists," Ambrus says. "Whoever sent them was relying on their mission leader for success."

"Fox," Ella growls. Ambrus nods in faint confirmation.

Rex gasps, realization feeling like an electric shock. "The plane crash. The second fucking plane crash," he whispers, feeling his heartbeat quick as adrenaline floods his system. "Shit."

Django turns around in his seat. "Rex?"

Ambrus sits up to look at Rex in concern. "What happened?"

Rex is trying not to let memory overtake him. He hates thinking about that stupid crash, and the shit flashbacks in the airport have made those events feel so much closer, so much more fucking real. "I woke up feeling pinned in place—I couldn't get up. Then I passed out and woke up again, and I wasn't pinned anymore. I thought—I thought someone must have moved whatever was keeping me trapped, but..."

Rex swallows, taking a breath that's just shy of a wheeze. "There were no other survivors of that crash. I wasn't pinned down. I just couldn't—it took a few minutes. It took a few minutes to get over dying from it."

"Fuck, Rex," Ambrus murmurs, and curls up against him, wrapping his right arm around Rex's chest.

"I'm fine. It's just—fucking flashbacks in the airport," Rex explains, swallowing again while trying to keep his breathing even.

Ella startles the hell out of Rex by bursting into loud, violent sobbing. "Baby girl, what the hell is—" Django starts to ask, and then his eyes widen. "No."

"What the fuck?" Brian asks, but Khodî's expression is starting to turn ghastly.

"They said I was crazy!" Ella gasps out, still heaving for breath as she cries. "They said I didn't have phantom limb syndrome, just phantom *twin* syndrome! I told them fucking no, I could fucking feel him! And all those psych quack asshole fuckers did was discharge me for being a nutcase!" Ella scrubs her face clean with both hands and then glares at them all in pure defiance.

"Don't you stupid shits get it? Eric is still alive."

Chapter 11

:⊃✕⊂✕⊃✕⊂:

"Can you still feel him?" Ambrus asks Ella, his voice gentle and full of respect. "The phantom limb-twin sensation they were being so callous about. Is it still there?"

"I—I haven't tried to find out in years. I'm supposed to be nuts, remember?" Ella replies bitterly. "I'd have to sit down and concentrate, maybe once we're somewhere relatively safe. It might take me a while to remember what it feels like."

"Then that's where we leave it for now," Django says, using the visor mirror to look at Ella. "If there's nothing to find, we keep on according to plan. If there *is* something? Ella, we'll find him. I swear."

Ella nods and wipes her eyes again before resting her head on the back of the seat next to Khodî. "All right. I can wait—what's another day or two at this point, right?"

Khodî half-turns around so he can run his fingers through Ella's short hair. "No matter what: it's going to be okay."

"Okay," Ella repeats, closing her eyes as Khodî keeps stroking her hair. Rex watches, trying not to feel like he's been kicked in the chest. It would be the best fucking thing in the world if Eric is still alive. It would also be the worst. The guilt of not looking for him, of not listening to Ella—that part, Rex isn't sure he knows how to cope with.

Wesley finally breaks out of heavy traffic, turning onto a smaller highway that runs east, away from the city. "Okay, Dad. Tell me where the hell I'm going."

"If we stick to the coastal routes, they'll either have roadblocks set up or they'll just...know. Sometimes they do, sometimes not," Django explains when Wesley turns his head to give his father a brief, baffled glare. "We go inland. Follow C101 until it meets AH1 west, and then hit QL-20. That will take us into Đồng Nai. We'll go south before we head east again to Bình Thuận Province. Then we drop southeast one more time to get to the coast."

"How long is that going to take?" Kai asks.

"Days," Ambrus mutters.

Django release a snort of amused laughter. "It's not fucking goat trails anymore, Euan. Six hours at most if we don't hit any more traffic."

"Six hours." Wesley looks like he wants to bang his head on the steering wheel. "Kai, I want you to hand me an entire strip of caffeine pills so I can stay awake long enough to get us there."

Rex falls asleep without realizing it not long after that. When he wakes up, it's fully dark. He glances around the van to find that everyone except Wesley is asleep or pretending to be. Ella's snoring again, so at least she's legitimately napping.

He thinks his father is sleeping until a streetlight temporarily lights up his face and glints off his eyes, cracked open just enough to see. "Dad?"

"Someone's following us," Django murmurs in response. "About ten miles behind."

"Trouble?" Rex yawns and tries to stretch without waking Ambrus, who has a death grip around Rex's waist.

"Can't tell." Django blinks a few times and then rubs his eyes. "That usually means that it's potential trouble, but not definite."

"Don't piss off the locals and everything will be fine, right?"

Django turn his head to look back at Rex, smiling. "Yeah. Something like that."

Khodî lifts his head, awake the moment he realizes he's hearing voices. "Where are we?"

"Finally out of Đồng Nai and into Bình Thuận, to my intense fuckin' relief," Django answers him.

"I thought Xāwuṭh was born in Đồng Nai," Rex says.

"He was, yeah. But some other shit went down in the province during the war that I don't like thinking about. Driving through this place brings a lot of it screaming back." Django glances out of the passenger-side window, where a store they're passing is still in the middle of putting away their wares for the night. "Day of the Nine Bullets levels of flashbacks, kids."

So much has happened in the last few days that it takes Rex a moment to remember the reference. "Euan almost died there. Glad he slept through it, then."

Django nods. "A lot of other people *did* die. It was one of the worst days among an entire decade of bad fucking days. That's when I knew I was done—retired from active service about a month later."

"Off-schedule," Khodî notes.

"Way off. How's the car sickness there, Khodî?" Django asks, blatantly changing the subject.

Khodî scowls. "I was fine right until you mentioned it."

They're heading south again on QL-55B, just on the southern edge of the Tánh Linh District, when Ambrus sits up. "Pull over. That sign has a bar advertising an ATM that spits out American currency."

Wesley glances back and forth along the roadside. "What sign? I don't see shit."

"Wait for it," Django says as they round a bend, revealing an actual eyesore of a billboard.

"Oh, the sign hiding behind a giant hill," Wesley grumbles under his breath. "Rex, your boyfriend is fucking creepy."

"And loaded," Ambrus replies, unoffended. "I have several dozen bank accounts that the department didn't know about. Before they're potentially found, I'd appreciate the chance to empty them. I don't know about the rest of you, but most of my rainy day stashes are elsewhere. We'll probably need the money."

"American cash, gold of the South Pacific." Kai lifts his head from where he'd slumped over to rest against the window while sleeping. "Is it safe to stop?"

Brian lets out a yawn. "I hope so. I need to water a bush like nobody's damn business."

"Yes, that. Gotta pee, Uncle Wes!" Neumia calls out.

"Fuck, I think we all do." Wesley smiles as he spots the bar that the eyesore billboard advertised. "Vietnam still doesn't have open container laws, right?"

"No, because your BAC behind the wheel is supposed to be zero," Django returns dryly. "No drinking and driving, dumbass."

"I have seen how people drive in this fucking country," Ella says, waking up without a single sound to give away the fact that she'd done so. "Bullshit that people obey that law."

"Just actually stop the car," Khodî begs. He's been resting with his head between his knees, hands over the back of his neck, for the last ten minutes.

The bar's parking lot is cracking, grayed-out asphalt, but it has a decent amount of traffic parked out front for a Thursday night in the middle of nowhere. Arc sodium lights paint the front lot in bright orange, so Wesley parks them off to the side, underneath a tree that offers them darkness and a hint of privacy.

Khodî opens up the back of the van and digs through Rex's luggage to find a t-shirt to change into. It won't do much to cover up the bloodstains on his neck and face, but if the bar is dark enough, no one will notice.

"It's too bad we still don't have that Veteran's shirt I got you," Kai says brightly.

"It's too bad I can't hang you upside down from a tree and leave you there, Kai." Khodî tosses his ruined coat, dress shirt, and tie into the trash bin out front as they walk in a bleary-eyed cluster to the bar's entrance. "Let's get this over with, huh?"

"What's on the sign?" Kai asks. "I can't read what the name of this place is supposed to be."

Django glances up. "Paint's faded. I can't make it out, either."

Rex's family crowds into a bar that was new before the war, actively seeking threats, other exits, the mythical American ATM, and bathrooms. What they get is a short, angry Vietnamese woman with iron-gray hair threatening them with a stainless steel cooking ladle.

"You! You no be here!" she shouts.

"Uhm—we only want to pee?" Wesley offers, and flinches away from her when she swats at him with the ladle. "Geeze, lady!"

Brian hefts Neumia up into his arms, sighing. "Look, is this about the airport thing?"

"Airport? No, not airport bullshit." Scary Ladle Lady turns her glare onto Rex's father...and Ambrus. "You two! YOU no be here!"

Django raises both hands, a peaceful gesture to show he's not armed. "Look, ma'am—"

She gives him a vicious prod with the ladle. "You no ma'am me! You drink me out of business!"

Rex glances over to see that Ambrus has an odd expression on his face, mingled remembrance and horror. "Uh. Django."

"Wait, what—" Django tries to say, but gets smacked with a ladle again hard enough that he grimaces.

"You leave!" Ladle Lady shouts again, glaring at each of them for emphatic good measure.

"Oh, she definitely owns this place," Wesley mutters under his breath. "In all senses of the word."

"Django!" Ambrus reaches over, grabs Django's head, and forcibly tilts it upwards. Rex follows their gaze and spies the handles of at least twenty military grade jungle-issue knives embedded in the ceiling.

Django's expression goes entirely flat in displeasure. "You have got to be fucking kidding me."

Ambrus releases Django, looking appalled. "I didn't know! The last time I was in this neighborhood, it was all bloody fucking dirt trails!"

"That is a lot of knives," Khodî observes. "It would take a hell of a throw to get them up that high, let alone make them stick."

"You drink too much, you damage my bar, you tip like shit!" Ladle Lady declares, and then swats Ambrus in the shoulder with the ladle while he's distracted by knives. "You NO stay!"

Brian looks like he's doing his best not to choke on his own laughter. "Can I at least take my kid to the bathroom?"

Ladle Lady squints at him. "You no pedophile?"

Neumia draws herself upright in mortal offense. "This is my *Dad*," she says scathingly.

Ladle Lady motions over her shoulder with her empty hand. "It that way, behind curtain, on left."

"Thanks," Brian says, giving the woman and her spoon a wide berth. Ella grins and bolts after Neumia and Brian, taking advantage of the distraction to get her bathroom time in, too.

"Look, I did not tip for shit," Django says, but he's hesitating. "I think I didn't, anyway."

"You drink too fucking much," their new friend replies, her face twisted up in a furious scowl. "How you know if you tip?"

"Now look—" Django audibly grinds his teeth before launching into Vietnamese. "*Chúng tôi chỉ muốn sử dụng máy ATM. Tôi sẽ cung cấp cho bạn một trăm đô la để bồi thường cho năm 1975.*

Sau đó, chúng ta để. Bạn không bao giờ nhìn thấy chúng tôi một lần nữa. Thỏa thuận?[1]

"No agree!" Ladle Lady retorts. *"Một trăm đô la không đủ. Bạn phá hủy quán rượu!"*[2]

"Destroy the bar—lady, this shitheap is still standing!" Django yells back.

"Oh, hey. Incoming." Khodî grabs Rex by the arm and pulls him back just as a knife falls from the ceiling. The blade embeds itself into the wooden floor where Rex's feet had been a moment ago.

"How the fuck did he get up there?" Wesley asks.

Rex looks up to find that his insane boyfriend has somehow scaled a smooth wooden column to climb around in the bar's thick bamboo ceiling joists. He's pulling rusty 1970s-issued knives from the ceiling and dropping them to the ground, one right after the other.

Ladle Lady stops waving her spoon around. "He no reach all of them," she says sagely. "My boys try. Stupid American drunks."

Ambrus glances down at her. "Sally, we were not that fucking drunk."

Sally of the ladle plants her hands on her hips. "Not drunk? You two make out like sloppy puppies in corner!"

"Oh, no." Rex groans in dismay as Khodî sprouts a huge grin that shows off almost all of his teeth. That definitely explains his father's reaction. "Sally, ma'am, I will pay you another hundred dollars not to fucking talk about that. At all. Ever."

Khodî slings his arm around Rex's shoulders, aiming his grin at Sally. "I'll pay you two hundred to tell this man here *all about it.*"

"Three hundred," Rex growls. "And if I get to beat my brother to death with your spoon, I'll give you another fifty."

Sally looks at Rex and Khodî, eyes Django, and then glances up at Ambrus, who is still retrieving knives. "Your son, he date your old boyfriend?"

"He was not my fucking boyfriend," Django tries to say, but it's too late. Sally roars with laughter, points her ladle at Django, and then laughs harder.

Khodî is still clinging to Rex, all but cackling under his breath. "I really did not think anything could make this day better." Kai is bent over, hands on his knees, laughing so hard that Rex worries his baby brother is going to rupture something.

"And this is me, being done with this level of awkward," Wesley announces, going straight to the bar. "Uh, *xin cho tôi một chai bia. Tôi phải quên đi những gì tôi vừa nghe.*"[3]

---

[1] Vietnamese: "We just want to use the ATM. I'll give you a hundred dollars to compensate for 1975. Then we leave. You never see us again. Agree?"

[2] Vietnamese: "One hundred dollars is not enough. You destroy bar!"

[3] Vietnamese: "Uh, please give me a bottle of beer. I have to forget what I just heard."

"Just any beer?" the bartender asks in English, most of his attention still on Sally.

Wesley buries his face in his hands. "If it kicks like an elephant, I want it."

"You no reach, I tell you!" Sally yells up at the ceiling, wiping tears of laughter from her eyes with one hand. "Central ones too far!"

Sweat is standing out on Ambrus's face as he studies the last five blades, which really do look like they're out of reach. "Hey, Sally? If I can get these last knives down, will you please never, ever talk about anything I did in this bar in the 1970s? At all? I mean absolutely never."

Sally is not impressed. "You fail, I tell *everybody*."

"Euan," Rex says, unashamed of the fact that he sounds like he's on the verge of a pathetic whimper. He does not want to hear those details. No. Never. At this point, unless Ambrus pulls telekinesis out of his bag of tricks, those knives aren't coming out.

"Ye of little faith," Ambrus murmurs. He grabs a rounded upper joist with both hands, letting himself slide off the edge of the lower support until he's hanging in the air, toes pointed at the floor. He takes a deep breath and then begins lifting his entire body in a slow, controlled motion until he's stretched out in a line parallel to the ground.

Rex watches in amazement as Ambrus grabs knife handles with his booted feet, twists them free, and lets them drop. "Holy fuck."

"I am so in awe of your sex life right now, little brother," Khodî whispers.

Rex nudges Khodî hard with his elbow. "Don't be creepy."

Ambrus frees the last knife and drops to the ground, landing in a crouch. "I win, Sally!"

"You cheating motherfucker!" Sally declares, but her scowl is gradually being replaced by a narrow-eyed attempt at hiding a smile. "Fine. You stay. You drink, but if you no tip? I take balls," she warns Django.

"Sally, I never skipped out on a tip," Django says. "Or a bill."

"Then you have thieving friends!" Sally insists.

Django glares at her while pointing at Ambrus. "The last time we were here, all of my friends were fucking dead except him and an asshole general you never got to meet! Blame your sticky-fingered kids, Sally!"

Sally glances in the direction of the bartender, who is watching Wesley in fascinated horror as he obliterates a second bottle of beer. *"Mày đã ăn cắp tiền của tôi, con?"*[4]

The bartender starts in surprise. "Uh, Ma—"

---

[4] Vietnamese: "You stole my money, child?"

"Sticky-fingered shit!" Sally yells, spitting on the old floor. "You no learn! He still steal from till, like grubby bastard," she confides before turning to Ambrus. "Thank you!"

Ambrus glances up from the knives he's examining with Kai's help. Despite the humid weather, some are still in decent condition. "I didn't remember doing this, or I wouldn't have left these here in the first place. Rude. Sorry about that—oh, hey. Django, this one's yours."

Rex tries not to flinch as Ambrus throws a knife at Rex's father. Django catches it by the hilt, like it's the most normal part of his day, and Rex stops holding his breath. Fuck. His father is insane, his boyfriend is insane, and...okay, he car-surfed down the interstate before he was old enough to drive. Rex is probably in perfect company.

Django tilts the blade to read whatever is etched into the metal. "I sometimes wondered what happened to this one." He drops it onto the nearest table. "Man, I was in a bad mood. Sally, sell them all to one of those creepy war memorabilia types on eBay." Sally's face brightens into a true smile.

"White Tigers Tavern. That's what the sign should read," Ambrus says. "If you still wanted to know, Kai."

Kai shrugs. "It's a cool name." Sally stops collecting old knives long enough to beam with pride.

Ella shoves her way through the curtain with a SIG already in her hands, which scares the utter shit out of the patrons in the bar who'd stayed to watch Sally yell at foreigners. "Oh, sorry, yeah, gun, no—I'm not shooting at you, you stupid fucksticks!" she declares, and then sighs as everyone runs out the door. "I keep forgetting normal people think guns are terrifying. We have a situation outside, by the way."

Wesley shoves the empty beer bottle at the sticky-fingered bartender, who takes it and then ducks down behind the counter. "They found us already? How the fuck did they do that?"

"Did we forget to say that the United States has branded us kidnapping, murderous terrorists?" Rex asks, keeping a bland look on his face. Khodî and Ella glare at him. "Huh. Guess we forgot to mention it."

"It was probably someone with a cell phone, a camera app, and a desire to earn a bullet to the head," Ambrus says in a tired voice as Brian and Neumia come out from behind the curtain. Neumia is behind her father, who already has his borrowed SIG in his hand.

"What should we do? Ditch out the back?" Wesley asks.

Sally rolls her eyes. "You no get far. Dunes behind the bar, not car. Dumb ass."

Rex notices when Ambrus suddenly lifts his head, his eyes flickering along as if he's trying to read the air. It's not the same act as his live-wire danger warning, but it's still enough to put Rex on edge. "What's up?"

"Something I need to deal with myself." Ambrus kicks the closest support beam hard enough to make dust rise into the air—and something falls down from the top of the post. Ambrus grabs it in his outstretched hand, revealing a sheathed sword. It's definitely old, with a curve to the blade that's mindful of the way Persian weapon styles migrated outwards.

"Where the hell did you get that *nguyen gươm*[5]?" Django asks.

"Took it off of a Việt Cộng officer back in 1971. Hid it in a bar. Seemed like the thing to do at the time." Ambrus takes it in a two-handed grip before sliding the sheath a few inches down from the sword's hilt, revealing age-darkened steel without a hint of rust.

Sally gives Ambrus an outraged look. "You hide that in my bar?"

"Yes, but I didn't leave it stuck in the ceiling," Ambrus points out, which leaves Sally mollified. Weapons must only be bad for business if they're embedded where they don't belong.

Kai grins. "Forgot it was there until you went knife-fetching, didn't you?"

"Utterly." Ambrus re-sheathes the sword and lowers it to his side, a grim set to his jaw.

"Talk," Django orders. "I know we were followed earlier. Are we in trouble or not, dammit?"

Ambrus's brows draw together for a second. He licks his lips, and then the determined cast comes back to harden his features. "We might have just gained allies, or I'm about to go slaughter two people I've considered friends since 1962."

"Slaughter?" Brian scowls. "They might get back up."

"Hence the fucking *sword*," Ambrus retorts, bleeding irritated sarcasm into the air. "It's a hell of a lot harder to heal if someone puts your torso in a dumpster and then drops your severed head into the nearest ocean!"

Ella grins, bright-eyed and pleased. "Rex, I like your boyfriend. Like, officially and everything: I like him."

"No poaching," Rex mutters at Ella. Not a complication he needs right now, thanks. "We're allowed to cover your ass, right?" he asks.

"Please." Ambrus hesitates. "Just don't shoot them, not yet, even if you get a clear shot. I'll give you a sign if things are going to hell."

"And that will be?"

Ambrus glances at Rex. He can see that his boyfriend is preparing for the worst. "I'll call her by her family name."

Rex tries not to wince. "Oh. Can you handle it?"

---

[5] Vietnamese sword; typically a curved saber.

"I'll handle it fine if someone else is the one shooting them," Ambrus mutters, and heads outside.

Rex pulls the SIG he kept in the waistband of his jeans and follows him. Everyone else is so close on his heels it's a wonder they make it through the damned doorway without getting stuck. The parking lot is almost empty of cars, but their van is still in place. One last car squeals its way out of the parking lot as Ambrus steps towards the center of the cracked pavement, his head barely moving as he uses his peripheral to check for danger.

Rex and family line up along the front wall of the bar before ducking down to minimize target presence. "What've we got, total?" Wesley asks.

"One full clip in each of the four SIGs, eight shells left for the sawed-off, and at least two boxes of .57 rounds for the sniper rifle," Django replies. "A full box of .22 full jacket for the bitty rifle. We *might* have another box of .357 left for the SIGs, but I didn't get the chance to double-check before we left Ho Chi Minh."

"And we only have the SIGs out here with us. Fifty-two rounds," Brian says, flicking the safety off the compact pistol before his finger rests along the trigger guard.

"If we're dealing with these damned Specialists, we may need every single round." Django's finger is on the SIG's safety, but he hasn't disengaged it yet. "If you take a shot, make sure it fucking counts."

"Nari, baby, fingers in your ears and stay behind me," Brian orders. Neumia scooches further back into her father's shadow.

It's really damned annoying when every single overhead arc lamp in the parking lot goes dark.

"What the shit?" Khodî hisses as Rex raises his weapon into the air. He just went from no clear targets to not being able to see a fucking thing. He blinks his eyes, trying to get them to adjust to the dark, but there's no damned moon right now to help out.

"I don't have a fucking shot—" Brian begins to say, and is cut off by the distinct and *loud* clang of metal striking metal.

Kai starts to laugh. "Someone actually brought a sword to a sword fight. This is awesome!"

"It'd be even better if we could fucking see!" Django growls.

Rex opens his eyes and catches the glint of starlight shining off metal. The sword twists through the air; sparks fly when the blades meet. He can just make out two forms moving in the dark at full speed. One is definitely Ambrus, the other is a hair shorter...and they're actually fucking dueling.

"We can finally make *Highlander* jokes now, right?"

"Kai, please shut up, or I will shoot you in the foot," Khodî snaps.

"Only if you carry me like a princess afterwards," Kai sings back.

Rex has to bite his lip against a hysterical bleat of laughter. Their lives have never, ever been normal, but today has seriously pushed the envelope, and possibly also set it on fire.

Rex sees his father raise his SIG. "I've got a shot lined up. What am I listening for, Rex?"

"For me to start shooting," Rex answers. He doesn't want to say that name, not yet. It feels like calling on bad luck, and he's Māori—he knows that shit exists.

"Damn. They're pretty good at this, aren't they?" Brian asks when another three minutes go by and nobody's landed a hit on flesh. Rex is starting to make out the other duelist's features. She's female, probably, with dark hair and dark eyes whose color he can't make out in the crap light.

That's not Ziba. Rex thinks she would be sensible enough to solve her problems by shooting them.

The arc lamps come back on all at once, blinding Rex again. By the time he's blinked spots out of his eyes, Ambrus has the sheath of the sword pressed against the breastbone of the woman he's been dueling, keeping her at arm's length. The sword is stretched out behind him, pointed at the woman who came in close on Ambrus's six while he was distracted.

Ziba Banner has a pistol shot lined up that will take Ambrus in the temple if she fires. Rex's finger twitches over the pistol guard, but Ambrus hasn't said a word. He can—he'll wait. Besides, if Khodî can survive a headshot and Ambrus can survive poisoning himself to death...

"Ambrus," Banner says in a rough voice, like she's suffering a head cold. She's wearing a thigh-length purple shift dress paired with what Rex's sister calls capris. Both match the metallic-threaded scarf wrapped around Banner's throat.

"Hello." Ambrus stares at his attacker, who isn't trying to use the distraction of Banner to chop his arms off. She's dressed in a dark blue tank top and jeans; if the lights aren't throwing everything off, her skin is a few shades darker than Banner's. Her hair is a bit longer, and her eyes appear to be brown, but otherwise she looks almost exactly like Ziba Banner.

Please be family. Please do not let this fucked-up day introduce cloning into my life, Rex prays.

Ambrus turns his attention to Banner again. "What brings you to Vietnam?" It hasn't escaped Rex's notice that Ambrus hasn't called Ziba by name—any name.

Banner steps back and lowers the Beretta 96, a model that holds .40 caliber rounds. Rex swallows down bile. That's definitely a weapon with stopping power.

"This," Banner says, and unwraps the scarf.

"Motherfucker," Ella spits in sudden anger. Kai's swearing is the choked sound of the medically offended.

Rex doesn't have to hear her name to lower his weapon. Oh, fuck.

There are livid purple bruises decorating Banner's pale throat. The shape is the perfect impression of a pair of hands that took hold and squeezed.

Ambrus is staring at the damage. "Oh, my God."

Banner nods, swallowing heavily. "I left him, Euan. We both packed up and left the night this happened. I swear if I'd known that he was going after you—"

Ambrus shakes his head. "It's not your fault. I'm just glad you're alive—they double-dosed him, Ziba."

"We know. Andi was watching the system remotely before they realized we were in the wind." Banner quirks an eyebrow at him. "Is there a reason you're still pointing a sword at me?"

"Because your cousin still has her kukri resting against my balls," Ambrus replies pleasantly. "Andi. Do you mind?"

Khodî whistles. "Shit, I missed that."

Andi smiles and draws the curved edge of her kukri back from its target, but not without making certain the blade crawls across denim with a sound like a pulled zipper. The only ones who don't cringe are Ella, Banner, and Neumia.

Ambrus lowers his sword and gives Andi a gentle prod in the chest with its sheath. She smirks at him in response. He sheathes his blade at the same time as Andi slides the military-issue-sized kukri into a wide leather sheath she's wearing on her back, hidden by the fall of her hair.

"Well, that was fun." Andi even *sounds* like Ziba, but she shares Ambrus's faded Oxford accent instead of Ziba's New York neutral.

"Are we allies?" Ambrus asks. "Or is this a chance meeting on your way through to someplace else?"

Banner and Andi glance at each other. "Ambrus, we've always had family to fall back on," Andi says. "We don't—"

"We have nowhere else to go unless it's to keep running," Banner finishes.

"Look, I'm sure we all feel very sad that you had to run away from the fucking department," Django calls out, loud and angry, "but I'd really like to know how the two of you found us in the first fucking place!"

"You mean like the bit with the airport?" Andi returns dryly. "And that very public gunfight?"

"They started it," Khodî points out. "We just happen to be very good at finishing it."

"Indeed," Andi murmurs, giving him a sidelong glance.

"I was the WAC glorified secretary who made Eugenes Amber a real person," Banner says, which makes Ambrus slap his hand over his face. "Oh. Not a deliberate slip?"

"No," Ambrus grouses through his fingers. "Motherfucker."

"I told no one, and the original paperwork is buried in a place I doubt anyone would ever think to look," Banner assures him. "The department finding you in the airport must have been the result of a seer catching a thread of possibility."

Ambrus drops his hand from his face. "Thread, hell, Ziba. What Jasper did probably created a fucking tsunami. It would have been the brightest potential in the entire region! Shit!" He turns around in a short-paced circle before looking at Banner again. "How did you find us so quickly?"

"We were still capable of monitoring the system for the first few days—we called in sick time to throw the department off our potential escape," Banner explains. "We hung out in JFK's terminal—and I never want to live in an airport terminal again, by the way. The moment Andi saw Eugenes Amber book a flight for Vietnam out of Philadelphia, both of us pulled our own false passports and hopped a flight to Ho Chi Minh. We arrived before you did, had no idea what to do—"

"So we rented a car and waited," Andi says. "We both know you well enough that once you were outside the disaster that became the capital, we could follow the sense of you easily."

"You were supposed to be shielding, you dumb shit," Django says, unimpressed. "I taught all the kids to do that. Common fucking sense."

"I thought I was, but..." Ambrus puts his fingers to his eyes, squeezing them shut. "Django, I don't know about you, but I do not sleep well on planes. Even I have limits."

"Yeah." Django glances at Rex. "Fair enough, Euan."

"They won't be the only ones, then," Brian guesses, sighing as he shakes his head. "Shit."

"We probably have a few minutes before more company arrives, yes," Andi confirms. "They will not be nearly as friendly as we are."

"You started a swordfight," Kai says.

Andi smiles. "And it was fun!"

Khodî glances at the van. "We should probably get the fuck out of here."

Rex looks over to see Ambrus biting his lip. His eyes are taking on that thoughtful glaze he gets when he's trying to consider about a thousand possibilities at once, an expression that's become more and more familiar as this clusterfuck of a week has progressed.

"No matter where we stop in Vietnam, we're going to gain police attention. Too many people have cell phones with cameras and Twitter access. I need to hit those bank accounts now, using Sally's ATM, before the department does the digging it's known for and stumbles over them. No one is going to feed us just because we're all pretty," Ambrus says dryly.

"We have enough—" Wesley tries to say, but Ambrus interrupts him.

"Yes, but for how long? We have no idea how long we're going to be off-grid and cash dependent." Ambrus looks at Banner and Andi, who are staring back at him with the battle-ease of professional soldiers. "We haven't seen the news since leaving the airport. What were the casualty counts?"

"Fourteen civilians," Banner answers. "Plus an entire standard ops team minus the lead, but we don't have any way to know Fox's status."

"Is it Fox coming here? Are we already dealing with a healed-up nutjob?" Django asks, which makes Ella growl.

"No," Ambrus and Ziba both say. "We'd know."

Khodî glares at Ambrus. "How the hell can you be sure?"

"Long-term proximity," Ambrus replies, and looks grieved.

"I had sex with that man. A lot. I'd know if he was getting close, even if he's lost his goddamned mind," Banner adds, anger making it seem like sparks are dancing in her eyes.

Khodî holds up his hands, gun barrel pointed at the sky. "Hey, just curious."

"If Fox brought in a full ops team, and they're down, then it's a backup team to contend with." Ambrus rests his sword along his arm, hilt pointed outward and ready for a quick draw. Rex wonders if his boyfriend is aware of the fact that he's now referring to his ex-partner by last name instead of first.

"A Specialist team is always on-station in the country," Andi says, and Ambrus nods. "Four to five people maximum."

"You, uh, don't seem torn up about the idea about killing this batch," Kai ventures.

A tight-lipped, feral smile graces Ambrus's face. "Everyone I ever gave a damn about in the department is dead, insane, or standing right here in this parking lot. Anyone who stays in the department with this double-dosing shit going on will probably be more than happy to try and kill us all. I'd rather make *them* dead, first."

"Okay. Going for the bag." Brian sprints over to the van. Wesley might tease Brian over his knee surgery, but it sure as hell hasn't slowed him down. Django's eyes are locked on Brian, keeping watch for potential threats.

"Heard a car," Brian tells them when he gets back, tossing Khodî the bag. "About two miles away if I'm judging the sound right."

Khodî unzips the black duffel and pulls out the lightweight little .22. "It's not much, but it'll still punch a hole through someone's eye."

Andi plucks it from his grasp and reaches out for the spare box of shells. "I have no issues with shooting into the windows of another's soul," she announces, and Khodî smiles in approval.

They luck out; there are two boxes of .357 left. One is enough to fill a spare clip for each of the four SIGs. Kai takes his sawed-off back, counting out the eight .240 lead shells with a resigned look on his face. Then he pops the shotgun open, checks that it was already loaded with fresh rounds, and starts pocketing the others.

"Oh, you went very traditional," Banner comments. "An actual sawed-off double barrel twelve-gauge."

Kai holds up one of his shells. "Maybe I only get two shots at a time, but I can put really big holes in things."

"Ziba?" Ambrus asks.

Banner holds up her Beretta 96. "Full clip of twelve, Euan, but I don't have a spare. I thought it might attract too much attention to bring a full box of rounds, even in a properly checked bag, and some enterprising soul in the TSA stole my extra clip."

Andi shrugs when Ambrus looks at her. "I only wanted my kukri. Do you know how blasted difficult it is to get a sword this size through customs?"

Khodî gets out the case for the PDShP anti-material rifle and opens it, snapping the weapon together with the swift precision expected in the military—at least until he catches Andi watching him. "What?"

Andi smiles at him. "I do enjoy watching a man who is good with his hands."

"Andi!" Banner yells. Andi just raises both of her eyebrows innocently and wanders back down the line. Khodî watches her leave, a flabbergasted look on his face.

Django glances down at Khodî. "So, are you gonna finish putting that rifle together, or are you gonna ogle her ass some more?"

Khodî glares at their father, flushes dull red, and turns his attention back to the rifle. What he mutters under his breath is definitely not polite.

Rex realizes that he's grinning. Revenge is awesome.

"One and a half boxes left of .57 rounds, not two full boxes," Khodî says.

"Later, I am allowing myself the opportunity to fangirl over you, sir," Andi calls from her position, setting up shop at the corner of the one remaining parked car.

Django frowns. "Me? What the fuck for?"

"Why would I not fangirl over one of the original Twenty?" Andi replies. "There are only two of you left!"

"Just two—Euan?" Django pauses in the middle of loading his spare magazine to stare at Ambrus. "What the shit?"

Ambrus's eyes are on the approaching headlights of a car. "It's just us, Django. We're the only ones still alive."

"Shit," Django repeats before turning his attention back to the inbound vehicle. "Government cars get more fuckin' obvious every year."

Rex nods in agreement. They have maybe two to three minutes before they have guests unless the driver decides to increase speed, but if anything, the driver is slowing down.

Ambrus suddenly lifts his head, turns, and looks at Ziba. "Why did he hurt you?"

"What?" Ziba has taken up position on the other side of the car, flanking Andi.

"Fox," Ambrus repeats intensely. "Why did he hurt you?"

Ziba hesitates before she gives Ambrus a sad, tired smile. "I told him I was pregnant. We've been using birth control, so he—he didn't believe the baby was his."

"Aw, god," Django mutters.

Ambrus purses his lips before nodding. "You're lucky to be alive at all."

"And that is exactly why we left," Ziba says. Andi has a sober and potentially murderous expression on her face. "I wasn't in the mood to take another chance."

"A wise decision. Wesley! Bring Nari over here!" Ambrus yells. Wesley frowns but walks over with Neumia holding onto his hand. "Nari, this is Ziba Banner," Ambrus says. "She's still going to be shooting at people, but she's going to do it from a position that's actually defensible. You and your uncle are going with her to help."

"I am not!" Ziba retorts.

Ambrus's eyes drop down to Ziba's stomach, the shape hidden by the loose dress she's wearing. "Are you keeping or aborting?"

Ziba glares at him in sudden fury. "Am I *what?*"

"Terminating. Or keeping her," Ambrus says in a harsh voice.

"Her? Oh. *Her.* Oh, god. I—I hadn't decided yet," Ziba admits, her shoulders lowering.

"Then don't let a fucking bullet make the decision for you." Ambrus points at the bar. "There's a single window in the front with a blackout curtain. Take advantage of it!"

"You're gonna want to be on the stick for this, then." Khodî unscrews the PDShP from its stand and hands Ziba the rifle. She gives it a quick once-over and nods before handing over the Beretta 96 in trade.

"Keep my baby girl safe," Brian murmurs as Ziba walks past. "Or I will wait until after you give birth to gut you like a fucking fish."

"Noted," Ziba replies dryly. She disappears inside with Neumia and Wesley as the government sedan pulls into the parking lot.

"That's an embassy vehicle," Andi says. All of them watch as the car comes to a slow, deliberate halt, showing off tinted windows and well-lit government plates.

Brian snorts. "Great. The United States convinced the Vietnamese government to play ball."

One woman and five men, driver included, get out of the car. They shut their doors, moving with the casual ease of people who believe they have the strength, the will, to breeze through a firefight and emerge victorious. All of them, even the woman, are dressed in the same gray three-piece business suits that the other agents wore in Ho Chi Minh. The department has apparently chosen themselves a uniform, distinctive and ugly. It makes their agents easy to identify, and a hell of a lot easier to shoot at.

Three white men: one is younger and potentially albino, but he has black hair, and Rex can't make out his eye color under the vapor glare from the lights. The other is older, with wispy gray hair and a full beard, paired with a gaze that is ice-cold no matter what color his eyes turn out to be. The third is middle-aged, large-boned, and has drooping jowls like a fucking English bulldog.

A tall black man and a barrel-chested Polynesian are bracketing a woman who is maybe twenty—slender, blonde-haired and wild-eyed, with the sort of build that is meant for speed, pinpoint accuracy, and breaking things. She smiles in a way that gives Rex the creeping chills. That is a woman who is bugshit insane, and he doesn't think a second dose of the program's miracle serum made her that way.

The Polynesian is green around the gills. Maybe Khodî isn't the only military type who gets carsick all the time.

Rex glances at his father, and Django shakes his head. No, he doesn't recognize anyone in the lineup. Good. His father doesn't have to shoot anyone that he actually likes today.

Bulldog Jowls speaks first. "You shouldn't have run, Ambrus."

"Run from what, Kröger? From being shot, dissected, or possibly incinerated? Please do enlighten me," Ambrus replies in a sharp voice. "I'd like to know."

"I'm sure the dissection could have been arranged." Jowls smiles, and all at once Rex has his voice pinned.

"I know you." Rex points at Kröger the jowly asshole with the business end of his gun. "You're the fucker that didn't want to take no for an answer on the phone a few months back."

Kröger smile widens. "You should have accepted our offer."

Rex doesn't allow himself to think about it; if he had, the fucker might have ducked. He simply squeezes the trigger, nailing Kröger between the eyes and dropping him like a tubby sack of bricks to the asphalt.

"What the hell?" their Gothy albino friend yells.

"Oh, I'm sorry." Rex grins as four of the remaining five draw weapons. By the time they have guns pointed at the bar, Rex's entire family has kill shots lined up. "Was that premature?"

The gray-haired man clucks his tongue at the crazy woman when she takes a step forward. "No, Vargas. Be patient. We had hoped to do this without violence, Ambrus."

Ambrus gives the gray-haired Specialist a look of polite disbelief. "I think that's the biggest lie I've ever heard come out of your mouth, Thomas, and over the years I've heard many. How did you end up leading a team consisting of Kröger, Vargas, Marcus, Ventimiglia, and Barrel?"

"My name is Barry!" the big Polynesian barks indignantly.

Ambrus smirks and shakes his head. "Your name has been Barrel since you rolled your way through Basic on your parents' dime," he says, which makes the black man snicker. "Miss Vargas, I was not yet aware you were cleared for field work."

"The Director decided that I was ready, especially given the need to retrieve you from your...kidnappers," Vargas replies, still with that same lunatic smile on her face. Rex is fully prepared to shoot her next. She and the old man, Thomas, are the biggest threats out of the group of six. Anyone who doesn't draw a weapon is either stupid, or they believe they won't need it. Vargas is insane, not stupid.

"Raise your hand if you actually believe that line of shit." Ambrus doesn't look surprised when no one moves. "I didn't think so."

"That man Rex shot? He's twitching," Kai informs them.

Rex glances down at Kröger, who is indeed twitching. If Khodî's downtime in the airport is any indication, that's a target who might be standing up again at any moment.

"When do we shoot these pricks?" Ella asks, flicking the safety of her gun on and off. "They're boring as hell."

"I'm not so sure that shooting them will be enough," Ambrus murmurs under his breath, just loud enough for Rex and the family to hear.

"Then we shoot at them a fucking *lot*," Khodî growls. Rex notices Andi giving him an appreciative glance, even if Khodî doesn't see it. "We're better than a bunch of pretentious, dried-up fucksticks."

"We probably have more bullets, too," Kai says in easy agreement. "I mean, unless they have T.A.R.D.I.S. pockets, they're not hiding a whole lot in those suits."

"They're not worried about bullets." Ambrus runs his hand along the sheathed sword before glancing at Django. "How long has it been since you've called the lightning?"

Django gives Ambrus an undecipherable look. "1975. Why?"

"Because you're about to find out how rusty you really are," Ambrus says in a wry voice. "I'd like to live through this."

"Shit," Django mutters.

Ella is the one to catch Vargas reaching into her coat. "GUN!"

Rex, Khodî, Andi, Ella, Django, Ambrus, Brian, and Kai all fire as one, like they fucking rehearsed it. A second volley of armor-piercing rounds comes from the window of the bar as the Specialists return fire.

They have Barrel down, a shot to the eye that Andi definitely gets credit for. Vargas's sleeve is turning red from a nick to her arm. The black man has a red stain on his shin, but doesn't seem bothered by pain. The sedan has several flat tires and faint dents marring the paint-job; armor-plated doors and bulletproof glass protected the car.

No one on Rex's side was hit, which Rex thinks is a fucking miracle. Vargas emptied her entire clip at them. Rex is about to comment on the Specialists' shit aim when he gets the oddest sensation at his back.

That's Ziba. She's...deflecting bullets? Altering reality? Rex isn't sure, and while he's grateful not to be dead, he isn't going to think about that concept again until much later. If the creepy feeling keeps them all alive, he'll cope.

"Did they—am I imagining things, or did they just fucking *dodge?*" Brian asks in disbelief.

"*Tītoko māpuna, huaki rere, Te mangō taha rua...*"

Rex feels the hair stand up on his arms as he realizes his father is chanting in Māori under his breath. Rex knows some of the war blessings, but this one is damned particular.

"*I rere ai te tapuae, I nguha ai te tapuae, I taka toto ai to tapuae...*"

"Split the rounds!" Khodî orders in a low voice. He and Ella fire the first volley; Rex counts off six seconds and joins in with Kai; Django and Andi fire two seconds after that; Ziba and Brian wait three seconds and fire the last set.

"*Tēnei hoki te tapuae ka rūmaki Ko tapuae o Tū.*"

"Motherfucker." Khodî's teeth are bared, his eyes gleaming with anger. Barrel is still on the ground. Thomas has a disabling wound to the left shoulder, but Kröger is getting back to his feet, a positively vile smile on his face.

"That is officially creepy," Kai says. "I didn't bring dynamite. Did any of you?"

"*Hīkoia te whetū! Hīkoia te marama! Ka rere! Ka rere!*"

Ambrus glances at Rex. "Be ready."

"For what?" Rex asks.

"Django," Ambrus whispers.

Rex doesn't even realize he's been saying the chant in time with his father until they hit the gap. Rex glances at Khodî, Kai, Brian, and Ella. It feels like his breath is caught in his chest.

Django bows his head, closing his eyes for a second. "*Ko te atawhaia,*"[6] he hisses, and then he rounds on Ambrus. "The slaughter at Ninh Chu was your fucking fault!"

---

[6] Māori karakia: "The quivering spear, to surprise in flight, Like the double-sided shark, Is the fleetness of the footsteps, Is the raging of the footsteps, In blood are the footsteps, Here are the footsteps' headlong rush, The footsteps of

Rex feels the change like heat under his skin and pressure in his ears. Ambrus's expression morphs into burning rage as he raises his hand, palm out, towards Thomas and his playmates. A visible ripple in the air rushes towards them, a tsunami wave riding the wind.

Three of the Specialists simply collapse, parts of their bodies caved in like an oversized ice cream scoop came along to say hello. Kröger staggers forward a few steps before he faceplants onto the asphalt, gurgling out one last breath. The windows in the sedan shatter in a rain of glass. Bulletproof plating in the car doors groans in distress before buckling with sharp cracks that sound like more gunshots.

"Holy fucking shit!" Kai blurts out in a squeaky, high-pitched whisper.

"Yep, ditto that," Brian says, wide-eyed.

The only two still standing are Vargas and Thomas, who both just seem too damned stubborn to die easily. They're leaning against what's left of the government sedan, staying upright with sheer willpower. Thomas is bleeding from his nose and ears; a blood vessel burst in Vargas's right eye.

Ambrus drops to his knees, gasping for breath like he's been running for miles. "You—you—"

"I'm fucking sorry." Django stares up at the sky, a terrible expression of self-loathing on his face. "It was the first thing I thought of."

"I will kill you," Thomas whispers, smiling at them. "I will make you witness the death of every bastard child you've sired, and then—"

Rex stumbles back when a lightning bolt shoots down from the clear night sky and strikes the sedan. He feels half-fried, the bolt was so close.

While Rex is still trying to blink bright white spots out of his eyes, he hears Kai says, "What the hell? Talk about good timing!"

"Timing didn't have jack shit to do with it," Django rasps. *"Mauruuru koe, Te Uira."*[7]

Rex finally gets his eyes to cooperate so he can see the damage. "Shit," he gasps out, staring at the charred, smoking asphalt. Nobody is standing, not after being struck by lightning. "Okay. I guess I know what happened to the radio tower—"

"Dad!" Khodî yells. Rex whirls around in time to see his father slump in a dead faint. Khodî catches him before he can hit the ground, swearing under his breath. "What the fuck!"

Tū. Stride over the stars! Stride over the moon! Flee! Take flight! Now the death-stroke."
[7] "Thank you, Te Uira." (Māori personification of lightning.)

"Māori live by the whims of the weather," Ambrus replies in a hoarse voice, repeating one of the family maxims. "He'll be fine. He's just...out of practice."

"Fucking hell," Brian whispers. "Practice?"

Ella is almost prancing on her feet. "I want to learn how to do that, like, yesterday and a half ago!"

Khodî gives Ella a disgusted look. "Help me take Dad inside. You can try to figure out how to play with fucking *lightning* later!"

Satisfied that his father is already in good hands, Rex walks over to Ambrus. He wants to reach out and touch the man, satisfy himself that Ambrus is all right, but he can't quite figure out where to even begin.

Ambrus tilts his head up and smiles at Rex. He's white in the face, but his eyes are clear, though Rex can see hints of the rage that Django managed to evoke.

"You don't, uh—you don't look all that great, either," Rex manages.

"Perhaps not," Ambrus agrees, "but I'm still conscious and Django's not. I win."

"Win what?" Rex asks, completely baffled.

"I don't know." Ambrus frowns a little. "We never did quite decide what it was we were trying to compete over, and it's been a while." He shakes his head as if to clear it, and then looks over at the ruined sedan and the bodies surrounding it. "I wonder if anyone's feeling talkative."

"They just got hit by fucking lightning!" Kai shouts. "They're all probably more in the mood to piss themselves."

"If they're even still alive," Brian says, mouth twisting in disgust. "Ugh, crispy bad guys. You fuckers do remember that shit like this is why I didn't join the military, right?"

Sally and her son come outside to survey the damage. Her son looks offended by the mess, but Sally tilts her head as she contemplates charred bodies and the wrecked car. "For one thousand dollar, I call people, they make bodies disappear."

"I'll give you twelve hundred if it happens within fifteen minutes," Rex finds himself saying.

"Deal!" Sally agrees with a bright smile, pulling a cell phone out of her skirt pocket.

"Shit," Brian mutters. "Is everything about this country fucked up?"

Sally puts her hand over her cell's mic to give Brian a sympathetic look. "No. Just you."

"That's probably true," Brian admits. "Hey, where did Andi go?"

"Checking on Ziba, most likely," Ambrus answers.

"Why aren't you freaked out by this?" Ella asks Sally.

Sally snickers between snatches of Vietnamese, interspersing it with an explanation in English. "Those two asshole set bar on fire one night, then make rain to fix. Then next week they drop mound of horse shit on arrogant bastard officer's head without leaving table."

Brian shakes his head. "I want to know just as much as I don't want to know."

Sally finishes her conversation and pockets her phone. "Five minute."

Rex finally reaches out, glad when Ambrus takes his hand. He pulls his boyfriend to his feet and hugs him. Ambrus smells like discharged lightning, accompanied by a melted plastic odor that must be remnants from that weird-ass pressure wave.

"You're okay? With—me?" Ambrus asks him in a soft voice.

Rex nods. "Hey, why not. But if we ever break up, just shoot me instead of squishing me, all right?"

Ambrus's arms tighten around Rex. "I really doubt either of those options will ever be necessary."

When they separate, Rex notices that Kai is still watching the corpses. "I'm seeing more twitching," Kai reports. "They're going to get back up eventually, even if they really, really shouldn't. Maybe even before Sally's magic cleaning crew gets here. Give me your sword, Euan."

Ambrus glares at Kai. "You are not chopping at the pavement with a sword from the nineteenth century!"

Kai shrugs. "Any other ideas, then?"

Ambrus frowns. "Maybe. *Cụ-Ly, bạn đã có một dao nặng?*"[8]

Sally nods and looks at her son. *"Có được anh ta con dao thịt lớn."*[9] Her son grimaces and goes back inside, returning a minute later with a large, wide-edged meat cleaver.

"Yeah, I'm not taking any fucking chances." Kai reaches for the cleaver. "Gimme." The bartender hands it over gladly, starting to turn green.

"Uh, Kai?" Brian's eyebrows are climbing his forehead.

Kai gives him an irritated look. "I'm in fucking medical school, Brian! Do you really think these are the first bodies I've cut up?"

"Yeah, but these are, uh, still alive," Rex points out.

Kai shrugs again and heads over to the lightning-burnt mess. "Not for much longer, they're not."

"Annnnd I will be taking my ass inside now." Brian turns and rushes for the door.

"You all go," Sally instructs after Rex and Ambrus both flinch when the cleaver comes down with a solid thunk. "He know what he doing. You squeamish!"

"Squeamishness is not the problem," Ambrus mutters, but he goes back into the bar with Rex.

---

[8] Vietnamese: "Sally, you've got a heavy knife?"
[9] Vietnamese: "Get him a large meat knife."

"Plan?" Rex asks his gathered siblings. Their father is still out, his head resting in Ella's lap while Ella distractedly taps her fingernails along her SIG's compact barrel.

"We have to leave," Khodî says. "As soon as we can move, we go."

"ATM." Ambrus pulls a cotton sleeve from the back pocket of his jeans. It's a tiny construct meant to mimic the exterior feel of an empty pants pocket, and it fools most pat-down searches. Ambrus slides out one of the bank cards hidden inside, studying it like a man trying to remember how to function. "Feeding us is still a priority."

"Thank the gods," Andi says. She's sitting at a table with Ziba, who is resting with her head in one hand. The fingers of her opposite hand are brushing up against the livid bruises hiding behind her scarf. "We really don't have much available at the moment. Most of our funds are in India."

"I need a road beer," Wesley declares.

"Sure, but you're not driving, you've already had two," Brian says. "I'll take a turn at the wheel. Does this place have soda? Caffeine? Coffee? I'll even drink fucking tea at this point."

"We still have caffeine pills," Kai offers.

Brian shakes his head. "Those always just make me feel sick afterwards."

Khodî nods as their piece-meal plan comes together. "If you have to piss, do it now. We're not stopping again until we hit the water."

Brian gets a Neumia-shaped burr as he heads for the bar. He swings her up, settling her into his arms so she's riding his hip. She's almost too big to be carried that way, but at the moment, Rex doesn't think either of them cares.

"I'll go swap the plates on the van, maybe slap on a few bumper stickers to help change things up." Wesley rubs his face with both hands. They're all starting to wear down, and Wesley crashes faster than the rest of Rex's siblings. "We don't have time to switch vehicles, especially since we're now hauling around eleven people."

"Would you like some help?" Andi asks.

Wesley's face lights up with an exhausted smile. "That'd be awesome, and it saves us some time. Thanks!" He lets Andi lead him outside.

"Rex? Bag, please," Ambrus calls.

Rex picks up the empty black duffel that held the weapons. He doesn't see the point of packing the weapons away again, not with the department and its Specialists all trying to crawl up their asses. They're carrying most of the gear, even Ziba, who has the sniper rifle slung over her back with a carry strap she improvised from something in the bar. The hard-shell case holds the rifle stand and nothing else, which means she pocketed the ammunition, too.

The growing pile of U.S. currency sitting on the table next to Ambrus makes Rex's eyes widen. "Holy shit, you weren't kidding. You're going to empty this ATM, Euan."

"Probably," Ambrus says in absent agreement, pulling the card out of the machine before snapping it in half. "Two more accounts to go. Everything else is in lock boxes scattered around the fucking globe. If we ever get the means to travel safely, we're not penniless."

"No, we're not." Rex is thinking of his own randomly scattered accounts, trying to remember how much he's stashed away over the years, but can't come up with a concrete number.

Rex begins stacking wads of cash into the bag, which would be easier if any of them had thought about rubber bands. "What about daily withdrawal limits?"

Ambrus shrugs, snapping another card in half. "Bank with the right people, and you set your own withdrawal limits."

"Right." Rex is curious as to which particular banks are willing to do that. Probably banks used to Black American Express Card clients. "Hey, so what's it called if you're paranoid that they're out to get you, but they really *are* out to get you, and they're willing to kill you to prove it?"

Ambrus pauses, brows drawing together. "Real life?"

Rex sighs. "Yeah, that sounds accurate." He's worried about Ambrus, about himself, his siblings, his father, his niece—fuck, at this point, even Ziba and Andi. Rex knew they were in deep shit the moment Ambrus was shot in New Jersey, but the confrontation with Fox in Ho Chi Minh has set off a deep feeling of unease that won't go away.

The ATM goes dry with the last bankcard, leaving one of the two accounts attached to it half-empty and the other one untouched. Ambrus mutters curses under his breath as he helps Rex pack what he pulled from the machine.

Kai comes in while they're stacking the last of the money into the duffel, wiping his hands and face on a white bar towel that's swiftly turning red. "Three months," he grumbles as Wesley and Andi walk in the door. "Three months, and I would have had my residency. Three fucking months."

"You would probably have been the most terrifying doctor the United States has seen outside of sanitarium experiments." Khodî is making a disgusted face at the amount of blood Kai is removing via towel. "Fuck, I hope those assholes weren't diseased."

"Monthly bloodwork before field approval," Ambrus reassures them, still sounding distracted. "He's fine."

"I am honestly disappointed that I beheaded those assholes and there was no lightning," Kai complains. "I could have made so many *Highlander* jokes if there had been more lightning!"

"You had your chance when Dad electrocuted those fuckers," Ella tells Kai, who scowls in recognition of the lost opportunity.

"What did you get out of the ATM?" Brian asks, returning with Neumia. They have two plastic-ringed six-packs of Coke with labels printed in Vietnamese.

"Six grand." Ambrus rubs his mouth and then wipes his eyes. "Not a lottery-sized haul, but it'll feed us."

Sally comes to them with a pile of wallets and dog tags cradled in her arms. "We take money off bodies," she says, as if daring them to contradict her. "You maybe want see documents, or you want burned?"

"I'd rather touch none of it, but we need to know what's going on." Ambrus holds open the end of the duffel bag. Sally dumps her prizes inside next to the money. "Thanks, Cu-Ly."

"You pay me, we even," Sally replies with a bright smile.

Rex sighs and peels off twelve hundred from the dwindling supply of American currency in his wallet. "Done. Sorry about the mess."

Sally's eyes widen in mock-innocence. "What mess?"

Ambrus bends over and gives Sally a peck on the cheek. "Hope we never meet again, darling."

"I hope we do," Sally counters, reaching up to pat Ambrus on the shoulder. "You and Māori—always entertaining!" she proclaims, and goes to the bar to join her green-faced offspring.

"We need to wake up Dad," Khodî says, but none of them move. Waking Up Dad has never been a fun proposition.

"We could carry him out to the van," Ella suggests. "He did kill two people without lifting a finger. That ranks right up there with the cow and the landmine."

"Cow. I don't even want to know," Ambrus mutters before he walks over to Django and leans over to shout into Django's ear. "HEY, ASSHOLE! WAKE UP, OR YOU'LL HEAR REVEILLE IN YOUR HEAD NON-STOP FOR THE NEXT SIX WEEKS!"

Django jerks awake, wide-eyed, and sucks in a shocked breath. He glares at Ambrus the moment he sees him. "I fucking hate you."

Ambrus's returning smile is sharp-edged happiness. "Yeah, I know. Come on. We need to move."

It takes three of them to get Django onto his feet, and Rex is honestly worried about keeping him there. It's like watching a soldier deal with blood loss—that particular woozy, light-headed shamble that could lead to faceplanting onto the floor at any moment.

The van was a tight fit before they got to the bar. With eleven people, it's like sitting in a sardine can. Nari is already curled up on Wesley's lap, and Ambrus might as well be sitting in Rex's lap just from the need to make room for Andi and Ziba on the bench seat. Khodî and Kai cram themselves in next to Wesley; Brian and Django have the two front seats.

Ella shrugs and sits on the floor behind the passenger seat. "Nobody kick me in the face."

"Everyone good to go?" Brian asks while adjusting the rear-view mirror.

Django rolls his head over to glare at Brian. "Just get us to the fucking ocean."

अश्लेषा

Chapter 12

❖❖❖❖❖

Rex knows his father. Django meant to stay awake until they get to the coast, but he's out within a few minutes of dark travel at highway speed. He'll wake up irritated and with a crick in his neck, but that's always better than injured or dead.

"No police barricade," Andi observes a few miles east of the bar. "The Specialists must have told them that they would handle it."

"Can't have the government secret weapons becoming known," Ziba says in a dry voice. "I'm still wondering how they're going to attempt to cover up what happened at the airport."

"Doctor the footage, leave out the part where they fired first, and play us on loop firing at innocent American intelligence agents. Problem solved." Wesley rolls his eyes when Rex glances at him in surprise. "Some of us actually do watch the news to find out how they create and get away with that fuckery, you know."

"How long have you guys been with this department shit?" Ella asks, changing the subject with all the subtlety of a hand grenade. When the lights of the highway pass over her face, Rex can see that she's staring up at their new friends. He can't tell if the expression on her face is relief, impending crush development, or target evaluation. Maybe all three.

"1962," Ziba answers, which confirms what Ambrus told them in the bar. "Andi here—she's my first cousin. We both enlisted in the WAC because we wanted to do something with our lives, and the Peace Corps wasn't exactly what we were looking for."

"That does kind of make me realize that we've never been formally introduced," Kai says.

Andi smiles. "This is Ziba Kumari Banner. I'm Anandi Lilavanti Banner, though I desperately prefer Andi. We're also both giving serious thought to reverting to the original Bannerjee."

"Kai," their brother offers immediately. "Ki te Muri kā 'Aukai, but you can see why we stick with Kai."

"Yes, that is an awful lot of vowels," Andi replies, her teeth flashing in the light as she grins.

"Khodî Som." Khodî points at their sister. "Ella Som."

"Are none of you named after your father?" Ziba asks, amused.

"Nope. I'm Wesley Ngata. Up at the wheel there is my brother-cousin Brian."

"Brother-cousin." Ziba forces herself around in the seat so she can stare at Wesley. "What?"

"Dad had a drunken tryst with two sisters whose ovulations had synched up." Wesley grins. "We are the definition of redneck Māori, Miss Banner."

"Ziba, please," Ziba corrects him.

"I'm Neumia de Lacy," Nari introduces herself.

"Pleased to meet you," Ziba says, holding out her hand to take Neumia's in a gentle grip.

"Rex Tjin," Rex says to Andi after Ziba scoots back around to face forward again. "At some point in the next forty-eight hours, you'll meet our brother, Xāwuṯh Bùi."

"Beowulf." Andi is definitely restraining a snicker. "Of course. Why not?"

"Xāwuṯh," Kai repeats, slowing down the pronunciation. "A lot of us call him Wolf, though, for really obvious reasons."

"So, WAC—how did you get from there to the department?" Khodî asks.

"My cousin and I, we specialized in certain types of emergencies," Ziba says, ducking her head. The smile on her face is fond self-deprecation. "We were technically diplomatic staff, but fights had a bad habit of breaking out wherever we went, and we would handle it."

"We thought three years of consistent kill counts and hostage rescue negotiations would at least make the military consider putting us in for combat training, even if we would still just be secret guards among the overseas diplomatic set." Andi scowls. "No, we were too fragile. Too feminine. Can't let us get our dainty little hands dirty. Up until that point, I'd never wanted to shoot someone so much in my life."

"We did have supporters, but Andi and I—we put a lot of time into trying to figure out if we wanted to enlist for another four years, or give in and apply to the CIA, joining the ranks of the Cold War spies," Ziba says. "The department came to us first. Specifically, this jackass."

"This jackass is trying to *sleep*," Ambrus complains, which makes Rex realize that Ambrus hasn't moved in the last five miles except for the slight rise and fall of his chest. Ziba pats Ambrus's shoulder with the casualness of long-term familiarity.

"Euan sat us down with Ziba and myself, had us sign the biggest stack of confidentiality agreements either of us had ever seen, and then told us every single risk involved in accepting a position in the program," Andi explains.

"They had non-Specialist positions, of course, though nothing like those teams you encountered in the airport existed yet," Ziba says. "Euan was already aware of the fact that we didn't want to be anyone else's blasted secretaries."

"Fifty-fifty chance of being absolutely fucking nuts," Khodî points out in a mild voice.

"It was *1962*," Ziba retorts in an angry whisper. "With military careers, it was accepted, even encouraged, that Andi and I remain unmarried. Two single women without such a career, however...it would have been expected that we go home, get married, and become brood mares for the family. Even if we decided not to, it just..."

"A fifty-fifty chance at being insane still sounded better than our alternatives," Andi says quietly. "Thus, you greet the very first women the department ever allowed to join the ranks of the Specialists."

"How much of this are you not supposed to be telling us?" Wesley asks.

"All of it." Ziba shakes her head. "We would be branded traitors just for telling you the Specialist position exists."

"Oh, the loss of respect, the infamy!" Andi mock-gasps, her hand pressed to her breast. "Oh, wait. Never mind, we've already been dubbed traitors. Every single one of us."

"Okay, I can't fucking take it anymore!" Ella exclaims. "Why does Ziba sound like she's from upstate New York, and *you* sound like Ambrus the ex-pat Brit?"

"Scot-tish," Ambrus grumbles under his breath.

"We both went to school in London for a time," Ziba explains, grinning at her cousin. "I refused to adopt any sort of local accent. Andi here reveled in it."

"It was the early 1950s, and it was obvious that I was not lily white as the purest virgin snow. Drove a bunch of racist Londoners absolutely bonkers when the foreigner spoke to them as if she was a local girl," Andi tells them with obvious delight.

"Oh, you're fun. We're keeping you," Ella declares, smiling.

"Please, like that was in doubt," Khodî says, and Rex has to bite back another snort of laughter. Revenge. Is. Awesome.

*   *   *   *

They ditch the van in a quiet neighborhood and walk the rest of the way to the docks in Phan Thiết. Khodî wants to drag his damned feet, he's so tired, but he can sleep when he's dead.

Shit, that's a terrible pun. He'll settle for regular sleep, thanks.

Andi takes one look at the way they're all physically run down and hoists up the duffle full of Ambrus's retrieved cash, carrying it over her shoulder. Ziba pulls a single rolling bag that Khodî suspects holds the only belongings they both still own. Ziba isn't much shorter than her cousin, but she seems dainty compared to Andi, who walks tall and proud like an Amazon warrior, declaring everything she touches to be hers.

Rex keeps grinning at him, the fucker. He is not that obvious. He's *not*.

Fuck, he probably is. It's been a long time since Khodî's been interested in dating, or even the casual hookups he'd managed when younger, and Andi is—she's gorgeous. Also, she's probably a flirt who isn't interested in him at all. That's fine; Khodî is still worried about making sure they all live through the rest of the week.

"Plan?" Khodî asks Django, who keeps rubbing at his eyes in a desperate attempt to stay awake and alert.

"Get a boat, international waters, sleeping, shower, food, so much alcohol," Django replies, making Khodî smile. "Ambrus says he's got a drop box with a burner phone on the coast in Brunei. We can call Wolf that way."

"Two nights on a boat, if we can find one that'll take us across the sea at a decent speed," Khodî estimates. "Pretty sure we can all handle that." At least it's not another goddamn car.

They get a surprise at the docks. For the first time in days, it's a good one.

"Cha! Ở đây!"[1] a man yells.

"Xāwuṭh?" Django whispers, as most of them drop whatever they're holding to turn and face the shouter. Khodî knows he, Rex, Ella, and Django all have their hands on a weapon, ready to draw and kill if necessary. Ambrus doesn't go for a weapon, but he looks like he's going to murder whoever stops him from finding a place to nap. He just won't need a gun to do it.

To Khodî's intense relief, it really is his brother. Xāwuṭh is easily recognizable, a full head taller than pretty much everyone around him. If not, there is always the quarter-inch wide white scar that severs his forehead, his eyebrow, and one cheekbone in a straight vertical line, like he'd tried to compete with their dad for scarring and *really* overdid it. Standing at Xāwuṭh's side with one foot on the dock, one foot on land, is a much shorter but familiar blonde-haired woman.

"Mom!" Neumia shouts. Brian lets Neumia down so she can run to her.

Bonika de Lacy picks up her daughter, holds her close, kisses her hair, and then gives Neumia a sharp look. "Hurt?"

"Nope. Dad would so not let that happen," Neumia declares. Bonika's pleased look lasts all of two seconds before Neumia says, "And I got to stab someone in the junk!"

"Did you?" Bonika lowers her daughter down onto the wooden dock. "I do hope it was for good reason."

"Fuckin' asshole who thought kids made easy targets," Rex explains while Khodî is still trying to figure out Xāwuṭh and Bonika's sudden appearance. "What the hell are you guys doing here?"

"Are you kidding? That airport shit out of Ho Chi Minh City is all over the news." Xāwuṭh turns his head to spit in the dirt.

"No way you made it here from Maluku in...in..." Wesley grinds to a halt. "Oh, shit, I'm that tired."

---

[1] Vietnamese: "Dad! Over here!"

"The airport incident was about ten hours ago," Bonika says, and Wesley whimpers.

"I wasn't in Maluku at all," Xāwuṭh explains. "Bonika here had to swap flights to avoid a group of fuckers dressed in gray suits, so I picked her up in Cambodia. I knew that we were going to be collecting you assholes next, so I used some reserves from a job, called in a few favors, and bought a large fuckin' boat that can hold all of us. Had the feeling I should head out early."

"And he was right," Bonika adds with a small, pleased smile.

Xāwuṭh smirks. "Never been wrong yet. We were already in the water, about halfway here, when the airport shit came in over the news. You guys have multiplied—who are the new girls?"

"Ziba and Andi Banner. Cousins, not sisters," Kai says. "We do not have a repeat of the Brian-Wesley problem."

"Gotcha. Nice to meet you. Please do not try to kill me or my family, and we'll get along famously," Xāwuṭh tells them.

"Same to you, sir," Andi replies with a wide smile.

"Xāwuṭh, what the shit is the media saying?" Django asks.

"The American channels aren't carrying anything except more of the same stupid terrorist bullshit, but anyone who's international and leery of the States is, uh, having trouble making their local affiliates comply with the United States' directive to stow that shit." Xāwuṭh grins, showing off most of his teeth. "It's slowly disappearing from TV, but a lot of people got to see American agents fire unprovoked on suspected terrorists, endangering the public in a way that said suspected terrorists were currently *not* doing. It's probably still all over the internet, though."

"Of course, it's harder for that line of complete nonsense to take in a part of the world where the suspected terrorists look much like everyone else." Bonika smiles, but then the smile drops from her face as she glances around at them. "Wolf, we need to get these people onto the boat before we have to drag them aboard."

Khodî's is in full agreement with her. The darkness is pressing in, encouraging a rest it's not yet safe to take.

"Good idea. All right, come on, assholes—all aboard the SS *Gives No Fuhks*, flagged out of Malta."

Kai blinks a few times. "Did I hear that right, Wolf? You named your boat *Gives No Fucks?*"

"F-U-H-K-S," Xāwuṭh corrects, grinning again. "They can't keep me from using a family name on a boat."

"You are a delightful asshole, Wolf," Ella says in all seriousness.

Xāwuṭh gives his sister a mocking half-bow. "Someone has to be. Where do you want to go?"

"Brunei," Django answers as they start walking down the long dock towards deeper water, where larger boats are anchored. There are only three at the moment, and to Khodî's eyes, they're all huge. "Unless it's an unnecessary trip now, Euan?"

"A burner is a good thing to have. Besides, that's not the only thing I was keeping there," Ambrus says.

When Xāwuth leads them to the entertainingly named ship in question, Khodî stares at it. "Wolf, what in the actual fuck, man?"

Khodî is not an expert on boats. What he does know is that this is a fucking *yacht*, even if it's old enough for the hull's red paint job to be coming off, revealing a darker color beneath that he can't see—Xāwuth was smart enough to anchor the boat out where the dock lighting doesn't work. The yacht sits low in the water compared to the more modern boats anchored nearby, with sleek and subtle lines that Khodî appreciates, but he was still not expecting a fucking *yacht*.

Xāwuth looks at Khodî like he's stupid. "You think I could have crammed all of your asses into my tiny damned boat? No fucking way. Stop whining and enjoy the fact that there's more than one head to piss in."

"More than one bathroom and large enough to have individual berths." Ambrus is also staring at the large damned boat in blank amazement. "You will not hear any complaints from my direction."

"What kind of boat *is* it?" Kai asks, watching as Xāwuth grabs a rope and pulls. A narrow gangplank emerges from the rear of the ship in ridiculously phallic nature, but when Khodî puts his foot once it's resting on the dock, the ramp is sturdy enough to hold the weight of a small elephant.

"Flybridge yacht, older model out of Turkey. Kind of on the small side, so there aren't that many berths. You guys will have to double up," Xāwuth says.

"Oh, the horror," Ambrus drawls, which makes Rex choke on laughter before he puts his hand over his eyes.

"So: you're the boyfriend." Xāwuth grins again. "I can't wait to dangle your ass over the side and quiz you about your intentions."

"Liquor is quicker," Ambrus quips, "and far more effective."

"You've already won points by being sensible," Xāwuth replies, clapping Ambrus on the shoulder hard enough that Ambrus stumbles sideways. "Everybody onto the boat. Vietnam's made my skin crawl ever since I convinced Mom to move back to Thailand."

Khodî listens with half an ear as Xāwuth tells Kai all about the boat in a level of detail that he never wants to try and remember. He pays attention to the important parts, like interior air conditioning, plenty of fresh water aboard, a kitchen that supposedly has food in it, private bathrooms in the two large bedrooms, a single toilet and shower for the double-capacity twin cabins, a wet bar, and oh yes, the fucking air conditioning.

After they're all aboard, there's a lull as Xāwuth goes up to the bridge of the stupid-large boat. Khodî catches a glimpse of someone else on the bridge with his brother: slight-framed, looks like they have their hair buzzed almost to the scalp. Khodî can't make out any other details besides some obvious Thai ancestry and dark hair, so they're probably one of Malai's many niblings.

The engine starts up with a smooth, muted roar. Within minutes, they're cruising through Phan Thiết Bay at a decent clip. The wind catches at Khodî's t-shirt and tries to tug it away. He leans against the railing, enjoying the feeling. Polluted ocean spray tastes like freedom. "Are we clear?"

"Waiting for open water," Django replies in a low mutter. Khodî nods, watching as everyone who still has one drops their bags. Ziba and Kai find a padded bench at the same time and cram themselves into place. It's not big enough to share comfortably, but exhaustion wins; they slump inwards to rest their heads together.

Xāwuṭh comes back when they're sailing through the unbroken darkness of the open ocean. Ambrus straightens and gives him a cautious look. "Are there listening devices on this ship?"

"Not on *my* boat," Xāwuṭh replies, scowling. "Checked her out from top to bottom. Nobody knew I was going to be purchasing her, anyway—didn't announce my intentions, just showed up and offered the owner money."

"And your crew member?" Ambrus asks.

"Family from my mother's side. Hey, Sorrow!" Xāwuṭh yells. "Put a stick in the wheel and come down here!"

About a minute later, a thin-framed Thai appears on the outer edge of the bridge. They drop down into a crouch on the deck near Xāwuṭh with the ease of someone who grew up around boats.

"Šwạ̄sdî,[2]" the kid says, giving the entire group a cautious look. Khodî is reminded of a rabbit that's getting ready to bolt for cover the moment something twitches in the wrong direction.

"Guys, this is Sorrow Bùi, who won't breathe a word about our shenanigans to anyone. Sorrow, this is my father, my asshole siblings, Rex's boyfriend, and two new ladies who look like they can break things with their bare hands—which is awesome, by the way. Neumia's the little one. You met Bonika already—that's Neumia's mom."

"Nice to—to meet you," Sorrow stammers out in passable English with a heavy accent. "I—apologize. Unknown—strangers. They make me nervous."

"Hey, it's cool," Kai says in reassurance. "Do you prefer he, she, they, or something else entirely?"

Sorrow's entire face lights up. It makes their eyes brighten and their features turn near-elfin as they smile at Kai. "Kheā. Bāng khrậng phwk kheā. Bāng khrậng p̄hm k̒ mì thrāb ẁā.[3]"

Kai smiles back. "We call that *agender* at my college. *Agender ḥmāykhwām ẁā mìmī kār tậng khā.*[4]"

<hr />

[2] Thai: "Hello."

[3] Thai: "He. Sometimes they. Sometimes I do not know."

Sorrow glances around at Khodî's family and their accumulated hangers-on. "None of you...object?"

Django shrugs. "Kid, I was bisexual when it was still literally fucking illegal," he says, which makes Sorrow bite their lip against a smile.

"I like agender. He is still fine, and I do not mind...mistakes," Sorrow tells them.[4]

"Mistakes?" Neumia pipes up. "What kinda mistakes?"

"I am...*Chŭx keid khxng čhạn khŭx Dxkbạw.*[5] I was...born a girl. My parents—"

"My uncle Sunan kicked Sorrow out of the house and disowned him because he didn't want to be married off to some asshole like a good little Thai blossom," Xāwuṭh explains before smiling in vicious pleasure. "Mom walked up to Sunan, slapped him across the face three times, and said Sunan was no longer any family of hers, either. Then Mom adopted Sorrow so he didn't have to keep Sunan's family name. Sorrow practically grew up on my boat when I was in port, so I took him with me the last time I headed out from Laem Chabang."

"Oh. Sorrow. I understand." Ambrus gives Xāwuṭh's cousin a gentle look. "You have my sympathies."

Sorrow ducks his head. "*Mị cảpĕn txng khxthos.*[6] It is not your *khwām yāk.*"[7]

"No, I have an entirely different one of those," Ambrus replies dryly, and then looks at Bonika. "Hello, de Lacy."

"Ambrus." Bonika's lips are twitching. "So annoyingly in my life again."

"To be fair, I had no idea," Ambrus says, and hugs Bonika. Khodî realizes his eyebrows are stuck up near his hairline. Bonika does not hug people, not unless those people are Neumia Anari. "They always called you Bo. When Neumia said her family name in the van, I chose to believe I was hallucinating from sleep deprivation, or that it was some other de Lacey family."

Anger and exhaustion turns Django's voice into gravel. "You're fucking *department?*"

"No, I used to be," Bonika answers him in a mild voice, one eyebrow lifted in a faint hint of derision. "Unlike certain parties, I was sensible enough to retire when Director Irvine did in 1998."

Ambrus sighs as he steps away from her. "I was retiring, Bonika. This year. The process was half done."

"And what happened?" Bonika asks, looking at him in a way that suggests she's humoring Ambrus's supposed retirement claim.

---

[4] Thai: "Agender means no preference."

[5] Thai: "My birth name is Lotus Blossom."

[6] Thai: "No need for apologies."

[7] Thai: "Difficulty."

"My partner shot me five times in the chest, precipitating my leap from the sixth floor of a building." Ambrus shrugs when Bonika gives him a look of angry disbelief. "I didn't take it well, either."

"That same man tried to strangle the life out of me a few hours before that," Ziba says softly. "We were...we were engaged."

Bonika's head jerks around to stare at Ziba. "I'm sorry, I thought I heard—what the entire—has everyone lost their damned minds this week?"

"Our current director has begun double-dosing agents," Ambrus says. That should answer Bonika's question pretty well.

Bonika's hazel eyes turn a solid, shining green that often makes lesser men shit their pants in terror. "He is doing *what?*"

"Exactly what I said he's doing," Ambrus reiterates tiredly.

"That's unsustainable, never mind the casualty rate!" Bonika bursts out. "He'll eventually run out of agents—"

"We suspect he's begun mass recruitment drives from other departments within the DoD, given someone we dealt with earlier this evening." Ziba is shaking her head. "I don't think Phillip Stroud gives a damn about the body count, Bo."

Django follows the conversation before he turns around and glowers at Brian. "Department."

"Of course I fucking knew, Dad!" Brian snaps in response. "I had to sign so many damned NDAs, and she wasn't even department anymore!"

"And my retired status is also why Brian has primary custody of our daughter," Bonika adds, but she's glaring at Brian, too. "Of course, someone neglected to mention his own status as a child of the program until well *after* Nari was born."

"Sue me," Brian mutters, turning around to glare out at the ocean.

Xāwuṯh glances around, unconcerned by the emotional rise and fall. "So, for the most part, everyone knows everyone else. Great! That solves a hell of a lot of awkwardness about having to share berths, doesn't it?"

As one body, they all turn and glare at Xāwuṯh, who stares back, unfazed. "What? You're out in the middle of the ocean. Go shower and chill the fuck out. We've got this. If we're boarded, there's a working intercom system to warn everyone, and then we can all shoot our joyful way into attracting sharks as we throw bodies overboard."

Ziba smiles. "Not much really bothers you, does it?"

Xāwuṯh's relaxed expression drops away like a stone. "Seeing my little brother take a fucking headshot on the news? That fucking bothered me. If you decide to go to war against these assholes, I'm already waiting to help burn it all down and salt the fucking earth. If I hadn't seen Khodî get back up, D.C. would be a smoking crater this time tomorrow."

"None of us are in any shape to go to war, not tonight." Wesley digs his fingers into his eyes in a pathetic bid to keep them open. "Thought's appreciated, though."

"Besides," Ambrus says in a light, musing tone that makes the hair on the back of Khodî's neck stand up. "Revenge should never be rushed."

Django smiles. "Mayamiko Chisomo Mphepo."

"South African?" Ella guesses while Khodî is still re-running syllables through his head to try and pull a language.

"Mayamiko Chisomo of the Wind. His parents named him praise and grace, but on the battlefield he was an utter force of destruction." Ambrus's smile is faint, fond—tired. "I miss that asshole Malawi import."

"Another of the original Twenty," Andi says quietly. "I got to meet him. Very kind man, even if he could also be an utter asshole."

Khodî's father is starting to look like he's taken one blow too many. "What happened to him?"

"He was working solo, trying to do something about the cartels arising in South America in the 1990s—the nasty ones that relied on human trafficking. Machete to the base of the neck." Ambrus's eyes glint in the darkness with what Khodî suspects is a hell of a lot of angry grief. "Found his body several days after the fact."

Kai leans forward, putting his elbows on his knees so he can rest his chin in his hands. "Then I bet it's all about spinal cord disconnect. As long as the brain can still communicate with the rest of the body, it can tell that ETKC-whatever stuff to go hyperactive and heal the damage. No communication, the hyperactive healing doesn't happen, and boom—dead Specialist."

Ambrus shakes his head. "That's too simple. Kai, apply as much science as you can, and I applaud you for it, but we're still capable of things that existing science can't explain. Also, I've seen someone take a .50 caliber round to the back of the neck. Full vertebrae shattering, Kai. We wrote him off until the bastard got the fuck back up and killed his way through insurgents in Beirut."

"Huh." Khodî turns his head, the insouciant tone of Xāwuṭh's voice a perfect telegraph of impending trouble. Xāwuṭh doesn't do subtle unless he's really excited about something. That 'something' is not always fun to deal with. "Basically, you guys are used to weird shit," Xāwuṭh says.

Kai gives Xāwuṭh a flat look. "Wolf, today I beheaded six crispy-critter still-living corpses with a meat cleaver."

Xāwuṭh gives Kai a proud smile. "Cool. So, if you guys are still set on Brunei—"

"Seria," Ambrus clarifies.

Xāwuṭh nods. "Okay. If you guys don't mind a trip up and around the island afterwards, Mapun is a pretty nice place to visit."

Django narrows his eyes. "Xāwuṭh, there isn't jack shit on Mapun."

"Nah, not really," Xāwuṭh agrees. "Fishing villages, a few tourists. It's a good place to hide if someone's looking for you, though."

"Let's just—we'll confirm it after Seria," Django says.

Xāwuṭh shrugs. "Works for me," he agrees, but Khodî is still wondering what in the hell his older brother shoved up his sleeve this time.

*　　*　　*　　*

It turns out there really are enough places for them to sleep if they double up like Xāwuṭh suggested. With that in mind, Khodî skips the potential scuffles of people trying to figure out who's sleeping where and goes straight to the head off the passage for the double-occupancy cabins.

The shower is a bright white stall barely large enough to turn around in, but it supplies heated, filtered salt water. He gives no fucks; salt water and soap will clean him just as well as fresh water. Khodî is finally able to scrub the blood from his hair, neck, and back. Finding the shard of dry yellow bone, a tiny sliver trapped in the curls of his hair, is the worst part.

He's done this before. He never wanted to do it again.

Washing until no hint of red splatters onto the bottom of the shower stall fills him with a deep sense of relief. It makes him feel less like he's wearing lies on his skin.

Someone left a pair of jeans and a clean t-shirt outside the bathroom door while he was showering. Khodî's grateful, even if they forgot to add boxers. The shirt he was wearing went on after the blood dried, but now it smells like gunpowder and ozone from the bar shootout. Khodî slides on the jeans, not really worried about the lack of underwear. He plans to faceplant onto a bed as soon as he can wind down. He knows the jeans came from Rex when the pant legs are too damned long. Khodî has to roll up the cuffs so he can walk around without tripping.

Khodî meets Ambrus in the wood-paneled passageway. He's got an armload of clothes and has definitely staked his claim as next in line for the hallway shower. Khodî motions at Ambrus's red-stained hand. "Will that come off?" He hopes so—he's not fond of the idea of his blood marking someone else's skin, either. Not that way.

He does not regret why and how Ambrus used it, though. Fuck that crazy, traitorous bastard, no matter how many doses of chemical bullshit Fox swallowed.

"Xāwuṭh says that there is a bottle of peroxide in the bathroom here, and if not, pumice stones exist," Ambrus says. "It's you and Ella in the double-bunk cabin at the end of the hall, by the way."

"Thanks. Have a nice shower," Khodî replies, feeling awkward as hell as he escapes the conversation. The first door on his left is open, reveling one of the two full-size cabins. The bathroom door inside the cabin is shut; Khodî can hear the muffled, ear-splitting shrieking that is Neumia Anari de Lacy in the middle of Not Enjoying Bath Time.

Bonika and Neumia are going to be sleeping near the bridge in the double-occupancy crew cabin, which is the only reason there's enough room for them all. Someone always needs to be awake and at the wheel, so Sorrow and Xāwuth are swapping out on the captain's cabin's sole bed.

Ziba is sitting on the edge of the full-size bed, staring into her rolling bag and not seeming to hear the racket from the bathroom at all. Andi's kukri is sheathed and lying on the other side of the bed, claiming territory. "Something wrong?" Khodî asks her.

Ziba glances up at Khodî and smiles. "Everything." It's an honest answer that gives him a sharp pang of guilt, and this shit isn't even his fault. "But I'm still breathing, and right now, we're all safe. I've learned to be grateful for these moments."

Khodî tries to smile back. "Yeah. We grew up on that mindset, too."

The next door on his right is the first of the double-occupancy bunks. His father has already passed out face-up in one of the single beds, one arm dangling down to brush the floor. A SIG is resting near his fingertips, and a serrated boot knife that came from fuck knows where is in bed near his left hand.

Kai is in the room's other bunk, literally faceplanted and snoring, his hair still dripping wet from a very recent shower. Khodî smiles and pulls the door closed so they can rest.

Wesley and Brian are already bunked out in the next double-occupancy cabin. Brian is asleep on one of the single beds, one arm thrown over his face. Wesley's eyes are closed, but his lips are moving in what Khodî thinks is one of the Māori prayers for a safe journey. Khodî thinks about it for a few seconds before closing that door, too, but Wesley doesn't protest.

The next door on his left is open. Rex is sitting on the end of the room's double bed. No guesses as to who Rex is bunking with.

Rex is slumped forward, elbows resting on his knees, his head hanging down to get a good view of the thin carpet on the floor. His hair is growing back in with a vengeance, showing as a fine blond bristle all over his scalp.

"Hey," Khodî ventures. Rex lifts his head at once, proving he hadn't fallen asleep in such a miserable position.

"Hi. What's up?" Rex asks.

"I was wondering if you'd gotten through this mess with any books," Khodî says. "I am way too damned cranked to sleep. Also, who's in your shower?"

"Ella," Rex says, which pretty much explains Ambrus's retreat to the hall shower. "And yeah, you're in luck." He pulls over the laptop-sized bag he used for airport carryon and unzips the biggest pocket. "I've got four choices for you: *Queen of the Damned, Pandora, Pride & Prejudice & Zombies,* or *The Girl in the Ice.*"

"I can choose between the mass execution of vampires, ancient Roman sexism and vampires, zombies where zombies don't belong, or murder." Khodî gives his brother a sour look. "Thanks a lot."

"It was an airport fuckin' bookstore," Rex retorts. "You're lucky you have a selection at all, you whiny prick."

Khodî snatches *Pride & Prejudice &* goddamn *Zombies.* "Thanks. I'm gonna go outside and try to pretend I'm reading a normal book."

"You're welcome. Have fun with the zombies!" Rex calls out as he leaves. Khodî is a good man, and he does not chuck the butchering of a classic at his brother's head.

The final door on the right is the last double-occupancy cabin, empty except for the tiny beaded purse Ella managed not to lose between Philadelphia and the boat. Khodî remembers *starting* the journey with a carryon bag, giving him a place to put books or supplies for a layover. After Fox and his bullshit at the airport, Khodî can't remember what happened to it, and their checked bags are probably in government hands by now.

He climbs a short set of stairs and takes the narrow walkway along the exterior port side until he finds another padded bench seat built into a little niche along the outer wall. It even has a single overhead LED he can turn on, plenty of bright white light to read by. Perfect.

He makes it to the first mention of zombies—seriously, why— when Andi finds Khodî's hiding place. "Hello," she says, tilting her head. "Should I bugger off, or is company acceptable?"

In answer, Khodî holds up the book so that the light shines onto the cover. "It's you or this."

Andi grins. "Oh, dear. I'd heard about that, but I hadn't read it. Is it awful?"

"It's weird and annoying because this asshole makes it work." Khodî pats the bench seat next to him, which has enough space for a second, smaller body. "I bet you're more interesting than a book, anyway."

Even visually, Andi is far more interesting. She's wearing a long batik cotton skirt that flows in the breeze, paired with a spaghetti-strap tank top that doesn't seem to have a bra underneath.

Goddammit, behave, Khodî tells himself sternly.

"Maybe, but I'm a very nosy person," Andi replies as she settles down next to him. "I poke and prod, ask questions, and generally make quite the nuisance of myself. You'll wish to return to zombies again in no time."

"I doubt it." Khodî side-eyes her. "Try me."

"All right." Andi gives him a searching look that makes the light glimmer in her rich brown eyes. "Why are you out here reading when most of the others are already sleeping?"

That's an easy one. "I never sleep well during shit like this, even if we're safe and clear for the time being. I usually have to read myself to sleep."

Andi nods. "Ah. I walk. I have to—to move. Assure myself. Pace the perimeter. It takes me a while to calm down, too."

Khodî smiles in understanding. "The more intense the mission, the longer it takes, right?"

Andi returns his smile, but it's tinged with melancholy. "Always. You were in the service?"

"Yeah. Joined up in 1994, went into Special Forces. Thanks to, er, previous service to the country, I got out of Basic as a 2nd lieutenant without needing to hit college first, then started prepping for SFQC and qualified as an 18A," Khodî says.

"Previous service to the country," Andi repeats in a dry voice.

Khodî grins at her. "I'll tell you later. It's a fun story, and given what my crazy asshole brother did, I want Ambrus to hear it, too."

"All right, then. Special Forces," Andi prompts. "What rank did you attain before retiring?"

"Promoted to lieutenant colonel after twelve years," Khodî answers. "That was still pretty new when I decided it was time to get the fuck out."

"Iraq?"

"I was there, yeah." Khodî runs his fingers along the pages of his closed book. "My tour for that full round of fuckery began just after 9/11, on the twelfth, at Ground Zero. I was part of one of the few military units currently in the States who were trained in search-and-rescue operations for wartime conditions. We suited up and went in with the first responders. Spent a week on-site, took a nap, went back in for another week. It wasn't long before I got sick from it. Came home in October on medical leave, coughing up blood."

"I'm so sorry," Andi whispers.

Khodî shrugs, realizes he's trying to tear into the paper he's holding, and makes himself stop. "It was a job that had to be done. I—my dad, he assumed I'd gotten into the toxic shit in the air from the towers coming down, just like everyone else. I didn't—I let him believe that. I didn't want to...shit."

Khodî sighs and tries again. "There was a debris shift. One of my men lost his protective gear when a collapsing section of girder ripped it right off his face. Training in that situation says you don't pull your gear, you just get the wounded out. Instead, I took off my breather, made sure he was suited and sealed, and *then* I got him out."

"Brave man," Andi murmurs.

"Still just a job," Khodî replies.

"And you healed, too." Andi doesn't seem surprised by that. "Son of Django Whetū, proof that the magical cocktail in our blood can be genetically passed on."

Khodî lets out a brief laugh. "Yeah. That's all of us." He tilts his head forward and lifts up his hair, cut short but still long enough to curl under his fingers. "I can feel a scar back there, but I can't see it. Can you?"

Andi's fingers gently brush against the area in question, and Khodî fights back a shiver. "It's a red line, but it's faint. Unless you buzz-cut or shave your head, it's not going to be noticeable. What is it from?"

"That's Fox's gift of the .44 headshot from behind that they were playing on the local news." Khodî does a good job of not grinding his teeth as he drops his hand and lets his hair cover the scar again. He'd been so damned overwhelmed by that weird pressure wave that he hadn't noticed the danger. He woke up after the fact, his head aching, blood pooling around him...and knew exactly what had happened.

"I'm glad you're still here." Andi's words surprise him, as does the depth of calm acceptance in her voice. "What did you do after 9/11, Khodî?"

Khodî raises an eyebrow at the perfect Khmer accenting of his name instead of the standard Americanization. "Afghanistan. Iraq. Ella's twin brother—Eric, Ella, and I, we're not half-siblings. We have the same parents. We lost Eric during that last big roadside assault in 2005. It wasn't—things weren't good. I was due to retire out or re-enlist in the fall of 2006, and I was so goddamned angry. Losing Eric pissed me off, made me think that more time in the military was exactly what I wanted."

"And then something changed," Andi guesses.

"February of 2006." Khodî puts the book aside, or he's going to end up destroying it on accident. "My men and I were supposed to be in a pacified area, one friendly to soldiers and allies. We were careless, or maybe we were tired. We took for granted that it was true." They'd been running nonstop for months, usually for bullshit reasons. A good night's sleep in a confirmed safe zone seemed like paradise.

"The building we were in had already taken damage during the war. Sometime after midnight, someone fired an RPG at us while we were sleeping inside. It didn't even matter that there were men on watch—it happened too fast." Khodî swallows. "I got a hint, a feeling, right before impact. Threw myself off my bunk, rolled underneath it just before half the building came down. Crushed the bunk, but it saved my ass. I only had a few scratches and a hell of a lot of dust to deal with."

Andi's hand creeps into his. He doesn't say anything, but he's so damned grateful for the contact. Sometimes it's rote, when he tells this story. Sometimes it's so raw he can smell mortar, dust, and blood. Doesn't even matter how many times he's repeated it to shrinks billing him assloads of cash, some of whom were dumb enough to ply him with platitudes afterwards.

"I got my men through everything that Afghanistan and Iraq could throw at us, and then it's just..." Khodî gathers himself. "I get up. I get moving, and there's no point. Almost everyone died when the building collapsed. The few who survived the initial collapse bled out on me. I have decent first aid training from SFQC, but I didn't have the skill to—" Khodî sighs. "In less than ten minutes, I'd lost my entire team."

"I'm so sorry."

"Eh." Khodî still doesn't know how to accept sympathy for that moment. It was his call on where they bunked that night. His responsibility. Sympathy can't change that.

Andi surprises him by reaching out, her fingertips tracing the scar on the right side of his face. "You took it hard."

Khodî keeps his voice light. "Someone puts a .44 to their temple and pulls the trigger, you can be pretty sure they mean to check out."

"But just like the airport—you didn't die."

"Nope." Khodî gives her a tired smile. "Shit luck, right?"

"I don't think so." Andi has a thoughtful look on her face that makes her eyes seem darker, more mysterious and compelling than they already are. "It isn't something that was outright discussed among the Specialists, since it wasn't consistent across the board. Some of us could take wounds that should have made us so very dead, and we would just...as your brother Kai said, it was like the drug went into overtime, speed-repairing the damage and keeping us alive. Others would take similar injuries, but they wouldn't heal. Much like the formula of the drug itself, we have no official reason as to why some of us live, and some of us die."

"You think you know, though." Khodî turns off the overhead light, realizing that his eyes have adjusted to the darkness enough not to need it. "You have a theory."

"I think it's a matter of belief," Andi says, uncrossing her legs as she shifts, looking up at the night sky. Out here in dark water, the light from the stars is bright and intense enough to highlight her face in a pale blue glow. "Those of us who survive do so because we *want* to. Those of us who die, they do so because they have already given up on life."

Khodî frowns. ".44 caliber round to the temple, Andi."

"And I think if you had truly wished to 'check out,' as you put it, you and I would not be sitting here having this conversation," Andi replies. "What you did strikes me as the act of a man who'd been pushed too far, for too long, and simply doesn't know which direction to go—he just has to make a decision, something that will be certain when nothing else is."

"Maybe." Khodî feels like she's touching on something he's never been able to put into words. "You do have an interesting way of looking at life."

Andi smiles at him again. "Well, I am the older woman," she says teasingly. "That isn't a problem, is it?"

"No? Why would it be a problem—" That question is answered when she leans over and kisses him.

Khodî stares into her eyes for half a heartbeat before he shoves his hand into her hair and pulls her in for another kiss. That must be exactly what Andi wished for. She makes a needy little gasping noise and climbs into his lap. They kiss like it's the only way to breathe, rough and hard.

Andi breaks off the kiss to gaze down at him. Her eyes are intense, but there is a smile quirking up the corner of her mouth. "I like you," she whispers. "I know it might seem otherwise, but I haven't...liked. In a long time."

"Same," Khodî admits.

When she reaches for the fly of his jeans, Khodî stops her, even though every single fiber of his being is screaming for him to do the exact opposite. "I—I don't have anything with me."

"My bloodwork tested clean not two weeks ago," Andi informs him. "I haven't been in contact with another person, or their blood, since then. You?"

Khodî has to stop and think, trying to remember. Bloodwork, there had been— "Yeah. Traffic accident on the highway last year, had to pull someone out of the wreckage, didn't have gloves. Everything came back clean, and I, uh....no, I haven't contacted anyone else's blood except my own since then. Or body parts," he adds, grinning. "My family has a history of accidentally making people pregnant when we don't mean to."

Andi smiles and bends down, nibbling on Khodî's lower lip in a way that makes him squirm. "Not to kill the mood, dearest, but I can't get pregnant."

"No?"

"Long story, but surgically removed uterus. Do you still wish to go track down a sibling and ask for birth control?" Andi asks him teasingly.

"Fuck no," Khodî replies. Andi grins and proceeds to prove that she is an enthusiastic partner in every sense of the word. Khodî never considered himself a slouch in terms of sex, but this is...this is different, and not just because people have been trying to kill him since the eighteenth of March.

"That was amazing," Andi says a few minutes later, a burr of pleasure in her voice. "I think I desperately needed that."

"Same," Khodî replies, and realizes that there is a wide smile on his face.

God, he's actually happy.

*　　　　*　　　　*　　　　*

Ella isn't stupid. She's manic, manipulative, and according to the military, clinically insane, but definitely not stupid. All it takes is finding Khodî's bunk empty, and Andi absent from Ziba's cabin, to put those two particular pieces together—which is also probably what the pieces in question are doing.

She grabs her stupid tiny hippy purse from the bunk. It's not large enough to hold anything *really* useful, but it means she still has her flash drives along with a stupid tampon if her IUD decides to quit doing its job.

Ella raps on the door to the VIP stateroom, which really doesn't deserve such a fancy title. It's a double bed in a space barely large enough to hold it. The tub-and-shower combo attached to the room? That's what deserves the name.

"Hey. Want a roommate?" Ella asks.

Ziba looks up at her in confusion. "I already have a roommate. Andi—" Her brow wrinkles. "Andi found herself somewhere else to sleep, I take it."

"At least for the night," Ella says, trying not to grin. Andi is likeable nuts, and Khodî has desperately needed to get laid for at least a decade now. "I refuse to sleep in the same room my brother and your cousin are occupying, doing things that I do not wanna hear my brother doing. Roommates?"

Ziba smiles. It makes her look less tired, and a hell of a lot more like someone who wouldn't need a sniper rifle to put down an enemy. Maybe just a good glare.

Damn. That's hot.

Ella blinks a few times and buries that thought. No, no, no. This is not the love boat, and Ziba just broke up with an asshole fiancé.

"Roommates would be fine, Ella." Ziba's deep blue eyes are full of gratitude as she picks up Andi's kukri and places it on the floor on her side of the bed. Ella congratulates herself for asking; she really does understand not wanting to sleep alone. She's been doing it for years.

Ella doesn't have luggage—thanks, stupid airport and Fox—so she wanders in, puts her purse onto the nightstand, and drops down on the opposite side of the bed before stretching out. It's been a long day of shooting both cars and people, and she's tired. She's only wearing a t-shirt and skirt, anyway, so bedtime is now-time.

She misses her horses. Therapy had been kind of nice. Horses are assholes, but Ella understands that kind of mischievous behavior.

Also, there was the bonus of taunting Khodî, who's been leery of horses ever since one dumped him in Cambodia when they were kids. The fall wouldn't have been bad, but that particular dick of a horse had dumped his passenger on a rock pile. Khodî did not forgive or forget, not easily.

"Overhead lights are still on," Ziba says as she stretches out next to Ella, a polite hand-span of distance between them. Ziba's still wearing her loose shift dress, but the scarf and capris are gone. The bruises on her throat are starkly visible. Ella does her best not to look at them more than once. "Do you want me to get them?"

"Nah." Ella takes off one of her sandals and throws it at the light switch. Perfect hit; they get darkness broken only by the glow of stars coming in through the port window. She sheds her other sandal and puts it on the floor next to her gun, just in case she needs to throw something and then shoot a distracted fucker.

Ella is firmly settled, ready for sleep, when she realizes Ziba is sniffling. "Hey. What's wrong?"

"Nothing," Ziba lies, sniffling again. "I'm trying to be quiet. Don't mind me."

Ella scowls. "Look, I am like, the worst example of empathic humanity there is, but I'm not going to ignore someone crying. What's wrong, badass?"

"Badass?" Ziba's voice sounds watery. "You think I'm a badass?"

"Pfft, yeah," Ella says, making sure her new roommate can hear the smile in her voice. "You booked it out of a hostile situation instead of taking foolish chances, and when it came time to fight, you took a gun, no hesitation, and you shot at those motherfuckers like they were the enemy they'd made themselves. Bet you've known some of those people a long time, too."

"I had, yes." Ziba sounds better, but Ella can tell she's still weeping. "I don't want to say anything. He did terrible things to your family."

Fox. Aw, man. "He didn't exactly behave himself around you, either," Ella says.

"No, but he...he used to. I know all you've seen is what the department has done to him, the lengths Jasper is willing to..." Ziba hesitates. "I'm not even sure what it is they've tasked him to do."

"Bad shit," Ella says flatly.

"Yes, I suppose so, but...I was going to marry him." Another sniffle. "He was young, but he grew up so fast, so hard, that it didn't matter. He was only a few months out from losing the junior status and making full agent. We were going to get married, have children the way *we* wanted to have them, and we got along so well, and I *miss him—*"

Shit, Ella thinks in resignation. She might want Fox deader than dead, but he wasn't always a homicidal lunatic.

Ella scoots her hand along the floor until she finds her SIG and the sandal, stuffing them underneath her pillow. Then she rolls over to face Ziba. "Scoot in, okay?"

"Why?" Ziba asks as she shifts over. Ella bites her lip and then gently draws the other woman into a comfortable embrace. Ziba is stiff in her arms, uncertain and confused.

"Listen. Rex told us what Fox was like before everything went to shit and Fox went crackers. He sounded like a neat guy, but he's one I never got to meet. That doesn't mean you can't mourn him, Ziba."

Ella doesn't mention shooting Fox in the throat until the gun trigger clicked dry and the slide locked back. Not the best timing, even if Ella thinks that Fox deserved it. He's probably still alive, anyway.

She swallows hard, trying not to let her eyes prickle with tears. The idea that Eric might also be alive is something she's had to stomp down on, hard, just to keep functioning. "There's nothing wrong with grieving what you've lost."

"You sound like a therapist," Ziba says in a sad, broken voice.

"Well, according to Uncle Sam, I'm officially nuts, so I've seen a lot of therapists over the years. I might as well be an expert on grief and insanity." Ziba's wet-sounding giggle is muffled but genuine. "You hear a lot of bullshit, but every so often some dumb shit with a doctorate will say something useful." Ella tightens her arms around Ziba. "Mourn your kid's father, Ziba. None of us—I mean *none* of us—will ever hold that against you."

Ziba breaks down crying—deep, heaving sobs that sound like they're tearing her apart. Ella sighs and pulls her in close. Ziba curls up against her, sobs with her face resting against Ella's breast, and holds onto Ella like she's found a lifeline as she keens her heart out.

Ella hates crying, personally. She never saw the point of it, but she's well-versed in coping with other people and crying. Kai as an infant: crying; check. Eric, when he awoke from terrible dreams that he didn't know how to explain. Rex when he was so young he probably doesn't remember it, waking from nightmares that he was still living in Singapore, that he'd never been found and his life was so empty...

Ella pets Ziba's thick plait of hair and rubs her back. "For what it's worth, I'm sorry he's nuts, Ziba. But I'm not sorry that you're safe. Congratulations on the kid, by the way. Kids are fun."

Ziba lets out a strangled giggle. "How do you know?"

"Well, Dad fathered eight kids and then crammed seven of us into a farmhouse," Ella replies, grinning. "If he put up with all of us charming, well-educated, dangerous nutcases growing up in the same house, parenting must have had *some* kind of charm."

"I think I'll stick with only the one baby, thank you," Ziba says dryly. Ella wonders if Ziba is aware that she just made the choice she said she hadn't yet made before—one that means she'll be giving birth in seven or eight months.

It seems safer not to mention it. "Go to sleep, Ziba Banner...or Bannerjee. Whichever." Ziba giggles again. "I'm right here, and nothing's going to happen to you. I swear it by my own fucking blood."

"I believe you," Ziba whispers.

Ella keeps petting Ziba, long strokes starting at her forehead, passing over her hair, and following down the line of her back, until Ziba's breath evens out into what Ella is pretty sure is exhausted sleep. Ella stays awake, alert for nightmares or jumpy PTSD-like reactions.

She's still studying the boring-ass ceiling when two giggling idiots stumble into the berth across the hall. There are two beds, but Ella thinks Andi and Khodî are going to end up collapsing into a single twin. That'll be a tight fit.

Heh. Tight.

Ella waits until everything is quiet, until she hears nothing more than tiny Sorrow's light footsteps walking down the passageway. He's probably checking on them per Xāwuṭh's orders, making sure everyone is in a bed instead of punching each other or something. Then Ella finally closes her eyes and lets sleep come say hello.

*　　　*　　　*　　　*

Rex dries off from the shower he finally got to have after waiting for the boat's water heater to catch up from everyone trying to bathe at once. It's worth the delay; he smells like knock-off Zest instead of battle residue, and the hot water will help him feel less bruised in the morning. Yeah, he heals faster than your average asshole, but he hit the ground pretty hard in the airport.

Ambrus is asleep in their double bed, his much shorter hair still managing to fan out on the pillow. Rex can see hints of golden red roots, but the dark brown dye job is still holding up well enough to pass casual inspection.

Rex crawls under the sheet and light blanket to find that Ambrus also decided that sleeping nude is the most sensible option. It means Rex can curl up next to his boyfriend and feel nothing but bare skin sliding along his own. Oh, gods all, but he needed that.

Ambrus's eyes crack open. "Mmrrgh?"

"Everything's fine. Go back to sleep," Rex says, smiling at the grumbled nonsense query. "C'mere, octopus."

Ambrus's lips twitch in a brief smile before he rolls up onto his side so that their hands and legs can twine together, foreheads resting close, their breath mingling. Rex watches as Ambrus goes lax again with sleep except for the snug grip he has on Rex's fingers. Most of the blood came off Ambrus's hand, which is a relief. A few more washings should get rid of the rest.

"You know, all of this crazy shit aside? I love you," Rex whispers, which causes Ambrus to twitch in his sleep. "It's been worth all of it just to be lying next to you right now." Rex closes his eyes, forcibly shoves away a mental repeat performance of the day's events, and makes himself pass out.

April 3rd 1951:

Django hides a wince as one of their military watchdogs walks by, one of the biggest pricks he's ever seen wearing a military uniform with officer's brass on it. To top it off, he's also a bigoted, racist shit-stain of a prick.

Major Cooper picks a new target daily, under claims that he's trying to keep their pet program types from losing their cool in the field. It's complete shit, but the program's directors are turning a blind eye for some damned reason—probably a stupid one.

Dealing with the double-dosed crazies had been bad enough. They're weeks dead now, but Django has to say that, if given the choice between Cooper and the crazies? He'd take the crazies again, no hesitation at all.

There are faint whispers from their guards that everyone is taking bets on who's going to snap and beat the shit out of Cooper first. Django was pleased to discover that most of the bets are on him. Nice to have a reputation. He isn't a bad soldier, but he will only put up with so much bullshit before he makes certain that it stops. He's a combat veteran from two different wars. You do not maintain bullshit attitudes in the field, or people die.

Maybe it's because of those rumors, but for the most part, Cooper ignores Django. Instead, he marches right over to his chosen target of the day.

Django rolls his eyes when he realizes that it's Inali. Great.

The big Cherokee is sitting in the shade, doing what most of them are at various points around the base right now—filling out their daily batch of ridiculous paperwork. How did they sleep? Did they dream? Appetite? What have they heard? What do they *think* they've heard? Did anything explode or move in your presence?

It's so goddamn stupid. English is considering lighting his set on fire to make them stop, but Django thinks it would only make the program's directors hand out more fucking paperwork.

Cooper puts his hands on his belt, resting his thumbs inside the upper lip of the leather like some television sheriff from a Western. "How ya doin' today, Black Fox?" Cooper sneers.

Inali calmly puts his clipboard and pen aside before standing up. His shoulders come back, his chin rises. At his full height, Inali is easily four inches taller than Cooper. "I'm having a lovely day, sir," Inali says while staring past Cooper's left shoulder. "And how is your day, Major?"

Django has to give the man kudos for that one. That was fucking smooth.

Cooper scowls and gives Inali a sharp nudge in the breastbone with his first two fingers. Inali's eyes narrow in acknowledgement of the struck pressure point, one that probably hurt like hell. "Well,

Black Fox-Black Fox, I was havin' a great day until I saw your ugly red neck in my yard."

"If you have issues with my skin color, you should take it up with our respective employers," Inali replies.

Cooper's smile turns nasty. "Oh, I did. Desegregated Army—I don't know what those senile old bastards are thinking. Just like your dumbass parents didn't know what they were doing, giving their greasy Injun baby the same name twice."

Inali murmurs something under his breath. Django shakes his head and puts both pen and clipboard aside, waiting to see how this plays out. Aside from being one of the three that's going to make up Django's quad of agents, soldiers—whatever the hell they're going to be—Inali is also a friend.

"What's that? Are you speakin' Injun at me, you piece of shit? We don't speak Injun in this country, boy! We speak English!" Cooper shouts, acting like a pissant drill sergeant with a tiny prick. "You should learn the language of the place you live in, boy!"

"You're right, sir." Inali gives Cooper an amused look before he says something that Django can't follow in the slightest.

Cooper pushes forward and stands on his toes so he can shove his ugly beak into Inali's face. "What the fuck did you just say to me, Sergeant?"

"Oh, you don't know Cherokee?" Inali feigns surprise. "I'm sorry, Major. I know you're from northern Georgia, so I thought you must have mastered it by now. Gotta learn the language of the place you live. Isn't that correct, sir?"

Django is already on his feet and moving, on his way to make sure that Inali doesn't kill Cooper. Beating the shit out of each other is Army standard, but the brass frowns on making officers dead.

Cooper's fist is already up and back, ready to swing forward. Inali is watching him, but has yet to make a move. The man is fast when he wants to be; he's only waiting for the right moment.

He never gets that moment because Kellagh-Ambrus joins the party. Django swears as the scrawny little shit Brit import jumps up on Cooper's back, wraps his arm around Cooper's neck, and rides him down like he's just found the best thrill at the county fair.

"Goddammit, I wanted to do that!" Inali shouts, and then everything dissolves into complete chaos.

By the time the MPs have bashed heads and sorted things out, Cooper's in the infirmary with two broken arms, a bruised windpipe, two black eyes, a hunk of hair ripped from his head, and is mysteriously missing an eyebrow. Django, Kellagh-Ambrus, and Inali are in the damned brig. Worth it.

"That was fun!" Kellagh-Ambrus declares, grinning and making his split lip even worse. A fresh trickle of blood runs down his chin that makes Inali shake his head and dab at the kid's face with a bundled up handkerchief. Kellagh-Ambrus tolerates it from the big Cherokee when everyone else would risk broken fingers.

Django thinks it's because Inali never acts like a parent; he just reacts like the kid is the biggest tiny annoyance in the entire U.S. military.

"You are a crazy fuck," Django tells Kellagh-Ambrus. "And give me one of those," he adds as the kid unrolls a small bundle of cigarettes from his uniform sleeve.

"Yeah, sure." Kellagh-Ambrus hands them out. "Share and share alike, or some shite like that, right?" English is the best of them at acquiring that kind of contraband, even if the cigarettes smell like they're on the verge of going stale. The program directors frown on alcohol, tobacco, or anything else that would make this shit tolerable.

"That's probably a more accurate version of the saying, yeah," Django says. "What happened to the rest of the pack?"

"Needed them to bribe a guard into sending a letter out to my sisters," Kellagh-Ambrus replies. "I behaved myself and adhered to their ridiculous confidentiality agreements, but if Nessie and Moira don't hear from me often enough, they'll start wondering if I'm dead. I refuse to do that to them."

Django nods, but he doesn't have the same problem. His mother would know if he was gone. Mereana knew about her brothers before she got those infamous telegrams in 1917; she'd know if her eldest child was dead.

"I hope that letter actually gets out," Inali murmurs, rolling the aging cigarette back and forth in his hand. "They're such bastards about that."

"Saw the MP put it in the mailbox with my own eyes," Kellagh-Ambrus says. "And y'know, you could have stayed out of it, Whetū," he adds, smiling again. Inali lets out a put-upon sigh and dabs at the fresh dribble of blood. "Pretty sure Black Fox is capable of breaking Cooper in half whenever he feels like it."

"Then what the hell were you thinking, jumping on that prick's backside, English?" Django asks snidely.

Kellagh-Ambrus shrugs. "That I've been bored out of my mind, and I hate that bloody miserable fucker. Isn't that reason enough?"

Inali chuckles. "Back on the rez, we certainly tend to think so. But if I kill Cooper, where will I get my entertainment from? Stupid white pricks. No offense, English."

Kellagh-Ambrus shrugs. "I'm an import from Scotland. We hate white English pricks almost as much as you do. Need a hand with that, Black Fox?"

"If you have a lighter, then—" Inali's head jerks back in surprise when the end of his cigarette ignites on its own.

"We have our own personal lighter," Django says to Inali. Cat's out of the bag on that front. Finally.

"I was wondering what happened to Cooper's eyebrow." Inali takes a drag from the cigarette after giving it a cursory inspection.

Django thinks it's a wise precaution. "English, you should probably fuckin' warn people when you do that."

Kellagh-Ambrus pops the end of a cigarette into his mouth. The tip flares red as he kindles flame like it's nothing, as if it's not supposed to be *impossible*. "Where's the fun in that?"

"Please, next time, inform me if you develop the means to, oh, set everything on fire," Inali tells Kellagh-Ambrus in a stern voice. "That's useful, tactical information. You have to start thinking like a soldier."

"Scaring the shit out of people *is* a tactic," Kellagh-Ambrus retorts.

"Crazy shit," Django mutters. Maybe there is something to be said about going into this stupid program while barely old enough to shave. Kellagh-Ambrus is enjoying the hell out of the results. The only downside so far was watching half the men living in their barracks slowly lose their damned minds.

Django has no right to bitch about a little bit of fire, anyway. Two days ago, he accidentally called a lightning strike that destroyed the radio tower. Nobody knows it was him yet; it's been dubbed blue lightning because there wasn't a cloud in the sky at the time. Django knows better. Someone had done a thorough job of pissing him the hell off, and he'd focused his anger on the tower just to have a safe target if something...happened.

Well, something fucking happened.

"Well? Why didn't you stay out it, then?" Kellagh-Ambrus asks, prodding at Django with his pointy damned elbow.

"And miss out on the chance to stomp on that fucker's head? Not a chance in hell."

"You are very vulgar," Inali observes politely. "Not that it's uncalled for, it's just that I do hear more obscenities from you than most of the others."

Django shakes his head. "Inali, I'm a World War II vet who saw action in Europe, which included finding one of the fucking camps. Then I got eight months of Korean combat before the program pulled me out and shoved me into this guinea pig cage with the rest of you. You're fucking damned right I'm vulgar."

Kellagh-Ambrus purses his lips before blowing three perfect smoke rings, the little show-off. "Is what Cooper says true?" he asks Inali. "Did your parents name you the same thing twice?"

Inali laughs aloud, the sound echoing off the cinder blocks that make up the brig. One of the MPs on duty gets up and looks around the corner at them, frowns suspiciously at the smoke, and then shakes his head before returning to his post. Django, Kellagh-Ambrus, and Inali pull their cigarettes back out of hiding.

"Of course they didn't," Inali explains. "They named me once, properly. Black Fox—Inali—was the name of one of our great chiefs. On the reservation, the BIA doesn't give a damn what we do, or what we call ourselves, just as long as the money keeps rolling in so they can steal most of it. When I decided to sign up for military service, one name was not enough."

"And you called yourself Black Fox Inali. Black Fox-Black Fox." Django snorts out a brief laugh, smiling. That's fucking funny.

Kellagh-Ambrus is snickering. "Django, we have to make sure Chisomo knows about this."

"Oh, so we can truly have a quartet of people with unusual names?" Django asks.

"My name isn't unusual!" Kellagh-Ambrus protests.

Django rolls his eyes. "It's got a damned hyphen in the middle!"

The kid pauses and then gives Django a wide grin, which means more blood trickles down his chin. "Say Éoghan Beathan Kellagh-Ambrus three times fast."

"Fuck you, fuck you, and fuck you," Django replies, taking a heavy drag on the cigarette. It tastes fucking stale, too. "I'll stick with callin' you English."

"I fucking hate you," Kellagh-Ambrus says in a flat voice, but Django can tell he doesn't mean it. His eyes are too vibrant. Such a terrible damned liar, this kid. Django hates the fact that the military will teach him how to be a good one.

Inali's shoulders are shaking, his laughter silent as he tries not to attract MP attention again. "The two of you alone make all of this bullshit tolerable. Chisomo and I would be bored out of our minds without you. There are not many people in this camp I would be pleased to work with, bending spoons or whatever it is we're supposed to eventually do."

"Does anyone have any guesses at all?" Kellagh-Ambrus asks.

Django hesitates. "I think they are going to start prepping us for spying. Groups of four are usually too damned small for combat, even if it's combat infiltration. You want at least six people for that."

Inali shakes his head. "Then this stupid cocktail of theirs wasn't necessary. I didn't need a drug to hear my ancestors speak to me. If they had simply *asked*..."

"Yeah." Kellagh-Ambrus stares down at the floor. "I understand that."

"You heard your own?" Inali asks.

"I—not that I know of. I just, uh...I could do little things. Avoid notice." Kellagh-Ambrus's lips twitch, but no real smile forms. "I could have done their spy shit without the drug, too. But during the interview..."

"Oh. Him," Django says in a low growl. He'd done his best to embed that asshole into a wall the moment he'd felt tickling thoughts that were Not-His creeping into his mind. He is Māori; that was the wrong fucking button to push.

"Him." Kellagh-Ambrus swallows. "He kept trying to convince me to do things—that same bullshit they're trying to teach us, you know?"

"Yes." Inali doesn't sound pleased, either. "What did you do?"

"Got really fuckin' angry and convinced *him* to pick up his own chair and break it against the wall," Kellagh-Ambrus admits, his shoulders hunching as his head sinks down low.

"Good," Inali declares, before Django can figure out what in the hell he's supposed to do with that kind of confession. "That man is an asshole."

"I didn't know what they wanted," Kellagh-Ambrus whispers. "I just hate being pushed. I—what was your interview like, Black Fox?"

Inali stubs out the remains of his cigarette on the concrete floor and then studies the cell's iron bars as he thinks about it. "Mine was fairly simple. They asked me if I was the man who always knew when it was going to rain. I said yes, because it was well known in my company that I was their weather vane. Where I am from, that talent? That's *normal*. These program directors, these white men, they ask how I know. I told them that anyone would know if they would only stop to listen."

"My aunt thinks that way," Django offers. "She's usually right, too."

Inali nods. "What about you, Whetū? As long as we're comparing notes like jocks in the locker room—" Ambrus sputters out innocent, red-faced laughter— "what did they ask you?"

Django stubs out his own cigarette. There's still tobacco left, but he's sick of the stale flavor. "I've been shot five times in combat. They asked me how I could still be alive."

Part III

"Only if you stretch out your hand
can others stretch out their arm."

–Tamil Proverb

Chapter 13

:XXX:

Upon waking, the very first thing Django does is reach for his gun—part instinct, part dream-driven impetus. There's nothing wrong, no strangers in the bunk room, no cinderblock or iron bars. There's only a closed door, another bunk in arm's reach, and Kai still faceplanted and snoring, the same way he fell asleep last night.

Django slowly releases a breath and flips the SIG's safety back on. The faint noise is still enough to get an incoherent "Mmmph?" from Kai.

"Nothing." Django tries to shake off the dream, a memory of something that happened so long ago that he'd forgotten all of it. "We're fine. Go back to sleep."

"Kay," his son slurs, and is out again at once. If there was one thing college dorm life apparently did the same as Army life, it made certain that you could learn to fucking well sleep anywhere.

Django stands and stretches until his fingertips graze the cabin ceiling. Then he gets dressed, tucks the pistol into the back of his jeans, and leaves the room, gently shutting the door behind him. He stops in the head of the hall, feeling like eyes are on his shoulders the entire time.

Paranoia, not a threat. He thinks so, anyway. He skips shaving, settles for splashing lukewarm filtered seawater on his face, and climbs one of the narrow wooden stairwells to the deck.

It's not really surprising to discover that Ambrus is already awake. He's wearing Rex's borrowed clothes, the jean cuffs rolled up so that Ambrus doesn't trip, but the t-shirt fits all right.

It's always convenient when your significant other can wear your shirts, except for when your significant other steals them all, Django thinks, and is seized by the grip of stupid, stupid melancholy. He doesn't need that right now. He should be happy: all of his kids are currently safe; the sun rising in the east is painting the ocean a gorgeous pink-orange with violet highlights; it's still early enough that the remains of night in the west are showing the last stars of the previous night.

"You're up early," Django says.

Ambrus turns his head just enough to look at him. "So are you."

"Dreaming. Decided I didn't like it." Django joins Ambrus at the boat's railing, feeling gentle morning sunlight paint his skin in soft warmth. It's still so damned odd to have this man back in his life—especially since the scrawny ginger bastard is dating one of Django's kids.

"I was, too," Ambrus admits, his eyebrows drawing together in a slight frown. "I dreamed about Ivan Polzin."

"The original Twenty are coming up a lot lately. Inali," Django explains when Ambrus gives him a startled glance. "I dreamed about the time you, me, and Black Fox tag-teamed Cooper and put the bastard in the infirmary for two weeks."

Ambrus smiles. "I remember that. That was a fun day."

Django hesitates. He's not ready to ask about Inali's fate. The Cherokee had been a good man at a time when decent men seemed to be in short supply. "What happened to Polzin?" he asks instead.

"He met an untimely end in Vietnam, 1971." Ambrus frowns again. "I'd volunteered to babysit him. He'd been getting worse."

"Worse? He was an asshole in 1956. How much fuckin' worse could he be?" Polzin came into the program a little bit off, but by the time Django bowed out, Polzin had to go on missions with a full team who knew how to keep the bastard on a leash. Django had overheard idiots talking about how it was the Russian coming out, but Django knew a hell of a lot of decent Russians, even when Russia was supposed to be the ultimate Enemy of the United States. It had nothing to do with nationality and everything to do with the fact that Polzin was a bloodthirsty fucker.

"Worse," Ambrus repeats. "He wouldn't conform to military standard, department standards—hell, anyone's standard. There was an engagement that took my attention away from Polzin. He used the opportunity to vanish. I had to hunt him down. When I found him, he was raping a Vietnamese boy. The poor kid couldn't have been older than twelve. He was not the first, and the previous victims were…they were not alive."

"Goddammit," Django mutters under his breath. "I didn't think he was a good person, but I didn't know he'd sink that fuckin' low."

"If I'd known, I would have dealt with the problem earlier, but I didn't. None of us knew." Ambrus's head lowers. "After two decades of trying to cope with his unpredictable violence, that moment was the last fucking straw. I didn't care if I was censured or jailed for it afterwards—I put two .45 rounds in Polzin's eyes to drop him, cut off his head, severed his limbs. Dumped his head in the river, burned his arms and legs in four different fires, and then left his torso to rot where it fell."

Django whistles. "Took no chances on him getting back up, huh?"

Ambrus's smile is bitterness laced with satisfaction. "I might also have been a little bit pissed off at the time."

"No fucking shit." Django thinks about it. "Stayed dead, right?"

"Dead as a fucking doornail," Ambrus confirms as the sun rises high enough in the sky to set his hair alight. It's almost enough to hide the dye job. "Why?"

"It's something I'm going to be keeping in mind," Django replies. "Sounds efficient. Speaking of efficiency, I'm surprised you didn't set one of those assholes on fire last night."

"It's been a while. That didn't even occur to me." Ambrus shakes his head, wry smile on his face. "I guess I don't have to limit myself the same way anymore, do I?"

"Didn't know it was a limitation in the first place," Django says. It sure as hell hadn't been through 1956.

"I've been working under a department-sanctioned mandate and an official Presidential decree to never, ever do it again."

Django stares at him. It must have taken something extra-special to earn that one. "Why?"

"I got to meet our sitting President and his Secretary of Defense in February of 1991," Ambrus says.

Django raises an eyebrow. "Yeah?"

"I was only trying to set fire to the fucking mission briefing they were trying to pass off onto the department." Ambrus grins. "Turns out that two-hundred-year-old wood catches and burns pretty fast."

"Good," Django says, laughing. "Hope you put the fear of god into them."

"I was never invited back during that administration, but I did hear rumors that someone was a bit leery of open flame after that."

"Can't imagine why." Django glances at Ambrus. "What kind of mission were they trying to hand out?"

"The kind where I told Irvine that if he accepted it, ever, I would fucking kill him," Ambrus says in a flat voice.

"War-related?"

"Yeah." Ambrus drags his hair away from his face when the wind pushes it in the wrong direction.

Django nods. "Good for you."

Xāwuṯh finds them a few minutes later. "Hey Dad. Boyfriend."

Ambrus smiles. "I do have a name."

"Yeah, and I'll get around to using it eventually." Xāwuṯh yawns. "Sorrow's at the wheel, no bad weather is due for days, and I need to pass the hell out for a few hours. Do either of you assholes know how to steer a boat?"

Django glares at his eldest son. "Xāwuṯh, that is a dumb fucking question."

"I can," Ambrus says, politely ignoring Django's irritation. "At least well enough to ensure that the boat doesn't sink."

"Good enough." Xāwuṯh takes the stairs two at a time up to the bridge cabin.

"Do I fucking know how to steer a boat," Django mutters, still annoyed. He only helped the ungrateful little shit learn to navigate the ocean in the first place.

"Don't worry. If something goes wrong, I will let you steer the stupid boat," Ambrus says. "Those are your genetics at work, by the way; stop bitching."

Django grinds his teeth, but it's a fair point. His eldest kid just pushed his buttons like a professional. Jackass. "Xāwuṯẖ could have shown us where the damned kitchen is on this overgrown tub."

"If you call this yacht a tub in front of Xāwuṯẖ, do I get to laugh when he throws you overboard?"

They find the galley by virtue of following the smell of coffee. Xāwuṯẖ always brews it like tar, putting even military-grade coffee to shame. "Food?" Ambrus asks, after lunging for the pot and getting first dibs. Asshole.

Django opens a cabinet. "Cereal," he announces, finding five boxes of branded cereal with Malaysian script, plus two more that look like off-brand rip-offs. He opens the small fridge built into the wall. "A hell of a lot of eggs, no milk, lemon juice, tamari, sesame oil, and fresh ginger." The ginger is living in a canning jar with no rim to seal the lid.

"This is a terrible cruise line. I'm registering a complaint." Ambrus eyes the cereal thoughtfully. "Hey, those are Rice Krispies. I dare you to make a Rice Krispies Treat using nothing but cereal and eggs. Bonus points if you add the ginger."

Django turns to glare at Ambrus. "I don't know what's worse—the idea, or the fact that I'm hungry enough to actually fucking consider it."

"It can't possibly be worse than anything we ate in 1955," Ambrus points out, opening jars on the countertop as he hunts for sugar to put in Xāwuṯẖ's tar-coffee. He finds unbleached cane sugar, but also a pound of butter shoved up into the underside of a butter preserver.

Ambrus and Django look at each other. "Rice Krispies, butter, eggs, and ginger," Django says, trying to figure out if they're actually doing something this fucking stupid or not.

Then his stomach growls, reminding him of last night's bit with the lightning. Shit.

"Carbs, protein, and fat." Ambrus sings out the old mantra with a wide, merciless grin on his face.

Django sighs and gives up. "I really, really fucking hate you."

The worst part of the entire process is that they've *eaten* half of the horrific brick creation by the time Kai wanders in, bleary-eyed and hunting for coffee. Ambrus takes pity on him and puts a chipped mug directly into Kai's hands.

Kai glances up, spies an unopened box of cereal, and grabs it. He puts his coffee down long enough to tear off the top of the cereal box, shoves his hand inside, and puts a handful of Malay-scripted Kix cereal into his mouth.

"Bleah, stale," Kai reports, and spies the brick. "Hey, real food!" He grabs a square and shoves half of it into his mouth before Django can warn him. "Nom," he mutters, and takes off with his coffee, cereal, and the brick, still chewing.

"What the fuck does college do to people?" Django asks in honest bewilderment. He'd expect that reaction from his Army brats, but Kai?

"Don't know. Never been," Ambrus says. "None of them really offer courses on how to stop being a military asshole and become a productive member of society. How did you manage it?"

Django shrugs. "Pretty sure I didn't. I just learned to fake it really well." He smiles. "Having the kids around helped a lot, though."

Everyone except Xāwuṭh and Sorrow wander in over the course of the next two hours. Sunlight and scheduling—or Neumia—drives everyone out of bed by nine. Django gives Khodî a stern glare over Khodî's proximity to Andi Banner, but Khodî doesn't notice. Django frowns, takes a closer look, and then almost bites the end of his tongue off to keep silent.

Holy shit. He can't remember the last time he saw Khodî *happy*. Amused, sarcastic, biting, driven, and sly, yes, but happy hasn't been on the list in a long damned time.

"What's this?" Khodî asks of the brick's pathetic remains. Everyone gave it a try out of curiosity or desperation, but Kai held the only definite opinion on whether it was liked or not by coming back for seconds.

"It's breakfast quiche." Ambrus's delivery is bland, uninterested, and utter perfection, especially since he doesn't even look up from his coffee to answer.

Khodî has never been shy about trying anything once, but the mutant brick has him raising an eyebrow while he's chewing on it. "Why the fuck is it crunchy?"

"Must be the eggs," Ambrus says in the same tone.

Andi gives Ambrus a narrow-eyed visual dissection that he pretends to ignore. She steals the other half of the quiche-brick from Khodî and takes a bite. "Ah, yes," she mumbles in agreement. "It is definitely the eggs." Django can't help it—he loses his shit laughing.

Khodî dusts his hands off on his jeans. "I do not even want to know." He leaves the kitchen with a cup of coffee and nothing else.

"You are such an asshole," Andi tells Ambrus, smiling.

Ambrus looks up at her, a hint of a smirk on his face. "It's not that bad though, is it?"

"No, it isn't," Andi agrees. "But I can taste what's in it, which is exactly why I'm concerned about the fact that I'm still eating it."

Django also didn't expect to find Ella mooning over the other Banner cousin. "Fucking seriously?" he asks her the moment Ziba is out of earshot. Banner doesn't seem to have noticed Ella's attention, at least.

Ella gives Django a helpless shrug. "Shiny?"

"Ziba is pregnant with another man's kid, the same man who has already done his fucking best to try and kill us," Django says flatly. "Ella, you are barking up the wrong set of panties."

"Look, even I'm sensible enough not to be pushing for anything like that yet, but if we ever get that far? I am totally getting money from you if I get to use that line," Ella replies, grinning. "Besides, by wooing her—maybe—I'm spiting the absolute fuck out of Jasper Fox. Totally adding that to the list of reasons to flirt with the shiny lady. Thanks, Dad!"

Django rolls his eyes. "Goddammit," he mutters. Ambrus is hiding his face behind a kitchen cabinet so he can laugh without being seen by Ella or Ziba.

He's tempted to escape the kitchen when Rex finally wanders in. He has no idea what his tolerance levels are going to be for seeing...well, anything, especially given what Ella and Khodî have gotten up to overnight.

Instead, all Django witnesses is a brief hug and two men leaning in close to each other, existing in each other's spaces without making it a spectacle. He knows right then that Rex and Euan are permanent. Those are two magnetic opposites that have found each other, and they're not letting go.

Dammit. Django is going to have to come to terms with some really awkward memories.

"What the hell is this?" Rex asks after he's swallowed down the last cup of available tar-coffee. He picks up a square of the panned mutant brick disaster. Unlike Kai, he investigates it from all angles instead of just shoving it into his mouth without concern for personal safety or ingredients.

"Imported Rice Krispies, eggs, ginger, and butter," Ambrus tells him. "It's not nearly as horrific as it should be."

Rex shrugs and takes a bite. "Tastes better than the MRE I ate in Turkmenistan," he pronounces after he finishes the square.

Ambrus raises an eyebrow. "You mean the one whose wrapper was discovered with an expiration date of April 2014?"

"That would explain a lot." Rex wipes his hands on his jeans when he realizes there aren't any napkins, cloth or paper, to be found. Xāwuth doesn't know how to buy paper towels, or much of anything that doesn't revolve around fish or beer. Bonika can't have been on the boat long enough to notice the lack of provisions, or the galley would have been well-stocked with food instead of future breakfast bricks.

Ambrus hands Rex another cup of coffee when the pot finishes brewing up a new batch of less tar-like caffeine. "Go round up the others, would you? I think I've figured out something that's been bothering me all morning, and it needs to be discussed."

"You gave me coffee first. I'll do pretty much anything you want." Rex grins before giving Ambrus a dry peck on the lips, exiting the kitchen by climbing the stairs next to the fridge.

Django waits until he's gone. "Turkmenistan, Euan. Did the department know he was going to be on the ground with you?"

"No. It was entirely unrelated," Ambrus answers in a sharp voice, glancing at Django. "I investigated the hell out of it, trying to make sure that no one was attempting to use him against me, or vice versa, but it was a coincidence."

Django crosses his arms and gives Ambrus a flat look. "There's no such fucking thing."

"I know." Ambrus rubs at his face with one hand. "But if there are no coincidences, what the hell am I supposed to make of that, Django?"

Django thinks about a random gas station stop, a beautiful Hawaiian woman, and how his life had utterly changed because of a few brief sentences. "That some things are meant to be."

*   *   *   *

There is a giant, gaudy interior lounge near the front of the ship. The ceiling is purple, the carpet is white, and there's plenty of seating, all of it upholstered in wine-red microfiber. It's garish as hell, but Django doesn't care. The room's best feature is that it's inside the ship, where satellites overhead can't see them.

Neumia is sitting on the floor in front of her parents with her dragon perched on her knee. Django notes the way Brian and Bonika are sitting at a tolerable distance from each other. That's not going to be a fun explosion when it happens, but it's long overdue. They fit well together the first time. Brian was just too young and stupid to realize it, and Bonika has a short-fused temper.

He expected his kids to give Khodî a mound of shit over hooking up with someone he's known for less than twenty-four hours, and is surprised when there isn't a single comment. Maybe Django isn't the only one who noticed the emotional switch in Khodî's attitude. It's like dealing with pre-war Khodî again, not the broken man who came home from Iraq in 2006.

Ambrus can go about invisible and unnoticed, but when he chooses it, the man can also radiate a fierce intensity that gets him immediate attention. He came into the service with the talent in raw form, and the passing years have refined it into something that could easily be terrifying.

Case in point: Ambrus waits until everyone is comfortable before standing, and they all look directly at him. "How many of you dreamed about making choices last night?"

Django wants to lean back and beat his head against the wall. Choices. Shit.

"Me," Rex answers, frowning. Kai and Wesley settle for nodding.

"Same," Khodî and Ella admit at the same time.

313

Andi and Ziba glance at each other. "I wouldn't have classed it that way at first—" Ziba begins.

"—But it definitely fits," Andi finishes. "So: yes."

Bonika sighs. "I was hoping that was just nonsense."

Neumia raises her hand. "Uhm—I did, too. Dream about deciding on things, I mean."

Brian nudges his daughter's shoulder with his bare foot. "Same here, sweetie. It's okay."

Xāwuṭh stumbles into the lounge with a steaming cup of the coffee that Ambrus brewed. "The fuck did I miss?"

"Ambrus asked if we dreamed about making choices," Bonika explains, and Xāwuṭh turns pale.

"Yep." Xāwuṭh drops down next to Wesley. "Fuck everything."

Django shakes his head. "What about Sorrow?"

"Him, too," Xāwuṭh mutters, sullenly sipping coffee. "Freaked him the hell out. I put Sorrow at the till so he could calm down while doing something familiar."

That's enough for Django. "Talk," he orders Ambrus.

Ambrus nods at him before addressing the group. "In Brunei, separated by a distance of about three miles, are two very different types of drop boxes. Because there are two, we all have to make a unanimous decision about how we're going to proceed."

"And we're choosing what, exactly?" Khodî asks.

"The very real chance that we may be going to war against part of the United States government," Ambrus answers softly.

Django gets it first. He's torn between wanting to shake Ambrus, punching him, or weeping in frustration because he already knows exactly how this is going to go.

"It wouldn't be war," Brian growls as Khodî jerks back in surprise. "That's called motherfucking self-defense!"

"Much like the matter of Skywalker versus Vader in the old *Star Wars* movies, that depends upon your point of view," Ambrus replies. "Western media has already done a thorough job of painting us as the enemy, Brian Ngata. If we act against them, even if it's for the good of all..."

"One of those boxes has something that could get us assassinated just for knowing it's there, doesn't it?" Ella doesn't look concerned or manic, which is the only warning sign her enemies ever get. This is Ella in true assessment mode. It's the mindset that terrified her students during war games for Ranger schooling, and before that it soiled the britches of many assholes on Pennsylvania paintball fields. Django never exaggerates when he says that Whetū girls are always terrifying. Neumia might not have needed to use that tiny rifle on the rooftop to cover her uncle's back, but that didn't mean she *wouldn't* have.

"It does, yes," Ambrus confirms. "My seniority in the department is the only reason that I even know it exists, but I'm not supposed to access it without express permission. Given the circumstances, I don't think I'll be asking for it," he adds dryly.

"Would this clear our names?" Kai asks. "Getting our hands on this mystery box, I mean. Would it help?"

"That's not the point," Ella murmurs, prodding at the carpet with her bare toes. "Not for this. That's never the point."

"But it would be convenient!" Kai retorts.

"This could potentially clear our names, yes, though it would have to be accompanied by one hell of a PR campaign." Ambrus pins Kai with a stern look. "Chances are higher that it never will; that we'll spend the rest of our lives in Edward Snowden's shoes. What this *might* do is ensure that those most qualified to hunt us down no longer have the authority or means to do so."

Khodî stares at Django, a set, tight-lipped expression on his face. It's reminiscent of 1991, 1999, 2005—so many goddamned times the tide's been against them, and Khodî stood with the family against every single wave. Django can't sit here and ignore that fierce, competent stability, the same as he can't ignore the giant problem that's actively hunting them down. He gives Khodî a single nod.

When Khodî looks at Andi, she takes his hand and twines their fingers together. God, they're so in synch already. She also nods her agreement of the unspoken question.

Khodî lifts his head and starts quoting: "I, Khòi Khôn đi Som, having been appointed an officer in the Army of the United States, as indicated above in the grade of OF-4 Lieutenant Colonel, do solemnly swear that I will support and defend the Constitution of the United States against all enemies, foreign and domestic, that I will bear true faith and allegiance to the same; that I take this obligation freely, without any mental reservation or purpose of evasion; and that I will well and faithfully discharge the duties of the office upon which I am about to enter."

Wesley glares at Khodî. "I would like to point out that I never agreed to that shit."

"No, but a lot of us *did*." Ella's lips are pressed together, her eyes still cool, hooded darkness. Django knows she's thinking of Eric in that moment, and what the department might have done. "Tell us our choices, Ambrus."

"Our first choice is simpler: We can ignore the vows many of us made to our government, given said government's desire to make us very fucking dead. We retrieve the contents of the first box, kept safe with a grandson of one of the original Twenty. Rex's name is already on the very short list of individuals allowed to retrieve that box. It's Tyung's business to oversee the discreet storage of goods. Even under pain of death, that man will never betray a word of what he kept in trust for me, who retrieved it, or when.

"Between the skillsets we possess and the contents of that box, we can effectively disappear. We'll find a nice place in the South Pacific, lead quiet lives, stay the fuck away from the department, and kill anyone who tries to make any of us do otherwise.

"Our second choice would complicate things." Ambrus shoves his hands into his pockets. "The retrieval of the second box will be noticed immediately. The department will know within minutes. There are agents from the States in the area already, and their sole purpose is keeping watch over this particular bank-vaulted drop box."

"'I'll bite," Kai says. "What's in the box?"

"*Se7en,*" Wesley mutters under his breath.

"The fuck?" Kai asks, glancing at Wesley in confusion.

Ambrus seems amused by the exchange before his expression sobers again. "After the Snowden affair, federal security was tightened. Sort of like locking the chastity belt onto the virgin after she's had the baby, but regardless, it's been done. This means that previously available networked data can no longer be accessed remotely. You can call in a data request and wait. Or, you can ensure that updated copies of that data is always available in certain secure locations around the globe for easier field access."

"What's in the box?" Kai asks plaintively.

Brian snickers. "Still *Se7en*." Kai throws a cushion at him.

Ambrus's eyes flicker over to Django. "In that deposit box, recorded on flash drives with accompanying backup copies, is the entire history of the department."

Every single bit of humor about the situation shrivels up and disappears on the ocean breeze. "Holy shit," Django whispers.

"Exactly. Everything from inception to the department's creation, all personnel files and service records, living or dead, executive orders—everything. All of it updated as of the first of March 2016."

"Well, if we do decide to destroy an entire portion of the federal government, all of that would certainly do the trick, wouldn't it?" Xāwuṯh asks.

"Again: not necessarily," Ambrus says, and Ziba nods, her lips thinned out in an unhappy line.

"Come on. The department has probably gotten into so much shit that it would be an open-and-shut case," Brian insists.

Django shakes his head. "Tuskegee Syphilis Experiment. Salk and the Influenza bullshit. Stateville Penitentiary Malaria Study..."

Kai's expression falls into dismayed realization before he takes over the recitation: "The University of Chicago's Malaria Study. Guatemala's Syphilis/Penicillin Experiments. Operation: Sea-Spray. The University of Pennsylvania and the hepatitis study. Willowbrook State School. Ohio State Cancer Study. Frank Olsen and LSD. ETKC-51. Big Itch and Big Buzz. Project Shipboard Hazard and Defense..."

"None of that fucking matters," Rex says in a harsh voice. "That shit's in the past. The department is a problem *right now*. If those fuckers don't count as a domestic enemy, then I don't know what the hell actually would. I'm in."

Khodî smiles at Rex, the snide, angry expression of a man who's ready to go kill something. "You just want to shoot another agent in the head while he's still blabbering."

"And you don't?" Rex counters. Khodî shrugs in response.

"It has to be a unanimous decision," Ambrus stresses. "The DoD won't only focus their efforts on me for stealing the contents of that drop box. They'll go after every single one of us, and I refuse to do that to someone who doesn't wish to look over their shoulder for the rest of their lives."

"We're probably going to have to do that, anyway." Wesley puts his arm over Kai's shoulders when he still looks dejected. "I'm in."

"They were already trying to kill me," Neumia says in a small voice. "I wanna help. I know I'm just eight, and I can't do a lot of things yet—Grandpa says I *shouldn't* do a lot of those things yet—but I don't want them to hurt us."

"The department was very good to us under Irvine's leadership, but it hasn't been the same since his retirement. I wouldn't grieve over the thought of tearing down its foundations and nuking whatever remains," Andi says.

Ziba bites her lip. "The department did good work until Stroud made us fugitives in this odd public war."

"True." Ambrus frowns. "I have been wondering: why this way, and why now?"

"No idea. Ziba?" Andi prompts.

"Tactically, it's stupid," Ziba replies. Then she smiles. "I'm in, by the way."

"They tried to kill my daughter." Bonika's eyes are glittering with rage. "Anyone who sides with the Director or the department is dead to me."

Brian gives Bonika a searching look before he speaks. "I'm with Bo. The fuckers tried to hurt my kid. They've shot us and turned us into fucking terrorists. I'm in. Let's destroy them."

"I think I've already seen what happens if we do nothing," Xāwuṭh says in a low, unhappy voice. "Besides, if you're going to blow up United States property, you are not having that kind of fun without me."

"They blew up my fucking house." Kai shrugs when the others look at him. "Hey, that's totally valid reason to want someone dead."

"What's the population type in Brunei?" Bonika asks. "I want to know who we can send in to cover your back."

"They get enough tourists that none of us will be noticed as long as we have the material available to look the part," Ambrus answers, and then sighs. "The predominant religion is Sunni Islam, which is not normally an issue, but they've gone ISIS-levels of terrible on certain subjects. Brunei made homosexuality punishable by being stoned to death in 2014."

They all stare at Ambrus in horror. "No public displays of affection," Ella says at last. "Got it."

"It's 2016, and we're back to this shit," Django growls. "Fucking great."

Ambrus looks regretful, but resigned to the situation. "The pendulum keeps swinging, Django."

"Plan," Khodî insists.

"Plan: once we're all on the ground, Rex will retrieve my belongings from Lam-Pan, and I'll be retrieving the contents of the other box with the invaluable assistance of illegally-obtained C-4 via contacts in Seria," Ambrus explains.

"That's going to attract a hell of a lot of attention," Khodî says as Kai whistles.

"That's the point." Ambrus sits down in a chair, starting to look tired. "There is facial recognition software inside the bank. Blowing in the goddamned wall is the fastest way in and out at this point, but when that happens? I have to run inland. I can't take the chance of leading any agents back to this boat. Not to all of you."

Rex's eyes narrow. "That sounds an awful lot like 'running away' again."

Ambrus locks eyes with Rex. "I absolutely swear to you that I'm not. I'll meet you all in—Mapun, you said?" Xāwuṯh nods. "I'll meet you in Mapun in a week if I have to remain on foot; a bit sooner if I find a faster way to travel. If I don't show up after a week and a half, it means I had to backtrack and go elsewhere, for my safety and yours. If that happens, there is a phone in the equipment Rex is retrieving. I'll call you and tell you where I am the moment it's safe to do so."

Rex finally nods, accepting the stark truth in Ambrus's words. "All right. What am I going to be doing with whatever's in this box?"

Ambrus grins. "Don't worry; it comes with instructions." He glances at Xāwuṯh while pointing upwards. "Does that C-band on the roof still work?"

"Piece of shit, but it works," Xāwuṯh confirms. "Receiver's touchy, but as long as I can line up a signal, we've got television."

"Good. We need to be able to monitor the press worldwide, but particularly the United States," Ambrus says. "We'll need to know exactly what we're up against when it comes to manufacturing a counter-campaign."

Ella rests her chin on her clasped hands. "Social media. That's going to be our only real starting point."

"That waits until you've got a hardline and ways to keep from being noticed, even if we're only observing hashtags," Ambrus tells her. "Anything that bounces a signal off of a satellite can be tracked."

"Yeah," Ella replies glumly. "Stupid satellite tracking ruins a hell of a lot of fun."

Ambrus points at her. "I want to see a list of what satellites have stopped you from doing when I get back from bank-theft and jungle walkabout."

"That could take actual fucking days to write out," Rex says, grinning.

"You say that like I don't keep the stupid list backed up on my flash drive," Ella retorts.

"Social media, news, and planning, assholes," Xāwuṭh reminds them. "I can make sure the right stations get programmed into the receiver. I hate standing out in the rain, repositioning that dish by hand. If the receiver won't cooperate, there's a place in Seria that caters to old tech shit that is useful to, oh, criminals."

"Well, we killed a lot of mercs, some United States military employees, stole a taxi, shot a bunch of department agents, and Ambrus is about to rob a bank." Ella grins. "Pretty sure we are criminals, Wolf."

Xāwuṭh rolls his eyes. "I like being a pirate better. Hell of a lot simpler."

"Pirates actually remember to provision their crew," Django says, unimpressed. "Brian and Wesley, you'll be with me when we go into port. We're going shopping so we don't eat the fuckin' boat on our way to Mapun."

"Clothes," Khodî speaks up. "If you lost your luggage—" Ella makes a sound like a dog destroying a chew toy— "write down what you need and hand it over. I'll make it happen."

"I'll hit up a local pharmacy and expand on our medical supplies, then. The kit I put together in Ho Chi Minh is a great start, but if we're going long-term..." Kai pauses. "Fuck it, maybe I'll just knock over a hospital. It'd save me from trying to answer some really awkward questions."

"When do we arrive?" Bonika asks Xāwuṭh

"Tomorrow morning. I'll radio ahead and arrange for tourist day-passes for everyone," Xāwuṭh says. "You guys can play bodyguard, go shopping, blow shit up, steal things—whatever you need to do. Just be back by dusk so we can get the fuck out of there."

Andi smiles. "Tomorrow will be the most normal day I've had in quite a while."

"Did I miss anything? Anyone want to argue? Ask questions?" Ambrus asks.

Kai scowls. "Yeah, I have a question. What's this *Se7en* thing that Brian and Wesley keep referencing when I ask about boxes?"

Ambrus stares at Kai in disbelief. "Someone please buy this man a goddamn DVD player or a Blu-ray so we can educate him about movies from the last thirty years. Seriously, you don't know *Gremlins* or *Se7en*? The rest of you have all failed in your cultural educational duties, and you're fired."

"*Gremlins* was a terrible movie," Django says.

"It's still more believable than the fourth *Indiana Jones* movie," Rex says, which earns him several glares.

Neumia raises her hand again. "What's for lunch?"

Xāwuṭh grins. "Hope you assholes like fish."

* * * *

Fish, of course, means catching the fucking things in the first place. Xāwuṭh is an asshole.

Ella baits a hook with a long strand of what used to be some other poor fish's intestine, casts the line, and shoves the pole into its holder. "I hope that attracts something edible, and not, like, a shark. I don't want to eat a shark."

"You tried to eat a shark when you were eleven," Xāwuṭh points out. He's standing beside her with his arms crossed, his eyes darting around as he watches people either cast lines or talk while waiting for fish to literally take the bait.

"That's exactly why I don't want to eat one now. Tough fuckers." Ella leans against her mutant-tall brother. "You're a good man, you jackass."

"Oh yeah?" Xāwuṭh snorts. "What makes you say that?"

"Because this is normal." Ella smiles. "For just a little while, it's a bunch of us stupid fucks standing out on a boat in the ocean, trying to catch lunch, having beer and talking like nothing's wrong."

"Ella, right now? *Nothing* is wrong," Xāwuṭh stresses. "This is the breather between the bullshit. This is us. Now pick up that line. You've snagged something, baby sister."

"I'm your only sister," Ella mutters, grabbing the reel and testing the slack on the line. "Well, it's interested, but not caught—nope, there's the catch," she says, letting the line run out a few feet before gently pulling it to a stop. She gives the fish on the other end some time to argue with the hook in its mouth.

Please don't be a fucking shark.

"Hey, yellowfin," Xāwuṭh says approvingly after Ella hauls the giant fish into the boat. "That'll feed us."

"That'll feed three of us," Ella replies, gauging the appetites of the family members and their guests. "We need more."

"THAT IS A SHARK, PUT THE FUCKING SHARK BACK, WHAT IS WRONG WITH YOU?" Khodî shouts.

Ella turns around to see Kai and Khodî shoving a four-foot Great White back over the side. "Well, at least it wasn't me this time," she says, and Xāwuṭh starts chuckling under his breath. "Oh, you fucker. You gave Kai that bait on purpose."

Xāwuth plasters a really fake innocent smile on his face. "Would I do that shit?"

"Yes. Fucking duh."

They get two yellowfins, including Ella's victory catch, plus a mahi-mahi and a blue marlin. Ambrus refuses to let them overcook the yellowfin tuna, which gets just enough time on Xāwuth's makeshift grill to sear the sides.

"It's *raw*," Ella complains, poking at the slices of red fish with a hint of proper color on the sides.

"Rangers." Ambrus mutters the word like it's a curse. "You lot don't get out enough." He drizzles the raw tuna with tamari and lemon before holding out a slice for her to try.

Ella narrows her eyes. She refuses to back down from what is obviously a challenge. She grabs the slice of fish and shoves it into her mouth.

Holy shit. That is the most delicious thing in the history of ever. She's never eating canned tuna again.

"Told you so," Ambrus says brightly. Ella punches him in the arm before demanding more yellowfin.

Ella has to admit that while Xāwuth is bad at planning for breakfast, he's good at carrying around the equipment needed for lunch and dinner on a boat—as long as you like fish and beer, anyway. Neumia is a good sport about fish for lunch, but when she realizes that dinner is also going to be grilled fish with lemon juice or tamari, sesame oil, and salt, she defiantly gets a box of half-empty cereal from the kitchen and jams her tiny fist in it, eating corn flakes with the intense glare of a child set on mutiny.

Sorrow shows up long enough for lunch and then later, dinner, trading shifts with Xāwuth for half an hour so he can steal some of their food. Sorrow is a tiny little Thai thing that seems jumpy around them, but Ella gets why. She just doesn't know what to do about it other than be herself, or maybe threaten to go bury Sorrow's parents in some shallow graves. Sorrow also swaps back and forth between English and Thai at random, which makes tracking conversation harder. Ella used to be conversant in Thai, but listening to Sorrow lets Ella know that she's seriously out of practice.

Xāwuth comes back at dusk with a steel-string guitar that Ella knows her brother hasn't picked up very often in the last decade. He used to play a lot more, but after their stepmother's accident, he just didn't care as much.

"What's the occasion?" Khodî asks.

"Enough beer not to care," Xāwuth replies. He's emitting low-pitched whistles under his breath as he tunes the old guitar by sound and ear. "Besides, once you learn it, you don't really forget. Your hands and fingertips bitch at you for not practicing, that's all."

"Your fingertips are so thick that sharks are jealous," Kai says. "I don't think that's gonna be a problem."

"Guess not." Xāwuṯẖ begins strumming a song that Ella has known since childhood.

"Is that 'Frere Jacques' or 'Sarah Jackman?'" Andi asks. She and Ziba are seated on the same bench, leaning into each other with their hands clasped together. It makes Ella's heart ache, but it's not jealousy or anything stupid like that. They just read like two family members who haven't had the chance to be together under normal circumstances in a long time.

Xāwuṯẖ shrugs. "Pretty sure it doesn't matter. Any requests?"

"*THE HOBBIT!*" Neumia yells.

Xāwuṯẖ smiles at her. "Aren't there three of those movies now? You've gotta be a lot more specific than that, pumpkin."

"She means 'Song of the Lonely Mountain,'" Brian clarifies. Ella is pretty sure her niece watched that particular movie at least fifteen times, and those credits were rewound a lot.

"A Whetū liking the Tolkien-based equivalent of a war song? Not possible, I say," Khodî drawls.

"Don't be a turkey, Uncle Khodî! I like this song!" Neumia retorts.

"Fine. 'Song of the Lonely Mountain,'" Xāwuṯẖ says. "But you've gotta sing it, kiddo. I don't know the words."

"Lies," Ella see Kai mouth at Xāwuṯẖ. Xāwuṯẖ ignores Kai, using the guitar's hollow body to drum out the opening beat so that Neumia chimes in perfectly.

Ella listens, smiling, as tiny Neumia uses some well-developed lungs to project the song. Her voice is still child-pitched, but Bonika has been sending Neumia out for voice lessons from the moment Neumia announced that she wanted to learn to sing.

Ella glances around at her siblings and knows what they're thinking. At the right moment, they all chime in on the chorus, all but shouting it out. Neumia's grin is a mile wide, but she goes right back into the song when her temporary chorus abandons her.

Ambrus surprises Ella when he slips his voice into the song with Neumia for the last lines before the chorus repeats. "Fucker," Khodî mutters, grinning as they all launch into the chorus again. It's Ella's favorite part of the song, too. After this week, it feels so appropriate that it's making her skin prickle with awareness of things *coming*, of things *changing*.

She has never been more certain that her brother is alive. She knows it like the thrum in her bones, the blood flowing through her veins, the vibration of sound in her throat, sinuses, and ears as they all sing defiance at the setting sun and rising stars.

Then Xāwuṯẖ starts playing another melody. Ella watches as Ambrus and her father both straighten in their seats like they've been tasered in the ass. Xāwuṯẖ ignores them, strumming through certain chords when he's not using his fingers to pick out individual notes.

"You know it?" Ambrus asks, when Xāwuṭh repeats the same introduction set again.

"Yeah, I know it," Django replies, looking startled. "I met the guy once at a veteran's gathering Jason made me go to, back when his girl was still Nari-sized. I mentioned my kids are assholes, right?"

"It did come up once or twice." Ambrus says as they stare at each other. There is a moment of silent communication between them that nearly takes Ella's breath away. She sees so few who understand that kind of possibility, a bond so deep it's like the twin-bond she had with Eric.

Sometimes you don't need words.

Ella has vague memories of hearing her father sing, little tunes from infancy that sometimes haunt her dreams. This is entirely different, two voices twining together to sing Jim Moore's "I Have Seen the Rain." Django's voice gets stronger as the song continues, like he wasn't sure he remembered how to sing—or more importantly, how to *feel* it.

They both sound angry during the chorus, but god, it's melodic anger, and it gives Ella a fresh case of the chills. Sometimes she has to make herself remember that her father lived through hell several different times, but there is something about Vietnam that was worse than anything else. He never wants to talk about it; never even wants to hear the music from that era.

Ella feels that way about Iraq sometimes, but not often. Iraq was bloody and terrible, but except for Eric's loss, it ended for her when she got out of the service. Most Vietnam veterans she's spoken to talk like the Vietnam War never stopped.

Ambrus and Django glance at each other again. Ella can all but feel the click, a connection finally settling back down into true synch after too many years separated. It's not like Ambrus and Rex, which is a click so fucking loud it's a wonder strangers don't stare at them in the street. This is brotherhood, the kind you only get when you've watched each other's backs and worn each other's blood, and that's how they end the song.

There is a long, shocked pause, before Ambrus glares at Xāwuṭh with red-rimmed eyes. "You suck," he declares.

Xāwuṭh smiles, all teeth and bright-eyed amusement. "Yeah, but I never swallow," he replies serenely. As if he's ever done either, the overgrown liar.

Ambrus snorts out unexpected laughter. "Everyone has their preferences." Ella and her siblings all pretend not to notice their father wiping his face dry. Ambrus pulled that distraction card perfectly, something that would have worked on everyone except those who knew Django best.

Then comes more beer, and Xāwuṭh takes a guitar break. Khodî picks it up, arguing with Xāwuṭh about chord-strumming. Xāwuṭh tried to teach him at some point, and Khodî quickly demonstrates that while some of it stuck with him, quite a bit of it didn't. The results are hilariously bad.

Ella watches Ambrus and Django lean in close to each other, words passing between them that are too soft to be overheard. It's not the kind of romantic intimacy Khodî wouldn't stop teasing them about in the Vietnamese bar, just more of that same brotherhood.

Ella is starting to think Dad's needed this kind of connection for a long, long time. Hell, probably Ambrus, too.

"1956," she hears in a low voice. Rex sits down next to Ella, holding out a fresh beer for her to take. It makes her realize her current one is empty, so that's grand timing.

"What about 1956?" Ella asks, twisting off the cap before taking a drink.

"That was the last time Ambrus was at the house. Met our grandparents, our aunt, in what I'm thinking was probably late 1951," Rex explains. "Dad and Euan have known each other a goddamned long time."

"Does it bother you?"

Rex shakes his head. "Like Dad said in the bar—Euan wasn't his boyfriend. It was just something that happened. Probably after that Ninh Chu shit that Dad mentioned during the fight in the parking lot."

"Slaughter," Ella murmurs, and shivers. "They probably drank themselves into a blackout one-night stand."

"Thinkin' so, yeah," Rex agrees. "They fit together, but not that way."

"You do, though." Ella reaches over to squeeze her brother's hand. "You and Ambrus. I'm so happy for you, you stupid ass."

Rex smiles and squeezes back, a gentle press on her fingers. "Thanks, Ella. If you get anywhere with Ziba, I'll be first in line to congratulate you on becoming a mom."

"Mom—wait, what—no, that's not—shit!" Ella's eyes widen in realization. "Let's rewind and go back to the part where we discover if Ziba even swings that way first, okay?"

Rex grins. "Okay. Just thought I'd mention it. Something to keep in mind."

"Asshole," Ella grumbles, and shoves at him until he goes away. Rex walks straight to Ambrus, sitting down next to him and joining in on whatever conversation Ambrus and her father are having.

Ella doesn't say anything when Ambrus and Rex slip away from the group about fifteen minutes later. They deserve to have some time to themselves, even if they're only going off to shag like rabbits.

*   *   *   *

Khodî has no damned idea where Rex disappeared to until he realizes Ambrus is gone, too. Okay, that's kind of obvious. He's starting to wonder if Bonika and Brian are going to pull a disappearing act, too. Bonika is sitting in Brian's lap, gesturing with a beer in one hand and miming a gun with her other. Apparently, it's story time. Also, Bonika should not be more terrifying when sitting in Brian's lap like that, but somehow she manages it.

Khodî is considering going to Andi—for conversation, at least, if not other things—when his father's hand comes down on his neck. It's a gentle grip that still manages to be unyielding. "Let's go have a talk," Django says.

Khodî winces. "Okay."

Django escorts Khodî to the front of the boat. There is deck space up here, but it's small, meant for more personal gatherings or ocean observation. It's quieter, too, and the lights are off except for the bridge lights upstairs. The moon hasn't crawled up the horizon yet, leaving the stars to illuminate everything in blue.

Khodî decides to get to the point. "Is this about 2006?"

"And how you came home afterwards with a new scar?" Django leans against the deck railing, his eyes on the gentle rise and fall of the ocean waves. "Yeah, it is."

"Look, Dad—"

Django holds up his hand, and Khodî falls silent. It's a signal they all learned from toddlerhood onwards, and he obeys it on instinct. "I'm not demanding that you talk about it. I'm not asking why. This isn't—this isn't about your reasons."

That's unexpected...and weird. "Then what is it about?"

His father frowns. "Back in 1951, I was a lab rat. I always regretted that I'd gone through the program in the first place. I don't know how I would have avoided it, but I still felt that way.

"The first time I was grateful for what ETKC-51 did to me, you were three years old. Helen had just asked me about raising you. I realized that if it hadn't been for the drug, I wouldn't have been there, not the way you needed. I was in my fifties already. I might not have lived long enough to see you fucking graduate high school, Khodî. I was so damned glad that aging wasn't going to be an issue."

Khodî swallows. This is really not the kind of conversation he expected. He'd never even known that Helen Merrill discussed these kinds of things with his father, program included. "Dad?"

Django turns around to look at Khodî. "Hearing about what really happened on the twenty-eighth of February—that's the second time I've been fucking grateful that I agreed to be a guinea pig, and that ETKC-51 carries down genetically. If I hadn't done that, if you hadn't...you're still here. I'm so goddamned grateful that I don't even think I have the words to really explain it."

Khodî feels his eyes burn with tears. Dammit. No. No damned crying—shit. "I'm so sorry."

"No, no." Django strides forward and pulls Khodî into his arms, a strong embrace that makes Khodî want to cry harder. He clenches his jaw against it. His eyes can water, but he is not fucking crying!

"Tell me all about it. Never say a damned word. I don't care," Django says in a soft voice. "I'm just so fucking glad you're still here. That's the important thing. That's all I give a damn about. Okay?"

Khodî grips the back of his father's shirt, sniffing back stupid tears. "Yeah. Okay."

Maybe one day, he'll talk about it. Maybe they'll sit down together, and Khodî will tell Django about the aftermath of that fucking RPG hit, and how Khodî had stared at the .44 in his hands until it seemed like the most logical thing in the damned universe.

Maybe one day, but not today.

Chapter 14

:)(X)(X):

Ambrus's head is tilted up at the sky, his eyes tracking along the stars. Rex manages to be patient for about four minutes before he finally asks, "Are you okay?"

"Yeah. I didn't think I would be, but...yeah. I'm good."

Rex grins. "Well, it's great to hear that your brain isn't a fucking mess, but I meant physically."

Ambrus lowers his head to stare at Rex in momentary confusion. "Physically—oh! Right. Yes. Shot five times, jumped off a building."

"Yes, that," Rex replies dryly. "I've been waiting for the subject to come up."

Ambrus raises an eyebrow. "I'll just bet you have." He glances in each direction of the narrow exterior sidewall of the yacht they claimed for privacy, checking for prying eyes, before pulling off his borrowed olive green t-shirt. "Not perfect, but it's healing."

Rex traces each scar with his fingertips. They're faint dark spots against Ambrus's pale skin, smudges of violet under starlight. The bullet wounds look like they've been healing for weeks, not just seven days. "Did you speed-heal these at any point? You know, like you did my bullet-and-poison combo in Turkmenistan, or Khodi's house-staking?"

Ambrus shakes his head. "No, Rex. This is ETKC-51 at work. We all heal fast, even if we're not actively using our abilities."

Rex frowns. "You know you say 'abilities' like it's a dirty word, right?"

Ambrus takes ahold of Rex's hand, exploring Rex's fingers with his hands and eyes. "Did the flash flood make the news?"

"Yeah," Rex answers, refusing to be sidetracked. "Front page news right before we left the States, photos included. You didn't cause it, you know. It happened the night before we left, not at the time you predicted."

"Predicted." Ambrus smiles, a wan expression with a hint of humor lurking in it. "I've only been able to confirm those moments as true clairvoyance, not precognition, about ninety percent of the time. There are days when the unaccounted-for ten percent scares the hell out of me."

"Yeah, I get it." Rex laces their fingers together and rests their entwined hands on Ambrus's bare chest, right next to the two scars over his left lung. "Dad told me why he left."

"I thought he might." Ambrus uses his free hand to stroke Rex's arm with his fingertips.

"He said you were going to learn not to specify if people lived or died," Rex says, "and Euan? You did that. You weren't specific. Nobody in that flash flood died."

Ambrus bites his lip. "That doesn't necessarily make it right."

"No," Rex agrees. "To be honest, that's some scary damned shit, but at least you know you're not directly causing anyone's deaths. Not that way, at least."

"That's how I could keep working in the department," Ambrus admits quietly. "And it's how I trained others. Don't be specific; don't call on people to die. I know of other trainers, other sponsors of new Specialists, who weren't concerned about collateral damage. Under Director Irvine, that would be...that training fault would be remedied as much as possible, but no system is perfect. Under Stroud—it got worse."

"That's not your fault, either. C'mon." Rex pulls on Ambrus's hand as he leads them to the stairs that go down to the cabins.

"Where are we going?" Ambrus asks with bemused curiosity.

"You're leaving tomorrow for at least a week. You think I'm sending you off without sex?"

"Oh, that." Rex can hear the delight in Ambrus's voice. "I wasn't sure if I should say anything about it. Stockholm Syndrome from being kidnapped and all, you know."

"Stockholm Syndrome," Rex repeats, smiling. "One day, remind me to tell you how I met my step-mother. Go on ahead to our room. I need to raid Kai's stuff."

Ambrus smirks and nods. "I'll be waiting with bells on."

Rex opens the door to Kai and Django's bunkroom. "We don't have any fucking bells!"

"I kind of want to buy some now, just to make the pun literal."

"No!" Rex shouts back, grinning as he goes inside.

He finds Kai's backpack and pulls out the first of the two kits that his brother put together in Ho Chi Minh. The first aid kit has nitrile gloves, but also condoms and dental dams, because his little brother isn't naive. Besides, the condoms are good for keeping limb-wounds clean and dry, so it's double the excuse to keep them around. The dental dams...well, Rex has needed those for actual medical practices. He never wants to repeat that fishing expedition, either.

Rex thinks maybe Kai went overboard when he discovers latex, polyurethane, nitrile, *and* sheepskin condoms. Allergies are a thing, but Rex has never been all that enthused by the idea of feeling like he's trying to fuck a leather coat.

There's also an organic, water-based lube with a Vietnamese label that says it's good for windburn, but Rex knows Kai was thinking dual-purpose. Hell, Kai is probably hoping to get laid at some point during this insanity, too—not that Rex blames him.

He gets back to their room, shuts the door, and turns the lock. It won't keep out the determined, but it will keep Neumia from barging in.

Ambrus smiles when he sees what Rex collected. "Ah, yes, those. But not in kinky black this time."

Rex shrugs and puts the white gloves, lube bottle, and condoms down on the bedroom's nightstand. "I thought you might be worried about—"

"Branding someone's face does count as blood contamination, yes." A flash of grief shines in Ambrus's eyes before Rex watches him determinably put it aside. "Come here?"

Rex takes his shirt off and crosses the tiny space, letting Ambrus pull him in close. It feels like the first time they've done this in days. It's not; it's just the first time it hasn't also been fraught with danger, exhaustion, or pain.

Rex wraps his arms around Ambrus, feeling warm bare skin beneath his hands. "Euan, I don't want you to go."

"Bad feeling?" Ambrus murmurs, his lips moving against Rex's collarbone. He twitches at the ticklish sensation even as it sends a pleasant shiver down his spine.

"No." Rex tightens his grip on Ambrus, squeezing his eyes shut. "I just don't want you to leave."

Ambrus lays his hands flat on Rex's back, palms resting over Rex's shoulder blades. "I'm coming back."

"Take someone with you," Rex whispers. "I'd feel better knowing you aren't alone."

Ambrus smiles, bringing one hand up to lightly stroke the hard nubs of Rex's nipples. It makes him tense up in a good way, gritting his teeth at the sensation. "If I'd worked with anyone here recently enough, and long enough, to know that it would go seamlessly? Yes, absolutely, I would." Ambrus leaves off the nipple-teasing to trace Rex's collection of scars, which is as much relief as it is frustration. "I haven't done field work with your family aside from this particular escape, and I haven't worked with Django or Bonika in years. Andi will consider it her duty to stay and guard her pregnant cousin. That leaves me with zero options."

Even though it's a denial, it still makes Rex feel better to know Ambrus *would* do it, if the circumstances were right. "Okay. I just..."

Ambrus puts his fingers over Rex's lips. "Hey. Shh. No fears. No concerns over what might be. Not right now."

Rex nips at Ambrus's finger and smiles. "Okay. I'm convinced, Euan." When Ambrus drops his hand, Rex leans forward and kisses him. Ambrus opens his mouth at once, deepening the kiss into heat and tongue. Rex gasps into Ambrus's mouth, feeling an electric tingle awaken along his skin.

"God, that's sexy," Ambrus murmurs, and then sucks on Rex's lower lip. "No biting. No blood-drawing."

Rex pushes Ambrus down onto the mattress. "Yeah, yeah, shut up." Ambrus laughs, a sound of absolute delight that's so damned nice to hear.

He knows that Ambrus glories in the sensation of being pinned, held in place. Rex also knows that Ambrus has the strength to toss him across the room.

It's not about being pinned, Rex thinks idly, kissing his boyfriend, dry pecks to deep, heated exchanges that leave him light-headed, like he's held his breath too long. *It's about...*

"Safety," Ambrus says against Rex's cheek. "A rare sensation in my life."

Rex pulls back enough to stare at Ambrus. "Are you reading my thoughts?"

Ambrus winces. "No? Not on purpose, anyway. It's rude, without permission. You were, uh, thinking very loud."

Rex raises an eyebrow and thinks very hard about the fact that he wishes he'd turned off the fucking lights.

"Hard." Ambrus snorts out a laugh. "Hold on." He reaches down and snags the laces on his boots, pulling them loose enough to get one boot off. Then he throws it at the light switch, plunging the cabin into darkness.

"I'm pretty sure I heard Ella do that last night," Rex says dryly. "I think you might have broken that switch, though. Good job—" He's cut off when Ambrus yanks his head down and seals their mouths together again.

"Nnngh." Rex squeezes his eyes shut against a full-body shiver, arousal that feels almost like pain.

"Not pain." *Blissful agony,* Rex hears Ambrus's voice in his head. "*Sǐ de hǎo xìngfú.*"[1]

Ambrus is not the only one who can discover new kinks later in life. Mandarin whispered into Rex's ear in that moment is probably one of the sexiest things he's ever heard.

"I could listen to you all night. Every night. For the rest of my life," Ambrus murmurs, his teeth latching down on Rex's throat in a bite that is too gentle to break the skin.

"Same." Rex threads his hand through Ambrus's too-short hair. He misses Ambrus's long red, flaming locks, but hair grows back.

They tease each other until Ambrus finally growls. "Rex Vis Tjin. Major."

Rex clenches his jaw as he shivers. Fuck, but that still sounds so very right. "Yes?"

"Tomorrow, I'm going to go blow up a damned bank and then run through a jungle to escape determined pursuit." Ambrus pins him with a stern glare. "While we still have this area of the boat to ourselves, I'd like it *very* much if you would knock it off with the teasing and fuck me."

Rex laughs. "All right! Hint taken."

"Thank you. Major."

When Ambrus finally gasps out Rex's name and falters against him, Rex seizes Ambrus with both arms and holds on tightly as they

---

[1] C. Mandarin: Blissful suffering.

both try to catch their breath. Rex feels strung out, wrung out, and so goddamned good.

It takes Rex a moment to realize that Ambrus is shivering. "Hey—shit. Are you okay?"

Ambrus nods without lifting his head. "God, yes. I'm good. I'm amazing. I could probably fucking fly right now if you asked me to."

Rex grins. "I have to be honest here, Euan. I've been in three too many plane crashes to be all that concerned about joining the mile-high club."

"That was not supposed to be a pun," Ambrus grumbles, and then buries his nose against Rex's neck. "You smell *amazing*."

Rex jerks back, trying not to giggle like a kid. "Asshole! That's still a ticklish spot!"

"Oh, really?" Ambrus squirms against him, nudging that same spot with his nose and then licking it, which makes Rex laugh aloud.

"Quit it. We have to clean up," Rex says, but he's not really in much of a rush. He wants to enjoy this, to linger and savor this feeling of being...of being...

"Whole," Ambrus whispers in an awed voice.

Rex swallows and tightens his arms around his boyfriend again. "Yeah."

For the first time in his life, Rex doesn't feel like the core of his self is empty.

*   *   *   *

On the morning of the twenty-sixth, Django stumbles up onto the deck after a shower, heading straight to the galley for coffee and more coffee. He doesn't know why he keeps waking up at 7:00 a.m. on this stupid fucking boat, not when he's still so damned tired.

He finds Khodî and Andi already awake. Khodî must have been the one to make coffee, since it's military grade instead of Xāwuṭh's traditional tar-fuel. "Morning," Django says gruffly, pawing at a mug until he can hold it without dropping it.

"Morning Dad," Khodî replies. "We're making another breakfast brick, and it's your damned fault."

Django stares at them until Andi shrugs, a mischievous smile on her face. "We do have plenty of eggs. Protein, Mister Whetū."

"Django," he corrects. "Mister Whetū is way too damned formal for these living conditions, Miss Banner."

"Andi," she counters, smiling again.

Django glances over at Khodî and sees a clubbed-in-the-head besotted expression on his face. Django knows that look. He used to see it in the mirror whenever Makani was around.

Please wait at least another week before you ask her to marry you, Django thinks, and decides to go outside.

Out on the back deck, Rex, Ella, Ziba, and Kai have extended the table to its full length, and most of their available resources are stacked on it from one end to the other. "Good idea," Django says in approval, sitting down in an empty chair while still sipping coffee. "Is that everything?"

"We didn't put the fishing gear out because I didn't want Wolf to murder me if the lines tangled." Kai picks up one of the recovered bloodied dog tags and drops it back into the pile with the others. "Oh, you were not a pleasant person."

"And getting the luggage out of the cabins would wake people up," Rex says. "Euan is still asleep. Figured one of us should get the chance to sleep in."

"You couldn't sleep?" Django asks, curious.

Rex stops in the middle of counting out rounds, frowning. "I think we're close enough to Brunei that I'm getting mission-tense. The sun hit the window and I was awake."

That would explain Django's own early rising. It's been years since he's run a mission, and sunlight used to mean the same thing to Django: get up, get your shit together, and get moving.

They still have the second set of false identification documents for every member of the family, Xāwuṭh included, though Xāwuṭh probably has a stack of his own hidden somewhere. The extras were safely hidden under their clothes in thin layers to escape pat-downs from the TSA, and RFID chips in passports tend not to set off metal detectors. The identities that got them into Ho Chi Minh went into the garbage that Xāwuṭh is going to burn once they're in port. The department can backtrack those idents now, and there's no damned sense in taking stupid chances.

Ambrus cheated and added a cash withdrawal from the Black American Express card during his raiding of the ATM in Vietnam. Between that, the other account withdrawals, and their own dug-up leftovers, they have about twelve grand in liquid assets. Django, Ambrus, and most of the kids all have drop boxes in random places around the globe, so money isn't going to be an issue for a while. Most of those drop boxes also have a third set of false IDs, giving them another fallback if the fucking department somehow gets their hands on the current set.

Their flash drives are on the table, two from each of the three bug-out bags. Rex keeps backups on his keychain, like Django and Khodî do. Ella keeps hers in whatever place she deems best—fortunately *not* in her checked luggage. The family documents and photographs are safely preserved, if not in useful, viewable formats at the moment. The topographical map Django received of Vietnam, Cambodia, Laos, and Thailand might be useful later. He's against throwing out resources unless they're outdated and inaccurate.

The recovered dog tags and wallets from the dead Specialists sit in a separate pile at the end of the table. No one wants that shit to mingle with their stuff. Kai is right about how gods-awful it feels.

Hardware is at a depressing low. They're down to eight weapons for fourteen people, and one of those weapons might be permanently out of ammunition. That's something Django plans to correct as soon as they find a port that doesn't give a shit about what's being sold at the docks so long as you behave yourself while conducting business. Django makes a mental note to ask Xāwuṯh if Sorrow's ever been trained to handle a firearm. If not, he'll probably need to learn.

Wesley turns up with a mug, yawning and looking like he ran into a wall on the way to the galley. Khodî and Andi trail in behind him, holding hands. "Hello, fellow nutjobs," Wesley grumbles. "What are we doing?"

"Status review." Rex is frowning at the pile of wallets and tags. "I'd really like to find out more about what in the entire hell is going on."

"Gotcha." Wesley gives the bloodstained pile a disgusted look, taking a sip of coffee that makes his expression sour even further. He hates coffee, but they've all hit the point of complete caffeine desperation. "This might be a rude question, but pre-caffeine, so deal: is there anyone in this fucking department that we should maybe *not* shoot on sight?"

"Kayin Afolayan, maybe," Ziba says after a long, thoughtful pause in which she and Andi stared at each other. Django wonders if they've mastered the art of mental conversation, or if it's just long-term familiarity. "She's a recent African import, but she's Jasper's age. They were friends." Ziba bites her lip. "If she's been double-dosed, or still believes in following Stroud, I would appreciate it if she doesn't suffer."

Django glances at Ziba and waits until she looks at him. "If either of those things are true and she's a lost cause, I'll make certain of it," he promises.

"Tamir Berkowitz, perhaps," Andi adds, saving Ziba from needing to answer. "His parents were second- and third-gen members of the department, but they were also good people. Tamir grew up in the U.S. as an obvious mixed-race child during a time when it was not socially acceptable, so he doesn't swallow bullshit as easily as your average white bear."

"You're mixed-race," Kai says. "Hell, so are we."

"Yes, but Ziba can pass, and I was going under an Americanized name at the time. It was easy to sway people into believing it was my foreign Londoner ways showing, not my Hindu background," Andi replies serenely. "You were born in a much more optimal time, Ki te Muri kā."

Kai shrugs. "Yeah, true."

"Is that it?" Khodî asks when the girls fall silent.

"Two Specialists from the program were listed as MIA, but no bodies were ever recovered," Bonika says as she joins them, sharp-eyed and alert despite the early hour. "Sometimes that meant a desire to retire without department oversight, but not always. I had a friend—Naidoo, Lesdi F., Specialist First Class, out of South Africa. I don't believe it was retirement in her case, though. She was up for a promotion that she wanted. Lesdi would have been the first black woman with a Senior Specialist ranking."

"What about the other one?" Rex asks.

"Kasun, Damir A., Serbian descent, first-generation American if you go by birth and not immigration." Bonika frowns. "He was a bit nuts, like Ambrus, but I also doubt he's still alive."

"That's probably for the best. We have enough crazy people to deal with, including us," Ella says.

Kai notices Andi's glower as she studies the pile, disappears for a few minutes, and returns with a pair of white nitrile examination gloves. "Might help," he says.

Andi gives him a bright smile of gratitude and slides them onto her hands before she starts handling dog tags and wallets. The white fingers of her gloves immediately turn rusty red and brown.

The group is comparing notes about their plans for the day when Andi starts swearing, a vent of pure filth that she definitely picked up from the military. "Something wrong?" Django asks, amused to see that Khodî is staring at Andi in fascinated disbelief.

Andi pulls out a plastic card that looks innocuous enough, but there is a sense to it that makes the hair on the back of Django's neck stand up. The card is blank except for a wide, solid black stripe that runs parallel with the magnetic strip on the reverse side.

"Holy shit," Rex breathes out in shock. "That's an updated SAP clearance card."

"Shit on a stick and roast it on a bonfire." Ella has a wary look on her face. "Does anyone else have one?"

Andi's frown intensifies as she pulls a SAP card from each and every wallet, including Vargas's ladies' clutch wallet. "This...is not good."

"Despite my upbringing, I don't speak military acronyms. What's a SAP clearance?" Kai asks. He's the only one of Django's kids who hasn't turned some shade of pale. Django doesn't feel all that great, either.

"SAP stands for Special Access Program," Khodî explains in grim displeasure. "SAP is a step above the three highest federal security clearance levels you can be granted as a U.S. citizen, the one nobody is supposed to know about. It's Black Ops, Kai."

"Did you have one?" Andi asks curiously.

Khodî shakes his head. "No. Never wanted it. Never needed it. I did work with an asshole who had it back in Iraq. He was happy to demonstrate that SAP is the American equivalent of a license to kill."

Andi must hear it in Khodî's voice the same way Django can. One of her eyebrows quirks up, as does the corner of her mouth. "What happened to him?"

Khodî shrugs, affecting nonchalance. "No idea. He wandered out into the desert one day and never came back. Damnedest thing," he says, and Andi laughs.

Django glances over at Ella, who is grinning wide enough that he can see most of her teeth. "Baby girl."

"What?" Ella blinks at him in a show of innocence. "I didn't take anyone out into the desert and bury them alive."

Ziba shakes her head, but she's smiling. "It probably couldn't have happened to a more deserving individual."

"Back to the boring shit that Kai and I don't understand," Wesley interrupts. "What's the issue with all of these dead Specialist assholes having SAP cards?"

"The only person in the entirety of our department who is supposed to have SAP is the director," Andi tells them, still holding one of the cards in her gloved hands. "The proper breakdown is that Senior Specialists have Top Secret access; First Class Specialists have the standard Secret clearance. Junior agents have to qualify for Confidential clearance before they're approved for fieldwork."

Django stares at the six black-striped cards that Andi is stacking up on the table. "You can do some bad shit with SAP clearance. I'm talking toppling-governments levels of bad." Jason offered SAP to him once, short-term only for a single op; Django had declined. He didn't need that kind of temptation in his life.

Rex shakes his head. "What the actual fuck is going on?"

"What I can say for certain is that Director Stroud gave SAP clearance to some of the worst examples of humanity the department had to offer," Andi says in a quiet, angry voice. "First Class Specialist Marcus, Giordan R; Senior Specialist Thomas, William J.; First Class Specialist Ventimiglia, Abramo C.; Junior Specialist Vargas, Cecilia M.; Junior Specialist Whitewater, Barry P.; Senior Specialist Kröger, Hugh K."

"None of them ever advanced beyond First Class status under Director Irvine," Bonika says. "He recognized that while they were efficient at their jobs, they also didn't care about collateral damage. It was better to send them out with teammates who would keep them corralled. I'm guessing that changed after Irvine retired at the end of 1998."

"It did," Ziba agrees. "But it wasn't a swift changeover. Stroud did most of it on the sly. We would go out on assignments and return to find that agents previously in positions meant to restrain their bad habits were now in positions where Stroud was their only oversight. Under Stroud, Vargas and Whitewater were both on the list of agents who were never supposed to be cleared for fieldwork—Vargas was too erratic, and Whitewater was a terrible soldier. Everyone called him Barrel, but not for reasons most people assumed." She holds up her hand and rubs her thumb and forefingers together. "He rolled his way through Basic Training because his parents' wealth greased the way. Without that monetary bribe, Whitewater would never have made it through boot camp."

"Thomas was espionage, the nasty sort of handiwork that started wars," Andi says. "Ventimiglia was assassination, something that was supposed to be used only when all other opportunities failed."

"So this Director Stroud asshole is giving out Black Ops cards like they're candy to scumbags." Wesley rolls his eyes. "That's just fuckin' fabulous."

"Marcus is proof that Stroud is actively recruiting from other agencies, too." Andi is reading the printing on a blood-spattered dog tag. "He kept one of his old tags from his previous profession. Marcus used to be Special Forces. His military ID was reissued within the last month for the DoD with the alphanumeric code for the department. Hmm. That's quite a pay-grade jump, too."

"Bastard is making us fucking look bad," Khodî mutters. Django agrees, but they both know that being SF doesn't prevent someone from being fucking stupid.

"Stroud might be attracting new agents with money, but if the Specialists back at the bar are standard, not an exception, he's probably double-dosing everyone who signs up." Rex gives the tags Andi holds an intense, focused stare, one he had even as a child. He's a brilliant tactician, but it's not a consistent or practiced talent—that is ETKC-51 at work.

Andi's voice is a careful neutral when she says, "You don't think it's an exception. You think it's everyone."

"Yep." Rex tilts his head to one side, still staring at the bloodied tags. "How long does it take for someone to lose their shit, Dad?"

Django frowns. "It varied." Dealing with another poor bastard like Fox isn't high on his list of things he wants to repeat. That shit was harsh enough back in the '50s. "Two weeks is the maximum average you could expect from someone who was double-dosed before they became a liability."

One poor bastard had gone to bed relatively stable, if a bit jittery. He woke up the next day completely insane, killing six people before they put him down. Django had almost taken his gun after the program heads at that point. He'd liked that asshole, a stupid young man who'd been trying to learn how to be a better person.

"Back in the 1980s, they somehow raised that threshold to three weeks," Bonika announces quietly. "No one has ever admitted how, and they wouldn't repeat the experiment beyond the testing that proved their results. Three weeks is when a modern double-dosed victim loses recognition of friends and foes. More importantly to the department: they no longer have the ability to follow orders."

Rex frowns. "Maybe three weeks max of usefulness per double-dosed agent. Statistically, that's shit, but you can do a lot in three weeks."

"Rex?" Django glances over at Rex, who still has that same intent expression on his face. "What are you thinking, kid?"

"I'm thinking that just because I hate chess doesn't mean I don't understand it." Rex rests his elbows on his knees so he can support his chin with his clasped hands. "Set up your strategy. Move your pieces into positions where they can be most effective. Destroy the roadblocks in your way, or convince them to move out of the way if destruction isn't possible.

"This isn't about Stroud turning the department into his own personal war machine." Rex looks at Django. "This is a damned coup in progress."

"A coup of *what?*" Kai asks when everyone else goes still and quiet. "C'mon, someone actually fucking tell me. I'm starting to freak the hell out."

"They're in the Pentagon. The DoD, Kai," Bonika says, wide-eyed and rattled. "Stroud is going to gain control of the entirety of the Department of Defense by violence, bribery, or puppetry, and he has the army with which to do so."

"Yeah." Rex looks pissed. "He who controls the military controls the U.S., even if no one knows who's really pulling the strings."

"Uh—the President controls the military. Commander-in-Chief," Kai tries.

"Who is advised by military leaders from the Pentagon, Kai." Bonika shakes her head. "It won't matter who appoints the cabinet positions from one presidency to the next, not if they're immediately turned into Stroud's puppets. The department's Director has ETKC-51 in his blood. He could gain control and remain in power for a very long time."

Khodî glances at Django, both eyebrows raised. "This may not be about wiping out the department for our own safety, not anymore. We might need to convince the United States government that they want us to clean up their fucking mess."

Django lets his lips curl up in a hard smile. "Wouldn't be the first time, now, would it?" Khodî smiles back, fond and sharp-edged at the same time.

"We need to make Stroud disappear," Rex says. "Barring that, we're going to need a plan based on the data that Éoghan gets from that bank vault."

"It has to be the latter, then. No one with that much power and influence can simply disappear," Ziba replies scornfully.

Django can't help it; he starts laughing. How someone as intelligent as Ziba Banner worked in the DoD from the 1960s until this month and still maintains that kind of political naiveté is amusing as hell.

Ziba sighs before she looks at Django. "Who?"

"Admiral Scott Williams, Pacific Command. Remember him?" Django asks.

"Of course I do. Williams disappeared in 1991, a suspected suicide into the Delaware River—" Ziba breaks off, her lips pressed together as realization strikes. "Ah. Your work?"

"Last official DoD contract I ever took," Django replies. "Trust me, if the government wants someone gone for making too much of a mess, they'll even make a four-star admiral vanish."

"All right." Andi strips off her gloves and then laces her hands to crack her knuckles. "We're still in agreement that the department must be eliminated. However, Stroud has a long list of friends and connections in D.C. If the government won't accept the necessity of a clean-up operation, then whatever we do to undermine Stroud will have to be so public that they can't cover it up."

"That's not gonna be easy," Khodî says. "He's way too white for us to pull the terrorist card on him the way he did us."

Andi makes a noncommittal noise. "Before we discuss that, I'm afraid I have to sour the mood even further. Why is Ninh Chu a trigger, Django?"

Every single muscle in Django's body locks up. He has to breathe out remembered panic before he can relax and think again. Ninh Chu is responsible for some of his worst PTSD. It's a damned miracle he didn't have fucking nightmares about it for the last two nights, not after using Ninh Chu as a focus for calling the lightning.

"Please," Andi requests gently. "I have a feeling it might be useful later, and I trust those instincts."

Django lets out a humorless laugh. "Tactician."

When Django glances up, Andi inclines her head in a graceful nod. "Ziba was the pretty face that wrapped everyone around her little finger in public. I was the spy. We work very well together, but I will always be the one who thinks of weapons before words, and Ninh Chu might be a weapon that may one day save our lives. If any of us are to press that particular button in Euan or yourself again, we need to know why it's so effective. It's easier to soothe those wounds afterwards if we know what we're talking about."

Django nods. He understands that kind of logic, especially after the shootout in front of the bar. "Listen up, then, because I'm only telling this story one time."

"Ninh Chu was a village in the Đồng Nai Province back when it was still the Republic of Vietnam. Despite what I said, the slaughter wasn't Ambrus's fault. We just—he believes it is, and I..." Django bows his head. "Fuck."

He can do this. He can.

"After 1973, there wasn't supposed to be an American military presence left on Vietnamese soil except for senior officials in Saigon, helping the South Vietnamese Army to coordinate a failing war. That was complete bullshit, of course. There were several platoons still on the ground, one of mine included. Most of 1st Battalion of 1st Group SF went back to Okinawa in January of '73, but I pulled a group of volunteers who were willing to stay behind and help play clean-up crew. We still had POWs to find and MIAs to account for on the American side. The brass who were still allowed on-site couldn't do that from Saigon. While the CIA worked from satellite intel, we were out with our boots on the ground. Technically, that meant there were empty spots in our battalion that were going to be filled with fresh faces, but 1st Group was going to stall that process until our volunteer group in Vietnam returned to take up our positions in the ranks again.

"Of course, shit didn't work out that way." Django focuses on his coffee mug for a minute, swirling around the cooling dredges in the bottom. "I didn't know Ambrus was still alive, or that he was in Vietnam, until this foul-mouthed, hippie-haired and bearded asshole comes strolling out of the bush and into our camp, saying he's been ordered to help us find what we were looking for. Hell of a gut punch at the time."

Gut punch. That was putting it mildly. 1975 was eighteen years out from 1956, and the stupid shit was supposed to have been part of Django's life, not a damned disappearing act.

"Ambrus was a bundle of rage, which wasn't normal for him," Django says. Ziba, Andi, and Bonika all nod, though Bonika has a look in her eyes that says she knows full well that Ambrus *can* be a bundle of rage, and it isn't pretty.

"It took a few hours of traipsing through the fucking jungle for Ambrus to finally tell me why," Django continues. "He'd gotten a mental nudge that a village in the north was under direct threat of retaliation from the Việt Cộng. They were carrying out extreme vengeance against people who still supported the South Vietnamese government. The brass promised that the village of Ninh Chu would get a protective detail, then ordered Ambrus out to join us on POW hunts. Lucky us, we found one. No Americans in the prison camp, but the South Vietnamese POWs certainly appreciated the rescue. We cleared the area of Việt Cộng tunnels and encampments, made sure it would take a hell of a lot of work to make that a viable base of operations again." Django smiles in a way that probably looks like nostalgia, but it's grief, too. He misses all of those bastards, his crazy-ass tunnel rats included.

"I knew Ambrus was going to bug out to Ninh Chu the moment the camp was clear. The radio was conveniently broken, and we didn't receive new search pattern orders before it happened," Django says. Rex snorts his amusement over that convenient arrangement. "My men—we took a vote. A lot of us had been in Vietnam since 1964. We saw a lot of bombed-out villages. Lots of innocent people dead for no good fucking reason. Saving Ninh Chu would have made us all feel a hell of a lot better about the last ten years."

Django puts the coffee mug aside so he doesn't give in to the urge to smash it against the deck. "We didn't make it in time."

He is so damned glad that Ambrus is still asleep, that he's not here for this shit recitation. Django carries Ninh Chu in his heart as a terrible reminder that fucking hellhole disasters like Vietnam should never happen again. Ambrus carries Ninh Chu in his heart like it's his own personal failure.

"Brass lied, didn't they?" Kai has a somber, hurt expression on his face. "They never sent anyone to the village for protection."

Django shakes his head. "No. The Việt Cộng knew there was a South Vietnamese munitions depot in the village, and they'd somehow gotten themselves a working airplane with a small supply of good, old-fashioned American napalm. There was nothing left afterwards. Three hundred dead. No survivors."

Django doesn't realize Xāwuṭh has joined them until he speaks. "The place where Ninh Chu used to be is considered haunted by pretty much everyone and their goats," he says. "Nobody wants to go near it, even though it's good farmland. I went through there once with Mom during a trip to go bargain for supplies in the next village. I couldn't—all I could hear was fucking screaming. I made Mom go around the fucking place on the trip back."

Ella is looking at Django. "What made it worse, Dad?"

"Việt Cộng were still there, waiting to see who'd turn up to check out their work. They had someone with them who could alter perception enough to keep their squads from being noticed. Maybe someone who ditched from the department, I don't know," Django says. "What I *do* know is that the bastards took us all completely by surprise. I took three hits before I even realized what the hell was happening. Ambrus took two when he knocked my ass to the ground before I could eat more lead."

Django bites his lip before giving them all a humorless smile. "Ambrus was the insane bastard who got the rest of us down onto the ground. Some of my men were already hit, but still trying to find something to aim at. Others just—some of them were too startled to remember to find cover when the bullets started flying." It happened sometimes, even to the most experienced soldiers. By 1975, they were all worn thin as hell and so jaded that bullets just weren't frightening anymore. Shots fired were just signals telling them to find the enemy and engage.

"Ambrus pulled injured men into cover and out of the line of fire while the rest of us tried to fight an enemy we couldn't fucking see. By the time he'd done everything he could to save my platoon, he was out of the fight."

"The day of the nine bullets." Rex swallows hard. "Shit."

Django nods in confirmation. "Yeah, that was it. I didn't know if my dumb fucking friend was going to live or die. I couldn't even get to him to find out how bad it was."

"Shit," Khodî whispers in realization. "That's why you—fucking shit. No goddamned wonder you understood. I told you on the phone about losing my team before I came home in 2006, and you *understood*."

"Yeah. I lost all of them. Everyone. Forty-three men, some of the finest soldiers and most honorable bastards I'd ever known." Django stares down at the deck. "Eight to the initial ambush, and the rest to a firefight that lasted all fucking night. It got so bad that I knew there was only going to be one way to end it."

Django looks up at the sky, which is overcast and gray, not typical at all for the season. "Just before dawn, I called the lightning with such force that it burnt out a second crater in the ground next to Ninh Chu.

"You know how Euan mentioned back at the farmhouse that my healing talent is only useful if it's life or death?" Django smiles. "That's the reason why two men walked away from Ninh Chu instead of just one."

"Walk?" Bonika gives him a wry look. "No, I imagine there was a lot more whimpering and limping involved."

Django cracks a raw smile. "That, too."

Sorrow appears in his silent way, emerging from the side deck. He stops when he sees them gathered together. *"Thâmị khuṇ thuk khn mxng ħemụ̄xn thî khuṇ kâlạng wị̂thukkħ tāy?"*[2]

"We kind of are," Khodî replies. "C-band's all set for the American news channels?"

Sorrow gives Django a worried look, but nods. "Yes. My cousin taught me many new words while doing so. I need a dictionary or a translator with no embarrassment over the saying of foul words."

Kai grins. "I'll do it. Betcha it's fun stuff, Sorrow."

"Let's just—we should go see if we're still on the news, first," Rex suggests.

That was a terrible fucking idea. They are definitely still on the news. If anything, the American media has doubled down on screeching about terrorist cells in rural Pennsylvania. Django is really damned angry about it, but right now, the only thing to do is to sit, wait, and plan.

* * * *

Around mid-morning, Xâwuṭh guides the SS *Gives No Fuhks* up the Sungai Belait River into Brunei. They dock at what Rex suspects is a high-class boating club. The staff doesn't bat an eye at the yacht or its paint-peeling condition; they just hand over the tourist visas that Xâwuṭh radioed ahead for and begin to fuel up the boat.

---

[2] Thai: "Why do you all look like you are mourning the dead?"

It's the boat's name that makes the two men stare at the boat in bewilderment. "Seriously?" one of them asks, glancing at Xāwuṯh. Rex's brother is investigating the yacht's prow for potential damage from her first re-christened sea voyage.

"There was a time crunch," Xāwuṯh explains gruffly, shoving a sizable tip into the English-speaking man's hand.

"I know this craft is registered in Malta, and that Fuhk is a family name, but I still cannot believe they let you get away with that," the other man says, revealing that he speaks English, too. His head is tilted in puzzlement as he studies the hastily stenciled name on the yacht's red-painted side.

"Money talks, my friends." Xāwuṯh grins in his teeth-baring way that makes people nervous. "Hell of a nice day. You got beer in this place?"

"For the tourists. Alas, I cannot partake," the second man replies.

"I'll drink for both of us. C'mon." Xāwuṯh all but drags the club employees towards the main building. The poor bastards don't seem to know what to do about being kidnapped by a six-foot-two Thai-Māori man.

Ziba smiles as she walks over to stand next to Rex, who is leaning against the railing to watch the show. "That clears our path nicely," she says as Xāwuṯh disappears inside with his new friends. "Is he always so..."

"Insistent?" Rex grins. "Yeah. That's Xāwuṯh for you."

Ziba gives Rex a gentle nudge in the arm with her elbow. "Go get dressed. You have to be presentable for Lam-Pan, and salt-encrusted jeans won't do."

"Am I about to walk into a house that I'll never be able to afford unless I decide to become a drug lord or something?" Rex asks.

"If I'm recalling the family history after Tai Wei Lam-Pan's exit from the program correctly?" Ziba smirks at him. "I think there are actual drug lords who are jealous of this family's house."

Rex tries not to sigh. "Right." He goes back downstairs to his cabin to find the bed made and Ambrus missing. He probably woke up when the boat docked. The fact that his boyfriend slept in at all is practically a goddamn miracle, but they all have shit to do and a schedule to keep.

In his luggage, Rex finds the nicest clothes he grabbed from that nightmarish trip through Target back in the States: tan slacks that haven't picked up any stains, a pale blue t-shirt, and a darker blue short-sleeve button-down shirt. Rex was wearing his only other nice shirt during the airport incident. That one still has bloodstains on it and smells like gunpowder.

Rex waves at Bonika to get her attention when she passes by his open doorway. "You think that boating club has a laundromat? If not, there has to be one somewhere in this city."

Bonika smiles. "That's a good idea. Now I'm upset that I didn't think of it first."

Rex shrugs. "I'll pretend ignorance. Your brilliant idea, not mine."

"Flatterer," Bonika returns dryly. "Put aside everything you need to have washed, a pile by the door. I'll tell everyone else to do the same, bag it up, and pay someone to run it over to be cleaned. I'm sure the right amount of money will convince them to make it a rush job."

Rex nods in relief. Between that and Khodî's planned shopping trip, they should be set again for clothes without needing to share. Ambrus, Django, and Khodî are all about the same size, but Brian and Wesley can only share with each other. Kai is a damned beanpole; Rex and Xāwuth are too tall. Ella is on her fifth day of wearing the same clothes and has resorted to showering fully dressed to cope. She can borrow t-shirts, but pants and undergarments are another matter entirely. Ella also confided in blunt resentment that she, Bonika, Ziba, and Andi all have completely different bra sizes.

Rex looks at the tan slacks again. "Does this boat have an ironing board?"

Bonika shows him where one is hiding, tucked in with a travel-sized iron next to a washing machine that's not hooked up. "We should probably get that fixed while we're here. That will be very convenient if we have to spend a long time at sea," she says.

"Yeah." Rex raps his hands on top of the tiny little clothes washer. It's not a dual unit, which is a damned shame, but a clothes dryer would eat up the generator fuel. "If you see Khodî before he leaves the ship, tell him to add clothesline and clothespins to his shopping list."

Rex presses the slacks, which makes them smell clean instead of like stale sea water and airport, dresses in the t-shirt and button-down, and steals a belt from his beanpole brother to support the weight of a Glock SIG in a holster at Rex's back. Socks and black dress shoes with steel-toed inserts complete the outfit. Rex checks himself out in the bathroom mirror and makes a disgusted face at his reflection. He shaved that morning, and his hair is a short blond halo of fuzz on his head, but he still looks like he dressed up for a job interview.

Ambrus asked him not to do anything to make this Tyung Lam-Pan person nervous, but the Glock isn't negotiable. Rex isn't going unarmed into a town that already has agents on the ground. He does double-check that the black duffle bag that carried their weapons is empty, even turning it upside down and shaking it for good measure. Once he's confirmed that the bag is ready to collect whatever is in Ambrus's mysterious deposit box, he heads out into the passageway.

"Please be kind to her," Rex hears. He freezes just before the turn that leads up the stairs.

"Didn't think it was any of your damned business," Khodî retorts.

"I've known her for a very long time, and I'm not trying to be offensive," Ambrus replies evenly. "I don't care whether you're friends, fuckbuddies, or if you marry her tomorrow. All I ask is that you be kind."

"Why?" Khodî's tone isn't suspicious, which means there must be some telling expression on Ambrus's face.

"Did Andi mention that she can't bear children?" Ambrus asks.

"Yeah. It, uh, it came up," Khodî admits. Rex bites his lip to choke back laughter—that's probably not the only thing that came up. "Why?"

"Andi was engaged to an agent in the program at the end of 1964." Ambrus's voice has gone quiet; anger, not caution. "Ziba and I weren't sure about him, but he seemed to be over the moon for her, so we let it be. Then Andi told him that she couldn't have children because of an illness that pre-dated ETKC-51. Her uterus had to be removed to save her life."

"Cancer?" Khodî asks.

"Or something very much like it, but whatever the problem, it was slowly killing her," Ambrus replies. "Instead of being reasonable, Andi's fiancé said many unkind things to her, broke off the engagement, and publicly denounced her as a waste of womanhood."

"What the ever loving *fuck!*" Khodî hisses in outrage. "Is this bastard still around? I feel the sudden need to carve someone's heart out."

"Oh, it's a bit late for that. He, ah, disappeared about a month afterwards." Ambrus sounds grim and pleased. "Fens are so very useful."

"You're a good man, Ambrus," Khodî says.

"No, I'm not." Rex feels his chest ache at the melancholy tone in his boyfriend's voice. "But I'm trying to be."

"Hey, that counts," Khodî insists. "Trust me on that one. Also, I'm aware that adoption is a thing that exists if I ever decide I want children everywhere."

"Glad to hear it. Have fun in Kuala Belait," Ambrus says.

Khodî chuckles. "Have fun blowing shit up in Seria. See you in a few days, asshole."

Rex immediately retreats, acting as if he just came out of his cabin. He and Khodî bump shoulders as Khodî walks by on his way to the cabin he's been sharing with Andi.

Rex smiles and continues walking until he can round the corner and push his freshly showered boyfriend up against the wall.

Ambrus murmurs his approval before Rex kisses him, long and deep.

"We're in Brunei. No public displays of affection." Ambrus has a wicked smile on his face as he licks at Rex's lower lip.

"We're not in public yet," Rex points out.

"Nope." Ambrus rises up on the balls of his feet, grabs Rex's hip with one hand, and curls his other hand around the back of Rex's neck as he pulls Rex in until they're pressed together, hips to chest and then to lips when Ambrus kisses him again.

Rex smiles as he nuzzles against Ambrus's freshly shaved cheek. He really wants to drag Ambrus back to their cabin, but they don't have that kind of time. "God, I love you. Please be careful."

Ambrus nods, pressing his lips against Rex's hair, nosing along Rex's temple and forehead before planting a kiss there. "I love you, too. I promise, I'll find you on Mapun, or you'll find me elsewhere. Singapore, most likely. I have a safe house there that shouldn't have been discovered by the department, especially considering the means in which I acquired it."

"Singapore, huh? If Rin understood my message and went where I told her, I'll introduce you," Rex says, and Ambrus smiles. "It's traditional to introduce your boyfriend to your mother, right?"

"Usually," Ambrus agrees, eyebrow rising in delight. "I can't wait to meet *Also* Tjin."

"If you call her that, she'll slap you." Rex kisses his boyfriend again, warm lips molding against his, the occasional flicker of tongue, and he glories in it. "Euan?"

"Hmm?"

Rex swallows down a sudden case of nerve-ridden butterflies. "Will you marry me?"

Ambrus leans back to stare Rex in the face. "Are you—you're serious."

"Yeah." Rex smiles and lifts both shoulders in an awkward shrug. "I don't have a ring or anything, seeing as we've been running for our fucking lives, but yeah—I'm serious. Will you?"

"We would have to find a place where it's legal," Ambrus murmurs. He kisses Rex again, hard and deep enough to leave Rex breathless. "Yes."

"Awesome. I—uh—wow." Rex grins, feeling like he's trying to balance on a gigantic bubble of joy. He doesn't have a ring, but he wants to give Euan something. Something important, like—

Rex touches the dog tags hidden underneath his t-shirt. He does have something.

"Rex?" Euan raises an eyebrow as he watches Rex pull the tags out of hiding and then pop the chain open.

"It's all I have, and I want them to be with you," Rex explains.

Euan holds very still, but Rex's hands still brush against Euan's neck while Rex reconnects the chain. Rex steps back and takes in the sight of his fiancé—*holy shit, holy shit, holy shit*—wearing his dog tags. "Guess that will have to do."

Euan lifts the first tag on the chain, which lists Rex's name, birthdate, the new service number he received in November when the DoD finally veered away from using Social Security numbers (which was stupid in the first place), his blood type, and religious preference. Rex doesn't really have one, his family history is so crowded with options, so all he had engraved on the tags was *a te Māori*. That's enough for any surviving family to understand what his preferences are for funerals. The back of both tags is engraved with a simplified version of the Special Forces coat of arms—a sword covered by a lightning bolt.

"I don't have mine," Euan says in a soft voice. "I wasn't wearing them when I went out that night to meet Fox."

"Doesn't matter. We'll figure out the details later. I just..." Rex trails off. "I love you, I really do want to marry your stupid ass, and I wanted you to be certain of that before you go."

Euan swallows and nods before he tucks the dog tags underneath his shirt. He's wearing Rex's olive t-shirt, Django's dark green long sleeve button-down, unbuttoned with the sleeves rolled up, a pair of borrowed cargo pants, and his boots. Rex hopes everything fits well. Euan is going to be stuck in those clothes for the foreseeable future.

"I do. I love you, Rex." Euan's voice catches on Rex's name. "I'll keep them safe for you."

"Okay." Rex smiles. "What the fuck do we do now?"

"You mean aside from collecting our mutual deposit boxes and enjoying the benefits of C-4?" Euan's expression brightens as he gives Rex a wicked smile. "Let's go see what kind of face your father makes when we tell him."

"That's mean," Rex replies, but Euan is right. Django Whetū's expression runs an entertaining gamut of shock, horror, resignation, happiness, and what might also be an eye-twitching recollection of *awkward*.

"Congratulations," Django finally says. Rex can tell it's genuine sentiment, not forced politeness. Then Django smiles. "Fuzzy dice, Ambrus."

Euan grins back. "Just buy me some fucking tea, Django, and I'll call it even."

The moment his father goes to collect Brian and Wesley for what may be a potentially terrifying grocery shopping trip, Rex turns to Euan. "Fucking fuzzy dice?"

"He's a cheap shit," Euan says. "I told him he had to buy us a car, and that was his counteroffer."

Rex stares at his boyfriend. Fiancé. "Oh, god. You two discussed this already?"

"Well, I was lying on the kitchen table, bleeding and drugged at the time," Euan responds in an innocent tone. "Maybe we settled on silverware."

"Oh, god," Rex repeats as he shoves Euan towards the gangplank. "Please just go blow up a bank. I can't believe you did that, you absolute asshole."

Euan laughs, picking up Rex's carry-on bag from the plane and resting it over his shoulders in a cross-body carry. Inside he has a single change of clothes, money, a few non-perishable snacks, one of the Glock SIGs, and at Django's insistence, the last full box of .357.

Euan breathes out and quirks an eyebrow at Rex. "See you soon."

Rex nods, swallowing back more nerves and fear and god knows what else. "Yeah. Have fun, Euan."

Euan smiles and waves one more time before heading down the gangplank. He shoves a pair of sunglasses onto his face as he proceeds along the dock to the boating club's asphalt parking lot.

"I love you," Rex whispers.

He really isn't all that surprised when he hears a response in Euan's voice, an echo in his head that he knows isn't one of his own thoughts: *I love you, too.*

*   *   *   *

Andi looks over her options for inconspicuous clothing to blend in with Seria's crowds of tourists. What she has is not promising. She and Ziba packed in too much of a hurry, and even her most bland clothing could stand out here.

"Andi?"

Andi half-turns to see that Khodî pushed open the door and froze in place. The words are on her lips: warnings about knocking, and how it's not nice to barge in on a lady.

The expression on his face stops her. Shock and amazement is giving way to something she might possibly label worship.

Well. She is standing in full view, completely naked. That might have something to do with it.

"Can I help you?" Andi asks in a mild voice, only the tiniest twitching at the corners of her mouth betraying how amusing she finds this to be.

"By all the fucking gods, you are beautiful," Khodî whispers.

Andi bites her lip as she feels the intense belief in his words. Not false flattery, not words meant to retain favor. Just simple truth from a man stunned beyond belief.

Andi hides it well, but she's startled by the unexpected emotional response. She hadn't planned to initiate a relationship with Khodî Som, not to the same deep extent Tjin has with Ambrus.

Definitely not anything like the bond Ziba had with Fox before the poor bastard took a second dose and lost his bloody mind.

By all the dear gods of her childhood: she might be altering that assessment, pending immediately.

"Thank you," Andi manages to reply in a normal voice. "What do you think I should wear into Seria?" she asks. "I have a few options, but none of them seem right."

"Clothing?" Khodî blinks a few times and then grins. "Right, you actually do have to get off this damned boat and go into town. Shit. Uhm." He presses his hand to his forehead. "Should I leave? I—kind of—Miss Banner, you broke my brain."

"I can tell," Andi says, a wide smile on her face. "My options, Mister Som?"

Khodî shuts the cabin door behind him as he enters and comes over to inspect her choices. The gleam in his eyes is pure calculation. Andi approves of the way Khodî snaps back into mission mindset after a boggled few moments.

"The pale slacks, the tank top, and the long-sleeved shrug," he says, holding out his hands. "Bo sent this to help round things out."

Andi takes the white cloth, which unfolds into a much longer length of material than she expected. "Oh. A headscarf, one long enough to wrap—yes, that will do nicely." She considers it and then smiles. "Help me to dress, Mister Som?"

"As my lady wishes," Khodî returns in the same insouciant tone, his golden-hued brown eyes filled with delight. He is, however, an absolute professional during his task. His touch does not linger, exactly as a proper valet would behave...and yet that makes it all the more erotic.

Oh, lovely. No matter how this turns out, Andi is going to enjoy her time with Khodî Som.

"Help me with my hair? Or do you—"

"I have a sister, Andi." Khodî gathers her hair with gentle hands, collecting it in the back. "I also had a step-mother who kept her hair long." He braids Andi's hair in such a way that it appears her hair is loose at the top, but ties it so that the braid hangs in a twisted loop that falls only to her shoulder blades instead of its full length. Once Andi wraps the scarf properly around her body, all of her hair is hidden from view.

"Beautiful," Khodî says again, placing a kiss on her forehead. "And you look like a local."

"Excellent." Andi shifts a little bit in place, making sure her hair is not going to slip free and wander into view. "Will you be willing to unbraid my hair upon my return this evening?"

Khodî nods, smiling at her. "And anything else you wish me to undo."

"You are delightful," Andi murmurs, and then wraps her hand around the back of his neck to pull him into a kiss.

*   *   *   *

Neumia is over the moon because she gets to go with Rex. It's partly to keep her away from the bank job several miles away, and partly because Euan believes that having Neumia along will help give Tyung Lam-Pan the impression that all is well. Rex's niece received the promised teal dye-job at last, and her hair is back in her favorite collection of braids.

It's a long walk in the heat. Neumia doesn't seem to mind, but Rex feels like he's melting. He's used to Trenton weather, not the South Pacific. At least a desert only offers dry heat, not hot air thick enough to choke on.

The address Euan gave to Rex leads them to a nice neighborhood situated between Kuala Belait and Seria. Walking up the long paved drive to the house makes Rex nervous, and not just because he can sense that weapons are trained on them.

"That is a *big* house," Neumia says, staring up at the mansion they're about to enter. "Who needs a house that big?"

"No idea, kiddo," Rex answers. It looks Moroccan on the outside, a massive stone edifice definitely built to withstand the heat. Rex picks out at least three sniper positions and two well-hidden security cameras by the time they make it to the front steps. "I guess some people like to have lots of space."

Rex holds out his hand. Neumia didn't want her hand held for the entire walk, but now she grasps on tight as they mount the stairs. Neumia only darts forward once, so she can be the one to push the doorbell. Rex hears the faint echo of the sound inside the house, a bright chime that sounds welcoming instead of ominous.

They wait only moments before the door is opened by a man in full traditional Sikh dress. "Greetings, Rex Tjin, Neumia de Lacy. I am Teipal Singh. You are both expected."

"Thanks!" Neumia replies, warming to the butler's good manners and kind smile. Then she notices the huge room that they're standing in, and her jaw hangs open a bit. "Wow," she whispers. Even that faint sound bounces off the walls. The outside had a Moroccan flair, but the inside of the mansion is a blend of Westernized Chinese architecture. Rex would like it a lot better if it was on a much smaller scale.

"Thank you for greeting us." Rex ignores how much his own voice echoes around the large entryway. "Will you tell Master Lam-Pan that we've arrived?"

"No need; he is aware," Teipal replies. "Come. Sit and cool yourselves after your long walk from the pier."

Teipal escorts them to a smaller room to the right of the front door, where comfortable-looking leather furniture surrounds a low table. Already resting there are two pitchers, one filled with ice water, the other holding some kind of fruit juice. Two clean glasses are empty and waiting. In the center of the table is a tray of sliced fruit with two artfully folded cloth napkins bracketing it on either side.

"Please." Teipal gestures for them to sit. "It is 32 degrees outside, and most of your walk was in full sun. Master Lam-Pan will be along in approximately ten minutes. Young lady, I enjoy the vibrant color of your hair," he adds, and Neumia beams.

Rex waits until Teipal departs, closing the wooden double doors behind him, before he sits down and tries not to groan in bliss. "Oh, hell, I could live on this couch." The leather is soft instead of stiff, and unlike most modern furniture he's encountered, the cushion gives just enough instead of too much.

"It's really squishy," Neumia agrees, bouncing once or twice before reaching for the strawberries. They're the most easily recognizable fruit—probably expensive imports unless there's a greenhouse on Lam-Pan's property.

"Wait a second, kiddo." Neumia pauses in place with her hand above the tray, frowning. Rex wasn't paying attention before, and it almost got him killed. He inspects the fruit, but his instincts are staying quiet. Nothing on the table is poisoned. "Go for it."

Rex pours juice into one glass and water for Neumia into the second when she gives the juice a narrow-eyed glare. "What is it?" she asks once Rex has taken a sip.

"Pomegranate," he says, feeling his parched throat soak up liquid and sugars like it's going out of style. "Sweet—better than any version you're going to get stateside."

Neumia frowns and then holds out her hands. "Okay, lemme try."

They end up swapping back and forth on their drinks, water to juice and back to water again. The strawberries vanish and the kiwi fruit slices are decimated. The pineapple isn't fresh, but sun-dried and coated in sugar, which is delicious.

"We are definitely going to be well-fortified for the trip back," Rex tells her.

"That was the entire point," a new voice says.

Rex turns, a bit startled and creeped out that someone managed to sneak up on him without being noticed, especially since there are closed doors involved. Standing in front of the still-closed double doors—what the shit?—is a very short Chinese man with sleek black hair, laughing eyes, and a polite, refined smile.

Rex stands up quickly; Neumia scrambles to copy him. "Tyung Xun Lam-Pan," he says, bowing in greeting. Neumia mimics Rex so smoothly that Bonika must have coached her.

Lam-Pan responds in kind, his smile widening. "Welcome to my home, Rex Tjin and Neumia de Lacy. I am aware of the fact that your visit must be short, but it is always a pleasure to meet friends of Euan. He has so very few. My grandfather always worried about him."

"He is worth befriending," Rex says, hiding behind formal words. He has Neumia with him. Bullets and running would not be a great way to find out what the Lam-Pan family stance is on homosexuality.

"I like him," Neumia adds.

Lam-Pan nods. "That is good. I do hate to be crass, but before you explore the contents of Mister Ambrus's belongings, there was an agreed-upon arrangement."

Rex nods and holds out a plain white envelope, flap folded but not sealed. It holds a note from Euan as well as the contracted sum of money, the final "rent" payment on the safe storage box in Lam-Pan's possession.

Lam ignores the money and reads the note instead, his gaze softening. "Everything. Oh dear. I did suspect it might be. I won't ask questions that you cannot answer, then."

Rex can't think of anything to say except, "Thank you."

Lam-Pan only smiles again before clapping his hands. The door opens and Teipal reappears. This time he is accompanied by a woman who is also Sikh, one with the regal bearing of a queen.

Teipal clears away the table's refreshment. The moment his task is done, the woman places two large black cases on the table. She leaves the room and returns a moment later with a third, smaller case. Rex knows military construction when he sees it—all three of the lockboxes are constructed to be fireproof and bombproof.

"We will give you privacy now," Lam-Pan announces. He quietly ushers Teipal and the unnamed woman from the room, closing the double doors behind them.

Rex gives it a ten-count before he goes to the door and throws the sliding bolt home. Lam-Pan has made him justifiably paranoid. Then he turns his attention back to the three black lockboxes. Each is secured with a digital combination, but the codes are on a second scrap of paper in Rex's pocket. The boxes are different sizes, so it's easy to match code to case.

"What do you think is in them?" Neumia asks in a soft, worried voice.

"I don't know." They're not booby-trapped—Euan would have warned him—but Rex is still cautious as he enters the codes and opens each box.

Neumia peers around Rex after nothing explodes. "I can look too, right?"

Rex nods. "Yeah, just—don't get too adventurous yet, okay?"

Inside the medium-sized lockbox is a laptop, one of the heavy-duty modern military bastards that can survive literal explosions. The laptop might not power on any longer after said explosion, but the hard drive will still be intact, the data salvageable. Rex hopes the laptop doesn't have a thumbprint encrypt, or they won't get to use it until Euan comes back.

With the laptop are two new smartphones, probably unlocked and ready to be used on whatever service they damned well like. Two sets of power cords and USB connectors are in neat bundles sealed in a plastic bag. Outlet adaptors are included that will ensure the power cords work in pretty much every electrical outlet in the world.

One of the phones has a white stripe painted down the backside. *Emergency Contact* is written within the stripe in Euan's close-set, curling script. Rex thinks about it for a minute before he tucks that phone into his pants pocket.

"Uncle Rex," Neumia whispers in a stunned voice.

Rex jerks his head around to look, hand already reaching for a weapon, but she's not in danger. Neumia is holding an open box that she's taken out of the smallest lockbox. It's made of aged, oiled hardwood, about the same size as of one of her shoeboxes. Inside, kept in transparent woven pouches, are gold and silver necklaces, rings, broaches, and pins. Hell, Rex thinks that round length of gold might be an actual damned torque—the old kind, not the modern copies.

Neumia's fingertips drift along one of the woven bags. "They're so pretty. Mom talks sometimes about having material goods set aside to sell. Is this that kind of thing?"

Rex slowly shakes his head. The inside of the wooden lid is inscribed with what he's pretty sure is Scots Gaelic, which looks like beautiful gibberish. "No, sweetheart. I think these are the Kellagh-Ambrus family heirlooms. Euan's family. I don't think they're for sale."

"Good." Neumia puts the lid back on the old box and sets it aside. "He shouldn't. It—it has feelings."

Rex glances down at his niece and sees that her lower lip is trembling. "Hey, it's okay." He rests his hand on Neumia's shoulder. "It's okay to feel things. Just don't let them tell you what to do."

Neumia takes a breath and nods. "I'm all right, Uncle Rex. Hey, that's a gun box, isn't it?"

"Sure is," Rex confirms, pulling out an old wooden pistol case from the smallest lockbox. Inside is an exceptionally well-preserved M1911 .45 caliber pistol. He touches the grip and knows at once that it's Euan's first service weapon. Rex had to leave his father's original 1911 behind in the States, which makes him feel like he's holding a gift in his hands. Euan hasn't demonstrated any sort of prescience beyond the creepy flood thing and the foreknowledge of the attack on the house, but Rex hefts the pistol box and thinks that on some level, Euan knew that this was something Rex would appreciate.

What really makes Rex think he's right are the three new boxes of .45 caliber ammunition in the box. He flips one over in his hand to check the encoded manufacture date and finds that the shells were produced in the last year. He might not need to put down a bear, but a .45 will sure as hell make a Specialist think twice about getting up again.

Two small flash drives are stashed beneath the pistol's box, secured in a static bag. Rex pockets them on instinct that he doesn't question. The only other thing in the smallest lockbox is a large manila envelope. When Rex unwinds the string that keeps it closed, he finds it full of handwritten notes and letters, the papers yellowing with age. He takes a quick glance at the pages without rifling through them, but doesn't recognize any of the handwriting. He seals the envelope with the string again, wondering if he's holding something else from the Kellagh-Ambrus family.

The largest box contains a padded case holding a disassembled satellite dish, control box, and the leads to hook it up to a computer. It's self-aligning, able to connect to any satellite in orbit as long as it's told what to look for.

Rex stares at it for a moment, eyebrows raised and eyes wide. This satellite setup is worth a *lot* of money on the black market. The right computer user, if they plan their attack in advance and do it fast, can do terrible, awesome things with it.

"Hoo." Rex snaps the padded case closed. "We might actually have a chance at this, kiddo."

Neumia looks startled. "We didn't before?"

"Oh, we had one, but this gives us one more advantage that we might really need. We're going to have to be so damned careful, though."

Neumia gives him a quick nod of understanding. "Aunt Ella's good with computers. I bet she can use it."

Rex feels his chest ache. "Eric was the one who could really make a computer sing." Ella may be right about Eric, but they still have to *find* their brother.

Neumia suddenly looks crestfallen. "Uncle Rex, how come you can miss someone you've never met?"

"Stories make people live, kiddo," Rex says, picking Neumia up and hugging her. "You miss Eric because we've all told you about him. After so many words, you feel like you've met him, lived with him, laughed with him." Rex gives her a gentle squeeze and feels Neumia squeeze back. "I miss him, too. So much. Eric would have adored you, Neumia de Lacy."

Neumia wiggles to signal that she wants to be put down. "Let's put everything in the duffel bag, Uncle Rex. I think we should go."

Rex pauses for a moment, head tilted as he listens. He doesn't hear anything, not exactly, but he thinks they're about to be on a tighter schedule. "Good call."

Neumia holds open the duffel bag. Rex puts the heavy satellite case in first before he stacks the laptop on top of it.

When he glances into the lockbox one more time, there's something else there that the laptop had been hiding. Resting on the bottom of the lockbox is a plain white envelope. Rex's name is on the front; Major is underlined with two strokes of intense emphasis that translate very well.

"Keep packing, kiddo," Rex tells Neumia, picking up the envelope and tearing it open at the end when he hears paper sliding around inside. "I need to read this first, just in case."

"Okay, Uncle Rex."

Rex breathes out, steadying himself, before he unfolds a single sheet of white paper. Euan's handwriting. It's legible, but cramped and rushed instead of his more typical clear script. The letter is dated the twenty-first of January—right before Euan came home from the Turkmenistan incident.

> *Dear Rex,*
>
> *Well, this must mean that everything has gone to complete shit, doesn't it? I hope it's not a permanent situation—I was getting used to living in that apartment. I was getting used to you. Being there.*
>
> *Dammit.*
>
> *If I've sent you to collect these things, then you are already aware of the danger involved, and what, exactly, it all means. I hope that you and your family are safe. I hope your father hasn't declared war against the entirety of the United States government. Wars against entire governments do not typically end well, and I hate that I'm speaking from experience.*
>
> *The phone with the white stripe has a number that I've memorized. Introduce yourself (and the other phone) to the Bugs Bunny pun of an application that's pre-installed, a green icon on the main screen. As long as you have the phone moored to a hardline internet connection instead of a mobile phone provider, you can message and call anyone in the damned world for free with that app—and what's better, it's encrypted. A phone call bounced off a satellite can be intercepted and listened to, but anyone trying to interpret a call or SMS sent by that app is just going to receive gibberish. The app can also conceivably get you arrested in the United States, but fuck, what can't these days?*
>
> *Save the satellite kit for emergencies. You'll understand what sort of emergencies I mean. Satellite signals can be tracked, but sometimes there isn't much choice.*
>
> *Once you have hardline access, the laptop should prove useful. Set up a proxy-chain, and you can regain internet access without much concern about being observed. (Stay away from .gov websites. No, no, and also NO.) When you power up the laptop, more specific instructions, and some useful starting points, are in a document file on the desktop.*
>
> *The jewelry and the letters in the envelope are all that remain of my family's belongings. I put everything in storage before I left for Vietnam. While I was gone, lightning struck the facility, burning it to the ground. Those items were the only things to survive the fire—God*

knows how, not when the destruction of that building was so fucking complete. I'm fortunate that a firefighter with morals found the jewelry, or I wouldn't even have that.

I entrust both of these things into your care. I have no pictures of my family. I only have memories of faces that have become so blurred by time that I'm no longer certain I'm recalling them correctly. If worst comes to it, and needs must, sell the jewelry to ensure your survival, but safeguard the letters for me, I beg you. They're all I have left.

Remain safe, healthy, secure, and fucking well-armed. I will see you when you've finished retrieving these items, or I will see you as soon as I can.

Please be on the alert for poison-bearing bartenders and bullets, will you?

I love you,
Euan

Rex folds the letter, tucks it back into the envelope, folds that in half, and slides the envelope into the same pocket where he put the emergency phone. He takes a quick glance around to make sure Neumia got everything, and that the three lockboxes are truly empty. He even runs his hands along the inside edges, tops and bottoms, making sure there are no lumps where lumps should not be.

"Okay, Nari. We're good to go," Rex says, and Neumia looks relieved.

"If I believed you had time, you would dine with my family tonight," Lam-Pan tells them when they return to the vast entryway of the mansion. "But I fear you do not."

"I think it's going to be an interesting couple of weeks," Rex says neutrally. "In utter truth, we would accept your invitation if the situation were otherwise."

"I understand completely." Lam-Pan waves the female Sikh forward again, who smiles at Rex and Neumia both as she deposits a dark blue duffle bag on the ground before their feet.

"For your journey, and your safety." Her words sound like a blessing, but she departs before Rex can see her expression.

"And this is...?" Rex asks, not yet moving to take the bag.

"I can be told nothing, and I understand why, but I can make educated guesses. As Jaipal told you: this is a gift, for your journey and your safety." Lam-Pan bites his lip, which makes Rex finally realize the man is much younger than he'd assumed, maybe twenty-five at most. "When things improve, please visit again, and bring Euan with you. It has been too long."

Rex nods. He's always game for a free meal that doesn't involve imprisonment, and Lam-Pan seems to be a decent man. "We will."

He picks up the second bag and immediately knows he's carrying weapons. The smile he grants Lam-Pan as they depart is probably a bit gleeful, but hell, Rex can't help it. Best. Gift. Ever. It also makes him wonder what talents Tyung Xun Lam-Pan inherited from his grandfather.

They walk back to Kuala Belait with the evening sun trying to blind them. Rex drops the bags long enough to pull out his sunglasses and put them on, smiling when Neumia does the same with a pair of mirrored lenses sized for her tiny face. He checks his watch; it's after five, and sunset is in about an hour.

That's when the ground beneath Rex's feet trembles. He drops a bag and reaches out on instinct, grabbing Neumia's shoulder to keep her steady. The distant echo of an explosion reaches his ears in the same moment.

Rex and Neumia turn around to see a plume of dirty smoke rise into the sky. A second rumbling echo follows the first—one explosion for the wall, one for the vault. A good gunshot probably destroyed the lock on the box that Euan is retrieving.

Run, Euan, Rex thinks. *Run, keep running, and do not stop for anything.*

In Kuala Belait, they find a vendor selling cold fruit drinks on the street. Rex buys four in recognition of their shadows, handing them out as Bonika and Ziba melt out of the crowd to join them.

"Anything?" Rex asks while Neumia guzzles down fruit juice at a speed that makes him worry that she's going to vomit it back up.

"Clear path all the way there, and again all the way back," Ziba reports, sipping at her juice. Her dark hair is pinned up in sloppy curls, paired with a tank top and Andi's flowing batik skirt. It makes her look like a college-age tourist, whereas Bonika, dressed all in white with prerequisite large sun hat and dark glasses, looks like a tourist with money. One to attract attention; one to be ignored.

They all step aside with the rest of the foot traffic as sirens clear the street, allowing rescue and police vehicles to speed towards Seria. "That must have been quite a bit of C-4 to get those results. I want to know who Ambrus purchased it from just as much as I really don't. Ambrus has odd friends," Bonika says in a low voice, lips quirked in a smile.

"He must, as we count among that number," Ziba replies in a smooth voice, which just makes Bonika laugh.

"Do you need help with those?" Bonika asks, watching Rex lift both duffels.

"No thanks." Rex isn't letting go of that second bag again until he's on the boat. He has first dibs on whatever is inside.

They're the last group to return to the pier, leaving Andi as the only straggler. Wesley and Brian are speed-loading supplies from the dock, trucking them up the gangplank before returning for more. Django, Kai, and Khodî are grabbing the containers from the deck and taking them to the kitchen, storage lockers, or to the berths, depending on what's inside.

"It'll be nice to have some fucking clothes again," Khodî is muttering as they board. He looks up at Rex. "Are we good?"

"Solid," Rex replies, holding up both duffel bags. "Want a hand?" he asks, and receives several loud requests for assistance.

Andi doesn't arrive until the sun is vanishing below the horizon. She hurries up the yacht's narrow boarding ramp and pulls the scarf from her hair as she steps onto the deck, breathing heavily with one hand pressed to her chest.

"Apologies," she gasps. "They cordoned off the area faster than I anticipated, and it took me a while to get past the police."

"What happened?" Django asks. Ziba refills one of the juice containers with lemonade that someone was smart enough to purchase and gives it to her cousin.

Andi takes several long drinks, wiping her face with the scarf, before she continues. "I saw Euan get in and out of the bank safely, but afterwards I lost him in the confusion. The local authority's attention is definitely focused on him. We could wave banners proclaiming our fugitive status right now and no one would notice. Given how much noise they're still making, I'm certain that Euan's in the wind."

"That's everything, then. We're ready to go," Django says.

Rex nods. It's painful to say the next, necessary words. Everything within him wants them to stay, to wait for Euan—but Euan isn't coming back to the boat.

They all know the plan. Stick to it.

"Let's get the hell out of here."

अश्लेषा

Chapter 15

:)(X)(X(:

They're well out of port, back in the safe darkness of open water, before Rex unzips Lam-Pan's duffel bag. Their father whistles over the gift, both eyebrows raised in appreciation.

"This is fucking helpful. What did you say to that man?" Django asks.

Rex shrugs, pulling an SAR-80 from the bag and sighting down the muzzle. It's an old Singapore model that was never mass-produced, but it appears to be well-maintained, and there is plenty of .45mm ammunition in the bag. "I didn't tell Lam-Pan a damned thing other than exchanging pleasantries over the stuff I'd gone there for in the first place."

There is supplemental ammo for the Glock SIGs, Ziba's Beretta 96 .40mm—even Kai's .30 bore shotgun, and it's not easy to get #4 buckshot in this area. Between the ammo and the extra weapons, the duffel's contents put them back up to a squad's proper ordinance capacity. They'll be set for a while as long as they don't try to start another ground war in Asia like that airport bullshit.

Django pulls a Beretta M9 classic from the bag, drops the magazine, and fieldstrips it in seconds. "Not my favorite, but it'll be nice to have a .9mm again. This saves us from needing another port stop before heading out to Mapun, too."

"Right." Rex puts the rifle down on the table, making a mental note that it needs to be fully stripped, cleaned, and oiled again before he chambers a round. "Dad?"

His father is putting the M9 back together with his usual swiftness. "What is it, kid?"

"On the flash drive that has our photos...do we have anything from Euan's family?"

Django slaps the clip home before he answers. "I'm not sure. Why?"

"He doesn't have any. Photographs, I mean," Rex explains, which makes Django turn around and stare at him in surprise. "Euan had everything in storage during Vietnam. A fire burned the building down. He has an envelope of letters and a wooden box, but that's it."

"Goddammit." Django frowns. "I can't remember, not for certain. We'll have to use that laptop and check the drives once we're on Mapun."

"Okay. Dibs on the Glock 34, by the way," Rex adds.

"Fuck!" Django spits out, glaring at Rex.

He grins back. "My gift. I get to pick first."

Rex checks on Ella after he strips, cleans, and reassembles the SAR-80, rolling it back up in its cloth case. Once upon a time, it was definitely someone's beloved weapon; all it needed was oil and a fresh cleaning. "How's the new toy?"

Ella clucks her tongue as her fingers fly over the keyboard. "Wireless and Bluetooth were both disabled when I started it up, which was smart of your boyfriend. Got dual boot, too—Linux or Windows startup, your choice."

"Which version of Windows?" Rex asks, curious.

"Windows 7 64-bit. It's a beautiful beast of a machine. Sixteen gigs of RAM. She's mine."

"You can't have her, Ella. You have to share," Rex reminds his sister, who curls her arms around the laptop and glares up at him like a dragon guarding her hoard. "Okay. You can share it later," he allows, deciding to go find something else to do that doesn't involve watching his sister growl over technology.

Instead, he runs into an indignant older brother. "Why can't I have the damned Glock?" Khodî asks, scowling.

"Because I'm the only one of us outside of Euan and the Banners who's worked in the field recently, all the latest bullshit aside."

Khodî glares at Rex. "I was a sheriff, Rex. Technically, I never *stopped* working in the field!"

"You were on-mission for drunks and wandering cows," Rex replies dryly. "Cows don't have guns, Khodî. Also, finders-keepers, fuck your luck, the gun is mine."

"Asshole!" Khodî shouts, and chases Rex the full length of the boat in retaliation. Rex can't stop laughing the entire way, even though he's risking a fall into the ocean. Irritating Khodî is a sublime pastime, and Rex really needed some normal right now.

About an hour later, Brian and Bonika finally break down and have a shouting match that looks like it's on the verge of devolving into an actual fistfight. Ella finally pried herself away from her new precious, so she and Rex are the ones sitting on the boat railing. They're either audience members or referees, but neither task keeps them from placing bets on who would kick whose ass. The problem is that both of their money is on Bo, and they don't have a third person to sucker into putting money on Brian.

At least Neumia is in the lounge with Kai as they enjoy their first viewing of *Gremlins*. Neumia is a little freaked out about predicting the Saint Patrick's Day massacre, so Rex is glad she's not hearing any of this.

From what Rex can pick out of the angry, Irish-accented swearing—Bonika's precise American neutral accent always goes to shit when she's pissed—Bo is furious that Brian didn't tell her that EKTC-51's effects were genetic and inheritable, or that Brian was living, breathing proof of it. Granted, neither of them actually planned to have a relationship in the first place. Brian and Bonika were a one-night stand that led to Bonika calling Brian a month later, two hours before a game, to tell him she was pregnant.

Wesley recorded that moment for posterity—not the phone call, but the pre-game interviews when a reporter asked Brian how he felt about that night's game. Brian had given the woman a deer-in-headlights stare, blurted, "My girlfriend's pregnant," and just looked really confused when everyone nearby congratulated him.

They did try to have a relationship after that, if only for their future kid's sake, but Brian and Bonika were really, *really* bad at communicating back then. Cue the current conversation, where Rex and Ella hear for the first time that Brian was terrified as fuck about what kind of potential talents Neumia would express from a double-hit of ETKC-51.

That doesn't actually help. If anything, that just makes Bonika even angrier. "Dae ye regret our daughter, then?"

Brian rears back like he's been struck hard. "What—no! Of course I don't! I—" He shoves his hand through his hair, which is getting long enough to brush his shoulders. "Look. We were having a kid. You made me sign an actual assload of NDAs so you could tell me you used to be department, and *then* wanted to meet my family. I didn't stop freaking out until you either didn't recognize Dad's name, or pretended not to know him—he stayed away from the bastards for a reason, and I was afraid..."

"That I'd gie oot about yer Da, an' try'n get him back in," Bonika finishes, eyes narrowed.

"The fuck did she say?" Ella whispers.

"That I'd tell them about Dad and try to get him back into the program," Rex translates. "You are bad at this."

Ella scowls. "Fuck you."

"I played daft on that front," Bonika says. "T'wasn' me business, Brian, and tha's when ye shoou've foockin' tol' me. It's called trust, ya dumb shite—"

"I didn't exactly have my own stack of NDAs to shove at you!" Brian retorts. "You're right—I was only a dumb shit ball player, Bonika de Lacy. I had no idea what to do about any of it. Then you picked up on me not telling you about ETKC-51's shit, thought it meant I was keeping secrets about our relationship, and decided I wasn't worth your fucking time!"

"I told ye, I used tae be departmen' 'cause I worried aboot our daughter, too!"

"But I didn't know that, same as I didn't know what was going to happen to Nari!" Brian shouts back, and then his expression turns into angry regret. "Besides, by the time we'd hit that point? I already knew you were leaving. What would have been the fucking point, Bo?"

Bonika's eyes narrow to icy slits of emerald-chip green. She stalks up to Brian, slaps him hard across the face, and then pulls his head down into a kiss. Brian stands there with his arms spread out, looking like a traumatized eagle, before he finally wraps his hands around Bonika's waist and lifts her from the decking.

"Aww, I wanted to break up a fight," Ella grumbles as Rex takes her by the arm and discreetly escorts his sister the hell away from a potential romantic staging area. If Brian and Bonika forget that they have a cabin available, Rex doesn't want to witness it.

"I'd prefer that Neumia has her parents back together, thanks," Rex replies. "Though hey, that was one hell of a slap."

"I bet he has loose teeth," Ella agrees sagely. "Hey, what if that slap and kiss is just a precursor to Bo throwing him overboard?"

Rex shrugs. "Brian knows how to swim."

By the time they get to the lounge, the movie's credits are rolling on the flat-panel television mounted to the wall. "What'd you think?" Ella asks, flopping down on the couch next to Kai and Neumia.

"That was awesome!" Neumia gushes. "Let's watch it again! Like we should replay the blender scene. A lot!"

"Kai?" Rex prods when his baby brother doesn't say anything.

Kai finally looks up at Rex with a poleaxed expression on his face. "The '80s were fucking weird."

"Maybe, but it's the nineties that got us *Gremlins 2*. That movie makes this one look normal," Rex says.

Kai's expression folds up into a suspicious glower. "No fucking way. Nothing can make what I just watched look normal. Nari, do we have the sequel in that stack of DVDs your Uncle Wolf brought in?"

Neumia is already shuffling through a stack of disks with the titles scrawled across them in dark green Sharpie marker. Pirates, man.

"Maybe. I think I saw—yep, here it is!" Neumia exclaims, holding her prize up over her head.

"Awesome. Put it in. I have to watch this." Kai leans back against the couch, arms crossed in glaring defiance that says he refuses to believe it's possible. Rex doesn't have anything else to do at the moment, so he decides to join them. Besides, it's been a while since he's witnessed this insanity.

Django enters the room a while later, looking baffled and irritated. "Some people really need to learn that there are cabins on this ship," he says, glancing at the TV. "What the shit is this?"

"*Gremlins 2*," Ella replies. She has a huge grin on her face because Kai's eye-tic has gotten worse as the movie progresses.

"Why?" Django asks, but that's a question Rex has no idea how to answer.

Xāwuṭh walks in, sees which movie is playing, and immediately brightens. "Hey, this one's my favorite!"

"What the *fuck* is wrong with you?" Kai bursts out. One of the gremlins has just mutated into a bat gargoyle thing, because reasons.

Xāwuṭh frowns at them like they're missing the obvious. "Because transgender gremlin, that's why."

Rex blinks a few times as he tries to process that. "What? Wait, back up a minute."

Ella points at the screen. "Nope, there she is."

They all stare at the television in bewilderment except for Xāwuṭh, who is grinning like a happy maniac. Then Ella cackles under her breath. "Wet and fed after midnight."

"Right," Rex finally manages to say. "They don't need females. They breed with water."

"See? Transgender gremlin," Xāwuṭh repeats, pleased. "Culture needed the push. This was a *weird* push, but most of them are."

"I think what's getting to me is that she has the most serious role in the entire movie." Kai's eye-tics have stopped, but his face is frozen in horrified bewilderment.

Neumia points at the TV when the sort-of-title-character reappears on-screen. "Who's Gizmo dressed up as?"

"Rambo," Django answers in a curt voice. "A character from movies that none of us watch because it messes with half the family's PTSD."

"What does Rambo do?" Neumia asks.

"Runs around shirtless, shooting things." Ella pats Neumia on the head. "Trust me, if you ever decide you want to watch men run around topless while shooting at things, there are way better options."

Rex looks over Neumia's head to glare at Ella. "You did not just volunteer to become our niece's porn gateway," he hisses.

Ella shrugs. "I'm the bad aunt. It's my job."

"You're her *only* aunt," Kai says.

Rex gets whapped with several of Neumia's teal braids when she vigorously shakes her head. "Nu-uh! I have Aunt Zannah, too!"

"Bo has a sister?" Kai sounds appalled. "Her parents made more than one?"

"Shut up, some of us are trying to watch this travesty!" Django snaps.

"All right. You win," Kai says when the credits roll. "The first movie is totally normal. Fuck, they broke the fourth wall harder than *Deadpool!*"

Xāwuṭh stands up and stretches. "That was fun, but I promised I was coming back to the bridge, oh, an hour ago, so I'll see you assholes later." He scrubs the top of Neumia's head on his way past. She ducks away from his hand, giggling.

"We could watch *Se7en* next!" Neumia suggests.

"We could, but you're not." Rex picks Neumia up and tosses her over his shoulder. "Bedtime, miscreant."

They meet Wesley at the doorway. "I heard the magic words about a movie."

"They won't let me watch *Se7en* with them, Uncle Wesley!" Neumia complains from behind Rex.

"Good. You aren't allowed to watch that movie for at least another five years," Wesley replies sternly. "Trust me, you've already had enough trauma to last until puberty just from this past week."

"Why are you in such a hurry to watch this movie again?" Rex asks.

Wesley grins. "Are you kidding? I lost my virginity thanks to this movie."

"That's gross, Uncle Wesley!" Neumia declares.

Rex's face twists up in baffled distaste. "What she said, bro. That's gross."

"Not because of the subject matter!" Wesley protests. "Hell, no. That's cannibal-levels of messed-up. Virginity loss was a thing because scary movies and bad movies are saviors of date nights everywhere."

"Good point," Rex admits. Wesley's right about the bad movie part. Rex still has no idea how *Kingdom of the Crystal Skull* ends.

Neumia is still slung over his shoulder, loudly protesting the unfairness of not getting to watch *Se7en*, as Rex takes her upstairs to the double-occupancy crew cabin Neumia was originally sharing with her mother. He's pretty sure that Bonika is going to be sleeping elsewhere tonight. Rex doesn't exactly need that cabin, not when his fiancé isn't around. Besides, if Brian and Bo are going to reconcile, they deserve the chance to do it without worrying about waking up their kid.

"You stayin'?" Neumia asks, yawning as Rex tucks her in.

"Yep." Rex turns off the lights except for the little LED pod light over his bunk. Thanks to the department, his Kindle is a loss, but Rex always kept his book purchases backed up on his laptop and the lightning connector drive on his keychain. That will plug directly into the jailbroken knock-off iPad that Rex asked Khodî to find during his shopping trip in Brunei. Illegal as all hell, and probably gives the company fits to know that they exist, but pirates will always find a way.

"I'm just going to be reading for a while, Nari." Rex takes off his shoes and flops down on his bunk. He's been keeping himself occupied, trying not to worry about Euan, and books are a good distraction.

Rex only gets a few pages into the first book of the *Prydain Chronicles* when Neumia pipes up. "You're worried about Euan?"

Rex glances over at Neumia. She's rolled over onto her side to gaze at him, looking tiny, fragile, and far too sad. "Yeah, I am."

"Even though you know he's gonna be okay?" Neumia asks.

Rex swallows before nodding. "I'd worry no matter which one of us it was out there, no matter how many times we've done this kind of job. Your grandfather, your aunt and uncles, your parents—any of us."

Neumia's tiny eyebrows come together to create a worried frown line. "Even though Euan's not gonna make it to Mapun?"

Rex feels his heart give a painful jolt. It takes a hell of a lot of effort to keep his expression and voice neutral. "What makes you say that, kiddo?"

"Cause he's not." Neumia bites her lip. "I mean, he doesn't get *caught* or anything. But he's not getting to Mapun."

"How do you know, Nari?" Rex asks, making himself breathe normally. This *is* normal—all of it. He wants Neumia to grow up believing that, the same way Rex and his siblings did.

"I dunno. I just do. G'night, Uncle Rex." Neumia rolls over to go to sleep.

Rex rests the e-reader against his chest, closing his eyes as he convinces his heartbeat to slow down to a normal rate. Aside from the initial jolt, he's not really surprised. Disappointed, maybe, but not surprised. Rex just hopes his stupid boyfriend is watching his ass.

*   *   *   *

Kai finally gets a turn with the laptop after pretty much everyone else and their gremlins. Most of the boat's collection of warm bodies are in bed, sleeping or...nope, Kai doesn't want to know what Brian and Bo are doing. At least they took over Rex and Ambrus's cabin before continuing to do the thing they were previously doing *outside, oh my god.*

Rex and Neumia are upstairs, Dad's asleep, and Wolf is listening to J-pop on the bridge, which, what the fuck, Wolf. Andi and Khodî took the room Andi and Ziba were originally sharing, and Kai is determinedly not thinking about that, either. It's not that he's prudish or anything. He's only wondering when the *Gives No Fuhks* boat became the sexy cruising times boat. Seriously.

When he passed the last cabin before the stairs and laptop-claiming time, he saw Ella passed out in the bunk opposite Ziba. The ex-Specialist was still awake, so he waved; she waved back. Ziba didn't seem upset, at least—just thoughtful. Kai really hopes that "thoughtful" doesn't slide into "completely fucking depressed" because her boyfriend lost his damned marbles.

Ella also tried to read him the riot act earlier about No Internet, but Kai isn't stupid. He made a point of reminding her—in Latin, because fuck you, that's why. He wants to get the chance to use the pirate-copy of everyone's not-favorite office suite. Kai likes to type out his thoughts, and after the past few days, he needs a keyboard so he can spew out medical theories (interspersed with *Highlander* jokes) at full speed ahead, way faster than he could write it out.

Kai sits with the laptop out on the back table with most of the exterior lightning turned off, enjoying the peace and quiet after the madcap fuckery that was watching two *Gremlins* movies in a row, followed by *Se7en* before he gave up and walked out. He's a doctor trained to help and heal people, and that was too much suffering for him to handle. Fictional or not, he couldn't help those characters, and it was driving him fucking nuts.

He's been typing for at least ten minutes—maybe a lot longer—when he hears, "Hi there."

Kai glances up to find that Sorrow Bùi has joined him at the table. "Hi," he says, remembering to be polite, before he goes back to typing.

"What are you doing?"

"Uh—medical theories. Typing out ideas about improving certain surgical practices. Writing bad jokes. Uh, it's brain spew. I'm typing brain spew," Kai answers. He glances up, expecting a bored audience, and finds the opposite.

Sorrow looks intrigued. "Surgical practices? What is your job?"

"I was studying to be a doctor. Even when you finally get there, you don't stop learning." Kai reaches up to rub his eyes. He's been staring at the screen so long that he can see the LCD's refresh rate behind his eyelids. Ugh. Definitely way more than ten minutes of typing.

"You are dedicated." When Kai glances at him again, Sorrow has propped his elbow on the table, elfin-thin chin resting on his hand, and is gazing at Kai in what he's pretty sure is blatant interest. Or...maybe that's curiosity? Shit, he is so out of practice at social crap. School has come first for a very long time now.

"Why do you say that?" Kai's heart is fluttering, like he's either trapped or about to kiss somebody.

"I spoke to you in Thai, Vietnamese, and English. Not only did you not notice the language changes, you responded in kind." Sorrow gives Kai a broad grin, his white teeth shining brilliantly against his tan skin. "Kai is a nickname, yes?"

"Sure is." Kai holds out his hand. "My full name is Ki te Muri kā 'Aukai."

Sorrow takes Kai's hand in a gentle grip, his fingers rough and callused from life at sea. "That is many vowels for an American name. No wonder they call you Kai."

"Uhm, I didn't think you were the social sort," Kai says, trying to figure out how to extract his hand without being rude. Sorrow joins them for group meals, but only long enough to eat and give Xāwuṭh boating breaks. Sorrow spoke when he was around them, but it's...

Okay, so Kai had a lot on his mind, and he didn't track Sorrow's conversations very well. He'd noted Sorrow's tiny, lean-muscled body, realized he was staring, blushed, and went right back to trying *not* to catch another shark.

Sorrow is the one to release Kai's hand, as if they've touched for just the right amount of time. "My family, it...what happened to me makes me nervous about wishing to be friends."

Kai nods. "I'm sorry. I—you know Wolf is totally aromantic and asexual, right?"

Sorrow tilts his head. "He breeds like a plant?"

Kai slaps his hand over his mouth to hold back a wild snort of laughter. "Uh, no, uh—not quite. He just doesn't do sex. Or romance. Ever."

Sorrow thinks about it. "No, I think that cousin Xāwuth *does* do romance. He's merely in love with boats instead of people."

Kai gives up and bursts out laughing. It makes his chest hurt less, but it also makes him realize he hasn't had much of a reason to laugh since Saint Patrick's Day video game night was interrupted over a week ago.

"I—uhm, I'm really bad at this," Kai says, deciding to be blunt. "What I'm trying to say is that in this family? We really don't care if you're a girl, a boy, neither, both, or if you decide to be a tree." Sorrow grins at him again. "Also, are you hitting on me? Because I can't tell and I don't want to make assumptions and also you're pretty—shit, I said all that."

Kai puts his head down on the table next to the laptop. He hadn't just said that, he'd spewed it all out in one breath.

Sorrow doesn't laugh at Kai, which is nice of him. "I was perhaps, trying to, uh, 'hit on you,' yes," he admits. "I am not practiced at it, but you were the first to notice that I am *me*. Is that bad criteria for dating?"

"I have no idea," Kai slurs into the tabletop, which makes Sorrow giggle. "Can we not do what Khodî and Andi and Brian and Bonika did, though? Brian and Bonika used to be a sort-of-couple, Rex and Euan were already dating last year, and..." Kai trails off and lifts his head. Sorrow is nodding, listening with a quiet attentiveness that Kai really likes. Outside of family members, most people just humor his babbling, like he's the fucking Hawai'ian entertainment bauble.

Kai starts over. "So, last week I pulled five bullets out of Rex's boyfriend. Then our house gets blown up, and my brother got a piece of it stuck in his arm." He makes a disgruntled face. Bad mental image, and also, Kai has no idea what Xāwuth told Sorrow about what the family gets up to. That might be a fun and traumatizing conversation.

Dammit, he already lost the thread. "Okay: house blown up, hurt brother, collected sister, killed a *hell* of a lot of soldiers, spent three days on a horse, spent thirty hours on a plane next to someone who would not shut up even when I threatened to kill them, got off plane, some asshole shot my brother and killed a bunch of people and made me remember—" Kai breaks off with a gasp and buries his face in his hands. "Shit."

Sorrow reaches out and cautiously rests his fingertips on top of Kai's shoulder. "You have been busy."

Kai nods. "There was a car chase in there, too. Also, more weird shit, and I'm not processing it very well, and, uhm...do you hug people? I could really use one of those right now."

Sorrow smiles, his dark brown eyes taking on a warm, soulful glow. "No one has asked for my touch in several years. Yes, I hug people, Ki te Muri kā."

"Trust me, Kai is fine. The nickname came from a person I'm promised was hella nifty," Kai babbles as he stands up.

They meet at the end of the table. Sorrow probably tops out five inches below Kai's five-foot-eight, and is hesitating even more than he is. Kai finally gives in and pulls Wolf's tiny Thai cousin into his arms for a hug.

Sorrow whimpers and rests his head against Kai's chest, his arms wrapping around Kai's waist. Kai simultaneously melts and wants to go punch Wolf's uncle in the face. He can't really do either, so Kai settles for putting his arms around Sorrow's upper back, feeling wiry muscle and the faint ridged line of his spine hiding under his t-shirt. Sorrow's wearing a binder; Kai hopes it's a good one and not one of the bad circulation-cutting-off sort.

"It will be all right," Sorrow tells him, which makes Kai bite his lip. He's the one who's supposed to be saying that.

"Probably, but I'm not a soldier, Sorrow," Kai whispers. Shit, he's shaking. Great. "I don't know how to do this shit."

"I am merely one who knows boats." To Kai's surprise, Sorrow lifts one of his hands and runs his fingers through Kai's curled hair. Awesome blissful pettings are awesome. "But I know that even best soldiers need doctors. I think you are already doing exactly what you know to do."

That's kind of insightful, actually. "How old are you?" Kai asks in bewilderment.

"Eighteen," Sorrow answers. "In a few days, I will be nineteen."

Well, at least if this goes anywhere, Kai won't be cradle robbing like a creeper. "Why do you sound like you've been—I don't know. Around?"

"I always liked boats, but boats are...my parents did not consider that my career should revolve around them. Without boats, I did not know what else I wanted to do with my life. I read a lot," Sorrow explains. It hasn't escaped Kai's notice that Sorrow hasn't let go of Kai's waist, but then, Kai hasn't released his grip, either. Maybe they both really needed a hug.

"I read medical textbooks, warrior stories from the old days of my people, biology articles, even National Geographic after I learn to read English. I could never settle on any one thing. So, I read more and more, and maybe I learn a little bit about everything. That must be useful to someone, somewhere, yes?" Sorrow asks.

"Definitely. I'm finding it useful," Kai says, and tightens his grip around Sorrow's shoulders. "So, uh...Lotus Blossom. *Dxkbaw*[1]. It's still fitting, you know. Flowers aren't female. They're male *and* female, with weird extra bits that I don't get because I'm a doctor, not a botanist."

"*Star Trek*," Sorrow says in approval, before letting out a thoughtful sigh. "Perhaps one day I will consider the name without bitterness, Kai. For now, all I can remember of that life is sorrow."

"Okay. *Khwām ṣeřā ṣok*[2] it is."

"Your Thai is awful," Sorrow complains.

Kai grins. "Blame Wolf. He's the one who taught me to speak it."

*   *   *   *

Everyone else is still asleep when Django wakes in the morning, even Rex, who passed out with his new e-reader over his face. Django bites back a nostalgic snort of amusement and leaves him alone. Rex will wake up if Django touches anything, and everyone deserves to sleep.

He glances into Brian and Wesley's open doorway to discover he was wrong. Brian is still asleep, but Wesley isn't there. He's been replaced by Bonika. Brian and Bo really should have remembered that there is an empty cabin available instead of trying to fit onto a single bunk, but hey, not his problem.

Django thinks about it as he goes to get fresh tar-coffee (thanks, Xāwuṭh) from the galley before he paces along the sidewall to reach the front of the boat. He finds Wesley sitting there in one of the yacht's folding chairs, staring into the sunrise. "Morning."

Wesley nods and holds up his beer. "What do you call it when it's still last night for you?"

"Stupidity," Django replies in a dry voice. "Can I sit, or would you like to continue drinking until we get to the island?"

"Nah, sitting's fine." Wesley tilts his head at the bench built into the front wall. "Just had a lot on my mind last night. I still have time to nap before landfall, anyway."

"Like what?" Django asks, sitting down and cradling his coffee. At least now there are enough coffee mugs. It's a vast improvement over the war of the tiny Styrofoam cups back at the Philly roachstrip.

Wesley empties the last sip from his beer bottle. "Like being really fucking pissed off."

Django nods. "Not like we don't have a multitude of reasons to choose from." He gives Wesley a brief up-and-down look. "Blaming Ambrus?"

---

[1] Thai: Lotus Blossom; pronounced *Lah-ow-boo-wah*.
[2] Thai: Sorrow; pronounced *Kwahn sow-soh*.

"Nah. Not my style, and besides, Rex's boyfriend didn't ask for his best friend to try and murder him." Wesley starts peeling the label off his beer bottle, a strip that stays in an unbroken, precise thin line as it comes off the glass. "What happened to us sucked, but we're all okay. We have fallbacks, and we can take care of ourselves."

"True," Django says. Kai makes jokes about Wesley and his chill, but the thing is—Kai's correct. It takes a hell of a lot to stir up Wesley's temper. "Who's earned your wrath, kid?"

Wesley scowls. "I'm pissed off at the fucking department because of my patients. My clinic was the only one in the entire region that would take *everyone*. I didn't run the place for the money. I ran it for the people who needed it. I didn't care if people paid me in chickens as long as they could get the help they needed."

"Please tell me someone actually did pay you in chickens."

Wesley smiles. "More than once. They had a chicken farm, and that was what they could afford. Besides, free food." His smile drops away. "Most of my patients don't have anywhere else to go, Dad. Either they can't make the car trip to a place that will take their insurance because the other local assholes won't, or they don't have any way to travel to Philadelphia in the first place. That's why I'm pissed. The department screwed up our lives a little bit, but they completely fucked these people over, and *none* of them did a damned thing to deserve it!"

"No," Django agrees, feeling an echo of Wesley's fierce, justified rage. "No, they didn't."

"We can't let them fucking win, Dad." Wesley holds up the long, coiled strand of paper when the last of the bottle's label pulls free. "I don't know what we'll do if we end up being our own little group of Snowdens, but I refuse to let the department get away with fucking these people over in the first place."

*   *   *   *

They arrive in Mapun around noon. The boat isn't even leaving a wake in the water as it drifts into an inlet that Xāwuṭh says is called Gunboat Harbor. Rex puts his hands on the deck railing, watching a dock get closer and closer until the yacht's nose gently butts up against the old tire wrapped around the post, cushioning it against new arrivals. Xāwuṭh cuts the engines as Sorrow jumps over the side with a line in his hand, landing on the pieced-together dock and securing the first rope before the yacht has a chance to drift. Rex tosses Sorrow the second and third lines, watching as he slowly pulls the boat in snug against the dock, stem to stern.

"Nice job," Rex says.

"I've done this since I was twelve. It would be terrible to do badly now," Sorrow replies, grinning. "Welcome to Mapun."

There are other boats docked in front of the village, most of them houseboats that families live on. Their group gets curious looks as they traipse down the long dock in small clusters, heading for shore. Thirteen people arriving at once probably means that the locals will dub them tourists, and tourists mean money. Rex doesn't mind being labeled a tourist as long as they're willing to feed him in exchange.

Ella makes a startled gleeping sound and then shoves her way forward at a dead run, almost knocking Rex and Sorrow off the dock. "What the hell, Ella?" Rex starts to ask.

The words die in his mouth.

His sister is flinging herself into the arms of a man waiting on the beach. Her weight almost sends them both crashing down onto the ground. The cane her victim is holding is the only thing that saves them from eating beach sand.

He has dark hair, tan skin, and familiar features that he shares with Ella, but something's gone wrong. A scar paints his face from jaw upwards, a nasty, jagged line that turns his left eye and a streak of his spiky black hair a disturbing shock-white.

"Oh my god," Rex can hear Django whispering. "Gods of my family's ancestors."

"Easy!" Ella's victim shouts, a wide grin on his face. "I've only got one real leg, you crazy bitch!"

Ella draws back enough to glare at him. "IT'S YOUR OWN DAMNED FAULT, YOU ASSHOLE!" she shouts before darting back in and wrapping her arms around his waist. "You complete fucker. You absolute fucking bastard."

"Hey, cut me a little slack here. Some of us have been busy hiding from the U.S. government."

"Oh, god. You—you—" Ella manages before bursting into loud, angry tears.

Rex feels like he's going to break. No, fuck; he's pretty sure they all just broke on some level, and he doesn't have the faintest idea of what to do about it.

"Holy shit," Wesley breathes. "I can't—I could, but I still can't believe it."

Eric looks up and grins at them all. "Hi guys. How's things?"

The next thing Rex hears is a splash, followed by sputtering and cursing. Rex turns around to find Xāwuṭh treading water and their father glaring down at him. "Did you—did you shove Wolf into the ocean?" Rex sputters in disbelief.

"That is for not fucking telling me!" Django yells at Xāwuṭh, right before he runs down the length of the dock, hits the sand, and envelops the twins in a massive hug.

Rex tries to catch his breath, even though he's not desperate for air. This is just—possibility was one thing. This is—

Khodî walks up next to him and nudges Rex's shoulder. "C'mon," he says in a low, steady voice. "That's our brother. Let's go say hello."

Rex nods, numbly reaching back and snagging Kai by the sleeve to drag him along. Brian and Wesley are in their wake, with Neumia clinging to her father's hand. Bonika, Andi, Sorrow, and Ziba follow, even if the Banner cousins don't quite understand what's going on.

By the time they're all standing on Mapun's glittering beige sand, Django has let go, but Ella hasn't. Rex thinks it might take a pry bar to release Ella's grip on her brother.

Khodî clears his throat. "So. IEDs aren't enough to put you down, huh?"

Eric raises his right eyebrow, the one not half-obliterated by scar tissue. "Down? No, more like it sent me into fucking orbit, asshole," he retorts, and then gets smother-hugged by Khodî.

Rex feels like a scale has suddenly balanced itself. God, he can hardly believe this is real.

"Ella, let go for a sec." Eric gives his sister a gentle nudge. Ella glares at him, but the effect is ruined by the joy shining in her eyes. "I'm not going anywhere. I promise."

"Okay," Ella allows grudgingly.

Eric smiles at Rex. "Hi, bro."

Rex swallows and then blurts out the first thing that comes to mind. "I was supposed to be there, goddammit. It was my job to cover your ass, and I wasn't there for you—"

Eric shakes his head. "Your job? I found out that you went AWOL to join that highway fight, dumbass. It wasn't your job, and what happened to me isn't your fault."

"Yes it is," Rex whispers, feeling like shock has immobilized him.

"You've got Dumb Older Sibling Syndrome going," Eric returns, and then tears slip from his eyes. "Oh, god. It's so fucking good to see all of you, I can't even—" He breaks off and strides forward to hug Rex, his embrace as strong as it had been so many years ago.

"Eric Som," Rex chokes out. "I missed you so damned much."

"Love you too, you asshole," Eric replies, his arms tightening again before he lets go.

Rex nods. He has to step away, wiping his eyes with both hands because he can't fucking see. By the time his eyes are clear, Kai is staring at Eric, who is staring right back at Kai with his mouth hanging open.

"I've seen photos—web searches, secure encryption, bullshit, et cetera." Eric's lips are half-parted as he gazes at his baby brother in disbelief. "Fuck, you look just like Mom."

That's all it takes for Kai to break down crying. Eric wraps him up in a hug, swallowing hard. Then Eric's eyes widen as he realizes that Kai is two inches taller than he is. "Aw, goddammit." Eric's eyes are red-rimmed as more tears fall. "My baby brother is all grown up."

Kai punches Eric in the shoulder without breaking off the hug. "You fucker!" he yells in a snot-thickened voice.

"Yeah, I know." Eric glances at Xāwuṭh as he sloshes his way out of the water. "You didn't warn any of them? You asshole."

Xāwuṭh grins, pushing his hair back from his face. "I did warn them. Not my fault that nobody picked up on it."

Khodî glares at Xāwuṭh. "When you picked us up in Vietnam, none of us had slept well in days, you dick!"

Xāwuṭh shrugs. "Still not my fault, and hey—you're here *now*."

Ella latches back onto Eric the moment Kai is willing to let go, burying her face against his shoulder. "What happened?" she asks.

Eric grimaces as he puts his arm back around his sister. "That's a complicated story. Not a long one, it just sucks."

Kai rubs his eyes clear and then points at Eric's right leg. "That's a 3-D-printed replacement, right?"

"Hell, yes." Eric says proudly. Rex noticed the prosthetic at once, but kept his eyes away, his stomach twisted with too much guilt.

Eric's wearing a pair of swimming trunks that end at the knee, covering the place where plastic must meet flesh. The prosthetic replacement is a beautiful organic construct, twisting lines that are as much cosmetic design as structural support. The knee and ankle even have properly articulated joints. "It took some doing to get the equipment out here, but I've got the neural interface for it, too." Eric demonstrates by shifting his weight onto the cane before lifting his prosthetic leg into the air, wiggling his toes.

"That is so fucking cool." Kai starts to smile. "I mean, I'd rather you still had *your* leg, but that's awesome."

"Is that the worst of it?" Django's expression is a guarded neutral mask that Rex knows is hiding a hell of a lot of emotion. When he doesn't know how to react, their father does his best not to.

"Mostly." Eric lifts his right hand into the air, revealing two more prosthetic pieces. His ring and pinky fingers are composed of the same organic printed structure. Straps run along his hand, securing the paired black fingers around his wrist. He demonstrates that they also have the interface by waving his fingers at them, then curling his entire hand into a fist.

"How's that work?" Wesley asks, intrigued. "I could really have used those back at my clinic."

"The neural interface is in here." Eric runs his left fingers over the wrist strap that supports the finger replacements. "There are electrodes built in that read the signals from the muscles that are trying to tell my hand what to do, and then they send the signal along to the electric motors in the prosthesis. Awesome stuff."

"Robot hand," Ella translates. "Badass."

"Isn't that expensive?" Brian asks.

"No, it's fucking cheap," Kai retorts angrily. "The tech's been available for years, but since medical companies can't make an assload of money off of it, the printed prosthetics haven't spread like they should have. People do their research and find out the tech exists in the first place, and *then* they work with it, but it's all small-time stuff. Pisses me off. Most of the designs are being spread out by open-source projects and websites."

"Easy, Doc," Django says, and pretends not to notice when Kai's face lights up like a sun breaking through a cloud at the title. "Anything else, Eric?"

"Just a couple of scars. Y'know, like my face."

"Makes you look punk," Khodî says, and Eric grins. "David Bowie and *The Crow*, dude. You're on the right track. Now you only need a bird."

Eric bites his lip as his eyes start watering again. "Fuck you, too."

"It's nice to see you again, Eric," Bonika says, her words falling perfectly into the conversation.

"Good to see you, too, Bonnie Kay," Eric replies, and Bonika glowers at him.

"It's *Bonika*, you unbelievable undead jackass," Bonika retorts.

Eric smiles at her. "Hey, it's still nice to see that you and Brian managed to get beyond the grudge...fuck..." He trails off and stares down at Neumia. "And who do you belong to, kiddo?"

Neumia's eyes are huge as she points first at Bonika, and then at Brian. "Them," she whispers.

Eric smiles and kneels down. Rex winces when he sees Eric's wobbling balance. No wonder he still has a cane—that prosthetic has to be new. "I didn't know I had a niece. Also, Brian is the last of my siblings I would have expected to successfully maintain a relationship long enough to have a kid."

Neumia gives Eric a shy smile. "I was an accident. Mom says she yelled at Dad a lot."

Eric looks up at their father and then starts laughing. "I'll just bet you were. Nice to meet you, kiddo," he says, holding out his right hand. "I'm Eric."

"I'm Neumia de Lacy. Or Nari." Neumia shakes Eric's hand. Then she jumps forward to hug him. "I know you," she whispers. "Because everyone told stories. Stories make people live."

"Bonus, then." Eric hugs Neumia with one arm. "Because I was actually still alive."

Rex sniffs hard to feel like he can breathe. He glances around, feeling a huge lump in his throat. At this point, they're all crying, even their father. They lost their home, their good name, their careers...but they have Eric back. Rex swallows down the old grief and thinks it's a fair fucking trade.

Ella helps Eric stand back up. He looks torn between gratitude and absolute irritation by the necessity of needing help at all. "Well, is there anything else awkward that I need to know about? Might as well get it all out of the way at once."

Rex wipes his eyes again and then grins. "I'm engaged."

All of Rex's siblings, Sorrow, and the Banner cousins turn to stare at him. Eric actually blinks a few times in surprise. "Fucking seriously?"

"Absolutely serious," Rex confirms, still grinning.

"When the fuck did that happen?" Khodî demands to know.

Rex pastes an innocent expression on his face. "Oh, that was yesterday."

Brian shakes his head. "Yesterday? Why didn't you say anything *then*?"

Rex shrugs. "Timing is everything." He then gets a wet hug from Xāwuth, who's laughing while offering his congratulations.

"Where's the lucky bride? Groom? Person?" Eric asks, curious. "Your Thai friend there is already staring at someone else, so I know it's not them."

Rex glances over just in time to see Kai blush. Oh, now *that* is an interesting development.

"That's also a complicated story," Django says, before assaulting Eric with another hug that looks like it might be grinding bones together. Eric doesn't protest; he only holds on, making a noise that sounds like quietly restrained grief.

*   *   *   *

Eric and Xāwuth own a pair of stilt-raised houses on the beach. They're distant enough from the harbor to mute the noisy bustle of houseboats, beach houses, and shanties that make up the harbor's unofficial village, but still close enough to get there quickly if needed.

Eric introduces them to the place he's been living in. The central room has chairs hand-made from bamboo cane with a small, low table that hosts a hurricane lantern filled with clear oil. There's a very basic bathroom, just a toilet and shower with a water heater wedged into one corner. Two bedrooms: one with hammocks, one with a mattress on a wooden frame. The houses are built sturdily enough to be decent homes, but cheaply enough that it wouldn't be a big deal if they were lost to a monsoon. All Eric and Xāwuth would need to do is pack up what little they have, put it on the boat, and ditch until the weather calmed down again.

The third room in Eric's tiny little beach house is a laboratory that would make a tech geek come in their pants. Rex spies the 3-D printer and the schematics pinned to the wall, his gut clenching. Eric designed and built his own fucking prosthetics. It's both genius and goddamned awful.

"I'm tapped into the island's hardline and hiding behind so many delightful new types of encryptions that I can pretty much do whatever I want," Eric explains as he shows off his computer setup. "If you guys want internet access and phone calls, we can do it."

Bonika seems to sigh. "Can you do a mobile-to-mobile encrypt?"

Eric nods. "Easily. What's up?"

"I need to call my sister. Susannah and I don't get along, but she will appreciate knowing I'm still alive." Bonika's expression is flat and unhappy. "I wanted to tell her without putting her in further potential danger, but didn't have a way to do so before."

Eric tosses her a cell phone. "Don't let the wireless connection to the router drop below three bars. It's theoretically been neutered so it can't try and tether to a satellite, but don't take any chances. Use the green app on the first screen to dial out, not the phone's dialer."

"Come on. Let's leave her to it," Brian says, which moves the entire group along to Xāwuṭh's house. It's designed much the same way—two bedrooms and a third smaller room, this one devoted to the storage of black market goods.

"Fuckin' pirate," their father says, a lopsided smile on his face.

Xāwuṭh performs a deep, sweeping bow. "Aye, and arr," he replies, and Neumia giggles.

"Does this village even have a name?" Wesley asks.

"Depends upon the day," Xāwuṭh answers. "The whole section of the island is officially the *barangay* of Lupa Pula. If Nari needs to go back to school for the year, the best elementary school on Mapun is nearby."

"That's a thought," Brian says. He glances down at Neumia, who scowls at the idea of school.

Their kitchens are outside—propane tanks with proper, oversized woks on waist-high stands. Non-perishable goods are stored in a locking cabinet next to the house. It's sort of like a Cambodian setup, but without the cows trying to crowd everyone out.

"We've got enough places to sleep. You can all stay here with us, or go back to the boat, whichever," Eric says. "There are cots folded up somewhere. Plus, the bonus of sleeping right next to the ocean? Serious lack of insects trying to eat you alive."

"I'm hearing a Ranger whine about mosquitos. I'm ashamed." Ella gives Eric a mock-sour glare.

Eric shrugs. "I lost enough blood in Iraq. The rest of it is mine, mine, mine, and they can't have it."

"We could always vote," Bonika says as she rejoins them, giving Eric his phone. "Boat, hammock, mattress, or cot."

"I will sleep on the actual fucking sand not to have to spend another day sleeping on a boat," Khodî announces at once. "I want my bed to sit still."

"No, I don't think you really want your bed to sit still at all," Ziba teases in a mild voice. Khodî glares at her while Andi bites her lip, her eyes dancing with hidden laughter.

Sleeping arrangements get pushed off as a later decision when Neumia announces that it's lunchtime, and she's hungry. Food does sound like a good damned idea.

"More fish?" Neumia asks in dismay when she sees Xāwuṯh bring out fishing poles.

"Best get used to it, kiddo. It's the staple of the South Pacific, unless you wanna go hunting for wild pigs and feral chickens," Xāwuṯh tells her.

"Feral chickens." Wesley stares at Xāwuṯh. "What kind of fucking island *is* this?"

"Mapun," Xāwuṯh says, like that explains everything. It probably does.

It doesn't take long to catch lunch. Away from the main village, the water is teeming with fish of all kinds. Neumia appreciates it when Xāwuṯh rolls strips of fish in dried coconut before grilling them. "Texture issues," he says to Neumia, handing her a plate of golden brown strips that look sort of like fish sticks. "I totally get it, pumpkin."

They unload the boat for those who are willing to sleep on the island. Eric and Ella also want to consolidate the available tech. Brian, Bonika, Neumia, and Wesley decide to sleep on the yacht. Brian and Bonika cite the need for privacy, and wanting to keep their daughter nearby. Wesley cites the desire not to be eaten by feral fucking chickens.

Everything seems so goddamn normal that it's actually driving Rex up a fucking wall. It shouldn't be normal. It should feel odd, amazing, disorienting—but it doesn't. Eric fits back into their lives like he never left, even though Rex can still feel the gulf created by ten years of separation. It's like an open wound in his heart.

He keeps thinking: *My brother is alive. My brother is alive. My brother is alive.* Eventually, Rex is going to convince his brain that it's true, and everything is fucking fine.

Xāwuṯh conscripts Sorrow and most of the siblings into starting the construction of a beach bonfire for the evening. Rex escapes the bustle of activity, intent on borrowing Eric's computer lab. He wants to look at the flash drives he shoved into his pocket from Euan's lock box, feeling the desire like it's an itch under his skin.

Rex powers up Euan's laptop after plugging in to an available, American-converted power strip. He skips hooking up to the network with an available cable, not sure what Eric needs to do to make the laptop as secure as the rest of his setup. Rex doesn't need network access anyway, not to look at files. Besides, if the flash drives from the lock boxes are full of viruses, this means he only kills the laptop instead of the entire lab.

On the first flash drive are photos that run from September of 2015 through the middle of December. Rex smiles when he sees a couple of joint selfies he and Euan took together after one beer way too many, giggling and practically falling over each other while trying to keep the camera still enough to capture a decent picture. There are a lot more of Rex by himself, photos that Euan must have taken on the sly. Sneaky asshole.

The background in each photo is usually Euan's apartment, though a few are street shots. One was taken in Maritimes, the only joint trip they made together. Sometimes it's Rex's apartment in the background, pictures of one or both of them on the couch, in the kitchen, doing stupid, mundane things that makes Rex's heart ache. He has no idea if they're ever going to have that kind of life again, even with an official engagement. Fuck, maybe they can live on a boat. Xāwuṭh does it most of the year. Can't be that bad.

Some of the photos are architectural—his boyfriend capturing elements of the old design of Rex's apartment. Rex feels tears sting his eyes again as he realizes that Euan was photographing things that might stir up memories.

There are also photos from Turkmenistan, including a picture Euan took of Rex while he was still sleeping in the hotel in Uzbekistan. Rex can't figure out if he's embarrassed or flattered.

When Rex plugs in the other flash drive, a text file automatically pops up on the screen:

Rex:

I'm assuming it's you, at least. If it's not you, there aren't many left who it could be.

This drive contains the results of an investigation I squeezed in while still in Turkmenistan. I tried to figure out if the department had deliberately involved you in that fucking mess, but everything I found says that you just, as you told me, "Drew the lucky straw."

If you are reading this, though...I might have been wrong.

Oh, and reading or viewing anything on this drive is treason, but if you have this flash drive, I doubt treason is really high on your current list of concerns.

—Euan

The drive is full of files so classified Rex could be executed just for knowing they exist, let alone reading them. He doesn't bother with the text documents, not yet. Rex enlarges the thumbnails so he can see preview images of the surveillance photos that Euan pulled from various points. There's Newark on Rex's way out, his arrival in Turkmenistan, hotel check-in...

Nothing for the hotel bar. There must not have been a camera in the room.

There's surveillance for Rex's airline flight out of Uzbekistan and his arrival in La Guardia, which was a weather-crowded disaster. His father is in multiple shots in Lehigh International, waiting through the flight delays for Rex to get in from New York. Then it's both of them in thumbnail shots until they're outside, out of camera range.

Even without opening the images to full screen, Rex doesn't see anyone in the background of those shots showing up more than once. No one is lurking, no one looking his way, no one turning up in shots again and again when they shouldn't. If someone tracked Rex, they'd done it this way, through the cameras instead of standing among the crowds.

Then again, Euan can hide from cameras. Rex never got around to asking if that was only something Euan and his father could do, or if it's a trained skill for all the Specialists.

Ziba and Andi will know. Rex makes a mental note to ask later.

Rex pulls that drive and pops it back into the static bag, but the first drive with their shared apartment photos goes onto his keyring with the other family flash drives. He runs a virus check on the laptop that comes up clean before he dares to insert the flash drive that has the old family photos stored on it, the pictures filed by decade.

Rex goes straight to the 1950s folder, expands the file folder screen so that the preview images are large enough to be easily viewed, and starts clicking through photos. Most of them are of people he doesn't know, but his father does. Sometimes Django appears with these people, still so goddamn young. It's also a stark reminder that Rex might have the posture and body language, but Khodî is the one who looks the most like their father.

He almost doesn't recognize Euan. His fiancé is sitting on the old yellow couch in the living room with the couch facing outwards, away from the fireplace, meaning it's a summer shot. Euan looks fucking tiny sitting there, partially hunched in on himself with his arms crossed as he glances up into the camera. Even in black-and-white, his vibrant eyes are the most recognizable, full of grief that makes Euan's smile seem forced and sad.

Rex's father comes into the room, leaning against a filing cabinet that is half-rusted, definitely a scavenged find. "Is that the only one?" Django asks.

"Only thing I've found, so far," Rex says, and forces himself to move on, scrolling through the next few photos. That damned soul-hurt smile makes Rex want to wrap the stupid bastard up in a hug, and said bastard isn't currently available.

"Leave off for now," Django suggests quietly. "That's a search that could take a while, especially since you're going to want to try the forties and sixties, too. A lot of photos from those decades looked the same, and if there wasn't a year or a note written on the photo, Makani would have just guessed on where to file it."

"You think there is something?" Rex asks, pulling the drive before closing the laptop and looking up at his father.

Django is frowning. "I want to say maybe, but I'm not sure. Mom could have asked for photos of them all, just because she was so damned intent on adopting Ambrus."

Rex smiles. "Now that would have been awkward."

Django nods. "Yeah, and I've had enough of that. C'mon. We're setting shit on fire."

Outside, it's already dusk. The sun is turning the sky gold and violet in the west. The fire that Xāwuṯh bullied everyone else into building is burning a shining blue-green at the bottom before it blossoms out into a warm orange glow, attracting them all like moths to the literal flame.

The beer also helps in getting their attention. Xāwuṯh is an expert at bribing people.

They gather in a circle around the bonfire, sitting on chairs, towels, or in Khodî's case, the beer cooler. Andi leans against the side of the cooler so that Khodî can comb his fingers through her hair, her eyes half-closed in bliss. Bonika is propped comfortably against Brian. Neumia is cuddled in on her father's opposite side, holding her teal dragon in her lap. Kai and Sorrow are sitting a polite distance apart as they share a towel, but still radiate interest at each other.

God, Rex misses his stupid idiot boyfriend-fiancé. Then he glances over at his father and feels guilt coil up in his throat. Euan is still alive, if unavailable. Others are not.

Ella sits next to Eric on a paired set of old folding beach chairs, their knees touching and their hands laced together. "I can't believe you're engaged," she says to Rex.

"Right?" Rex grins at her. "I'm still kind of stuck on the disbelief part, too."

"Speaking of disbelief." Khodî glares at Eric. "Where in the entire *hell* have you been?"

Eric glances at his watch. "I'm impressed. It only took you six hours to give in and yell that question."

"Asshole," Khodî retorts. "Seriously—I want to know, and so does everyone else. 'Orbit,' while an entertaining answer, is not exactly an explanation for where the fuck you've been for the last eleven years."

"It hasn't been eleven years. It's been—"

"OH, GOD, SHUT UP, IT'S CLOSE ENOUGH," Ella yells at her twin, a wide grin on her face. "Just talk!"

"Well..." Eric frowns, resting his chin on his left hand. "Huh. I don't know if I'm drunk enough for this yet."

"Try anyway. I'm right here," Ella says, leaning over to bump shoulders with her twin.

"We need to know, Eric." Django's voice is quiet, barely audible above the snap-and-crackle of burning driftwood. "There are some fault lines that need patching."

Eric winces. "Right. Good point." He stares down into his beer bottle, firelight reflecting off the brown glass. "I wasn't kidding about orbit—I took a fucking flight when the IED hit. I didn't even have a chance to figure out if I was dead, dying, injured, or just half-deaf and confused when someone grabbed me by my bag straps and hauled me away from the fight."

"Shit. No wonder we couldn't find you afterwards," Rex says, horrified. "Things were so bad we couldn't even begin searching for another two fucking hours. You would have been long gone."

"Definitely long gone by then," Eric agrees. "I got kidnapped by three Iraqi soldiers. Two of them started arguing over who was going to get what from my kit. While I'm still trying to figure out if I'm *dying* or not, these two assholes are bitching each other out over a cell phone that was worth maybe five dollars.

"The third soldier was a Kurdish man conscripted from the north. Poor bastard was really not prepared for soldiering, or for his fellow soldiers to shoot each other in the face over an argument about war trophies."

Khodî frowns. "Well, that's fucking convenient."

"Seriously, two-for-one sale," Ella says, and Rex bites back a smile.

"I guess." Eric glances at Ella, Khodî, and Rex before he stares into the blue-green morphing flame at the base of the fire. "I blacked out around that point. Blood loss, probably. Stress. Self-defense—who knows. While I was taking a nap with my mouth still full of sand, Roj Yasin escaped north and brought me with him to his family's camp. He'd apparently decided to use the opportunity of dead superior officers to book it the hell out of the fighting zones. When I woke up, I was way the hell north of Baghdad."

Ella scowls. "Dude went home with his very own POW."

"Hey, ransom is a thing when your original sources of income have been destroyed." Eric takes a long swallow of beer. "Iraq was already rattling sabers about the Kurds. I didn't blame Roj for thinking about a ransom. I especially liked the part where he and his family kept me from fuckin' dying. Roj, his wives and their kids—they all helped me heal up. First they claimed to need a live soldier to ransom, and not a man dead of infection. Fair enough. I get a crutch and have to re-learn how to walk with only one leg so I can move around, because they're not carrying their ransom object to any agreed meeting point. Still a fair point. They were also feeding me—can't starve your ransom object to death, after all."

"Where's the loss point?" Wesley asks. "For your leg."

"Mid-thigh," Eric says, and Wesley huffs out an irritated sigh. "Yeah, I know. It's a crap loss point. It's easier to cap a joint with a prosthetic instead of a stump."

"Far easier, but still not fun," Wesley mutters.

Eric smiles. "By the fourth month, we all knew that the family was full of shit about the ransom, but they were also afraid that if I left, I'd turn them in. Took another couple of months to earn that kind of trust. That's also about how long it took my eye to finish healing, anyway. Started out blind, and now it's just fucked up, but at least I can see things."

"How bad?" Brian asks.

"I have pristine twenty-ten vision in one eye, and the other provides me with a black-and-white blur of moving shapes," Eric says dryly. "Ask me how much fun it is to use binoculars.

"Around the first of January, Roj got me a caravan ride back to Baghdad. My plan was to report in, let everyone know that I wasn't dead, get an honorable discharge for missing most of a leg and being legally blind in one eye, and go the hell home." Eric shakes his head. "Yeah, that worked well."

"The fucking department," Django growls.

"Yeah. Them," Eric says. "I didn't know what was going on, not at first. Everything seemed fine, even though I didn't see anyone I knew. Got into base, confirmed my identity. Threatened to beat an MP with my crutch for being a dick. You know—usual army shit."

Brian points at Eric. "And hello, listen to all the reasons why I never wanted to be military, summed up beautifully."

"That's because you would have actually attacked the military police officer, bro," Wesley says.

"Exactly my fucking point," Brian retorts, and swigs down the rest of his beer before gesturing for Khodî to get him another.

Eric waits out the beer handout before turning serious again. "I talked to a paper-pusher, found out that Rex and Ella were already out of the Army ballgame, but nobody knew where Khodî's team was working. I figured I'd at least get to scare the hell out of one sibling before the news went home that I was still alive.

"The weird shit started when I didn't get a medical exam. A soldier comes in missing limbs and half-blind, that's SOP. Tended to go hand-in-hand with a debriefing, but it's usually considered a good idea to make sure your soldiers aren't about to drop dead on you.

"Instead, I get a nice little room inside a commandeered building downtown," Eric says. "Also not SOP, but the Kurdish family I stayed with didn't have television, and the radio was unreliable for news. For all I knew, the war went to shit and turned everyone paranoid. I asked for a phone, since I wanted to call home. No dice. Asked for my superior officer in the company—still a denial. That's when I got a bad feeling about things. Probably should have been aware of the problem sooner, but you want to trust your commanding officers—and I was still tired. Hell, probably still shell-shocked."

Eric glares down at his beer bottle. "They made me wait two hours in a stifling office with only a single window open for air. No fan, no water. I'm feeling like a prisoner instead of a soldier.

"Finally, a CO walks in, some two-star general named Stewart I'd never heard of before. There isn't a base or battalion affiliation on his uniform, which at that point? Creepy as all hell," Eric says, taking another drink.

"Stewart tells me that it's his job to debrief me and find out why I'm not dead. I told him I was never dead, that I'd spent six months in the north of Iraq as a POW."

Eric hesitates. "It wasn't that he didn't believe me. I realized pretty fast that he didn't care what I had to say. Stewart was only a warm-up for someone else, this ginger-haired man with some hard blue eyes."

Rex feels every muscle in his body seize in sudden, agonizing fear before Ziba says, "Phillip Stroud."

Eric nods at her. "That'd be him. Slimy motherfucker."

Rex breathes in and out a few times and then chugs down most of his beer. Fuck, he did not need that kind of shock.

"The slimy asshole introduces himself as the Director of *the* department," Eric says. "And that's when I'm told—not asked—that I'm joining up. I politely decline."

Eric's eyes narrow, reminding Rex that he was part of a *pair*, two of the most aggressive and effective Rangers that school has ever seen. "Stroud tells me I don't have a choice. Says that since I've been declared legally dead, they can do whatever the hell they want. It burned, god, it did, because he was right. It's right there in the military paperwork. The Army gets to choose whether or not they release our bodies back to our families. We're their property until the day we discharge, or we're smart enough to stay dead."

Andi lifts her head in realization. "He wanted to see what would happen if you dose someone who was born with ETKC-51 already in their system."

"Yep." Eric looks at his empty beer bottle and sticks it upside-down into the sand. Khodî gets up from the cooler and gets Eric another without saying a word.

"Kids, I'm calling dibs." Django's voice is a low, angry snarl. "When we find this motherfucker, I'm ripping Stroud's head off."

"As long as we get to take photos or record it for posterity, sure," Ella agrees. "But I get to shoot him everywhere else."

Django smiles, but it's not a pleasant expression. "Just as long as he lives long enough for me to deal with him, you just shoot that bastard all you like, baby girl."

"Double-dosing makes you fucking nuts. You aren't nuts, so I'm guessing that Stroud didn't get what he wanted," Rex says.

Better to focus on that than on the stupid panic he'd felt upon hearing ginger hair and blue eyes. He also *really* hopes that's as far as the similarity goes.

"Stroud and General Stewart say they're gonna leave me alone in this nice little hot-box of an office, let me think about it for a little while." Eric rolls his eyes. "Like sweating my ass off is going to make me willingly swallow their bullshit.

"I gave it about ten minutes before acting. See, something about missing a leg means they stop thinking you're dangerous. Nobody thought to disarm the one-legged man."

Khodî glares at Eric. "That is an awful fucking pun."

Eric holds up his right arm and wiggles his two bionic fingers. "Totally worth it for the look on your face."

"Yeah, yeah. What the hell did you do next?" Khodî asks.

Eric grins. "Used the crutch to break out the window, frame and all. Gave me just enough space to squeeze through and climb out of the building. I gotta tell you, it is *not* fun to jump into a garbage bin when you only have one leg. I'm really glad someone ditched a mattress there instead of a hell of a lot of broken glass."

"Mattresses have springs," Kai says, wincing.

"I might have taken some puncture wounds in inconvenient places," Eric admits. "Still better than a lot of other options. I crawl out of the trash and—well, the Iraqi insurgents we'd been fighting for the past few years? They saw me trying to escape a U.S. military installation. They saved my ass."

"Holy shit," Rex murmurs while Ella and Khodî stare at Eric. "I just—I can't tell if that's irony, or the universe's idea of a fucking cosmic joke."

"Iraq wasn't a Good versus Evil fight," Django says, glancing around at Rex, Ella, and Khodî. "You were there. You fuckin' know this."

The words chime in Rex's memories for some reason, but he can't quite pick out why. It's true, though. The only reason Rex, Ella, Eric, and Khodî were still on the ground in Iraq in 2005 was because of the bullshit notion that the U.S. military's presence was needed to maintain the peace. Peace, his entire ass. It's 2016 and the United States military is *still* in Iraq.

"The insurgents saw that I wasn't white, that I wasn't in uniform, and that I was...oh, god. I was scared." Eric's voice drops to a whisper. "There wasn't anyone else I could go to, anyway. The insurgents knew that the U.S. had labeled me a threat—fuck, I might as well have been a terrorist, and these men and women understood that so goddamn well. They were fighting for their homes, for their right to be free Iraqi citizens, and all they got for it was a fucking label slapped on them so that Americans would have an excuse to call them Enemy."

Ella wraps her arm around Eric's shoulders, shushing him in a gentle undertone as he cries with both hands plastered over his face. It makes Rex feel broken inside again, and for so many different reasons that he doesn't even know how to count them all.

Eric finally drops his hands from his eyes, wiping his face clean. When he speaks again, his voice is rough but steady. "They adopt me for a little while. Long enough to get me re-hydrated after that office bullshit, keep me hidden while military teams search for me. Get me different clothes so I blend in. Racism was so damned rampant in the ranks at that point that all it took was some facial hair and a head covering, and I wasn't American anymore. I was Iraqi. Even more damning in those bastard soldiers' eyes—I was *a disabled fucking towel-head*," he seethes. "Maybe Ella and I lucked out with our company, but the shit I heard—you can't bring fucking peace to people you don't even respect!"

"Truth," Xāwuṭh says, nodding. "Hey, I grew up in Vietnam, assholes," he reminds them when the military quartet looks at him.

"I limped right through a military checkpoint with a couple of women who had guns hidden beneath their robes. Nobody gave a damn. I never got asked for identification, or where I was going." Eric shakes his head, bitter expression on his face. "At that point, I fucking hated myself. I hated what I'd been doing for the last few years. I just—I hated that there was no damned point. We were being used and just—fuck."

Eric rests his chin on his hand again as he collects himself. "I probably shot at those same people at some point," he says softly. "Maybe more than once, and they're the ones who saved my life."

"And we're all damned glad that they did," Wesley says fiercely.

"Once we're outside of the city, there's a ride waiting to drive me across the border into Jordan. I thanked them, and I gave them my tags. Told them that I owed them my life, if they ever needed anything, if I survived and they figured out how to find me... "

Eric bites his lip. "All they have to do is ask. Any time they need to."

Django gives Eric a soft look that still has sparks of fire in it. "Why the hell didn't you come home?"

"Home. Yeah. I wanted to, believe me." Eric smiles at his bottle, a green-glassed rice beer. "There's the complicated part. First I had to steal my first prosthetic so I could get around easier. Did you know those things are sized to fit?" Wesley makes an extremely unhappy noise. "Nope, I had no idea. They were looking for a one-legged soldier, though, and being able to wear a pair of jeans meant it looked like I had two legs, even if it was really uncomfortable. I wore sunglasses. So many hats. I hate hats so much now, it's ridiculous."

Eric takes a breath and lets it out in a long, slow exhale. "Sorry, I get a bit, uh...that wasn't a fun time. Since I knew the department and Director Creepy were involved, I needed to know how closely they were watching for me. I did a test: found a hardline internet connection in Amman, Googled my own name, and walked out of the building right afterwards.

"A military team had the place surrounded and locked down in less than ten minutes."

Khodî whistles, shaking his head. "That is fucking fast."

"They had to have been sending teams across the entirety of the Middle East. Every city," Bonika says, her eyes narrowed as she gazes at the fire. "An operation of that magnitude—I was already retired, but I still imagine that the Banners heard nothing about it."

"Not a whisper," Andi says.

Ziba shakes her head. "Not a word. We were senior agents, and we knew nothing of this."

"Stroud," Brian growls.

"They had overkill in mind, too," Eric says. "Actual, legit terrorists weren't getting that kind of military attention. On to test number two. I take a ride down the road and hook up to a hardline in Maan. It's February of 2006 at that point, but I don't remember the date—a lot of shit blurred together on me that year, that month in particular."

Khodî grimaces and turns his head away. "Yeah, we'll uh— we'll discuss that later."

Eric glances at him before deciding not to push. "Okay. Anyway, I wrote a basic encryption and hit up my military records in a library. In and out before booking it back to an observation point. Almost didn't make it."

"Christ," Django whispers.

"Third test," Eric says, ignoring their father. "Got into Tel-Aviv and found a friend of ours. You know, from our, uh, punishment detail for 'accidentally' blowing up that asshole general's car."

Ella smiles like a gleeful crocodile. "I remember."

"I talked to Akiba, told him what was going on," Eric continues. "He was appalled, and agreed to a sob story cover to test out how far this shit was going. If anyone asked, he'd say that he only just heard about my death in Iraq, wanted to confirm the details, blah, blah, blah. I was smart enough to be at a safe observation distance before he hit the files through properly secured Israeli channels."

Eric chugs down the rice beer and looks at Khodî. "Get up off of that thing and get me another, huh?"

Khodî does so, tossing over a bottle that's dripping ice and water. "That bad?"

"They killed him." Eric twists off the cap and takes a long swallow. "It should have been a fucking diplomatic incident—Akiba was doing really well for himself. Instead, they covered it up, said he died in a car accident." Eric scowls. "Yeah. Sure. A car accident. One that earned him a bullet to the face for trying to help me."

"Shit. I heard about that," Rex says, startled by how close he'd been to Eric at that point. "I was in Jordan at the time."

Eric swirls the beer around in the bottle before taking another drink. "That's what convinced me that going home would get one of us killed—maybe all of us. I didn't dare try anything like that again. Losing Akiba was enough. No more. If I'd given any of you a hint that I was alive, you'd have tried to find me, probably succeeded, and the result would be the same. The fucking department would have been right there waiting for us."

"Maybe. Maybe not," Django says.

"I know we're a family of crazy badasses," Eric replies in a soft voice. "But I couldn't—I'd rather it was only me 'dead' than all of us. We lost Mom. You guys lost me for a while. That...I didn't want the family to shrink any more than we already had."

"I didn't notice anyone from the Specialist ranks off on long missions to the Middle East. We were in and out of that area often, but nothing like this." Ziba's eyebrows are drawn together in an angry frown. "Stroud must have been using the non-specialist teams in the department, or maybe even utilizing outside forces."

"Mercenaries," Andi says. "Maybe even DoD contractors."

Rex puts his hand on the two flash drives in his pocket. "Ziba. Andi. Do you guys know how to hide from cameras?"

Both cousins turn to stare at him in surprise. "No," Andi says, while Ziba looks confused. "Is that possible?"

"They didn't teach it." Django shakes his head, a bitter smile on his face. "Son of a bitch. Ambrus didn't tell you, either."

"He didn't tell anyone—no one from the remaining Twenty told anyone—because you can't track bastards who you can't capture on camera," Rex says in sudden realization. "If a Specialist went rogue and could hide from cameras, they would be very, very hard to find. Damn. That's why Euan concentrated on the CCTV so much. If anyone had been following me around Turkmenistan, they might have been on camera."

"What the hell are you talking about?" Django gives Rex a piercing, Dad-like and demanding, "Tell me" look.

Rex pats his pocket, where the Turkmenistan flash drive is living. "Euan kept all of the surveillance from the Turkmenistan incident when he was trying to figure out if the department was playing games. Nothing conclusive, but we can always go through it again while we're waiting for him to turn up. Lots of government files, too."

"I'd love to see that later," Eric says. "The files."

"Sure," Rex agrees. "We can all commit treason together."

Kai rolls his eyes. "We've been doing that since the eighteenth of March. Might as well continue along the treason train."

"It took me until 2013 to get to Xāwuṭh in a way that I was certain wouldn't attract the department or the military," Eric says, pulling their attention back to him. He's smiling, but it's not a happy expression. "Xāwuṭh almost killed me when I turned up on his boat unannounced."

Xāwuṭh grins at Eric. "You're still lucky I had a knife instead of a gun, dumbass."

"If you'd carried a gun, I wouldn't have jumped you. I can dodge a fucking knife," Eric retorts.

"You dodged, yeah. Then you fell down and started laughing," Xāwuṭh says dryly. "It wasn't that fucking funny."

"Bitch, I'd been on the run from the United States military for over seven years. It was *hilarious.*"

Khodî reaches over and shoves Xāwuṭh to make him shut up. "What happened then, Eric?"

"Then? Oh. Well, then I was safe on a boat in the middle of the Pacific Ocean, so I had a long overdue nervous breakdown," Eric says cheerfully. "I don't remember a lot of that, either."

"Aw, fuck," Kai says as he, Wesley, and Brian all glance at their older siblings. Rex understands the nervous breakdown bit, and he knows Ella is aware of what that shit is like—Khodî, too. Now they're a four-pack set of nutcases.

"Hey, it's fine." Eric shrugs. "I'm the mostly-recovered nuts type who just has to worry about some interesting PTSD. I'm doing much better. I used to wake up mid-blackout to discover I was trying to kill everyone in a blind panic."

Xāwuṭh snorts in amusement. "Yeah, there was one crew member who didn't last long."

"Some people just don't handle having a gun to their head very well," Eric agrees.

Khodî flinches, his hand automatically going to the scar on his face. "Yeah. That's one way to put it."

Eric doesn't notice Khodî's reaction because Ella is glaring at him. "Something you want to fess up to, jerkface?"

"You mean the fact that I contemplated suicide? Often?" Eric's smile is gentle. "Because I did—I spent a lot of time exhausted, running around the whole of fucking Southeast Asia to avoid department mercs. One of the few things that kept me from eating a bullet—I was afraid the department would somehow Frankenstein's monster me back to life. Then I'd be shit out of luck, dealing with an entirely new set of problems. No thanks." Eric reaches out and takes his sister's hand again. "It got better, after I found Wolf. I don't...I didn't want that anymore. After today, I really don't want to. Okay?"

Ella purses her lips, visibly unhappy, but she nods. "Okay."

Django gives Xāwuṭh another glare. "You still should have told me."

"I did try to, once," Xāwuṭh replies, unconcerned. "Worked one of the old call-signs into a radio conversation we were having, said the signal was echoing pretty bad on my end. It was 2014, though. You took me literally."

Django's brow furrows before he looks away. "Dammit! I remember that. Fuck!"

"Hey, I'm serious about being glad you guys didn't come looking for me," Eric says. "Look what kind of circumstances it took to get you guys here safely! I spent half the day yesterday laughing my ass off, watching network messages pop back and forth on military channels as they talked about how they'd missed a satellite overhead shot of Kuala Belait in Brunei by five minutes. They knew you guys were there because of some bank theft, but they still don't have a boat profile to look for. They have jack shit, and it's *awesome.*"

Khodî lifts his head from where he's been contemplating the coals in the fire. "You were telling Wolf where to go, and when to go there."

"Pfft, no. Wolf knows where the hell he's going. Like I could stop him." Eric grins. "No, I told him *when* to go. No overhead satellite shots. No boat tracking. Utter win."

"How the hell are you doing this?" Andi asks. "They'd find you, tracking satellites directly."

"That's the great part," Eric says. "See, the U.S. getting its panties into a twist about Snowden, renewing the Patriot Act—well, it pissed off a lot of other folks who don't want the government up in their business. If you know your programs, stick to hardlines, and never bounce off a satellite, they can't find shit. Any transmission they pick up is nothing but noise. I can sure as hell watch them, though. It's like having an orgasm without the mess."

"Gross," Neumia announces. "I am okay with the Adult Words, but Uncle Eric, please no with the grossness."

Eric stares at Neumia for a few seconds. "Gotcha. Sorry, kiddo. I'm not used to having actual kiddos around anymore. I'll try to remember to avoid the gross. Okay?"

"Okay." Neumia snuggles back in against Brian's side.

Andi pins Eric with a stern glare. "I didn't need to concern myself with this sort of avoidance before. Satellites and hardlines. Details, please."

"Proxy-chains. Linux login, access to an account in, say, Sweden, and then you bounce that line from server to server until it's a web wrapped around the fucking globe. I don't link up to the satellites directly to watch them—I slip into the computer of someone *else*, someone whose job it is to track those things. That's how I know where they're going to be." Eric smiles, proud of himself. "I have to say, having a hell of a lot of free time enhanced by the intense desire not to be caught? It really builds your skillsets."

"I'd like to learn that 'hiding' trick that Rex mentioned, Django," Ziba says, glancing over at him. "If you don't mind teaching it."

Django shakes his head. "I don't mind—I already have to teach it to this lot here, anyway."

"As long as nobody does anything stupid, we have the internet back," Ella says, and Eric nods. "We have news sources. Social media. We can get information that isn't filtered through the entire three companies that control all visual media in the United States."

"It's down to fuckin' three companies now?" Xāwuṯh looks irritated, disgusted, and resigned, all at once. "Hello, oligarchy."

"We're aware." Ziba says, another frown marring her face. "It's one of the multiple branches of forming oligarchy that many of us within the department were working to try and prevent."

"Well." Andi looks down at the sand, regret written large across her features. "Not anymore."

Chapter 16

There's a minor shuffle for beds when everyone finally gives up on talking and the beer is gone. Xāwuṯ takes one look at Andi and Khodî before giving them his bedroom. Rex and Xāwuṯ set up cots in the main room; Kai and Sorrow fight with the hammocks in the other bedroom. Ella sticks to Eric like glue, but somehow convinces Ziba to join them in Eric's house for the night. Rex has no idea what that's about, but Ziba looks relieved by the offer. Their father says he's taking one of the hammocks in Eric's other bedroom. Wesley, Brian, Neumia, and Bonika retreat back to the yacht, with Wesley still muttering about feral fucking chickens.

It's too hot to sleep in his clothes, but really damned impolite to sleep naked right now. Rex settles for pulling his t-shirt off and resting in his shorts. The front door is standing open, and the salt-tang ocean breeze helps a lot.

He glances over to see Xāwuṯ ditched his shirt, too, and is sitting cross-legged on his cot in a pair of denim cut-offs that are so sun-bleached the original blue is all but gone. "You sleeping?"

Xāwuṯ glances up, his knife halting in place, half-embedded in another piece of driftwood. "Not yet. Thinking for a while. I'll put the lights out, though, as long as you don't mind me burning the lamp so I can see what the hell I'm doing."

"Lamp's fine." Rex lies down and blinks to adjust to the dark after the electric lights go out. Then the lamp flares into temporary orange brightness as his brother strikes a match. Xāwuṯ lights the tip of the hurricane lamp's wick and then turns it down so the fire burns low.

Rex can hear Kai and Sorrow talking in the bedroom, a murmur of mutual Thai quiet enough to be indistinct, like a radio playing far away. Each pass of Xāwuṯ's blade seems to blend in with their voices. Khodî and Andi are polite enough to shut the door, even though Rex suspects that they aren't up to anything. Tonight just feels too emotionally crammed.

He misses Euan fiercely, like it's a physical ache in his chest. He had no idea anyone could care like this, feel like this, about another human being. No one ever fucking warned him that love is also pain.

By military standards, Rex didn't do enough to be so exhausted, but he feels drained and done in. The quiet drone of the ocean waves finishes him off, pushing him into sleep.

Rex doesn't lucid-dream on his own, or at least he thinks he doesn't. If he ever has, he's never remembered it later. However, sometimes he picks up on other people's dreams, and that's why he knows what lucid-dreaming is like. Rex is used to getting caught up in his siblings' nighttime shenanigans—they're so tight-knit, it was hard not to when they all still lived at home. Khodî and Kai dream in flashes and feelings unless it's a nightmare, which are always sharp-edged and painful. Ella and Eric are both lucid dreamers, every time, and that led to some interesting talks the day after when they resume a conversation they were having in their sleep with someone else who may or may not actually remember it fucking happening. Brian and Wesley most often shared dreams with each other instead of advertising to the entire house, but since they were smart enough *not* to join the military to pick up an assload of PTSD, their dreaming minds are often full of either the very weird or the very mundane. Makani and their father were always quiet in comparison.

It was one thing to share dreams with family. The military was an entirely different basket of fuckery. Basic training and cramped military confines taught Rex how to wake up if he stumbled into someone else's head-related crap. After a few years of that kind of unwanted practice, Rex got pretty good at keeping to himself.

The scenery Rex finds himself gazing at is so realistic that it actually takes a little while to realize he's stumbled into someone else's lucid dream. Not a sibling, either; he'd recognize the feel.

Instead of jerking back and waking up out of politeness, he sticks around, fascinated by how clear everything is...and because he's curious as to *where* this is. It sure as hell isn't Mapun.

Whoever is dreaming is looking at a sign in Malay script. Stray Not-His thoughts are interpreting the words as Sandakan Shipping & Supplies. Rex frowns in his sleep, remembering that Sandakan is the port on the northeastern tip of Malaysia. It's the only way to cross miles of open water to get to Mapun unless you own a boat.

The docks are under watch. There are military boats in the water with searchlights.

Fuck. He's not getting to Mapun. Not that way.

Swimming eighty-four miles is also not the way to get to Mapun, Not-Him thinks sourly. He does not need to be eaten by sharks, or miss the island entirely. That would be embarrassing.

It won't matter if he retreats using the Malaysian coastline or the Indonesian one—they're going to notice him. White thumb, sticking out, horrible jokes, must avoid. He's going to have to travel straight overland. Seven hundred eighty miles through hellish, mountainous jungle terrain. Great.

Not-Him sits next to a garbage bin, posing as one of Sandakan's easily overlooked homeless men. The patrols ignore him while he calculates travel times in his head. He got lucky on the way here, catching a ride on a truck with a lead-footed driver. If he has to walk the entire way back, that's...fuck, that's seventeen days if he's making good time. With the mountains in the way, thirty-five days is a hell of a lot more realistic, and that's just the time it takes to get to Pontianak.

Vehicles aren't the solution. He needs a horse. Mule. Pony. Donkey. If he finds the right trails, he can get his travel time down to two weeks. Food shouldn't be a problem; it isn't the first time he's relied on a jungle to feed him. He's worked under these conditions often over the years. It's just not fun.

Pontianak and its direct route to the sea via the Kapuas River can get him illicit passage on a cargo ship. Depending on the weather, it's only two days' travel between islands, three if the weather is shit. He's either going to be traveling for about sixteen days, or well over a month.

Fuck that. If he can find one, he's stealing a Batak pony.

Please, please, let his malaria vaccination be up-to-date. He can't remember. He is not letting his asshole fiancé's charming words become prophecy.

Rex feels a sour taste in the back of his mouth as shock-fueled adrenaline floods his system.

Singapore. Fiancé. Malaria jokes.

This isn't a stranger's dream.

Euan?

Not-Him jerks in place. Suddenly it's as if an actual, physical line connects them, stretched from Mapun to Sandakan. Rex can sense stunned confusion, recognition, joy, and fear. He can feel eyes on his skin, as strong as a physical presence.

OhmyGod—Rex?

That's what makes Rex snap himself awake. He swings his feet over the side of the cot as he sits up and buries his head in his hands, trying to figure out if he's going to start vomiting.

His stomach settles after that initial burst of nausea. He breathes through it, rubbing his fingertips through his bristly hair while trying to calm the hell down.

He can't. He can't stop hearing things.

Words. Language. Indistinct voices. Loud shouts.

He recognizes Filipino. Malay. Thai. English.

Rex bolts through the house's open doorway, running down to the shoreline until warm ocean water surges forward, covering his bare feet before it retreats.

There are so many conversations. They flow over each other like the waves flow over the sand. Each new string of words covers the previous and changes the shape of what once lay below.

He can't understand it, can't track any of it. It's just so much goddamn noise, and it will not stop!

Rex blanks out and comes back in to find a strong arm around his waist, dragging him away from the ocean. "Wha—?" he manages, and then starts coughing out salty water. He's drenched, water running off his arms and face in thick rivulets.

His head is still a fucking stadium of people, all of them talking at once.

"Trust me, this is not how you make that shit be quiet!" Xāwuṭh barks at him. "Fucking ocean, are you fucking nuts?"

Rex grasps at Xāwuṭh's arm. "Xāwuṭh? I didn't—I wasn't trying to—"

"Fuck. You didn't do that on—shit. DAD!" Xāwuṭh shouts, but Rex doesn't only hear his voice. It's also in his head, the word *DAD* reverberating around in Rex's skull before it sinks into the morass of voices clamoring for attention. It feels like they're reaching out to drown him.

Rex clasps both of his hands to his head. No, no, no. *"Bùkè, bùkè, bùkè..."*[1]

*   *   *   *

Django awakens with a start when he hears someone call his name. It only takes him a second to realize he didn't hallucinate it, and he knows the voice. Xāwuṭh.

He flips himself out of the hammock with the easy motion he mastered by the end of his first year in Vietnam. He grabs the M9, tucks it into his jeans, and exits the house, bare feet churning in the loose sand. He doesn't sense trouble inbound, not the sort that would mean he needs a gun, or that they need to run—

He halts for a moment in shock when he sees his kids. Xāwuṭh is kneeling down on the sand, holding his brother. Rex is soaking wet with his hands clamped over his ears. His eyes are squeezed shut, his mouth open in a jaw-clenched grimace.

Django can hear Rex chanting under his breath, one continuous denial, over and over: *"Bùkè, bùkè, bùkè..."*

Shit. Not this; not right now, dammit!

Breathe. You've done this before. It's just been a while, Django reminds himself, and then runs to them.

"Dad, what the hell?" Xāwuṭh looks up at Django in wide-eyed desperation. "I caught the dumb fucker faceplanting into the ocean. I don't even think he realized it!"

"No, he probably didn't." Django kneels down on the ground next to them, resting his hand on the side of Rex's face. "Aw, goddammit."

Every single mental pathway Rex has is standing open, blazing in all directions. It's not just output—it's input.

It's everything. All at once.

Django swallows. "Remember when you were a kid, and you told me it felt like the world was shouting at you all the time?"

Xāwuṭh nods. "Yeah. You had to teach me how to shut most of that out. Not perfect, but hey, that's why boats exist."

---

[1] Mandarin: v. "Can not (cannot)." 不克

"Imagine going from zero to full blast with no warning," Django says, and Xāwuṭh goes pale.

"But he *was* at full blast!" Xāwuṭh protests, helping Django pick Rex up from the wet sand to take him back inside the house. Rex is still chanting *Can't, Can't, Can't* in a way that has always been chilling to hear. "When we met him in Singapore the first time, Rex was used to hearing and listening and reaching out—fuck, I was jealous because doing that wasn't making him nuts!"

"Just get him lying down again," Django orders as they put him down on the cot. Rex immediately rolls over to curl up on his side in a fetal position. He's not aware of anything they're doing, his hands still clasped to his head as he mutters that same fucking denial under his breath.

Xāwuṭh starts turning on the lights. Seawater becomes bright sparkling droplets against the *moko* on Rex's back, making it look like the *manaia* is watching them.

Django's heart feels like it wants to splinter and crack. All of his kids picked up expanded gifts because of their inherited ETKC-51, even if they don't use them for much beyond useful intuition. Django never wanted to push their awareness beyond that—not out of fear of the talents themselves, but a defense against the fucking department.

Rex is different, and it's Django's damned fault. He wasn't there when Rex needed him—he couldn't have been, he hadn't known, but...

Khodî pushes the bedroom door open, sees what's going on, and swears a blue streak. "I'll go get the twins," he says, leaving the house in a mile-eating sprint.

"What's going on?" Andi asks. Django looks up long enough to see her emerge from the bedroom, wrapped from the chest down in the long batik cotton she usually wears as a skirt. Her hair is falling in thick, loose strands almost to her waist, making her look a Hindu goddess.

Django kneels down and brushes his hands over his son's face, trying to soothe back what must feel like an agony of noise, fire that can't be escaped. "C'mon, kiddo," Django murmurs under his breath. "You can do this. You can shut this down."

Andi asks a quiet question that Xāwuṭh answers: "Blown open mentally." Django has no idea Andi is approaching until she's kneeling by his side.

"May I?" she asks in a gentle voice. Her dark eyes are soft with concern.

Django bites his lip against the protective growl that wants to emerge. This has always been family business, but—but they need help. They've needed it for years, but literally had no idea where to find it. "Yeah. Just don't...don't prod. It makes it worse."

Andi nods, doing nothing more than brushing her fingertips along Rex's temple before her brow furrows together in bafflement. "He has no natural shielding. This is all construct."

"We know," Django replies tiredly.

Andi gives him a sharp look. "I've never met anyone without any kind of natural shielding."

Django resists the urge to roll his eyes. "Well, now you have."

Ella bursts into the house and drops right down next to the cot. Eric is only about thirty seconds behind her, shadowed by Khodî, who still looks worried about his brother's stability. "I'm good," Eric says, waving Khodî off before sitting down next to the cot in an awkward sprawl. "Fuck. When is the last time—?"

"When we were all still in fucking high school!" Ella snaps. She places one of her hands over Rex's, which has gone white-knuckled with tension. "Aw, baby, no. Not this again."

"That long, huh?" Eric rests his hand over his sister's, the shine from his prosthetic fingers reflecting the overhead light. "What triggered this?"

"No idea. Caught him taking a header into the ocean at the shore," Xāwuṭh answers.

"Usually it's a dream." Khodî sits down next to him so he can place his hand over Django's. "Come on, Wolf. It's a family activity."

"What the fuck," Xāwuṭh mutters before sitting down close to Rex's head. "What the hell is going on, guys?"

"I was gonna ask that," Kai says, coming into the room and rubbing at his eyes. "The hell—oh. Shit. Oh, shit," he whispers. Sorrow follows him in, stops, and stares at what's going on like everyone has lost their damned minds. Django thinks that's probably pretty damned apt.

The moment Django sees Ziba grace the doorway, looking tired, frazzled, and confused, he gets her attention and then tilts his head at Sorrow. Ziba understands at once, leading Sorrow from the house while speaking to him in a low whisper. An explanation, perhaps, or maybe instructions to keep his mouth shut. Django doesn't give a fuck which option she chooses, not right now.

"Is he—I don't know how to—"

"It's fine, Kai!" Django barks, and then flinches at his own harshness. "Dammit. Sorry, Kai. Have a seat and put your hand somewhere. Touch is reassuring."

Kai nods, taking a few steps forward to put his hands on Rex's feet, which are still dripping seawater. "Ow," Kai says a moment later. "How does someone function like this?"

"We don't function very well at all," Xāwuṭh tells Kai wryly. "What are we doing to help?"

"That's what I'd like to know." Andi gives Django a questioning look, receiving a curt nod of permission before she rests her palm over Django's other hand. Her mental touch is delicate where she herself is not, like petals dancing on a spring breeze.

"The only thing we can do—soothe all of those open pathways, all those shining lights," Khodî explains. His eyes are closed, his voice soft, but there is coiled strength lurking there. He's the best of the kids at finding and tracking; he is the absolute best man Django has ever known for being able to see. "Wolf and Rex are the ones who have the worst trouble filtering out the background noise when they decide they really want to listen to something."

"Fuck the hell out of you, I do too know how to make things shut the fuck up," Xâwuth growls. "Mostly, but mostly is still better than this—I could drop every shield I have and still it wouldn't be like this!" Xâwuth takes a breath, teeth grinding together as he forces himself to calm down. "What the hell went wrong, Dad?"

"The first time we brought Rex home to Pennsylvania, we knew it was going to be a shock," Django says. The explanation is as much for Xâwuth as it is for Andi Banner, who is still baffled by Rex's lack of natural shielding. Rex's litany of refusal has quieted with so much tactile reassurance, but they're not done yet.

Django looks at Andi. "Rex had no shielding when we found him with his mother's family because he kept reaching out for emotional connections that refused to reach back. He never built walls to keep anything out, not when he couldn't get anyone to connect with him in the first place."

"Oh, gods, the poor dear. How old was he?" Andi asks. "When you found him, I mean. I cannot imagine any one of you unwilling to reach back."

"Not quite one-and-a-half," Khodî answers. "I was almost five, and—god, Andi, Rex was amazing. He was communicating on my age level, soaking up languages and ideas. He was so used to having those channels blown open all the time that he absorbed everything like a fucking sponge."

"Amazing," Andi murmurs.

"Rex's family let me formally adopt him. We were in Vietnam first, then Cambodia, trying to cushion that upcoming cultural shock by giving him emotional connections in places that were still vaguely familiar: me, Khodî, Xâwuth, Khodî's and the twins' mother, Chanthavy—even the twins, though they weren't even a year old yet." Django closes his eyes for a brief moment. "It wasn't enough. We went home to Pennsylvania, and Rex completely and utterly shut down."

"It was everything." Khodî's voice still holds a hint of grief. "He slammed those mental channels closed, refused to speak or gesture or—it was like someone pressed a goddamn mute button."

"He got better, but it took a while. Rex never lost self-care, he never stopped...functioning." Django hates using that word. It sounds too sterile for what they went through during those agonizing few weeks.

"Singapore," Xāwuṭh growls, like it's a curse. "And then he never opened any of it back up. None of it."

"No. Not consciously, never again." Django swallows in relief as he feels Rex's mental pathways starting to close, curling up in tight furls like flowers hiding from the night.

Kai frowns. "That's weird. I can feel what he's doing, but none of us ever close up to that extent. Shit, it's a wonder he picks up on anything."

Django shakes his head, running his hand down Rex's face as his son's harsh expression begins to ease. "Rex has some amazing filters for what he wants to come through, but when this happens? He never remembers blowing everything open. Something will hit him hard, and all of his shields fucking drop. Half the time he doesn't even remember what caused it."

"It reminds him too much of before we found him." Ella is biting her lip as she caresses Rex's shoulder. "He'd wake up from nightmares when we were kids. He'd tell me that the house was empty, and we were gone. He'd say that everything, everywhere, was just empty."

"His brain rewired itself to tie the bad shit in with the good." Kai sighs. "Man, I haven't taken enough psych courses for this. Would he remember those, at least? The nightmares?"

"Sometimes," Ella replies just as Rex's eyes flutter open.

"What the actual fuck," Rex rasps out.

"You had a flashback and took a dive into the fucking ocean," Xāwuṭh says flatly. Django is grateful for his eldest son's quick response. He has no idea how he would have answered that question.

"Wait—seriously?" Rex blinks a few times and then groans. "Oh, shit, who parked a boat on my head?"

"And that would be my cue to go find the good painkillers." Kai disappears into the bedroom before coming back with his medical kit. "How big a boat are we talking about?"

"Fucking container ship," Rex answers, pressing his fingertips against his temples. "Help me up, okay? If I'm going to throw up, I'd rather do it on the floor and not on myself."

Django and Khodî help Rex sit up. Khodî gives Rex a gentle nudge when he veers to the left; Andi does the same on the right side when Rex tries to lean in that direction.

"Fuck everything," Rex mutters. He closes his eyes and slumps forward so he can at least keep his balance.

Kai tilts his head, studying his brother. "Yep, skipping the pills, going straight to the liquid injection. You good for that?" When Rex manages a terse nod, Kai pulls out three different bottles and fills a single needle from each one. "Anti-nausea, migraine wonder juice, and a dose of Calm The Fuck Down."

"I *am* fucking calm!" Rex snarls, and then grimaces in apology. "Okay, maybe I'm not." He winces as Kai uses hand-pressure to find a vein in his arm before sliding the needle home. "That shit burns, Kai."

"Damned well better," Kai replies. "If it doesn't burn, I didn't do it right."

"Mad fuckin' scientist doctor," Khodî mutters, and Kai smiles.

Once he's sure Rex can remain upright on his own, Django finds a chair to sit in. Khodî plops down in the other cot next to Xāwuṯẖ, who glares at him for sitting there without asking. Kai sticks near Rex, sitting cross-legged on the floor, while the twins cuddle up on either side of their brother. Andi also stays nearby, a mix of curiosity, polite intrigue, and genuine concern keeping her seated close to Rex.

Khodî's gaze is flickering between Andi and Rex. Django has to admit, there are far worse people his son could have fallen in love with.

Django is fucking concerned about Rex—it's literally been twenty years since Rex broke himself this badly—but he's also constantly getting hung up on the fact that most of his kids are all in the same room. He never once believed that they would have Eric back, not after that hellish funeral and Ella's broken heart. Django faced the reality that they would never be together like this again...but they are. If Brian and Wesley weren't sleeping out on the boat with Nari and Bonika, all of his kids would be crowding into the same space.

Django resolves to have a quiet breakdown about that later. Rex is more important right now. "You all right?" he asks once most of the tension is gone from Rex's face.

Rex nods, rubbing the bridge of his nose. "Sorry. Didn't mean to be a pain in the ass."

Xāwuṯẖ snorts. "I'm glad I was still awake, or you would have woken up choking on salt water."

"Right." Rex gives his brother with a wry smile. "Thanks, Wolf. I'd probably have drowned myself on accident. Now there's a stupid way to go."

Django trades glances with Khodî and gets subtle confirming nods from the twins before he decides to push. "Bad dream, Rex?"

Rex slowly shakes his head. "Uhm—no. Informative, actually, not bad. It was just, uh..." He swallows. "You guys know how we used to share each other's dreams?"

"Used to?" Eric rolls his eyes. "No, that talent is still alive and well, and I would desperately like Ella to dream about something else because that was *so awkward*."

"She's pretty," Ella mutters defensively.

Eric puts his hand over his eyes and makes a frustrated noise. "Yes, but I have literally just met this person. So. Very. Awkward."

Andi smirks at the exchange, well aware of where Ella's attention has wandered.

Rex smiles a little. "Might as well get used to the idea, Eric. But no, not—okay, has anyone ever dreamed someone else's conscious actions?"

Django sits up ramrod straight, feeling his gut curdle and bile sour the back of his throat. "Yes. It's a tactical skill the Twenty were taught. Those of us who'd put up with that, anyway. It's invasive. Usually requires a hell of a lot of specific training, too."

Rex lifts his head, open-mouthed shock branding his face. "Oh."

"Only a few of the Specialists can do such a thing." Andi rests her chin on her clasped hands. "And I've never known anyone who ever did so on accident."

"That is really not helping," Rex says. "What's the trigger?"

"You go looking for someone," Andi replies. "The process is more complicated than that, but that's the gist of it. I can't do it. Ziba can, but for her the process usually requires sedation."

"Great." Rex sighs as he pinches the bridge of his nose. "I went to bed worried about my idiot boyfriend. So I found him. In Sandakan."

"Holy shit, bro." Khodî whistles. "That's a hell of a long way to pick up on a dream."

Rex whirls on Khodî, glaring at his brother. "Dream, my ass! I snapped out of it because there was conscious recognition at the end. Khodî, we fucking spoke to each other! By name—Euan recognized me!"

"What's the intel?" Django asks in a composed, steady voice. That gets Rex to look at him. "If you got it, we might as well hear it and use it. The how part doesn't matter, not right now. You're just going to have to be more careful."

"More careful. How?" Rex whispers, anger turning into shocked dismay.

"Go to bed with your thoughts focused locally," Andi suggests. "I know it's harder, especially when you wish to reach for someone, but I was told that it helps."

"Locally." Rex sighs again. "Right: Euan can't get to Mapun. The department has teams patrolling the northern ports and coastlines in Malaysia and Indonesia. They know we went north, but not where."

"We'll have to post satellite crossover times, then," Eric says. "Make sure everyone's indoors when they happen."

"And cover the boat," Xāwuṭh adds, scowling.

Rex nods in response to both suggestions. "Yeah, that's probably a good idea. Sandakan was pretty much jam-packed with assholes. Euan's retreating overland, back to Singapore. He estimated his travel time at just over two weeks if he's lucky, and over a month if he's not."

"Straight over the middle of the island." Django shakes his head. "Some poor fucker is going to be lacking a pony by sunrise. You can't get a vehicle through that mess."

"Averaging that out, we'll be on Mapun for about two weeks as long as the department doesn't figure out where we are," Khodî says.

Kai shrugs. "It's not a bad place to hang."

Eric smiles. "They won't find us. I've been working out of Mapun for over a year now. Trust me—as long as you play by my rules when it comes to the phones, computers, and satellites, the department isn't finding jack shit."

Ella brightens. "That means I'll have plenty of time to practice calling lightning!"

Eric leans around Rex so he can stare at his sister. "You want to do *what*?"

Kai raises his hand, revealing the lightning tattoo that wraps his right wrist. He got it when he turned eighteen, done in Makani's favorite shade of blue. "Betcha I do it first."

"You are so on," Ella replies, grinning.

"Later," Django orders them before giving Rex a level stare. He doesn't want to ask this, but it has to be done. "Do you remember what happened after the dream? Do you remember waking up?"

"I—" Rex frowns, the faintest hint of distress in his eyes. "No. I don't even remember—Euan said my name, and then we were all here in the house."

"Full PTSD blackout. Damn," Kai says. "I haven't seen any of us pull that in a while."

Rex hesitates, his eyes darting around the room to briefly study Django, Khodî, Kai, Ella, Eric, Andi, and Xāwuṭh. "Was this like—was it like high school? Was it that?"

Ella nods and leans against him. "Yep, sure was. But we were here, and you're fine."

"No bullshit, right?" Rex asks, reaching out to grab Eric and Ella's hands.

"No bullshit," Eric promises as he takes Rex's hand in a firm grip. "Have we ever?"

Rex glances at Eric out of the corner of his eye. "Do you really want me to answer that question?"

Eric looks thoughtful. "Statute of limitations is way up at this point, right?" he asks. Ella starts giggling as the stress in the room finally breaks.

Andi's curiosity has intensified. Whatever she wants to ask, Django hopes it's something easy to answer. Rex still looks like his head hurts, even with Kai's injected cocktail. "Is *Ashlesha* your *lagna*?" she finally asks.

Rex blinks at her a few times in confusion. "What the hell is a *lagna*, and what's an *ashlesha*?"

"Ah." Andi shakes her head. "I'm sorry. I made an assumption based upon the serpent on your back."

"It's part of my *moko*," Rex says, brow still furrowed in pained confusion. "It's my *taniwha*, the serpent who lies in wait."

"Why did you choose it?" Andi asks, her gaze shining and intense.

"My job was about stealth, about choosing the right moment to strike." Rex accepts his t-shirt when Kai hands it over. Kai is thinking about the same thing Django is—extra insulation to help prevent shock. It's not likely at this point, but no one expected anything that happened after everyone went to bed, either.

Rex pulls his shirt on over his head and tugs it down into place. The fabric develops dark splotches as it soaks up saltwater. "My cousins and I—and Khodî—we thought it was a good choice."

Andi nods thoughtfully. "To answer your question: a *lagna* is the closest celestial body to break the eastern horizon at the place and time of your birth; the Ascendant. The *Ashlesha* are two *naga*, the great serpents entwined. The *naga* themselves are creatures of cunning as well as divine links to other worlds. Those born under the stars of *Ashlesha* in the constellation of Hydra are intuitive and fearful—or fearless."

"Like a horoscope," Ella says.

Andi's mouth twists in displeasure. "Yes, but it's nothing like the ridiculously staid Western horoscope you find in every bloody American newspaper. Jyotisha Astrology is far more accurate, and it's based on science as much as it is on knowledge of the old Vedic texts and their stories."

Khodî grins. "She's like a walking damned calculator for this. It's terrifying. I told her my birthdate, place, and the time, and she didn't even need to look it up to confirm it. She says I'm *Uttara Bhadrapada* and *Punarvasu*."

"What the fuck does that mean?" Rex asks before Django can voice the question. He doesn't know enough about that part of the world to even remotely grasp what the hell Andi's talking about.

Andi smiles. "*Uttara Bhadrapada*. That is the warrior's star, and Khodî's Ascendant, the house of the body. *Punarvasu* is the star of renewal, the house of the moon, which represents the mind. There is also a house of the sun that represents the one's course of action, the choices one might make, but even I have limits for what I can remember."

"And man, did all of that feel weird to hear," Khodî admits. "It fits in a fucking creepy way."

Andi's voice and gaze turn somber. "I've studied Vedic Jyotisha for a very long time now. To calculate true astrology, one must have the equivalent of a doctorate in astronomy—you must know of the stars and their movements in order to correctly predict another's traits. Knowing your *lagna*, and what celestial bodies were dominant when you were born? That's merely the start. There is so much more, all of it changing as the Earth moves through space and the stars move along their own paths." Andi tilts her head as she looks at Rex. "When is your birthday, and where were you born?"

Rex still looks bewildered. "Singapore. Around dawn, somewhere in Sungei Kadut. Nineteenth of September in 1979."

The intriguing thing is that Django can all but see the gears turning in Andi's head as she takes those fragments of information and translates them into something more. "You are *Punarvasu*, Rex."

"Star of renewal," Django reminds Rex when his son gives Andi a blank look. Django is Māori and he is of the Whetū; he knows better than to disregard the stars. "What does that mean, Andi?"

"*Punarvasu* can mean many things, but to briefly summarize, it represents things that are good in our world," Andi clarifies. "It also exemplifies a fresh start, or freedom from restrictions and limitations."

"Oh," is all that Rex says, but Django feels his blood try to freeze in his veins. Freedom from limitations. Fuck, that is not the kind of thing he wants to hear right now.

"Okay, after we sleep? I wanna talk about this more," Ella says. "I want to know my *lagna* thing, because so far? This is all creepy accurate."

"Well, you all are children of the stars," Everyone turns to Andi in confusion—except for Django, who covers his face with one hand. "*Whetū* is the Māori word for stars. Of course you all find truth within them."

"Now I'm also creeped out," Eric says. "Rex, you're coming to bed with us."

Rex stares at Eric in drug-addled exhaustion. "What?"

The twins continue to badger Rex until they convince him to sleep with them in Eric's bed, all but hauling him out of the house. Ella brackets Rex on his left side; Eric paces alongside Rex on his right, using his cane to keep his balance as they walk along the sandy beach. Django watches their progress, not satisfied until he sees all of them disappear into Eric's house.

Khodî blows out a long breath before he turns around and goes back into the bedroom without a word. Andi seems to consider the matter before she joins him, pulling the bedroom door closed.

"I'm gonna go the fuck back to sleep, I guess. Dad, do you mind if we swap out?" Kai asks. "I'd rather stick close to Rex. He's never had a bad reaction to anything I gave him before, but just in case, you know?"

Django nods. "Yeah, go ahead. I'll sleep here."

He waits until Kai is gone, and Xāwuth is distracted by putting out most of the lights in the living room, before he wanders out to the shoreline. Django sits down at the edge of the water, keeping his jeans dry while his bare feet rest on wet sand, his toes kissed by each incoming wave.

Salt helps, sometimes. Django doesn't know why—some sort of mystical bullshit that none of the program's early teachers could ever really explain. He doesn't care as long as it helps him calm the hell down.

Any help is enough. A single hand may place the stone that diverts the flood. Be at peace, man who awakens the stars.

The memory of Chosa's words sends a chill through him. The old Khmer midwife helped birth Ella and Eric in Cambodia, and she told Django that not long afterwards. He didn't know what Chosa meant at the time, but he sure as hell understands her now.

Xāwuṭh comes out to join him, dropping down onto the sand next to Django. "What's wrong, Dad?"

Django rubs the bridge of his nose, realizes he's copying Rex's gesture from a few minutes earlier, and smiles. "For the first time since 1974, I want a goddamn cigarette."

Xāwuṭh chuckles. "That can actually be arranged."

Django shakes his head. "No thanks. It's just a stress reaction. I don't really need one."

"That, I get." Xāwuṭh is worrying at the meditation bracelet on his wrist, sliding the wooden beads along the elastic strand but never letting them audibly click together.

Django stares out at the dark ocean. "You weren't afraid of your gift when you were young. You handled it well, even if you didn't know how to muffle what you heard when we first met. I was able to teach you how to shield, how to build walls."

"Yeah, I remember." Xāwuṭh looks at Django from the corner of his eye. "And?"

"I can't teach Rex." Django presses his fingers into the pressure points along his forehead, warding off a tension headache that wants to form. "I've tried, but the kind of teaching he needs—I don't even know where to begin. He needs natural fucking shielding, but those constructs have to be open for that to happen, and when he manages it, we get shit like tonight."

"Maybe we should start with therapy," Xāwuṭh suggests dryly.

"His entire childhood was therapy against fucking Singapore and his damned grandmother," Django retorts. "Xāwuṭh, I gave him shielding lessons, the same ones I taught you. Hell, that's the way *I* was taught. Rex took those lessons and did something completely different. The people I know of who would be able to help him learn to control that consciously—they're all dead."

"Well, let's make him consciously blow those shields open," Xāwuṭh says.

Django drops his hand and looks at his eldest son. "We tried that once. It didn't go well."

Xāwuṭh frowns as he makes the connection. "That would be the high school incident they were talking about."

"Yeah." Django looks out at the ocean again. "Makani had been studying psychology when we were still trying to figure out how to help Rex—things like tonight used to happen a lot more often. We tried to experiment, to talk him through remembering the actual event. He fucking shut down on us again. Just for a few hours, but hell, that was terrifying enough.

"Rex blocked that out, too," Django says. "He knows about the event because we told him, but he doesn't have any conscious memory of it."

"And that's why you're worried."

Django nods. "If he's starting to reach out, if he's dream-sharing with someone who's conscious? Xāwuṭh, I'm not just worried. I'm fucking terrified."

"Then what the fuck do we do?" Xāwuṭh asks.

Django smiles. He's an eighty-eight-year-old man, and he feels so old right now. He buried his parents and his sister. He oversaw his wife's cremation. He witnessed the funeral rites for his aunt and grandfather. He thought he'd buried one of his children in Arlington by memorial proxy.

"When Makani died, I didn't listen to the wind, not as much as I should have," Django admits. Losing her had hurt so goddamned much. He kept waking and reaching out those first few years, certain that he'd find her lying next to him. Each time he found nothing, Django's heart fractured a little bit more.

"I still listened to my instincts, kept us all alive, but it was harder to fucking care about it," Django says. "Then the military reported Eric dead and I—I stopped listening. The instinct was still there, but I didn't want to fucking hear it, not when it hadn't saved Eric or Makani. I shut it out."

"Christ on Buddha's lap," Xāwuṭh mutters.

Django smiles again, a faint, humorless expression that makes him feel even older. "Ambrus said I was out of practice, and he's right. I've only just started paying attention again. We need to know what the hell to do next. I need to open all of those paths back up and listen to the wind."

"Then I'm staying right here." Xāwuṭh glares at him when Django tries to say no. "I already pulled one stupid asshole out of the ocean tonight."

"This doesn't require moving at all," Django insists. "It's just..."

"I remember," Xāwuṭh says quietly. "But I'm staying. And Dad? Practice doesn't mean shit. Just do what you already know how to do."

Makani, Django thinks, and his senses feel alive just from saying her name. For the first time in almost two decades, he tilts his head and truly listens to what the wind has to say.

He has no idea how much time has passed when he blinks awareness back and realizes that Xāwuṭh's hand is on his shoulder.

His head feels crowded with far too much; his heart feels at peace for the first time in years.

"You all right?" Xāwuṭh asks.

"We need to be in Singapore by April thirteenth." Django puts his hand to his head as he tries to sort through it all. Fuck, he didn't expect to pick up on this much shit.

"If the weather's good, travel time from here is about four days," Xāwuṭh tells him, which is reassuring. It doesn't cut short their potential two weeks—it extends it by a day or two.

Django is less happy about the next bit. "Ella's right. We all need to practice, even though I really don't want my baby girl calling lightning from anywhere."

"Like Ella needs to be any more terrifying than she already is," Xāwuṭh agrees in a mild voice. "What else?"

That's the part Django *really* doesn't like. "I need to make a phone call."

*   *   *   *

Xāwuṭh shows him how to use an application on a cell phone—one tethered to Eric's wireless network—to make encrypted calls that can't be tracked back to Mapun. "Skips out on the satellite," Xāwuṭh explains. "Even if the signal's intercepted? Anyone trying to interpret it will get gibberish."

"How far can I wander without it being a problem?" Django brings up the dialer under the app in question, a terrible pun based on a classic Bugs Bunny catchphrase.

"Just watch the wireless signal," Xāwuṭh answers. "Don't let it drop below three bars. Satellite network access is supposed to be disabled on the phone, but smartphones sometimes try to actually be fuckin' smart."

"Right. Thanks." Django takes the phone outside, paces the perimeter around Xāwuṭh's house until he's certain of his signal range for the wireless, and then dials.

"General Merrill," he hears a man say in a clipped voice. "Make it fast. I'm busy."

"General? They promoted your ass?" Django smiles. "I thought they didn't do that for you Marine types who spent so much of your time out doing crazy shit."

There is a long, shocked pause. "Holy fucking shit—Django?"

"Hi, David. How the hell are you?"

"Currently terrified that I'm giving away your position!" Jason's son snaps back. "Are you clear?"

"It's a secured line," Django reassures him. "We're okay. Is your father—?"

"Dad's still with us."

Django lets out a relieved sigh. He knows cancer is a bitch, but goddammit, he wants to be able to attend Jason's funeral when he goes, not drop by with a half-assed flower years from now.

"I'm assuming that you need something," David says.

"I do, and it's going to sound like the request of someone who's lost their damned mind," Django replies. "I need you to get me the cell phone number for the man who was Secretary of Defense in 1991."

David snorts. "You're right. You do sound like you've lost your goddamn mind. For God's sake: Why?"

"Because that man still has his fingers in a lot more pies than most of D.C. would be comfortable with if they knew." Django can't help smiling again. "Besides, think of how much it would piss him off if I once again put myself in a position to help him."

"You take a hell of a lot of joy out of irritating that man. It would be simpler just to punch him again," David suggests.

"But then I'd have to be physically present. No thanks."

"Good point," David admits. "Has to be a cell?"

"Yeah."

"Okay. Your number's coming up as unknown. How do I contact you?" David asks.

Django rattles off the number; he wrote it on his hand when Xāwuṭh gave him the phone. "Text it to me. I'll take care of the rest."

David doesn't give in to the urge to sigh, but Django gets the impression that he wants to. "Am I going to be seeing body bags in D.C. again, Django?"

"Maybe. Hell, this time it might even do some good."

"This isn't like that shit in 1991," David replies. "You and I both know that we're sitting on an oligarchy in all but name at this point."

Django watches a crab trundle by on its way back to the ocean. "Yeah, but if that asshole goes for this, we might be getting rid of one of the bits of rot that help that shit fester."

"Goddammit." David goes quiet for a moment. "I can get it, but it'll be a few minutes. The rest of you are okay? No one else is hurt?"

"We're all fine," Django says, even if he's not sure about Rex being one hundred percent. "And...David?" He swallows. "Tell Jason that Eric's alive."

Django hears David choke on his own spit. "Jesus Christ. Are you fucking serious?"

"Damned serious. He was a POW first, and then the department went after him," Django tells him. "Eric didn't hit a safe point until 2013, David."

"Fuck. Okay. Well, I guess that tells me what bit of rot you're going after. God, please be careful. You're practically my brother, asshole. I'd like to see you again when this shit's clear."

Django smiles. "Same to you. Behave, you traitorous Marine."

"Hoo-rah," David retorts, and the line goes silent.

Django puts the cell phone down on the steps of Xāwuṭh's house where Xāwuṭh is sitting. His eyes are hooded as he watches his father.

"What are you planning?"

"Sanctified destruction," Django replies, and Xāwuṭh grins wide with gleeful pleasure.

Django walks over to Eric's house and quietly goes inside. Kai is in the hammock in the first bedroom, his arms and legs hanging out of it, sound asleep. He's going to wake up in the morning literally tangled up in that bed. Sorrow looks like he's far more used to sleeping in a hammock. Maybe he'll be nice enough to untangle Kai in the morning. If they do anything else, Django doesn't want to know about it. There's enough shit going on in his life right now. He doesn't need to worry about them, too.

In the next room, the twins are bracketing Rex in at the center of the bed. They're lying in an intertwined pile that reminds Django so much of when they were tiny children that he has to lean against the doorway, a sob trying to work past his throat.

He never wanted this for his kids. He never wanted the training he gave them to be anything but a fucking precaution, and yet here they are...on the verge of war.

It does not escape his notice that Ziba's cot is as close to the bed as it can be placed without blocking Ella's exit. They're facing each other, and one of his daughter's hands is reaching in Ziba's direction.

Django goes back to the other house, mounts the steps, and passes Xāwuṭh, who's keeping an eye on the phone. No messages yet. He hears nothing but silence behind the closed bedroom door and slowly pushes it open.

Khodî is asleep, lying on his stomach with the left side of his face pressed against a thin pillow. Andi is awake, curled up next to him as she runs her fingers through his hair and along the scar on Khodî's face. The bedsheet is resting high enough on her body to preserve some sense of modesty.

Their eyes meet for a moment. What Django finds in Andi's gaze is protectiveness, patience, unyielding steel, and utter understanding. Django gives her a slight nod and shuts the door. There's another arrangement that's starting to look permanent.

When Django goes back outside, Xāwuṭh hands him the phone. "Text."

He memorizes the number and brings up the encrypted app again as he walks down the steps. Xāwuṭh will probably hear everything, but he wants to be standing in the water when he makes this call.

Django double-checks that the wireless stays at three bars as water comes rushing in over his feet and ankles. He can taste salt in the back of his throat, borne on the wind and crammed into his senses. He dials the number and puts the phone to his ear.

His kids deserve to have their lives back.

अश्लेषा

For my Family

Begun April 3rd 2016, along with all of *Awaken the Stars*. *Ashlesha* manuscript completed June 14th 2016.

ABOUT THE AUTHOR

Jer Keene lives in Maine and would desperately like to live in Florida again. (Send help.) The author shares living space with a mate, their two Podlings who are approaching terrifying teenage-years, five cats, and the author's Henchperson.

The author has been actively writing since age fifteen. Despite hearing nothing except, "That's nice, dear" throughout adolescence, the author kept doing both, because crazy people keep doing the same thing and expect different results.

She is also a part-time artist who likes flamethrowers and can cannons. Sometimes emits caustic sounds. Should be approached with caution.

Updates on upcoming projects and confirmation that the author is still alive can be found at jer-keene@tumblr.com.

Book II:

Vishakha विशाखा

Will Be Released

~~Summer 2017~~

Winter 2018

(Schedules are great until life intervenes.)

By 1975, Django Whetū has seen enough of war. He started with World War II, saw action in Korea, got inducted into the hell known as the program, and then pretty much ran from its special blend of awful the moment he had the opportunity.

Django returned to regular service and jumped (literally) at the chance to join Special Forces as it became an official branch of the U.S. Army. One of that decade's only bright points was standing with his brothers-in-arms, refusing to obey the order to cease wearing the Green Beret until Kennedy finally gave up and let them have it.

Then the war in Vietnam made him hate the service more than the damned program ever did.

Taking contracts from the Department of Defense—contracts Django can make the call to take or pass along to someone else, contracts he can handle his way, without direct oversight? That is an entirely different story. He's always been good at his job, even if it has its downsides. The Khmer Rouge, landing on a dead cow during a night jump, accidentally fathering multiple children despite using all the damned birth control available...

All right, so that last part isn't a downside. It's just not what Django Whetū expected from his life.

Fortunately for everyone involved, he doesn't have to stop being a soldier to be a father.

Turn the page for a preview from *Vishakha*:

April 21st 1975:

"Saigon is going to fall in seven days. You need to not be here."

Jason Merrill glances up at the man standing over his desk. Django Whetū doesn't look like he's seen the inside of a proper Vietnamese bathhouse in over a month, but hell, no one knew where the man took himself after the goddamned disaster that was Ninh Chu up in Đồng Nai Province. Three hundred civilian villagers and forty-three American soldiers dead. To say Colonel Whetū hadn't taken it well would be the understatement of the goddamn century.

Command tried to get Whetū declared AWOL. Jason made certain it didn't happen. The Congressional dickery from Washington doesn't make him happy, but since Jason is supposed to be a diplomat, not a military presence, it does give him a certain amount of leeway.

"Are you sure?" he asks Django, only lifting a polite eyebrow at the man's unclean state. "About Saigon, I mean." He knows *something* is damned well going to happen, but the Republic of Vietnam has pulled miracles out of its ass before.

"Yeah." Django drops a folder onto Jason's desk. "I can smell it on the wind."

"Are you sure that's not just you, Colonel?" At least the paperwork is clean, even if the soldier presenting it is not.

"Been a rough few weeks, General."

The local brass who'd made the shit call on Ninh Chu ended up dead before Jason could get to him. He knew it wasn't Django's work; Django would have dropped a corpse on his desk and dared Jason to say boo about it. Jason suspects it was Kellagh-Ambrus, who he's seen a few times in Saigon in the past couple of weeks. They still pretend not to remember each other, which keeps Jason's hands clean of the insanity that was the old program. When a much younger captain named Django Whetū had left that same clusterfuck, Jason took a look around and decided that Django had the right idea.

Ever since leaving, though, Jason has only ever heard it referred to as the department. Not even any capital letters—just "the department." Creeps him right the hell out.

Jason opens the folder. "I won't argue with you there—holy shit." He stares down at the documents in his hands. "Are you sure about *this?*"

When he looks up, Django's head is turned to the window, his eyes tracking the progress of traffic passing back and forth outside. There's a hard set to his jaw, but an empty, grieving look in his dark eyes that Jason has seen only once before.

Django heaves out a long breath and turns back to him. "Yeah, Jason. I'm—I know you're still in the game, but I'm—"

"Hey, no. You stow that, right now. We have two different kinds of jobs, Django," Jason says, checking the calendar on his desk before scribbling his signature and the date on every necessary line. "I've been a paper pusher for a long time. You've been out there dealing with that shit in the jungle for ten years now. If you say you're ready to get the hell out of the Army, then you're ready."

"There going to be a problem with me not being on the four-year mark for a discharge? Or about Ninh Chu?"

"Those in charge of that blunder have already been dealt with," Jason says in a harsh voice, checking through the rest of the folder to make sure he hasn't missed a signature line, or that Django hasn't missed a form. As expected, everything is where it should be, even the briefing paperwork for the separation counseling that Jason knows full well Django would sooner cut off a limb than attend. "And there will be no issue with the timing of your discharge."

"Kellagh-Ambrus?"

Jason glances up. Django's eyes have that slight narrowed edge that Jason recognizes; Django is either righteously pissed off or righteously worried about someone.

"Oh, I imagine Kellagh-Ambrus at least assisted with the blunder's clean-up," Jason says. "No more than that. He doesn't want to complicate my life. Nice of him."

Django's brow furrows. "Yeah, guess so. We done here?"

"Technically, you have to hand over your service revolver," Jason says, shutting the folder. "Among any other Army-issued ordinance." There's a mulish look on Django's face in response to that, which isn't a surprise. "Or I can suggest an alternative."

"I'm listening," Django replies. "You've never deliberately steered me wrong, General."

Jason grimaces. Deliberately? No. Accidentally? Far too many times for his conscience to be comfortable with. "Sign one more form, agreeing to be an available contractor for the Department of Defense."

"Contractor. You mean mercenary." The edges of Django's lips turn down in a frown that scares the shit out of the kids just entering the service. It's a hell of a lot of fun to watch. "Thought that was company work or a cover term for our continuing operations here. Didn't think it was a job for individuals."

"Sometimes they are little more than mercenaries, yes, no matter if you're a company or working solo," Jason says, "and there *are* solo operatives. Just not very many of them."

Django's eyes narrow. "Go on."

"Unlike direct service to the military, you have the option of turning contracts down if they don't suit your morals, or if they smell like so much bullshit." That earns Jason a faint nod. Still on the right track, then. "Turn down too many contracts in a row, and the DoD might get cranky, but you can also terminate your employment at any time you like and retire in truth."

Django thinks about it only a moment before nodding. "Give me the form."

Jason has to go to a stack of filing cabinets to search for a copy. There aren't many men in the United States Army he'd even make this sort of offer to. Django's right; it's mercenary work, but if Jason is going to employ a mercenary, he wants one that at least has some sense of right and wrong still rattling around in his head.

When Django hands back the signed form, Jason looks up at him. "This is dated for six months from now."

"Yeah. I figured I was due for a vacation before I started up again," Django says with a faint smile.

"Understood. Going home?"

Django shakes his head, smile vanishing. "I'm not ready to go back to the States yet, Jason. Maybe in a few months."

"You should," Jason says, giving Django a concerned look. "You need to sit your ass down in that farmhouse for a while, Django. Home is good for the soul."

Django shrugs. "My mother's people are from this part of the world, Jason. Technically, I am home."

"Fair enough," Jason admits, smiling. "Going to go on walkabout, asshole?"

"I'm Māori, not Australian, dickhead." Django grins. "Something like that, though. Maybe I'll head out on horseback. Play tourist. I've never been to Cambodia."

For some reason, a sour feeling settles in the pit of Jason's stomach. "Be careful. Nobody's confirmed anything, but there have been rumors coming out of the capital that don't sound right."

"Good reason to make sure I go in armed, then," Django replies, and then hesitates. "I—Jason—"

Jason shakes his head, gets up, circles his desk, and hugs the stubborn motherfucker. "You take care, all right?"

Django's arms are tight around him. The man Jason is holding is a shade too thin to be healthy. He also smells like he's been rolling around in a pigsty, which means Jason now gets to share in the wondrous odor until he changes clothes.

"I will. Thanks, Jason."

"No need to thank me. Just keep your head down and your ass in one piece." Jason draws back and rests his hands on Django's shoulders. "And for God's sake, man, take a fucking *bath* before you go."

Django rolls his eyes, gives him a lazy salute, and leaves. Jason doesn't sit back down until the door closes behind him, a terrible weight on his shoulders. Django isn't his kid—Jason is only ten years older—but after the program, Jason somehow wound up in the role of pseudo-parent to Django Whetū. It's a job that has as many perks as downsides, and right now it feels like he's just watched one of his own two kids walk out of his life for good.

Fuck, Django, Jason thinks. *Please do not go off and lose your shit.*

When evening comes and it's almost time for dinner, Jason is signing off on yet more paperwork when one of his adjutants knocks on the door. "Excuse me, General?"

"What is it, Lieutenant?" Jason asks without raising his head. News of President Thieu's resignation came to him two hours ago, and he has to get this shit done. Tomorrow, everything will need to be packed up or shredded. Thanks to their brilliant ambassador, Jason is going to have a fight on his hands the entire damned way. Nobody will want to admit that Saigon is lost until they're fleeing into the damned hills.

"Well, sir, it seems that one of our men stole this man's horse," Lieutenant Green says.

Jason glances up in surprise. "Come again?" Lieutenant Green is standing at parade rest, and next to him is a younger Vietnamese man with a scowl on his face. "One of our men did *what?*"

"He say you pay!" the man declares, pointing at Jason. "He say General Merrill give money for horse!"

"That son of a bitch," Jason whispers, and startles both Green and the horseless man when he bursts out laughing.

When Saigon is overrun in the twenty-eighth, just as predicted, Jason isn't surprised. Annoyed, frustrated, and saddened by the utter fucking disaster this entire war has turned out to be...but not surprised.

ACKNOWLEDGMENTS:

To Gail again, a great bloody artist available for commissioned work at tuntematonkorppi@tumblr.

To Jeremy Keene, technical advisor for this book and lovely mate whose kidneys warm my icy feet at night. Yes, you really can do all of the stuff described in this book. No, you really, *really* shouldn't.

Editor Joy Demorra is available at www.joydemorra.com. She's editing and writing her own damned good erotica, available soon.

Editor Jules Robin is available at editorjules@gmail.com for helping to shape-up anyone's writing endeavors.

All the love to FULL30.com for providing excellent resources on firearms and how to use them safely, as demonstrated by trained professionals. Also, blown-up watermelons. Blow up your own watermelons responsibly!

Translations for Mandarin were provided by Bern. Please remember that there are many spoken dialects of Mandarin, and some of what you read may be unfamiliar, but still correct for their region. Language is hard. (Mandarin is insane.)

Translations for Japanese provided by Mr. Prime & Mrs. Memprime.

Translations for Thai provided by Google Translate, and have been verified to be mostly correct. Mostly.

Translations for Vietnamese provided by "a friendly neighborhood internet lurker, who ambushed a friend with random translation questions." They're being modest; they were really helpful.

Translations for Māori come direct from a grand Māori online dictionary available at http://maoridictionary.co.nz/.

Acknowledgments, Continued:

A lot of people helped me survive long enough to get this written by providing financial, emotional, or food-based support—or just sending me shiny things and fan art. They are, in no particular order: